LA FOG

Arthur Swan

LA FOG is a work of fiction. Names, characters, business, events and incidents are either products of the author's imagination or used fictitiously. With the exception of public figures, any resemblance to actual persons, living or dead, is purely coincidental. Any opinions expressed belong to the characters and not the author.

This work is dedicated to the millions who come
to Los Angeles to create,
who believe in LA as an idea,
who believe creativity is not a right but hard work,
the hardest work.
who take risks,
unwilling to compromise their passion,
because passion is life itself.

Prologue

Yucatán Peninsula

Although the men were paid through a shell corporation, they all knew where the money came from, and they never expected to see the man in person.

Someone said officials had been bribed to clear the area surrounding Chichén Itzá where, below the central pyramid known as Temple of Kukulcán, ground penetrating radar had revealed a sealed-off passage that led to a secret chamber.

The men tunneled through coralline dust and limestone rock day and night for a week. When they finally reached the passage, they were ordered to stop digging, return to the surface, and wait.

The stadium lights surrounding the dig site and the makeshift runway created a dome of light like a giant bubble, breached only by the pyramid, its massive stone steps ascending into the black void of the night as if they went on up forever.

The men kicked around between the tunnel entrance and the runway until finally one of the diggers marched up to the foreman, Malcolm, and asked, "What the hell is in that chamber?"

Not a new question. Nor was the answer. "No idea," Malcolm said. They were paid not to ask. They were paid exorbitant wages to come here on short notice and work around the clock. What could possibly be worth so much?

The archaeologists—there were three among them—had described all kinds of Mayan ruins and artifacts. Interesting, but not worth venturing into the passage and jeopardizing their bonus.

At two a.m., a Pilatus PC-24 touched down. *Evan York's plane*, Malcolm thought, though he doubted it actually contained Evan York.

The man who emerged from the plane had dark stubble. He was thin, average height. Hair cut short at the sides, parted, and styled back into a wave.

Not old or young. Not Evan York.

It was Niles Anderson, York's representative, whose first words were to remind them, again, of the agreement they had signed: *no one was to enter the chamber.*

Niles nodded toward the plane. "Evan York."

Malcolm nearly stepped back. "Evan York is here in person?"

He was. Evan York was on the plane. And he waited there while the men returned to the tunnel to disassemble the remaining wall of white ostra stone that sealed the entrance to the passage.

Malcolm was curious too, of course. He had hoped to see something. But the passage was too long, too narrow. The light diminished quickly, as if swallowed by the darkness in the passage. An absolute wall of blackness cloaked the chamber.

The men stared into it and then looked toward him. He knew what he had to do. Evan York was up there in his private plane, waiting for them to finish. Malcolm ordered the men back to the surface and followed them out of the tunnel.

Outside, they lined up like soldiers as another man, who was not Evan York, emerged from the plane. He was younger and brawny with a shoulder holster strapped over his pressed white shirt. His neck bulged against the collar. He looked them over, nodded to Niles, and waited at the bottom of the stairs…

Evan York stepped out.

He wore tan cargo pants and a long-sleeve, athletic shirt that seemed tailored to his broad shoulders. Malcolm had seen pictures, of course, but pictures failed to capture the spry energy coiled in every step Evan York took. He was sixty-seven but looked fifty-five, maybe fifty. His white hair was coifed back. His smile, genuine. His teeth, perfect.

He was often described, by the media, as *present, effervescent, charismatic and irresistible*, and it was clear why.

One by one, he shook their hands. Malcolm's palms were sweating from the humidity and the heat. Evan York maintained his smile. He looked Malcolm deep in the eye as if he knew him, not just who he was but who he wanted to be—the best part of himself.

Evan York gave a slight wink. "It's Malcolm, right?"

Malcolm choked on his words and barely managed to nod.

Evan York stood back and addressed them all, in his upper-class, British accent. "Really great work, guys. We're going to double the bonus."

Malcolm straightened. Who cared about the chamber? All he cared about was getting hired again, doing another job for Evan York.

At the tunnel entrance, Evan York removed a hard hat from the rack. Niles reached for a hat too, but Evan York placed a hand on his shoulder.

Niles paused, slumped. He stepped back beside the bodyguard.

Evan York donned the hat and entered the tunnel alone.

Once he was out of sight, Niles ordered the men to pack up. Malcolm glanced at the tunnel. No point in asking.

"Another crew is on the way," Niles said. "By tomorrow afternoon there will be no trace we were here."

—

It was a squat, single-story building. There was no sign, not even an address stenciled on the bare stucco. Just an aluminum door with a two-way mirror reflecting harsh sunlight and the Latino man on Lincoln Boulevard. He had gelled hair, a white shirt, and black pants. He moved an orange cone aside and motioned the black sports car, a brand-new Tesla Roadster, into the swath of red curb in front of the building.

The man who unfolded himself from the Roadster was Evan York. He left the door open for Ernesto to valet and frowned at the nondescript building. Next door was an artisanal water store. Across the street, parked beside a carwash, a pink van advertised Topless Maids $99. North of the carwash was Checks Cashed and a Starbucks.

The door to Starbucks swung open. A bearded hipster cruised out with a four-pack of grandes. He was wearing jeans, a black T-shirt, and a red cape. It was Halloween. Evan had almost forgotten. The hipster slid on a pair of black shades and gawked at the Roadster pulling away. Then at Evan.

Evan turned toward the mirrored door, hoping he hadn't been recognized.

Niles, his COO, held the door open. His gray shirt accentuated his all-day five o'clock shadow.

"I'll have a macchiato," Evan said, "plus whatever you want."

"We've got better beans here," Niles said. "Trust me. I'll have an assistant make you one."

"Never mind," Evan said. Niles didn't get it. Evan liked Starbucks. He hated that he couldn't just go in without his personal detail and a big fuss, so he was having his own Starbucks installed at his house. His own friendly baristas, espresso machine, his own milk frother.

Inside the building was a narrow lobby flanked by white doors. A thick, dull paint coated the cinderblock walls. The floors were rustic, unfinished wood. Evan had asked Niles to lease this place because there were too many people in the Santa Monica office lurking around, looking to get involved in things. This project required absolute secrecy. No leaks.

"Does Luis Luna have it?" Evan asked

"He's got something," Niles said, "but he'll only show it to you."

It was crazy, the stunts people pulled to get a meeting with Evan. But this time his hopes were up. Despite the bad phone photo, Luis Luna appeared to have the artifact Evan had been searching for.

Evan followed Niles into a narrow hallway. On the left was the room full of Mayan artifacts Evan had purchased. Many were fakes, but even the real ones were worthless to him.

"Amelia is asking about the procedures," Niles said. "She needs to know what to do after we put the test subjects to sleep?"

A sleep study was the cover story. Like everyone else, Amelia was unaware of the artifact and the ritual, which Evan would have her add on as some kind of coordination test. Even doctors stopped asking questions once there was enough on the table.

"I'll fill her in after I talk to Luis." Evan wished he knew more than what he'd gleaned from the wall paintings in the secret chamber. In the ritual they depicted, two men were lying down, each with one hand on a device. Their eyes were closed. He assumed they were sleeping, but who knew? There weren't subtitles.

At a turn in the hallway, Niles slowed. "This is crazy."

"Yes, it is, Niles, my friend. Indeed, it is."

He passed Niles and turned down the hall as if he were familiar with the place. He knew that by "crazy" Niles meant "a waste of time" which was worse. Though no one said it to his face, of course, everyone thought he was wasting his time. Why wouldn't they? They had no idea about the legend he was pursuing. But so long as the checks cleared, no one complained.

But crazy ideas had made InGenetics into a Fortune 500 in less than four years. Evan loved making big bets on crazy ideas, riding the thin line between bankruptcy and his island in the Caribbean. It took vetting. Deciding which ideas to pursue, who to listen to, who to ignore. Everyone had eyes and ears, but few actually observed. Listening had made Evan rich.

And this legend, far-fetched as it was, sounded like the real deal. Luis Luna's voice had trembled as he explained how his mother brought the artifact, which he called the Encanto, from Guatemala. Something about his story rang true. The Encanto might just be the object depicted in the ritual, the object missing from the chamber below the Temple of Kukulcán. Certainly, it was worth Evan's time to find out. If the legend was true, it would blow away everything else at InGenetic.

Evan had offered Luna five hundred thousand for the Encanto, though he'd gladly pay more. If the device actually worked, it was worth all the money in the world.

Niles sprinted past Evan and stopped a door on the left. He pulled his phone. "I'll have Amelia bring the first test subject—"

"Let me talk to him first." Evan waved him aside. "He's alone, right?"

The test subjects made Evan uneasy. If there was any chance the Encanto worked, letting a third party in on the secret was risky. Although they had signed an NDA, in the words of Ben Franklin, *three can keep a secret, if two of them are dead.*

Evan raised his hand to knock.

What if Luis held back? The Encanto was useless without knowing how to use it. The wall paintings depicting the ritual left a lot of questions unanswered.

But Evan knew how to get what he wanted. *Be prepared. Give yourself options.* He turned back to Niles. "Give us twenty minutes, and if I'm not out, knock on the door and say there's a problem."

"What kind of problem?"

"Just follow my lead."

"If you tell me what's going on, I can prepare some contingencies."

Evan trusted Niles as much as anyone of his staff, but this was too preposterous even for Evan to admit out loud. He first had to prove it to himself. "You'll be the first to know."

Evan entered. As he glanced back, Niles was trying to peer in behind him. Evan closed the door.

Luis Luna slid to his feet from the left of two hospital beds. It was a windowless examination room, with high-end monitoring equipment and all kinds of cords, dials, and screens. Bolted to the wall was a medicine cabinet. To the right of the door was a chair.

Luis wore a brand-new dress shirt, still creased from the package and bloused around the narrow belt line of his jeans. He had a round face with deep lines grooved into his forehead. Probably forty-five, possibly fifty. His teeth were stained and worn. Before shaking Evan's hand, he placed an object wrapped in a royal blue cloth on the far bed.

Evan's phone chose this moment to buzz in his pocket. Intending to decline the call, he pulled his phone out, but it was Ashley, his daughter. She was the one he was doing this for.

"I have to take this," Evan said.

Luis nodded.

Evan turned his back and answered the call. "Baby-love! Mind if I call you back?"

"Of course." Despite the extra layer of cheeriness infusing her voice, her disappointment was obvious. "So, does it work?"

"I'm checking it out right now." He wasn't about to say anything within earshot of Luis, and until he knew for sure, he had to wait. InGenetic was successful, wildly successful, yet so far it had failed to achieve anything memorable enough to capture her interest. He yearned to tell her how the Encanto could change the world. If it worked, she'd be proud of him. She would want to get involved.

"I'll call you back in one hour, I promise." He would make it up to her. He'd make up for all the times he had focused on work instead of her.

He ended the call and turned to Luis. "Alright, let's see it."

"What about the money?" His Latino accent was thick but clear.

"I'm good for it." Evan smiled. He knew the score. Once he issued payment, Luis Luna would vanish. But first, Evan had to learn everything Luis knew about this *Encanto*, and everything his mother or friends might know. "Give your account number to Niles."

"I need to get paid today."

Evan shook his head. "It will take some time to verify you're not selling me a fake. If you're telling the truth, the deposit should hit your balance in two days—a week at the most."

Luis's shoulders sagged. "That's not soon enough."

Evan shrugged. "Sorry to hear that." As he turned and reached for the doorknob, he forced himself not to glance at the blue cloth on the bed. "Didn't mean to make you drive all the way down here for nothing."

"Wait," Luis said.

Evan turned back.

Luis's face had tightened into a pained expression. "My mother... she has cancer."

"Sorry to hear that." Evan repeated, trying to mean it, but if not for the cancer, Luis might never have stolen the Encanto from her.

"Just promise me you'll pay as soon as you can. She needs treatment."

"Not a problem. We'll prepare a document of intent. Hospitals don't expect payment the same day." Evan would have Niles find out about this treatment and maybe pay for it. A hospital could consume the five hundred grand in a matter of hours, and Evan wanted Luis to walk away with a life-changing sum.

Luis bit his lip. His hands trembled as he picked up the cloth bundle from the bed and slowly unwrapped it. He held it out in the nest of cloth, just beyond Evan's reach.

It was a white stone, three inches in diameter and unnaturally round, aside from a flattened area at the bottom and top shaped like a tear. Coral-like holes spiraled around toward the bottom. The stone was pumice, probably, and mounted on top was an elongated *S* of chiseled obsidian with a head with nostrils and fangs, and a forked tongue. The feathered snake deity, Kukulkan. It matched, almost exactly, the wall paintings in the sealed-off secret chamber below the temple. This *was* it. What he'd been searching for. *The Encanto.*

"*Beautiful*," he said. "Beautiful." He reached for the device.

Luis pulled back. "You don't want to touch it."

"What does it do?"

"Do? You didn't tell me it has to do something." Luis held the Encanto off to the side.

"Relax. You'll get paid." Evan held out his open palm.

"Careful," Luis said. "It's really fragile. Just hold it by the cloth, okay?" He rewrapped the stone. Inhaled. Placed it gingerly on Evan's palm.

As he released it, his shoulders relaxed.

"Do you know where it came from?" Evan asked.

"Guatemala, like I said."

Over the phone, Luis had relayed the story of how his mother had smuggled the Encanto across the Mexican border only to keep it hidden in a drawer. Like an emergency fund. A drawer! An insane place to keep it, given the risk of fire or robbery. It could have been lost forever in shoddy apartment where Luis lived with his mother and daughter. Had she brought it along on the arduous journey across Mexico just because it might be valuable, or because she knew of the ritual?

She had to know. She must. And *if* she knew the ritual, then she must have tried it. Of course she had. And if she had performed the ritual and it didn't work, then why keep the Encanto?

And the way Luis was acting, she must have told him. Maybe not everything but he knew something about it. That was for sure. Evan's confidence surged. He couldn't wait to show Ashley.

"I mean, where is it from originally?" Evan said.

Luis shrugged. "You tell me."

Evan studied the feathered snake. It was a thousand years old, maybe two thousand. "This is Kukulkan, the Vision Serpent. He acted as a messenger between the king and the gods."

Luis furrowed his brow. "What gods?"

Was he trying to play Evan for a fool? "Mayan. There are legends of Mayan technology that surpassed ours."

"Like what?"

Evan had eyes. He'd seen how Luis held it like a hot potato. *When they play dumb, you play dumber.* Play right into the natural human tendency to correct mistakes.

"It's an ancient GPS," Evan lied. It did sort of look like a compass, though it was more—so much more—if the legend was true. "It can point to any city in the Mayan Empire."

Luis made a thickened sound in the back of his throat. He looked doubtful, and for good reason. Ancient Mayans had only Earth's magnetic field to work with. Aside from the poles, it would have been impossible for the snake to point at any particular location.

Luis said nothing. He set his jaw like he'd arrived at a decision. *Had he bought the GPS-lie?*

Evan's heart thrummed. What if he was the one living person in the world who understood the true purpose of the Encanto? The only one who had seen the paintings in the sealed-off chamber below Temple of Kukulkan?

He lifted the Encanto from the cloth. It was a work of art. An amazing piece of craftsmanship, especially given that the Mayans had no access to metal tools. It felt surprisingly light. Must be hollow inside. He turned it over. The little holes spiraled into a ring on the bottom.

He turned it back upright and traced a finger along the jagged edges of the black snake.

"No!" Luis grabbed his hand. "Don't."

Evan hadn't planned on turning the snake-dial until the test subjects were sleeping with their hands on the device, like in the ritual, but why not test it? "If it breaks, you'll still get paid. Don't worry."

"It's not that." Luis swallowed. "It... My mother says... it contains an evil spirit."

Evan hadn't seen or heard anything about a spirit in any of the legends. Maybe she'd invented a story to scare Luis away from messing with it. Maybe, for some reason, she didn't trust him?

"You mean like a ghost?"

Luis glanced at his feet. "I don't know."

"Have you seen it?"

"No."

"Have you seen any evidence of one?"

"No."

"What did your mother say?"

Luis glanced down and to his right. "She said it killed my father."

"The spirit in the stone? You believe that?"

Luis's jaw clenched. "No. He was a dirty cop. He got himself killed by the army."

Evan nodded. He understood. She wanted her son to think highly of his father, to spare him the truth. And if Luis didn't believe her, there was her granddaughter to think of. Hell, maybe the old woman even had convinced herself, preferring to blame a ghost for the sins of her dead husband.

So then why all his nervous energy around the Encanto? "What do you believe?" Evan asked.

Luis blinked rapidly. "I don't know... Look, I made a mistake." He reached for the device. "I never should have taken it from her."

Evan backed away.

Luis lunged toward him, his eyes dark. Determination on his face, and... something else. Sweat beaded on his upper lip. He was afraid.

Evan turned, shielding the Encanto with his body. No way would he surrender it. It was finally his.

Evan had an idea. Maybe Luis would calm down if he thought the Encanto was useless. If Evan just twisted the black snake, nothing should happen. In the wall paintings both men were holding the device. And it seemed like they had to be sleeping.

And Evan wanted to turn the dial. The chiseled snake looked so easy to turn. Its bulging eyes seemed to dare him. Twisting the snake was the right thing to do, the only thing. A need. He *had* to turn it.

And yet still, he hesitated. Why? Because of Luis? No.

With his forefinger, he flicked the head of the black snake.

Luis grabbed the Encanto, and they both clutched the device. Both afraid to pull harder. Both refusing to let go.

The snake spun clockwise, like a well-oiled compass. Half a turn.

Then, abruptly, it stopped. The tail pointed at Evan. Its head, the forked tongue protruding from its open mouth, at Luis.

Luis gulped.

Within the device, something clicked. A sound like two stones slamming together with the force of a spring. Evan pictured an ivory pistol, its hammer cocking.

Searing pain shot through his palm.

He screamed and nearly dropped the Encanto. He examined his hand. In the center of his palm was a puncture, no bigger than a pinprick but reddening. Something had stabbed him from the base of the white stone.

And it burned. It burned all out of proportion.

Luis had backed up to the wall beside the medicine cabinet, his eyes darted around the room.

Evan showed him his palm. "It stabbed me."

Luis gave no indication that he heard Evan at all.

Evan looked around. "I don't see any ghosts. Do you?"

Luis snapped into action. "I need that money as soon as possible." He lunged toward the door.

Evan casually blocked it. He couldn't let Luis leave. Not after they had started the ritual. Evan's palm still stung, though not as bad as before. But what if? What if, sometime after Luis left, the results of the ritual came to fruition? It would be an amazing experience. He hadn't planned on trying the ritual himself, not the first time, but now that they had started it, he hoped it *would* work. And he had to take precautions.

There was a knock on the door. Niles, and not a moment too soon.

Evan opened the door and stood to the side, letting Niles block Luis from exiting.

Niles glanced from Luis to Evan. "Problem. One of the test subjects cancelled."

Evan made a show of rolling his eyes. "For fifty grand just to sleep, you'd think they'd show up. We only needed them to nap for an hour."

Luis's eyes widened. He glanced from the Encanto, in Evan's hand, to the beds.

"I know," Niles said without missing a beat. He'd had years of practice following Evan's lead. "Especially since we're paying in cash."

Luis rubbed his cheek. "Fifty grand? Just to sleep?"

"The FDA won't approve our drug therapy without a study," Evan said. "It's a small price to pay if we can beat our competitors to the market." He could almost see the wheels turning in Luis's head. The best way to get someone to do what you want is for them to come up with your idea on their own.

Luis squinted. "What's the drug do?"

"It helps you sleep."

"You can't be telling him this," Niles said. "He hasn't signed the NDA."

Evan winked at Luis and smiled. "I trust him." He went to the medicine cabinet, removed the unlabeled spray bottle, and brought it over. "It's all natural. You just spray it on your skin, and it triggers sleep hormones in your body."

Luis tried to look doubtful but couldn't quite stop his lips from curling into a smile. "What are the side effects?"

"None that we're aware of," Niles said.

Luis scratched his head. "I guess I can help you out, but... I'm going to need a hundred grand."

Evan gave Luis his best smile and slapped a hand on his shoulder. "That's great, Luis. You'll be helping a lot of people desperate for this product."

"I'm going to need that in cash," Luis said. "Today."

Niles raised his hand. The closest he ever came to protesting. "That—"

"Is no problem," Evan said. If they didn't have the cash, Niles would figure out where to get it. He always did.

"I'll call Amelia," Niles said.

"That won't be necessary. I'm going to do the trial, too. Right here with Luis."

Niles's hands shot up in protest. "You? Uh—"

"It will be great advertisement." Evan smiled and glanced at Luis. "Excuse us for a second."

He ushered Niles into the hall and closed the door behind them. Niles glanced down the hall as if hoping for backup.

"Can I count on you?" Evan asked.

Niles straightened. "Absolutely." He seemed to forget whatever protest he was about to make.

"Call Dimitri." Evan's personal guard followed orders without question and would come as fast as he could, but he was at the estate in Palos Verdes, and with the 405 always jammed, he might not get here in time. "Get Ernesto in here too. He's discreet, right?"

Niles's eyes widened. "Of course, but—"

"I'm not to leave this room without the secret password." Evan glanced behind him at the door. Niles leaned in close, and Evan whispered, "Excalibur."

"You got it," Niles said.

"Luis is free to come and go as he pleases. In fact, I want you to go in and wake him up in an hour."

"O-kay." He obviously wanted to ask why but knew there was no point. Evan wasn't going to explain.

Evan returned to the examination room, sat on the bed by the door, and rolled up his sleeves. He squirted each forearm three times with the cream. Passed the bottle to Luis. Rubbed the cream into his skin.

He felt exposed. He was taking a big risk here. No telling how Luis would react. What if Evan's safeguard with the password didn't work? He needed Luis to trust him completely. And more money, at this point, would only raise his suspicion.

"Come work for me," Evan said.

Luis applied a meager squirt to one arm and smeared it lightly. "Doing what?"

Evan smiled. The half-squirt was more than enough to induce an overwhelming drowsiness.

"What's your current line of work?"

"Maintenance."

"We need maintenance. Who's your employer?"

Luis clenched his jaw. "An apartment."

Was he undocumented? "I'll talk to Niles after our little nap. We've got all kinds of openings. If you need a work permit, we can get that no problem. If you're qualified, we'll sponsor your H1B."

Luis's lips tightened. He nodded. "What if I can't fall asleep?"

Evan shrugged. "Then it doesn't work. Not your problem. We'll do a blood test and try to figure it out."

Luis laid back on the bed beside Evan's, seeming satisfied to close his eyes and ask no more questions.

No need to bother with the motoring equipment. Evan dimmed the lights and rolled onto his side. He watched Luis's regular breathing, wondering how he'd spend the windfall after his mother's cancer treatment.

Evan had long ago passed the point where money could change his life. He had more than he could spend in many lifetimes. Money was just a tool now. Useful, but not everything.

He closed his eyes and exhaled, feeling a certain sense of nostalgia, and loss, for the time in his late twenties when he sold his first company. To be young, suddenly rich, but still anonymous. To be able to walk into a Starbucks without personal security and an entourage of assistants.

Because of him, Ashley had never experienced life as a normal human being. He had failed to provide her this privilege—but maybe now he could.

Gray

Gray was quitting, so the incessant din of his coworkers clicking away on their workstations no longer made him feel hopeless. In fact, he felt sorry for them. He almost skipped down the aisle between the cubes and then up the three steps to the raised platform where Brad lorded over them from his all-glass corner office, the only office on the floor.

Brad was sitting behind his oversized desk, which was also glass, staring at his phone, as usual.

Gray knocked on the door.

Brad slapped the phone face down and leaned toward his monitor. "Just a minute."

Behind him on the glass wall, he'd mounted a large digital clock—the kind you'd normally see at a sports event—so that the engineers coding away in the cubes below merely had to look up to see the red numerals marking the time: 2:07:31, 2:07:32. Behind the clock, LA sprawled eastward, the buildings ascending like an irregular staircase to downtown, where the tallest cluster of gleaming monoliths was still dwarfed by the backdrop of mountains. The peaks clustered with antennas and towers.

Brad clicked his mouse and punched his keyboard. His thin, colorless hair, spiked up with some kind of gel, always looked wet. His face was unnaturally tan, his cheeks flat, and his eyes were too small for his face. His mouth twisted into a bothered expression whenever someone came up to his office uninvited, and now was no exception.

He motioned for Gray to enter, making a performance out of the next four keystrokes.

I quit, Gray wanted to say. He couldn't wait to see the look on Brad's face. But first, he had to tell Claire. "I need to leave a little early."

Brad blinked as if the request was outlandish, way beyond anything anyone had ever requested throughout his vast career as a supervisor, which was all of two years.

13

"I need to take my kid trick-or-treating," Gray added. Which was true. It would be Mindy's first time, and Gray was looking forward to it, but it wasn't until six.

"O-kay," Brad said. "How early?" Surprisingly, he passed up the opportunity to remind Gray, yet again, about the sprint, the arbitrary milestone Brad had probably invented himself in order to pressure the team into working unpaid OT.

Gray glanced over his shoulder. Below Brad's office, the arrayed cubes were occupied, all except for his. The thought of returning to his desk made his throat tighten.

"Now."

Brad's eyes widened. He stared at his watch. Then, as if his watch might be mistaken, he checked his phone and turned in his chair toward the digital display behind him.

2:07:47. 2:07:48. 2:07:49.

Wasted seconds clicking by.

Gray could agree with Brad on this, because every second he spent standing there was time he could be painting. Creating art was a need. The food of his soul. Without it, he was hardly human at all, just a code-writing robot. This job was standing in his way. He couldn't take it.

Brad swiveled back to face Gray, his brows raised. "You're coming in this weekend, right?"

"Maybe Sunday," Gray lied.

Brad's brows slammed together. "You know the sprint is due Wednesday."

There it is, Gray thought. *2:07:58. Almost thirty whole seconds without mentioning it.* "My stuff is basically done."

"It's in code review?"

"Not yet." No point in submitting any earlier than he had to just so some stickler, of which there was one on every review, could eat up all the available time with an endless stream of unnecessary changes for Gray to implement.

Brad exhaled a long breath. "Do what you've got to do, I guess... but you're the only one leaving early."

Brad's little jabs used to anger him, and so did his insinuation that this was all a contest to see who could put in the most hours, but now he just felt sorry for his coworkers, most of them single men (or "goldmines" as he'd overheard Brad refer to them on occasion), who would no doubt toil for decades before realizing they were going nowhere.

In his performance review, Brad had said Gray needed to focus on priorities, basically implying (though not in a provable way) that Gray's family had cost him a raise. Well, he was focusing on priorities now: *his* priorities. Brad could think whatever the hell he wanted. *What's the worst he can do?*

If Brad fired him, it would be a favor. If he was fired he could collect severance, and he wouldn't have to worry about convincing Claire that he could quit his job to become an artist and yet still, somehow, continue supporting her and Mindy and Tyler. It would all be out of his hands.

Gray pulled out his phone, careful to obscure the lock screen from Brad. "It's Claire," he lied. "I'm already late."

Lifting the phone to his ear, Gray turned his back on Brad. "On my way."

He descended the office steps and strode past the cube farm to the little hallway with the elevator. He pressed the down button for the next to last time.

Saul

Would a cloud be too much to ask? The afternoon sky had thinned out and surrendered to the relentless sun. Saul parked on Lincoln Boulevard near the mob of looky-loos pressing in around the barricades on the sidewalk. Behind the crime scene was a carwash with faded fin-toppers that might have looked stylish in the sixties.

He left the engine running for the AC. In front of him was a pink van advertising *"Topless Maids $99"* and then a squad car. Beside it, Hernandez was talking to the uniforms. She was five foot two and lithe. She only saw him as a partner, but Saul was hoping for more.

He couldn't bear for her to see him heave his huge belly out. If she would just get in here with him, they could crank up the AC and talk like human beings. Forget all the politics and procedure of the LAPD.

He motioned her towards his car, but she looked away.

He flashed his lights.

Useless signal against the sunlight. He sighed. Grabbed his trench coat from the backseat. Climbed out of the car and put it on. It did little to hide his girth. If anything, the coat made him more conspicuous.

Instantly sweating, he tried to ignore the murmurs from the crowd, the mouths gaping open, all the phones pointing at him as he plowed his big belly toward Hernandez.

She glanced at him from the corner of her eye but continued joking with the uniforms, as if unaware of his approach. Her skin was perfect. She would look twenty-five if not for the clump of gray hair always falling across her forehead.

"What's the status?" he asked.

"Where you been, *Barker*?" She trotted out her Chicana accent, pronouncing the *P* in his last name like a *B*. She was pissed.

"Traffic's a bitch," he said.

She pointed inside his coat. "Is that the evidence you were looking for?"

16

He glanced down. A dollop of ketchup stained his shirt. He hadn't noticed it escape his burger. He should have told her he was going to the Castle for lunch. She knew he belonged to the clubhouse for the Academy of Magical Arts, but she had no idea how much he loved going there. The ornate wood and crystal chandeliers. The deliberate lack of windows which made it feel like stepping out of LA and back in time to an alternate world where the air seemed to spark with possibility.

He'd only lied because Hernandez was working through lunch, and what if, like his ex, she hated magic?

He buttoned his coat over the stain. They needed to focus on the case. At least Saul did. Not that Lieutenant Levy had actually told him in so many words, but she'd called Hernandez with the assignment instead of Saul when he was the lead detective, or he was supposed to be. If Levy had demoted him, she should have at least told him, but Saul wasn't surprised. She was passive-aggressive and still held a grudge against him for the Brown shooting. Although he'd been cleared of wrongdoing, the fallout had stalled her career.

Hernandez led him away from the uniforms to the black-and-white on the curb in front of Checks Cashed. In the backseat, a middle-aged man with a box-shaped head, shaved almost bald, stared at the crowd with a sour expression.

Hernandez turned toward Saul and combed back her shock of white. "Look. I don't care if you take a long lunch, just let me know where you're at, okay? We're partners. We're supposed to trust each other."

Her eyes caught the sunlight like honey. Saul tried to memorize every detail. He could gaze into them for hours. "I went to the Castle. If you want to come next time—"

"Hollywood is too far for lunch."

Was she suggesting somewhere else? A real sit-down meal instead of their usual takeout? Or maybe dinner? The Castle would be ideal for dinner.

Before he could ask, she slapped the roof of the squad car. "We've got the bastard dead to rights, and get this: he can't move his legs."

"He's a paraplegic?"

"Exactly. His wheelchair's in the trunk."

Saul peered through the back window of the car. The man inside had a potbelly. His arms were cuffed behind his back. He looked up at Saul, his face blank and his eyes, shadowed by a massive brow, just dark hollows.

Saul shuddered.

"Sheesh. Is he talking?"

"Not really. He's demanding the right to clean himself, but I'm thinking, you bash someone's head in, you wear the blood-splatter, am I right?"

Saul shrugged. The streaks of dried blood on the man's cheek were of little concern to him.

Hernandez held out her phone. "Check this out. Some woman actually filmed the whole thing."

As he took the phone, his knees trembled under his weight. He looked around for somewhere to sit. But they were pinned into the stretch of sun-bleached sidewalk between the crime scene and the makeshift barricade holding back the crowd.

Pushing his way through the crowd was Chu, the assistant chief coroner, who tended to assign the high publicity cases to himself. Having Chu on the case meant an autopsy with no delay, so Saul was fine with the showboating. He motioned for the uniforms to move the barricade.

As Chu approached, Hernandez asked, "How's my favorite coroner?"

"Good, good. Who's the vic?"

"Luis Luna," she said, "Latino, age forty-seven."

Chu glared at Hernandez.

"I only took out his wallet. Didn't touch anything else, I swear."

Chu snapped on a pair of latex gloves and motioned his crime-scene photographer, who had just arrived with all his gear, through the barricade.

They approached the yellow tape surrounding the blood splatters on the sidewalk and Luna's body, a white sheet was draped over him.

Chu frowned at the sheet. "Who covered the body?"

"One of the unis," Hernandez said. "He's new."

"I can see that. I'll need his shoes. Yours too, Hernandez."

"I wore booties," she said.

Chu frowned again. He activated a digital recorder and kneeled by the body. He peeled the sheet back, revealing Luna's face. The whole right side was beaten beyond recognition. His left eye glazed over. Chu parted Luna's lips. His mouth was full of blood. His teeth broken.

Chu spoke into the recorder. "Severe blunt-force trauma to the right side of the head. Victim's air passage is blocked."

He paused the recording. "So Parker, when are you going to get me in at the Magic Castle?"

"Anytime," Saul said. "Just let me know."

"Next time you're on stage."

"That could be a while." Saul hadn't performed in over a year. For him, it wasn't about performing. He enjoyed watching other magicians, watching the impossible occur right before his eyes. Riding the thrill for a few seconds before mentally deconstructing exactly how the trick was performed. Knowing the method behind the magic gave him a certain assurance.

"You've got to look at the video," Hernandez said again.

Saul had almost forgotten he was holding her phone. He moved beside her and held it up so they could both watch. It began with Luna already lying face down. Near his head, a toppled Starbucks oozed brown liquid onto the pavement.

The wheelchair was on its side. The perp pulled his torso and potbelly up onto the chair, his legs trailed limply behind him.

Luna managed to turn over. To raise his arms in defense. But it was useless. The man reared up on his wheelchair and slammed a baseball bat into Luna's skull. He repeated the beating. Luna's hands fell limp by his side.

Finally, two Latinos ran into the frame, snatched away the bat, and wrestled the crazed paraplegic down on the pavement. He screamed in a language Saul didn't recognize.

Saul lowered the phone and stared through the back window at the perp. They had the right guy, yet he seemed different somehow. His shoulders sagged. His head lolled on his neck. He stared up at Saul with eyes that seemed to have nothing inside them. Like he was a spent shell, a remnant of the man in the video.

"I made the woman delete it from her phone," Hernandez said, "but I bet you dinner she tweeted it."

Dinner. Saul felt his face redden. "You're on." Regardless of who paid for the meal, dinner was a win for him.

"So what's the motive?" he asked.

"Who cares? We've got him on video."

"It'll make a difference in court. The DA will insist on something."

"How about: he's a psycho."

Saul mopped his brow for the third time. "Even psychos think they have a reason."

Chu concluded his preliminary examination and motioned for a pair of EMTs to place Luna's body on a stretcher. Saul wished he'd close the lifeless eye, but Luna was no longer a man to Chu. He was a thing to be studied. And a vehicle to rocket Chu into the headlines.

"You don't look so good," Chu said. "You should take off that coat."

"It's my knee," Saul lied. "I strained it chasing a perp." No way he was removing his coat with all the bystanders behind the barricade pointing phones in their direction. His shirt was soaked through and clung to his belly. Couldn't be more wet if it rained. Although, he would certainly be cooler. He shielded his eyes to sun and gazed upwards. Endless blue sky. Could be hours before marine layer rolled in.

Saul turned to check the other direction. Same deal. The crowd extended a full block north, up to Rose. Beyond it was a gas station, and beyond that a restaurant named Casablanca beckoned like an oasis. Air conditioning. Food. No windows.

A place where he and Hernandez could escape all this. A place they could talk.

He was cooking inside the coat—he had to take it off. Chu was right about that. But now a van from Fox News was rolling up beside the black and-white, not even bothering to park, hardly even slowing before unleashing its crew, including two cameramen, recorders on their shoulders already rolling.

As senior detective, Saul was expected to handle the reporters, make the standard neutral-non-statement. But at this stage, even saying they had a suspect in custody could backfire.

He faced the window of Checks Cashed and frowned at his reflection. "We need media relations. I'll call the L-T."

"Already spoke to her," Hernandez said. "She wants us to punt."

Saul searched her face. She looked away. Earlier, she'd acted like her conversation with Levy was perfunctory, more of an oversight that Levy had called her with the new assignment instead of him. But now it was clear. Levy had cut him out of the loop, and she lacked the balls to inform him.

"Then I guess you should do it," he said, which was fine with him. He had no desire to appear in the news looking like an eggplant in a trench coat. Hernandez would look amazing on camera. Even if all she said was *no comment*, it would come across more positive from her than from him.

"We could just leave." She said it like he had a choice, like maybe this time it wasn't an order, but next time, who knew? "Let's take the perp downtown. Maybe he'll talk in the box."

Fine. Saul was glad to get out of the sun. "I'll follow you."

Gray's Lie

At the intersection of Rose and Lincoln, Gray was stuck in his car, almost choking on exhaust, and basically, it was Claire's fault. He'd suggested coming to the beach how many times? She never said no, not exactly; she just had this way of procrastinating to some unknown date in the future.

He rolled up the windows. If he'd just paid the twenty-two dollars for beach parking, he could be walking on the sand right now. But instead, here he was, stuck—at a green light—with no one moving and not even a chance of street parking. Across Lincoln, a mass of people crowded around an ambulance and three police cars.

Finally, the T-bird in front of him moved. He turned right onto Lincoln, hoping for a better view of whatever was going on the left side of the street. Dumb. You couldn't see anything from the road. He made it maybe ten feet and then had to slam the breaks.

Time to get out of here. He nudged his Camry into the bike lane and turned down an alley. Also jammed. But there was parking: a single open space behind the Fringe Salon marked with "*Customers Only.*"

Screw it. He could use a cut. Anything was better sitting in his car stuck in the gridlock.

He parked and entered the salon through the back. It was a narrow room with three barber chairs and a sink. At the front was a reception desk with a large fern and a shelf of products. Gray was the only customer.

A stylist, a black man with neon-yellow hair, introduced himself as Devan. He led Gray to a barber chair, faced him toward a mirror, and stood behind him. "So, what can I do for you?" He spoke with a lisp.

Gray's dull-brown hair was unkempt, as usual, but thinner than he remembered. "Something different," he said. "What do you think?"

Devan ran his fingers through Gray's hair from different angles. His brows furrowed. He smacked his lips. "Who cut it last time?"

Gray shrugged. "Supercuts, I think."

Devan shuddered.

While washing Gray's hair, Devan recounted what he'd learned from Twitter about the police presence outside, "Some lunatic bashed a guy's skull in with a hammer."

Gray shuddered. "Oh man."

"I know." Devan smacked his lips. "Someone shared a video, but the link was dead by the time I clicked it."

"I thought it was safe over here."

"I don't know if it's safe anywhere. The guy who got killed was in a wheelchair, can you believe that? What kind of psycho kills a disabled person?"

Gray grimaced. A guy in a wheelchair. Anyone could die, anytime. There was no guaranteed tomorrow. Next time it could be him. His pulse started racing as he thought of all the time he'd wasted. He had to do something with his life. Now or never.

Devan wrapped a towel around Gray's neck and ushered him back to the chair. He checked his phone. "OMG. Ashley York might costar in a One Direction biopic!"

"Great." Gray hated Ashley York. If she hadn't been born rich, no one would care what she was up to, and she wouldn't be costarring in anything.

Devan opened a drawer and chose a pair of scissors. "You don't follow her?"

Gray groaned. "No, but my wife does. You'd think her life depended on it."

"Ooh. What does she think of August Grant?"

"Who's that?"

Devan smacked his lips. "He's Quantum-Man, silly. Although, if you ask me, he's too hot to wear a mask. Anyway, Ashley's dating him. Wouldn't surprise me at all if they're the next Kunis and Kutcher."

In the mirror, Gray noticed how much grayer the stubble on his chin had become. And his eyes were more than a little bloodshot, probably from all the late nights, trying to make time for himself before he had to get up and do it all over again. The cycle of dread. How did he get here?

His whole life he'd always been drawing. In college, he'd started painting without much thought about what he wanted to do with his life, aside from the fact that he knew he'd spend it with Laura. And then, after they broke up, it was Claire. When he almost lost Claire, all he could think about was how to build a life with her. He wanted a family, and in order to provide for them, he need some kind of job. The tech industry was paying well, so he'd changed his major to comp sci. He and Claire moved in together, and the years clicked by in a blur.

He'd sort of forgotten how much he enjoyed painting. Until last year. Mindy got into coloring books, and one night, while drawing with her, it all came back. He sketched her sleeping in her little bed. He drew portrait of Claire, who was eight months pregnant with Tyler at the time, holding her belly.

He then bought some acrylics and an easel, and now he was begging Claire just for a few hours alone in the garage. They had agreed on Saturday mornings as his designated time to paint, but there was always something else going on. And Saturdays weren't enough. He needed to paint full time.

Quitting his job would be easy—he looked forward to that—but he dreaded telling Claire. Quitting his job, their only source of income, was a bad decision, a terrible decision, and yet the only option he had. His dreams would not be denied any longer.

But how to tell her? The whole reason he'd driven down to Venice Beach was to find a place to think, to come up with a plan. He needed a way to pay the bills.

What he needed was a drink.

"What do you think?" In the mirror, Devan presented Gray's hair with his palms. The sides were buzzed flat, and the top was coiffed up with product. It looked thicker than ever.

"I look like a new man." Gray smiled. Things were going to work out, somehow. They had to.

—

There were plenty of bars around, but Gray had to move his car from behind the salon, and anyway, it would be a bad idea to have alcohol breath when he explained to Claire how he was quitting.

From the alley, he saw Fox News and NBC vans adding to the to the jam-up on Lincoln, so he tacked through a neighborhood down to Venice Boulevard and turned east, toward home. The sun sunk into the clouds behind him as he waited through one light after another.

A block past Helms, the Library Bar practically beckoned him into its lot. If he stopped for a while, traffic might thin out and he'd get home at the same time anyway. It would be a good idea to at least spend a few minutes thinking through what he was going to say.

Inside, the lighting was dim, and the air thick with the smell of beer and the distinct aroma of old paper from the hardbacks that lined the walls. The bar was polished wood and at the far end, a shaggy-haired man in a plaid shirt was arguing with the bartender.

Gray grabbed the nearest stool. The bartender approached. He had a lantern jaw, and it was set with a look that said Gray had to order fast, and it better be something besides water. So Gray ordered a Corona, because he hated beer and would be less tempted to drink it.

The bartender popped open a longneck. Placed a napkin in front of Gray, centered the bottle in the square, and returned to his argument with the shaggy guy at the other end of the bar.

Gray's phone rang. He pulled it out. In the photo on the screen, Claire was smiling. It was from before the kids, maybe eight years ago, but she looked fifteen years younger and much happier.

He answered, and she opened with, "Where are you? I thought you were leaving an hour ago."

In the condensation on the bottle, he sketched a zigzag. "There's a game at Dodger Stadium. Traffic is jammed."

She sighed. "Just get here."

Gray promised he would and ended the call.

More and more, he'd found himself living in borrowed moments like this. It had started one night after the 10 crawled to a dead stop. He'd pulled off into a neighborhood to wait it out, and yet it seemed like he got home around the same time, so he started doing it every night. Just for a while, at first, and after getting away with it, he snuck an easel into his trunk. He stopped at a park a few times and setup his easel, but he couldn't really focus on a painting. He felt too guilty stealing time when he should be helping Claire with the kids. So, to take the edge off the guilt, he began stopping at bars. For a quick drink, at first, which soon became two. And now, more often than not, he couldn't say how long he'd been sitting there or for how many drinks before Claire had texted. He'd done it so many times that his lies about working late were wearing thin.

But it was an adventure. A new bar each night. He was anonymous. Didn't matter if it was a pub or a cantina, if it was packed or empty, if the bartender had tattoos or a suit. No one cared how long he stayed. Bars were more than just rooms full of booze; they created a kind of slowness. An easy space where he could sit in silence. Like now.

Behind the shaggy-haired man, a door swung inwards to a brightly lit office. A man with glasses and spiky hair emerged and perused the shelves of hardbacks lining the back wall of the bar. Moving toward Gray, he ran his finger along the spines and settled on a novel with bold letters on the dust jacket, "*Tim O'Brien.*" He nodded toward the bartender and returned to his office, where he eased onto a leather couch.

An idea dawned on Gray. This was exactly what he needed: a bar with a back room. He could convert it into a studio, a space where he could paint. He would hire some hip bartender to handle the day drinkers, and then at night Gray would emerge from the studio and sling drinks himself. He could hang his best works out in the bar. Kind of like a gallery. Maybe even sell a few.

Maybe, once he had his own bar, he would stop drinking. He was sick of the headaches anyway and had been intending to cut back for years, but then something always went wrong between him and Claire, and he just needed to take the edge off.

Above the bar was a flatscreen. The bartender powered it on without consulting Gray, even though he represented fifty percent of the customer base. The Dodgers were playing the Giants, the announcers shouting. The manager kicked the door shut to his office.

Gray just needed ten minutes of silence, but instead he got a commercial for a Ford F-150 with a frenetic beat even louder than the game.

He stood up, and the bartender ignored him. Shaggy was jabbering, yelling above the TV volume about who should pitch the second inning while stuffing peanuts into his mouth.

Gray slapped a ten down on beside the napkin, now soaked with condensation from his full longneck.

At the exit, he stalled, pretending to examine the books near the door, but his mind was locked on the Corona, the bubbles rising into the neck…

He turned back. Snatched the bottle from the bar, and tilted it back. He took a long pull. Gulped so hard he almost choked.

Now, the bartender took notice. He paused midsentence to watch Gray slam the half-empty beer back on the bar, then turned back to Shaggy. "Look, all I'm saying is the Dodgers don't have to win, so long as the Giants lose…"

The muscles in Gray's shoulders loosened. All the tension eased out of him. But the glide of the alcohol brought with it the guilt. Which would fade, if he drank more. *Who cares if I finish my beer?* He wanted to drink the whole damn bar. But it wouldn't be enough.

That was the problem with drinking: it was never enough.

—

Outside, a solid mass of low cloud had swept over the city. People liked the marine layer because it cooled LA down, but to Gray the gloom was oppressive. He stood there. The drone of traffic surrounding him. He should just go home, but what to tell Claire? If it not for the kids, he would just quit regardless of what she thought.

Gray got in his car and sat in the parking lot watching the mist grow denser around the streetlights. The road blurred out of focus, fading away. He checked the rear-view mirror. Nothing but fog.

Nothing to be afraid of, he told himself. *It's perfectly safe here.* But his heart was beating faster. He was spooking himself out again. Claire would laugh if she had any idea how easily he was frightened.

He'd always been like this, ever since the *Trollenberg Terror,* which he had watched way too young. The second half of the movie, after the one-eyed alien came out, was no problem (it had looked cheesy even when he was a kid), but the beginning, before he even realized it was a horror flick, when the rock-climber fell out of the fog…decapitated. The scene still sent a chill down his spine, even now.

Near the front of his car, something scuffed the pavement. A boot?

He flicked on the high beams… Beyond the hood, the fog was solid white.

He started the engine, dimmed the headlights, and rolled out of the lot.

—

The traffic had gotten worse. The 10 was jammed. The surface streets, jammed. It took a mind-numbing hour of grid lock just to travel the ten miles to Silver Lake, and, of course, Claire's car was in the driveway. He had to park two blocks from their house. He ran through the fog, and as he reached the front door, he felt a rush like he was digging himself out after being buried alive.

He opened the door.

From the living room, the TV was blasting, a commercial for Sit N' Sleep. "I'm home. Claire?"

She was on the couch with Tyler in her lap, chewing on his rattle. She wore the same sweatpants as she had this morning. Her raven hair was tangled and oily, her skin so pale it almost shone, except for the bruise-like shadows around her eyes. Her eyes had many colors. When he met her, they were blue like the Pacific in the summer sun. Tonight, they were slate-gray. They flicked up toward Gray then back to her phone.

She said nothing.

"Mind if I turn this down?" Gray moved the towels off the coffee table and began rifling through the magazines for the remote.

"What's with the haircut?" she asked.

"My barber quit." Gray glanced at her. "Like it?"

"It's your hair."

The commercial break ended, and the news came on. They showed clips of Lincoln Boulevard. Gray froze. If they showed his car, Claire would recognize it. They cut to a carwash cordoned off with yellow police tape, the crowd pressing in around it. According to the anchor woman, a guy in a wheelchair, a man by the name of Edward Saroyan, had done the killing, and with a baseball bat not a hammer. But it was hard to imagine how a guy in a wheelchair had managed to bludgeon a man who could run away. To Gray, Devan's version sounded closer to the truth than what the NBC was saying.

He found the remote and turned it off.

"I was watching that," Claire said.

Gray sat beside her on the couch and tried to look cheerful. *Start positive.* "How was your day?"

"What do you mean, *my* day?" She plopped Tyler on his lap.

"I just…" Bad question. He knew how her day was, just like she knew about his, and it had been so long since either of them had asked the other that now it seemed weird to ask.

A stench curled Gray's lip. Tyler's diaper needed changing, and it couldn't wait. Gray carried him to the nursery and unfastened his diaper. "Oh man, little man."

Tyler started crying.

No big deal. All he had to do was get through tonight. Telling Claire was going to be hard, no doubt about it, but he *would* get through it. Then tomorrow was Saturday, his day to paint.

Lifting Tyler's ankles, Gray gingerly wiped the goo from his butt. Clearly too much for just one wipe. He went to the box for more wipes.

"Don't just dab at him," Claire said from the doorway. "You've got to get in there." She snatched a wipe, pushed Gray aside, and scooped the poo out from between Tyler's legs.

"You got some on your hand." Gray pointed.

"It's just poo."

"Exactly, excrement." His least favorite thing about babies.

Claire wiped her hands and left.

Gray secured Tyler in a fresh diaper. Then made rocket noises while lifting him above his head. Tyler laughed and pumped his arms. It was so easy to make them laugh, sometimes. Gray's favorite thing about babies.

Mindy edged into the doorway, the pink princess dress she got for her fifth birthday still a size too big. Locks of cocoa hair curtained her face as she leaned against the door frame, hugging a doll to her chest.

"Are you ready to go trick-or-treating?"

She looked down. "I guess."

Her level of enthusiasm would go way up once she learned about the candy. Gray couldn't wait to see her face when she learned that all she had to do was knock on a neighbor's door and they'd give her sweets.

"Well, you need to wear a costume."

"I am."

He smiled. Any day of the week he could come home and find her dressed like a princess. "Oh, I thought those were your normal clothes."

"No. I wear girl clothes when I'm a girl."

"So you're not a girl, tonight?"

"I'm a princess fairy-girl." She laughed and spun.

"Well, alright, then." He ushered her forward.

Tyler started to sob.

Gray tried the rocket ship again, but this time Tyler only wailed.

Claire appeared from the other end of the hallway. "Give him to me." She took Tyler in her arms and swayed him with a practiced tenderness. "Who's my baby boy? My bubble-baby-boy."

He stared up into her placid face and seemed to relax.

She carried him into the living room and said over her shoulder, "We don't have anything to make for dinner."

Gray glanced at the door. He didn't feel like to going back out in the traffic but this could be the opportunity he needed to talk to Claire. He followed her to the couch. "I'll call Belinda," he said. "We can go out, just the two of us. She can make macaroni for the kids."

Claire shook her head. "I can't deal with her anymore."

Gray glanced at Mindy, who had no doubt picked up on her mother's animosity toward the one decent sitter they had. Sure, Belinda was a little nosy, but it wasn't that big of a deal.

"I'll deal with her. You can just wait in the car when she comes."

"Won't work," Claire said. "She'll want to talk to me."

Claire was right, of course. Gray shrugged. "I'll make up an excuse."

"No, you won't. She'll ask you something you don't know the answer to, and I'll have to get involved."

"So, what do you want to do? I promised to take Mindy trick-or-treating."

"Elmo's, Elmo's, Elmo's," Mindy chanted. She loved Elmo's because of the chocolate-chunk pancakes they let her order for dinner, which she smothered syrup.

Claire sighed. "Too much effort to get ready."

"Delivery?" There wouldn't be dishes, and after they'd put Mindy and

Tyler to bed, they could sit down, just the two of them, and he could finally explain to her why he had to quit his job.

"No." Claire sighed. "I'll just go to Elmo's."

"Great, I'll call Belinda."

"I don't want macaroni," Mindy said.

Claire shook her head. "We're all going."

Mindy clapped. "Elmo's!"

That decided it. Elmo's would be crowded, too crowded to talk, but maybe while the kids were distracted, he could at least lay down some groundwork so it wouldn't be a complete shock later on when he dropped the bomb.

"I have to take a shower," she said.

Gray reached to take Tyler, cupping his fuzzy little head. Amazing that something this small would grow into a man.

Claire pulled him away. "You'll wake him. I'll go put him in the crib. You get the car packed. There's no time to go trick-or-treating."

As she carried Tyler to the nursery, Gray kneeled down beside Mindy.

"Can I get the chocolate chip pancakes with maple syrup?" she asked.

Claire calling off the trick-or-treating had hardly even registered. But next year Mindy started kindergarten, where she would for sure learn that people gave out candy on Halloween. Claire didn't get it. He had to take her tonight. He just had to.

———

In the driveway, Gray took Mindy by the hand and stepped out from the porch light into the fog. Tyler, strapped to Gray's chest in a Bjorn, woke up and dreamily looked around.

Mindy halted at the curb. "Elmo's."

"We're just going while Mom's in the shower. Don't you want to show off your princess outfit?"

"I'm a fairy-princess!" Mindy jerked her hand free, launched into the road, and spun around.

The street appeared empty, at least from what he could see in the thick fog. "Mindy, you have to look first." He grabbed her hand and led her across.

Lining the walkway up to the neighbors' were rows of jack-o'-lanterns with carved expressions alternating from ecstasy to fear and fury, all lit up with orange lights meant to look like candles. Shadows flickered on the pavement.

In the center of the yard a trio of stuffed witches perched on a haystack, held their brooms out like weapons. On the hedge, a black cat arched its back, its tail sticking straight up. On the roof, an orange light silhouetted a group of crow cut-outs.

One squawked. Gray jumped, and Tyler laughed at the sudden movement.

The ebony bird abandoned its wooden brethren and flew off into the night.

"It's just a bird," Mindy said, "and those witches are fake."

Gray pretended to laugh. He glanced back toward their house. It had faded into a shadow behind the fog and the haloed porch light.

On the neighbors' front stoop was a chalk outline of a body, which they had to stand on to ring the doorbell. Gray worried that maybe this house was too scary for Mindy, but then again, she seemed less scared than him. He pressed the button.

Organ music bellowed.

Gray racked his brain for the names of the couple who lived here. They had hardly spoken since he and Claire moved into the neighborhood four years ago.

The organ reached a crescendo. The door creaked open. An elderly man in a brown suit peered out at them. The suit hung limply off his stooped shoulders.

Mindy hid behind Gray's legs.

"And who do we have here?" The old man grimaced, or maybe he was trying to smile, but the way the wrinkles twisted on his face made the expression look painful. As he bent down, his body shook.

Gray gently prodded Mindy out from behind his legs. "We have a very shy fairy."

"A princess fairy," she said, almost too quietly for them to hear.

Gray smiled. "So, what do you say, Mindy?"

"Trick-or-treat."

The old man produced a bowl heaped with packets of Skittles and M&M's. Mindy's eyes went wide. More candy than she had ever seen.

Gray handed her the bag he'd brought for her, which she took as if in a trance, her eyes on the candy as the old man dumped it in.

Gray reached out to stop him. "That's plenty."

"I've got more in the kitchen," he said.

Gray laughed. "No, I mean, that's more sugar than she eats in a year."

"Well, I'll be here all night if you change your mind." He reached for the door.

"Wait." Gray introduced himself and they shook hands. But the old man didn't mention his name.

Gray assumed he must be the father, possibly the grandfather, of either the man or the woman who lived here. "So where is the rest of the family?"

The man's eyes narrowed. "Out of town."

Gray motioned toward the yard. "They set this up and missed the big night?"

The old man's eyes flashed. "You think I'm too old to celebrate Halloween?"

"Of course not, I just—"

"These are my decorations," the old man shouted.

"Wow," Gray said. "Amazing."

The man tilted his head toward the ground. "Yeah."

"Have you had a lot of trick-or-treaters?"

The old man swallowed. "You're the first."

If he was disappointed, Gray could understand. "This isn't a popular neighborhood for Halloween, and most people don't go out when it's foggy."

"The fog ain't nothing," the man said. "It's the crazies. People don't feel safe."

"The crazies?"

"You see the news?" The man's voice went hoarse. "LA is falling apart."

"We don't get much time for news." Gray patted Mindy on the head, signaling for him to keep the conversation age-appropriate.

"The air makes people's brains go haywire. The wheelchair-crazy is just the beginning."

The murder on Lincoln was definitely not something Gray wanted Mindy to hear about. "We should get back." He turned toward the road.

The fog was closing in. The row of jack-o-lanterns faded off into the whiteness.

"Elmo's!" Mindy took Gray's hand and pulled ahead of him.

"Be careful," the man called after them.

As they crossed the street, Mindy tried to pull her hand free, so she could dig into her candy, but Gray held on. "Wait until we get inside."

"Are you afraid of the crazies?" she asked.

"No, that guy was just talking about people who like to party a lot, in places like Hollywood. We're safe here," he said, but he was afraid, afraid that if he let go of her little hand, she might vanish in the fog.

As they reached the driveway, the outline of their Craftsman house came into focus.

"When we get inside, I want you to put your candy away until tomorrow. Okay? Let's keep this trick-or-treating our secret for now." He knew Claire would eventually find out, but better to keep it from souring the night.

Inside, Mindy ran ahead toward the living room, clutching the bag to her chest.

"Let's put it in the kitchen," Gray said. But it was too late. Claire was on the couch with her phone, her damp hair pulled back. She looked from Mindy to Gray and clenched her jaw.

"Mindy," he said, "show your mother what you got from just one house."

"But, you said—"

"Never mind. Let's just show her."

Claire's eyes were a dangerous blue. Electricity swirled inside them. Mindy held the bag out, but Claire remained focused on Gray. "I can't believe you did that," she said. "I told you I'd be ready quick."

Mindy veered off to a corner, dumped her candy, and began sorting it.

Gray swallowed. He kneeled down and pretended to tie his shoe. "The car is packed if you're ready." He glanced up at her.

"I still have to dry my hair." She sighed, and then threw off the blanket and heaved herself up from the couch. "Screw it. Let's just go."

Ashley

The tires squealed as Ashley turned her Mercedes into the driveway. She gunned the engine and slammed the brakes, skidding to a stop just short of the gate. While waiting for Sammy to open it, she tapped the wheel with her thumbs. She felt his eyes on her, but if she turned toward the guard booth, if she so much as glanced in his direction, he'd smile that big friendly smile of his and yell her name like she was so awesome, and then she would break down.

She did not get the part. During lunch, the dickwad director had been texting the whole time while the producer droned on about how he'd clawed his way up from nothing into a Hollywood bigshot. She had gone in confident, heather-blue culottes and a satin crop top, but when she asked about the film, the producer suddenly noticed his food and the director looked up from his phone and began drilling her with random questions like, "What's your favorite childhood memory", to which she'd answered honestly: playing Marco Polo with her dad. But was that the wrong thing to say? Don hadn't told her what to say. She must have said something wrong, or maybe they had decided already, because after the check came, the producer said, "You don't want this role."

And the director, while sipping his espresso, basically left the conversation and went back into his phone.

The producer began to go on and on about what a great big favor they were doing her by casting someone else. She should have walked out right then, but for some reason she sat there like a little girl being lectured. He had another part in mind for her, of course. Still too early to talk about, of course. And when the time was right, his people would talk to her people. Of course.

But they both knew that call would never happen.

And now she had to shield her eyes, like her shades weren't enough to block the sun. The tears were coming. No stopping them now. The gate finally opened.

"Thank you, Sammy," she choked.

———

In her parlor, she collapsed on the couch and screamed into the pillow.

After a good long cry, she rolled onto her back. Haze-filtered light poured through the wall of windows. She called her dad.

It rang and rang. Finally, his personal assistant answered.

"Where's Dad?" Ashley asked.

"He said not to disturb him," his PA said in a terse whisper.

"Seriously? What's going on?"

"I was going to ask you. He skipped the interview this morning. And now everyone's panicked something's wrong with the new drug."

Weird. It wasn't like him. He wouldn't have scheduled an interview he didn't want to do. And yesterday, he had promised to call her back but didn't, and he always kept promises, at least up until now.

"Put him on."

"But—"

"Just put him on, okay. It's urgent."

Through the phone speaker came a timid knock and a muffled conversation. Then her dad picked up. "Ashley?"

Weird. He *always* called her "baby-love." Had he finally realized she was a grown woman?

"I didn't get the part." Her voice wavered. It echoed almost shrilly in the big, open room, and she wanted to cry all over again. But she was done with crying.

"Sorry to hear that. Is there something I can do?" He sounded a little off. Not the tone of his voice but the way he was speaking. Slower, and maybe… what happened to his self-confidence?

Maybe because this time there was nothing he could do? She wasn't about to let him executive produce again. Last time, all he kicked in was a couple mil for *Butcher Shop*, which was a waste because the script was so shitty, and then the reviews blamed her acting and accused her of sucking so bad that her dad had to buy the role for her, which was worse than not getting cast at all.

"So what happened with the artifact?"

"What artifact?"

"Are you kidding me?" Yesterday, he'd been all excited about finally getting his hands on some artifact he'd learned about from a cave painting in Mexico. He'd thought it would do something spectacular and had sworn her to secrecy without even explaining what the secret was.

"Ha ha. Yeah, the artifact. Guess I told you about it yesterday?"

"Are you feeling okay?"

"Yeah. Uh… No, actually I think I'm coming down with something."

"Well did it work?"

"What? The artifact? No, it doesn't do anything."

"Bummer. I guess you're too busy for dinner?"

"Yeah." He sounded almost relieved. "I am really busy here."

"So what happened? Today was the big launch for Endo—what was it again?"

"Right. They told me it launched this morning."

"Then why skip the *Good Morning Show*?"

"I had to take care of something."

Why was he being so vague? He must have realized that it was hard for her to care about InGenetic with so much tragedy in her own life. It was great that he was so passionate about his business and all, but... "So, I'm not your baby-love anymore?"

"What do you mean?"

"You called me Ashley. You never call me by my name."

"Oh. You'll always be my *baby,* love." He didn't sound too convinced. "But I should go."

They said goodbye, and he disconnected.

"Love you too, Dad," she said to the silence on the end of the line.

On the glass coffee table, Andrea had stacked the issues of *Vanity Fair* in some random order again. Ashley went ahead and ordered them chronologically. Then fanned them out in an arc so at least her cover issue from six months ago was still partially visible.

Then she called August, put her phone on speaker, and centered it in the arc of magazines on the table.

As it rang, she curled up on the couch.

"What's up, babe?" he said.

"Want to come over? I'll have Andrea cook us a special dinner."

"Can't do it. What time does she leave?"

"Seven. But I could ask her to stay if that's too early."

"Let's just get together later on tonight."

Ever since they had hooked up, last week, August had been avoiding her. She was almost positive it had something to do with the sex, which she hadn't really been ready for, but what choice did she have? Every heterosexual female in the world wanted August Grant, so why wouldn't she?

Now they were dating, apparently, at least according to the tabloids, where the buzz on August had gone high-key ever since the announcement that he would star in the nine-figure *Quantum-Man*. Dating August, real or fake, certainly boosted her popularity on social media, which helped her career. And she did kind of enjoy making women jealous.

"Want to talk dirty?" he asked. He asked every time, but she had no idea how to talk *dirty*. Raquel would know, of course, but that 'friend' was the last person she wanted to ask.

"Not right now."

Ashley agreed to meet him at the Standard later, which meant he would be there with his entourage, and she couldn't stand hanging around his entourage with all their in-jokes that she didn't care to get in on. So, she would have to bring Raquel. Better to bring her along than to deal with her badditude if she found out Ashley went without her anyway. And she'd find out pretty quickly.

Ashley couldn't go anywhere without someone tweeting her location.

She changed into a bikini and stopped in the kitchen on the way to the pool. Andrea was cleaning the counter. From her ponytail, a strand of hair fell across her cheek. She looked up and tucked the strand behind her ear. "Going to soak rays?"

Obvious question. Ashley spread her arms and held them up. And why did Andrea always have to sound so cheerful? Probably because she was thin as a toothpick.

"Can you make me a juice?" Ashley asked.

"Yes, I will do."

"Something with carrots. And bring my robe out."

Ashley opened a drawer in the counter and pulled out one of many vapes. She stepped out into the garden and inhaled a long drag. Exhaling as she walked to the pool, feeling lighter with each step.

She lay in a lounger facing the sun and closed her eyes. She couldn't keep running to dad every time something went wrong, like a kid. He might love her—she *knew* he loved her—but his work came first, always had. Instead of attention, he had provided her with this high-end lifestyle, which he must know was no substitute because almost every time they talked, he gave her more money.

What she needed was someone she could talk to. *Really* talk to. Someone who was there for her no matter what. But her wealth—technically, her dad's wealth—isolated her like a giant golden wall built between her and the real world. Not that she was alone, not physically. When you're Ashley York, everyone's your friend. *Friends*—more like leeches. Especially Raquel, but at least Raquel she could count on to be there.

Ashley texted her.

Ashley:
What's up bitch?

Raquel:
Yo bitch, how did it go?

Ashley never should have told Raquel about the lunch, but last night Raquel needled it out of her. She basically guessed that Ashley has something big the next day when she didn't want to party. No other reason not to party. If Raquel ever managed to attach herself to someone more famous, she would go public with every private detail that Ashley had ever revealed about herself. She had no doubt that Raquel would gladly shit all over her if it would raise her own celebrity status, which wouldn't exist at all without Ashley.

What Ashley needed was some dirt on Raquel, some kind of a bomb to hold over her. Pity that the only way to end their friendship was with blackmail.

Ashley:
Director was a dick.

Raquel:
Yeah, they're all 🥿🥿🥿

Raquel thought she was an expert because, as a kid, she was on Disney TV, but she hadn't landed anything since then, whereas just last month Ashley was in a music video, which of course, according to Raquel, didn't count because the video was only online.

Raquel:
What's happening tonight?

Ashley:
The Standard

She looked around for the vape pen. It was on the little table beside the lounger. She took another drag.

Raquel:
August going?

Ashley:
Later

Raquel:
TD. Warm up drinks at my place. 7?

There was the sound of sniffing, and then something licked Ashley's face. She sat up and screamed.

A black, furry thing lunged toward her crotch.

She dropped her phone and stood on the chair. A brawny, black dog of some kind slobbered all over her foot.

"So sorry, Ashley," Sammy shouted as he sprinted down the lawn toward the pool.

"Where did it come from?" Ashley yelled back. It didn't have a collar or anything.

Sammy jogged through the half-open gate. "I don't know." He made his way around the pool and grabbed the dog by the scruff and pulled it back from Ashley. "She sure likes you though."

As if in agreement, the dog wagged its tail, staring up at her with its big wet eyes.

"Well, I'm all covered with fur now. Get it out of here."

"Sure thing." His eyes flicked from the vape to her body and scanned up and down, which she would have been fine with if it wasn't for the dog fur on her leg. She brushed it off, but there was still the slobber on her face. She needed to wash.

"So, did you get the part?" Sammy asked.

Damn it, who hadn't she told? Tears welled up in her eyes again. She blinked them away but there would be no holding them back if she told him how they didn't even give her a chance. "Don't know yet."

"My fingers are crossed for you, Ashley." He held up the hand not holding the dog to show that indeed his fingers were crossed. "You deserve it."

On the chair, Ashley's phone buzzed. She grabbed it and glanced at the screen. Another text from Raquel. This one demanding she commit to the pre-drinks at seven.

Ashley:
I was just nearly mauled by a dog.

Raquel:
OMG!!! Seriously?

Ashley:
I was laying out by the pool and it got in somehow. Thank god for Sammy.

Raquel:
When you going to bone him?

As Sammy ushered the dog through the gate, his arm muscles bulged beneath the tight shirt of his security uniform. The white fabric looked good against his dark skin, and she liked the way he hadn't told her that the dog was no big deal. If there was anyone genuine in her life besides her dad, it was Sammy. And, if she was honest with herself, she would love to bone him. But...

Ashley.
I'm with August now, biatch.

Raquel:
As if that's exclusive.

Ashley:
What are you talking about?

Raquel:
Are you two seriously dating?

Ashley:
You jealous?

Raquel:
True dat!

But what if Raquel actually knew something? She did have other sources of gossip besides Ashley. If it came out that August was seeing someone on the side while publicly dating Ashley, it would look bad for her image, which could set her back years from being cast in a serious role. So now she had to go to Raquel's for the stupid "pre-drinks" she didn't want to make sure Raquel didn't really know anything about August.

———

Streaks of white light. And red. So many lights. And Ashley can't focus on any of them. Hollywood Boulevard slides past in a blur. They're in the backseat, and Raquel is leaning forward, saying something about Beyonce and Jay Z to her driver, Raul.

"I'm too wasted," Ashley says.

But Raquel can't seem to hear her.

How many cosmos had she had? Too many. She'd said it was too many, but Raquel kept pushing for more. And there were the hash cookies, which Raquel insisted they try even though Ashley was already blasted when she got to Raquel's, and, of course, it had turned out that Raquel didn't really know anything about August. Just the same pop-news gossip Ashley has already heard. Trash news. That's what it is. No reason to believe what they say about August given all the shit they make up about her. And why does she care if he's seeing other women? Are they even dating? Dating August Grant might be great for her image and all, but she doesn't really like the way she feels around him.

Right now, what she wants—what she *needs*—is to go home and sleep. She leans her head against the window. The car comes to a stop, but the street keeps on moving. They're at the front entrance of the Standard. Cameras swarm toward the car.

"God, they're like flies!" Raquel opens her door to the barrage of flashes. She lasciviously extends her legs from the car and rolls her shoulders back.

"You called them," Ashley says.

"I would never." Raquel glances back toward Ashley with an expression of hurt that, even in Ashley's delirious state, looks like bad acting. The corner of Raquel's lip twists upward. She would and, in fact, had, and this wasn't the first time she'd broadcast their whereabouts to the paparazzi.

Raquel is out of the car now, and Raul holds the door for Ashley. As she slides across the seat, the car sways beneath her like a boat in a storm-tossed sea. She catches herself on the headrest.

Outside, Raquel is on the sidewalk, basking in the dizzying array of flashes, adjusting her posture, obviously getting off on the attention.

Ashley tries to focus, tries to find an anchor in the cacophony of light, but even Raul's face is a blur. She swings her leg out toward the curb. Raul extends a hand to her. "Oh my god," someone screams. Gasps. "Ashley!" Her name is repeated again and again. They're all coming at her—the cameras and the phones—and in that instant she remembers her sexy Catgirl costume that she never changed into because Raquel insisted she looked amazing in the sweater dress, and how, after all the cosmos, Ashley hadn't felt like changing anyway so she'd just taken off her underwear, because the dress showed panty lines—the dress that was now up to her waist with her legs spread for all of Hollywood Boulevard, and nothing on underneath.

The flashes accelerate into a frenzy as the cameras close in like predators to a fresh kill. Ashley just wants to curl up in a ball and disappear.

Raul shouts and body-blocks paparazzi, shoving them back.

Raquel takes Ashley's hand, smiling as if it's a performance. That's really all it is, Ashley decides: a performance.

She swings her other leg out of the car, pulls down the dress, bats her eyes and smiles her best coy smile.

Using Raquel's arm for support, Ashley attempts to strut, but she can feel how awkward it looks. Vodka and sling backs—bad combination. At least Raquel is also walking stiffly with her leather fuck-me boots zipped up over her knees. Between the top of the boots and a nearly nonexistent skirt, an indecent expanse of thigh jiggles with each step—practically modest though, compared to what Ashley just exposed.

As they reach the bouncer dressed in black, who holds aside the velvet rope, the shouts of Ashley's name grow desperate. They want to see her face, to photograph her shame for all the world to see, and if she doesn't turn, they'll just show her from behind. So, she stops. She puts on a smile. Aping Lady Gaga at the Grammys, she turns her more photogenic left side toward the cameras and waves.

In the lobby, another bouncer ushers them past the long line of people in costumes waiting to get in. There's a Shrek and a group of *Star Wars* geeks, but mostly it's the Avengers, whose names Ashley can't remember.

The bouncer uses the card on his lanyard to open the VIP elevator and helps them inside. Ashley doesn't stop smiling until the metal doors close and it's just her and Raquel. She leans against the back wall and lets her eyes close.

"Crazy biatch!" Raquel says. "You should have told me you were free-balling it!"

"I—" Ashley hoists her lids back up so she can stare at Raquel, who kept pushing the cosmos. *Just one more*, she kept saying, when she knew Ashley was well past her limit. Such that now the elevator seems to be spinning off its axis as it whirls up to the club. She just wants to go home and pretend it never happened. *But no.* No point in telling Raquel it was an accident. No point in saying anything when it takes so much effort just to stand here and not be sick.

Raquel, admiring her reflection in the doors, drapes her hair back over her bare shoulders. She pulls a strand around her cheek, carefully arranging it so it dangles from her collarbone to her cleavage. She pushes her breasts together. "They better show my picture too."

Claire Wilson

If Claire had known Elmo's would be this crowded, she would have insisted on somewhere else. Or they would have just stayed home and ordered take out, like Gray suggested. She's too tired to be sitting here jostled by the ocean of people on their way to the bathroom. If not for that and the pots clattering in the open kitchen, she could fall asleep right here in her chair.

Claire stifles a yawn, but her eyes stay closed, the darkness tugging her down.

How? How is it possible she can feel so sleepy here yet never in her bedroom?

But truth is, she can't sleep anywhere. She knows that. It's the insomnia—this feeling that sleep always feels just a moment away and yet remains always out of reach.

Every night she collapses into bed, sleep crashing over her like a wave, and then it recedes, leaving her lying there in the darkness, waiting just a little longer before checking the time, just a little longer. Useless.

She has tried it all. Melatonin and magnesium, yoga and meditation. Six months ago, she'd tried pills, only to end up addicted with dizziness and dry-mouth, and still...terrible sleep.

Life feels far away, like nothing can touch her and she can touch nothing. Each day more tiring than the last.

"You okay?" Gray asks.

Claire opens her eyes. But he's not looking at her; he's watching the bar.

If she had slept, she might enjoy the costumes, the people out to see and be seen. Her family are the only ones in the restaurant not dressed for Halloween. Probably why the hostess stuffed them back here near the bathrooms where Gray, of course, said the table was fine. And she is too tired to care.

The bathroom door swings open. A heavy man in a Superman T-shirt two sizes too small bursts through. The door is going to hit Tyler, so obliviously content in his booster seat it's almost cute. Claire stands to block the door...

too late.

The door catches two inches from Tyler and retracts. Heavyset Superman trods off without noticing, trailing a stench of industrial soap.

Gray slumps, as if embarrassed by Claire's reaction rather than concerned. His eyes dart to the adjacent table. The couple pretends not to notice, but of course they did. The tables are practically touching.

If Claire wasn't so tired, maybe she'd have seen the door was no danger.

"Daddy, look." Mindy shows Gray the scribble she made on the paper tablecloth.

"That's great," he says. "A horse."

"No, silly. It's a unicorn."

Tyler snivels. Not bad yet, but he'll be wailing soon if someone doesn't hold him.

Gray grabs a purple crayon. "Want me to draw him some friends?"

"Draw Piglet." Mindy assigns him a small circle to draw in.

Claire, left to deal with Tyler, unstraps him from the booster seat. He coughs and starts to cry.

How did I get here? She bounces him in her lap.

She loves him, of course she does, and Mindy too, but when she was working, she slept so much better. She actually *slept*. The need for constant attention drains her, like she knew it would, and yet still she had let Gray persuade her to have kids. His relentless intensity, which had attracted her at first, now exhausts her. Once he latches onto an idea, she might as well just agree to it instead of fighting and fighting, only to end up agreeing anyway.

When they met in college, she'd no idea what she wanted, and Gray had a head full of dreams. He possessed this passion for life that seemed to be missing in her, and the way he tried so hard to reach through all the barriers she constructed, the way he relentlessly pursued her, made her feel…it made her *feel*. Like him, believing she was more than she was made her a better person, bigger somehow, more alive.

She should have dated other boys. Margo, her roommate, drew them in one after another with the way she let them talk about themselves. She was outgoing, easy to be around. Why had Claire judged her so harshly for just trying to discover what she wanted?

Until Gray came along, no one had showed interest in Claire, so how was she supposed to know how far away he was from what she wanted? Or if she even wanted to be with anyone at all? But now Gray is all she has. It was just too much effort to keep in touch with Margo and everyone else and their perfect lives on Facebook. Maybe if she wasn't so exhausted all the time she could post some cute photos of Tyler and Mindy.

A waitress dressed like Princess Leia plops jars of water on the table. "What can I get for you?"

"We haven't had time to look at the menu," Claire says.

"Dewar's. Neat," Gray says with the usual longing in his eyes. And already Claire can hear the whiskey in his voice.

Every time the waitress returns, he'll order another, until it's finally time to go, and then Claire will have to drive. Doesn't matter that she's too tired. He just assumes she'll drive without asking, like he always does. Tossing them back, while his mood inflates beyond all reason, until talking to him is like staring straight into the sun. And the more he drinks, the more his intense energy focuses on her, the more he tries to pry something out from a place inside her where there's nothing, only exhaustion.

Tyler's getting fussy again and he'll start bawling soon if she doesn't do something.

"So," Gray says with that look in his eyes, his volcano of thoughts about to spew.

Can he not hear Tyler?

"Not now, Gray." She digs around in the bag of baby supplies, finds the bottle and gives it to Tyler. As he suckles the rubber nipple, gazing up into her face, his sobbing subsides. Bad idea to feed him this late past his bedtime. He'll be cranky tomorrow.

Claire checks her phone. Forgetting again that the battery had died. She opens the menu. Still the same as last time she looked. Is she even hungry? Insomnia makes her feel disconnected from her own body, like she's puppeteering it from some great distance away, disconnected. Unable to think. And with Gray watching her every move, obviously not going to leave her alone about whatever is on his mind.

"What?"

Gray runs his fingers through his hair. "I just...I wanted..." He glances toward the waitress who still hasn't brought him his booze.

"Just spit it out already."

He plants his hands on the table, inhales, and glances at the menu. "How about we split the bisque?"

Really? That's it? She hates bisque. He knows she hates bisque. She picks up the menu and holds it in front of his gaze. She's not even hungry. But it doesn't matter; she still has to sit here, take care of Tyler, and watch Gray drink.

Gray's Dream

After they came home from dinner, Gray tucked Mindy into bed and read her the story of her choosing, *Where the Wild Things Are*. After he finished, she insisted he read it again. Halfway through, her eyes were closed, so he tested if she was awake by changing the story. "And Prince Spinach parachuted down, and the wild things played twelve string guitars in homage to their new king—"

"Daddy, you're reading it wrong."

He squinted at the page as if in disbelief, and tried not to smile but couldn't help himself.

"And the wild things roared their terrible roars!" she said.

By the third read, her breathing was soft and regular with the intervals of sleep. He closed the book. He turned out the light and stood in the doorway and watched her sleeping beneath the moons and stars projected onto the ceiling from her nightlight. In her little bed, she looked bigger than she was, and he felt wistful, wishing her childhood could go on forever.

He checked the nursery and found Tyler in his crib, sound asleep, beneath his spinning mobile of smiley flowers.

The sound of the TV seeping down the hallway meant Claire was on the couch. He went into the kitchen and closed the door.

He was still stuffed from Elmo's yet craved something more. Something with flavor. He opened the pantry and stared at the cans, the jars, and the bags of chips. He opened a bag of BBQ chips and stuffed three into his mouth and chewed them into a tasteless sludge. Not food.

What he wanted was an escape. A drink. And why not? The two drinks at dinner were nothing. The second one he hadn't enjoyed at all, what with Claire glowering, ratcheting up the intensity with his every sip, and if he'd tried to explain how the trendy thick glasses made the stingy pours look like more than they were, she would have said he was an alcoholic.

His temple throbbed. It would be a full-on migraine if he didn't have a nightcap, just a few swallows to wash him into the sweet release of sleep.

He ducked into the garage for a quick round of the Dewar's he kept on the workbench by his easel. For the most part, the garage was unusable space thanks to all the junk he and Claire were too lazy to get rid of. Bins and boxes filled the shelves along the walls as well as the parking area, where among the boxes stood a foosball table and a pair of bikes that hadn't been ridden since college. A narrow path, which tonight was blocked with a laundry basket, led from the kitchen door to the workbench by the outer door. Beside the workbench, Gray had hollowed out a cubby for Tyler's playpen and his easel.

The easel was covered with a white cloth, which he considered removing. But the half-finished landscape would fall so short of his expectations for the image that he yearned to paint—that tomorrow he *would* paint—but tonight was too depressing to consider. At least if he left it covered, he could pretend the painting looked like he imagined. Because there was still time.

He didn't want to drink. Not really. Alcohol never gave him the release that he yearned for—that he got from painting, each stroke of color on canvas. That feeling of flow, the current of inspiration.

The feeling that never lasted. It left sometimes as quickly as it came. And when it wouldn't come back, he drank.

But being drunk was no better than being sober. In truth, it was worse. If he could drink successfully then his meaningless job wouldn't matter. He could endure another year, and if he could do another year then he could do five. He could make it until Mindy and Tyler went to college, and then what difference would it make?

He took a long pull of the Dewar's.

He swallowed until his throat burned, until he felt like he would choke or vomit or both. He slammed the bottle down on the workbench and tightened the lid. On the way to the kitchen, he stumbled over the laundry basket, caught himself on the door. He glanced back over his shoulder at the half-finished painting on the easel he was afraid to uncover and then turned out the light.

Charlie Streeter

Earlier that night, at Charlie's daughter's house, after eating four bags of the disgusting skittles, he brushes his teeth in the dark. Outside the bathroom window, the street is completely devoid of trick-or-treaters. Not a sign of life. A porch light illuminates the empty drive across the street. That dolt with the cute little princess packed her up in the minivan along with his wife and their baby, and they all went out somewhere, when anyone who knows anything knows better than to go out on Halloween.

Back in Charlie's neighborhood in Fullerton, they close down the street for Halloween because the hordes of trick-or-treaters, who drive in from who-knows-where, can't be bothered to walk in an orderly manner along the side of the road. The twenty pounds of candy he bought for tonight would have gone in an hour in Fullerton. *What am I going to do with it all now?* Seems like Lynda could have at least mentioned that Silver Lake doesn't give a damn about Halloween before she and her husband left him watching their house for three months.

He stands on the front stoop looking down the hill. No one else is coming. He bends down carefully—the last thing he needs is to lock up his back again—and unplugs the strings of orange lights on the house and the hedge. The jack-o-lanterns, he decides, can just burn themselves out. Not worth his bending over to turn them off one by one. He's not even sure he can. Why had he wasted his money paying the landscaper to put up decorations? Who was he trying to impress? Not the slouchy dolt from across the street. His daughter was cute enough, but she saw only the candy.

Charlie shuts the door and stands in the foyer. The emptiness of the house rings in his ears. He needs to get out, go somewhere, but he can't drive, not with his back hurting worse than ever. How did he end up like this? In Vietnam, he'd humped the heaviest pack in the squad. In addition to all his own gear, including a canteen and spare boots made from alligator skin, he carried an M79, extra grenades, and the praise of his men. They called him

Hulk, Hulk, Hulk.

He needs one more Oxycontin. Then he'll quit. But how can he quit if his back won't stop aching?

———

He drives slowly toward the 101 freeway. Headlights appear behind him, and he pulls over to let the vehicle pass. Normally he spends his afternoons people watching in Grand Park, but today he'd wasted time getting ready for the trick-or-treaters who didn't come, and now he feels off. What good are routines if you don't stick to them?

Of course, anyone who knows anything knows better than to drive downtown on Halloween, where it's overrun with crazies, but someone has to keep an eye out. Keep the crazies in check. In addition to the typical homeless crazies who talk to their imaginations, tonight there will be all kinds of young crazies who only come out on Halloween, using it as an excuse to prance around in next to nothing, all drunk or high or who knows what.

He should go to Santa Monica Boulevard, the height of debauchery, where —if he believes the *LA Weekly*—the most outlandish crazies parade the street. But there won't be parking. Anyone with a lick of sense would know that. Better to stick with Grand Park, stick to the familiar, on a night like tonight.

There goes his exit. Too late to take it.

Lynda had tried to get him a smartphone, but he wouldn't fall for it. He is not about to become another moron who can't even take a crap if his phone doesn't say so. "If you won't get a smartphone, at least get a navigator," she had said.

But he wouldn't be nervous at all if it wasn't dark out. He's not used to driving at night.

He takes the next exit and, right away, finds himself among the crazies. The homeless ones camped under the overpass and all along the sidewalk. They stare at him funny. And he stares back. As he rolls up to a dimly lit T intersection, one of the more deranged crazies yells at his car.

Charlie scans from right to left, unsure which way to turn. At the bottom of the hill is a building with slits for windows: a jail.

Movement.

In front of the jail, a derelict warehouse casts a shadow on the street, and within that shadow the figure is almost hidden.

It's a crazy alright, and he's striding up the hill...toward Charlie's car. Did he escape from the jail? The bums huddled on the sidewalk go still in their blankets as if petrified.

Past the warehouse, he emerges into the dim beam of a streetlight. Tan shirt. Olive pants. The star of a sheriff. Charlie almost laughs with relief. He'll ask this officer for directions the old-fashioned way. Not like the millennials who would rather look at their phones than talk to anyone.

Still, he waits in his car.

Ten yards away from him, a bum hunched in blankets climbs out of the shadows toward the officer. Charlie lowers his window. The bum murmurs garbled nonsense at the officer, probably his deranged way of begging for money. The officer makes a wide arc around him, but the bum lunges toward him, trying to get his attention.

The officer jerks back as if stung. He snarls, unholsters his weapon, and swings it with demented determination. With the butt of the gun, he clubs the bum in the head.

He drops to the ground. Drops his blankets. Raises his arms in defense. The crazy officer speaks to the bum, too softly for Charlie to hear. The bum struggles to his feet and hobbles into the road in front of Charlie's car.

Through the window, Charlie locks eyes with the crazy officer. He strolls toward Charlie's car as if nothing happened at all, as if he is a perfectly safe, upstanding officer of the law, smiling, like Charlie could be his new best friend. Mucus runs from his nose into his mustache. His eyes are opened wide, wide open. Charlie has never in his whole life seen anyone crazier than this officer, who is holding his gun not quite pointed at Charlie. But a threat, no doubt about that.

Not much more than a step away, he reaches for the door, which is, of course, locked, but the window is down. The officer raises his gun.

Charlie slams the gas and spins the wheel right, turning uphill and away from the crazy officer.

Thump.

Charlie rips his gaze from the officer just in time to see the bum collapse on his front fender and slide down out of view. Why was he still in the road?

Charlie should stop, should call 911, but the mirror shows the officer is still approaching, undaunted.

He slams into reverse. In front of his car, the bum lies in the street, in a heap just like Private Birdsong back in 'Nam, when Charlie kicked the tripwire which he should have seen—*would* have seen, if he wasn't adjusting his fucking pack.

The rear window shatters. The clap of gunpowder rattles his chest—mortar-fire from the brush—and he shoves the car into drive.

His tires squeal. He clenches his teeth so hard they almost shatter. The bum, lying on the blacktop, flails an arm. As the tires gain traction, Charlie fish tails around him.

He speeds up the hill. The sound of gunfire ricochets all around him.

He speeds toward the skyscrapers looming behind the warehouses. Silver Lake is north—everyone knows that—but which way is north? If not for the crazy officer shooting at him, he might have some idea where he was.

He stops at an intersection. Beside him, an LAPD cruiser eases to a stop at the light. Charlie looks straight ahead. *Just an old man in a Taurus. No need to look any closer. No need to notice the shot out rear window or the dented front fender. Look ahead. Look at the crazy costumes in the crosswalk, crazy kids hardly wearing anything aside from makeup and spandex.*

Was that crazy who shot at him a rogue officer? They're probably all in cahoots. Regardless, no one will believe Charlie. Of course, if he had one of those damn smart phones people are always gazing into and missing the world around them, he could have filmed the crazy officer bludgeoning the bum. But who could he show it to? They're all crazies. They're all in on it. And now, they're probably all after him.

When the light turns green, he turns right, away from the copper beside him. He turns and turns again, until he sees a sign for the freeway.

As he speeds up the on-ramp, cold air blasts through the shattered rear window. What if that officer got his license plate? There was plenty enough time for a good look—if the officer had half a brain in his crazy head.

Fortunately, Charlie's car is still registered to his old address in Fullerton. Good luck finding him there. But still, with a busted window and dented fender, he might as well paint a target on his car.

Charlie only hopes that the crazy has forgotten his face, with the way his eyes were gaping open like they weren't seeing Charlie at all, and that mucus running into his mustache, which he did not wipe away.

Worse was the bum, who Charlie had left in a heap on the black top. His arm flailing uselessly. Helpless and injured, with the crazy, and his gun.

But what else could Charlie have done?

He'll have to hide his car. He'll park it in the garage when he gets back, which means he'll have to move Lynda's car to the curb. Hopefully, the neighbors won't ask why her car is parked on the street instead of his. The mom won't even notice. She's always staring into her phone while pushing the stroller when she should be watching for traffic. But what about the slouchy dolt—he might think it's suspicious. And his little girl: she might point it out. She's a smart one, that little girl.

To switch out Lynda's car, Charlie will have to find the keys. After managing three weeks alone in the house without snooping, the thought of searching their bedroom turns his stomach in a knot. But what choice does he have?

He'll just poke around until he finds the car keys and that will be it.

But then what if he can't stop himself? What if once he starts looking, with nothing but time on his hands and nowhere to go until the heat dies down, he ends up going through everything? Lynda and her husband seem ordinary enough, but everyone has something to hide. Charlie does. Charlie has lots to hide. His Oxycontin, for one thing. His habit out of control, and now… Now, Charlie had hit a man and left him to die in the road.

Saul Versus the Armenian

Earlier, when Saul had checked his watch at 5:53 PM, Saroyan was still sitting placidly behind the two-way mirror in the box. This was interview suite three, which had the broken chair that usually made perps squirm, but not Saroyan. He just sat there. His gray hair was disheveled. He had sallow skin, jowls that sagged down a double chin. A broad shelf of brow over pure black eyes too small for his head.

Saul jacked up the heat to ninety-five.

Behind the glass, Saroyan's lips curled. He hadn't requested a lawyer. Not even a phone call. His one and only demand had been to have the blood wiped from his face. Saul had obliged, if only to lighten things up with Hernandez, which had basically worked. He'd produced a handkerchief with a wave of his hand and a snap, and she half-snorted, half-laughed.

But Saroyan had said nothing more, and he was still just sitting there, staring straight ahead.

Saul's stomach twisted. Something worse than hunger.

Hernandez entered the observation room and stood beside him. "Think he's ready?"

"Hard to say." Saul tilted his head. Saroyan hadn't even asked for water.

She started the video camera. "Let's give it a shot."

Guess it's her call, he thought, since it seemed like Lieutenant Levy had decided to make her the lead investigator without telling him. Probably hadn't told Hernandez yet, either. She would have said something by now.

"In a hurry to get home?" He regretted the question even as he asked it, the bitterness that leached into his voice. But it was a double standard. How could Hernandez give him a hard time for a long lunch at the Castle when four days out of five she left early?

"It's Halloween," she said.

Saul looked away. He should apologize. After all, she had a son to go home to. The Castle was all about him.

He nodded toward the break room next door. "Coffee?"

"That's more like sludge than coffee," she said. "I'll meet you in there."

She wasn't kidding about the coffee. It was a no-name variety, too low-end to be sold in stores, that the city bought on the cheap. It tended to burn in the pot and was almost undrinkable. But it contained caffeine and it did sort of smell like coffee, which was sometimes enough to tempt a perp.

In the break room, Saul triple-stacked wax paper cups. Poured in the black sludge. Carried it to the box.

The heat hit him like a punch in the gut. He gulped at the stale air and wedged himself between the table and the wall across from Saroyan. Saul sat and sipped the coffee. Bitter. But he pretended to enjoy it.

Saroyan stared blankly. The cans in the ceiling cast harsh light on his face. He did not blink.

Hernandez came in. Took the seat beside Saul and crossed her arms.

"Mr. Saroyan," Saul said. "Mind if I call you Edward?"

"I am called Wayob," Saroyan said. His face remained stolid.

"Way-ob. Is that spelled w-a-y-o-b?" Saul wrote it down.

"In your language, I suppose."

"Okay, Wayob, I'm Detective Parker and this is my partner, Detective Hernandez."

Wayob pressed his lips together, as though he was trying to frown but the corners of his mouth twisted toward a smirk.

"You don't need us to tell you," Saul continued, "you're in a lot of trouble here, Wayob, but maybe we can help. What happened, from your point of view?"

"You will not believe me."

"We've got an eyewitnesses, and we've got the whole thing on video," Hernandez said, "so you'd better give us something if you want to see daylight again."

Wayob leaned back in his chair and stretched his mouth far too wide for a genuine smile, like a child impersonating a cartoon.

Saul would have laughed if not for the obvious hatred—and pain—welling in his dark eyes. "We know there's more to it," Saul said. "There are always two sides."

"There can be only one truth," Wayob said, and he was right about that. If they could lock him into a confession, it would make the case even tighter.

"I agree," Saul said. "If he provoked you, if he was bullying you, that's a form of abuse you know. You can prove it with a lie-detector test. It will help your case."

Wayob's attempted smile vanished, his face hollowed. "You cannot help me. I know of your primitive technology." He enunciated the last part with an air of disgust.

The statement surprised Saul. "You're aware of something better?"

"The Ancient Mayans had a magnet, which, held next to your head, would tell for sure if you were lying."

"Sounds like magic." *Or mindless babble*, he thought, *but at least he's talking.*

"No. It was real," Wayob said bitterly, almost shouting. "Those abominable priests isolated the engineers so they could claim to have the power of gods."

"How do you know?"

Wayob slumped. The energy drained from his voice. "I was there."

"I thought you were Armenian," Saul said.

"I am not the man you see before you."

"Okay…, so who are you?"

"I am Wayob. This I told you."

"Right."

They were wasting time. Nothing that Saroyan, Wayob, or whoever he thought he was said made any sense, unless this was an act for an insanity-plea-defense. Regardless of what the justice system said, Wayob was responsible for his actions. He would not get off with insanity, not if Saul could help it.

"Let me guess," Hernandez said. "You were jealous Luna could walk, so you decided to whack him."

Wayob laughed bitterly. "You understand nothing."

"You won't be laughing in prison," Hernandez said. "Doesn't matter you're in a wheelchair, just makes you easier to rape."

Wayob looked from Hernandez to Saul. "You cannot keep me here."

"Oh no?" Hernandez asked. She had this way of pouncing in interviews then shrugging it off as if it were nothing. "Want to call a lawyer? Go ahead. I'll get you a phone."

"You are wasting my time."

"Oh," she said. "So, you've got somewhere else to be?"

He slammed the cuffs on the lacquered mahogany and turned his palms up. "Release me now or I shall take my revenge."

Since good cop, bad cop seemed to have had no effect so far, Saul changed tactics. He slid the two extra cups off his coffee. Turned them upside down on the table. He fished a quarter from his pocket. Showed it to Wayob. Set it on the table between the cups.

"Wayob, I'll make it easy. Guess which cup the quarter is under, and you're free to go. Hell, I'll even drive you anywhere you want to go."

"*Barker!*" Hernandez said.

If he believes he can roll out of here, then he really is crazy, Saul thought, hoping Hernandez was more playing bad cop than angry.

Saul placed a cup over the quarter and began sliding them on the table in slow circular motions, moving one in front of the other. Hernandez shook her head.

Saul stopped and presented the cups to Wayob.

"I know it is there." Wayob pointed to the cup on Saul's left.

Saul nodded. "So where do you want to go?"

"East." He glowered at Saul. "I shall go on my own."

"Oh?" Saul lifted the cup…. It was empty.

Wayob lunged his cuffed hands toward the other cup, but it was out of his reach. He leaned back in the broken chair and tried to straighten his back. "A cheap trick."

"Perhaps." Saul restacked the cups under his coffee.

The two men stared at each other. Saul let the silence hang there like a void that must be filled.

"Release my hands," Wayob said. "I shall show you what I can do."

"I think we've seen enough." The thought of Luna's pulverized face made his stomach tighten.

The heat was unbearable, perspiration had wicked through the pits of Saul's shirt, and yet Wayob's skin was dry, his face ashen in the can lights.

"You have not seen anything yet."

Saul barely registered the threat. He was used to them. "Why?"

"Why what?" Wayob asked.

"Why kill Luis Luna?"

Wayob's brows furrowed and his eyes squeezed shut. His mask had slipped away, and behind it was sadness and fear. Maybe even regret. It looked genuine.

"I had no choice." His chin trembled. "I had to kill him or suffer a fate worse than death."

Saul hoped the video was still recording. *Keep him talking.* "He threatened you?"

Wayob studied his hands as if they were new to him. He looked up and straightened in the chair. "He set me free."

"Sounds terrible," Hernandez said.

Saul glanced at her. *Let him do the talking.*

She got it. They waited for Wayob to fill the silence.

His bleak eyes showed no emotion.

"Come closer." He attempted a smug grin. "I shall give you a taste."

"From where I sit," Hernandez said, "looks like you're the one who gets a *taste*, and a whole lot more, once you're in prison."

Wayob scowled. "You cannot contain me."

"How did you know Luna?" Saul interrupted, hoping to catch him off balance.

"I can become anyone, even you, Detective Parker, or your pretty assistant."

Hernandez crossed her arms and set her jaw. The comment seemed to bother her but he had heard her called worse.

"Don't piss us off," Saul said. "We don't have time for games."

"And here I thought you were the sort of man who enjoys tricks."

"Murder is no trick."

"No," Wayob growled. "It is not. I do not do tricks."

Saul stood and placed his hands on the table, exposing his sweat-soaked pits as he leaned toward Wayob, who still gave no indication he'd noticed the excessive heat.

Saul stared into those beady eyes that seemed to possess an energy all of their own. His massive brows were slack, his face empty, no longer any trace of the emotion that had flickered across it when Saul mentioned murder. As if Wayob felt nothing now and never would.

Hernandez scraped her chair back and went to the door. "Let him cook, Parker. He's useless."

Wayob shrugged, as though he could snap his fingers and disappear into the night.

Hernandez was right. No sense in humoring him. They should investigate Luna. A connection between him and Wayob could prove premeditation, making an insanity defense all but impossible.

"You cannot keep me here." Wayob stared at Saul with no tells, no sign of lying. Could he be so delusional?

Saul squeezed past Hernandez out the door.

"You shall see, Parker. You shall see," Wayob shouted.

Hernandez pulled the door shut behind him, and he turned to face her. She rolled her eyes. "We've got a psychopath who beat someone to death—from a wheelchair, no less, and of course, you entertain him with magic."

"At least I got something."

"You got a lot of bullshit. That's what you got."

"Maybe."

Her shock of white fell across her eye. She shoved it back. "What if he'd guessed the right cup?"

Not possible. But he didn't say it. Already he regretted getting defensive; this was Hernandez. "We should do the death notification." It was the last thing he wanted to do, but talking to Luna's next of kin was their best hope of finding a connection.

"His license is an old address," she said. "He left no forwarding."

"We'll find him. He had to live somewhere."

Hernandez turned abruptly toward the elevators. Was it really the coin trick? He knew she liked magic, which he found even more attractive than her physical appearance. And on top of that, she had brains. She had the whole package. And his gut fluttered every time he saw her.

He entered the observation room to check the recording.

Wayob Versus Bruce

The guards had issued Wayob a wheelchair, if one could call it that. Looks more like a lawn chair fused onto a shopping cart. He cannot reach the tiny wheels. Does not matter. He shall not be here long. Not like this. Fucking Parker. Thinks he can lock Wayob in a prison, but he shall see. He shall see. They roll Wayob like a sheep to slaughter into a dormitory cell with endless rows of sagging bunks.

Wayob can work with this. These men in ragged orange scrubs he can understand. They are like animals, malicious eyes like lions ready to pounce.

"How about a hand?" Wayob shouts.

They stay back. *Perfect.* Let an alpha make his move. Just one brave, foolish alpha is what Wayob needs. But first, he needs leverage.

He reaches for the nearest bunk. Leaning forward, almost falling out of the chair, he manages to reach the chipped-green iron frame.

"That's Bruce's bunk," says a shirtless man with ribs protruding from his tattooed chest.

"Not anymore," Wayob says. He heaves himself out of the chair, trying uselessly to kick his immobile legs.

The shirtless man scurries away, down the corridor of beds.

Wayob's arms are strong at least, strong enough to lift his potbelly from the chair to the bottom bunk. But as he leans forward and pulls himself from the chair, it rolls out from under him. He must flounder himself onto the bed.

Exhausted, he lays face down to catch his breath.

"De-tec-tive Par-ker," he laughs. Wayob shall show him a trick, a real trick. Once he gets out of here. Once he finds Abuela Luna.

His blood boils at the thought of the old woman who somehow resisted setting him free for so many decades. So much agonizing time spent focusing his mind on her mind and yet he was unable to tempt her. He screams with rage.

The other inmates gather to watch, closing in on him. They should be afraid, and soon they shall be. Soon Wayob shall have his hands around Abuela's wrinkled weak neck. He shall look into her eyes as her life drains away, and she shall know it is her own weakness that has killed her, killed her whole family.

Wayob sits up and locks his arm around the metal bar of the bed frame to anchor himself against whoever approaches first—probably this 'Bruce' who the shirtless, skeletal man went to inform of Wayob's trespass. All that matters is to overcome Bruce before this crippled body Wayob is controlling becomes damaged beyond all usefulness. He must win. Time is running out. Luna's weakness will not last.

Wayob must free himself from this prison, and this time he shall have a good pair of legs, a strong vessel.

"Hey, pal, that's my bunk." A bull-chested man, also shirtless, marches toward him. His scalp is shaved. SIN tattooed across his forehead in bold black letters.

"You must be Bruce." All that matters is the next ten seconds. Wayob shall fight and fight to win.

"Only friends call me Bruce."

"So what shall I call you then? Shit-face?" *Come closer.*

Bruce takes a step forward. "Kiss my feet and maybe I'll pretend you didn't say that."

"This is not your bunk anymore, Brucie-Bruce-Bruce-shitty-Bruce. You sleep on the floor now."

Closer.

"Over my dead body, motherfucker."

"Not dead, just unconscious," Wayob says from his perch on the bottom bunk.

Bruce rushes forward, leaning down to punch him, and Wayob turns his head to absorb the blow. Anchoring himself with an elbow around the bed frame, he reaches down and scoops Bruce's legs out from under him.

Bruce falls backward onto the concrete and lands with his hands behind his back. Wayob launches down onto him and locks an arm around his thick, filthy neck. He slams his head into the man's nose.

Bruce presses a hand to his nose, blood gushing between his fingers. "Motherfucker!" He punches Wayob in the ribs. Then head butts, his skull hard as a boulder.

Wayob ignores the pain and Bruce's mucky blood. He does not listen to ringing in his ears. He must fight through the blackness narrowing his peripheral vision. He forces his eyes to focus on the bloody mess of Bruce's face. Must stay conscious.

The other prisoners around them climb up on the beds, shouting, "Fight, fight, fight."

Bruce shoves Wayob off toward the bed and tries to get up.

All or nothing. Wayob grabs onto his awful head. Wayob forces his torso up. Then, with all the weight of his upper body, he shoves Bruce's head into a of the bed frame.

.. .... no way to catch himself, Wayob face plants into the concrete floor beside Bruce, who has fallen limp, unconscious or dead. *Please not dead. Not again.*

He uses his last remaining strength to pull himself partially onto Bruce. Enough to feel the blood pulsing through his thick neck. Bruce will regain consciousness soon. A good vessel for Wayob.

The other men shout for Bruce to get up, shout for more blood. And Wayob laughs. He is still laughing as he presses his forehead to Bruce's tattooed temple. As his body goes limp.

Magic

Homicide Special had cleared out except for Saul. As a peace offering, and because it was Friday night and Halloween, he had volunteered to finish the paperwork on Saroyan so Hernandez could go home to her son. Of course, she wasn't going to fawn all over Saul because of some paperwork. But he could hope. Plus, the Castle would be filled past capacity and Saul couldn't get into the spirit.

With the video of Saroyan committing the murder, not much detective work was required. They had gone back to using his real name after finding no mention of Wayob in his background. The case had been assigned to Homicide Special because of its high-profile nature. The media was out for blood, the public demanding justice. Once Saul buttoned down the paperwork it would be up to the DA to make sure Saroyan wasn't released on some technicality. Almost certainly, he would plead insanity and vie for a stay at a mental health facility until he could convince the doctors he was no longer a threat. Cases like Saroyan's often had an unsatisfying outcome, if not an outrageous one.

Homicide Special was a windowless room containing four rows of desks. Saul and Hernandez occupied two desks side by side near Levy's office. The room was divided by an invisible wall of rivalry between the detectives who reported to Lieutenant Delrawn and those who reported to Levy.

Lieutenant Levy's team, Saul and Hernandez in particular, tended to draw the media headaches like Saroyan, even though Levy had a decade more experience than Delrawn. Captain Malone, who oversaw the Robbery Homicide Division including Homicide Special, was punishing Levy for backing Saul on the Brown fiasco. Though, of course, he never said so. Nor did Levy. Nor did Hernandez or anyone else. But Saul knew. They all knew.

Three years ago, Saul shot and killed Felix Brown. Saul had tried to keep Levy out of it by saying he'd acted alone, but she'd had to back him or risk losing respect from the other detectives under her supervision. A lieutenant

was ineffective, and ineffective lieutenants didn't last, not in
ial.

ia made Brown's case about another Black man shot by a white
er, with little mention of Brown's own actions or the gun he'd drawn.
After the Police Commission reluctantly ruled that Saul had followed
procedure, a group of protesters blocked traffic on the 110, which didn't
bother Saul because they didn't know what he knew. They hadn't been there.
What bothered him was that the LAPD settled the lawsuit from Brown's
family without a trial. It was like admitting to a wrongful death.

As a distraction from the paperwork, he went to YouTube to watch videos
on magic. Bullet Catch, Quarter-Through-the-Cup, Asrah Levitation, trick
after trick. He knew them all. It was comforting. And also depressing. He kept
on watching though. Some were good, like David Copperfield flying inside a
glass box, but Saul knew how the invisible wires fit through the lid. What he
was looking for, he realized, was a trick he didn't know—which at this point
would have to be real magic. *Real magic.* He laughed.

It was almost midnight when his desk phone rang. The caller ID said,
"*Blocked number.*" Strange.

He answered. "Parker here."

"Ah, Detective Parker," a man said in a gruff and vaguely familiar voice. "I
hoped to catch you."

"Who is this?"

"It is me, Wayob. Strange, is it not, how such a warm day becomes a cold
night?"

"Where are you?" Saul asked. He didn't sound like Saroyan, and yet he sort
of did.

"You see? This is why I have called, Parker. This is my warning. Do not
concern yourself with my whereabouts. Do not interfere."

"Did Hernandez put you up to this?"

"I believe tricks are your forte."

Hair bristled on the back of Saul's neck. Saroyan must have found an
inmate with a phone to whom he was feeding lines.

"You'd better tell me who this is if you don't want to get busted."

"Busted? What do you mean?"

"Let me guess. You're in the cell next to Saroyan?"

"Okay. Go ahead and 'bust' me. I am looking forward to this."

"If you think you can hide the phone up your ass, don't bother. They'll find
it."

"Disgusting. I would never. In fact, I shall stay on the line."

"Your funeral."

Saul muted his audio on the desk phone and used his cell to dial the night
captain at the Metropolitan Detention Center.

"This is Banks."

"It's Detective Parker with the LAPD."

"What can I do for you, Detective?" Banks said with a certain amount of sarcasm. There was a long-standing rivalry between the Sheriff's Department, who ran the MDC, and the LAPD.

"You've got an inmate with a cellphone."

"That's a negative. We run a tight ship here."

"I've got him on the other line. Go check the cells near Saroyan. He's telling this jerk what to say."

"Hold on," Banks said. "Sierra Alpha Romeo Oscar Yankee Alpha November?"

"Right. Detective Hernandez booked him this evening."

"He's in the ICU."

Saul almost shouted. "What?"

"Ten bucks says he doesn't wake up," Banks said.

"How could this happen?" Saul said.

"According to the snitches," Banks said, "Saroyan started the fight."

Saul rubbed his temple. "Why wasn't he in solitary? He's a violent offender. We were still questioning him."

"What do you think we are? The Hilton? We're way overbooked, and Saroyan is no worse than half our population. But feel free to take it up with the county supervisors. I'd consider it a favor."

"Maybe I'll take it up with the warden."

"Good luck with that."

"Look, I get it," Saul said. Banks was right. Despite having the world's largest jails, California lacked the budget to properly house the swelling population of inmates. "Just tell me what happened, okay? Saroyan can't walk. Why did he pick a fight?"

"He had a death wish, I guess." Banks still sounded annoyed, but words quickened with eagerness. "He took down an Aryan Brother, mean bastard too. He knocked out one of my guards."

"Saroyan?"

"Bruce Dunn, the badass Saroyan jumped. We had him handcuffed to the stretcher, but he dislocated his own arm in order to attack Aleman and kicked him into a pipe."

"Sheesh."

"Dunn says he didn't do it, but the prison doc saw the whole thing. Aleman, too, but we can't get in touch with him."

"What do you mean?"

"After he came to, he walked off the job."

Victor Aleman had booked dozens, maybe a hundred, criminals that Saul had delivered to the MDC. He was a squat, mean little man. The sort who struck back. Walking away was out of character.

"Was he hurt bad?"

"We don't know," Banks said. "He didn't even take his car. Probably plans to sue over working conditions."

Saul couldn't help feeling that somehow this was related, that maybe it was more than just the cadence of the gruff monotone on the other phone that sounded familiar. "What's his mobile?"

"I can't give out personal information. You know that."

"I just want to make sure he's okay."

"He's not answering."

"Maybe he'll answer my call," Saul said. "I've known him longer than you."

"If you're such best buds, then why don't *you* have his number?"

"You know how guys are," Saul said, but truth was he didn't care much for Aleman, and he doubted Aleman liked him either.

"You mean he's not into *magic*?"

Saul rubbed his forehead. How did everyone know about the Castle? He'd told Hernandez because she was interested in magic, but she knew better than to spread it around. Guys like Banks, once they find out how you're different, love to lord it over you.

"I can get you into the Castle," Saul said, "if you want?"

"Yeah, thanks but no thanks."

"Look," Saul said. "I just want you to listen to this guy on the other line. You tell me you think."

"Why should I listen? He could be anywhere."

"If you don't listen, then it's your ass when someone gets killed."

Saul put Banks on speaker, set his cell phone down next to the desk phone and unmuted the audio. "Wayob, you still there?"

"So, do you believe me now? I can be anyone. You cannot stop me."

"So who are you now?"

"Leave me alone Parker, or more shall die. I regret the life I must take, but I deserve a *life* in the world."

Saul stopped the audio.

"Aleman doesn't talk like that," Banks said. "But I'll give you his number just to cover my ass. I've actually got real work to do."

He was right: it was almost impossible to imagine Aleman speaking like that. Could Saroyan have dictated what he should say?

But then, why would Aleman comply?

Banks ended the call and texted Aleman's number. Saul called the mobile. But it rang through to voicemail.

Maybe Saroyan wasn't as unconscious as Banks thought. Saul decided to go to the hospital and see for himself.

His gut tightened. He should call Hernandez and give her the update, but why wake her? What did he really have here? If Saroyan was awake, Saul would make him explain. And then it would be nothing.

—

Saul sat at Saroyan's bedside in the ICU shuffling a deck of cards to the beat of the heart monitor. He'd spent the night in the worn polyester chair, shifting his weight around on the deflated cushions, waiting for Saroyan to wake up. Saroyan had a skull fracture, four broken ribs, and one broken arm and the other one was handcuffed to the bed. He wasn't going anywhere, but Saul couldn't give up and go home—not after the phone call. How the hell had Saroyan pulled it off?

He pulled his phone. Tried calling Aleman again. And again. Still no answer. Saul texted that it was Detective Parker and to call him back immediately.

Whoever had called Saul had threatened to kill someone. And to Saul, the threat was credible. Maybe not enough for a warrant or even a BOLO but Saul had a feeling—Aleman must have seen something, he must know something.

And so did Saroyan. A lot more, probably, than what he'd said in the interview and now he was lying there. Probably more asleep than unconscious. Saul reached for his shoulder. Perhaps he could shake him awake?

The back of Saul's neck prickled. A signal from the amygdala—someone was behind him. He glanced over his shoulder.

Hernandez stood in the doorway. His pulse quickened.

"Why didn't you call me?" she asked.

He felt the blood rush into his cheeks as he lowered his hand, hoping she hadn't seen that he was about to shake Saroyan's shoulder. "Didn't want to wake you."

She glanced at her phone. "It's nine-thirty."

"It was three when I got here."

She nodded toward Saroyan. "I hear he got a taste of his own medicine."

Saul felt bad for sitting in the one chair but if he stood now, with Hernandez right beside him, it would call attention to his belly. He began spreading the cards face down on the bedside table.

"What are you doing?" she asked.

"Pick a card."

The heart monitor beeped.

She combed back her shock of white bangs. "We don't have time for this."

"My feeling exactly. But all we can do now is wait."

"We can go to Luna's last known address. We need to locate his next of kin."

"According to the building manager, he moved out years ago" Plus, right now, Saul was more worried about the phone call than Luna's family. "Let's give Saroyan a little longer to come out of it."

"Last night, you were hot to trot on the death notification. What changed?"

"He called me from a coma."

"What?" She glanced at Saroyan.

He pointed toward the foot of the bed, where a clipboard was attached with Saroyan's information. "Apparently, he was comatose an hour before I got the call. It was someone pretending to be him."

"So now you're conducting the investigation alone?"

"Not at all. This was at midnight. I was going to call you this morning..." How did it get to be nine-thirty? Must have dozed off in the chair after all. "I didn't realize how late it was. Anyway, it was only threats. Nothing to act on."

She frowned. "A prank?"

"I wish. Whoever it was knew details about our interview with Saroyan and spoke just like him. Maybe his voice was deeper, but remember the arrogance? It was the same. At first, I thought Saroyan had bribed an inmate somehow, or maybe a custody assistant—Aleman walked off his shift last night—but it was like speaking to Saroyan and yet... it wasn't him."

"You get the number?"

"Blocked. I've got someone on it though." He'd have to change the subject if she asked who or how. He had gone a little out of bounds by calling Mark Chen, a systems engineer at Verizon, who owed him a favor. Tracing a number didn't require a warrant, technically, but Verizon would have insisted on one if Saul had asked through official channels.

Hernandez furrowed her brows, as though deciding not to ask. "So, why call you?"

Saul shrugged and turned up his palms. "He claimed to be warning me. I'd better not interfere with his plan to kill someone or else..."

Hernandez snorted. She chose a card from the middle and cupped it in her hand.

He slid the cards into a stack, split it, and shuffled. With a flourish of his hands, he presented the deck. "Put the card back anywhere you like. Don't let me see it."

She slid it in near the top. He shuffled again, then put the cards in his front pocket. "You chose the ace of spades."

"How the hell?"

Saul waved his finger. "A magician never reveals his secret."

"Of course."

He reached for the cards. "You know what? This time, I'll show you."

"Actually, I prefer the mystery."

The notion caught him by surprise. They were detectives. Eliminating mystery was what they did. "Cool," he said. Maybe not knowing made the simple trick seem, to her, like real magic?

Saroyan coughed. They stood over him as the beeping of the heart monitor accelerated. He opened his eyes. Attempted to lift his head and grimaced. His eyes darting around the room. "Where...am I?"

"You're in the ICU at Good Samaritan," Saul said.

Saroyan groaned and tried to sit up. The handcuffs clinked against the bedrail. "What happened? Why am I restrained?"

"You started a fight, which, apparently, you lost."

"Impossible." His eyes went wide. He jerked the cuffs, testing their hold.

Hernandez turned toward the door. "I'll get the nurse."

"You killed a man," Saul said. "We have to take precautions."

"No. I would never." Saroyan's brows furrowed. He squeezed his eyes closed.

"Last night you admitted it. You don't remember?"

His eyes flicked open. "Last night..." His eyes widened. "No. I didn't." He began breathing heavily.

"Perhaps your head injury has affected your memory, Wayob."

"Who is Wayob?" Saroyan sounded more Armenian now. He blinked at Saul with disbelief as if seeing him through a fog.

"You are."

"No. My name is Edward Saroyan. What is going on?" He rattled the cuffs again.

"Okay, so it's Edward now. Good. What is the last thing you remember, Edward?"

"I remember…" Saroyan's gaze went off into the distance. "I was at my carwash. At the register. It was slow day. Maybe I fall asleep. And then—I don't know, something happened—and I woke up here."

"You don't recall killing Luis Luna?"

"No, I—" His brows twitched. His breathing accelerated, short raspy breaths. What was he hiding?

"You bludgeoned him with a bat," Saul said.

"No!" Saroyan moaned.

A pulsating alarm sounded on the bio monitor. It grew more intense, and Saroyan flung his head from side to side, as if trying to ward away his memories.

"Edward?" Saul said. "Please, help us help you. Help us make sense of this."

But he'd withdrawn inside himself. He twisted and flopped in the bed. No way he was acting. He was recalling the murder, Saul was almost positive, and it was as if he were rejecting the memory with every cell in his body.

Saul placed a hand on his chest, ignoring for a moment that he was a murderer and not just a human being in pain.

A nurse in his mid-twenties, wearing blue scrubs, rushed in followed by Hernandez. Saul got to his feet and stepped back. The chair cushions slowly reinflated. The nurse reset the alarm and checked Saroyan's vitals.

"I'll get the doctor," he pulled his phone and swiped the screen.

Saul leaned toward Hernandez. "He prefers his own name all of a sudden."

The doctor was thin with mousy hair. She looked over the equipment and injected something into Saroyan's IV. "Mr. Saroyan isn't ready for visitors," she said.

"We just need to ask a few more questions."

"I'm afraid he's not in any condition to answer." Saroyan's pulse slowed.

Saul flashed his badge. "Lives could be at stake."

"Our responsibility is to the patient."

"We get it," Hernandez said. "You've got to do your job, but we've got to do ours too."

"I remember," Saroyan said weakly.

Saul exchanged a look with Hernandez.

"You've got two minutes," the doctor said, "after that he'll be out. At least until tomorrow."

Saul thanked her, took out his phone, and began recording. Given Saroyan's condition, whatever he said now might not be admissible in court, but still—it could be useful.

The doctor turned to the nurse. "I'll check back in twenty minutes." She hurried out.

The nurse scribbled a note on the clipboard.

With heavy lids, Saroyan gazed up through his drug-induced haze, pupils dilated, eyes out of focus.

Saul leaned in close. "What do you remember?"

"It seems like a dream. It had to be, but then...how do you really know?" He trailed off.

"He'll be asleep soon," the nurse said. "We gave him a heavy sedative."

Saul wanted to shake Saroyan to keep him awake.

But Saroyan was fighting the tiredness on his own, shaking his head from side to side. "It's strange," he said. "Dreams make no sense after waking up. But when you dream...it's real. Usually, I don't remember my dreams. Only the feeling...

"It was terrible." His eyes blinked fast and wouldn't open all the way. He slid the cuffs down the rail and clutched Saul's arm. "I don't want to sleep, please..."

The nurse squeezed between Saul and Hernandez and tried to elbow them back. "He's suffering from blunt-force trauma. He needs to rest until he stabilizes."

Hernandez moved back a step but Saul wasn't budging. He weighed twice as much as the nurse and he needed information. "Tell us what happened," he said to Saroyan.

"It was like you said. I hit him with a bat. But...it wasn't me."

The nurse glanced at Saul, his eyes wide. He lowered his arms and took a step back himself.

Saul stood there in silence, hoping Saroyan would continue speaking before the drugs overtook him.

"It was like my arms and hands were someone else. I would never...I tried to stop myself, but I couldn't.... It was not—I was like a prisoner. Watching... my hands.... I felt the wood as it struck—that part is clear. Nightmare—" His eyes closed. "Please...make it go.... I don't want to remember..."

"Mr. Saroyan?" Saul asked.

The interval of the heart monitor slowed.

Saul gave Saroyan's arm a tentative shake. The nurse touched Saul's arm, not forcefully, but enough to make it clear that he should stop. When he glanced back at Hernandez to see if she would back him up—they had to know more—she shook her head. Bad idea.

Saul withdrew.

The beeping of the bio monitor slowed. Saroyan's face relaxed. He was asleep now, deeply asleep.

Hernandez clawed back her shock of white.

The room seemed to be shrinking. Too crowded for him and Hernandez and Saroyan, and what he claimed to have happened. The nurse and all the equipment around the bed. And the one chair, its slumped cushion, leaking yellow foam from a coin-sized tear.

New Direction

Gray woke to the sound of sirens winding through the city. Beside him in the bed, Claire's spot was empty. He pulled the covers over his head. The sirens faded, and the sound that replaced them was a percussive swooshing, which it took him a moment to realize was rain. The first rain of fall.

He closed his eyes and rolled onto his side and let the sound of water wash over him, the patter on the roof. Outside the bedroom window, it was pouring into a puddle, probably a clogged gutter.

So far, the kids were silent, and he hoped it would be a while before they stirred. Hopefully, the rain and the moist in the air would calm the whole morning.

He drifted to a place where he could see the dream he was having, like it was waiting for him. He's a freshman, and he's sitting beside Laura on the lawn in the quad listening to who-cares-what-band, sitting closer and closer, high on hormones, hearts pounding double time to the drums. Where can they go afterwards? Because, in this dream, she wants to stay with him all night.

—

"I can't handle everything by myself." The sound of Claire's voice ripped him awake.

He opened his eyes. She stood over him holding Tyler, her hair disheveled, in the same sweatpants and T-shirt she'd been wearing last night.

"Mindy won't get dressed," she said, "and I need to feed Tyler again."

Above Gray's right eye, the remnants of last-night's Scotch tightened like a vise in his skull. "What time is it?"

"It's after eight. I've been up all night."

Gray sat up. Beside the bed, his clothes from last night lay crumpled on the floor. He dragged over his jeans and pulled them on while Claire complained about his snoring and about how then Tyler had woken up and she'd had to sit with him for the rest of the night because every time she tried to put him down he started crying again.

He rubbed his forehead. "How about I feed him?" He reached for Tyler.

Claire shook her head. "He still needs breast milk. You just get Mindy dressed."

He found Mindy in her room, wearing only pink underwear, arranging dolls on her bed as she sang to herself.

Gray opened her closet. "So many beautiful dresses. How about this yellow one?"

"No! Princesses wear pink."

She led him to the garage and dug her pink dress out of the laundry basket, the only thing she would wear. Gray tossed it in the dryer to fluff out the wrinkles. As they watched it spin, he hugged her and rubbed his throbbing forehead.

Once in her pink dress, she launched into the kitchen. Gray glanced at his easel with the cloth still draped over the landscape, which today he would finish. He swallowed.

In the kitchen, Claire had Tyler in his highchair and was cutting up an avocado for him.

Mindy climbed into the chair beside him and snatched a piece with her fingers.

"I told you not to let her wear dirty clothes," Claire said.

"We, uh…cleaned it." Gray winked at Mindy. "Who wants pancakes?"

Claire groaned.

Mindy raised her hand. "Macaroni, please."

Gray smiled. "That's not on the menu."

Claire spooned a green chunk of avocado into Tyler's mouth, which he gummed around and maybe swallowed some, but mostly it ended up on his chin and bib.

"Guess that's like dessert?" Gray asked Claire.

"He's not hungry. I don't know why." She piled avocado on his tray and took out her phone.

Tyler swept the green chunks off onto the floor and squealed. Gray kissed his head and let the avocado remain on the floor for now. If he was going to cook, he couldn't get caught in an infinite loop of pick-up-the-mess with Tyler.

"Oh my god!" Claire said to her phone.

Gray could hardly hear her over the hammering in skull. Food would help, at least a little. But he knew the monster pounding against his frontal lobe. He knew it well. It would never be sated until he quenched its thirst.

He opened the fridge and looked for the butter. It wasn't on the door where it belonged.

"Did you hear me?" Claire asked.

"What?"

"Ashley York pulled a Paris Hilton!"

"What's that?"

"She flashed her cooch!"

"Amazing," Gray said, but if he never heard Ashley's name again it would be too soon.

Claire retreated toward the living room.

Gray found the eggs, but if there was butter in the fridge, he just couldn't see it. He slammed the door.

He followed her to the doorway. "You remember it's Saturday?"

She collapsed on the couch and swiped her phone. "So?"

"It's my morning to paint."

Claire looked up. "What do you mean?"

But she knew. How many times had they talked about it?

"Remember, last Saturday you went out with friends." *And came home drunk*, he might have added.

"God," she threw her phone down on the cushion. "You're like my third baby." Once upon a time, she might have said it playfully, and once upon a time, he might have laughed at himself, because maybe he was whining a little. But not now. Now there was nothing but bitterness in her voice. She meant it. She thought he was being a baby.

She heaved herself up from the couch, a storm brewing in her eyes.

He braced himself in the doorway. He had to stand his ground, had to at least finish this one painting so he would have something to show her, something to justify quitting his job. When he opened his mouth to try and explain how much he needed this morning, just a few hours to paint, she turned away from him and marched toward the hallway.

"I'm taking a shower," she said.

—

An hour later, Gray opened the garage door. Outside, the street, washed clean by the rain, was drying in the sun. He drank in the moist air and angled his easel into the sunlight.

Claire had taken Mindy and Tyler, and her icy comments about his painting, to the park. It was like the ground between him and Claire had cracked open, and the crack had gradually widened such that now they were standing on opposite sides of a chasm of unknowable depth, with a cold wind blowing between them.

But when had it started? Years ago, it seemed. Certainly, Mindy's birth had changed things, and more dramatically than they had expected. It had ended the evenings of laughter on the balcony of their old apartment as the lights of Hollywood came alive below them. But the cracks were there, even then. Even before Claire was pregnant, the lazy mornings of lying in bed making love had tapered off, and Gray wondered if it had more to do with him than with her. Maybe she'd sensed the disappointment seeping off him. Maybe once he got out of his job and into painting, things would be better.

It didn't have to be his own art, not all the time. Album covers, even ads would be fine. Anything beat writing code no one cared about.

He lifted the cloth, tossed it on the workbench, and considered his painting. Beside the Malibu Lagoon, a bush was burning. Fire spread toward the dry hills behind it. Burn down and start anew, start over—like he wished he could do with his life—but the painting on the easel, yet again, fell short of his imagination. The strokes were haphazard, unorganized, as if only by coincidence they had formed an image. If he was kind to himself, the painting was competent—the proportions and colors matched the photograph taped to the easel—but competent wouldn't cut it. Competent was not going to feed Mindy and Tyler.

What he needed was a passive source of income, some kind of insurance in case it took longer than expected to reach to the point where he could earn enough from art to support his family. But right now, he needed to focus on his painting. He needed to wash away all these negative thoughts like the rain had washed the city clean. Music, loud music. And, of course, a nip of Scotch.

As the oaky liquid warmed his belly, he turned on the radio. An old song by the Smashing Pumpkins was playing. He turned it up and let the music course through him. This was the feeling he was trying to capture in his painting. He darkened the sky with charcoal-colored smoke. He loved acrylics, the way they layered—no need to start over. He made the sun a glowing red disk on the horizon. As he transformed the scene from the reference photograph into a whole new image, he wondered if this could be his masterpiece.

If he could make a name for himself, people would come to him. They would buy his art, and the more he could produce, the more he could afford to spend time painting.

All he needed was time—uninterrupted, continuous time. If he was going to make it, if he stood any chance at all, he had to give all he had. He had to open a vein and bleed his life's blood into his art.

A news blurb came on the radio with an update on the murder of Luis Luna. The wheelchair-guy, Saroyan, was the killer after all. Now he'd been hospitalized after starting a fight in prison. Gray shivered. A man had been bludgeoned to death, and no one knew why, and he had been right there.

As he leaned over the radio to change the station, a hoarse voice behind him almost shouted, "Hi, neighbor."

Startled, Gray shut off the radio and turned.

Standing in the doorway of the garage was the old guy from across the street, his pale skin almost transparent in the sunlight. His charcoal-colored suit hung almost flat from his bony shoulders, as if it were still on the hangar. *A truly unique-looking man*, Gray thought. Beautiful yet fragile, like a malnourished pug.

"Sorry to scare you," the old guy said. "Halloween *is* over after all."

"You didn't. I… thought I was alone."

He pointed toward Gray's painting. "That's really pretty, aside from the fire."

Gray swallowed. The fire was the whole point. It was the instrument of change, otherwise it would be, at best, just another pretty landscape, unlikely to grab anyone's attention. But now Gray noticed the scale of flames was out of proportion with the foliage they were consuming. The fire didn't fit.

"You're right," Gray said. "I guess it needs a lot of work."

"I think you're onto something though. Reminds me of the way sunsets looked in seventy-three when I came back from 'Nam."

Gray loved the way art was more than the piece itself. It existed in the mind of the viewer, and each person, from their own point of view, experienced it in their own unique way.

He selected a liner brush from the rack on the workbench and began trying to work some more detail into the flames.

He felt the old man staring over his shoulder. He seemed content to stand there all day in the doorway to the garage, watching him paint, which would be fine if Gray could focus with an audience. He needed to make progress. He put down his brush, and turned back to face the old man and his glassy eyes.

"I'm sort of busy, but thanks for stopping by."

The old man stepped inside the door. "I didn't introduce myself last night. Name's Charlie. Charlie Streeter."

Gray carefully shook his bony hand, afraid it would break. Charlie began a tedious explanation about how was housesitting for his daughter, who was on sabbatical with her husband in El Salvador.

Gray felt trapped by the conversation. He wanted to be alone with his painting, his music, and the Dewer's, which Charlie was staring at as he spoke. "I wanted to explain," he was saying, "why my car is in the garage and Lynda's is on the street."

"O-kay," Gray said. "Thanks." He picked up his brush and squinted at his painting.

"They asked me to drive it while they were gone."

Gray glanced toward the kitchen. *Would he follow me inside? Or just stand here and wait for me to come back out?*

"So the battery wouldn't go dead. So, I'll be driving Lynda's car for a while. Just didn't want you to think anything of it."

If Charlie hadn't called attention to the blue Prius on the curb, Gray wouldn't even have noticed. What was the big deal? Perhaps he was going senile. Probably irresponsible of Lynda to leave Charlie alone in their house.

"Anyway, I just wanted you to know." Charlie glanced over his shoulder toward the Prius.

Gray stepped into his personal space, hoping to herd him out. "Sorry, but I really need some alone time so I can concentrate on my work."

Charlie's eyes widened. He shuffled backward, nearly falling. Gray, feeling like a bully, reached out to help him, but Charlie scuffed his feet back into the sunlight of the driveway, sweat glistening beneath the few hairs combed across his spotted scalp, and pretended as though nothing had happened. "Mindy was a cute little princess fairy. If you ever want me to look after her, just say the word. I've got nothing but time on my hands."

Gray nodded. "We'll keep that in mind." *Never going to happen.* They had their issues with Belinda, but at least she could keep up with Mindy.

Charlie shuffled across the street, each step slower than the last, seeming to shrink under all that dark fabric in the sunlight.

—

Later, Gray stood behind his easel, relishing the energy pulsing through his veins, the flow that only came when he was alone with his music and just the right amount of alcohol, an ephemeral inspiration that begged for more—more Scotch—but more would only ruin it. Gray had been here and done this. Many times. It produced sorry work, and it was his fear of the letdown, of all the sloppy-Scotch paintings he'd thrown out, that stalled his hand from lifting the bottle again. He pounded the cork in with the side of his fist and turned off the music.

He streaked more red into the horizon. Like the blood that must have been on the sidewalk. It must take incredible strength to shatter a man's skull with a bat and from a wheelchair.

Focus. He stepped back to consider his work. It was colorful, but color was not enough—color meant nothing without emotion. It was emotion that drew people into an image and captured their imagination. He could stare for hours at Van Gogh's self-portrait. The way the lines, which up close were rough and irregular, seemed to actually move as you stood back, as you focused on the depth of his eyes. Art granted you permission to observe a subject, someone who would never allow such scrutiny in person. Someone so different from ourselves, yet the same underneath. A universal human essence which could only be captured in a portrait. A window into a soul.

That's what Gray needed to paint.

Forget landscapes. He should paint someone with character, personality. Charlie. He should paint Charlie—the way he had stood there. The sunlight streaming in around him—the deep furrows weathered into his face. The lines told a story. A story Gray could capture in a portrait.

Gray leaned the incomplete burning landscape against the workbench to dry, though he might not even keep it. His unfinished paintings were stashed in the crate hidden below the workbench, but it was nearly full.

He placed a fresh canvas on the easel. This was his favorite part of painting. The unblemished canvas held every possibility for the image he might paint, the image as flawless as his imagination. He wanted to just stare at the blank canvas, with maybe just a token nip of Scotch, and bask in his imagination of how good it could be—how good it *would* be. In his mind's eye, Charlie came into focus. Gray had to get started before it faded away. He had to hurry.

He used a charcoal pencil to sketch the underpainting... But the man standing in the doorway didn't quite look like Charlie. His face was a little too narrow, his eyes sunken, and the lines around his mouth were tightened into a cruel smile.

Gray had never been any good at drawing from memory. He should just ask Charlie to pose, maybe not for the whole portrait but at least for a reference photo. He might be happy to. He must have been lonely to come over here with nothing more important to say than whose car was in the garage.

Gray stepped outside and shielded his eyes in the sunlight. Charlie's house, with the witches, the jack-o-lanterns, and all the crow cut-outs, would make an excellent backdrop.

Claire's minivan sped over the hill into their neighborhood. She swerved into the driveway and stopped just short of where he was standing. Her window started down, and then—probably because it was taking too long— she flung open the door and practically leaped from the car.

"I thought you wanted to paint."

"I am." Gray glanced back toward the open bay of the garage, where the sketch he'd started was hardly visible, and unimpressive.

"Mindy threw up on herself."

Gray opened up the back passenger door. Mindy was buckled into her booster seat, eyes cast down. Dried orange chunks of curdled vomit on the front of her dress.

"It's ruined," Mindy said.

"I told her to get off the merry-go-round."

Gray looked back at Claire as she went around the car to get Tyler out from the opposite side.

"It'll be fine," he said to Mindy. She wouldn't look up at him.

He lifted her out of the car, pretending not to smell the vomit. "We'll just put it in the wash after we wash you."

As he turned toward the house, Claire stomped past him with Tyler, heading for the easel. Gray hugged Mindy to his chest, bracing himself for Claire's reaction. But she passed right on by as if there was nothing there at all. Did she see it? She had to have seen it. The sketch was rough, of course, and it hardly looked like Charlie at all, but still... it was the start of Gray's first portrait, and those eyes, those sunken eyes... it had potential. He hoped.

And Claire had deliberately ignored it, which was worse than if she hated it.

———

After he bathed Mindy and fed everyone, it was nap time. Mindy said she wasn't tired but agreed to stay in her room for an hour of quiet time.

Claire wanted to take a shower, so Gray carried Tyler, who was sound asleep, out to the playpen in the garage and covered him with a blanket. The door was closed, and Gray kept it that way. He covered his would-be-masterpiece with a cloth, uncorked the Dewar's, and drank in silence, in the dim bulb mounted to the workbench. More than anything, he wanted to get back to that feeling from this morning, ride the swell of inspiration. He wanted to blast the stereo. And not through headphones, which were inside, and he didn't feel like getting up, so he opted for another drink.

From across the garage, Gray heard the water sluicing through the pipes from the hot water heater squeal to a stop as Claire finished her shower. He slumped forward on the stool, his eyes closing. The Scotch had dropped him.

The kitchen doorknob rattled, and the door slammed open into the counter. Gray had to force his lids up, force himself to look at Claire. She was standing in the doorway, wrapped in a white towel, dragging a comb through her damp hair.

She flicked on the overpowered fluorescents in the unfinished ceiling. "What are you doing in the dark?"

Gray squinted and as he jerked open the top drawer of the workbench and began raking in tubes of paint. "I was just closing up."

"God, you're so weird." She turned back toward the kitchen and threw the door closed behind her, leaving Gray in the harsh light from the four exposed tubes, with Tyler whining as he woke.

He rubbed his aching eyes, got to his feet and shut off the fluorescents, which he'd been meaning to replace with LED mood lighting. He lifted Tyler from the playpen and rubbed his back until he quieted down.

"Am I weird?"

Tyler had nothing to say on the subject. His eyes were closed again.

True, Gray was drinking... alone... in the garage. And Claire probably knew it. But she didn't know why, how much he'd rather be painting, how hard it was to focus with all this weighing on his mind. He'd planned on waiting until Sunday to tell her how he was quitting his job, but why wait?

He found her in the bedroom. She was lying on the bed, still in the towel, with a second one wrapped around her hair. Her eyes were closed, but he knew she wasn't sleeping. He sat down beside her, on the bed.

Her brows tensed. His timing couldn't be more obviously bad, so instead, he lay back, holding Tyler against his chest.

She forced out a breath, a heavy burst of air, as if it had broken free from her effort to contain it. She rocked herself up off the bed.

Gray's eyes closed, and this time he found them too heavy to wrench open. The darkness behind his lids pulling him down. Claire's hairdryer whirred. Sleep.

———

Claire launches through the kitchen door to the garage where Gray is working on his portrait of Charlie. He can't let her see it. Not like this. It's not finished yet, and there is nothing worse than a bad first impression. He jerks from the workbench, sending tubes of paint flying across the garage.

But it's too late.

Claire comes to a complete halt. Her mouth falls open. Her eyes widen. Gray follows her gaze to his unfinished painting...which is... not Charlie at all. It's a dark figure, an indistinct man on a sidewalk in the fog, emerging from a shadow between streetlights.

Gray's heart pounds in his throat. He's terrified. The image has nothing to do with the portrait he started. It's a masterpiece. The indistinct face of the man contains all the pain of Munch's Scream coiled into short, perfect strokes. It's like Monet, or Monet's impression of Dali, more beautiful and haunting than anything Gray has ever painted, more than he's ever even hoped to paint.

With no explanation as to how this masterpiece materialized on the easel before him, he turns back to Claire, but she is not Claire—she's his mother. And they're not in the garage anymore; they're in the kitchen he grew up in. He is a boy, and she is standing over him. "Do not want what you cannot have," she says.

"I don't want anything." He chokes at the sound of his nine-year-old voice. "I just want to paint."

"Wake up," his mother says, her face harsh, leaving no room for discussion.

And so he runs—that's all he can do. If he can make it to his room and lock the door behind him, he won't have to listen to her. He can paint if he wants.

As he passes, she grabs his shoulder. He tries to wrench out of her grip, but he cannot free himself.

"Wake up," she says again. Her eyes flicker with such a cold shade of blue that it hurts to look at them.

He blinks. He clenches his eyes closed.

When Gray opened his eyes, he found himself staring into the cans in the ceiling which were dialed up to full brightness, and it was Claire standing over him, shaking his shoulder.

Immediately, his head started pounding. The lights seemed to amplify the pain in his skull. Still on his back, he felt around for Tyler, who had been on his chest when he fell asleep. "Where's Tyler?"

"You slept all afternoon," Claire said. "What's wrong with you?"

He sat up and groaned. The hangover tightened like a vise on his skull. He closed his eyes and tried to remember the masterpiece from his dream. The dark man. Gray caught a fleeting glimpse before the whole image blurred into darkness itself.

"It's almost five," Claire was saying. "So much for the Day of the Dead thingy."

Gray opened his eyes. According to the clock by the bed, it was 4:18. The Dia De Los Muertos parade didn't start until seven. "We can make it."

Claire wrinkled her nose. "Do you really want to go?"

Last weekend, he'd convinced her to go for Mindy's sake while secretly hoping that Claire would enjoy it too. Occasionally, she had fun when he convinced her to leave the house—though not so much lately.

Now, with the way his head was pounding, he hardly cared about going anymore either. But what else were they going to do? Not like he was going to get any more painting done tonight, and his head would be pounding regardless. At this point, his hangover was the only sure thing in his life. Maybe getting out of the house would clear the air between them, so they could finally talk.

He climbed out of bed. "Let's just go."

He trudged past her, ignoring whatever excuse she shouted after him as he left the room. He needed a shower. If he could just stand under the hot water and not think for fifteen minutes, he would be fine.

In the hallway, Mindy latched onto his leg. He rubbed her head and pretended to smile as he bent down and wiggled his fingers near her armpits. Her head jerked as she giggled—the threat of tickling worse than the act itself. He tried to pry her off, but she clutched on tighter.

"If you don't let go, I'm going to tickle you." He wiggled his fingers some more, then made good on the threat.

Remarkably, her laughter seemed to ease the throbbing chaos in his head. As he started toward the bathroom, she remained latched to his leg.

"Time to let go, Mindy, so I can get ready for the parade."

He dragged her along the carpet. She couldn't stop giggling.

"Don't you want to go? There might be ice cream."

He dragged her into the bathroom and turned on the shower. "You're going to get wet if you don't let go."

She didn't let go, so he bent down and hugged her. She squirmed out of his arms and ducked into the narrow gap between the toilet and the counter, still giggling uncontrollably.

He motioned her out. "That's enough."

She made for the door, then sidestepped and latched onto his leg again, writhing around on the tile, desperate for a tickle. He placed a hand on her head. "Daddy needs to shower, Mindy, okay?"

Her giggling tapered off as she gazed up at him with her doe eyes. She released his leg.

Gray's heart melted. Suddenly, he hardly cared about taking a shower.

Mindy left the bathroom without another word, shutting the door behind her.

Ashley's House

Ashley was up early that morning, hoping for a miracle but knowing her crotch would be all over Instagram… and it was. It was everywhere, trending on Facebook and Twitter. She wanted to tweet back that it was an honest accident, that her dress had slipped up on the leather seat, but in the photos she looked so wasted that any comment from her would only fan the flames of the trolls. God, the names they were calling her.

She turned up the volume, trying to drown shame with reality TV while waiting for the inevitable call from Don, her agent.

She hoped her dad wouldn't find out. He was huge on social media, of course, but he let his PR people handle it for him. The question was, would they tell him? Would they show him the photos of her wasted in the back of Raquel's Escalade, her dress riding up as she tried to get out, her legs spread and crotch exposed for all of Hollywood?

Her phone vibrated with the expected call at the expected time: nine a.m. Cue Don. She muted the TV, stood, tightened her robe, and answered the phone.

"Ashley, darling," Don said. "What were you thinking?"

But Don worked for her. She didn't have to explain herself to him. "Any publicity is good publicity, right?"

"No. It's like bad advertising. Your public image has a huge impact on the marketability of your films."

"But I'm not in any films, remember?" If she'd gotten the role, which Don had basically guaranteed her, she would never have gotten smashed in the first place.

"Ashley, baby, I'll get you a part. Give me a chance and I'll make you a star. But please, help me do my job here. No one will cast you with a bad reputation."

Ashley rubbed her forehead. "Look, I didn't mean to, okay? Yesterday was kind of a bad day, remember? That jerk-wad producer you sent me to lunch with?"

"I get it. You needed to blow off some steam. Just let us help you next time. That's why we hired Clayton. If he'd driven you to the club, nothing like this would have happened."

But she didn't need a babysitter, what she needed was a role. On the still-muted TV, a reporter stood in front of a jail downtown. Inset in the upper corner was the car wash she'd seen in an earlier blurb, the sidewalk cordoned off where a man had been murdered. "I don't understand why my crotch is going viral," she said, "when people are being beat to death in broad daylight."

"That was yesterday," Don said. "Today is all about you."

She turned off the TV and closed her eyes. She felt boxed in. "What can I do?"

"I hired an internet-cleaning service. They can't get everything, of course, but these guys are the best. They'll get the pictures of your little wardrobe mishap taken down. And once there's nothing to look at, it'll stop trending."

But the damage was done. Even without pictures, people were going to remember. *I'll never live it down.*

And Don, predictably, decided to trot out his catch phrase. She could have said it along with him. "One step at a time."

"Yeah, but I'm walking backward."

"Not for long," he said. "I've got something for you."

"What?" She was almost skeptical.

"The biggest opportunity of your career, that's what."

"Seriously? Why didn't you say that to start with?"

It was a Charlie Kaufman film directed by Sean Penn. She leaped up from the couch and paced below the wall of windows. Outside, West LA stretched out to the blue expanse of Pacific. The morning rain had washed the city clean, and Catalina Island seemed closer than ever.

"You'll costar with Zac Efron," Don was saying, "if you get the role."

"So, what do I have to do?"

"Not much. Just a reading."

"So it's an audition?"

"No, no, of course not. They want you. They just need to check your chemistry with Zac. Without someone like him attached, it will never get funded. You know how it is."

Ashley could hardly hear over the sound of her heart pounding. "I guess."

"They want you in costume. They're going to do a full lighting test. Who knows, they might even use it for publicity."

Ashley's stomach lurched. She wasn't ready.

"No need to thank me," Don said. "Just keep a low profile. I'm begging you. I put my ass way out on the line for this."

"Of course." She wasn't going anywhere. She would practice every minute for the next two days before the screen test.

After hanging up with Don, she called Sammy in the guard booth and made him promise to bring her the screenplay the second it arrived.

With nothing to do but wait, she paced around the house. In the dining room, the glass tabletop had streaks on the glass. Circular arcs of dried cleaning solution distorted her reflection.

"Andrea?"

No answer.

Where was she? Not in the kitchen, unless she was ignoring Ashley.

Ashley returned to the TV. For some reason, she felt guilty asking Andrea to do her job, despite the fact that Ashley was paying her double the usual rate for a housekeeper. The problem was that Andrea—who was trying to make it as an actress as well—was too damn cheerful. Almost sarcastic, the way she said yes to everything, and it had gotten so bad lately that Ashley was considering hiring another housekeeper to do the actual cleaning and cooking. But then, if she hired someone else, what was she paying Andrea for? She couldn't just let her go.

A text came in from Raquel.

Raquel:
How's my favorite biatch?

Ashley set the phone to the coffee table. She had nothing to say to Raquel, but her screen displayed a new notification.

Raquel:
Lunch at the Ivy

Bring underwear 😒

What Ashley needed was an excuse to keep Raquel off her back while she focused on the screen test, which she certainly couldn't tell Raquel about, because Raquel would blab it all over the place and somehow ruin it. The last thing she needed was for Sean Penn to find out and think she was bragging about it.

Her phone lit up with a notification from Twitter. Raquel had just tweeted, *Lunching with Ashley York at The Ivy.*

Ashley:
WTF! I saw your tweet. I've got yoga.

A white lie. Ashley would feed her one after another, and even if Raquel suspected Ashley was up to something, she'd have to just chill, because after all, Raquel couldn't afford to piss Ashley off. She needed Ashley more than Ashley needed her.

Raquel:
Skip it, girl. You're more famous than Lady Gaga! We've got to smoke this

while it's hot.

Ashley could have guessed this whole lunch thing was yet another way for Raquel to use her to bolster her image for the wannabes on her feed.

A call came in from August, his perfect face filling her screen—never a hair out of place. Even in his profile pic, he had his eyes focused and lips tightened in a way that came, she knew, from hours of practicing in front of a mirror. He was calling with FaceTime, so she smoothed her hair and loosened her cashmere robe before answering, "Hey, you."

"What's up, it-girl?"

"It-girl?"

"Yeah, you created a sensation."

Last night, she'd been too embarrassed to admit it was an accident, and now it was too late. "I don't know about that."

"Are you kidding me? You're so lucky you're a girl. If I sunned a crowd, they'd put me in jail."

New subject. "Are you coming over tonight?"

"Probably not until after midnight," he said. "Boys' night."

'Boys' night,' she knew, was basically his entourage plus as many girls as they could round up, which hardly mattered to her because he was coming to see her afterwards.

———

Ashley was in the sunroom when Sammy's deep voice bellowed through the house. "Knock knock."

"In here," she said.

He strode in with the screenplay she'd been waiting for all morning, his stark white smile widening with each step, showing off his always-positive outlook on life. Something surged inside her and she leaped up and hugged him, and only then did she remember how she had loosened her robe as a tease for August, to which he'd hardly reacted.

But now she felt something.

As she pulled out of the hug, her hand raked Sammy's neck, and his gaze slid down her cleavage. Blood rushed through her body, headed south, perhaps because it was such a bad idea in so many ways to even be thinking about Sammy when she had August Grant coming over. Any other woman in the world would think she was crazy.

"You okay?" Sammy asked.

Was he talking about now? Okay with him looking at her? She frowned. If she answered honestly, it would start something—bad idea—but she didn't exactly want to shut it down either, so she told him what she'd been dealing with all morning. "I'm trending."

He scrunched his brows together, mirroring the gravity of her expression. "That's not good?"

"I didn't mean to."

"Didn't mean to what?"

Was it possible? Was Sammy the one person in the world who hadn't seen the photos from last night? He must have seen them. Of course he had. He was being a gentleman to pretend.

"Well, it was an accident. Don't believe what's online."

"I only believe what I see with my own two eyes." And as he said it, his two eyes swept over her boobs again, this time too obvious to ignore.

Bad idea. In so many ways. She pulled her robe closed. She wanted him to know that she hadn't intentionally flashed her crotch last night as some kind of a ploy for attention, which as pathetic as it was, wasn't half as bad as the truth: that she'd let herself get so wasted it had happened by accident.

Sammy glanced away. The room felt cold.

She wanted his eyes back on her. "I wish more people were like you, Sammy."

He flashed his white smile. "You'd be surprised, Ashley. People are getting tired of living in their phones. They want something real."

She nodded, wanting to believe him. Maybe once the pictures were gone, the rumors would be just rumors, which maybe people knew about but didn't really believe all the way, like all the porno sites claiming to have movies of her but they were of other girls—girls who looked nothing like her except maybe they wore an outfit like one she'd worn once, before they undressed and screwed some man whose face remained offscreen.

"So..." Sammy said, "um, about that dog..."

"It's still here?" She didn't mean to snap, but she had specifically told him to get rid of it. This was first time he had ever disobeyed her.

"I can't find the owner. I've got signs up at both gates to the neighborhood, but no one has called."

As if on cue, the dog barked. And it was a deep bark, loud and close.

"Oh my god—is it in the house?"

"No." Sammy glanced toward the door. "She's outside, but I thought you might want to meet her again. She's calmed down a lot since yesterday. I swear."

"Sammy, I can't. I have to get ready." How was she going to focus with some dog barking? She held up the screenplay. "This is Charlie Kaufman. With Sean Penn directing."

"Way to go, Ashley!" Sammy flashed his smile. Did he know how endearing it was? Hard it was to stay mad at that smile.

"They haven't cast me, yet, but I've got a screen test, and I need to nail it."

"I'm sure you will." He stepped toward the door. "I'll leave you to it then. You won't hear a peep out of us. Don't worry."

But she would hear the dog if it barked, even from all the way up at the guard booth. It was that loud. And even if Sammy kept it quiet, just knowing the dog was there was a distraction. She did sort of want to meet it though, and if she did, she'd want to play with it. She'd be thinking about it when right now she needed to focus more than any other time in her life.

"Isn't there some shelter or something you can take it too?"

"Shelters kill dogs. I mean, you wouldn't believe—"

"Just figure something out. I can't have it here."

"Will do." He turned toward the door. "Call if you need anything, anything at all."

He meant it. Ashley knew he did. She could count on him, and it didn't matter that she was paying him; he wanted something more than money. The only one in her life who didn't want something from her was her dad.

Overcome by a sudden bout of weakness, she snatched up her phone. She had to know if he knew.

Ashley:
Hey, Dad. You there?

She stared at her screen and waited. She couldn't straight-up ask him if he'd seen the photos without tempting him to go look, but she had to talk to him. He'd say something if he knew. He would have to say something. And then she could tell him how it had been a horrible accident, maybe without mentioning how messed up she had been at the time. If anyone would understand, it was her dad.

She called him.

His phone rang twice and went to voicemail. She ended the call.

Ashley:
Give me a call, okay?

The little animated dots in the blue bubble appeared, showing that he was typing. She waited.

And waited.

Dad:
…

Eventually, the bubble with the dots disappeared. Now it was just her text at the bottom of the screen. After another minute, she refreshed the app.

Still nothing.

"What the hell?"

Death Notification

At 2:11 p.m., on the 10 east from downtown, an overpacked pickup cut in front of Saul. He hit the brakes. Beside him in the passenger seat, Hernandez rocked forward, her neck tensed against the decrease in speed. Her eyes remained on her phone.

He swallowed back a belch. "I give up," he said. "How did you do it?"

"Do what?"

"With the neighbor. How'd you get her talking like that when she wouldn't even open the door for me?"

Hernandez shrugged. "I speak Spanish."

"Yeah, but you had her feeding us tamales."

"I told her your blood sugar was low."

Saul felt his cheeks flush. He pretended to laugh. "I only ate to be polite." In truth, he'd been starving, and the tamales were so tasty, he'd eaten four in spite of himself. "I'm actually on a diet."

Hernandez chuckled but she looked serious. She combed back her shock of white bangs. "It was just to get us in the door."

Saul nodded. "Much appreciated." The elderly woman knew where the Lunas had moved. And now, thanks to Hernandez, they were on their way to do what should have been done yesterday: notify Luis Luna's family of his death.

Like all cops, Saul dreaded death notifications. They weren't trained for it. No amount of experience made it any easier. And this time would be particularly bad because unless Luna's family lived in a total news blackout, they had by now seen the horrific images of his death. They'd know how he was murdered, and they'd demand to know why. A death needed to be understood in order to move on. People could not accept murder as some random act that defied explanation, and neither could Saul. There had to be a reason, a story behind it. That was his mission: to make sense of the madness.

In front of them, in the truck bed, a tilted stack of wooden chairs bounced against an inadequate length of cord.

It had been twenty-four hours since the murder, and Saul and Hernandez were even further from a motive than when they'd started. They had the perp, Saroyan, chained to a bed in the ICU, but he had changed. Last night he'd confessed to the murder, but now he denied it.

Saul couldn't help feeling like they'd only glimpsed the tail end of a monster who had shed Saroyan like some insignificant appendage it could regenerate.

Keeping one hand on the wheel, Saul pulled out his phone and hit redial.

"Who you calling?" Hernandez asked.

"Aleman."

"I still don't think it's related," she said.

"I don't believe in coincidences."

"They happen every day. Statistically unlikely, I'll give you that, but odds are Aleman needed a break after what happened."

"Maybe." It *was* hard to imagine that Aleman would want anything to do with Saroyan, but Saul had to find out for sure. "Aleman's not the sort of guy who runs off with his tail between his legs."

"He got knocked out. Maybe he wasn't thinking straight."

"So where did he go? His car's still at the MDC."

"Where does he live?" she asked.

"Highland Park. A ten-mile walk, if there's even a way over the 5."

"Maybe he got a Lyft."

"Possible, but then why not answer his phone?" They had been over this already, and as much as Saul wanted harmony between them, he couldn't let it go.

She shrugged. "Heard of Occam's Razor?"

"Is it any better than Gillette?" he joked, rubbing his bristled chin, hoping to make her smile.

Her lip twitched slightly. "It means stick with the simple explanation."

"Which is what? At this point we have no explanation at all for Aleman's behavior."

"I don't see how it makes a difference. Saroyan killed a man, and we've got it on video. Case closed."

"But he claims to have had no control over his actions." And he claimed it with such conviction that Saul knew he truly believed it.

Hernandez shrugged. "So, he's a psycho."

"You think he has multiple personalities?" He'd never encountered such a case, but even if it were true, Saroyan was still responsible—at least a part of him was—and Luna still deserved justice.

"No," she said, "I think he's a good actor."

"That's what I thought at first, but then why change it up?"

"Yeah." She brushed back her shock of white. "That was weird. I didn't like his new accent any better."

"If he can pull off an act like that while heavily sedated, he should be working in Hollywood. Not at a carwash."

"I'm thinking it's because of the drugs that he dropped the performance from last night. But don't worry, we'll talk to him again when he wakes up. I just don't see a reason to go chasing irrelevant leads."

Ahead, the overfilled truck slowed down. Saul swerved around it and accelerated.

Hernandez went silent, gazing out at the blur of palm trees and warehouses below the freeway.

"Must be a tough commute," Saul said. "I can't believe people live out here."

"Some people can't afford to get closer."

She was right. Even middle-class families had been forced further and further out by the inconceivable sums of money in Hollywood and Silicon Beach. The city of LA had a budget that topped ten billion a year, and the chief of police alone pulled down more than three hundred grand. Although Saul was barely scraping by, he was rich compared to the majority of people they dealt with: people like the Lunas, the ones who couldn't afford to live closer.

Saul exited onto Loma Avenue and followed the road as it passed derelict warehouses and veered right, turned again, and then dead-ended into the parking lot for the Lunas' apartment building, almost underneath the freeway. A two-story stucco affair, typical of urban blight apartments built during the 1950s boom. Designed to last maybe thirty years at the most. Now the stucco was discolored and cracked. The roofline sagged, and a blue tarp had been tied down over a corner as a cheap patch for a leaky roof.

"Depressing," Hernandez said.

Saul rolled to a stop in front of a sign with faded red letters: *TENANT PARKING ONLY*. When he opened the door, the hiss of the freeway filled the car. He climbed out. Shattered safety glass sparkled on the asphalt as they approached the rusty, metal stairs attached to the exterior of the building. When they reached 2B, Saul knocked on the faded blue door.

Behind it, a female voice asked, "Quién es?"

"La Policía," Hernandez said.

Saul buttoned his coat and sucked in his belly as the locks clicked and a chain unlatched. The door opened.

Behind it was a girl with sepia-colored skin and furrowed brows. She was short, five feet at the most, with high cheekbones and salon-perfect hair combed down over one shoulder. She turned toward the apartment's interior and shouted, "Abuela!"

"Do you speak English?" Hernandez asked.

"Of course." She stepped back for them to enter.

Inside the door, a series of photographs lined the wall portraying the girl as she grew from a child into nearly a woman now. Whether the background was a church or a beach or a park, she stood between Luis Luna and an older woman, Luis's mother, probably—same chin, same penetrating eyes—who seemed to shrink as the girl grew taller. The one outlier was a black and white of a young man with a striking resemblance to Luna. In the photo, he wore a dark uniform with light trim and lapels. Insignia like a sun. Like Luna, he had prominent cheekbones and shiny, dark hair. Maybe two inches long. Brushed but a little tousled, with a clear tendency to wave. He was Latino, but as much Aztec or Mayan as Spanish. Plenty of Native American in him. That was for sure. All the Lunas had indigenous features.

The old woman from the photographs touched the wall of the inner hallway as she approached the main room of the apartment. Her eyes were glazed white.

As the girl went to help her, Saul looked back at the photos, and this time he saw the change: as the old woman's hair lightened from gray to stark white, her eyes lost their clarity and focus. He had missed it before because in every shot, she still knew where to look, right toward the camera. A proud, knowing expression on her face.

Saul and Hernandez waited by a shelf of ceramic owls near the entrance to the small, overheated room. Bright Mexican blankets draped the couch. Dark fabric curtained the one window. Below it, marigolds were scattered on a small shelf illuminated by flickering prayer candles that flanked a framed photograph of Luis Luna.

Saul introduced himself and Hernandez to the old woman, but she didn't mention her name, and they didn't press for it. She was undocumented and they didn't need to know it.

At the end of the hall, she reached out a trembling hand for the recliner that faced the couch. The girl took the woman's other arm to help but she pulled her arm away. She could sit on her own. She settled back into the recliner and pulled a red and blue blanket across her lap, as if unaware of the heat.

"I know why you're here," she said in a thick Latina accent.

Saul nodded toward Luna's shrine. "Was he your son?"

Her face hardened. She said nothing. Her glazed eyes stared straight at his chest.

The room felt too small for his massive frame. He was towering over her, and already he was sweating. If he weren't so fat, he would take off his coat. He sidestepped around the shelf to the couch.

The dark eyes of the ceramic owls sparkled in the candlelight. As he sat, the cushions sagged from his weight. Hernandez wedged herself between him and the armrest.

The girl pulled a wooden chair out from the dining table and turned it toward them. "Abuela doesn't speak English. And you're right, he was my father."

The old woman inhaled deeply, as if gathering her strength. "Rosa, por favor, ir a su dormitorio."

Rosa argued with her in Spanish. Before Saul could interject, Hernandez placed a hand on his knee. They had worked together for more than a year, and this was the first time they had touched. And it felt as natural as if it happened every day.

"Sentimos mucho su pérdida," she said. "We're very sorry for your loss."

The woman pulled out a worn handkerchief from the bag beside her chair. She mopped her eyes and blew her nose. Then, with slow trembling hands, she folded the cloth into a neat square.

With his limited Spanish, Saul couldn't follow what was said next, but there was something more than grief in the lines on the old woman's face. And Hernandez, who was never at a loss for words, seemed taken aback.

"She doesn't think we can help," she said.

"Did you tell her we've got the perp?"

Rosa's eyes darted to the floor, and she straightened, gripping the bottom of her chair.

"No, es imposible," the woman said.

Saul heaved himself up from the couch and showed Saroyan's DMV photo to Rosa. "Do you recognize this man?"

"No." Her eyes darted from the photo to Saul and back to the floor.

"He must have known your father, somehow. Anything you can tell us would help with the investigation."

Rosa looked at the photo again and described Saroyan to the old woman.

Saul's phone buzzed in his pocket. He was tempted to check who it was, but right now it was crucial to study the woman's reaction.

She shook her head. "No era ese hombre. Es mi culpa que su nieto está muerto."

"She says it's her fault," Hernandez said.

Saul slid the photo into his pocket, rubbed his temple, and returned to the couch. He couldn't follow much of the ensuing conversation between Hernandez and the woman, but he understood she was in a lot of pain—that much was clear from the strain on her face. After every few words she gasped for air—short, raspy breaths.

Hernandez paused, and then asked a question.

The woman's milky eyes glanced down and to her right. A jolt of current surged through Saul's gut. People glanced to their left when recalling a memory. To the right was the imagination center. Right and down was a lie.

The woman looked up at Saul. Her eyes seemed to focus on something inside him. She spoke carefully measured English. "Leave it alone."

Hernandez inhaled. "We should go."

"What else did she say?" Saul asked.

"She says Saroyan is not our guy."

"Then who killed Luna?"

"Era yo," the woman said. "I did. Y mi corazón va a estar en una terrible prisión para siempre."

A wireless handset on the counter rang, startling Rosa. She leaped up from her seat.

The woman abruptly started coughing. It sounded like a lot of fluid in her lungs. She turned sideways, pulled out a handkerchief.

The phone kept ringing.

The woman waved Rosa toward it, and they argued in Spanish.

Rosa answered the phone as the woman climbed out of the recliner. "One moment." Rosa carried the phone to her Abuela.

The old woman wiped her mouth and guardedly folded the handkerchief. She took the phone and shook it toward Saul. "Es importante." She turned toward the hallway.

Saul glanced at Hernandez, who stood up. "Entendemos," she said to the woman.

The old woman, clutching the phone, touched two fingers to the wall on her way to the back room.

Saul asked Rosa, "Mind if we ask you just a couple more questions?"

She slumped back into the chair. "I don't know why she's acting like that. Normally Abuela is the sweetest woman you ever met."

"She's grieving." Hernandez combed back her shock of white and sat on the armrest beside Saul. "As I'm sure you are too."

Rosa nodded and looked at the floor.

Saul leaned forward. "Do you know what she meant by 'things aren't as they appear'?"

Rosa bit her lip and shook her head. "Something's wrong with her. She won't go to a doctor."

It would be easy to dismiss the old woman as senile, if not for the phone call last night—the man who had claimed to be Wayob, but who had sounded like Saroyan and yet, not like Saroyan at all. The old woman wasn't crazy; she was scared.

Why blame herself? They all knew how Luis Luna had died. Maybe he'd gone to Venice for her. Maybe she'd sent him on some errand, but... it seemed like more than that. Like she knew Saroyan herself. And maybe she knew about Wayob.

She knew more than she'd said. That was for damn sure. Perhaps much more. But she'd said all she was going to say, for now. So the only question left was, what did Rosa know?

"I believe your grandmother," he said. "There's something more going on here."

Rosa's eyes widened, and she looked directly at him. "Like... what?" Like she wanted to know as much as he did.

He heaved himself up of the couch. Went to Luna's shrine. Picked up the silver frame and examined the dark-skinned Latino. Luna's penetrating eyes seemed to be peer out from the photograph, staring at Saul. Had Luna known Saroyan? "That I intend to find out."

He lifted the curtain and squinted into the sunlight. Behind the glass, the window was secured by vertical bars with patchy, white paint surrendering to rust. Beyond them was the freeway. Sunlight glinted on the cars careening past. Their case against Saroyan remained the same. Hard to imagine what could change it. Saul closed the curtain and turned around.

If Rosa knew anything, this was her chance to fill the silence in the room. But she had withdrawn inside herself, smoothing her long hair between her hands, looking down at the floor.

Hernandez was already standing. She tilted her head and Saul agreed. They should leave, let Rosa and her Abuela deal with their grief. Try again later. Hernandez gave Rosa her card. "If there's anything we can do to help, please call."

Wayob

After trudging all through the night and half the day, Wayob is thirsty, so thirsty. So annoyingly, utterly, thirsty. And so sick of this vessel, this body of Victor Aleman and all its petty, physiological needs, which Wayob would shed himself of, except that he is so close, so very close. He can almost hear the hum of the old woman's mind, even without entering a state of meditation.

Why is Wayob still free? For if anyone knows how to recall Wayob to the Encanto, the miserable stone which imprisoned him for so many centuries, it is Abuela. *Abuela.* Who held the Encanto for decades and refused to use it, despite all the effort Wayob wasted whispering into her sleep. She kept Wayob imprisoned in the utter darkness, alone and disembodied. She forced Wayob to suffer in the awful torment contrived by the despicable priest, because she blames Wayob for the death of her husband, when it was her husband's own fault. Out of utter desperation, Wayob whispered into her deepest stage of sleep—as if the idea was her own—that if she destroyed the Encanto, Wayob would die along with it. Although, in truth, destroying the Encanto would set him free. He would have one life left to live in the first vessel he finds. Yet, she had failed to act.

Ignorance?

No, she knew. She must have known, like she must now know that Wayob is free. So, unless she has become benevolent in her old age—for Wayob does not deserve such torture—she must be using the Encanto. Finally, after all this time, Abuela is just as greedy as everyone else. And her greed shall be her demise.

Wayob should thank the man, whoever he is, who returned the Encanto to Abuela. For her mind rings out louder than anyone else who has ever held the wretched device. So loud it's almost annoying.

Despite all the agony she inflicted upon Wayob, he still does not wish to kill her. But he must. After all he has suffered, Wayob deserves to be free. But Wayob shall not repeat the mistake of killing the one who holds the Encanto without first finding the wretched device. Abuela must surrender the Encanto before Wayob kills her. This vessel, Aleman, is unacceptable. Wayob must find someone else, and he requires the Encanto to transmigrate, and then he shall destroy it and be free. Abuela would not even have to die, if she could be trusted to let Wayob live the life he deserves, after all he has suffered.

Wayob's feet are so heavy, almost too heavy to lift in the awful boots Aleman wears. Wayob groans and drags his feet along the pavement, across yet another street.

An iron fence blocks his path. His eyes hurt from the sun as he forces his gaze up along the wretched iron fence, which seems to stretch on for miles to the north and just as far to the south, but Wayob must go west. Beyond the fence, Abuela is near.

A block to the south, sun glints on a gate. Wayob trudges toward it. Perhaps this miserable vessel shall prove useful after all, for Wayob learned, decades ago, of the power a man in uniform commands from the chief of the police of Guatemala City, Miguel Arredondo Sosa, who tracked Wayob down when Wayob was finally almost free. Sosa—so like Parker—with his misguided notion that Wayob should suffer for those who died, who had to die. And why should Wayob suffer? What for? Killing Wayob cannot bring them back. So Sosa, the meddling bastard, he had to die too. Ironic that, so many years later, it was Sosa's son, little Luis Luna all-grown-up, who released Wayob from the Encanto. *Karma.*

As Wayob approaches the gate, an electronic trill rings out like a demented songbird, the phone in his pocket again. Wayob contains his impulse to hurl the wretched thing away, to smash it into the sidewalk. The phone might prove useful. He reaches into his pocket and squeezes and presses the wretched device until finally its incessant chirping ceases.

From the metal box mounted by the gate, a deep voice bellows out, "State your name and the nature of your business."

Excellent, Wayob thinks, *no wasting time.* "My name is… Victor Aleman. Let me through."

"Where's your car?"

A reasonable question. Wayob should have driven, clearly. Would have, if he'd known how far he must travel. He prefers to let Aleman live, but in order to find his vehicle, Wayob would have had to peer into Aleman's memories, which would have exposed Wayob's own memories to Aleman.

Like with the crippled vessel Saroyan, who Wayob only peered into out of utter desperation to escape Parker's unwarranted treatment—odious Parker— all Wayob found was Saroyan as a child, his mother using her own body as a shield against Saroyan's drunken father, his father hitting her, over and over again, the vein bulging in his temple, his neck red against the white collar of his shirt.

Saroyan's memories proved a colossal waste of time during which Saroyan might have gained some dim knowledge of the Encanto, so now Saroyan must be dealt with, unfortunately. No choice.

"Still there?" the voice barks through the metal box.

Wayob glares at the camera mounted above it on the fence. "Of course I am still here. Let me through. I am an officer of the law." Approaching the camera, he points to the to the badge on the uniform that belongs to Aleman.

"No one here called the cops."

"My business is elsewhere. I need only to pass through your fence."

Laughter bellows through the box. The voice laughs at Wayob. "That's a new one."

Wayob grinds his teeth and forces his face into a smile. Just a peaceful officer in need of a shortcut. For official police business.

A motor engages. The gate rolls open. Behind the fence, a parking area stretches out to a rectangular building composed of metal, concrete, and glass. From the building, a man with a huge upper torso emerges. He has square shoulders, and a uniform of his own. Dark blue. A rectangular device affixed to his belt. A weapon? *We shall have to find out.*

For Wayob can tell by the way this man is marching toward him that he must be dominated, immediately. Wayob has traveled too far to back down.

Wayob steps through the gate. Draws the gun from his pocket.

The man slows down. He reaches toward his belt... then withdraws. Holds his hands out by his sides. "What's this about?"

"I do not wish to harm you," Wayob says, and he means it, "but I shall, if you make me."

When Wayob shot the man in rags, it was a mercy kill. It had been the deranged old man who hit the ragged man with his vehicle. Wayob merely ended his misery. A favor for the ragged man and for Wayob, who simply could not afford witnesses after all the effort he had expended freeing himself from jail and the crippled vessel of Saroyan.

Too bad the old man escaped. He must have reported the encounter, probably blamed Wayob for running over the ragged man. Thanks to the meddling old man, this officer, with his disproportionate upper torso like an upside-down triangle, now takes a step forward. He means to challenge Wayob—live or die.

Clearly, this man holds the same barbaric notion as Parker and Sosa that Wayob should suffer for those that died, when Wayob never wanted to harm anyone. The priest made him like this. The vile fucking priest.

"It was the priest." Wayob fires into the air. The force kicks his arm back so hard he nearly drops the weapon. As he struggles to remain in control, the gun fires for a second time.

The man falls to the ground.

Then he climbs to his knees, raising his hands. This time high overhead. "Don't shoot. Take whatever you want from the warehouse."

"What is in there?"

"I don't know, man. They don't tell me shit."

Wayob levels the weapon. "How many people inside?"

"No one."

"Do not lie to me."

"It's Saturday, man. No one works weekends."

"Keep your hands up," Wayob says, "Take me to your vehicle."

"Aw man. Not my ride." The man rises, his hands still in the air. "Take one of the trucks. I won't call it in, I swear. It probably won't even be missed until sometime next week."

Cooperation is good. Cooperation is key, since Wayob has little experience with vehicles. He allows this man to lead him around the warehouse to one of the white trucks parked in a row.

Wayob climbs into the driver's seat. "How do I drive this contraption?"

"Are you serious?" the man asks.

Wayob shoves the gun barrel into his ribs.

The man leans into the vehicle and shows Wayob how the gears are on the steering wheel. Just forward and reverse. No clutch. Driving seems easier now than the last time he tried it in Guatemala.

Wayob takes the key from the ignition and climbs out. "Get in and show me."

The man gets into the truck and shows Wayob the controls for a second time, speaking as if Wayob is an idiot.

Wayob withdraws the cuffs from his belt. "Keep your hands on the wheel." He cuffs the man's wrists to the wheel.

"You can't leave me like this. I thought we had a deal."

Wayob shrugs. "This is the deal."

"Come on," the man begs. "You can't leave me here. I need to use the bathroom."

"Disgusting," Wayob says. "But you have already delayed too much as it is."

Wayob chooses another truck, identical to the one with the man chained to the wheel, and drives out through the gate.

The man's directions prove accurate: just a mile and a right turn, and then Wayob is cruising east on a freeway elevated above the sprawl. He should have obtained a car sooner. He is moving so fast. Too fast. He slows a bit and closes his eyes. Just for a second. Just to get the bearing of Abuela's mind, which he can hear even without slipping into a trance. The sound of her mind grates on his nerves.

Almost right below him.

Wayob opens his eyes. The barrier wall along the side of the road rushes toward him. The highway had veered to the left. How was Wayob supposed to know that? He spins the wheel and slams the brakes—too late.

Wayob sees it happen and then hears it. The crunch of the truck against the wall. Wayob squeezes his eyes shut as he is thrown sideways.

When he opens them, he is facing the opposite way. Cars zooming toward him. Squealing tires. Slamming horns.

His head throbs.

The smacking sound he'd heard, he realizes, was his forehead thrown against the glass. The windshield remains intact, as does Aleman's skull, it would seem. Wayob gingerly traces with his fingers the swelling lump on his skull. The flesh is tender, but the skull served its function. Will Aleman remember how this happened? Unlikely. The sooner Wayob finds a new vessel the better.

Wayob pulls the handle, but the door refuses to open. He shoulders into it. The metal groans. Using both hands, he shoves with all his might.

As if to spite him, the door suddenly swings open, spilling him out onto the pavement. He lands on his shoulder in a puddle of brown filth.

Pain.

He has never felt pain like this before—inside the Encanto, there is no such thing as pain—but these wounds are not mortal. He struggles to his feet. Muck has soaked through his sleeve. He tears off his outer shirt and uses the dry part to clean his hands and face.

He looks down over the barrier wall. Below the highway is a derelict building, blue plastic on its roof. Inside the building is Abuela. So close. He can almost jump down upon her.

Wayob laughs.

Wayob jogs along the freeway. Wayob laughs and laughs.

Saul and Hernandez

The 10 was jammed. Saul and Hernandez were halfway up the on-ramp when the car in front of them slowed. Saul hit the brakes. Too late to turn back. "Should have checked traffic."

"It's an accident," Hernandez said.

Sure enough, on the opposite side of the divider, a white truck had hit the barrier wall, spun out, and was now facing the wrong way. Its front bumper missing. Grill crunched into the engine. Oncoming traffic had all but stalled. Cars snaked around the truck one or two at a time.

By the truck, looking over the barrier on the opposite side of the freeway, was the driver. He wore a wifebeater and olive pants, both smeared with dark grime, maybe oil. A mechanic, probably, or a landscaper. Something about the stocky man triggered a sense of *déjà vu*.

"Should we stop?"

"Not our beat." Hernandez pulled her phone. "I'll notify dispatch."

She was right. They would only end up directing traffic, and he would look ridiculous climbing across the divider.

He eased forward a few feet then had to stop again, despite there being no obstruction on this side of the freeway, only lookie-loos craning their necks as if they had never seen an accident on the side of the freeway.

The driver remained standing there, looking down over the barrier. His shoulders trembled like he might be crying. Probably shaken from the accident.

"Unis on the way," Hernandez said.

As they passed the accident, traffic accelerated. Sirens wailed in the distance.

Saul's phone buzzed in his pocket and he pulled it out. On the screen was a text from Chen, the engineer at Verizon who owed him a favor. Chen had traced the blocked number which had called Saul last night: Aleman's cell phone.

Saul relayed this to Hernandez. "It doesn't make any sense," she said. "He was really acting like Saroyan?"

"Almost exactly. He claimed he was Wayob. I'm thinking we should stop by his apartment."

"Okay," she said. "I guess it can't hurt."

They exited the 10 onto the 5 north.

"It's sad," she said.

"Aleman?" If he wasn't such a mean little man, Saul might feel sorry for him.

"No, Rosa. She's going to have to drop out of school now. They're undocumented, so it's not like she can get financial aid or anything."

"Terrible..." Saul racked his brain for something more to say, but in truth he had been so concerned about Saroyan and Aleman that he hadn't considered the long-term ramifications of Luis Luna's murder on Rosa and her grandmother.

He took the 210 to Highland Park. Aleman lived in yet another example of cheap 1950s construction, but given the proximity to downtown, his rent was probably three times more than the Lunas'. His building had been renovated. A stone facade built over on the stucco around the entrance. White letters mounted on the stone spelled out "The Avalon," like inside was somewhere better than LA.

The entrance door was unlocked. Saul held it open for Hernandez and immediately regretted it when she had to swerve around his belly. Might as well put a sign on it.

"Front bumper," he said.

She stopped in the entrance and squinted at him.

Not funny. "Never mind," he said.

The interior floor was some kind of faux wood. They took the hallway on the left toward Aleman's. 112. They knocked on his door.

No answer.

Saul glanced at Hernandez. She shrugged. He knocked again. "Police!"

Behind them, a door opened. A man with a bushy beard leaned out into the hallway, mid-twenties, sporting a Dodgers T-shirt with a torn collar, a brown stain on his belly.

Saul asked, "Have you seen Aleman?"

"Who?"

Saul pointed with his thumb at 112. "Victor Aleman."

"That guy." The bearded man shook his head. "He's usually not back until like five on Saturdays."

Saul checked his phone. It was 3:10. He waited for the man to close his door then pulled out his lockpicks.

Hernandez frowned.

"Exigent circumstances," he said. "Aleman has been missing for fifteen hours. We need to make sure he's okay."

She shook her head. "No indication he's in danger. He ditched work, but maybe he's just out on a bender."

"He threatened to kill someone."

"But who, when, and where?"

"That's the problem. All he said was 'Another must die,' but if you'd heard *how* he said it—"

"Doesn't matter. He's got a clean record."

She was right, of course. No judge would sign a warrant based on what Aleman could claim was some general statement about the human condition.

"Let's wait outside," she said. "This isn't worth your career."

Saul's career had stalled, and he didn't really care, but hers he had to consider. If Aleman had passed out or was hiding in there, then no big deal if they waited. At least she would see for herself how he was acting.

They re-parked across from the Avalon, with a clear view of the entrance and the alleyway to the tenant lot. What if, while they sat here, Aleman was stalking his victim? What if there were clues in his apartment as to whose life he meant to take?

Without a warrant, the evidence might be useless in court, but Saul could worry about that later. He just had to slip in and out unseen. And if he found nothing, he could relax, because he'd know waiting here for Aleman was the best they could do. He could enjoy his time with Hernandez instead of staring out the window, worrying uselessly.

The longer he sat there, the less he cared about Aleman because here he was with the woman of his dreams incarnate. And he was blowing it.

Think, man, think!

"Why don't we use first names?" he asked. "I mean, cops are supposed to be friends, right?"

"We're supposed to think rationally," she said.

"And friendship prevents that?"

She crossed her arms. "Emotion does."

Saul rubbed his chin. "I don't know. Emotion helps me make connections. You can't always follow the evidence."

"That's intuition. Not the same thing."

A Prius pulled out of the alley and turned. The driver, an Asian woman, strained to see over the wheel.

"I wouldn't mind if you called me Saul."

"Okay, *Saul*. You know Aleman might have just pranked you, right?"

"Mind if I call you Rhonda?"

She raised her eyebrows. "Yes," she said, like maybe she was kidding. But she wasn't. That was clear.

"Aleman doesn't strike me as a prankster," he said. "Wish you could have heard his voice."

She flipped back her shock of white. "Maybe Saroyan bribed him somehow to waste our time. I bet he'd get a kick out of that."

There was more to it. Saul was sure. There was more than just a casual connection between Saroyan and Aleman. Hernandez would have to see it for herself. She had come this far.

He changed the subject. "Why do you think the grandmother is blaming herself for the murder?"

Hernandez shrugged. "Maybe she sent him to Venice. Maybe he was doing something for her."

"That makes sense. But seems like she'd still want justice. She told us to leave it alone."

"Yeah. That was weird. If Saroyan murdered my son, I'd want the bastard put down."

Saul recalled the old woman's glazed-over eyes, which rotated down and to the right as she spoke, even though she was blind. A force of habit. She was hiding something.

"How did she hear about the murder?"

"I got the feeling she just knew, you know? Like she felt it."

"You mean... clairvoyance?"

"Not exactly." Hernandez gazed across the street at the row of palms rustling in the wind. A wistful look came into her eyes. "Socrates said the soul is made of energy, separate from matter, and this energy creates a vibration that impacts all living creatures."

Saul was dumbfounded. Here he was suspecting the Luna elder and her son of something nefarious, while Hernandez was suggesting something so far out there it might as well be magic—real magic.

She turned to face him. Her brow furrowed. "You don't think it's possible?"

Realizing he was squinting, Saul smoothed his expression. "It's possible, I think." He wasn't about to disagree with her belief. But magic was real only to those unaware of the trick. And he knew all the tricks.

What he didn't know was science. Science was real. Science he could get behind. "I read that at a sub-atomic level, everything is energy. You think it's all connected some way we can sense?"

"We're capable," she said. "We're probably taking it in, subconsciously, but the logical part of our brain drowns it out. Maybe if we slow down and really concentrate, we *can* feel it." She smiled. "Like *deja vu*. Maybe this energy is what causes *deja vu*. It's all connected across time and space."

Maybe she was right. Who was Saul to say? Maybe it explained the sparks he'd felt earlier, when she placed her hand on his knee. Had she felt them too? If she had, maybe she would fancy a kiss? (Just as an experiment. Just to prove her own theory.)

It should be so easy. All he had to do was lean across the seat and plant one on her. If he did, and *if* she kissed him back...

But if she refused, then it was game over. Forget about a relationship.

He glanced down. His belly lay in his lap like a sack of old clothes that needed to go. What did he expect?

She squinted out the Avalon. Her streak of white fell across her forehead. She pulled out her phone and glanced at the screen. "I need to get home for dinner with Rumi and my mom. Mind dropping me at the PAB?"

"Not at all." Saul started the engine. The Police Administration Building was only ten miles away. In less than an hour, he could be back here searching Aleman's apartment on his own.

As he merged onto the 210, Hernandez's gaze raked over his belly. He tightened his grip on the wheel and pretended to focus on the road.

"You going to the Castle tonight?"

Was she just making conversation or, maybe, fishing for more? "I'll put you on the guest list," he said. "If you want to stop by for dessert or a show, or something."

"Can't tonight."

Saul's chest tightened. He stared out at the Prius to their left, like it suddenly required all his attention.

"It's just…," she continued, "on Saturday nights, my mother and I watch our telenovela, and I've hardly been home all week."

He tried to sound upbeat. "I get it. I'll just put you on the list in case some other night works. Whenever, you know? Anytime."

Hernandez swiped on her phone. "Sure."

Saul merged the 5 south. A bank of low clouds pushed in from the coast. Darkened out the setting sun.

By the time he reached Elysian Park, the sky was a solid gray mass. Lights were on at Dodger Stadium. On the 110, traffic slowed to a halt. He exited on Broadway. While waiting at the light, he tried calling Aleman again. If Hernandez could just hear for herself…

Five rings. No answer.

When they rolled up to the PAB, it was dusk. The lower floors were lit up. The glass building was shaped like a boat moored among the taller buildings behind it. Officers coming and going. A hive of activity. Light from the lobby spilled down the steps to the sidewalk. Saul parked by the curb.

"See you later." Hernandez smiled slightly and turned to get out. Did her smile have something to do with him? He sure hoped so.

She took her time getting out. As she approached the wide steps to the lobby, her broad hips swayed in her cotton slacks. Saul felt lightheaded.

Later, she'd said. Later when?

He could have asked. He could have at least waved goodbye instead of just sitting like a silent lump of lard.

His phone buzzed, and he checked the screen.

Victor Aleman.

As Saul answered, he flung open the door and heaved himself out.

"De-tec-tive Par-ker." That same mocking cadence.

"Where are you?" Saul asked.

"I am closing in."

Saul scanned the dozen or so pedestrians within sight. The only one with a phone was a guy in a suit, crossing First toward City Hall. Too lanky to be Aleman, too tall.

"Where are you?" Saul asked again, as he bounded onto the sidewalk. He had to keep him on the line. Hernandez had to hear this.

"My concern, Parker, is that you keep calling this device. I told you to leave me alone."

A man in three layers of dirty coats steered his cart of belongings toward Saul. He pointed at the no-parking sign. "Twenty bucks and I'll watch your car."

Saul swerved around him. No way Hernandez could hear him through the glass. Saul charged up the steps.

"So, who are you this time?"

"Wayob," said the gruff voice on the phone.

Saul shouted, "What happened to Aleman?"

Just as Saul made it to the entrance, on the opposite side of the vast lobby, Hernandez stepped into an elevator. As the doors closed in front of her, she raked back her shock of white.

"Aleman shall be fine," Wayob said. "Many decades ago, I encountered a man just like you, a *policia* who refused to leave me alone. He died, and it was his fault for meddling with my freedom. Do not repeat his mistake."

Hernandez was headed to her car, Saul knew, but there was no cell service in the garage, and no way he could catch up to her now, so he lumbered toward Main, the closer of the two exits to the garage, hoping to flag her down as she left.

"Who died?" Saul asked.

"I do not have time for another of your *interviews*, Parker. Leave me alone or there *shall* be retribution. I shall have no choice." Wayob ended the call.

Saul halted, chest heaving. He leaned forward, hands on his knees, to catch his breath. No point now in racing to catch Hernandez.

Was that Aleman pretending to be Wayob? Or someone else with Aleman's phone?

Saul called Mark Chen.

"You get my text?" Chen asked.

"I'm going to need a little more." Saul doubled back toward his plain wrap. "I need a location on that number."

"Whoa. I can't do that."

"Can't or won't?"

The homeless man held his hand out, wanting payment for watching Saul's car.

Saul stepped into the street to avoid him.

"It would mean my job," Chen said.

Saul stuffed himself behind the wheel of the plain wrap. "I'm not asking for more than what you guys are already handing over to the NSA."

Chen went silent for a long moment. "I don't know anything about that."

"Look, I get it. But lives are at stake. If someone dies…"

"I'll be covered. I don't mean to sound ungrateful or anything, but I've already gone way out on a limb for you. Verizon has official channels for coordinating with law enforcement."

"Vicky around?"

"Aw, man. Don't go there."

The Chens had promised—Vicky, emphatically—that they would do anything to repay Saul for recovering their stolen artwork.

"I'll go where I have to," Saul said. "Nothing personal. Like I said—"

"Alright, alright. I'll hook you up—this one *last* time. Then we're even."

"Of course," Saul said. As far as he was concerned, they were already even. More than even. There was no quid pro quo for doing his job. He just lacked any other option. Verizon would demand a warrant. A warrant required the signature of a judge. And judges required more than some vague threat from a public servant with a clean record. Hernandez was right about that.

Chen sighed and ended the call.

———

Saul turned from Cesar Chavez onto Main. The Olvera Street Plaza was packed. Some kind of festival. He swung a U-turn and parked beside the plaza, behind the row of cars already lined up along the red curb.

He pulled out his phone and clicked the link from Chen. It opened a map with a red pin indicating the location of Aleman's phone. He was on Olvera, the cobbled street between the plaza and Cesar Chavez.

A dotted line traced backward in time showing the movements of Aleman's phone over the last twenty-four hours. Last night, after leaving the MDC, Aleman had traveled east—on foot evidently, moving at less than four miles an hour. At around three in the afternoon, his speed increased suddenly and his path moved off the surface streets and onto the 10. Where it stopped for a while, almost exactly where Saul and Hernandez saw the accident.

Maybe it was a coincidence?

One coincidence was possible, but then Aleman had circled the Luna's apartment. Two coincidences? Impossible. He must have known, somehow, that Saul would be there. Or maybe his strange trip had something to do with the Lunas. However, he hadn't gone to their apartment; he'd zigzagged to a Metrolink station in El Monte, where he took a train to the nearby Union Station and then walked here.

After traveling all night and day, Aleman must have a reason to attend the street festival, and Saul very much wanted to hear it.

A crowd was gathering around the gazebo in the plaza. As Saul pushed his way through, he called Hernandez on impulse—then cancelled the call. She would ask how he was tracking Aleman, and avoiding telling her would be the same as lying. This much he had learned from his failed marriage, from all those nights he had let his now ex-wife assume he was working late when he was really at the Castle. And then she had blamed her affair on his secret life. She had said magic turned her off, but still. He should have told her.

As Saul swiped back to the map, Hernandez appeared on the screen, her LAPD profile pic, dress blues and classy smile. He had to answer. If he screened her out now, she would know.

"What's up?" she asked.

Saul hesitated. If they were ever going to be more than just partners, he had to trust her—all the way. "I've got a bead on Aleman."

"Where?"

"Olvera Street."

"*El Pueblo?* How did you find him there?"

"Would you believe I just happened to stop by for the Day of the Dead festival?"

"No."

"I'm tracking his phone," he said.

She inhaled. Saul knew, just from the sound, that the corners of her mouth were drawn in.

"I'm just going to hang up," she said. "We'll pretend I never heard this."

The crowd was bunching up. A pair of uniforms were sweeping people back to make way for the parade. Holding out his badge, Saul shoved through the human barricade while keeping the phone to his ear. "That's why I changed my mind about calling you."

"Why are you jeopardizing your career? Aleman's not worth it."

"This is bigger than Aleman. I don't even know for sure if he's the one calling me."

"Look," Hernandez said. "Levy's asking if you're pulling your weight. If she finds out—"

"She asked you that directly?" If Levy came out and actually said that, then Saul was in the shit for sure.

"Nah, she beat all around the bush. You know how she is."

"I see."

"I didn't mean like you're fat or anything."

"No, I know." *Freudian slip.* He had been on Levy's shit-list ever since the Brown shooting, and he doubted she would ever let it go. "She's going to make you lead detective, and I want you to know there's no hard feelings. You deserve it."

"Oh, I doubt that."

"Trust me—it's already happened. She just doesn't have the balls to tell us, and by us, I mean me."

The buildings of the historic pueblo flanked Olvera Street. At the entrance was a stone pedestal with a giant cross. Behind it, a row of kiosks divided the street, forcing the crowd into two separate lanes. Saul took the left fork, heading for the location of the red pin—the last ping from Aleman's phone.

"We're off topic," Hernandez said. "My point is, you're going overboard, like you always do, for what might be a prank call."

At least if it was, then no one would be in danger, but finding Aleman, or whoever was pretending to be Wayob, meant more to Saul than his career— what little might be left of it.

"Better to go overboard for nothing than to do nothing if someone's in danger." The way he spoke left little room for doubt.

"True," she said with more than a little hesitation in her voice.

"He called me again. And this time he basically confessed to killing an officer."

"Why didn't you say so?"

"He said it was decades ago and didn't give any other details, but he threatened me again."

"Alright. I'll be there in thirty."

"No, let me find him first. You've got family night." Saul ducked under a low awning.

"Dinner's over. It took Rumi all of two minutes to wolf down his dinner and then he asked to be excused."

"Teenagers," Saul said, like he knew anything about teenagers. He had been one once, thirty-five years ago. "What about your soap opera?"

"You don't want me there?"

If she wanted to come, then he was happy to have her. More than happy. "Oh, I want you," he said. *Too obvious?* "When I find Aleman, or whoever the bastard is, you're going to want to see for yourself."

After she agreed to come, Saul ended the call.

The sight of a kiosk selling churros triggered a vast hollowness in his stomach—*churros*. He forced himself past the almost overwhelming scent. Cinnamon, sugar, fried dough....

In a shop window, Mexican blankets similar to the one on the Lunas' couch were arrayed over a railing. Saul stopped and checked the map on his phone. The blue dot representing his location was almost right on top of the red pin. He scanned the crowd. Mostly Latino. Aleman's pale complexion would stand out. Unless he was one of the dozens of men wearing masks. Plenty were stocky enough but most were too short. Aleman was medium height... the same height as the man in a big sombrero, dressed like a mariachi, facing away from Saul. He plowed toward the man. A woman in a formal red dress clung to his arm.

Saul tapped him on the shoulder.

They both turned at once. The woman's face had been painted like a sugar skull with a colorful pattern around her eyes. The man's upper face was hidden behind a half-skull mask, only his eyes peering out at Saul through sockets of the skull. Below the mask, he frowned.

Too much chin. And his face was too lean. Not Aleman.

Saul backed away. He surveyed the mass of people. There were too many. Aleman was slipping away. And with each ticking second, so was the truth.

Something bumped Saul's leg. A stroller. Behind it, a woman in her mid-thirties tightened her grip on the handle as if preparing to mow him down. "Excuse me." She had mocha hair and steely eyes ringed with dark circles of exhaustion. Her skin was so pale it was almost blue.

Saul stepped back. Behind her, a little girl in a pink dress paused, enthralled by the woman in the red.

"Mindy." The woman with the stroller tugged the girl's arm.

"I'll help you get through," Saul said.

Using his girth, he plowed through the crowd, still scanning the faces for Aleman. The woman trundled her stroller behind him on the uneven bricks, towing her little girl. Saul led them through the tightly packed crowd and emerged into a more free-flowing throng of people milling to and from the plaza. He stepped aside and motioned the woman ahead.

She pushed past him. No eye contact. But her little girl looked up at Saul. He smiled and waved goodbye, and she gave him a big grin. Two missing teeth.

He checked the map on his phone and found that his blue dot had moved a bit but not the red pin. He called Aleman's number. As the ringtone played in his ear, he scanned the crowd. There were phones out all over the place, people taking photos or texting, but no one seemed to notice a call.

Aleman's voicemail picked up. Saul ended the call and swiped back to the map. The red dot jumped. Must be some kind of lag. Aleman must have passed on the opposite side of the street behind the kiosks. Now he was near where Olvera met the plaza.

Saul marched toward the location, watching his phone the whole way. The pin placed Aleman in the restaurant on the corner, La Golondrina.

Saul wedged himself through the crowd. He passed by a table just as a waiter delivered a steaming pan of fajitas. His stomach rumbled. The tables were jammed together, each with a platter of chips and salsa. Margaritas. Guacamole. He swallowed. He tried to focus on the faces. They stared back with glassy eyes.

An arched doorway led to a dimly lit interior. A split-level with terra-cotta tile and exposed brick preserved from the former pueblo. Saul tried to concentrate on the faces, not the food going into them. Chicken mole. Enchiladas. Quesadillas.

A hostess intercepted him. "How many?"

"Two." He gestured toward the back wall.

She seated him at an empty two top next to an elderly couple. The man nodded his fedora at Saul then turned back to his wife who was dressed all in red.

The table hid much of Saul's girth, but a fat man at an empty table looked suspicious, so, just to blend in, he ordered the nachos grande with cheese, sour cream, and carnitas. Not to eat—the last thing he wanted was to be stuffing his face when Hernandez arrived—but she might want some. Maybe they could eat together.

At the bar, a man with his back turned had the same squat torso as Aleman, the same oblong head and thinning hair. Though the plaid shirt, untucked over faded jeans, seemed out of character for Aleman. Saul had only ever seen him in uniform.

The nachos arrived. The bottom dropped out of his stomach. He had every intention of waiting for Hernandez. He was on a diet, after all. Yet, the nachos were going in his mouth. Almost involuntarily.

Basically, he had to. He would look suspicious just sitting behind a platter of nachos grande and not eating. He tried to slow down but his body demanded fuel.

The man was doing no harm at the moment, just drinking Tecate and reading his phone. If he was Aleman, then Saul should wait for Hernandez.

But what if he wasn't Aleman? What if, while Saul was sitting here gorging himself on the nachos he already regretted, Aleman was closing in on his victim?

Outside, drums hammered. Tambourines rattled. The sound of the parade moving closer. People rose from their seats.

The man who might be Aleman stood. Aleman's height. He merged into the crowd already shuffling toward the exit. Saul had to catch him before he was lost in the crowd. Time to find out if he was Aleman or not.

Saul plowed past the tables, into the crowd. Once he was in earshot, he shouted: "Hey, Aleman."

The man kept moving, out into the plaza, toward the performance at the gazebo. He seemed in no hurry.

Saul caught up to him, grabbed his shoulder, and spun him around.

"What the hell?" The man was clean shaven with a big nose, expansive forehead, and a receding hairline. Aleman's brow was narrow. And he had a mustache.

"Thought you were someone else," Saul said.

The man grumbled and turned toward the gazebo.

Saul checked his phone. The red pin was still on La Golondrina. He hurried back, and was glad to find his table as he'd left it. Still, a large portion of the nachos grande remaining for him and Hernandez to share. The table beside his had been cleared. Aside from a cellphone. The old couple must have left it.

The nachos Saul had eaten burned in his stomach. He called Aleman's number.

On the neighboring table, the phone buzzed. It chirped.

Saul snatched it up and stared at it, stared at his own number on the screen. The phone continued to vibrate and chirp in his hand.

He flagged over a waitress. "Who left this phone here?"

She reached for it. "I'll take it to the hostess in case they come back."

"I'll do it." Saul marched to the hostess stand.

He showed her his badge and pointed out the table, next to his, where the elderly couple had been sitting. "Do you have their number?"

She swiped the screen of her iPad, and showed Saul the number they had used when they made their reservation.

He dialed. It rang four times.

The woman answered.

"Where's Victor Aleman?"

"Who?"

"Victor Aleman."

"Who is this?"

Saul introduced himself and described Aleman.

"I'm sorry, but we haven't seen him. We don't know anyone like that."

Saul wasn't surprised. He thanked her, ended the call, and returned to his table.

He pocketed Aleman's phone, hunched over the nachos and plowed in.

Gray's Dilemma

Earlier that night, on the way to Dia De Los Muertos, Gray merged into the left lane, just to do something, but all four were equally slow. The alcohol had left his system and taken with it the fluid in his skull, shriveling his frontal lobe. It felt like all the cars on the 101 were plowing over it.

He checked the rear-view. Tyler was strapped in and sound asleep. Beside him, Mindy frowned. She'd complained about going to the celebration, but once she saw it, she would change her mind. They just had to get there.

He glanced over at Claire in the passenger seat. She looked up from her phone. "What?" Her thumb kept right on swiping the screen.

His chance of finishing a painting this weekend—let alone of finishing a good one—were dwindling down to impossible, and with nothing to show, not even one worthy painting to back up his plan, how could he give notice at work? How could he tell Claire? Realistically, it might take months to finish his masterpiece, and months become years. Even if his painting was amazing, even if the world agreed, Claire might not be into it. The way she had breezed right past the portrait he'd started without saying anything, said *a lot*. She might be the last person in the world who would recognize him as an artist.

He had to think from her point of view. Maybe she'd be supportive of his new direction in life, if there was something in it for her. She had griped often enough about how lucky he was to go to work, so maybe she could get a job while he stayed home to paint. He wouldn't mind more time with the kids.

"You ever think about maybe going back to work?" he asked. "You know, maybe after Tyler's old enough for daycare."

"Seriously, Gray?" Her eyes seemed to spark from the headlights in the oncoming lane.

He looked straight ahead. The car in front of him slowed to a stop, and so did he.

"Do you know how tired I am?" she continued. "I can't think about anything but sleep."

Ahead, the 101 stretched out like a serpent of red and white lights tightening around the skyscrapers downtown. He eased forward.

By far, the biggest problem was the mortgage. $4,200 a month was a tough pill to swallow, and on top of that, property tax was $950. Plus insurance premiums, utilities, car payments, and cell phones added up to another $1,500 at least. $6,700 wouldn't be a problem considering he made $12,400 per month, except after all the taxes, plus withholdings for Medicare and Social Security, his actual take-home was more like $7,900. Add then after food and daycare, most months they ended up in the red. Next fall, Mindy started kindergarten at a public school, but then he and Claire had already agreed on daycare for Tyler—$1,200 a month. And they should be saving for college, and retirement.

Even if Gray kept on working, he wasn't making enough, and there was no opportunity for a raise. He'd been passed over for enough promotions to know it would never be him, and no matter how fast he coded, Brad merely compressed the schedule such that Gray was always struggling just to keep up.

And if he quit working, their savings would be gone in four months. Kids came with responsibilities. He knew that, and he wanted them, of course. He was the one who had to convince Claire, but somehow, in the midst of all his convincing, he'd never considered that having kids might mean sacrificing his dreams. He'd assumed he could have it all.

Gray was barreling forward when the car in front of them stopped. He slammed the brakes.

Claire grabbed his shoulder. "Shit, Gray!"

He stopped just in time. He swallowed and adjusted the rear-view mirror. Mindy's lip quivered.

"You ready to see the parade?" he asked her.

She shook her head.

"Did I mention the chocolate-covered churros?"

Mindy's lips betrayed her with an almost smile before she managed to suppress it with a clown-sized frown.

"I can turn around if you want," Gray said. "I guess we don't have to go."

"Yeah, let's just go home." Claire said. "By the time we get there, the parade will be over."

Gray shot her a look. He knew she hated downtown, but staying at home was like living in a pressure cooker. Why was it always up to him to drag them out? By the time they were driving home, they would be laughing, maybe singing, or at least everyone would be so exhausted that when they got home, he could paint.

"It's up to Mindy," Gray said. "But I should point out we don't have churros at home, and we're all out of chocolate sauce."

Now Claire shot Gray a look. *Touché.* Maybe he was being manipulative, but it was true.

"Keep going, I guess." Mindy straightened her pink dress beneath the seatbelt.

Gray chuckled, raised his eyebrows, and winked at Mindy in the mirror.

Half an hour later, he exited the 101 and rolled into a long line of cars waiting to park at El Pueblo de Los Angeles. Complete standstill.

Claire sighed deeply.

"I'm thinking I should open a bar." He just blurted it out, without even intending to say it but now that he'd said it, a certain looseness sank into his shoulders. He felt almost relieved.

"Seriously?" Claire practically shouted. "Our house *is* a bar... and you need more to drink? Seriously?"

"It's not about that. It's my job... we can't get ahead." And it was true. A bar that doubled as a studio and gallery would not only give him the time and space to paint, it could even turn a decent profit.

Claire crossed her arms. "Bull. Shit."

Gray did not want to argue in front of Mindy. In the mirror, she looked already close to losing it, and if she started crying it would upset Tyler, who was awake now and looking around.

He lowered his brows at Claire and nodded toward the back. "We should tone it down."

She rolled her eyes, like he was the one and only baby in the car. "Right." She leaned back in her seat and shut down.

Gray pulled out his phone, opened Candy Crush, and handed it back for Mindy to play under the condition that she let Tyler watch.

The primary parking lot was full. It took another twenty minutes to inch along to a dimly lit secondary lot. At the entrance to the secondary lot, the attendant, whose shaved eyebrows had been replaced by tattoos of braided barbed wire, wrapped Gray's twenty around a fat wad of bills and peeled off three ones for change.

Gray parked and unstrapped Tyler while Claire set up the stroller. He took Mindy by the hand and they followed the crowd as it wormed around a busker with long, gray hair, his guitar case opened for donations, which so far consisted of about seven dollars and some change.

Adjacent to Olvera Street was a restaurant. A barker shouted from the door, "Tacos, burritos, tamales, es deliciosa! Tacos, burritos, tamales."

Gray salivated. A burrito and basket of chips would cure his hangover, and, although he was a Scotch man, he could stomach a decent tequila. Maybe even a wine or sangria. Too bad there wasn't time before the parade.

They followed the crowd funneling into Olvera. Mindy tugged his hand and pointed out the bricks. He explained how it had been paved by hand, and how Olvera was the oldest street in LA. He hoisted her up to his shoulders and made his way toward a kiosk selling sugar skulls and fresh baked churros.

"Ice cream!" Mindy pointed toward a window between shops. She could find ice cream in the Sahara.

"You don't want to try a churro?" Gray asked. "They're really good."

"Ice cream!" Mindy said. "They have sprinkles. I can see them from here."

Gray glanced back at Claire, who was a few yards behind with the stroller. "We're getting ice cream."

She groaned. "Of course."

At the window, Mindy ordered chocolate with extra sprinkles. When he attempted to lower her from his shoulders, she clutched his neck. "I can't eat standing up. Please, Daddy."

He laughed. "I wish someone would hold me up above the crowd."

He wrapped the cone in a stack of napkins and handed it up to Mindy.

Ahead, a face-painting booth encroached on the sidewalk, creating a narrow passage through which navigating the stroller would be difficult. Claire had stopped just short of it and parked the stroller outside a store selling Mexican blankets. She watched him approach with an expression of such intense exasperation that Gray might have laughed if it wasn't exactly the wrong thing to do.

"Want to trade?" Gray asked her, pointing at the stroller where Tyler seemed content staring up at the faces in the crowd.

Something landed on his chest and slid down his shirt. Wet, cold. It was Mindy's ice cream.

This time, she was too ashamed to protest as he lowered her to the ground.

He patted her head. "I know you didn't mean to."

He glanced up at Claire. "I'd better go wash this off," he said, already salivating for the drink he would snag on the way, and maybe a quesadilla.

"It's fine," she said. "It's dark. No one's going to notice."

"It'll stain."

She rolled her eyes. "Just hurry."

Gray started off, pumping his arms like he was jogging, though there were so many people he could hardly walk at a fast pace. While scoping out a bar, he noticed a long line for the men's room. *Better join it and see how fast it's moving.* He knew better than to come back with ice cream still on his shirt or Claire would right away know he had had a drink.

The line descended a short flight of stairs and made its way into a stone alleyway with a low, arched ceiling. The air in the alley was cold, and the ice cream on his shirt wasn't helping.

From the restaurant above, a mariachi band trumpeted, like sirens calling him. The margaritas were flowing. Tequilas, sangrias, and cervezas. A full bar, probably. Maybe even Scotch.

"Sounds like fun up there," Gray said to the guy in front of him, who was dressed like a skeleton, all black with white bones, skull mask, and top hat.

He grunted and kept right on scrolling his phone.

The line inched forward. Tucked under the stairs to the restaurant was a fortune booth with a modest sign, "El Fortunas Cinco Dilores." Below the sign was a black curtain through which a thin Latina emerged, dressed all in black. She leaned against the doorframe and looked directly at Gray.

The trumpets blasted.

She was awkwardly beautiful, with gangly arms and a nose just a little too long for her face, which made her more interesting as a subject. And she showed no reaction to Gray staring at her, so maybe she was focused more on the line than on him. Hard to tell. Her eyes were shadowed by drapes of black hair. She yawned and rubbed her eyes.

Behind her, through a crack in the curtain, candlelight flickered. Gray had a feeling it was warm back there. And he needed an escape, just for a minute, and since there wasn't time for a drink, a quick fortune couldn't hurt—nothing for Claire to smell, and better for his ego. Fortunetelling was basic psychology, right? She would ask leading questions, predict a change in his future, and then he could finally tell someone that, yes, he planned on becoming an artist, somehow, full time. And, of course, she would *foresee* that he'd find great success (and a generous tip for herself).

If nothing else, it would give him a chance to study her up close. Maybe she'd let him take a photo with his phone, from which he could compose a portrait.

He tapped the skeleton guy on the shoulder.

The guy glanced up from his phone.

"I'll be back in a minute," Gray said. "Mind saving my place?"

He grunted affirmatively, sort of nodded, and went back into his phone.

Gray stepped out of line and had to restrain himself from leaping across the alley. He didn't want to scare the girl, who for sure saw him now. She averted her eyes and lifted the curtain for him to enter.

He stepped inside.

And was met with the smell of burning sage. Its smoke curling up from a ceramic smudge pot, half-encircled by prayer candles, on a small, wooden table in the corner of the narrow rectangle of a room walled in with black cloth. Through a break in the curtains, a narrow split, Gray glimpsed another room, more candlelight.

"Have a seat," the girl said. "Abuela will see you in a sec."

Gray turned to face her. "Abuela?" He felt almost duped. He wanted the girl to tell his fortune.

"My grandmother." She snaked her hands through her hair, glanced up at him and laughed. "You'll be glad when you meet her, trust me."

He swallowed his disappointment. But he was here already, so he might as well.

He paid the girl his five dollars. She parted the curtain to the inner room and slipped through.

———

Gray waited in the narrow room walled in by black cloth. He sat in the chair nearest the curtain through which the girl had disappeared, the girl who hadn't said her name. He leaned his head toward the cloth and listened hard, but the fabric dulled the whispering on the other side. He wasn't sure what he heard, if it was even words.

He inhaled the sage. The candles flickered in a draft.

What was he doing? Quitting his job? A fantasy. Nothing more. That was why he hadn't told Claire, why he couldn't tell anyone. No way to say it out loud without hearing how ridiculous it sounded.

What he had was a hobby. To think it could be something more was a pipe dream with no basis in reality. Who does that? He had not even one finished painting. It was like jumping from a plane with only some rope and nylon, and a vague idea to build a parachute on the way down.

The room felt smaller. Like the walls were drawing in.

What was he doing here? A fortune-teller? Please. Like that was going to help.

As he stood to leave, the girl slid through the inner curtain, tripped, and caught herself. "Abuela is ready for you."

He opened his mouth to say he was leaving—Claire would be boiling over by now—but the girl held the curtain aside. Warm light poured in from behind her. It shimmered from hundreds, possibly thousands, of candles. His mouth remained open but no words came out. He was out of the chair. Practically floating toward the light.

Beyond the curtain, there were only fifty candles, maybe a hundred, arrayed on two shelves flanking the room. An ancient woman with hunched shoulders sat at a small, wooden table in the center. The room wasn't much bigger than the waiting area but somehow it seemed more spacious, the walls of black cloth even darker, as if they were empty space. The woman sat over a white, bowl-shaped candle, a pool of wax around its wick. The flickering light cast deep shadows between the wrinkles etched into her face. A wattle of loose skin sagged from her chin to her neck, and her eyes were milky white.

Gray had to paint her. This was more than want, more than desire... this was a need. He felt it in his heart. Would she pose for him? She was obviously blind, so he could snap her photo and she would never know.

He glanced over his shoulder. The girl had vanished behind the curtain, leaving him alone with her abuela.

"Sit, sit," she said, her voice raspy and wet. Her body was shrouded in a colorful shawl. From beneath it emerged two meaty arms sleeved in black. She reached across the table toward him, palms extended on either side of the candle.

He pulled out the chair across from her. It was low to the ground, as was the table. When he sat, he bumped his knees on the table.

As she cackled, the lines around her mouth and her eyes stretched up in pure joy. He felt warm inside, and then he started laughing, too. All he'd done was bump his knees on the table, but now it was more than that. Something had passed between them. They had shared a moment.

Her cackle sputtered into a cough. She tried to contain it as she snatched a white cloth from her shawl and covered her mouth. The cough spasmed up from deep in her chest. She shook. She had blotches on the skin on the back of her hand.

She coughed and coughed all while her eyes seemed to probe into him. He could almost feel her gazing in. He looked away.

On the shelf to the left, marigolds had been strewn among the candles around a photograph... which at first Gray doubted. The Latino smiling out from the silver frame bathed in flickering light—it couldn't be—but there was no mistaking that cleft chin.... It must be him. It had to be him, the man whose brutal death he'd almost witnessed on Lincoln Boulevard: Luis Luna. Here, in the black-curtained back room of a fortune booth, surrounded by candles and flowers.

Gray gulped for air. The fortune-teller and her milky eyes... Somehow, she had known he would come here. She had placed this photo on the shelf for him to see, as if this were his future. A cruel fortune for five dollars.

But this was impossible. There must be some other explanation. Maybe she knew Luis Luna. Maybe he'd been a member of the community who took part in this celebration of Dia De Los Muertos. Maybe, if Gray looked around, he'd find the same photo displayed in other shrines on Olvera tonight.

After her coughing jag ended, she stuffed the handkerchief back in her shawl.

Gray asked, "Did you know him?"

She said nothing. The deep grooves in her face were like weathered rock, thousands of years old, maybe older. Why did the girl have to leave them alone?

He smelled incense. When he looked around for the source, he noticed the photo seemed to have changed. Luis Luna was still sort of smiling but now his eyes were sad, and all the color had drained from the marigolds, like an overcast sky at dusk.

"Su nombre." The fortune-teller had produced a scrap of paper and a pen. She pushed it toward him on the table.

Was this a joke? He squinted at her.

Her milky eyes seemed to gaze right through him. Maybe she would show his name to the girl, who would look him up online and find something real to put in his fortune.

He scribbled his name, sort of curious what the trick was.

Her brows furrowed. She pressed her lips tight, and a powerful emotion crossed her face, whether it was remorse, pity or a deep sadness, Gray wasn't quite sure. "I'd love to paint you," he said.

She snatched his hand and held it palm up.

"I'll do it for free," he continued. "What's the best way to contact you?"

She said nothing. With her fingertip, a hard bloodless thing of leather and bone, she traced his palm.

The silence was intense. He felt the need to say something. He swallowed, preparing to ask if he could take her picture, for reference for his portrait of her, when finally, she spoke.

"Tienes..." She seemed to struggle. "You have... eye."

Like an eye for painting? She was following the clue he'd given her. Gray chuckled, awkwardly, despite the dead serious look on her face.

"Tienes un buen corazón."

"I don't understand Spanish," he said. "No comprendo."

"Todos se aprovechan de un hombre con un buen corazón, y lo siento, pero ahora yo también debo hacerlo." She reached inside her shawl and produced a round, white, porous stone the size of an orange, flattened on top where a snake was mounted, carved from obsidian. Rows of jagged ridges chiseled into its back looked like feathers. A pair of fangs protruded from its wide-open mouth.

She placed the stone in Gray's palm. It felt cool and somehow right, like it belonged there in his palm. She folded his fingers around the stone and twisted the snake a half-turn counter-clockwise. Its fangs pointed at him.

A tingling sensation nettled his palm as though his hand was falling asleep.

She spoke in soft Spanish, her voice catching on the wetness in her throat, the wattle below her chin trembling.

He nodded, not understanding a word. Her hands were cold and leathery, like mitts pressed around his hand that held the stone.

She began singing in an unfamiliar language. Her eyes closed. Beyond the candlelight, a deep blackness seemed to open up, as if the room were floating in space.

The stone warmed in his palm. The tingling sensation slid up his arm, along the back of his neck. The candles faded away.

He drifts on a cloud. Below him is LA...

He sees a garden, a grassy hill warmed by the setting sun, overlooking the city and the sea. And now he's standing at an easel. His easel. His painting of the dark figure is nearly complete. The figure comes into focus: a short man with brown skin, not much older than a boy, standing in the shadow of an immense stone temple. His expression is placid, but his eyes... his eyes are solid black, deeper than night. Not eyes at all—they're holes.

Behind Gray, a door closes. He spins toward the sound. Above the garden, stands a modern looking house with a wall of dark windows and a turret. The old woman descends the steps from the patio and approaches him with a glass of deep-red wine. She hands it to him. Her expression is somber in the waning light, which seems to smooth the wrinkles on her face, and her eyes are now dark pools. They take him in, all that he is, as he drinks the blood-red wine.

It tastes of nothing. He gulps and his mouth remains dry. He holds up the glass. Instead of wine, it contains a milk-like vapor that swirls like fog in the glass.

She extends her wrinkled hand and takes the glass from him. She drinks.

Gray opened his eyes. He was seated again before the fortune-teller, back among the black curtains and the candles. She had stopped singing. Her pupils were frosted again. Seeing nothing.

The marigolds were bright orange and red, but as he watched, they faded. Incense burned his eyes. He blinked. "I must have drifted off..."

She had withdrawn her hands from his fist. The stone felt cold in his palm. The snake had been mounted such that it could rotate like a dial, and he had a vague notion that if he did so, the stone would somehow pull him back into the dream. *Was it a dream?* It had felt like one, yet he'd been wide awake. He wanted another look at the painting—his painting. If he could recreate what he'd seen and maybe give the man some eyes, it could be his masterpiece.

Gray traced his finger along the snake, along the ridges of the feathers chiseled in the obsidian. He nudged the head, which gave only a token resistance and then started to turn.

"No!" The fortune-teller's hands pounced on his, gripping his hands with surprising strength. Her milky eyes remained fixed, unfocused. How had she known he was twisting it?

It was a foolish notion anyway to think this thing could help him see what he'd obviously dreamed. She pried his fingers from the snake, although there was no need. He was going to give it back to her. But when he tried to, she jerked away.

"Lo siento, lo siento," she said. "Destroy! Nada vale la pena abrir las puertas de Xibalba. Lo sé, créeme. Lo siento." Tears streamed down her weathered cheeks. She balled her fist and brought it down like a hammer above the charm, which was still in his palm. She repeated the motion, then mimed twisting the snake-dial and fiercely shook her head.

"No entiendo," he said. "I don't understand. No hablo."

"Abuela! No se puede dar!" the girl said.

Gray turned in his chair. The girl had emerged through the curtain.

"Hice!" the fortune-teller said.

"What is it?" he asked.

The girl shrank away from him. "She should not have given it to you. You must destroy it."

If they were so afraid of this thing, why keep it around? "Do you have a hammer?"

The fortune-teller shouted hoarsely in Spanish.

"It is yours now," the girl translated. "You must do this yourself."

"Uh…" Gray looked down at the stone charm in his palm. Didn't he have enough to deal with already?

"Time for you to go." The girl held open the curtain.

She was right about that. How long had he been here?

He considered just leaving the charm on the table. It looked like it was worth more than the five dollars he'd paid for the fortune he hadn't received.

The fortune-teller set her jaw, and the girl avoided his eyes. He had the feeling they would freak out if he tried leaving without it.

As he stepped out through the curtain, the fortune-teller shouted after him, "No te utilizarlo!"

Outside the booth, he was assaulted by the sounds of the parade, which somehow the curtains had muffled. His hangover, which he'd almost forgotten about, returned with a vengeance. The drums pounded in his skull, making him dizzy. He leaned against the cobbled wall.

Was that all a performance? The fortune-teller had seemed for real. Her tears had been real. If that was acting, she should get an agent—she and her granddaughter.

Gray clutched the porous stone and hefted it in his hand. It was surprisingly light.

The line for the bathroom was just as long as before. No sign of the skeleton guy who was supposed to hold his place. He'd have to tell Claire that he waited but the line just wasn't moving.

He pushed off the wall and turned toward the street, colliding with a stocky man whose head hit Gray's chin.

They both stepped back. The man had wild eyes and dried mucus in his mustache. He was dressed as an officer, his uniform disheveled and untucked. He apologized and asked for the time.

Gray checked his phone. Texts from Claire filled the screen:

In the plaza near gazebo.

Ready to go.

Where are you?

"It's 7:30," Gray said.

"Where are we?" The officer looked around like he'd just dropped out of the sky. His badge featured the California golden bear encircled with the words "*Sheriff Los Angeles County.*" It looked too real for a costume.

"Are you okay?" Gray asked.

"Yeah, I'm fine. I just..." He wiped sweat off his forehead into his thinning hair. "I was... in an accident."

"I'll call an ambulance."

"No no. If you could just show me where I am?"

"You're lost?"

"I don't know. I was walking, and... I don't know. I spaced out, I guess."

Gray showed him the map on his phone. "You're basically downtown."

"That's what I thought. It's the parade. You know? I got turned around." He stood there with his mouth half open as if trying to remember what he was about to say.

"I've got to go," Gray said. Claire was already upset. "Sure you don't want me to call anyone?"

"I'm fine," he said, still looking confused.

Gray exited the alley. The main part of the parade had passed, and the crowd was joining up behind it, some carrying tambourines and gourd rattles. Paper mâché skeletons bobbed and swayed to the beat.

Gray drifted into the procession milling toward the plaza. He rubbed his thumb along the porous stone.

It fit in his pocket, but Claire would notice the bulge.

She might not be mad anymore. He could picture them in the plaza: Mindy in awe of the parade, Tyler asleep in his stroller—he could sleep through anything, the louder the better—and Claire on her phone scrolling through the endless feed of Ashley York.

He could spare two minutes to figure out what to do with this thing he didn't want but which felt wrong to just leave in the street. He slipped out of the procession and into a gap between kiosks to study the snake. It must have taken hours to carve, maybe days.

It was a shame to destroy it. And why should he? Why him? If they wanted it smashed so badly, why give it away? Why advise against twisting the snake-dial yet also show him how. The fortune-teller had placed it in his palm and turned it herself.

He was never going to get ahead in life doing what other people told him. If he lacked the nerve to turn a dial, which probably did nothing at all, how was he ever going to quit his job?

With his index finger, he traced the S of the snake. A sense of dread welled up inside him. He clenched his jaw. No old woman's hands to stop him now. He had to do this. Or he'd never change. He might as well keep living his life the same old way.

The snake faced him, almost grinning. He poked it in the head. It spun from the six o'clock position to the twelve, where the flattened tear shape on top came to a point.

Inside the stone, something clicked.

Something stabbed Gray's palm.

He flipped the charm over. On the bottom, little holes in the stone traced the pattern of a spiral. He rubbed his palm on his shirt and examined the wound. It looked minor—just a tiny streak of blood in the meat near his thumb—and yet it burned all out of proportion, as if his whole hand were in flames.

The shutters slammed shut on the kiosk beside him. The person inside it switched off the lights.

Hair prickled on the back of his neck. Across the street, a blackness filled the alley so dark it swallowed all nearby light. He shivered.

He marched toward the crowd amassing at the plaza, with a fear growing inside him that someone was watching, which made no sense, but what if they were? He couldn't just lead them to his family.

He forced himself to stop. To turn his head. To look around.

No one seemed to notice him. They were all absorbed in the festivities, or their family and friends or their phones. The fortune-teller had spooked him was all. Nothing to be afraid of.

He shuddered and started to run.

A Different World

Ashley awakens to a pain in her right hand. Like something pricked her palm while she was sleeping. How could that have happened?

She stretches her legs, which feel oddly big, and something blocks her feet. She rolls on her side and feels an unfamiliar fabric on her legs—jeans? Is she wearing jeans? After having sex with August last night, he'd mumbled something about being on set early and left, and she specifically remembers slipping on a pair of black panties. That's all she ever slept in.

She opens her eyes... and is greeted by beige carpet and kids toys strewn all around a coffee table, which is covered with a mishmash of magazines and coloring books, as if deliberately disarranged to get on her nerves. On top is the *Vanity Fair* with Jennifer Lawrence.

She leaps to her feet. Above her, a low ceiling hangs unreasonably close. Her legs are wrong, way, way wrong. Too thick and long, and the jeans are baggy. She doesn't *own* baggy jeans. And it's not just her legs: her whole body feels off. She stumbles back onto the faded gray couch she'd woken up on and has never before seen in her life. *What the hell? What is going on?* Her hands are man's hands. She holds them in front of her face. Dark, unsightly hair on every knuckle, even the pinky. And on her ring finger, a wedding band. Yellow gold. Who wears yellow gold?

She rubs her eyes. Her cheeks feel like sandpaper. Is that stubble? And her nose... it's too wide. Her brow is bony. Her whole face feels unfamiliar, wrong, wrong, wrong-wrong-wrong.

She leaps off the couch again, and it's like these legs, which are definitely not her legs, know what to do. They take a step forward, a wide stride, unsteady. She forces her next step to be shorter, like her normal walk, and stumbles. Catches herself on one knee and rises again. *Just focus on where you're going.* One step, then another. She lets this awfully wrong body lope along in its strange, gangly way, an unnatural stiffness in the right knee.

She reaches a dim and depressingly narrow hallway with an even lower ceiling than the den where she awoke, if she's even awake, which she better not be. *I can't be. No way.*

The door on the right is half-open. It's a minuscule bathroom. She pushes in and flips on the light.

The man in the mirror has thin, brown hair and frantic eyes that widen as she raises her brows. She shakes her head, and he mocks her by mimicking the action—he *is* her.

She falls into the wall and screams. But the pitch of her voice is too low, as if she's screaming with his voice. She pinches her forearm. *Time to wake up....*

She doesn't wake up. Instead, she feels pain. She squeezes the skin between her fingertips. More pain. Real pain. This man—she is this man!

"What the fuck, Gray?" A woman with dark tangled hair shoves in through the door, her hands balled into fists and her eyes electric, practically sparking with blue light, like she's super pissed, like any of this is Ashley's fault. "You woke up Tyler."

Who the hell is Tyler? "Who the hell are you?" Ashley asks with the stubbled face in the mirror and the voice that's not like her voice at all.

The woman crosses her arms over her shapeless blue night shirt. "Why are you acting so weird?"

"Are you kidding me? What the hell is going on?"

"Did you throw up?" the woman asks. "I told you not to eat that burrito."

"No, I—" Ashley raises the pitch of her voice, struggling to make her voice sound normal. "I'm Ashley York." Her voice cracks.

"Are you trying to be funny?"

"No! Who is he?" She points at the man in the mirror. The man points back. *This is not real. It can't be real.* It's a nightmare, that's all. So why can't she wake up?

As Ashley tries to leave the bathroom, the dumbfounded woman stands in her way. Ashley plows past her, willing this man's body in this nightmare to run. It strides into action down the narrow hallway, and she's carried along inside it, feeling the exertion in the legs that aren't hers. They feel heavy. Her whole body feels heavy and slow and out of shape.

She flees through the front door and stumbles around the minivan, which barely fits in the short driveway. The street is unfamiliar. She looks up and down the hill. Where the hell is she going? Where is she?

From the house across the street, an elderly man emerges and cuts across the lawn toward Ashley. "Morning, Gray," he shouts.

"I don't know you," she says. *Gray?* Does everyone see this man's body instead of her?

The old man keeps on coming. He's frail and stooped and wearing a brown suit so old it looks retro.

He steps off the curb. "I should have told you yesterday, but I moved Lynda's car to the street because there was... It was an accident... and this crazy officer, I think he's after me."

Ashley backs away.

The old man creeps toward her. "I didn't mean to. Okay? Alright?"

Ashley runs. From the man, from everything, from this person who everyone seems to see instead of her.

For lack of anywhere else to go, she dashes back into the house she woke up in, through cluttered, claustrophobic rooms condensed into a floor plan smaller than her den, until she finds a bedroom. She locks the door, kicks her way through the wrinkled clothes strewn all over the floor, and plops down on the bed.

I just have to go back to sleep. If she goes to sleep, this nightmare will end. Obviously. Sleep put her here into this body, into this life, this world, that isn't hers, and sleep will get her out again.

But as she climbs under the covers, someone pounds on the door. "Gray?" the woman calls. "Gray, I know you're sick, but I still need help with the kids."

"Go away."

"Why is the door locked? *We don't lock doors.* You're breaking your own rule."

"I need to sleep."

"Take some Ibuprofen. It's too late now."

Ashley ignores her, and her hammering on the door. She imagines herself in her own house—her immaculate house—in her big white bed where she belongs.

A baby screams through the thin walls of the house, and the woman stops pounding on the door. Ashley would scream too if it would do any good. Tears stream down her cheeks. She closes her eyes and focuses on how she should look in the mirror: blonde hair and unblemished skin, the woman she's always been and still is.

She can't relax. The linens on the bed scratch her skin, like they have a thread count of like yarn. She throws them off. The awful underwear she's wearing fits like it's two sizes too small.

The baby stops crying and is replaced by the sound of the woman cooing through the wall. The din of cars on a highway sound like they're right behind the house.

She had made this body run, more or less, but she can't make it sleep—or make herself sleep. She can't even settle on how to think of herself now, just like she can't focus on remembering how she looks, because she's in a man's body now. *What the fuck?*

The woman returns to the door and pounds harder, as hard as the heart that isn't Ashley's is pounding against her ribcage, pumping someone else's blood through her head. Sleep is not an option. Not now. Anyway, who ever heard of going to sleep in a nightmare? She has to face this, somehow. She's got to do something.

Ashley climbs from the bed and jerks open the door.

The woman's eyes flash. "Don't ignore me, Gray." She clutches her phone in her fist like a weapon, like she might actually use it to club Ashley.

Ashley snatches the phone, ducks around the woman, and lunges down the hallway.

"What the hell?" the woman yells after her. She pursues Ashley into the living room. "Who are you calling?"

The Face ID refuses to unlock. The phone demands a passcode.

She holds the phone toward the woman's face, hoping to unlock it. The woman grabs her arm and tries to wrench the phone away. "What's got into you, Gray?"

"I told you. I'm Ashley York. I need to call someone to come get me."

The woman, with surprising strength, pries the phone from Ashley's fingers and steps back. "Are you making fun of me? Yeah, I'm into celebrity gossip, so what? At least I'm not shutting myself in the garage all the time." The baby has started crying again and the woman turns toward the hallway. "Why don't you help instead of acting like a jerk?"

"Oh, so you won't let me make one call and I'm the jerk?" Ashley says, but the woman has already hurried away.

There's got to be another phone here. Ashley looks around the couch where she woke up, or dreamed she woke up, or whatever. On the cluttered coffee table, on top of a coloring book right next to the *Vanity Fair* is an iPhone.

Ashley holds it up to her face that isn't her face. The phone unlocks.

There's only like four contacts: Claire, Dad Wilson, Leonardo, Mom Wilson, and Steve... and, of course, Ashley doesn't know who any of them are. She also doesn't recall the numbers for anyone she knows. Not even her own number, which she just changed because some jerk posted her old one online. She'd always had everything she needed right there, synced across her devices, people she could call would come help her at a moment's notice. But now she's lost access to her life?

What if this is real? It seems like it's going on too long to be a dream. What if she's stranded in this strange body forever?

She collapses on the couch and rubs her face in her hands, then pulls her hands away in shock when she feels the coarse, bristly cheeks. She closes her eyes and tries dialing her dad's personal line on an imaginary keypad. She pretends she's a girl again, calling him at work. She can see her little finger pressing buttons, but she can't visualize the numbers. They're lost in the past. She must have been seven or eight the last time she manual-dialed, before he gave her her first phone, a pink flip-phone with his number programmed as contact number one.

She opens her eyes. Still under the claustrophobically low ceiling—still in this man's body. The question is, what happened to her body? Does it even still exist? What if this Gray dude has it?

She has to find a way home.

She glances at the wrinkled shirt she's wearing. A black T-shirt with a stain of what looks like chocolate down the front. Dream or not, she can't go out like this.

She hurries back to the bedroom. The clothes on the floor are all women's, as are those in the closet, which won't do. Everyone will think she's this Gray dude, won't they?

In the hall closet, she finds a stack of t-shirts, a few button downs on hangers, and three pairs of dark blue men's Levi's—who still wears Levi's? Better than nothing. She grabs a pair and tugs them on over the awful underwear. She chooses one of the least offensive button downs, a brown one, and impulsively checks the tag, which is faded and unreadable, and anyway, who cares?

She yanks off the stained shirt and ducks into the bathroom to line up the buttons in the mirror. Gray—or is it her?—looks pretty good in the shirt. *Him.* She can't start thinking of this body as herself. She needs to get *her* body back —and she's going to do that how?

She opens the door and inhales a deep breath. *One step at a time, Ashley.*

What she needs is a car. She searches around and finds a set of keys on a little table by the front door. As she snatches them up and heads out, the woman storms after her. "Where are you going?"

Better just to play along with her narrative. The last thing Ashley needs is this woman freaking out and trying to follow her or something. "Work."

"It's Sunday."

This situation is so ridiculous that she hasn't even considered the day of the week. She snatches the keys. "Yeah, well, doesn't matter."

She steps outside, ignoring whatever the woman says, and closes the door behind her.

Gray Day

The sound of water splashing. The hum of bugs all around. A pillowy bed perched on the bank of a river. Dark water flowing languidly through a warm afternoon. The long slow notes of a bird. Gray leans his head back in the pillow, scans up the banana tree above the bed, and finds a yellow bird. Its song trails off. Then, from higher up, the song is continued.

He sits up. Beside the bed is a table with a bottle of wine and a papaya sliced in half. Beside that, on an easel, is a painting, which he must have started before drifting off. It's the scene right before him, except standing by the river is Laura, smiling, just like when they'd arrived in Paris for the summer of their sophomore year.

And then he hears her. He actually hears Laura laughing—she's here. She's in the river, splashing with three umber-colored boys. She beckons for Gray to join her.

He pats the bed beside him. *Come up and dry off.*

She laughs.

Gray picks up a papaya half, holds it out, and with his other hand, motions her toward the bed.

She shouts that the water is perfect, dives under, and disappears below the dark water.

Gray wants, no *needs* more than anything, to be with her there in the water when she comes up for air. He runs toward the bank. The boys cheer. He dives in.

The water is cold.

It wakes him up. He blinks in the harsh sunlight.

No wonder you can't sleep. "Why did you open the curtains?" he asks Claire.

He closes his eyes, but even through his lids the light feels too bright. He turns his head away, pulls up the covers, and nestles into the pillow. If he could just go back to sleep, to Laura... but there's too much sunlight on his face.

Yet even with the curtains open, their bedroom doesn't get direct sunlight until late in the morning, almost noon. He bolts upright.

"Claire?"

She's not beside him. And this bed, it's giant. It has a plush white comforter. He's in a vast, airy bedroom. Cream-white curtains frame cathedral-sized windows, six of them. Outside, a green hill rises to a blue horizon. Sunlight fills the sky.

Across the round room is a chaise lounge, also white, and a daybed buried beneath neatly stacked pink pillows.

This cannot be real.

Last night, after they'd put the kids to bed, he'd decided a drink was in order, which was followed by an argument with Claire—about what, he can't remember. If not for the Scotch, they probably wouldn't have argued at all. He has no memory of going to sleep, or leaving the house. Certainly not of coming here. Which is where?

He climbs off the bed, expecting to find his clothes on the floor where he'd normally leave them, but the floor is bare, blond wood, and his feet... they're slender, too tan—not his feet at all!

Dizzy, he breathes fast with seemingly no air reaching his lungs.

Slow down. Breathe slow. He must be hungover, more than ever before. The alcohol leaving his system is making him see things that aren't real, some kind of short-circuit in his synapses. That's what this is. A waking dream.

He rests his hands on his hips—but they're not his hips. They're wide, curving out from a slender waist. *This cannot be! What is happening?*

Heart pounding, he looks down... Protruding from his chest is a pair of breasts—naked breasts. He cups them in his hands. *Must find a mirror.*

As he lifts his right foot, his leg feels unexpectedly limber. His heel hits the wood. His foot pivots, and he bounces—too high—and tries to correct as his left foot lands, sending him stumbling. He starts again. By giving into the movement, although it feels foreign to him, it works—left-foot bounce, right-foot run. It's automatic, controlled by some part of the brain that operates below his level of consciousness.

The bedroom has three doors. He opens the middle one to find a tiled bathroom the size of a spa, blue and white mosaic on the floor.

He approaches the mirror above the sink and sees not his reflection but a brown-eyed blonde, a girl he knows but can't quite place. *Is this a dream? A lucid dream?*

He admires her half-naked figure—flat stomach, bony hips supporting the thin straps of lace panties. He grabs a lock of long, salon-perfect hair and pulls, half-expecting a wig to come off or maybe a mask, maybe a whole suit. It hurts, like pulling his own actual hair—it *is* his hair.

This somewhat familiar girl in the mirror is him, somehow. Although she's not him. Or is he her? Are they her breasts or his?

He pinches a nipple—it stiffens. It hurts. These breasts are definitely a part of his body. He squeezes them, and the sensation of the skin from the touch of his hands is unreal—it's amazing.

Intricate.

Vivid, in every detail.

In dreams, things seem to change every time you look, but this is solid, real. And he feels more awake than ever. He never knew a dream could be like this... but perhaps they all are? Perhaps they only fade upon waking.

He's dreamed of women, of course, but *being* a woman? Crazy. And then to know he's dreaming while still dreaming—insane!

He leans toward the mirror and gazes into her-his chestnut irises. So clear.

Gray's mouth goes dry. When he tries to swallow, his front teeth are too big. He slides his tongue over them, and they feel too big, too. These are not his teeth. This isn't him.

He leaves the bedroom and follows a hallway to an interior balcony that overlooks an immense living room. Sunlight filters through a wall of windows, across polished wood floors. He descends the curved stairway and passes a loveseat, an ottoman, and a white-linen couch submerged, almost entirely, by pastel-colored pillows.

In front of the couch is a glass coffee table framed with silvery metal, on which dozens of lifestyle magazines are fanned out in a neat arc. This house should be featured in one of them. Hell, it belongs on the cover.

Outside the windows, an expansive lawn stretches out between rows of palms and slops out of sight. A distant ridgeline rolls down into a brownish haze which almost obscures the city below. LA, probably, SoCal for sure, from the looks of the dry scrub on the ridge, but not his neighborhood—not even close.

He crosses the room to the French doors and steps out onto the patio, where he can almost taste the moisture in the air from the lawn sprinklers. All he needs is an easel and this will be like his dream from last night in the fortune booth. Crazy—he's remembering a dream within a dream. But then, doesn't everything seem familiar in dreams? Because you always dream of things you've seen before.

So, where is he?

Claire probably has every one of the magazines on the coffee table. So maybe this place is in one of them? As he turns to go check, the sound of whistling rises above the swish from the sprinklers. A familiar tune.

From around the corner of the house strides a muscular, black man in a security uniform, his head shaved bald. When he notices Gray, he stops abruptly and shields his eyes to the sun. His mouth drops open.

He cuts across the lawn, jogging through a sprinkler to reach the patio. *Mission Impossible*, Gray realizes. The security guard was whistling the theme song to *Mission Impossible*.

"Ashley," he shouts, "is everything okay?"

Ashley York. Gray remembers now: he should have known right away. It was definitely her face in the mirror, Claire's idol, Ashley York. Somehow, he is in her body.

"Ashley?" The guard runs a hand over his scalp, his wet shirt clinging to his torso, and stares—at Gray's chest.

Gray wonders if he should feel embarrassed since it's not actually his body that's practically naked, but still, he crosses his arms over his breasts. "I'm fine," he says, with a voice that's not his.

If this is a dream, he *should* be waking up in a cold sweat right about now.

The guard inhales. Places a tentative hand on Gray's shoulder. "Girl, let's get you inside."

Gray allows himself to be steered back in through the French doors. With each step, he can almost feel the guard's eyes on his butt, the revealing lace panties.

Inside, the guard releases Gray's shoulder, and follows close behind, almost too close. *Where are we going?* Gray stops and turns to face the guard.

The man's eyes dart from Gray to the floor to the kitchen. "Where's Andrea?"

"Andrea?" *Who's Andrea?*

The guard whistles. "Girl, what did you get into last night?"

Last night, Gray got into the Scotch, nothing unusual about that, but, of course, there was also the white stone with the snake mounted on top, its fangs practically sneering. The old fortune-teller had begged him to destroy it, but instead of heeding her warning, he'd spun the chiseled snake, expecting nothing to happen. And nothing had happened... at least, not until now.

Had she known he'd awaken in Ashley York's body? And if so, how could this have caused her so much distress? *This is incredible.* It could be an even more amazing experience if not for the guard's eyes probing the lace panties and then crawling up Gray's midriff to hover around the breasts, which are technically Ashley's.

The guard lifts his gaze, and they lock eyes. His brows mash together. "Do you want me to... I don't know?"

Gray swallows, his heart hammering in his ears. "I should get dressed."

The guard's eyes dart to the floor. He starts toward the kitchen. "I'll find Andrea for you."

Gray hurries toward the stairs.

In the bedroom, he grabs the phone by the nightstand and opens Instagram which comes up on the account for Ashley York and now there is no doubt. He is her. In her body. So, if this isn't a dream, what does it mean for him? For his life? His body?

He dials his own number, but who does he expect to answer?

The question staggers him. He's seen enough science fiction to guess it could be another version of himself, like from a parallel universe, or maybe he and the Ashley York swapped bodies. What will he say? What can he say? *Hello, I am the real Gray Wilson. Who the hell are you?*

After five rings, when his voicemail picks up, he releases the breath he's holding and ends the call.

But what if no one answered because there *is no one* to answer? What if his body vanished in the night? Or what if, it's like *It's A Wonderful Life*—to everyone else he never existed at all?

He has to know.

After another full ring, with phone-glued-to-hand Claire still not answering, he begins to worry. What if his whole life doesn't exist?

She answers the call. "Who is this?"

He swallows. He can't speak with his own voice, but he has to know if his life as he knew it still exists. "Is Gray there?"

"Who is this?" she asks again.

What can he say? He can't get side-tracked trying to convince her. He just needs to know. "May I please speak with him?"

"I'm going to hang up if you don't tell me who you are."

"I'm—" He was about to invent a friend from work, but Claire would see through the lie in an instant. "He's there, right?"

"Why would I tell you?" She sounded annoyed and maybe a little suspicious.

If he had disappeared, she'd be freaking out. That meant his body is there, but who is it? Some parallel-universe version of him, or is it Ashley, or maybe it's just on autopilot? It wouldn't take much to slog through a Sunday without raising Claire's suspicion.

"How would you like to earn a thousand dollars for five minutes of your time? I'm conducting a survey—"

"Nope." Claire hangs up.

At least his life is there, but how can he get back to it? The charm. When the fortune-teller placed the porous stone in his hand, she'd dialed the obsidian snake a half turn. Maybe that's all he has to do and then everything returns to normal. It would be easy to try, if he had any idea where he put the damn thing after the parade.

He could also sneak around the side of their house and spy in, but then what? Claire would freak if she saw Ashley York. And what was that show in which a guy from a parallel universe came in, took over the real guy's life, and murdered him? Is that what the fortune-teller was worried about?

Tomorrow, the house should be empty when Claire takes Mindy to daycare, but how can he wait until then?

He glances around the circular bedroom with all the sunlight streaming in through the drapes over the matching white furniture. On the nightstand beside the bed is a pink vape pen with a silver mouthpiece. He reaches for it. Presses the button. The heating element glows electric blue.

He inhales just a little of the steam it produces. It tastes vaguely of peaches... no, definitely peaches but with a musky aftertaste.

He flops back on the bed, closes his eyes, and exhales as he nestles into the down comforter. His scalp tingles, like his hair is lifting off his head.

I needed this. A day for himself. For so long, he'd needed a break from his life where Claire hardly cared if he came home or not and couldn't give him ten minutes alone. He never had time to paint. He needs a break from all the wasted hours of working and writing code, which only gets rewritten by someone else anyway.

He takes another drag.

It all seems like a dream, now. How can you ever really know for sure that you're awake? He runs his fingers through his hair. It's long, sleek, and thick, as though transformed by some styling process into golden Taklon.

Is he really a woman? He doesn't actually feel any different.

"Ms. Ashley?" A waif-thin woman, who looks to be in her early twenties, appears in the half-open door to the hallway, her brown hair pulled back tight into a ponytail.

Gray launches to his feet, pulls the comforter from the bed and covers himself. "What's up?"

"What shall I make for breakfast?" The woman, who must be Andrea, asks with an accent that sounds somewhat European.

"Right," Gray says. He could get used to this. "I'll have an omelet."

Her eyes flicker, but her oval face remains blank. "You do not like eggs."

Gray scratches his head. "What do I normally eat?"

She leans forward and squints. "Maca smoothie-bowl."

Since she thinks he's Ashley, it means she works for him, so she'll make whatever he wants, right? But maybe he should try the bowl. Could be better than an omelet for all he knows.

"Sounds good," he says. "Are there any paint supplies here?"

She glances around the room. "You are tired of white?"

"No, I mean acrylics. It's a beautiful day. I want to setup an easel on the lawn."

She squints at him and then at the vape on the bed. She laughs, dryly, as if obligated to laugh.

"No, I'm serious," he says, but then he starts laughing too. He can't help it. It's the expression of pure bewilderment on her face. *She has no idea.*

She laughs for real this time, her face turning beet red, then she regains her composure and backs out through the door. "You need to eat before your massage," she says and shuts it behind her.

To resist the temptation of another toke, he opens the nightstand drawer and shoves the vape inside it. While it's open, he notices a remote control. He presses the power button, and a screen descends from the ceiling, lit up with icons for all the various streaming platforms.

He opens Netflix and chooses an episode of *Black Mirror*. When it starts playing, he realizes he's seen it before, but now the idea of a fabricated human, who looks and acts exactly like your deceased loved-one, no longer seems far-fetched—not after he's awakened in the body of Ashley York.

He can't relax. Instead of the show, he keeps picturing the look of distress on the fortune-teller's face, and his mind keeps racing. He should try and find her—but what's the point? He's sure he needs the charm, and didn't he already decide to wait until tomorrow to go home? Doesn't he deserve to enjoy himself? Just for a little while?

He goes into the bathroom to splash water on his face. He dries off by the giant tub sunken into the tile. Claire always took baths to relax. If he's ever going to try it, now's the time. He turns on the faucet and adjusts the temperature. He bends over and slides the panties down his legs, and as he does so, the lack of his usual anatomy disorients him, and he almost falls. He plops himself down on a white stool by the sinks.

A thin line of white skin cuts between the deep tan of his stomach and legs. He runs his finger over it, pausing at the trimmed strip of light hair leading down. His pulse throbbing.

He feels guilty. He wouldn't want Ashley toying around with his body. And what if she can see what he's doing? What if she's trapped in the back of her mind with him in control?

He sighs. Just a bath. That's all. Nothing wrong with that. He'll just relax for a few minutes and that's it.

He eases himself into the hot water. Ashley's nipples peek above the water. The controls for the tub are conveniently located by his right hand. He activates the jets. A current gushes between his legs, surprisingly well-aimed. It creates a tingling sensation that almost tickles, but in a good way. He turns up the pressure of the jets.

It feels… amazing.

All over his body.

He slides his fingers down his side, across his hips. The sensation of touching a woman and feeling his touch as a woman is overpowering. He hadn't planned on reaching down—he really was just going to take a bath, but now—now-now-now—now he must. Doesn't matter if Ashley can see this. Probably she's in his body, probably right now fondling his erection, enjoying it as if it's hers.

Ashley's legs are his legs now, and the slipperiness between them—that's his. He slides his fingers into it… and draws upwards. Grazing the nub of flesh, he inhales sharply. Sensitive. And the feeling isn't just there at the surface, it goes deep inside. Is this the way Claire feels when they make love? Do all women feel like this?

The sensation builds and builds throughout his body. Not like the out-of-control-all-at-once male orgasm. He moans, and his moan is her voice—begging for more. With one hand, he increases the pressure of the water jets and with his other, he increases the rhythm.

His fingers keep moving, keep pressing as the pulsing energy builds from deep inside… Waves crash through him from his thighs to his head. He screams, gasps.

Water splashes onto the floor.

His pelvis shakes uncontrollably.

A wave of relaxation washes through him. Every muscle in his body seems to loosen.

His throat burns and then he chokes back a sob. *What am I doing?* Here he is with the time to finally do whatever he wants, and what does he do? Abuse a body that's not even his.

He climbs out of the tub, towels off, and dresses as fast as he can.

Sammy

The dog, which looked to be mostly pitbull, licked Sammy's hand as he scratched under her chin. He slid open the window to the guard booth, popped his second Red Bull for the day, and leaned back in his chair. The dog raised her big, black head and sniffed at the air.

Sammy gulped the fortified soda, but the rush of sugar and caffeine only served to perplex him. He'd fantasized countless scenarios in which Ashley came onto him, yet he'd never in a million years imagined that she might just walk out of her house practically nude.

He would've taken her too, right there on the patio, but she hadn't seemed to know where she was. Of course, he could have pushed the situation, but he didn't want to push. In the long run, he knew that pushing would get him nowhere. He wanted to be pulled into her. She was the boss, and it would have to be on her terms.

So here he was, day after day, telling Greta that he was close to his big break when he wasn't close to anything like that. All he cared about getting close to was Ashley York, with her skin tanned to the color of honey—probably tasted like honey too.

She'd stood there with her breasts out, but the look on her face had been pure confusion, and when she noticed him running toward her, it became fear. After all the effort he'd put in, always smiling and kind, for her to be afraid of him... nothing could be worse. He downed the Red Bull.

His phone rang. *Greta.* He crushed the can, tossed it in the recycle bin, snatched another from the mini-fridge, and answered.

"What are you doing?" Greta asked.

"Working."

"Working on making something of yourself or sitting there staring off into space?"

"Right now, I'm trying to find a home for this dog."

"It's still there? Ashley told you to get rid of it. This is what I'm talking about."

Sammy closed his eyes. "Look, I was thinking, she's a friendly girl—part black lab, I think—we should adopt her."

"Adopt a dog? Are you serious? I'm going to have your baby. And you think I have time for a dog too?"

He rubbed his forehead. "You're not even pregnant."

"Who's fault is that?"

Maybe it was his fault, technically, but she wasn't exactly helping the situation. "We agreed the extra OT was a good thing."

"Yeah, six months ago. It's time Ashley sees you as more than just another Black ass in a uniform."

Greta wouldn't be pushing so hard if she had any clue that the OT was just an excuse to spend all his waking hours at Ashley's. If he could just sleep here—probably, no one would notice if he slept in the guest house, and he could tell Greta it was a promotion—then he wouldn't have to drive all the way back to their the shitty duplex in Inglewood, where she was always pushing him to rise above a life he hardly lived.

But she was right: you had to push to make something of yourself—at least, they did—and he wasn't pushing hard enough. That was the problem. He didn't care.

All he cared about was Ashley. He should not be thinking these thoughts, but he couldn't help it. They were consuming him.

"You hearing me, Sammy? Ashley York tells you to get rid of a dog, it's gone. Just drive it off somewhere and let it go. The dog's not your problem. Your problem is getting noticed. If you can't even handle a simple order, Ashley will never hook you up. How are we supposed to support a child on your shitty paycheck? I quit my career for this!"

"I gotta go," he lied.

He was sick of hearing about all Greta's unrealized expectations for him. All the trying so hard, for so long, to get nowhere. Why couldn't things just come easy for him like they did for Ashley? As she had appeared on the patio in those panties, hardly more than a scrap of black lace.

He hung up and crushed the third Red Bull of the day.

Maybe he didn't mean much to Ashley now, but there was a reason why she wanted him on OT and not Franco. And maybe he could ride that good vibe. Maybe she *would* hook him up with some kind of big-league gig where he wore a suit and had his own people who answered to him... and then she'd see him differently.

A Camry turned into the driveway. Unannounced guests were rare, and Sammy doubted that anyone Ashley knew would drive a Camry.

As it slowed toward the guard booth, the dog leaped up on the windowsill and started barking. The guy behind the wheel lowered his window. His hair was tousled, and he looked stressed. Ashley's fans who found their way here were usually women from somewhere in the Midwest, thinking they could hang with Ashley just because they were friends on social media or whatever.

Sammy stood and patted the dog's head. "Good girl," he said softly. "I'm thinking Ashley will change her mind once she sees you're a guard dog."

The guy in the car frowned. "Why is that dog still here?"

Sammy furrowed his brows and pulled the dog back from the window. *How does he know?* Ashley must have posted something, obviously. She shared everything on social media.

"Are you just here to check on the dog?"

The guy leaned out the window and raised his brows. *"It's me,"* he said emphatically, and pointed at his face. "I'm Ashley."

Sammy had encountered his share of stalkers, but this was a first. "And here I thought I was having a crazy day, but you just took it to a whole new level."

"I know it sounds crazy," he said, "but I am Ashley. How else would I know about the dog?"

"You've got a phone, don't you? How many times did she post about it?"

"None. And how would I know your name is Sammy Johnson? You've worked here for three years."

"Uh huh. I already know who I am. Thanks for telling me, though. You seem to be the one who's challenged in the identity department."

"But I am Ashley." The guy rubbed his hands over his face, through his thin brown hair. He glowered at Sammy. "I'll prove it if you let me in, please."

"I'm sorry," Sammy said. "You need to back out, all the way to the crazy house." He decided against extending the usual courtesy of opening the gate so he could circle forward and around the booth.

The guy clenched his jaw. He tried to get out of his car, but Sammy leaned out of the booth and held his door closed. "Sir, this is your last warning."

"You can't keep me out of my own house!"

"You're from those tabloids, aren't you?" Sammy was sick of the way they tried to make Ashley look bad. "I'm calling the police. You don't want a harassment beef on your ass, trust me." Ashley had a strict policy of not talking to the press, and he had probably said too much already.

He shut the window to the booth and held up the phone.

The guy who claimed to be Ashley screamed.

Sammy made a slow performance of dialing.

The guy slammed his Camry in reverse. On his back way up the drive, he clipped a palm.

Sammy sat back in the chair and shook his head. The dog sat on the floor and stared up at him.

"What a loony-bird," he said. "I should have let you bite his ass."

The dog glanced at the window.

"What's you're name, anyway? Alice?... Ariel?... Shera?"

She perked her ears and tilted her head.

"Shera. Your name is Shera."

She nuzzled her head between Sammy's legs and wiggled her butt. He laughed. His heart swelled. "You're not going anywhere are you, Shera? No, you're not. I'm thinking we keep you in the guest house."

Hostage Exchange

"What do you want?" Aleman sounded more annoyed than surprised, when Saul finally caught up to him in the cinderblock hallway of the MDC. His forehead was bruised and swollen above his terribly narrow brow, which made his whole face look too small. His mustache was frayed and underlined by chapped lips.

"You hung up before we finished talking last night." Saul said.

"I don't know what you're talking about." Aleman's gruff monotone lacked the cadence from last night, but the pitch was the same.

"You don't remember calling me?"

Aleman ratcheted his brows down and glanced to the right. "I never called you."

"The call came from your phone."

On the second call, Aleman had forgotten to block the caller ID, so now Saul could confront him without admitting to the trace.

"Yeah, well—" Aleman glanced over Saul's shoulder, down the hallway. "I lost my phone. So, whoever called you, it wasn't me." He shouldered past Saul and continued walking.

Denial or amnesia? Saul could have predicted his reaction. It was just like Saroyan.

"Hold up." Saul started after him. "I might know who has your phone."

"This had better be quick," Aleman said without looking back. "Only ten minutes left on my break."

He led Saul to a windowless break room that was almost an insult. Five foot by ten, most of which was consumed by vending machines and a two-seater table. Aleman slouched into the chair by the machines.

Saul bought him a Coke then squeezed into the narrow gap across from him, between the table and the wall. He tried to sit without bumping his belly on the table. And failed. The table's metal legs groaned as they skidded a few inches on the polished linoleum.

Aleman snorted and pushed back on the table.

Saul pretended not to notice. "I went by your apartment yesterday."

Aleman looked down and said nothing. In the harsh fluorescents, his skin looked sallow, highlighting the bruise.

"Where were you?" Saul asked.

Aleman blinked rapidly. "What's it matter to you?"

"We're friends, right?" He didn't care much for Aleman, but it was worth a try.

"I don't know about that."

"I get it," Saul said, hoping Aleman's ill will was more due to the rivalry between the Sheriff's Department and the LAPD. "I'm a Montague and you're a Capulet."

"What are you talking about?"

"I was worried about you. I heard you left your car here."

Aleman clamped a meaty hand on the Coke can and frowned. "Guess I needed some air." Seemed he had no intention of mentioning his trek out to El Monte.

"Totally understandable," Saul said. "So, what happened with Saroyan?"

"Who's that?" Aleman said guardedly.

Did he really not know? "The one who took down the bastard who attacked you."

"Dunno," Aleman said. "Wasn't my fault."

"Saroyan's a paraplegic," Saul said. "So, help me understand how he took down Dunn."

Aleman wiped the perspiration from the unopened Coke. "Must've had help."

Another dead end. Saul changed direction again, hoping to catch Aleman off guard. "How did you get that bruise?"

Aleman gingerly touched the swollen knot on his forehead. "Dunn kicked me into the wall, remember?"

"According to the doc," Saul said, "it was the back of your head that hit the pipe."

"Yeah? Well." He pointed at the bruise. "What's the evidence say?" He stood. "I've got to get back."

Time to lay down some cards. "Hold on." Saul reached into his coat, pulled out Aleman's phone and slid it across the table.

It skidded to a stop in front of Aleman, whose eyes went wide. He grabbed it, pressed his thumb to the screen and unlocked it. Now there was no denying it was his phone.

"Who else has access to the phone?" Saul asked.

Aleman swiped the screen. His brows furrowed.

Saul waited a few seconds. "Do anyone else's fingerprints unlock it?"

Aleman didn't look up. "No..."

"Check your call log." Saul recited his number.

Aleman's eyes darted from the phone to Saul and back. His mouth fell open. "Impossible."

Saul shrugged. "You were identified."

Aleman reached out and steadied himself on the chair. "Where?"

"Ever been to La Golondrina?"

"What's that?"

"The restaurant on Olvera where you left your phone."

Splotches of pink appeared on Aleman's throat. He tore open the Coke. Swallowed hard.

"The hostess identified you from a photo," Saul said.

"Guess I didn't notice the name. Something happen... after I left or something?"

"Like what?" Saul asked as casually as he could.

Aleman blinked. Then his face hardened. He started toward the door.

Saul heaved himself up after him, his belly bumped the table back again. He lunged into Aleman's path. "What happened last night?"

"I don't know what you're talking about."

He tried to shoulder past, but Saul shoved him into the wall and stared down into his terribly narrow eyes. "What happened? Tell me."

"This is bullshit." Aleman's brow wrinkled around the bruise. He looked more confused than defiant. "Nothing happened."

Bullshit alright. Saul was sure now: it was Aleman who had called him.

"You saw me there, didn't you? Did you think I was tracking your phone?"

If he had left his phone on the table to throw Saul off course, then why report to work as if nothing had happened?

As Aleman glanced down, Saul could almost see the wheels turning in his head. Aleman was a mean little man, and mean little men, when cornered, always went for the groin. Saul caught Aleman's knee as it came up for the blow. He should have stopped there, but he had to retaliate. Violence was the language of men like Aleman, so he shoved Aleman's knee away and rocked forward with his huge upper torso, swinging his head like a bowling ball. It could have been a knockout blow, except Saul needed Aleman awake and submissive, so at the last instant he pulled back and merely knocked foreheads, smacking the swollen flesh of Aleman's bruise.

The back of Aleman's head thumped the wall. He slid sideways and caught himself on the snack machine. He cradled his forehead in one hand and shoved his phone into his pocket with the other. As he withdrew his hand, his elbow stiff, his next move was equally obvious, which left Saul no choice— Aleman was dumb enough to tase him, no doubt about that. As Aleman reached for the taser on his belt, Saul slipped a hand into his coat, freed his Glock 22 from the shoulder holster, and swung it out, aiming at Aleman's center of mass.

The taser shook in Aleman's hand. "You're not going to shoot me," he shouted.

"Only if you make me." Saul held the gun steady. "Muscles contract when a four volt electrical stimulus is applied. A taser delivers fifty thousand. Guaranteed contraction of all muscles in the body. In the case of joints rigged with opposing muscles, such as my trigger finger, the stronger side, would be the curling motion, wins. So go ahead, tase me. You'll be shooting yourself."

Aleman clenched his jaw. He lowered the taser. "Now what?"

"I'm arresting you for murder."

Aleman's eyes went wide. "What are you talking about?"

"You confessed to killing a cop yesterday."

He shook his head slowly. "Who?"

"I'm giving you a chance to tell me. If someone put you up to it, maybe I can help."

Aleman snatched the Coke from the table. He gulped the soda and coughed.

"Don't you think I would remember?" His eyes found Saul's and then he looked away, down and to the right.

Maybe he'd experienced something like what Saroyan had described—some dreamlike memory of losing control. He certainly remembered *something*. Something bad. And whatever was going on seemed bigger than just Saroyan and Aleman, two of the most unlikely men to work together. Yet they had both spoken with the same cadence, both claimed to be Wayob.

Saul holstered his Glock. "Tell me what you remember. I'm trying to help you here."

Aleman chuckled dryly. "I don't need your help." He slammed the can on the table and crushed it with his palm. "I'm going back to work now. Do what you've got to do."

Saul dug through his overstuffed wallet. Handed Aleman a business card.

"What's this for?"

Saul tapped the pocket where he kept his phone. "That's my personal number. For when you're ready to talk."

Aleman crumpled the card and dropped it on the floor.

"Just tell me who Wayob is," Saul said.

Aleman stepped on the card, shouldered past Saul and out the door.

Saul flattened a five-dollar bill and fed it to the snack machine. He punched in the number for BBQ chips. The steel coil jerked into action and took five full seconds to release the bag. As Saul squatted to retrieve it from the slot at the bottom of the machine, he groaned from the strain.

He sat at the table and opened the chips. If Aleman wasn't talking, what could he do? His only other possible lead was the Lunas, and they weren't home. He'd spent the night in his car outside their apartment, listening to the din of the cars careening up the 10 freeway, wondering where Rosa and her blind, sickly grandmother could have gone.

Fifteen minutes later, Saul was still sitting there in the break room when his phone buzzed. He pulled it out and glanced at the screen. Lieutenant Levy.

"What's up, L-T?"

"Parker." She enunciated the second syllable harshly. "We need you at the

Beverly Hills Library, now."

On a Sunday? He held the phone to his shoulder as he opened his second bag of chips. "I'm kind of in the middle of something." The chips rattled in spite of his effort to keep them quiet.

Levy snickered. "I can hear that," she said. He pictured her sarcastic half-smile, the closest she ever came to laughing. "A gunman has taken Bob Jaggar hostage, and we've got media up the ass."

The name sounded vaguely familiar. "Should I know who that is?"

"He was in a couple eighties sitcoms," Levy said. "Remember *Houseboat*, the *Full House* spinoff?"

"What's this got to do with Homicide Special?" The unit investigated only serial and high-profile homicides. Saul had no experience with kidnappings.

"Nothing," she said. "Except the shooter is requesting you by name."

A chill shot through Saul's gut. "Who is it?"

"Robert Rydell."

The name drew a complete blank. "How does he claim to know me?"

"He said you were following him last night."

Saul's stomach churned. He snatched up the bag of chips and started down the hallway. "I've never heard of Rydell. Last night I was looking for Victor Aleman, a custody assistant at the MDC. There's a connection between him and Saroyan."

"Saroyan?" Levy said. "I closed that case. It's with the DA now."

"We don't have a motive."

"We've got video of the murder. Move on."

"So who's Rydell?" Saul asked.

"He's a rich guy in his mid-sixties, white, with no prior record, and now he's killed a man. You really don't know anything?"

"No." Saul held the phone away from his mouth so she wouldn't hear him panting as he jogged down the hall.

"Well, he's holed up in the library. If you can't break the stalemate, we're going to have to send someone in."

Saul hit the button for the elevator, which from the fifth floor should be faster than the stairs. "I'll call Hernandez."

"She's already on the way."

He restrained his chuckle and tried to sound surprised. "You called her first?"

Levy hesitated. "High brass is up my ass to put a good face on this. The media is all over it, and now some asshole is live-streaming outside the library."

The elevator arrived and Saul stepped inside. He understood. The image of the LAPD mattered more to Levy and the high brass than the fact that the shooter, with one confirmed kill and a hostage, was requesting Saul by name. He was the status quo. A fat, white male. A statement from him would sound like bullshit. Especially after the Brown shooting, which the media would dredge up all over again if they discovered he was assigned to the case. And

Hernandez was a Chicana who spoke with authority and intelligence. And she was slender.

But Saul was glad for Hernandez. The exposure would be great for her career.

Meanwhile, the bag of chips in his hand was going stale. Better go ahead and eat them, better now than while driving. He held the phone away from his mouth while he chewed.

"So," he said, "what you're saying is that Hernandez is in charge now?"

"Well, you're still the senior detective, of course. I just can't make you lead on this."

Saul released a strained laugh. "You weren't going to tell me, were you?"

"It's out of my hands. Anyway, Rydell knows you, somehow. You can't lead a case you're involved in."

Chickenshit. He crunched hard into the phone. Not enjoying the chips at all.

The elevator doors parted. He marched out into the parking deck toward his plain wrap, glancing at his phone to make sure he still had reception.

"Rydell picked up the landline," Levy said. "I'll transfer you."

There was a click. A hiss came on the line. He climbed into the car and transferred the call to the car's audio system. "This is Parker." He started the engine.

A nasally, male voice blared through the speakers, "Par-ker." That voice—not the tone but the enunciation—was familiar.

Saul checked the mirror and hit reverse.

"Who is this?" he asked.

"Why it is Robert Rydell."

Hair prickled on the back of Saul's neck. "Do I know you?"

"No, but I know you, Parker. Yes, I do."

There it was. That cadence, unmistakable, and he pronounced Saul's name with an air of disgust. Rydell pretending to be Wayob, Saul assumed. He wanted Rydell to admit it, wanted Levy and whoever else was listening to hear it for themselves. If Rydell implicated Aleman and Saroyan, they would have to grant Saul some leeway for his investigation.

Saul turned out of the garage toward the 101. "So it's Rydell... not Wayob?"

"Ah, very clever, Parker. Clever, clever."

"So which is it?"

"I don't have time for games. Tell these imbeciles to release me."

"Funny. I'm supposed to tell you to surrender."

"Don't waste my time, Parker. Release me, or people shall needlessly die."

"And why is that?"

"They say I am surrounded and they will shoot if I do not surrender, but as you know, for me, death is a mere inconvenience, whereas those that I slay shall cease to exist. Same with Rydell, if they shoot me. Does no one care about his fate? No one has to die here. I would prefer not to harm anyone, of course, but I am running out of time."

Saul accelerated up the ramp toward the 101. The freeway was jammed. As Saul tried to edge between a Range Rover and a white Audi, the Audi sped up and blocked him. He had to swerve onto the shoulder.

The Audi driver flipped him off with both hands. Her blonde hair flapping in the wind.

"Are you listening to me?" Rydell almost screamed.

"How do you know Edward Saroyan?" Saul asked.

"Are you toying with me, Parker."

"No, I just— I don't get it. Friday night, Saroyan said *he* was Wayob. How do you explain that?"

"That was me, you dullard."

There it was. Rydell had just implicated himself with Saroyan. The connection was not surprising to Saul, but it baffled him. Why claim to be Wayob?

"Believe me or not," Rydell continued, "it makes no difference to me. Just tell them to let me to leave in peace, or Bob Jagger's death shall be your fault."

Saul engaged the blue strobes in his grill. "I don't see why you need to kill Bob Jaggar. You're immortal, right?"

"I can find a new vessel, and I shall if they shoot me. Wait and see, Parker. I am done wasting my breath. Either they let me walk out of here with Bob Jaggar or he shall die."

"We can't let you leave with a hostage," Saul said. "Take me instead."

"Are you outside?"

"I'm almost there," Saul lied.

"I am done with waiting."

The car in front of Saul moved aside. He gunned up behind the white Audi. The driver noticed the strobes and slowed down. Saul bleeped the siren. "I know who you're looking for." Yesterday, Aleman had walked practically all the way to the Lunas' apartment, so Saul assumed Rydell shared Aleman's interest, just like they had shared the same act.

Silence on the line.

"I'll take you to them," Saul said, although in truth he had no intention of allowing Rydell anywhere near the Lunas.

"How can you know?" Rydell asked, suspiciously. "Where is he?"

He? Rosa and her grandmother were on their own now that Saroyan had murdered Luis Luna. So who was this he?

Aleman's words from last night echoed in Saul's mind. *Another must die.*

Saul exited on Beverly. "Once Jaggar is safe, I'll show you."

"I do not need you, Parker. I shall find him on my own."

"But how long will it take you? I know exactly where he is."

Rydell said nothing.

"Rydell?"

Levy came on the line. "He hung up."

"Clear the unis out of there," Saul said.

"We can't do that."

"He's going to kill Jaggar if you don't give him some space. At least make it look like they're packing up. Buy me some time."

"With all the cameras on the scene, we might as well make an ad for kidnapping."

The Audi driver pulled over at the exit for Vermont, hands locked on the wheel. Saul sped past.

"Then clear the media, at least. Say it's for their own safety. Think about how it's going to look with the LAPD standing around while Jaggar gets murdered."

Wayob Takes Parker

Wayob slams the phone down on the counter. Parker does not know. How can he? He cannot. If he knows about the Encanto, if he knows where it is, he would take it for himself. Of course he would take it. He would leave Wayob trapped here in this miserable bright space lined with books, and Jaggar with all his whining.

Jaggar is sitting against the semi-circular, white counter centered in the large room, arms tied behind his back with a cord.

"Stand up," Wayob says.

Jaggar glances toward the inner door, beyond which officers are, of course, still lurking, in the main part of the library, in spite of the warning shots Wayob fired. At least the bookshelf he barricaded the door with seems to have held them back so far. And they do not dare shoot through the shades.

The emergency exit, labeled "Alarm Will Sound," is also barricaded with a bookshelf. He'd got it there just in time too, just as police cars flooded the parking lot outside in a chaos of flashing lights.

"I can get you out of this," Jaggar says. "I'll hire you the best lawyers money can buy." He flashes his stupid smile, as though he has power over Wayob.

Above Jaggar's head, the side of the counter is inscribed with the phrase, "*I have answers.*" But Wayob knows the answer, not Jaggar. It may seem as though Wayob is trapped here in this hideous tomb of books with no potential vessel sleeping within in range—he has tried to transmigrate, twice—but there is one vessel, one means of escape, so brilliant that it makes Wayob laugh.

"Pay me this, hire me that. You think that I care?" Wayob raises the gun. "Stand up."

Jaggar's eyes widen. He pushes himself up on his knees and rises slowly.

"Do not fear," Wayob says, "I only need you to sleep. Turn around."

Jaggar shakes his head.

"They all want me to set you free," Wayob lowers the gun. "Turn around, and I shall untie you."

Jaggar kicks him in the shin and dances backward.

"You fool." Wayob rubs his shin and raises the gun. But shooting Jaggar would be idiotic when Wayob must be smart to overcome Parker and his minions.

Jaggar lunges forward. Wayob attempts to dodge, but Jaggar head butts Wayob in the side. They topple to the floor. Instinctively, Wayob catches himself with his hand, the hand with the gun, leaving himself vulnerable to Jaggar's next offense, which is unbelievable. Deplorable. Jaggar's teeth sink into Wayob's arm.

"You vile, filthy man," he screams.

As Wayob rolls onto his back, he clutches the gun so hard the metal hurts his hand.

Jaggar, with his arms still tied behind his back, worms onto Wayob's chest.

Wayob slams the butt of the gun into Jaggar's head. "Get off." He slams it again. And again. The metal smacks Jaggar's skull. Something gives.

Jaggar, at last, stops moving.

Wayob rolls Jaggar off him. He scoots backward on the hard, white floor.

Jaggar just lies there on his side, his head facing away from Wayob, lolling against the floor.

Wayob gets to his feet. He creeps closer. He jabs Jaggar's back with the gun.

No reaction.

Wayob crouches and presses the gun barrel to Jaggar's ear. With his other hand, he slowly reaches over Jaggar's mouth, careful to avoid touching him.

No air coming out. No air going in.

"No!" Wayob leaps around to face Jaggar and falls to his knees.

Jaggar's eyes are open. The life has gone out of them.

"No." Wayob grabs a handful of Jaggar's cheek. The skin is loose, clammy. Jaggar's neck has gone completely limp. His gray-colored hair flops across his forehead, the furrows gone from his brow.

Wayob swallows back the bile in his throat. "No."

He shoves Jaggar away.

The words on the counter practically scream at him. *I have answers.* They mock him. For there are no answers, not anymore. Only one option remains.

Wayob grabs the gun. The officers lurking in the library probably heard Wayob scream, little that it matters now.

Let them gun him down. He shall awaken in some other vessel. Wayob should have allowed them to shoot him an hour ago instead of wasting so much time. This is Parker's fault.

"What are you looking at?" he asks Bob Jaggar. "You are dead already. Easy for you."

Wayob should make a run for it. He should just go. *Go now.* But dying hurts. Dying is utter agony, and worse than the pain is the uncertainty. When shall he awaken in his new vessel? Where? Presumably closer to he who holds the Encanto. But he does not really know. The black-hearted priest banished Wayob to this atrocious existence without explaining a thing. Of course, he probably presumed Wayob would never escape the Encanto. The barbarian, his foul breath and tiny chin.

Blood pounds in the head of this vessel who Wayob must shed himself of but cannot, not here in this awful room with the corpse of Jaggar, who now seems to be smirking.

"Wayob."

Is that Jaggar's voice? Jaggar's voice in my head?

"Way-ob."

No, it is Parker. Parker mocking him.

The pounding subsides for a moment. "Rydell?" Parker says. "Open up."

The knocking starts up again. And Wayob realizes it is not in his head.

The phone on the counter blares. From outside, Parker yells again, "Rydell."

Wayob laughs and sprints toward the outer door. *Parker, my savior.*

Wayob drags the bookcase back a foot and peers behind it. Outside the window in the door, Parker's massive trench coat hangs over his stomach and his shoulders on top of which sits Parker's fat face.

"Parker."

"Send Jaggar out," Parker says. "I'll come in."

"No, I shall come out. You shall drive me away from here."

"Whatever you want. Just leave the gun inside."

Wayob laughs. "You think I am a fool, Parker?"

"No one will shoot you if you're unarmed."

"Oh, I know, Parker. I know all too well, all about your fetish for unjustified confinement. But not this time. This time, you drop your weapon and turn your back to the door."

"Not until Jaggar is safe. I'll drop my weapon if you send him out. If I don't surrender, you can shoot us both."

"No. Jaggar stays inside, and if you refuse to comply, I shall end his life."

"Then you'll get the death penalty for sure. If you release him, you'll serve a few years at the most. The guy you shot at his place is going to live."

"I welcome death," Wayob lies. "Just make it quick."

"That's not how it works. You'll be on death row for years. Or... I can get you out of here right now. My car is right there." He points behind him and steps aside, revealing a brown vehicle backed up onto the curb, facing away from the library. Behind it, dozens of police vehicles are fanned out, flashing blue lights, and behind them a crowd of officers with guns all aimed toward Wayob.

Parker steps in front of them. "We'll go together and find the guy you're looking for, I promise."

Parker knows something, Wayob realizes. Not everything, probably, but enough. What if Parker's plan is to have Wayob lead him right to the Encanto?

Wayob slams his fist into the bookcase. *Fucking Parker.* He screams, "I shall shoot Jaggar and then I shall shoot myself."

"Don't."

Wayob should just do it. He should have, earlier, but now he has wasted so much time. "I am counting to ten."

"Be smart, Wayob. Let's work something out."

But Wayob *has* worked it out. "Two." Parker will not wait for a countdown, Wayob knows. The officers will blast their way in here, with Parker leading the charge. "Three."

The phone on the counter starts ringing. Wayob marches to the counter, answers the phone and yells into the receiver, "Four." He slams it down.

"Five," he shouts at the inner wall, then hurries back toward the outer door.

When Parker barges his way in here, attempting to be a hero, Wayob shall take him by surprise. He lays prone by the wall and extends his arms, holding the gun with both hands. He braces his wrists in anticipation of the awful kickback and the noise, hoping only to wound Parker severely. No need to kill him. Wayob just needs to escape.

"Okay," Parker yells from outside. "We'll do it your way."

"Do not be fooled," Wayob says to himself.

"I mean it," Parker says. "I'm unarmed."

Wayob scoots forward and peers out the door. Parker stands there, the back of his giant coat filling the window. *Too easy.*

"Remove the coat," Wayob says.

After glancing around, Parker removes the coat. He points out that his shoulder holster is now surprisingly empty. He raises his hands. "Okay. Come on out."

Using Parker's immense size, Wayob can easily shield himself from the other officers's guns on the way to the vehicle, at which point Wayob will have to climb in first and duck down, which is probably what Parker is counting on.

Wayob smiles. "What happens when we get to your vehicle?"

Parker removes the handcuffs from his belt and clasps his left wrist. "I'll cuff myself to the wheel." He dangles the other manacle in the air.

"That could work, but first we must get there. Where is your gun?"

"I threw it in my trunk while you were counting."

"You expect me to believe that?"

"I'll show you." Parker's voice has an edge, a certain earnestness. He probably would love to show Wayob the trunk, where there is almost certainly a gun. But is it his only one? *No.*

"Clever, Parker," Wayob says, "but you should know that I have experience dealing with men such as yourself." Wayob cringes at what he is about to suggest. Hard to imagine anything more vile, but Wayob has come too far to allow Parker to outsmart him. "Unfortunately, I must insist that you undress."

Parker's eyes widen. "What?" He steps back, exposing Wayob to the crowd of officers with their guns all aimed toward Wayob.

Wayob lowers himself down from their view. "Undress."

Parker crouches down, exposing Wayob again and causing him to draw back behind the wall. *Will it stop a bullet?* "You are trying to get me shot," he shouts.

"No," Parker says, "I had another weapon. You were right. I'm getting rid of it."

Wayob peers around the wall.

Parker has hiked up one pants leg where, strapped just above his ankle, is a little gun. *Parker, you trickster.*

"What are you doing?" Hernandez shouts. Detective Hernandez, who had tortured him with her ridiculous questions when he was in the vessel of Saroyan, trapped in that hot little room, is marching towards them. She raises her gun.

Parker removes the gun and slides it away on the sidewalk. "This is the only way." He stands with his back to the door, just like Wayob ordered.

But Parker might have a dozen more guns hidden beneath the voluminous layers of his clothing, and Hernandez is right there, blocked by Parker from Wayob's sight.

"Tell Hernandez to back away," Wayob says.

"Hernandez isn't going to be a problem. Don't worry."

Wayob agrees that Hernandez shall not be a problem, because Wayob shall use Parker to shield himself, and she will not risk her partner's life.

Wayob stands. "But, Parker, you intend to be a problem, as we both know. Remove your clothing."

Parker looks down at his enormous belly. "This is a waste of time. Aren't you in a hurry?"

Wayob clenches the gun in his hand. It would be so easy just to shoot Parker, but then he might as well shoot himself. "You are the one wasting time. Would you like me to shoot you?"

"Go around to the other entrance," Parker says to Hernandez.

Although her response is muffled by the glass, and the massive amount of meat on Parker's body, it's clear from her tone that she is refusing.

Wayob presses the gun barrel to the glass. Time to take charge. If he shoots Parker in the shoulder, just a hole through the fat on his arm, Parker should be able to drive just fine.

"Don't look," Parker says to Hernandez. "There's no way to unsee this."

He faces Wayob and begins unbuttoning his shirt. Hernandez is fortunate to be spared from this agony which Wayob must endure for the sake of his own safety.

Beneath Parker's shirt is another shirt, a tight one, which clings to the immense roll of his belly. Parker unbuckles his pants.

Bile rises in Wayob's throat. The human body is revolting. What has Wayob gotten himself into? He groans.

"Want me to stop?" Parker asks.

Wayob wants to scream, *yes!* But he cannot allow Parker to see him suffer. Wayob swallows back the bile. "Keep going."

Parker's pants fall.

Suddenly, Wayob returns to the most awful night of his life, all those centuries ago, when his bride performed that deplorable act on the odious priest. When Wayob caught them together, the priest banished Wayob to this miserable existence. *Odious fucking priest.*

Nausea overtakes Wayob. His throat burns. Whatever filth Rydell consumed before Wayob took him as a vessel is about to spew up. Wayob bends over, falls to his hands on his knees, and retches. "Enough, enough!"

Obviously, Parker has no other weapon or he would not have undressed down to the thin T-shirt and white garment covering his groin. Whatever awfulness lies beneath it, Wayob cannot bear to look.

"Turn around!" Wayob shouts. For this, he shall take revenge. *Oh Parker, we have just begun.*

Parker glances behind him and then just stands there with his shoulders slumped, looking ridiculous in his awful underwear and his stupid silver watch.

Wayob inhales. "Turn around. I said turn around."

Parker crosses his arms over his belly and attempts to cover his groin with his hands. Finally, he turns around.

Wayob wedges himself between the bookcase and the door and presses the red handle with the "Alarm Will Sound" warning. Hardly matters now.

Wayob shoves the door open. The alarm blares. Wayob covers his ears, the alarm seems to grow louder. So loud it hurts.

Endure. Must endure. Wayob withdraws his hands from his ears and marches out with the gun extended. He presses the muzzle to the back of Parker's head.

"Walk," Wayob says.

Parker lunges forward, and Wayob trots after him.

He must not allow any distance between them for Hernandez and all the other officers who wish to shoot Wayob, though their bullets would almost be easier to endure than the proximity to Parker's body, which Wayob must suffer though because he cannot afford the time it takes to die and find a new vessel. If he waits too long, he who holds the Encanto might turn the dial, trapping Wayob back inside the awful device. And there he would remain, disembodied in the darkness with only his thoughts churning around in the void, and no way of knowing when if ever he shall be released again.

Parker stalls.

Wayob smacks into the awful expanse of his back, just a thin layer of fabric between Parker's flesh and Wayob's face. The nausea returns. Wayob punches the gun barrel into Parker's neck. His finger twitches on the trigger, but right then, the alarm finally ceases.

Wayob shoves Parker forward. "Walk at a steady rate."

Wayob trails Parker the last few steps to the vehicle, staying close. At the rear door, Parker stops and turns unexpectedly.

Wayob's heart slams against his ribs. He cringes back, which exposes him to Hernandez, who stands near the hood of the vehicle, seemingly undaunted by the awful sight of Parker in his undergarments. With one hand she raises her gun while with the other she flips back the mismatched clump of gray hair on her forehead. "Let him go," she shouts.

"Get back." Wayob moves closer to Parker, putting Hernandez out of his sight and therefore Wayob out of hers. If she was going to shoot through Parker, she would have by now.

"If you hurt him, you're dead," she says.

"I doubt that," Wayob says. "Do not attempt to follow us. Or I shall shoot Parker and drive for myself."

Parker motions Wayob to get in the vehicle. Almost too easy.

"I shall ride up front," Wayob says.

"Suit yourself." Parker opens the driver's door. "I assume you'd rather climb across than trust me to walk around."

Wayob backs into the car, keeping his gun trained on Parker while lowering himself to avoid giving Hernandez a shot through the windshield. But when Wayob peeks over the dashboard, she is not even watching. She is staring at Parker. Why? Wayob has to watch Parker for the sake of his own protection, but Hernandez could so easily look away, yet for some reason she is transfixed by Parker's elephantine body, which he is trying to conceal behind the vehicle door, a useless endeavor.

Wayob struggles across the divider between the seats. As soon as there is space, Parker, in his abdominous T-shirt, crams himself behind the wheel and cowers down, a hangdog look on his face. Wayob has won.

Parker starts the engine and cuffs his wrists to the wheel. Wayob does not even have to prompt him.

The exit is blocked by a police vehicle. As Parker accelerates toward it, the officer behind the wheel leaps out to safety.

"What are you doing?" Wayob braces himself for impact.

Just before colliding, Parker swerves up onto the curb. The vehicle plows through some shrubs, over the sidewalk, and bumps down into the road.

"They won't pursue us," Parker says. At the intersection, he swerves left and right at the next. "So, where to?"

Wayob smiles. "I thought you knew."

"Yeah, well, pretend I don't."

"Go north," Wayob says.

They must find a safe place for Wayob to meditate on the sound of the mind who holds the Encanto. But Wayob shall not take Parker to him. *Parker knows something. Perhaps not everything, but enough.* Wayob shall leave Parker restrained in the handcuffs, alone. Let Parker suffer the same torture he inflicted upon Wayob.

"So what's with *Wayob*?" Parker asks. "Is that like a codename?"

Codename? "What do you mean?"

"Someone put you up to this. Tell me who you're working for and you might not have to serve any time at all."

Working for? Wayob had been afraid for nothing. "You know nothing at all." Wayob laughs.

And he laughs.

Whatever Parker says next, Wayob ignores it. Parker is merely a nuisance. No more than a fly to be swatted away.

And the problem with flies is that you swat them away, and they come back, again and again. They always come back. They keep bothering you until you squash them.

Gray's Painting

The first floor room in the turret has high ceilings, wooden floors, and three vertical windows punched through the curved stone wall. Three cushioned chairs are angled toward one window each. Gray sets the Michaels bag on the wooden desk situated between the windows and the chairs. The desk is barren, and the room is mostly empty space, staged to look like an office even though it seems to serve no clear function at all.

He sets up the easel by the desk. He'd wanted to set up out on Ashley's field-sized lawn, like in his dream, but with her security guy circling the house every ten minutes, probably hoping for another glimpse of Ashley York's boobs—Gray still can't understand how they're his—he can't concentrate. If he could get into the flow, this uneasiness would fade away, as would this feeling of judgment, which seems to fill every room of Ashley York's enormous house, even down here.

Andrea had bought him the art supplies only after asking a lot of questions, apparently doubting he'd ever use them. He should have just gone to Michaels himself. He'd wanted to. He wants to go check on Claire and the kids too, but what if leaving Ashley's is like leaving a dream? What if there's no coming back?

He stares at the canvas.

Where to begin? In his mind, he knows what the fortune-teller looks like, but when he tries to picture her face on the canvas, all he sees is white.

A white wall.

He opens the brushes. For some reason, Andrea purchased Beniccis, the most expensive set in the store, instead of the Princeton Select Black Taklons he requested. But they'll do. He pulls out a #2, round and dabs it in raw umber. As he turns toward the easel, the image of a wall returns to his mind. He poises with his brush above the canvas, closes his eyes, and concentrates on the old fortune-teller's face....

He sees the wall, bathed in intense light. He has the unmistakable sense of being watched, as if someone is standing behind him. He's afraid to open his eyes... but he has to.

He lowers the brush.

Standing in the doorway, Andrea crosses her arms. "Still haven't started yet, huh?"

"I can't concentrate if you don't leave me alone."

"I was just checking to see if you need anything." She sounds genuine except her eyes flick to the side.

"I'm fine," he says.

She stands there and tilts her head. A lock of hair falls over her left eye.

"What?" he asks.

"It's just... I don't understand why you're starting a new hobby all the sudden? Don't you have that screen test on Tuesday?"

Gray glances down at himself in the body of Ashley York. "Right."

"Aren't you nervous?"

"Maybe I need to take my mind off of it."

"You don't need to rehearse?"

"Tomorrow."

Her eyes bulge almost out of her head. "O-kay." She closes the door.

Here he is with no obligations, no interruptions from Claire or the kids—he can paint all day and all night, if he wants—and yet all he can paint on the canvas is a wall. A blank wall. Here he is in this vast house effectively all for him, with personal staff and a pool, a view of LA and the ocean—the dream of any artist come true—and he is unable to paint.

Why?

Maybe he needs a little lubrication for his creativity. At home, he usually has a Scotch, just to clear his head. Has it gotten to the point that he can't paint without it?

He trots to the living room to check out the wet bar. The cabinet below the bar contains about ten different kinds of schnapps, two tequilas, and one bottle of Pappy Van Winkle. Gray uncorks the Pappy and gulps two swallows, probably four hundred dollars' worth, but it has the same oaky flavor as any other bourbon, the same burn as it slides down his throat.

His shoulders loosen. Ashley's body is feeling more comfortable, more like his own. If there was some way to know for sure that the charm could return him to normal, he could relax. But he couldn't find anything on the internet about the charm or the old fortune-teller. He could go looking for her but, he reminds himself as he takes another pull of the Pappy, she doesn't speak English and seemed to want nothing to do with him after she'd given him the charm and told him to destroy it.

On the subject of body switching, Google had only suggested movies in which people trade places by wishing on a star, magic altar, doll, or genie. But Gray had not made any wish. If he had, he'd have chosen someone other than Ashley York to body swap into: maybe her father, since Evan York has all the real money. Maybe he'd wondered, for a brief moment, what Ashley's life was like, but only because Claire is obsessed with her.

From behind the wet bar in the living room, he hears Andrea speaking from somewhere in the back of the kitchen but can't see her. "Ashley thinks she's an artist, all the sudden."

"No way," a male voice responds. The security guy? Gray hadn't seen him circle the house in a while.

Gray carries the Pappy along with him as he sneaks back to the easel. He doesn't have to justify himself to Andrea—he's not even Ashley—but he still has to paint at least one portrait that he's happy with, just to prove to himself that he can.

He stares at the canvas, and there it is again: the wall. He wishes he could punch it. Punch the image in his mind, little good that it would do. He's been stuck before. He just has to get through it, just has to paint something, anything. Anything would be better than standing here staring at a blank canvas.

He grits his teeth and traces a curve on the page. A thin line… Suddenly, it comes into focus. The line is the edge of a counter. It's not a wall; it's a counter. He sketches its geometry… and slowly it forms as a semi-circular counter inscribed with the phrase, "I have answers."

Weird.

It's as if his hand has a mind of its own. Perhaps he has imbibed too much. That certainly wouldn't be a first for him, but never before has he painted something so specific without first seeing it somewhere else.

Behind him, a voice says, "Hey, that's my Pappy."

Gray whirls around. A short guy with jet-black hair styled into a wave, strides toward him. He looks familiar. He has a chiseled chin and boyish cheeks, and before Gray can resist, the guy's hand is around his waist. He pulls Gray in for a kiss, but Gray doesn't lower his head, so the guy pecks him on the chin.

August Grant, Gray realizes, the Hollywood heartthrob Ashley is dating. Claire would be so jealous. Too bad she'll never believe it.

August steps back, lowers one brow and arches the other, an expression which seems to mean that Gray should explain himself. How did he even get into the house?

"Guess you normally just show up?" Gray asks.

"When Franco's working."

"Franco?"

"I know. You like Sammy better." August grabs the bottle of Pappy from the desk. "But it's demeaning the way Sammy makes me wait while he calls you every time I come over. He knows who I am. It's demeaning. You should get rid of that guy."

August tilts the bottle from side to side, as if it's some big mystery how the level of brown liquid has sunk below the label, which was more than Gray meant to drink.

"Now Franco, he gets it," August says. "He has the gate open by the time I roll up to the booth. All he says is, '*Alright.*' I love the way he says it. *Alright.*" August glances around as if something is missing, then fixes Gray with the mismatched brows. "Did you drink from the bottle?"

"So what if I did?" Gray says. Even though it's clearly not something Ashley would normally do, she shouldn't have to take shit from August, not here in her own house.

"You bought it for me." August takes a swallow and returns the bottle to the desk. "Since when do you like whiskey?"

"I'm developing a taste."

August returns the bottle to the desk. "So, what's with the painting?"

"It's just something I have to do." Gray motions toward the door. "And I'd like to get back to it, if you don't mind."

August twists the nearest chair around and plops into it. "'I have answers.' Are you starting an advice blog or something?"

Gray faces the canvas where, instead of the portrait of the old fortune-teller he'd meant to paint, his sketch of the counter with the odd inscription almost mocks him. "It's supposed to be art."

But it's not. It's too technical, architectural. He's never painted anything like this before in his life.

"Weird," August says. "It's hard to picture you as an artist."

"Well." Gray inhales deeply. "People change."

"You should paint celebrities—like me. Who wants to look at a painting of words?"

Gray swallows. "I don't know."

"Stick to what you're good at," August says.

Which would be what? Gray wonders. Art is all he has.

August pulls his phone out and motions Gray toward the arm of the chair. "Check this out."

Gray wonders if he can have August removed from the premises. Franco works for Ashley, right? His number must be in her phone.

"Where are you going?" August asks as Gray starts toward the door.

"I need my phone."

"You found it? Wait?"

Before Gray can escape, August is out of the chair and in Gray's face with his own phone. On the screen is a video of the murder Gray nearly witnessed in Venice. The killer, perched on his wheelchair, swings the bat down on the victim's head. Gray grinds his teeth. Someone had been this close and all they did was film it?

Gray backs away, feeling lightheaded.

"They've already hired a screen writer," August says. "You think I should I play the victim or the homicide detective?"

Gray stares at him in disbelief. It's like he doesn't get it. "That was a person—a real person, murdered on the street."

"I know." August steps in close, too close. "If I play the victim, I'll win an award."

Gray steps back and collides with the chair. The armrest catches him behind the knees, and he falls backward into the chair. He swings his legs around, but before he can get to his feet, August leans over him, his hand on the armrest, blocking Gray's escape.

Gray opens his mouth to tell August to back off, but August leans forward and shoves his tongue into Gray's mouth, his two-day-old scruff scratching Gray's lips.

Gray turns his head away and shivers at the abrupt transition from murder to sex. How can August be so detached? It's like he's actually turned on by it.

August starts unbuttoning Gray's shirt. Gray wants to shove him away, but maybe he should try to enjoy this. It might be his only chance to experience sex as a woman, which could be amazing if he can just detach himself from the fact that it's a man who has his knees between Gray's legs.

He closes his eyes. August grabs one of Gray's breasts and with his other hand, guides Gray's hand to the bulge in his jeans, which turns Gray off, probably more due to the abruptness than the male anatomy itself.

He drops his hand, lays his head back, and imagines it's Andrea unbuckling her belt.

At the sound of the zipper, Gray squeezes his eyes shut…and waits.

Nothing happens.

He opens his eyes.

Inches from his face, August's semi-hard snakes out from a bush of black curls.

Gray jerks away and pushes August back.

"What the hell?" August says.

Gray was thinking the same thing, but for the opposite reason. Does Ashley just go to town on August with no foreplay whatsoever?

"Look. Um… I just need to take it slow. Okay?"

"What do you mean 'take it slow'? Look at my face. You're not turned on?"

Gray wants to experience sex as a woman, but not like this. At least, not with August Grant. "I guess not," he says. "Thought I was. Sorry."

August jerks up his pants and snarls his zipper. Slams his belt through the buckle and parades out of the room.

Escape

Before surrendering to Rydell at the library, Saul had activated location sharing with Hernandez on his phone and hid it under the spare tire in the trunk.

Rydell had threatened to kill Saul if anyone followed. Hopefully, since Hernandez could track their location, she would keep the LAPD out of sight long enough for Saul to find out who the hell Rydell was after. He might just reveal the whole plot, so long as he believed he had the upper hand, which obviously he did from the way he was laughing at Saul, leaning against the passenger window and waving his stolen Ruger LCP.

The light turned green, and Saul accelerated up Beverly, both wrists cuffed to the wheel. It was a dangerous game. He'd never have surrendered if he'd known Rydell was going to humiliate him in front of Hernandez. Nothing could have been worse than standing there in his sweat-stained T-shirt, his enormous belly hanging over the waistband of his too-tight tighty-whities, the quarter-sized hole over the left butt cheek, which years ago, his wife (now ex) had insisted he throw out. He'd only kept them to spite her and was only wearing them today because he'd been too busy to do laundry. His chili pepper boxers, or maybe the dachshunds, might have detracted from the awful sight of his sagging belly.

At least now that Hernandez had seen how fat he was, he didn't have to keep wearing the damn trench coat when it was eighty degrees out. Nothing was going to happen between them. Not anymore.

"Par-Par-Parker," Rydell said. He would be handsome if not for the arrogant arch to his brows. His disheveled gray hair shook when he spoke. "Parker-fucking-Parker."

Saul returned his gaze to the road and said nothing.

"So," Rydell continued, "how did you know I would be there last night?"

Saul's heart hammered against his chest. Only Hernandez knew that he'd tracked Aleman's phone. "And where was that?"

"*El dia de los Muertos,*" Rydell said with perfect Spanish. "Do not insult me, Parker. I saw you."

"Why were you there?" Saul asked.

Rydell grimaced. "Is this one of your tactics? Pretend to know nothing and see what I say? What did she tell you?"

"Who? Hernandez?"

Hernandez was the only woman Saul had spoken to last night. By the time she arrived, he'd already lost Aleman in the crowd. She'd accused him of inventing the Wayob calls as a way to lure her out for dinner, though she said it with a hint of amusement in her voice, like maybe if he really had, it would be fine—like maybe he should ask her out for real. And he'd planned to, before Rydell humiliated him. Now that she'd seen all that, all he could hope for was pity—and there was no path from pity to love.

Rydell grinned. "You have no idea, do you, Detective Parker?"

"How about you enlighten me?"

"No. Be grateful you know so little. Perhaps now I can allow you to live. If you get me where I need to go and stay out of my way." He waved the Ruger. "Think you can do that, Par-ker?"

"Of course," Saul lied.

"I do not wish to harm anyone," Rydell said, his voice cracking. "But I have no choice."

Saroyan had said the same thing.

Saul nodded as if the notion made sense. "So then, who's putting you up to this?"

"A sadistic priest. Unfortunately, he died long ago."

What could Rydell possibly gain by blaming his actions on a dead priest? At least he was talking, and maybe if Saul could keep him talking, he'd say something useful. "So why take Jaggar hostage?"

"I needed a vehicle."

Saul turned right on Sunset as if uninterested in where they were going. Rydell fell silent and closed his eyes. The smirk remained on his face.

"You have a Jaguar and a Ferrari," Saul said. "Why bother with Jaggar's car?"

The smirk fell away. "This is exactly what I'm talking about, Parker. No questions."

Saul shrugged. "I was just thinking that if it was some kind of emergency, it might help your case."

Rydell pointed to the right. "Pull over. There in the grass."

"No parking," Saul said. "If I stop here, it'll raise all kinds of attention."

"Then stop somewhere discreet. I do not care where. Just make it fast. You are going the wrong way. I know it."

They crossed Sunset, and Saul turned left into a neighborhood, drove a block, and parked beside the vast lawn of a mansion.

In the passenger seat, Rydell crisscrossed his legs. "I must meditate. Say nothing, or I shall end your life." He rested the Ruger in his lap, aimed at Saul.

His finger remained on the trigger as he closed his eyes and leaned back in the seat.

In the rear-view, Saul watched a familiar red Mustang turn the corner and pull to the curb a half-block behind them. Hernandez. She'd acquired the city-owned ride somehow while at Rampart Station and had managed to retain it when she got the bump up to Homicide Special. The other detectives all drove Crown Vics.

Beside Saul, Rydell's eyes remained closed. The corner of his mouth gradually wound back into a smirk.

Meditation required concentration. It required relaxation, especially in the face, Saul knew, because he'd started meditating in the hopes of curbing his near-constant compulsion to stuff food into his face. Acid roiled in his gut. Rydell was planning something. Probably thinking he didn't need Saul anymore, now that they had evaded the police. Rydell was about to make a move.

In the rear-view, all Saul saw of Hernandez was dark hair hanging down from her head. She was probably looking at her phone. *Look up.* Although it went against protocol to confront an armed gunman with a hostage, she would act if she thought Saul was in imminent danger.

Saul glanced at the Ruger in Rydell's hand and back at the rear-view. *Look up. Look up.*

She looked up.

He signaled for her to buzz by them in her Mustang by tilting his head and swiveling it forward. Saul needed Rydell distracted, just for a second, so he could gain the upper hand.

In the rear-view, Hernandez shook her head. She hadn't made sense of his signal.

He repeated the motion.

Through the windshield, she mouthed, *no.*

Maybe she didn't understand what he was asking, but she knew him well enough to assume he was about to try something dangerous.

But he had to. Regardless of Rydell's intentions, Saul needed to gain the upper hand to gain back the respect he'd lost back at the library, along with his clothes. Beauty, after all, was half confidence.

Saul removed the paperclip he kept wound around the band of his watch. He straightened it with his fingers.

Rydell's eyes remained closed. The smirk remained on his face.

With his left hand, Saul slipped the paperclip into the lock on the cuff on his right wrist. He used the lock as a fulcrum to bend the end of the paperclip into a *L*. Pushed it down into the lock. Turned it like a key against the ridges inside.

Rydell's eyes flicked open. His nostrils flared.

Saul jerked his wrist free just as Rydell shoved the Ruger toward his chest —impossible to miss.

Saul couldn't imagine a worse way to die with Hernandez right there to see it. His plus-sized body slumped in the seat. His already sweat-soaked T-shirt stained with blood. Belly hanging out over his tighty-whities, which wouldn't be white anymore after the bullet had pierced his heart and his bowels emptied out. And then the last thing she'd remember about him was the smell of his shit.

Unacceptable.

Rydell squeezed the trigger.

The Ruger didn't fire.

It couldn't fire, because Saul had shoved his finger into the trigger guard and blocked the trigger.

Rydell screamed, wrenched the Ruger to the side and might have broken Saul's finger off in the trigger guard, except Saul, with his other hand, had latched onto Rydell's arm.

Rydell froze.

Saul had to hold onto to the gun, which meant he had to hold onto Rydell, which meant he couldn't leverage his weight advantage. Instead, he pulled Rydell toward him.

Rydell winced. His grip loosened on the Ruger, and for a moment, Saul thought he might just let go.

No such luck. Saul clutched the Ruger with his right hand, his finger still wedged through the trigger guard. With his other hand, he released Rydell's arm and—before Rydell could react—released the Ruger's magazine. He tossed it into the footwell by Rydell's feet. A wasted effort if a bullet was in the chamber. Except, just as Saul had hoped, Rydell followed the motion with his eyes.

Saul pried out the takedown pin. Tossed it over his shoulder. Pulled the slide forward and off the frame. A bullet was in the chamber. Saul shook it loose, reducing the Ruger from a deadly weapon to a harmless piece of metal.

He'd disarmed Rydell, but that was the easy part.

Now he had to find pants. Hernandez hadn't seen him from behind, and he intended to keep it that way. But his pants were back at the library, and Rydell was a size thirty, thirty-two at the most. Even if the geometry worked, there wasn't time for Rydell to strip off his khakis and for Saul to put them on; Hernandez was already out of the Mustang and approaching the passenger side, Glock extended.

Rydell opened the door. So far, he hadn't looked back in Hernandez's direction.

Saul lunged across the divider between the seats, reaching for Rydell's arm. Rydell dodged. Before he could leap from the car, Saul grabbed his belt.

Rydell screamed.

Saul pulled him back. "Relax. Or she'll shoot you."

Rydell clutched onto the doorframe and stared out at Hernandez. She stood ten feet back, on the lawn Saul had parked beside, legs apart, Glock aimed at Rydell.

"Hands on your head," she said. "You have the right to remain silent.

Anything you say can and will be used against you—"

"Shoot me," Rydell said. "I dare you."

Hernandez continued mirandizing and kept her weapon trained on Rydell in case Saul lost his grip, which meant it was up to him to subdue him. Which meant Saul—in his underwear, with Hernandez standing right there—had to climb on top of Rydell and pin him against the passenger seat.

He considered letting Rydell charge out of the car so Hernandez could shoot him. She would have to. And Rydell deserved to die.

But Saul couldn't allow it. More and more, he was starting to suspect a third party behind the whole Wayob act, and Rydell likely knew who it was.

So, dreading that Hernandez had to see this, Saul climbed on top of Rydell and pinned him face down in the seat, his belly pressed into Rydell's back.

Rydell screamed.

Heat flooded Saul's neck and face. He clung to the hope that although Hernandez could see his big, hairy back and his shoulders, maybe from where she stood, the roof of the plain wrap blocked her view of his butt.

Saul grabbed Rydell's left shoulder and pulled his arm behind his back. Rydell screamed in Spanish and then in some other language, which Saul had never heard before. Probably just gibberish.

He cuffed his wrist to Rydell's. "We're doing this the hard way," Saul said, "unless you want to tell us who Wayob is?"

With his right arm, Rydell was still trying to pry himself free. Hernandez holstered her Glock and approached. She was going to see.

"Stay back," Saul said. "I've got him."

"You see how Parker tortures me?" Rydell screamed. "I do not deserve such treatment. I was merely defending myself from Jaggar. Look at my arm. See the marks from his teeth?"

"So he bit you," Hernandez said, "and you bashed his head in? Sounds like a great defense you've got there."

Saul pressed forward, grabbed Rydell's right arm, and wrenched it free from the doorframe. But now all he could do was hold it behind his back. He needed another hand.

"Come in through the back," Saul said. "Help me cuff him."

Saul managed to hold onto Rydell while sliding back enough to get his butt down into the driver's seat, out of view, while Hernandez climbed in through the back. She reached between the seats and unlocked the cuff on Saul's wrist.

"Do not touch me, vile woman," Rydell said.

Hernandez transferred the cuff from Saul's wrist to Rydell's other arm. In the mirror, she locked eyes with Saul and brushed the shock of white from her forehead. "I'll drive him downtown," she said, her voice lower than normal, absolute.

She had a thick skin, Saul knew. But whatever her reason was for wanting to drive Rydell, Saul was happy to oblige. It would give him a chance to grab clothes on the way.

Unfortunately, it required him to get out of the car to cover Rydell while

Hernandez escorted him to her Mustang.

"You are wasting my time," Rydell said as he walked. But he climbed right in before she could shove him.

After securing Rydell, Hernandez presented Saul with his clothes. They were in the front passenger seat, folded neatly, suit on top of his trench coat. Saul held the stack over the lower part of his belly in a way that he hoped looked natural, like he wasn't consciously trying to hide it.

"Good work," she said.

"I had hoped Jaggar might be alive," Saul said. Although, in truth, he had suspected the real reason Rydell had agreed to the exchange.

"He was dead before you got there. But thanks to you, we got Rydell alive."

Saul nodded. "If he starts talking, call me. Someone else is behind this whole Wayob thing, and I bet he knows who."

"Want to follow me? I'll wait."

No. He wasn't about to let her watch him pull his pants up over his butt, his belly hanging over the belt line. "I'll meet you at the PAB."

"Suit yourself," she said.

Saul chuckled. "Exactly."

As he stood facing her, the stack of clothes in front of his belly seemed to shrink. She got in the car. Sparked the engine. And sat there.

She was waiting for him to move.

But if he turned toward the plain wrap, she'd see his butt, the tear in his too-tight tighty-whities. And if he walked backward, she'd know how awkward he felt. And, probably, he'd fall on his ass.

So he turned. He strolled like he hardly cared that she saw (because beauty, after all, was half confidence). And he vowed to lose the butt—and the belly —whether or not she ever looked at him again.

Back To the Beginning

Ashley swings open the front door to the claustrophobic mid-century where she'd awakened in the body of a stranger, closes it behind her, and leans against it. The nightmare started here, so this is where it has to end.

At Oakhurst Academy, where she'd been shipped off to at age six when her nanny married her father, escape rooms were huge. When you get stuck in an escape room, you have to go back to the beginning and try something else. The obvious thing never works. That would be too easy.

Of course Sammy didn't believe she was trapped in the body of some guy. She wouldn't believe it either. But here she is.

After Sammy had denied her access to her own house, she'd gone to Don's, because she always went to Don, but his gate might as well have been a wall. It was Don's new wife, Connie, who'd answered the intercom. Connie, only two years older than Ashley, gets off on acting superior, like there's any chance she'll be granted some of Don's power and influence in the inevitable divorce.

"I'm sorry, who are you?" Connie had said.

Ashley had looked into the camera mounted above the gate and tried out a disarming smile, like a guy who might be Don's buddy. "I'm a friend of Don's." As soon as she says it, she recalls that Don doesn't have any male friends.

Don's voice booms through the speaker. "Have we met before?"

"Many, many times." If she could look into Don's eyes, maybe she could reach him. "Let me in and I'll explain."

"Explain what?"

"Just let me in."

"I'm hanging up."

No way being Gray Wilson would get her through the gate. She had to work with what she had. "I'm Ashley York. I know, hard to believe—"

"Whoa, buddy. I need you to leave."

"You got me the screen test with Sean Penn for the Kaufman film. Please let me in. Just for ten minutes—"

"Who are you with, *Variety*? I'm not confirming anything."

"No. It's me, Ashley. You said I could count on you—for anything, Don. You said to come to you first. One step at a time, right? Like you always say. Just let me come in and we can talk, you'll see. I need help."

"Look, this is my house. This is where I live. You have no right to be here."

"And how do I know where you live?" she asks, although she knows at this point it's useless. What could Don to do, anyway?

"What's your number?" he asks. "I'll find someone to help."

But he wouldn't. She knew he wouldn't. He just wants the crazy man away from his house.

"I needed you, Don. Remember that." Ashley slams the car in reverse and speeds away, seething through her teeth that when she gets back to her own body, she'll fire his ass and find some other agent.

But how would she get back to normal? She can't drive around forever with no money and no one believing who she is. And, damn it, she's hungry. Going back to Gray's house is basically her only option.

As she grinds through the stop-and-go on Santa Monica Boulevard, she can't shake this feeling of being watched, which is weird because she's so used to people staring at her. But no one would know her in Gray's body. She's anonymous, now—incognito. The only car behind her is a green Jaguar, two people inside, their features obscured by the reflection of sky on the windshield. Still, she feels something like sinister eyes on her back.

That had given her another reason to return to Gray's. She'd never been alone in LA after dark.

"Is that you, Gray?" a woman shouts from the living room.

Ashley opens her eyes. "That's me." She'll play along. She's an actress, after all. She can fake her way through this.

Ashley parades to the living room, where the TV is on, and the colossal mess of magazines and coloring books have overflowed from the table onto the floor. On the couch, the woman Ashley now knows is Claire, the only favorited contact in Gray's phone, is sporting a faded green T-shirt and sweatpants. In her lap, the baby coos and when Claire ignores it, staring at her phone, the baby coos louder.

"Thanks for the advance notice that I'd be a single parent today," Claire says without looking up.

It occurs to her that Claire might have noticed the real Gray do something out of the ordinary, something to cause Ashley to wake up in his body—something Ashley can reverse. She hopes so. "Sorry about that," she says. "Thank you. I appreciate you."

Claire looks up from her phone. "Huh?"

"I was just wondering, did you notice anything unusual yesterday? I did something weird, right?"

Claire's brows furrow. "What are you talking about?"

That's the problem. She doesn't know what she's talking about.

Claire turns up the TV. An anchor woman with painted-on eyebrows stands before a gate wrapped in yellow police tape. The gate looks familiar. As the camera pans, Ashley recognizes the street. It's Don's street.

"At eleven a.m.," the anchor woman says, "Martin Rydell stormed through this gate and assaulted Tommy Morello, a food delivery worker. According to a source in the Beverly Hills Police Department, Morello was armed in spite of regulations, and shot and injured with his own gun. Rydell then took Bob Jaggar hostage. We're still learning the details, but sometime after police cornered Rydell at the Beverly Hills Library, he allegedly murdered Bob Jaggar."

"Holy shit," Ashley says, "I could have been killed."

"What are you talking about?" Claire asks.

Ashley doesn't want to go there. Explaining to Claire how she had left Don's probably minutes before the kidnapping is more than she can manage right now. "It just makes you think is all."

"Huh?"

Ashley puts a finger to her lips. On the screen, a montage of Bob Jaggar's career is cut to a soundtrack of cheesy guitar with a raspy male singer. His most notable roles appear to be cheap-looking sitcoms from before Ashley was born. She sure hopes her career sums up to something more meaningful.

The anchor returns to say the police have apprehended Martin Rydell. A mugshot pops up on the screen of an older white man, his skin so pale it looks like he's never seen sunlight.

Ashley shivers.

The news cuts to the police building downtown. A Latina detective with gray bangs promises justice for the senseless killing of a beloved Angelino.

Claire mutes the volume. "Are you making dinner? I did breakfast and lunch."

Ashley hasn't eaten all day. Maybe with something in her stomach, she could think. She's never actually cooked before, but she knows how to heat stuff up.

In the kitchen, she opens the fridge. Its meager contents are all piled onto the middle shelf, as if thrown in with no consideration for arrangement. Bags of wilted green stuff that might have been salad some weeks ago, a block of bright orange cheese, a Tupperware of some white, clumpy stuff that makes her gag. Good thing there's nothing in her stomach to throw up.

She checks the cabinet between the fridge and the pantry. It contains several bottles of brown booze. She moves one aside to see if they have anything good. Behind the booze, at the very back of the cabinet, she spots a round, white stone with a black snake on top. A stone with a spooky, black snake is a strange thing to have. Stranger still to hide it in the back of the cabinet behind a bunch of booze.

She slides the booze aside and snatches up the stone. A pattern of tiny holes spiral from the side to the bottom. The chiseled snake is mounted at the center of its belly. It looks eerily similar to the cave painting her dad showed her on his phone. But how could that be?

If only she could remember his number.

She runs a finger along the *S*-shaped snake, which seems rigged to turn, but when she applies pressure, it won't move. She tries the other way.

It turns.

A half-turn. Then it sticks, with the snake's forked tongue pointing directly at her.

She shivers. If she believed in magic, which now maybe she has to, this would be just the kind of thing some idiot who should know better would mess with—and mess up her whole life in the process.

Does the stone have something to do with her presence here in Gray's body? If so, and if her dad has any idea of what it can do, then his obsession suddenly makes sense. Evan York doesn't waste his time on anything less than spectacular. That would also explain why he'd refused to tell her what it could do, because who would believe it without seeing proof?

Could this really be one of the artifacts he'd been searching for?

The one he'd bought Friday didn't work, he'd said. What if this one does? What if this was what he'd been searching for all this time, and here she is holding it in her hand with no way to tell him she's found it?

Ashley marches back to the living room. Claire is still on her phone, still watching some crap reality show, a big-haired actress complaining that some bitch tried to slip in the shower with her boyfriend, the bad words bleeped over but obvious.

Ashley stands in front of the screen and holds up the artifact. "How does it work?"

Claire glances up at her. "How would I know? What's it supposed to do?"

Maybe it doesn't do anything at all. "What did you see me do with it?"

"I saw you try to hide it when we came home. How much did it cost?"

Ashley turns it over again, like maybe there's a price tag. "I don't remember. Where did I buy it? I'll check my credit card?"

Claire slaps her phone down in her lap. Her eyes widen. "Are you kidding me? You told me you were going to the bathroom. What's going on?"

Good question. Ashley stares at the snake. She'd woken up this way, so maybe now that she's turned the snake, she just has to fall sleep, and when she wakes up, everything would be back to normal.

Ashley starts toward the bedroom.

Claire shouts after her. "Where are you going? What about dinner?"

In the hallway, out of nowhere, a little girl with cocoa-colored curls ambushes Ashley's legs. Ashley stumbles and throws her hands out reflexively to catch herself on the wall, dropping the artifact. She just manages to restrain herself from shoving aside this girl, who is now clinging to her leg, swaying as she giggles, her curls bouncing.

She's quite endearing. Ashley smiles in spite of herself.

A few feet away on the worn, beige carpet, the artifact is on its side, the snake sticking up at an angle. It looks intact.

From the other room, Claire yells over the din of the TV, "Mindy, you'd better not be out of your room."

Mindy blinks and stares up at Ashley. She has chestnut eyes and surprisingly thick lashes. "But Daddy's home!"

"Do you need to go back to your room?" Ashley asks her.

Mindy frowns, then giggles. "Tickle me."

"What?"

"Tickle me."

"Wait. So, you *want* me to tickle you?"

"No." Still holding onto Ashley's leg, Mindy leans back. She *does* want to be tickled, and if Ashley tickles her, maybe she'll let go.

Ashley bends over and digs her fingers into Mindy's ribs. "Tickle, tickle, tickle."

Mindy releases her leg and falls back on the floor. She rubs her side. "You hurt me."

Ashley's never tickled a kid before. Why did she think she knew how? She squats down beside Mindy and strokes her hair. "I didn't mean to." She really hadn't tickled her all that hard.

Mindy's lip quivers. She turns away and, without another word, goes to her room and shuts the door.

Ashley picks up the artifact. The snake and spindle its attached to are carved from black glass, which could easily have broken, but it seems intact, fortunately.

Ashley returns to the master bedroom and wades through the piles of clothes to the less messy of the two matching pine nightstands. She sets the artifact beside the metal Ikea lamp, lays back on the bed, and closes her eyes.

She inhales slowly. Exhales. "I am in control. I am in control," she repeats again and again like a mantra.

A few minutes later, she feels better. But she's not tired at all. What if she does somehow wake up back in her own body? Will she ever have a chance like this again? That moment with Mindy back there in the hallway, that was a gift. Ashley should have enjoyed Mindy's giggling, the way she was so ecstatic to see Ashley, even though she thought Ashley was her father. Mindy is like the daughter Ashley has always imagined herself having, except instead of blonde hair like Ashley's, Mindy has amazing brown curls, almost begging Ashley to brush them.

It's only Sunday. Ashley still has until Tuesday before the big screen test. And, for all she knows, this could be a dream—a very, very real dream. She hasn't really spent any time exploring what the hell this is. All she did all day was freak out about her body, her whole life lost behind the gates of Beverley Park.

She yanks down the jeans that are not hers and then the awful, black underwear she woke up in. She squeezes the limp sausage... Nothing happens.

She rubs. It is sensitive, but nothing like her clit—her lost clit. *Stop... Be here. Own this narrative.*

She unbuttons the shirt and rubs her abs. They have some potential. Maybe with some manscaping and a training regimen this bod of Gray's could look better than August's, which is too buff for his height. He won't admit it, but she knows the reason he always insists on meeting at wherever they're going out is because he's nearly a head shorter and doesn't want to be photographed walking in beside her.

She sniffs her armpit. Baby powder and man sweat, which she actually prefers to the overpowering deodorants men like to wear.

She cups the sack. Rolls the right ball between her thumb and forefinger and gently squeezes. It hurts. Even with this tiny pressure, it's clear that if she squeezes any harder, the pain will be unbearable. At Oakhurst Academy, her roommate thought squeezing a guy's balls was a huge turn on, and all this time Ashley had believed her, but damn was she wrong. Way, way wrong. Now Ashley understands why whenever she went for August's balls, he pulled her hand away and placed it on the tip.

But something is happening.

A swelling sensation.

She squeezes the shaft. It's growing... getting stiffer. As she strokes, the head becomes more and more sensitive. It feels good.

And at the same time, weird.

This urge to keep touching; it's just too weird. She wrenches the jeans up and belts them over the bulge. Buttons her shirt down over it.

Takes a deep breath. Gets up from the bed.

Solitary Confinement

It was Sunday, so the PAB was mostly empty. On the fourth floor, Saul wheeled a chair from a conference room, dropped his to-go bag into the seat and pushed the chair down the hall. The bag contained two burgers from The Counter, one for him, a half-pounder with provolone and bacon; and one for Hernandez, chipotle turkey with cranberries and jalapeño jack. But it had taken him too long to get here. She was already at the press conference, where the media was going to love her as she exuded competence to all the citizens of LA and demanded justice for Bob Jaggar, as if the murder of a once popular TV star mattered more than all the others.

And as thanks for her good performance today, Hernandez could count on more media headaches, and probably, at some point, a promotion. Did she want that? He hated to lose her. She was a damn good detective. And every time she looked at him, something fluttered in his stomach.

But now that she had seen his double-wide butt, the best he could hope for was pity. Maybe it was better if she got promoted. No reason to torture himself by being around her and her pity. He shoved the chair forward. Its wheels skidded on the linoleum.

He yanked his burger from the bag. Tore off the wrapper. Took a big, honking bite. The beef was cold. He hardly tasted it before taking another bite.

As he approached the holding cell, Rydell sat on the bunk and leaned back.

"Par-ker. I knew you would come."

Saul stared at him through the bars and chewed.

Rydell tried to look placid, but his jaw tightened. The slant of his brows betrayed him.

Saul ate the last bite and now that he wasn't focused on himself, he tasted it —Angus beef, cheese, bacon, and bread. Blended together. Perfect harmony.

"So." He swallowed. "You're telepathic too?"

"No, I have experience with men like you, Parker. You are like a fly. I swat you away and swat you away, and yet still you return. Only one way to get rid of a fly."

Saul pulled his phone from his pocket and started an audio recording. "Mind if I record this?"

Rydell said nothing. Maybe if he made a clear and credible threat, the DA would add it to the long list of charges.

"It sounded like you threatened me," Saul said.

"It was a promise. Your fault that I am here. Release me now, or I shall have to take revenge."

"And how, exactly, do you intend to carry out this revenge of yours?"

Rydell sat up. "I have the means to free myself. As I have demonstrated to you."

"Are you talking about Saroyan?"

"You are still not seeing me for who I am, Parker."

Saul wasn't sure how to handle this. Maybe humoring him would lead somewhere? "It's hard to see you when you look like someone else, Wayob." Saul tried to follow his delusional line of logic. "So you're saying you escaped from Saroyan's body to Aleman's, and now you're Rydell?"

"He is my vessel, yes."

"Well, it won't happen again. We have ways of preventing your 'escape.' Very uncomfortable ways." Saul hoped Rydell wouldn't call his bluff.

He shrugged. "Chain me to the wall. Go ahead. But soon I'll be free. You should be careful, Detective Parker."

The burger bricked in Saul's stomach. It wasn't Rydell's words. It was the way he spoke that got under Saul's skin.

I'm done with him, Hernandez had said, a fierceness in her voice like Saul had never heard before. She'd asked Saul to book Rydell into the MDC, where, according to protocol, he should be held until arraignment. But Saroyan had nearly died there, and now with Aleman back on duty and somehow involved in whatever the hell this was... *No, I'm not moving him. No way.* Rydell was going to spend the night right here. Saul could count on the watch commander to let it slide.

Now that he had Rydell behind bars, maybe he could press his advantage to make him talk. He rolled the chair up to the bars. Lifted the bag containing the one remaining burger and held it out. Hernandez wasn't going to eat it. After the press conference, she had to get to home to her son.

"What is that?" Rydell asked.

"Turkey burger," Saul said. "Might be good."

"Severed bird flesh and bread. Get that filth away from me."

Saul sat in the chair and looked in the bag. The burger was wrapped in white paper. His mouth watered. He wanted to try it, but he shouldn't. He should give it to the watch commander for keeping an eye on Rydell.

He closed the bag. Rydell's lips stretched into an unnatural grin. A film of dry skin on his upper lip cracked and split.

In the car, Rydell had asked, *What did she tell you?* before he clammed up, no doubt realizing he'd slipped. But now Saul had an idea who this *she* was.

"What did you think she told me?"

Rydell's grin became a grimace. "What are you talking about?"

"You know."

Rydell glanced down and to the right. "Why would I care what some vile woman told you?"

"Are you talking about Hernandez or Mrs. Luna?"

Rydell said nothing. His face turned from pale to ashen.

"Why did you kill Luis Luna?"

Rydell said nothing.

"Maybe you want to let Saroyan take the blame after all?"

Nothing again, but this time Saul waited him out.

Rydell glanced around the four by ten cell. "I do not know what it is you are talking about."

Without realizing it, Saul had unwrapped the second burger and bitten into it. The turkey was quite tasty, although he would always be a beef man. Since it now had a bite missing, he might as well finish it. No big hurry to get thin now that Hernandez had seen how huge he was. No way she could forget.

He'd eat the rest, but not in front of that smirk and the arrogant arch of his brow. Saul rewrapped the burger, stuffed it in the bag, and stood up.

"Sleep tight."

Rydell leaped up and grabbed the bars. "Hernandez said I must bed down with the worst of your prisoners, like before."

Now Saul had no doubt about keeping Rydell in the holding cell. Maybe a night alone would loosen his tongue. "I decided to spare you."

"Then do not leave me here." Rydell's pitch shot up as he spoke. He pressed his face against the bars, tears welling in his eyes. Crocodile tears. "Please."

Saul dropped the bag in the chair. "I've got work to do."

"You forget your occupation, Parker—serve and protect. I am the victim. I *am* the victim."

"And how is that?"

Rydell's face reddened. "It was the priest." His lip curled. "The odious, fucking priest."

Last time Rydell mentioned the priest, he'd also mentioned the priest was dead, and now Saul had a growing suspicion who had killed him. "What was his name?"

"Ajau Kan Kakzik."

A strange sounding name. Too strange for Rydell to have just made it up.

"Where's the body?"

"I did not kill him," Rydell said. "But you would not blame me if I had, if you knew the torture he had inflicted upon me. He locked me in darkness—for centuries."

"Sounds pretty bad," Saul said. "And also like a load of nonsense."

"Did you speak to the old Luna woman? I am curious why she said her poor son had to die."

Saul's stomach lurched. Mrs. Luna had claimed responsibility. Though there could be a lot of misguided reasons for her to blame herself, she had refused to explain why. She was hiding something. That had been clear. Hernandez had picked up on it, too.

"The way this works," Saul said, "is I ask the questions and you answer them."

Rydell's trademark smirk flickered at the corner of his lips. "She did not tell you anything. Of course. You would be wasting your time to even talk to her, because you know she is senile. Out of her head."

"Where is she?"

Rydell laughed. "You cannot find her? Some detective you are."

"You have anything to do with that?"

The grin vanished. "Do not blame your ineptitude on me."

"She didn't come home last night."

Rydell's brows launched up his forehead. His eyes widened. Maybe he didn't know where the Lunas were, but he knew something. And he was afraid.

"I get a phone call. Do I not?"

Saul shrugged. "Maybe tomorrow."

"I need my call. You cannot keep me here without my phone call."

Technically, he was right. He was allowed a call within a reasonable amount of time. But Saul would get away with delaying it. He had recorded more than enough to justify his concern that Rydell might use his call to place more people in danger.

"You're doing this to yourself," Saul said. "Tell me what's going on and we'll work something out."

Rydell turned his back on Saul. He grabbed the bunk and shook it. It held fast against the wall. "I cannot stay here."

"Then give me some reason to let you out."

"I shall take my revenge. An equal measure to the torture you have inflicted upon me."

"Good luck with that." He had better things to do than to stand here listening to Rydell talk in circles. He had to find the Lunas. He rolled the chair back down the hall.

"Parker. Parker!" Rydell's voice echoed after him. "Parker?"

Saul rolled the chair back to the conference room, and hefted the bag from the chair, the last burger with all but one bite remaining.

"Parker!"

At the elevators, Saul pressed the up button.

"Be careful out there in the fog," Rydell shouted down the hall.

Saul stepped into the elevator and waited as the doors closed. Then he called the watch commander to request a welfare check at the Lunas apartment in El Monte.

Ashley and Mindy

Mindy, now in pink pajamas, pulls a book from the shelf by her little bed and hands it to Ashley. It's *Where the Wild Things Are*. Mindy snuggles under the pink comforter. Ashley sits beside her and starts to read. She finds herself enjoying the story, more than Mindy, apparently, who is frowning.

"What about Prince Spinach?"

Ashley glances at the shelf where books are jammed in and twisted sideways. She moves a stack to her lap and begins shelving them from biggest to smallest. "Help me find it."

"No," Mindy says. "He's a Wild Thing. *You know.*"

Ashley wishes she did, but she doesn't. She skims the rest of the story. No hint of Prince Spinach. "Prince Spinach took a vacation," she says. "Hopefully, he'll be back tomorrow." She continues reading where she left off.

"You're reading it wrong," Mindy says.

Of course she is, but what can she say? She's not Mindy's father. She doesn't want to freak Mindy out. She tries reading Carol with a deep, silly voice.

"Quit it. Read it the right way." But Mindy's laughing now.

After Ashley finishes the story, Mindy insists on a second reading, during which she falls asleep. Ashley shelves the book neatly and lays back, her long man-legs draping off the kid-sized bed. She shuts her eyes and listens to Mindy's peaceful breathing beside her, feeling closer than she could have imagined. On some level, Mindy must sense her dad is different, but she doesn't hold back, not at all.

As Ashley moves to get up, Mindy snuggles into her chest. Unconditional trust. Ashley melts back into the bed, not wanting to disturb her innocent sleep and so exhausted, she might soon fall asleep herself.

Her attempt at macaroni and cheese had turned into a trying ordeal. Not because it was hard in and of itself but there were too many distractions from

Mindy and Tyler. Tyler had literally cried over spilled milk—screamed, actually—and the juice she'd poured for Mindy had been the wrong kind and needed ice, but not that much ice. The macaroni had almost burned, and then Tyler mushed it around more than he ate it. He'd laughed at Ashley's attempt to wipe his face, raked the macaroni from his tray onto the floor, and started crying again as if some great injustice had occurred. Then, finally, Claire entered the kitchen. Smirking as if *of course* she had to bail Ashley out. That had made Ashley feel better because obviously the real Gray couldn't even handle both kids on his own.

Now she understands that all the help her own dad had employed had nothing to do with him not wanting her. Raising a child is a lot for one person on his own, and with everything else on his plate, especially after the second marriage ended, he had needed the help. No wonder Claire is cranky. She's probably overwhelmed from managing Tyler and Mindy alone all day. She looks exhausted. Her lids are dark and puffy but her eyes have a depth. Maybe if the corners of her mouth weren't tightened down, she would be beautiful. Maybe even more beautiful than Raquel. Maybe, after some rest and a spa-day, Claire would be interesting.

Claire and Sex

Claire is lying on the couch when Gray bursts out of Mindy's room and makes a beeline toward her. She pretends to focus on her phone. As Gray's eyes dart around the mess of magazines she's been meaning to sort through, her body stiffens. Why can't he just leave her alone?

Gray rakes the Legos aside on the floor by the couch and plops down by her head, seemingly unaware of Mindy's drool on his shirt. Claire stares at her phone but it's just the icons on the home screen. She doesn't even know which app to open.

"Are you okay?" he asks as though he might really want an answer this time, his voice lacking the usual, bitter undertone.

"I'm tired," she says, like he couldn't just guess. "If I could just sleep…" If the insomnia would just stop crawling under the covers and itching in hard to scratch places.

"I wish you could," he says. His stoic mask is missing, and behind it, there is no sign of the sadness she knows he's been hiding. If anything, he looks worried, maybe even scared. Probably, he's wondering what she's been thinking. They both know their marriage is crumbling.

"I'm sorry," she says.

"Me too?"

Why is he saying it like a question? Like maybe he isn't sorry for the argument he started last night? She can't even remember what it was about now. She swallows her anger. He is trying to bridge the canyon of crap between them. She should make an effort, maybe even take it a step further, because he is apologizing. Probably he has no idea what she's saying sorry for. "For last night," she says, but she means for everything, for the way they've become. "You didn't have to sleep on the couch."

At least if he hadn't, she wouldn't have stayed awake all night wondering if he'd ever get into bed beside her. She had tried counting backward from a hundred, promising to fall asleep by fifty, then twenty-five. But of course, it didn't work. It never did. When Tyler started crying, it was almost a relief. It gave her a reason to get out of bed.

"Maybe you should have come to get me." He smiles, and his smile seems different, or maybe she just forgot what it looked like. She hasn't seen him smile in so long.

He leans toward her, like he might kiss her, but then he stops.

"What?" she asks, although she knows. "It's too late." She's known it for weeks, months, maybe longer. Yet they keep going through the motions, as if their marriage might suddenly spring back to life.

"No," he says. "It's not like that." An intense mix of emotions swirls across his face as he stares at her, as if deciding which one to react to. He leans over her... and kisses her.

His lips flounder around, like it's their first kiss. She pushes back on his shoulder, but with little effort. She opens her mouth to tell him to stop, to tell him it's too late—it's over—but their tongues touch, and when he pulls back to breathe, she can't say it.

He looks into her eyes, like he is seeing her all over again for the first time.

She wants him to stop, but if he does then it's for sure—their marriage is over. And just by thinking this, she knows it's the last thing she wants.

She climbs in his lap and massages his shoulders. He rubs her neck. His touch shoots electricity up and down her spine. This new way of pressing his fingertips into her muscles is exactly what she needed, after all these years of begging him to try something different, now—finally—he gets it.

And she has been withholding herself, spending all that time on Instagram trying to tune out of her life—their life. That must be why he said he was Ashley York. It was a plea for attention.

He kisses her again. It feels new, somehow, different.

"Maybe we should stop," Gray says.

"No," she says. She might even get some sleep if they have sex. "But, not in here."

She leads him to the bedroom, where in the doorway she pulls her shirt over her head and throws it to him.

He shuts the door. She lays back on the bed, her hands behind her head.

He leans over her, bathed in the rectangle of dim light streaming in through the window. Kisses her nipple. Just the tip. His lips are like tiny sparks, a current she's never felt before.

What was the point she'd been making by giving him the cold shoulder for so many months? Whatever the reason was, it was stupid. What a waste. All this time that she was punishing Gray she was really punishing herself, because she needs this more than he does.

She runs her fingers through his hair. Pulls his head to her other breast. As he takes it in his mouth, she arches her back. Her pulse quickens. The need rises in her body. She slides out of her sweatpants, embarrassed for him to see that she didn't even bother with underwear today. She pushes his hand down. Over her stomach and further down. Presses his fingers into her. *See how ready I am.* She unbuckles his belt.

As he struggles out of his jeans, they tangle at his ankles. He falls to the bed.

It reminds her of college, their first time in her dorm. Just like that night, he now sits on the bed with one foot free and the other still caught in his pants. She swallows a laugh. It's the funniest thing she has seen in weeks.

She flexes her hips. "Hurry up."

When he finally climbs over her, his face looks younger, and the way he touches her, she feels alive. Awake. When he slides inside her, he sighs, and the vibration of his voice resonates all over her. She moans.

He shoves his fingers into her mouth. All she needs right now is for him to keep moving. She arches her back.

His rhythm is uncontrolled. He closes his eyes, and he's off. Gone. Somewhere else. And that's fine. Just don't stop. *Do. Not. Stop. Never stop.*

But then she feels his slickness, and he falls beside her on the sheets.

She throws a leg over his sweaty stomach and straddles him. "Is that it?"

His eyes remain closed.

She pulls on her sweatpants and leaves the room without bothering to turn off the lights.

Death Is No End

Wayob rips a ribbon of cloth from his shirt. There is no way to silence the tearing threads. He cannot stop. Can. Not. Stop. If he stops, he might never start again, and he must—must, must, must—finish before Parker returns.

This is all Parker's fault. All of it. Wayob has to die because Parker— Parker!—has isolated him in this cell and prevented him from taking a new vessel.

Parker thinks he is so smart. Parker has no idea. He suspects. Maybe, Parker suspects, but he does not believe. He shall though, and by then it shall be too late. Wayob will see to that. He shall laugh in Parker's face.

Is Wayob immortal? He certainly feels no different than he did all those centuries ago before the odious priest banished him into darkness, disembodied inside the Encanto.

Egregious priest.

What can stop Wayob from living forever? Not Parker. Certainly not Parker.

Truthfully though, Wayob had not meant to kill anyone.

Jaggar truly was an accident. He did not deserve death any more than Wayob deserves to be locked up. Not his fault. Wayob wishes he could take it back. He would if he could.

He who holds the Encanto was the one who drove away in a vehicle, leaving Wayob no choice but to pursue him. This happened just after Wayob awakened in the vessel of Rydell. He had been trying to meditate on the sound of the mind of he who holds the Encanto—so much harder to hear than Abuela's—when his concentration was broken by someone yelling somewhere outside Rydell's palace. Since it seemed the yelling was not ceasing, Wayob went outside to insist that it did.

And that was when he heard the words of the man. His man. Across the street, he was in a vehicle outside a gate, yelling into a metal box that he was someone else. And then Wayob knew, he was the one who holds the Encanto.

He had to be, because when Wayob had felt himself being pulled from the Encanto, he concentrated, really concentrated on the man who holds the Encanto, who Wayob must kill. Though truthfully, he would prefer not to, but kill that man Wayob must. Wayob would kill a thousand times if he had to. The death of one man no more than a grain of sand to the ocean of darkness inside the Encanto, where minutes pass like hours, days like centuries. A torture worse than death—the injustice of the abominable priest. Anyone would kill to save themselves from such agony.

Before Wayob could reach him, the man pulled away from the gate, leaving Wayob no choice but to obtain a vehicle and pursue, and he had previously learned better than to try and drive at the same time. If he had not wrecked, he might have reached Abuela before she gave the Encanto to this man, and Wayob could have spared himself another night of agony disembodied in its darkness.

So he had needed someone else to drive, and he found someone right there at the palace next to Rydell's. But the man with shaggy hair pulled a weapon on Wayob, leaving Wayob no choice. If Wayob had known the delay it would cause taking Jaggar hostage, he would have just shot himself right there and then. Wayob could have found a new vessel. Someone close to the man who has the Encanto.

But no, thanks to Parker, now Wayob is locked in this filthy cell.

Parker cannot keep Wayob trapped alone like this forever, can he? Wayob will not risk waiting, not this time. If he who possesses the Encanto turns back the dial or gives the Encanto away, Wayob shall be pulled back inside, trapped in an agony much worse than the death he must now inflict upon himself. Total deprivation of all senses. Trapped in rumination with no way out, waiting and waiting and waiting and waiting and waiting for someone to use the Encanto…, Wayob shall go insane.

A magic as strong as Xibalba, as Earth itself. Pity the atrocious priest who banished Wayob to this miserable existence died centuries ago, his flesh no doubt rotted in the jungle along with the whole Mayan Empire. The priest deserved to die a miserable death, which Wayob would have enjoyed carrying out. But Wayob shall still have his revenge when he destroys the Encanto and frees himself forever.

Unfortunately, Wayob must first kill himself. Though not exactly himself —he must not think like this or he will never get it done—only this body that Wayob occupies must die. It will feel like Wayob is dying. Thanks to Parker, Wayob only has this horrible, painful means of escaping this terrible place. But Wayob would die a thousand times before returning to the Encanto.

He knots the cloth strips into a makeshift rope. His hands slow and become unsteady. It is Rydell, his subconscious desire to live impeding Wayob's progress, making Wayob doubt his actions. But Wayob has been through this before. So long as he who holds the Encanto still owns it and still occupies a body other than their own, Wayob shall awaken in a new vessel, another body to control.

Wayob hopes. For he does not really know. Not for sure. It's not like the wicked priest bothered to explain how the Encanto works before banishing Wayob into this tortured existence.

Though Wayob's mind has dominated Rydell's, he is not powerless, and he seems to be awakening, breaking free from the paralysis through which he has witnessed Wayob's actions in his body. Every muscle strains against Wayob's effort to move it. But Wayob shall overcome him. Rydell's life shall end. Pity. This is Parker's fault. Parker killing Rydell. Not Wayob, not really.

Wayob has seen the inside of many minds. He knows that in the reverse situation, Rydell would kill Wayob. For Wayob is no worse than anyone else. In fact, Wayob is better. At least Wayob is honest about his desire.

Not like Abuela, who must have wanted something. She must have had some reason for keeping the Encanto all those years. She is so strong to be able to resist Wayob's whispering for so long, and also smart, Wayob must concede. Somehow, last night, she had known how near Wayob was, for just as he finally fought his way through the mob—his skin crawling from all the many people he had to shoulder past—and her little hut where she performed her fortune-telling-charade was finally within Wayob's sight, she gave the Encanto away. And by doing so, she forced Wayob out of Aleman's body and back into the darkness. The nothingness. Alone.

Does she know what she did? Does she have any idea? Wayob shall tell her —no, he shall show her—that all her effort served only to delay his freedom, and for this she must pay. He does not wish to harm her. Wayob would never harm anyone. No, they bring it upon themselves. They torture Wayob and leave him no choice.

And now Parker—fucking Parker—seems determined to follow in the footsteps of Abuela's dead husband, Sosa. Despite the distance and all the time, so much time. Glacial time. Parker, who hunts Wayob, when Wayob should be helped. Needs to be helped. Why does no one care about Wayob? Wayob does not want any trouble. Does not wish to harm anyone. Wayob is the victim, the one who for centuries has suffered the egregious torture of the revolting priest.

Parker knows nothing compared to what Sosa knew, would know nothing at all if he had not tricked Wayob, angered Wayob into admitting... what? Wayob cannot remember what he said to Parker. No matter, the swine shall suffer. Wayob shall see to that. Wayob shall not let Parker get the best of Wayob again.

With so many obstacles, it is a miracle Wayob can make any progress at all. So many people who care only about themselves regardless of how their actions serve to further Wayob's suffering. Like Saroyan, who almost certainly discovered the power of the Encanto while Wayob was probing his mind for an escape from Parker's false imprisonment. Saroyan's memories were useless, and now, if he knows of the Encanto, he will stop at nothing to gain for himself a new body, one with legs that function as they should. He will try to obtain the Encanto. He will get in Wayob's way.

So now Wayob must go out of his way to put Saroyan down. No choice. Maybe Wayob can take down Saroyan and Parker both in one swoop? Losing focus. Wayob must do this deed. This time—once he awakens in a new vessel—he shall take care of Saroyan, Parker, and end the life of the man who has the Encanto. Then Wayob shall take the Encanto for himself, ensuring his freedom, forever.

Does he not deserve at least one life to live, maybe two, after all he has suffered? Even Death would be better than the dark, the dark-dark-dark and alone.

Wayob tightens the makeshift noose around his neck, and the other end he ties to the metal bar between the posts of the top bunk. But it lacks enough height. Aside from the bunk, the only other item in the cell is a sink combined with a toilet. So, Wayob must kneel. He must lean forward against the noose, feet back and knees above the floor, in order to create enough pressure to stop blood flow to his brain, to restrict breathing…

It is not working.

Reaching up, Rydell fights Wayob's will. Forcing the arms to pull against the noose.

Stop, Rydell. Stop. Wayob controls your body.

Wayob screams, mustering all his willpower. He twists the knot tighter. Twist. Twist. The bed creaks as though it might topple forward despite being bolted to the wall. Wayob fights Rydell in his mind. Arms release the noose, but now feet come under him, taking his weight.

No. No, no, no. No no no no.

Wayob controls. "You are nothing Rydell. You are powerless," Wayob says through gritted teeth.

Strain. Straining. Strain.

Wayob forces his hands that are Rydell's hands down to his ankles. Wayob lifts his legs off the ground. All his weight held by the torn strips of cloth tied around his neck.

Straining… No. Stay…

Arms locked around legs. Unable to breathe. If he can just pass out, gravity shall take care of the rest. Gravity will help Wayob, unlike everyone else.

And it is not just Rydell fighting to live, Wayob realizes—it is himself. Wayob. His own instinct for self-preservation which must be suppressed.

Think of the freedom. Now, think of the darkness… never again.

Wayob shall be whole—a whole true person, as he once was. Human. Finally and forever free of the Encanto.

Freedom shall come from dying now. His reward. His revenge on Parker. Parker, who has forced Wayob to kill himself. Parker must suffer himself.

Wayob almost smiles as the cinderblock wall before him fades into darkness.

Parker… One more minute. Just one more. Unconsciousness…

Parker. Parker. Parker.

Saul and Marla

Saul parked by the line of palms, trunks like gray pillars rising into the clouds. Using his phone as a flashlight, he found the gate in the hedge. He held his lockpick out and ready... and useless.

His shoulders dropped. He felt suddenly heavy and needed to sit.

He'd found nothing in Rydell's background to explain his actions. No connection to Saroyan or Aleman or Wayob. Or to anyone. Rydell had no living family or friends. It was almost sad the way the man seemed to move through life with as little impact as possible, subsisting off the fortune he'd inherited from his father's grocery store chain.

Saul would feel better with a guard watching Rydell, but the holding cell wasn't approved for overnights and the cameras were blocked up in court, the ACLU arguing they violated a prisoner's right to privacy. Still, the holding cell beat checking Rydell into MDC where Aleman was on duty and Saroyan had nearly gotten himself killed.

Soon I'll be free. Rydell's voice echoed in Saul's head. So long as Rydell believed himself capable of walking through walls, the threat of prison was useless. Saul had to find some other leverage to make him talk.

His only other leads were the Lunas, who were stonewalling him as badly as Rydell and Aleman were, maybe worse. The uniform who performed the welfare check had put Rosa on the phone, and she had insisted they were fine and claimed they'd simply spent the night with a friend.

"Who?" Saul had asked.

Rosa hesitated. "I can't say."

"Can't or won't?"

"It's just..."

In the background, he'd heard Rosa's grandmother speak harshly in Spanish, and from the determination in her voice, he knew there was more to the story—more than some undocumented 'friend' who was wary of the police. Perhaps a lot more. The old woman had started coughing, and then

Rosa said, "I have to go." She'd returned the phone to the uniform, and there was nothing more Saul could ask him to do.

Tomorrow, he would drive to El Monte himself. Maybe if he showed Rosa some photos of Aleman and Rydell, she would start talking. But he doubted it. He needed a lever, some kind of incentive for her and her grandmother to reveal whatever it was they were hiding.

He was too exhausted to think anymore. Tonight, he needed sleep.

He sliced his pick through the air like a wand, wishing it had the power to shatter steel. But as he knew better than anyone, there was no such thing as real magic. The lock remained intact. It glinted obstinately in the light of Saul's phone: a solid steel U hooked through the latch between the gate and the fence, anchored into a fat dial numbered from zero to thirty-five.

The only thing more ridiculous than a grown man of fifty-two years having to break into his own place was that his landlord, Marla, had upgraded the padlock to a combination job.

He had thought they'd come to an understanding that from time-to-time, when he was too tired, he could just sneak in through the back gate. Why choose tonight of all nights to replace the lock? It had been a long day. He was spent, drained, and he just couldn't deal with Marla, not tonight, and whatever 'emergency' she had in mind.

Above him in the fog, something rustled. The palms, probably. The air was still. The fog descended toward him.

He leaned his ear to the lock and turned slowly. Listened hard, imagining the tumblers clicking open.... Turned the dial back and forth. Nothing happened. He was out of patience.

He grabbed onto the gate and lunged up. And couldn't even lift his feet off the ground.

He sighed, backed off and started up the sidewalk. His footsteps fell heavy on the pavement. Fog closed in around him like all the unanswered questions. *"Who is Wayob?"*

The street had almost vanished as he trudged on through the mist, rounded the corner, and took the driveway.

The house was dark space. It loomed ahead in the gray. Floodlights cut through the fog. Saul braced himself and waited for his eyes to adjust. The floodlights were on a motion detector. The house remained dark. Was Marla actually sleeping for a change? He took one hopeful step. Two... A light came on in Marla's living room.

Saul started marching. Beyond the house, at the end of the driveway, was the converted garage where Saul lived. As he passed the house, Marla threw open a window.

Saul froze, wishing he could wrap himself in the fog like a cloak of invisibility. Although the garage wasn't much more than a stucco box with a bed and a shower, it was all he needed. It was close to the Castle. It would be ideal, in fact— if not for Marla.

"Saul," she whisper-yelled.

He was caught in the floodlight. No way to avoid her. She leaned out the window maybe three feet from his face.

"Hey, Marla. I'm beat tonight."

"I need your help."

He gazed longingly toward the darkness beyond the floodlights. His garage apartment waited in the haze. "We'll deal with it tomorrow."

"I think it's a rat," she said. "I can't sleep with that nasty thing in here."

"You have two cats." He had intended to end the conversation there but found himself turning toward her. His shoulders slumped. The rat didn't matter—*if* there even was one—she was just lonely. She'd won this property and two others in a messy divorce, and now it seemed like Saul was the one person in her life who paid her any attention at all.

As he stepped to the window, he surreptitiously slid the rose, which he'd been saving for Hernandez, from the trick pocket in his sleeve.

Marla stood from the couch backed up against the inner wall just below the open window. As usual, she was dressed up, and tonight she wore black, her short hair neatly combed. She hadn't been sleeping; she'd been sitting in the dark, waiting by the window.

"The rat's in the kitchen," she said. "I'll let you in the back."

"Hold on." Saul leaned in through the window. He reached down and made a big show of checking behind a cushion on the couch. He jerked his arm out as if snatching the rat.

Marla screamed, jumped back and landed hard, rattling the window in its frame. She was heavyset, though not as big as Saul.

"It's right here," Saul said. "Right where you were sitting." He flourished his hand, snapped his fingers, and produced the red rose. He held it out to her. "And now your rat is a rose."

Her cheeks brightened. She took the flower and smelled it.

Gray Reversion

The fortune-teller's eyes are black holes. Gray cannot look away, not even a glance just to see where they are, before her eyes swallow all the light around them and there is nothing left but darkness. She screams, her breath stale and smelling of death. He reaches out to shove her back—but all there is, is darkness. Darkness so thick he can almost feel it. And when he tries to breathe, the air tastes like ashes. Too thick to breathe. Not air at all.

The sound of gushing water. A familiar sound. The toilet in the master bathroom, in his and Claire's bathroom, in Silver Lake. He'd been meaning to call a plumber about it because every time you flushed it, the toilet practically erupted. Had he actually heard it, or was it just a memory? A sound which had splashed into his nightmare just to let him know he was dreaming. He was only dreaming. As he drifted off toward unconsciousness, now someone was talking.

Claire.

Gray opened his eyes, and it was Claire. She was standing over him. "I can't make breakfast and feed Tyler at the same time," she said, as if nothing at all had changed.

Gray leaped from the bed, which was their bed. The clothes under his feet were his. And it was his body—completely naked—and his. He slapped his boring old hips, his chest. Yes! Him. He was back.

Claire was backing away, brows furrowed, like *what the hell's wrong with you*, but her right lip was curling toward her patented wry smile—which he hadn't seen in a long, long time. He hugged her.

She broke free. "Thanks, but not in the mood, right now." She wasn't mad, not yet, but she had that spark in her eye like don't push it or she might be.

"What day is it?" he asked.

She squinted at him. "November... second."

"So, it's Monday?"

"Have you lost your mind?"

He rubbed his temples and glanced around at all the clothes on the floor, and just above the baseboard were the little handprints, from when Mindy was a toddler, which they still hadn't scrubbed off. Their bedroom was the same as always, only now, somehow, it looked worse.

"I don't know," he said.

"Well, get dressed," she said. "We have to get the kids ready." She left him standing there.

He pulled on some clothes and sat on the bed. Had he really been Ashley York? His memory lacked the indistinctness of a dream. He would check online, though he was certain she looked exactly like his recollection of her face reflected in the mirror. He could probably paint the exact arch of her brow, the slope of her nose, her chestnut eyes, her lips, her hips.

So, assuming he was actually Ashley yesterday, then had she been in his body? Or had his body made it through the day on autopilot, like it seemed to do whenever he drank past the point of blackout.

Whatever had happened yesterday, he felt more alive now than he had in months, maybe years. That's when he saw the eyes. The eyes of the obsidian snake now seemed beady and cold. It sat on the nightstand, perched on its white stone, its head—its gaping mouth—pointing directly at him. He had no memory of placing it there.

After Dia De Los Muertos, he had hit the Scotch pretty hard. His memory had blurred almost to the point of blackout, but he was sure that the last time he'd seen it, the mouth of the snake had been pointing in the opposite direction, toward where the flattened top of the stone came to a rounded point.

Had the snake turned on its own? Like some kind of reset?

He picked it up and examined it. There was nothing apparently mechanical. The stone was cold and smooth, aside from the spiral of tiny holes that converged at the bottom where something had pricked him and retracted after he turned the snake. The small scab in his palm had healed some, but it was still ringed by red flesh.

He wouldn't have risked turning the snake again. That he knew for sure.

But what if he turned it now. Would he become Ashley York again? It was a crazy notion. And yet, now it seemed possible. But why Ashley? If Claire wasn't following Ashley on Instagram, checking her feed dozens of times a day, Gray would hardly know who she was. Could it relate to one of the recent images of Ashley he'd seen on Claire's phone?

What if he rotated the snake-dial back to the twelve, and instead of Ashley York, he found himself in some horrible life far away and stranded there. Why risk it? He couldn't stand losing Mindy and Tyler and Claire.

The fortune-teller had told him to destroy the charm, and maybe he should. It seemed too dangerous to keep around the house, especially with kids. But for now, he decided to hide it in the hall closet, where he kept his clothes.

As he was covering the charm with a pile of old t-shirts, Mindy startled him from behind.

"What are you looking for, Daddy?"

He spun around. *Did she see it?* He didn't think so. Her face was pure innocence and curiosity, her hair tangled from sleep. She looked adorable in her pink nightgown. A sob welled up in his throat. He swallowed it back. "You." He swept her up in his arms. "I missed you."

Her brows furrowed. "Mommy said I have to get ready."

"Yeah. We're late, I guess. Can I help you get dressed?"

"No. I can do it myself."

He put her down. "Better hurry."

She ran to her room and stripped out of her nightgown without closing the door. Gray chuckled to himself.

In the nursery, Claire was swaying Tyler in one arm while with the other she spread a towel on the changing table.

"Let me take him," Gray said.

As she passed Tyler to him, her mouth—though not quite smiling—lacked its usual tightness, and there was a gentleness in her eyes. More like she was sharing rather than dumping off a load she didn't want to deal with.

"So, yesterday," he blurted out as he laid Tyler on the table and began removing his diaper. "What did you think of it?" Awkward. But he couldn't say what had happened. No way she was going to believe that he spent a day as Ashley York.

If Claire reacted at all, he missed it. When he looked up, she was standing in the doorway. She tilted her head, and then a great distance came into her face, as if traveling away. "I'll get Mindy ready," she said as she turned away. "We're running late." She started down the hall.

Gray had to let it go for now because he knew that the more he asked, the less likely she was to answer. He'd have to wait for her to reveal something, which she almost certainly would, if anything odd at all had happened here yesterday.

After dressing Tyler, Gray carried him to the kitchen and belted him into his highchair. Mindy was already eating cereal. "You ready for daycare, pumpkin?" He combed her hair out of her face.

"I've got it from here," Claire said. "You're late for work."

Work was just about the last thing on Gray's mind, but at least in his cube, there would be plenty of time to search the internet. If Ashley's house had a turret like the way he remembered, then he'd know for sure that yesterday was real.

He went into the bathroom, started the shower, and let the hot water stream over him.

Ashley's house had an amazing view, but it was too big, too empty, and he hadn't liked all the people barging in on him. At least Claire knew how to give him some space. And he didn't mind when Mindy interrupted him. She was only five, and yet she was more polite than August Grant showing up out of nowhere and trying to shove his crotch in Gray's mouth.

After experiencing the kind of life so many people aspire to, now Gray knows how little he cares about fame and fortune. The life he'd always wanted was right here where he'd left it. Were there problems? Of course. Who didn't have problems? How many people throw their whole life away for a change they later realize isn't worth it? At least now—thanks to the portrait he'd finished last night at Ashley's—he finally had the confidence to quit his shitty job.

He turned off the shower and got dressed.

In the kitchen, Claire was at the sink. Her back was to him. From the basket beside her on the counter, he grabbed a bagel and said goodbye.

She turned off the water. "Hold on." She dried her hands and, to Gray's surprise, walked him to the door.

She kissed him.

Not a long kiss, but not quick either. Her lips were somewhat dry. They lingered as she withdrew. A hint of a smile brightened her face.

He wanted to say something, more than some platitude like *I love you*.

She turned back toward the hallway.

"I see you," he said.

She didn't react.

He might as well head into work, where he could check on his COBRA benefits and maybe clue Brad into the fact that he was quitting, or, really, he should tell Claire first, but now wasn't the time for a big discussion, because it would make Mindy late for daycare.

Tonight, he would tell her, and he had a good feeling about it. It was going to go better than he'd thought.

He stepped outside into the cool morning air so thick with moisture it tasted fresh. A familiar stiffness in his right knee shortened his stride as he walked down the drive. There was something satisfying about it, like every step he took was spaced exactly the right distance apart.

Sure, he had enjoyed himself in Ashley's body, of course he had—but damn, was it great to be back.

Connection

Saul rolled up to the gate just inside the parking deck below the PAB. He strained his arm out the window toward the electronic box. His card wouldn't reach. He had to back up and pull in closer.

As the gate lifted, he noticed Hernandez's red Mustang backed into the second row. And beneath the glare on her windshield, the profile of her face framed in a shadow of hair crowned by her shock of white.

He nodded to her and rolled past. Though there was a spot right beside her, he parked three spaces down between identical Crown Vics, buying himself a few more precious seconds to come up with what to say. Probably she felt just as weird as he did about her having seen him in his threadbare briefs. If he could joke about it, maybe he could at least salvage their professional relationship.

As he climbed out, she came to meet him. "You're late," she said.

He glanced at his watch. 9:04. He'd meant to arrive at eight, before Hernandez, in order to move Rydell to an interview suite where, he hoped, Rydell would say something useful after having spent the night in the holding cell. He didn't want her to find out about the holding cell, not after she'd specifically asked him to book Rydell into the MDC.

But as he was leaving home, Marla had ambushed Saul with an omelet, pancakes, sausage and potatoes, all setup on the patio outside his garage apartment.

"I had to help my landlord," he said to Hernandez, which was basically true. He had to help Marla eat breakfast. She had the rose he'd given her last night in a glass vase on the table, and then after breakfast, he'd felt obligated to look for the rat she was still pretending was in her house.

Hernandez curled her lip. "When are you going to move out of there?"

"As soon as I find somewhere better," he said. The converted garage was the best he could afford that close to the Castle.

"Let's get coffee." She turned abruptly and started marching toward the elevators.

Saul jogged to catch up, the pancakes ballooning in his stomach. He should check on Rydell. Yesterday, Hernandez said she was done with Rydell, but what if now she wanted to question him too?

It would actually be good for her to see how he was acting, and it would be great to get her input on whatever he said. The truth about the holding cell would go down easier, Saul knew, after she'd had her coffee. And plus, they still had to clear the air.

At the elevators, Hernandez pressed the button and glanced around, her eyes briefly catching his. Awkward silence. Saul studied his shoes. He needed a joke. *You saw me in mine, so now it's only fair you show me yours, right?* Wrong. *Don't piss her off; make her laugh.*

He felt her eyes on him, no doubt picturing him the way he'd looked in his underwear. When he glanced up, she looked away and bit her lip.

He reached behind her and pressed the button again.

"I almost didn't recognize you without your coat," she said.

"I'm kind of trying a new look." He glanced down at his belly, which protruded, in the white button-down, over the belt line of his pants. Why the hell did he have to tuck in his shirt? But now that she'd seen him in his too-tighty-whities, the trench coat would only draw attention to what he'd been trying to hide. It wasn't out in the media—at least, not yet. Civilians had been cleared for their own safety before Saul had exited the library. Still, a uniform might have snapped a photo with their phone, which by now would have been forwarded around to at least half of the LAPD.

Hernandez frowned and looked up at him. Brushed back her shock of white. "I liked the way it looked on your shoulders."

His mouth fell open. She held his gaze. Something surged in his stomach. Not hunger, no… She liked the way it looked on his shoulders—*on him.* This was hope. He wanted to run to his plain wrap and get the damn coat right now.

The elevator chimed. The doors whooshed open. He steadied himself, motioned for her to enter first, and followed her in. He stood in the back.

She hit the button marked *L.* "Levy didn't tell you, did she?"

"Chickenshit," she whispered and then louder. "You were right. She's making me lead detective."

Saul nodded. He'd seen it coming, and yesterday when he pressed Levy, she had passively admitted that Hernandez was the lead on the Rydell case, but she'd repeated that it was only because of Saul's personal involvement. But Saul knew the truth.

Over the years, Levy had ostracized a half-dozen detectives under her command by gradually lowering their responsibilities until they had nothing to do. Then she transferred them out of Homicide Special, as if purely due to some lack of work and not at all her opinion of their performance.

Saul couldn't let that happen to him.

"I tried to turn it down," Hernandez said, "but apparently it's not optional."

"I get it," he said. It was all about image. Media relations meant more to the high brass than actual results. "You look better on camera than I do." Even as he spoke, the words ricocheted in his gut.

Lame joke.

Hernandez's eyes widened. Then narrowed. He'd struck a nerve, even though he'd only meant to insult Levy, who was afraid to stand up to the high brass, and himself. Here he was making a self-deprecating joke, which even if she had gotten would have only garnered pity, right after she had just complimented his oversized shoulders. What was he doing?

"No, I, I mean—" he stammered, "Yes— You are great with the press... But, more importantly, you're a damn fine detective. And if that's not Levy's reason for promoting you then shame on her. It's been a privilege—"

Hernandez punched him in the shoulder. "We're still partners."

She smiled.

The doors slid open. Sunlight poured in. Saul shielded his eyes as they stepped out into the lobby. He veered toward the cafeteria. She wasn't beside him.

He squinted and found her silhouette heading for the main exit. She motioned for him to catch up. "Come on."

Saul groaned. "You and your gourmet coffee."

"It's not about gourmet. That sludge in cafeteria is not coffee. It's not even drinkable."

Outside the PAB, Hernandez launched down First. Saul had to almost run to keep up.

"We still make decisions together," she said, "just like always. Levy wasn't even clear if this is a permanent role change or just for this case or what."

"Not surprised." Already, Saul was sweating. Good thing his coat was in the car. He'd wear it again, of course—*I like the way it looks on your shoulders*—but not while they were practically jogging in full sun.

"When she asked me to tell you for her, I nearly lost my shit. I told her she could just go ahead and handle the press briefing by herself."

Saul knew Levy would agree to almost anything to avoid confrontation, especially with Hernandez, and especially right before a press briefing where she was counting on Hernandez to make her look good.

"I'm guessing that ended the conversation," he said.

"Yeah. She said she would, but, of course, she didn't say when."

Hernandez launched across San Pedro, roughly the border between the glass monoliths behind them and the new-old part of downtown where historic buildings were renovated rather than bulldozed. Saul lagged behind in the crosswalk, panting.

Hernandez waited on the curb. When he caught up, she said, "Levy closed the case on Rydell."

Saul shook his head. He shouldn't be surprised—Levy had done the same thing with Saroyan—but still. "We don't have a motive."

"Doesn't matter, according to Levy. We've got him dead to rights."

"Sure, but juries want a reason. They want to know why."

Hernandez flipped back her streak of white. And he saw it in her eyes, how much she hated his need to find the explanation behind every single detail. Levy, too. Saul took longer than anyone else in Homicide Special to close cases. It didn't seem to matter that when Saul closed them, they stayed shut, thanks to his thorough investigation. And now, with Hernandez effectively his superior, he knew what she was going to say....

But he was wrong.

"You're right," she said.

Saul almost fell backward into the street. It was all he could do to contain his shock.

A slight smile brushed her lips. "We should keep digging into it."

She turned and started walking again. Saul bounded after her. His heart hammered in his chest, and not just because of the strenuous pace she was setting but because right now, he loved her. They were on the same page. This was huge.

"I'm thinking there's a third party behind this Wayob thing. I just can't imagine what the endgame is."

"We'll find out," Hernandez said. "Rydell is more than just crazy. You're right about that. Once we have something definitive, then we'll take it to Levy. Who knows? She might be grateful we saved her ass from having to explain to her superiors why she closed the case, prematurely."

"If we can find the connection between Aleman, Rydell, and Saroyan," Saul said, "we'll be on our way. Can you imagine three people less likely to be involved in a conspiracy, or whatever the hell this is?"

"They could be fanatics who saw the same video on YouTube."

Saul was lagging behind again, but they were almost at Starbucks. Next shop on the right. "It's got to be more than that. Rydell knew where I was Saturday night."

Hernandez snorted. "No secret there. One of the unis could have tipped him off."

"But I never made it to the Castle. He knew I was on Olvera."

"Who else knew you were there?"

"You're the only one I told."

She glanced over her shoulder at him. A fiery look in her eyes. "I didn't tell Rydell shit."

"I know," Saul said. "Anyway, this was before you even met him. He must have been there." *But why?*

"What about Aleman? Maybe he saw you."

"That's what I thought, at first, but he seemed confused when I questioned him, like he had no idea where he was Saturday night."

"Like he was lying?"

"No. I don't think so. He was scared. It doesn't make any sense."

"You've got that right." Hernandez blasted past Starbucks and continued down the hill.

Saul shouted after her, "Starbucks not good enough, either?"

"Just a little further," she said. "Race ya."

He wiped the sweat off his forehead. There was instantly more. He was out of shape and she knew it. She was a foot shorter than Saul, yet somehow walking at a pace which Saul couldn't maintain even at a jog, even though it was downhill. It was so hot. He might as well be wearing the coat. At least it would hide his belly. It bulged against his shirt, threatening to pop a button with every step. Perspiration soaked his pits.

Finally, she stopped (a couple blocks past Starbucks but it seemed further on foot). Heaving to catch his breath, Saul slowed to a walk.

She held open the door to Ground Down, the cafe which had been closed every time Saul had driven past.

"I thought they were out of business."

"Let's pray that never happens," she said.

Affixed to the window, a card listed the hours: "*8 AM to 1 PM, Tuesday–Friday. Closed Saturday–Monday*". Inside, it was packed.

Hernandez ordered Sumatra. Saul asked for the same. She went to get seats. He poured the top inch off his coffee to make extra room for the cream. Hell, he'd earned on the sprint here. He poured it in and sipped... It was good but needed something more. And since he was skipping sugar, he added more cream.

At the high counter by the window, Hernandez had saved him a stool between her and a guy with long hair hunched over a laptop, but the gap had room for maybe half Saul's girth. And after the sprint down here, he needed to sit.

The couch in the corner, the one place he could fit, was occupied by a couple. The girl spoke in earnest as she leaned against the boy, her leg crossed over his, their feet propped up beside crumpled cups that dripped dark remnants on the faded mahogany table.

There must be some kind of etiquette. Once you're done, you should leave.

Saul stood beside the stool he was too fat for, sipped his coffee, and tried to look natural. Hernandez turned sideways to face him. His belly filled the space between them. He backed up.

She held up her phone. "Check this out."

On the screen was a video shot from a traffic cam at the intersection of Beverly and Santa Monica. As the light changed, a silver Camry turned left. A green Jaguar sped after it, ran the red, and careened onto the curb.

"That's Jaggar's Jaguar," Hernandez said. "He was driving, but we assume Rydell had a gun on him at that point. This was just a couple of minutes before the responding officers intercepted and pursued them to the library."

Saul felt his stomach go to work on the cream and the caffeine. This changed everything. He restarted the video. A text notification came up on the screen.

Levy.
Are you with Parker?

He swiped it away. "You get a read on that Camry? Rydell admitted he was pursuing someone."

Hernandez held out a folded piece of paper. She traded him for her phone.

Saul unfolded it. A printout of a driver's license. Gray Wilson. White male, thirty-six. Height: 5-11. Weight: 182.

She said, "His silver Camry is registered to the address on his DL."

The first connection was the hardest, and now, thanks to Hernandez, they had it. She was the best partner he'd ever had. When he was stuck, she always found a way through it.

"So let's go talk to him," Saul said. "Maybe he'll tell us what the hell is going on."

She didn't seem to hear him. She was staring at her phone. Her brow furrowed. She dabbed and swiped.

Was she texting with Levy? Saul, looking for an excuse to glance at her screen, reached across the stool to set his cup on the counter.

She blacked the screen. Clipped her phone on her belt. "We have to go see Levy."

"What for?"

Hernandez stood. "Wouldn't say."

Saul chugged the coffee and nearly choked on the thick liquid. After effectively demoting him, Saul had expected Levy to avoid face-to-face at all cost. Whatever the hell she wanted, it must be huge.

"Let's question Wilson, first," Saul said. "Maybe he'll give us something. It might be enough to convince Levy that we need more time instead of just taking whatever she's about to drop on us."

"Takes too long to get to Silver Lake." Hernandez's voice shot up an octave. This was an order, which must have come out harsher than she'd intended because she lowered her voice before continuing. "I mean." She grimaced. "Maybe if I say we're stuck in traffic, we can buy an hour. We could stop by the MDC and see if this video gets us anywhere with Rydell, now that we know who he was chasing."

The coffee curdled in Saul's stomach. He had to tell her.

He started toward the door. "We could split up," he said over his shoulder. "If you want to go see what Levy wants, I'll take a pass at Rydell."

"I wish," Hernandez said. "I'd take Levy over Rydell any day, but I can't show up without you."

Saul pulled the door open and motioned her through. His gut roiled, but what could he do? This was Hernandez. He couldn't refuse. Before this was all over, he had the feeling he'd need her help. Levy was going to drop a new case on them—he just knew it—and there wasn't time. He had to find Wayob.

He stepped out into the sun and stood beside Hernandez. "Rydell's in the PAB."

She blinked rapidly.

"In a holding cell—"

"Shit, Saul. You didn't book him?"

Saul shielded his eyes. "Rydell actually wanted to go to the MDC. You should have heard him. And Saroyan ended up in the hospital the night after we booked him. I couldn't risk it."

"Shit." She tossed back her shock of white. "Well…, I guess now it's easier to have a go at him before Levy."

He nodded and gazed at the daunting hike back up First. Almost certainly, it would land him in the hospital. "Let's Uber it."

"No." She launched up the sidewalk. "Race ya."

Saul sucked in a breath. And trudged after her.

Ashley Revision

Sunlight. Ashley awakened to the warmth on her face. She opened her eyes and squinted at the sunlight streaming through the window. Two windows— no, four. The wall was curved...

Her bedroom! She struggled free from a tangle of covers and felt her face, her hips—it was her body. It worked!

She sprung out of bed. Ran to the dressing room. Stood before the mirror.

Never before had she felt so relieved to find herself in such an awful pair of shorts. She stripped them off and threw them in the trash, like she should have done in the first place after whatever company had sent them hoping she'd wear them. As if. The powder-blue top was not something she would ever wear either. At least it matched her complexion.

Was it a dream? Gray's body? Impossible, right? She must have dreamed about the artifact with the snake after her dad showed her a painting of one like it on his phone.

She found her phone in the bedroom. According to the screen, it was Monday.

It couldn't be Monday.

But it was. On her phone was a day's worth of unread texts from Raquel. Ashley had never slept through a whole day before, not even that time when she had pneumonia. So if yesterday wasn't a dream, then what was it? If it was like that cheesy movie where Ryan Reynolds switched places with Jason Bateman, then Gray might have been here—in her body. She should have memorized his number. She'd had his phone all day. If she could call him, and he answered, then she would know for sure.

But she _could_ call her dad. She could ask him what was really up with the artifact he was looking for. Maybe he would believe that she had spent a day in Gray's body. If it was even real at all.

His phone rang and rang, and then there was a click as the call was transferred. Niles answered right away. He had a big title but basically Niles was her dad's right-hand man, who followed her dad around like a puppy. The fact that it was Niles answering and not some assistant meant that almost certainly something was wrong.

"Where's Dad?" Ashley asked.

"Ashley! Do you have any other way to get in touch with him?"

"What do you mean?" She'd called his personal phone. What other way was there?

"I am not sure," Niles said, "but since he's not answering our calls, I was wondering if his phone is working."

"When was the last time you heard from him?"

"Friday." Niles sounded almost embarrassed.

"Friday? That's two days ago!" *What the hell?* Her dad got busy, sure, all the time. Sometimes she didn't see him for months, but he always took her calls. And he was always, always was in contact with Niles.

"It was a weekend," Niles said. "But now there's this crisis brewing at InGenetics. I need to know how to handle it."

"I can't believe you're worried about that." Ashley marched out of the bedroom. "What if he was kidnapped? Did you call the cops?"

"No. Dimitri saw him at the house yesterday."

"Weird," Ashley said. "So then, he is around?"

"Apparently, but I don't know what's going on."

"Well… tell him to call me."

Whatever was going on, her dad would call her when he could, and she had the feeling that he would call her before Niles.

After ending the call, she descended the stairs, sliding her hand along the redwood rail.

The house was eerily quiet. She stopped and listened… But for what? What did she expect to hear?

Downstairs, sunlight softened by a dissolving layer of cloud streamed in through the windows. On the coffee table, her magazines were all out-of-sorts, and after she had shown Andrea—how many times?—how she liked them fanned out in an arc.

"Andrea?"

No answer.

An intense stillness hung in the air. It was almost lonely compared to the near-constant cacophony at Claire and Gray's.

Down the hallway, the office door, which she always kept closed, was ajar. She peered inside, and almost jerked back. An easel had appeared. Slowly, she approached it. On the easel was a large painting of a man sitting behind a table facing the viewer, his back to a wall. A cheap-looking trench coat stretched over his massive shoulders. He had thinning hair, a boxy head, his brow was deeply creased. And his eyes—they stared right out of the canvas, right at her. It was mesmerizing. The bold lines of the painting seemed to capture the man exactly. Even from a distance Ashley would recognize him in a crowd. It was amazing, really, but also disconcerting. Someone had been in her house.

Could Gray paint like this?

Beside the easel, a disarray of paint tubes, two of them open, were scattered on her desk. They were on a rag, but the rag was thin and the paint could easily soak through to the sandalwood.

A vibration startled her. Her phone, which she'd forgotten was still in her hand. She glanced at the screen.

Raquel.

Ashley declined the call. What could she say to Raquel?

She screwed the caps on the paints. Ten seconds later, Raquel called back. Fuck it. Easier to just to answer.

"Yo biatch," Raquel said. "Where the hell you been?"

Trapped in a man's body, getting busy with his wife. "Long story," Ashley said.

"I got an audition for *Quantum-Man.*"

Seriously? "What role?" The real question was why hadn't Ashley heard they were still casting? Some kind of an agent Don was if Raquel got to audition and not Ashley, who was already well known and, in theory, beyond auditions. Maybe her name was hurting her more than it was helping. She needed to change that.

"I did a scene with August," Raquel said. "We really have great chemistry together—on camera, I mean."

"That is so great," Ashley lied. She didn't like the way Raquel flaunted the 'chemistry' she supposedly had with the guy Ashley was supposedly dating. Why was she even friends with Raquel, anyway? And August, he could at least have told her they were still casting for *Quantum-Man.* Even if it was only some bit part, he still could have told her.

"Pretty sure I nailed it!" Raquel said. "You just know when you get it right, you know? Sergei Ratnikov said I have serious potential."

Gratuitous name dropping—nice. Ratnikov was a terrible director and everyone knew it.

"I've got to go," Ashley said.

"Cool, I'll be over later."

"No," Ashley almost shouted into the phone.

"What? Why not?"

Ashley started back toward the living room. It was a bad idea to tell Raquel about the screen test she needed to rehearse for. Raquel would repeat it to the wrong person and somehow ruin it. Deep down, Ashley had always known that Raquel hated her for wealth and her notoriety, which all came from her dad, like she could help it. But now Ashley was going to make her own name for herself. Maybe the Charlie-Kaufman-Sean-Penn film wasn't destined to be a blockbuster, like *Quantum-Man,* but the role was an almost guaranteed Academy Award nomination.

She couldn't get caught up with what might have happened yesterday, crazy as it was. Whatever explanation existed for everything—the portrait in her office, the disheveled magazines, the dream that she'd spent a day in the life of some guy named Gray Wilson, which had seemed so real—she could only control tomorrow. And the screen test was the best shot she'd ever had. She had to do whatever it took. She had to be better than her best.

"I need to focus on acting now," Ashley said.

"Right, we're actors. So, what are you saying?"

Raquel was a distraction. Worse than a distraction, she made Ashley feel ugly inside. "The other night I was too wasted to go out, but you kept feeding me cosmos. You and your driver practically carried me to the car."

"You're mad about that? You were dying to flash your cooch and you know it."

Raquel would never admit that she had insisted on going to the Standard because she had wanted to be seen there with Ashley, and to be seen looking better than Ashley, with Ashley almost too drunk to stand.

"I told you I wanted to go home."

"Seriously? When?"

Ashley was pretty sure she had said it. Even if she hadn't, Raquel should have known. She must have known.

Ashley sat on the couch and leaned forward. "I need to make some changes in my life. It's time we went our separate ways."

"Seriously? I'm your best friend, Ashley."

"I know," Ashley said, but friends like Raquel were worse than no friends at all. "I can't be around you anymore."

"August told you, didn't he?"

Ashley was curious but knew she didn't have to ask. She just pressed her phone to her ear and waited.

"Put yourself in my shoes," Raquel said. "He was all over me, and it's not like you have an exclusive relationship, right? That's what he said, and I guess I just got caught up in the moment. No big deal. At least not for me. I was one and done—but I think he wants more. I bet he didn't tell you that, though, did he?"

Ashley leaned back into the couch. Was their relationship exclusive? They hadn't discussed it, but she had assumed so. But with her best friend? *Come on.*

She wanted to feel hurt. But instead, it was relief that washed over her. She had known that August didn't care about her. Not really. And she hadn't really cared about him. They were using each other to boost their images, and it seemed to have worked. August had been cast as Quantum-Man, and on social media, Ashley was more popular than ever. Not that she cared anymore. From now on, she was going to make it on her own merit or not at all.

"You still there?" Raquel asked. "So, I'm all you've got. Keep that in mind while you're going around making all these changes." Raquel ended the call.

Ashley tossed her phone on the cushion and began sorting the magazines on the coffee table, which were not nearly so disheveled as the pile at Gray and Claire's, but eventually they would be, if she let it go. It had bothered her before that sorting them in chronological order meant the latest issue of *Vanity*

Fair covered her photo on last month's cover, but now it hardly seemed to matter.

Not a Toy

In the nursery, Claire rocks Tyler in her arms. He won't stop crying. His diaper is clean and he's not hungry. By the afternoon, he's usually asleep, so probably he's just crying because he's tired, which Claire can understand. She's tired enough to cry herself despite that she actually slept last night.

Thanks to the sex.

Finally, for the first time since Tyler was born, the first time Gray had so much as touched her since that morning, months ago, when he snuggled up to her under the covers. It was just before dawn, and she, of course, was already awake. They'd started caressing, and just as things were heating up, Tyler started bawling. And she had to get up. She was the only one who could feed him.

Afterwards, she saw herself in the mirror, the dark bags under her eyes, her tangled hair, her saggy breasts. How could anyone want her?

She almost never cries, but that morning she did. And by the time she got it under control, Gray was up, helping Mindy get ready, and neither one of them had tried anything since, not even a kiss, until last night. There just isn't time for sex, and she needs to feel needed.

Like last night.

The way Gray came onto her, like there was no choice. Like he *had* to have her. He was a different person. He'd never turned her over like that before and in the moment it was exactly the right thing. His fingers in her mouth, and she came, and then he came, and she would have again if he hadn't stopped. If he hadn't fallen beside her on the bed and fallen asleep.

Afterwards, she had a nightmare in which Tyler was screaming and she couldn't reach him—couldn't get out of bed because her legs wouldn't move. She called out for Gray, but he wasn't there. She was alone.

But he was right there beside her, mouth breathing, when she jolted awake at three a.m. Tyler was sleeping soundly in his crib.

Now, Tyler's tears have run out and his wail is weakening, like he's forcing himself to keep crying because he knows she'll stop rocking him once he falls asleep. His fat little cheeks are red from the effort, and his eyes are staring up at her, like he's waiting for her to say something.

She keeps rocking him. "What's up with your dad?"

The sex last night was one thing. She wouldn't mind some more of that, and maybe if they did it more often it would last a little longer. But Gray has become such a space cadet lately. When his car got towed this morning, because he'd parked by the hydrant right down the hill from their house, she shouldn't have gotten mad—but come on, she had to drive him to Pomona!

And what's with the new haircut? How did he even have time with all the extra hours he's been working? Or so he said.

Any other man she might suspect of an affair, but Gray is probably just sneaking off somewhere to drink. Or to paint. Probably both.

And she can hardly blame him with how she's been so tired lately. All she can ever deal with is what absolutely must be done in the moment, and she can't even do a good job at that. She can't give him the love he deserves; she can hardly take care of herself. All her energy goes to Tyler and Mindy, and then there's none left.

But the problem isn't all her. They've been avoiding each other because whenever they go deep, whenever they try to talk about something that isn't immediate, he inevitably asks about the night before he proposed—always wanting to know where did she go. It doesn't matter. Why won't he let it go? It was years ago. It's got nothing to do with anything now. *I need him to trust me.*

But how can she expect him to know what she needs when she never tells him. She hadn't wanted another baby, but did she ever really say it out loud?

That's the problem with insomnia. Thoughts are like little moths always flapping around in her head. Never landing.

Tyler's eyes blink closed. His mouth yawns open. Innocent. She has to stop blaming Gray and just tell him she needs to go back to work.

She lays Tyler in his crib and clicks on the baby monitor. Tonight, she'll talk to Gray—really talk to him.

She'll shower, fix up, make a nice dinner and—*who am I kidding?*—order take out. Once the kids are in bed, she and Gray will sit down, and she'll explain how she needs something outside the house, how she needs to be more than a mom, how it doesn't matter if daycare costs more than her paycheck.

In the hallway, she listens outside Mindy's door. Typical silence. Most likely, Mindy's in there coloring for her usual audience of stuffed animals, which is always entertaining, but right now Claire's so exhausted she's happy to take the quiet as a sign that all is well.

She goes out to the garage where, after glancing over her shoulder, she uncovers Gray's easel. She'd half-expected him to have started something new, but the sketch looks the same as Saturday when she breezed past it, pretending not to notice how much life Gray had captured in the stark lines, in this portrait of the man who looks like Charlie's evil cousin. She can already tell it will be amazing if he ever actually completes it. It's a leap above the collection of landscapes he's hidden below the workbench, as if she can't find them there. And even the landscapes have potential—if he'd just finish one.

She should encourage him. It wouldn't kill her to say something positive every now and then. No secret how desperate he is to hear it. It would be easier if he wasn't always traveling off somewhere inside his head. His body might be right there beside her, but his mind is always off in some secret world he'd rather be painting.

And on top of that, he goes to work every day. He gets to be a software engineer *and* an artist, and meanwhile, what is she?

A mom?

She wouldn't trade Mindy and Tyler—not for the world—but being a mom is not enough. And it never will be.

Once she gets her own job and their marriage is on equal ground, it will be easier to act supportive.

She trudges to the living room, collapses on the couch, and closes her eyes against the sunlight blasting in so bright it almost makes a sound. She could dark it out if they had the curtains that Gray wants, but what good are curtains against the tornado churning through her head?

What to do, what to do? Her old job at Wastewater was better than being trapped here all day, but after wasting so much energy convincing Gray that her job was worse, she can't just capitulate now. So, what else is out there? Who would even hire her after a five-year hiatus?

She needs some kind of a plan before talking to Gray. She'll lay it all out for him such that he'll have to go along. But what's she going to figure out when she can't even think? If she could just get one whole night of decent sleep...

Mindy's laughter reverberates down the hall.

Claire leaps up. Her pulse kicks through the fog in her head.

Mindy's just laughing. What's wrong with that? She's a little girl, and she should laugh more than she does. That's the problem with insomnia: either Claire overreacts or can't react at all.

Outside Mindy's door, Claire stands listening to her daughter laughing. Must be a sugar high. Mindy must have gotten into the desserts again.

But... there's a sharpness, a tone to her laughter that's not quite right. Not quite like Mindy, who as far as Claire can recall has never laughed out loud alone in her room.

The laugher abruptly stops. Mindy whispers.

Claire presses her ear to the door but can't make out what Mindy is saying.

She cackles. Her laughter lacks all sound of fun. It sounds... malicious.

Claire turns the knob... then hesitates. Maybe it's the insomnia. She's not hearing things right.

Mindy screams.

Claire throws open the door, expecting to find her hurt.

Mindy is sitting on her bed, legs crossed, staring down with eyes opened wider than Claire has ever seen them. In her lap is the stone thingy Gray got at the Day of the Dead.

"What happened?" Claire crosses the room and kneels beside Mindy.

Mindy lifts her pale, little palm. A drop of blood in the center. Claire wipes the blood away. A little hole the size of a pinprick. The skin surrounding it is red.

She snatches the stone thing from Mindy's lap and runs her thumb over the snake's fangs. Too blunt to have pricked Mindy's palm, and the stone is round with a flattened top and bottom. "How did you hurt yourself?"

"I—" Mindy's lip quivers. "I didn't mean to."

Claire sits on the bed and hugs her to her chest. "It's okay." She rubs her back.

Obviously, Gray doesn't know it's dangerous or he wouldn't have left it out for Mindy to find.

After Mindy's stuttered breathing returns to normal, Claire asks what she was laughing at.

"I don't remember."

Claire pulls back and tries to catch her eye.

Mindy looks down.

"You don't remember?" Claire asks.

Mindy shakes her head.

Claire glances around at the usual disarray of Mindy's room. On the floor, a pair of white bears sit in front of a coloring book as if studying it. Nothing odd about that. Nothing surprising at all, aside from the stone thingy with the evil-looking snake, which Claire suddenly wants away from her daughter, out of her house. If Gray wanted a souvenir from the Day of the Dead, why not just buy a sugar skull like everyone else?

"Want a Band-Aid?" Claire asks.

Mindy nods, her mouth small and pouty.

After fetching a pink Band-Aid and applying it to Mindy's palm, Claire carries the stone thingy to the kitchen and opens the cabinet to the trash. Gray won't miss it. Probably, he's already forgotten all about it.

Before tossing in, on a whim, she holds the stone with her fingertips, away from her body, and swivels the snake.

It spins, and some internal mechanism clicks. The snake abruptly stops 180 degrees from where it started. Its head points at her chest.

Weird.

She waits for something to happen…. Nothing does.

She drops it in the trash.

The Key to Your Dreams

What went wrong? After Wayob endured dying, endured killing himself in the awful vessel of Rydell, instead of awakening in the new vessel Wayob deserves, he finds himself here, trapped alone in the black nothingness of the Encanto, his thoughts going around and around. How much time has passed? Hours? Days? A week? There is no sleep, here. No dreams, nothing. Only Wayob, reduced to nothing but a mind.

And why? Because he who held the Encanto had ceased using it. But after he learned of its power, how could anyone lose his nerve?

Wayob would take anything over this disembodied nothing, even Rydell's miserable body, which had always been too hot or too cold, his skin chafed by itchy garments—miserable, so miserable Wayob could retch....

And yet, to have a vessel, to see the world around him, to feel anything other than this.

What Wayob needs is a strong vessel. A body to instill fear in others. *Stand back.* Give Wayob the space he deserves. For Wayob no longer tolerates weakness. Not anymore. Not after what happened with his young bride, after he tried to reason with her when he should have done something the instant he discovered her vile desire—anyone else surely would have—but he was so young himself at the time, so naive, and no one had told him what marriage meant. He had hoped. He had trusted... foolish.

Over his centuries of imprisonment, Wayob has rolled out his hopes again and again, and as always, they got smashed, like berries on a well-traveled path.

Again today, after the little girl took the Encanto for herself, Wayob thought she would free him. Foolish. When Wayob realized she could hear him whispering to her, he had felt almost disgustingly giddy. Never before has Wayob managed to reach the holder of the Encanto so quickly. Even Abuela, who seemed highly attuned to Wayob, only seemed to hear his whispering while asleep.

Of course, Wayob is getting better, but there could be more to it. Perhaps this miserable little girl is special. Perhaps her young ears have a predilection to his whisper, little good that it does Wayob. The brat unlocked the Encanto, but just as Wayob felt its dark magnetism begin to loosen, it tightened again. The little imbecile must have turned back the dial. Why oh why, why would she do that? To open a door just to slam it in Wayob's face. Does she think the Encanto is some toy? This life she is screwing with is Wayob's life.

She shall learn.

Now no one can blame Wayob for slaying this child, who holds the Encanto, for she deserves it.

Wayob concentrates on the sound of her mind. Come closer. Closer. *You want to use the Encanto.*

Useless. She is too far away to hear him.

Wayob must wait. Wait and wait and wait in the darkness. Like always. Sooner or later, she shall give into the temptation to become someone better than herself.

Surely, this child does not possess such willpower as Abuela, who resisted Wayob's whispering for decades. Abuela had heard him—she had to have heard him—but she refused to use the Encanto. Even though it would have returned her sight to her, still she refused. She blames Wayob for the death of her husband, when it was the army who shot him. True, Wayob was using him as a vessel at the time, but Wayob was just trying to escape. Just trying to be free. Does Abuela care? No, she does not care about Wayob.

She ignored him for decades, even after Wayob began whispering while she was in the deepest stages of sleep, when surely it must have seemed like her own idea to destroy the Encanto and Wayob along with it. No way could she have known that destroying it would free Wayob into one final vessel, so why? Why refuse Wayob even this mercy?

Wayob laughs. *Ironic.* After suffering through all the decades of her resistance, it was Abuela's son, Luis, who set Wayob free. All that time, Luis must have lived there with Abuela and within reach of the Encanto, with Wayob so close and yet a million miles away, because despite all his centuries of trying, Wayob can only reach the mind of the one who holds the Encanto.

Stop distracting yourself, Wayob. Concentrate. Must concentrate. Yes, Wayob can whisper. He can and he will. Little brat must want something. Over the centuries, alone in the darkness, Wayob has learned how to hear the desires of she who holds the Encanto—no thanks to the barbaric, fucking priest, who doubtfully had any idea of what Wayob could achieve.

Wayob concentrates on the mind of she who holds the Encanto. She desires to… what? Wayob cannot hear. Focus, Wayob, focus.

Think, my precious holder of the Encanto, why wait to grow up? You can become a princess, right now. You hear me?

Hear me. Come closer. Pick up the Encanto.

The Encanto holds the key to your dreams.

Where's Wilson?

The door was open. The mattress bare. Aside from the toilet and bunk bolted firmly to the cinderblock wall, the holding cell was empty.

Saul had fucked up, that was clear. How badly depended on who found out that he'd left Rydell in the holding cell instead of booking him into the Metropolitan Detention Center.

But it wasn't just that. It was the way Rydell had begged to be confined with the other inmates. Just like Br'er Rabbit. He should have kept an eye on him instead of going home and lying awake, watching the shadows churn on the ceiling, while a tornado tore through his head.

Who was Wayob? And why would Saroyan, Rydell, and Aleman all claim to be him? How were they connected? Saul looked at Hernandez. She had all but ordered him to book Rydell into the MDC.

Her eyes seemed to darken. She brushed back her shock of white bangs.

"Don't worry," he said. "You're not accountable."

"You should've told me he was in the holding cell," she said. "We're supposed to be partners."

"I get it." No point in excuses. If he had any hope of recovering the way she'd seemed to soften toward him, he had to rectify the mistake. Maybe it wasn't as bad as it looked. Maybe someone else had simply moved Rydell or even booked him into the MDC like Saul should have done, which would be embarrassing but soon forgotten.

Saul pulled out his phone. The watch commander would know.

The elevator chimed.

Lieutenant Levy stepped out, her starched shirt strapped down by red suspenders, hair like fluffy curtains flapping against her cheeks as she marched toward them. Levy never left her office. She avoided conflict at all costs. Yet here she was. A soldier marching to the fray.

"Where's Rydell?" Saul asked her. No point in playing dumb.

Levy had the sort of plaster-pale skin that burned from a minute of direct sunlight, which made her flushed cheeks all the more dramatic. Her answer was an octave lower than normal: "The morgue."

The hallway seemed to sway. Saul's legs felt like guacamole. He grabbed the door of the holding cell, the steel cold in his hand.

Hernandez straightened. "Shit. How?"

Levy crossed her arms and stared at Hernandez, her eyes burning with an intensity he hadn't known she possessed. "Strangled himself with his shirt."

"This is on me," Saul said. "Hernandez told me to book him."

"I could have guessed," Levy said. "Wish I could shield her from the blowback."

"What's the big deal?" Hernandez asked. "Rydell could have offed himself in the MDC just as easily."

Good point, Saul thought. To him the big loss was that Rydell had taken the easy way out when he could have led them to Wayob.

Levy explained how Lieutenant Mayfield, commanding officer of the Jail Division in the sheriff's department, was making a big deal about Rydell's suicide in the hopes of sweeping the Saroyan fuckup under the rug.

Hernandez snorted. "Good luck with that."

"Mayfield has friends in top brass," Levy said. "They're looking for blood."

Saul held his wrists out toward Levy. "So, take mine."

Levy wasn't about to stick her neck out for him, nor did he want her to. Despite Saul's seniority, she'd promoted Hernandez to lead detective and then blamed it on politics, as if the decision were above her pay grade. But they both knew she was punishing him, still, because when he'd shot a Black man on her watch, the fallout had stalled her career.

"You'd better hope this doesn't get out in the press." Levy turned toward the elevators. Then added, "I'm putting you on cold cases."

Saul's stomach churned. *Cold cases.*

Hernandez marched after her. "Both of us?"

Levy pressed the up button. "Sorry." The doors opened, and she hustled inside. End of the conversation, as if he could just let it go.

He reached out and blocked the left elevator door from closing as Hernandez grabbed the right. In his haste to reach the back of the elevator, where his belly would be less obtrusive, he bumped her aside. She pretended not to notice.

Instead of standing by the door, she squeezed in beside his plus-sized frame, her compact stature accentuated by his size.

The doors closed. Levy pressed the button for the sixth floor. Saul was already sweating. She pressed it three times and then stared at the numbers above the doors, as if she could ignore him and Hernandez into non-existence.

Saul glanced down at Hernandez. She was looking at him. His fuckup. His chance to justify his actions.

"Rydell wasn't working alone," he said. "If we don't continue the investigation, more people could die."

Levy frowned. No eye contact.

Saul continued, "He knew things he had no way of knowing, like where I was Saturday night."

Levy crossed her arms. "Like that's some kind of a secret."

Saul kept his life at the Magic Castle separate from work—like the Castle itself seemed separate from LA, an alternate world of ornate wood and crystal chandeliers where possibility sparked in the air—but sometimes his enthusiasm boiled over. On multiple occasions, he'd invited Hernandez to join him, though she'd never accepted, and now there was no point in asking again.

"He wasn't at the Magic Castle," Hernandez said. "We were on Olvera."

Levy chuckled. "At the Day of the Dead festival? How many people were there?"

"I doubt Rydell was one of them," Saul said. "Wrong demographic." As a white male, he'd received more than his typical share of odd looks.

"So why were you there?"

"Working the case," Hernandez said.

True, technically, though at the time Hernandez had been skeptical. She'd even teased him about inventing the whole thing about tracking Aleman there as an excuse to lure her out for dinner—and with a twinkle in her eye, like it was a good thing, maybe. But now that she'd seen his huge, hairy belly hanging over his too-tight tighty-whities, he could forget all about ever asking her out for real. He'd seen the look of pity in her eyes, and there was no path from pity to love.

The elevator doors opened. Sunlight poured in from the hallway that ran along the outer wall of the glass building. Levy marched out into the brightness, her figure blurred into a silhouette.

Saul motioned for Hernandez to go first, then trailed after.

Bad idea to mention Wayob, Saul knew, but he had no other card to lay down. "Saroyan and Rydell both pretended to be the same person," Saul said to Levy. He pulled out his phone and started the recording he'd made of Rydell. "...your fault that I am here..."

Outside Homicide Special, Levy paused and glanced back.

Saul turned up the volume. "Release me," Rydell was saying, "or I shall have to take revenge." Saul paused the recording.

"It was freaky," Hernandez said. "We've got Saroyan on video acting like that. You should see it."

Levy shrugged. "Weird's not enough." She pushed through the door.

Saul charged after her into the windowless room. As he reached for her shoulder, the half-dozen detectives at their desks fell silent. Saul held back. No hard evidence. No hope of convincing her.

Levy slinked through the desks, slipped into her office, and locked her door with its papered-over window behind her.

Detective Williams smirked up at Saul from his desk. Saul stepped closer and glowered back until Williams looked down at his screen.

Hernandez motioned Saul back to the hallway.

He shut the door behind him. "It's not fair for Levy to punish you too," he said.

"That's not how this works. We're partners." She smiled with her lips but not her eyes.

"I get it. And I'm sorry. But...I can't give up until we catch this Wayob bastard."

"Don't apologize. I'm with you. We have to catch him. Levy might even be grateful once we do and she takes all the credit."

Saul shook his head. If they ignored her orders, Levy would hold a grudge regardless of the outcome. "You've got a big future in the department," he said. "Better if you work the cold cases for now. I've got nothing to lose."

In a couple of years Hernandez's son, Rumi, would be going to college. She needed this job, and so, as the lead detective, she couldn't permit Saul to go off and investigate Wayob. Which meant he'd have to go behind her back, which would probably shred whatever remained of their relationship, but what choice did he have?

Hernandez swallowed. "You go check out Wilson," she said. "I'll keep Levy off our backs."

A current of energy surged through his chest. She was going out on a limb because it was the right thing to do. "Wish you could come with me."

She lifted her head. Her eyes sparkled in the bar of sunlight streaming down the hallway. "You owe me one."

He almost hugged her. "That I do."

—

It was half past eleven by the time Saul turned onto Gray Wilson's street. As he rolled up the hill, he scanned the cars parked along the curb for Wilson's Camry. Not there.

Wilson lived in a single-story Craftsman with pale wood siding. Its driveway was empty. As Saul heaved himself out of the car, a crow squawked from a nearby power line and flew off.

He knocked on the door.

No answer.

He went around the side of the house and unlatched the gate. A narrow path led to a back deck shadowed by a palm. The yard of scraggly grass, surrounded by a tall gray wooden fence, sloped down from the house. He stepped up onto the deck and approached the double sliding doors. Blue sky reflected on the glass. He shielded his eyes and peered through.

Inside, a disarray of toys and magazines lay strewn across the carpet. Beside a couch was a plate of what looked like dried marinara. The house was as still and silent as the aftermath of a storm.

Saul returned to the front yard. Across the street, an elderly gentleman in a brown suit stood on his lawn, hand tented over his eyes.

Saul waved.

The man turned away. Staggered on rickety legs toward his house.

"Wait," Saul yelled. He hurried across the street. Instantly out of breath.

As he pounded up the front walk of the man's home, the man shuffled inside and slammed the door. A solid clap of wood on wood.

Saul lumbered onto the stoop and knocked. "I'm Detective Parker with the LAPD."

No answer.

Saul held his badge to the peephole. "I just want to ask a few questions. It's about your neighbor, Gray Wilson."

"I don't talk to crazies," the old man shouted through the door.

"Smart," Saul said. "I'm trying to stop one the crazies, and I'm hoping you can help me."

There was a long pause. The old man's voice trembled. "You know about the crazies?"

"That's why I'm here," Saul said, unsure if the man was referring to the Wilsons or some product of his own dementia. But he had to find out, unlikely as it was that the old man had seen Wilson do or say anything that would explain why Rydell had been so desperate to follow him. "Mind opening the door?"

The door unlocked. Inched open a crack. Behind it, the old man's eye was open wide above a dark bag of sagging skin. "Gray's not home."

"Any idea when he'll be back?"

"His car was towed."

"When was this?"

The door opened wider. The man's face was sallow, lined with deep crevices. "I'm Charlie Streeter." He held out a hand for Saul to shake then led him into the house. His suit still had the creases from where it had been ironed and it flapped around when he walked, like it was staked up by seven or eight frail bones and nothing else.

They reached a dusty living room with drawn curtains, lit by a table lamp with an incandescent bulb. Streeter sat stiffly in the wingback beside the lamp.

Saul sank into a catty-corner loveseat across from Streeter and waited. Give people silence and they tend to fill it.

Streeter snatched a prescription bottle from the side table. He clawed it open. Emptied two big pills into a trembling palm. "For my back." He dry swallowed. He leaned back. His face slipped into the shadow behind the lamp. "So, what do you want?"

From his coat, Saul pulled a deck of cards and a handkerchief. Magic tended to relax people. Something about the mystery made them want to open up. "Do you like magic?"

"No."

Saul folded the handkerchief around the cards and squeezed them in his fist. With his other hand, he pulled out the handkerchief with a flourish. He opened his palm.

The cards were gone.

No reaction from Streeter. His eyes were glassy, out of focus.

Whether or not he'd even seen the trick, Saul had no idea.

"I want to ask about your neighbor, Gray Wilson."

"Good painter," Streeter said. "Sweet little girl."

"Anything unusual?"

Streeter exhaled. "He's not a crazy, if that's what you're asking."

Saul folded the handkerchief and creased it, stretching out the silence for Streeter to fill.

But he said nothing more.

Saul slid the handkerchief into his coat pocket and leaned forward. "I'm just covering the bases, you know? It's probably nothing to do with Wilson, but I've been dealing with these perps—crazies, you might say—who are all connected somehow."

"Crazies." Streeter nodded as if he knew exactly what he meant—how three different people had all acted like Wayob, and all spoken with that maniacal-musical cadence.

"Yeah. Do you know where Gray Wilson is?"

"After his car got towed, he and his wife loaded the kids in the minivan. I'd have told him not to park by the hydrant, if he'd asked me, but some people never learn." Streeter swallowed. "If they don't suffer the consequences." His hands were shaking, perhaps from guilt of not warning Wilson but more likely it was the blue pills.

"What you should be worried about," Streeter continued, "is crazy officers."

"What do you mean?"

"I'm talking about guys who attack people for no reason."

"I hear you."

"Yeah, you hear me, but what are you going to do about it?"

Was he referring to some incident in particular? Now it was Saul's turn to swallow. Had Streeter read about the Brown shooting? Saul never should have confronted him alone, and for that he accepted the consequences, but it had been Brown's play. He was the one who drew what Saul confirmed, after he shot him, was a gun. Saul had followed procedure. The shooting was justified. Not that anyone in the press cared to mention that. They had made it about another Black man shot by a white officer.

"Do about what?" he asked.

"About the crazies," Streeter growled. "What do you think we're talking about?"

"I work homicides," Saul said. "But I want to help."

"What if you had a body? Then what would you do?"

Saul didn't want to go off on a tangent, but if Streeter had witnessed a crime… "Is this hypothetical? Or—"

"What if someone was killed in an accident caused by a crazy officer?"

"Then I'd call it in, same as with anyone else."

"But the officer might blame someone else. Like an innocent person who was just driving by in his car."

"There would be an investigation. Internal Affairs would jump on something like that."

"With all that bureaucracy, it's a wonder you guys ever solve anything at all."

Saul nodded. "I know what you mean. Did this happen to you, or someone you know?"

Streeter glanced down and to the right, all the wrinkles on his brow clenched together. "Can't a man ask a question?"

"Was Wilson involved?"

"Gray doesn't have anything to do with anything. He's going through a tough time and doesn't need you asking a bunch of questions and making things worse."

"Like what kind of a tough time?"

"How would I know? I only just met him Friday night."

That wasn't too surprising. In LA, neighbors rarely had time to be neighborly. Saul still hadn't met his.

"So, what makes you think he's going through a tough time?"

"Well." Streeter clasped his hands together. They kept shaking. "For one thing, he ran outside in his underwear."

Saul's gut churned. Rydell had forced Saul to strip down to his underwear before taking him hostage. Could this be related?

"Did you see who made him do it?"

"No one made him do it. He was out of his head."

Saul squinted. "So, you're saying Wilson is crazy?"

"Meh." Streeter coughed dryly. "I was married once. There's a reason I'm not now." He looked down, and light glinted on the sparse oily hairs combed across his sun-spotted scalp.

"You think it was an argument with his wife?"

"What else would it be?"

Good question. If Rydell hadn't tried to take Wilson hostage, then maybe this was just a coincidence. Saul was skeptical of coincidences, but the flip side of the coin was the human tendency to invent patterns where there were none. Coincidences *did* happen.

"Where did Wilson go in his underwear?"

"What? No. He went back inside. And don't ask him about it, either. What goes on between a man and his wife is his business. Besides, you only care about homicides."

"I care about all crimes. It's just a matter of priority. Did anyone else witness Wilson's unusual behavior?"

"In this neighborhood? Of course not. If a jetliner landed in the street, no one would notice unless they saw it on their phone."

"It's great you're here, then, to keep an eye on things."

"Meh. If they knew anything about anything, they would setup a neighborhood watch. I don't even live here. I'm just staying while my daughter is out of town." Streeter eased himself up out of the wingback. "Now, you'll have to excuse me."

Was Streeter holding back? Or was this feeling in Saul's gut just his own desperation to know why Rydell had been following Wilson?

Saul heaved himself up. "Where you headed?"

"Why would I be going somewhere?"

"You're all dressed up."

"Grand Park." He pointed at his eyes with his index and middle fingers, and then at Saul. "That place is swarming with crazies."

"Keep an eye on them. Good idea." Saul snapped his fingers and revealed a business card as if it had appeared out of the air. "Give me a call if anything else comes to mind about Wilson."

Streeter blinked, back hunched, but did not reach for the card. His arms seemed lost in the loose sleeves of his coat.

Saul placed the card on the side table beside the pills. "Don't worry," he said on his way out. "I'll do my best to stop the crazies."

No Such Thing

No sign of the marine layer. Not a wisp of cloud. Nothing. Just the giant ball of burning hydrogen stuck stubbornly above the horizon, its heat amplified by the windshield.

Saul was desperate for AC, but that required starting the car, and the kick of the engine would almost certainly draw Wilson's attention.

Finding him had been easy. He'd pulled up Wilson's LinkedIn profile and found his current employer, Intrepid Solutions, right at the top. After driving to the office, a tower in West LA, he found Wilson's Camry in the lot and waited nearby. Having an officer show up at work tended to put people on edge.

At three thirty, Wilson emerged from the stairwell and approached his vehicle. He had a determined, maybe even desperate, look on his face. Saul decided to follow him. Maybe a domestic dispute was the reason Wilson had run out of his house half-naked, but what if it was something more?

Wilson drove to a residential street in Beverly Hills, parked, and then just sat alone in his car. Saul parked a hundred yards behind him and waited. Was he meeting someone? Stalking someone in one of these multimillion-dollar houses? Ahead of the Camry, the street widened into a cul-de-sac where a formidable gate restricted entry to the exclusive neighborhood of Beverly Park.

As Saul waited, people returned to the other parked cars and departed, along with the shadow of the eucalyptus tree, which had provided some respite from being cooked in the heat. He sloughed off his jacket, took out his cards, and began shuffling.

Now that Rydell had offed himself, Saul's only hope of finding the truth was if Wilson knew something about him. It was hard to imagine what Rydell would have wanted with a software engineer, but then it was also hard to imagine how he'd have gotten tangled up with Saroyan and Wayob. If Wilson was involved too, would he admit it? That was the question.

Perhaps he'd just happened to be there when Rydell sped through that red light.

Since Wilson was Saul's only lead—besides the Lunas, who were stonewalling him—he wasn't ready to blow his cover just yet. Not until he knew what Wilson was up to.

He pulled out his phone and called Hernandez. After everything that had happened, he'd neglected to tell her that the Lunas never came home Saturday night and that Rosa claimed they had stayed with a friend—one she refused to identify.

Hernandez seemed unfazed. "Maybe their friend is illegal as well."

"It's more than that. They're hiding something. You saw how Rosa's grandmother acted at the death notification."

"Maybe, but we can't make them tell us, and it's probably unrelated. Let them mourn in peace."

"Maybe if you talked to them without me around, they'd open up? Use your Spanish powers."

Hernandez sighed. "They'll never trust me. I'm a cop."

"Just try," Saul said. "Please. I'll owe you one."

"You already owe me for covering for you on the cold cases."

"Indeed, I do. And now I owe you two."

"I charge interest."

"I'd expect nothing less."

After ending the call, he reclined his seat and prayed for the marine layer to roll over the city and cool things off. He squinted through the glare on the windshield at the dark shape of Wilson in his car.

The boom of an engine woke him. He'd dozed off with his mouth hanging open. He sat up, wiping the drool from his chin, just in time to see a black Maserati, the gate closing in its wake. The Maserati squealed as it hot-dogged down the hill.

Wilson's ignition kicked. As he U-turned, Saul slouched down and waited for him to pass. Then he started his own car and followed at a distance.

At Sunset, Wilson turned east toward his house in Silver Lake. Traffic was heavy. Saul closed the gap. They inched forward. Gridlock.

Low clouds rolled across the sky: the marine layer, at last. The temperature dropped, and Saul opened all the windows and inhaled the moist, coastal air. It felt good.

After half an hour of stop-and-go grind, they reached Hollywood as the sun pierced the clouds on the horizon. Wilson turned right on Highland and parked a few blocks down. Saul cruised past. In the rearview, he watched Wilson enter The Woods, a dive bar with a stone and wood facade sandwiched between a liquor store and a Middle Eastern joint. Saul circled back, found a parking spot two spaces behind the Camry, and walked to the bar.

He opened the door to darkness. Peering inside was like looking into a cave. The Woods was the trendy sort of establishment that would be packed by midnight, but as his eyes adjusted he saw that right now there were only three patrons, including Wilson. All men, all at the bar, all turning toward Saul in the doorway.

He pretended to receive a call and retreated.

He understood the allure of booze. He'd tried on drinking after his marriage ended, but all he found at the bottom of the bottle was more misery and exhaustion. And despite eating less, he'd gained weight. After depositing countless paychecks into the Castle bar, it got to the point where he couldn't follow even basic sleight of hand, and that's when he finally gave up the booze. Because he lived for magic. Not to be fooled by it but to understand it. To learn the method because there was always a method.

But there was no such thing as real magic. No such thing as Wayob remotely controlling someone else.

The bottom dropped out of his stomach. He needed a snack. Wilson might leave while he was gone. This was a test, an opportunity to finally start his diet. His stomach would just have to wait. Maybe burn some of the excess baggage he was wearing.

Then, as if to try his resolve, a burger truck rolled to a stop in front of him. The Patty Wagon, its name decaled in a loopy cursive, hit reverse and wedged into the gap between his plain wrap and Wilson's Camry.

A line of customers materialized along with the smell of the grill. Saul swallowed. He could almost taste the fries. Sprinkled with bits of bacon and malt vinegar. Smothered with ketchup. Gourmet buns brushed with butter, toasted on the grill. Cheddar cheese melted over grass-fed beef, medium-rare.

More people got in line. They blocked his view of The Woods. So he basically had no choice. The only way to keep an eye out for Wilson's exit was to get in line. And if he got in line then he had to order.

Distance

Outside his front door, Gray paused. On Saturday, he'd parked in front of Charlie's house—he was quite sure—and Claire never drove his car. So the fact that it had been moved, and not only moved but parked in front of a hydrant, which he'd never do, meant that yesterday while he was in Ashley's body, someone else had been in his.

He took a deep breath. If he was going to find out what had happened with his body, he had to tell Claire the whole story.

Inside, it was dark. The TV illuminated the living room with a dancing tampon commercial. Claire was on the couch, hunched over her phone as usual, in her usual sweatpants and the green sports tee whose white letters had mostly peeled off after so many washes.

He stood in front of the TV until she noticed him.

"Where were you?" she said without looking up.

"Had to stay late," he lied. Though he might as well have worked late. Leaving early had hardly helped him come to terms with the insanity of spending a day in another person's body, and the three drinks had done little to prepare him to tell Claire.

As she glared up at him, her eyes sparked in the blue light of the TV. At the beginning of their relationship, her unfathomable gaze had made him feel drunk. They had spent hours staring into each other. A turn on, a dare. Who could last longest before diving into the other, before tearing off their clothes? But as the years slogged by, the charge in her eyes when she looked at him had changed. It felt dangerous.

She raised her brows. "Really."

Did she think he wanted to stay late?

"You heard Brad this morning," he said. She'd been in the car when he called his supervisor to say he'd be late since his car had been towed to Pomona. Brad had given him a guilt trip about the big sprint for the deadline on Wednesday—a deadline invented by Brad.

Her nostrils flared. "Were you actually doing something or just avoiding me?"

"I wasn't avoiding you..." But he had been, at least in part. He forced himself to hold her gaze, like a soldier under fire, as she pressed her lips together and waited for him to speak. "It's just..." He had to tell her the truth, the whole truth, or as much as he knew. "Mind if I sit down?"

"Just tell me," she said.

How could he say he'd been Ashley York without sounding ridiculous? "So, yesterday—"

"I called your office. And your supervisor said you left early *again*."

"Yeah, well, Brad thinks leaving before nine is leaving early."

Claire crossed her arms. "I called at like four thirty."

"I was just driving around, okay? The point is—"

"You were just driving around? Every single night? You expect me to believe that?"

It was a double standard. She'd disappeared all night once, and here he was just a few hours late. "You expect me to believe you about your little drive."

Her eyes darkened. "That was college. You want to go *there*?"

"You want to tell me where you went?"

She rifled through the magazines on the coffee table and dug out the remote. "I'm watching my show." She ramped up the volume. A hardness came into her face.

Gray clenched his teeth. They were too charged up to talk. No sense in trying.

—

In the kitchen, he jerked open the fridge. Bottles of condiments clanked in the door. There on the center shelf was a bag from Sharky's, his favorite. He stared in disbelief. Claire rarely ordered delivery, and when she did it was Noodle World, never Sharky's.

He took out the bag and opened it up. It contained chips, salsa, and a giant burrito wrapped in foil. A Fiesta burrito, his favorite.

He stood over the sink and devoured it. Outside the window, fog drifted through the beam of the streetlight. Maybe he should quit worrying about whatever had happened yesterday—it wasn't like it changed anything now. He should focus on the future. If anything, he felt more confident than ever about quitting his job. He decided to give notice tomorrow. Only, he really should tell Claire first.

He chased the burrito with tap water and then checked the pantry where Claire stashed chocolate behind a box of old orzo. A single square of Special Dark remained. Tempting, but he couldn't eat the last of her supply. He should get some Godivas, like the ones Ashley had had, and hide them here for Claire to find, as a peace offering.

He balled up the burrito wrapper and opened the cabinet to the trash can. When he saw what was inside, his pulse quickened. It couldn't be—but there it was, right on top, half-covered with wilted lettuce. The charm. What the hell? He snatched the stone from the trash and examined it. Aside from some oily substance that might have seeped into the little holes on the bottom, it appeared intact.

He marched back to the living room. In flickering blue light, he held the stone out toward Claire's face, which remained an expressionless mask.

"Why would you throw it away?"

"That thing almost sliced Mindy's hand open," she said. "You smell like alcohol, by the way."

Gray glanced toward the hallway. Mindy's door was closed.

As he rushed down the hall, Claire called after him, "Don't you dare wake her up."

Gray flung open the door. *Please, be Mindy.* Her bedroom was dark, except for the spinning moons and stars on the ceiling projected from the nightlight. She was swaddled under pink covers, lying on her back. *Please be Mindy. Please be Mindy.*

He flicked on the overhead light and kneeled beside her bed.

Her eyes came open.

"Mindy?"

"What's the matter, Daddy?" The inflection of concern in her voice, the innocence in her eyes. *It was her. Had to be her. His Mindy.*

He threw off the covers, drew her up into his arms, and hugged her. Tears welled in his eyes. *Thank god.* "Were you asleep?"

"It bit me." She was looking at the charm, which he'd dropped on her bed. She showed him the pink Band-Aid, with a cartoon princess, on her palm.

He brought her hand to his lips and kissed it. "What happened?"

She shook her head. "I didn't do anything."

He picked up the stone, avoiding the oil on the bottom. The head of the obsidian snake faced him. The tail was aligned with the flattened area on top, at what he thought of as the six o'clock position, just as he'd left it this morning. On Saturday, when he dialed the snake to the twelve, something inside the stone had pricked him.

He glanced at Mindy. She was staring at the stone in his hand. Her eyes were wide.

He asked her, "Did you turn the snake?"

She looked down. "No."

She was lying, obviously, but why? "It's okay if you did. I just want to know."

"What difference does it make?" Claire was in the doorway, glowering, her arms crossed.

It made all the difference in the world. But Gray couldn't explain it right now. Mindy was scared enough. Since the snake was still at the six, she should be safe from waking up in the body of a stranger.

But...how could he be sure?

And the snake, perched on the porous white stone, its mouth half-open, forked tongue lashing out beneath the fangs, seemed to mock him. Its beady eyes looked malicious. Hard to believe that turning the snake had caused him to spend a day in Ashley's body—but it must have. The way the fortune-teller had refused to touch it after she gave it to him, like she had finally rid herself of some great burden she could no longer bear, made him suspect it only worked on one person at a time. And her granddaughter seemed to reinforce the idea. "It is yours now," she had said. After all, if it worked on multiple people at once then why was he the only one who could destroy it? So he had to make sure it was still his, for Mindy's sake. He gripped the stone in his left hand, avoiding the spot at the bottom where it had pricked his palm, and rotated the snake. *For Mindy,* he thought as he flicked it to twelve o'clock.

It stabbed him anyway—what felt like a needle pierced the flap of skin between his thumb and forefinger. He yelped and dropped it on the bed. But whatever had stabbed him had already retracted into one of the stone's many pin-sized holes.

Mindy scooted away from the charm on her bed. "That's what happened to me!" She hugged a pillow in her lap.

Gray sucked the wound. Beneath the iron in his blood, he tasted something sour, something foreign. He examined the spot. A dot of red the size of a pinprick. It had stopped bleeding.

"Can you come out here, Gray?" Claire, still in the doorway, had that look in her eyes. "It's past bedtime."

Gray gingerly moved the charm from the bed to the bookshelf and helped Mindy under the covers. She stared at the stone.

"Think you can go to sleep?" he asked.

"If it stays quiet."

No doubt she was well aware of the impending argument between him and Claire. "It'll be okay." Gray stroked her hair and kissed her.

He picked up the stone and turned out the overhead light. In the softer light of the stars spinning on the walls and ceiling, Mindy's face relaxed.

He closed the door behind him as he stepped out into the hallway and whispered at Claire, "Why would you let her play with it?"

"I didn't let her play with shit."

Too loud. He motioned her toward the living room. And now he remembered that when he was hiding the charm, Mindy had asked what he was doing.

At the end of the hallway, Claire spun to face him. "Why would you leave it out where she could find it?"

"I can't believe you threw it away."

"How much did it cost?"

"Nothing." He smelled the greasy spot on the bottom. Olive oil, stale cheese.

"You mean you stole it?"

"No."

Claire snatched it from his hand and marched toward the flickering light of the TV.

"Careful." He launched after her. "There's something sharp in there."

"Yeah, no shit." With her shirt, she cleaned off the goo. "So, what is it?" She held up the stone and examined it.

"I don't know." He wasn't sure how to explain and didn't know *if* he still wanted to. Would she believe that it had somehow transported him into the body of Ashley York?

"Then why do you have it?"

Gray shrugged. "A fortune-teller gave it to me."

Claire rolled her eyes. "Please don't tell me that all these nights you've been seeing a fortune-teller."

He shook his head. "At Dia De Los Muertos, there was a long line for the bathroom. She was right there and insisted I take it."

"So, wait. You were in line, and she came along and gave this to you?" Claire shook the stone. The flattened head of the chiseled snake seemed ready to strike.

"No. I got distracted." He reached for the charm.

She snatched it away. "Right. So while I was waiting for you, you went off and did your own thing, like you've been doing every single night." She collapsed on the couch, closed her eyes, and exhaled.

He sat, leaving a cushion of space between them. What could he say? "Have you ever wished you could wake up as someone else?"

"What are you talking about?"

"What if you could wake up with a totally different life?"

"Like?" Her voice softened. "How?"

"That actually happened to me yesterday."

"If you're talking about the sex, I don't want to talk about it."

Sex? Gray felt like he was falling. It had been months since that morning when he and Claire had managed to find each other in the pre-dawn darkness—the warmth of her body under the covers when, almost the instant they started touching, Tyler had started crying. Claire had launched out of bed, and Gray had waited an hour, maybe two. He'd watched a beam of sunlight coming through a crack in the curtains as it worked its way down the wall. She never came back to bed, and nothing had happened since. Neither of them had even mentioned it.

And now he was jealous. Jealous of what his own body had gone and done without him. He reached for his drink. But on the side table was only the baby monitor and a pile of Claire's magazines.

Almost on cue, Tyler started wailing.

"I'll go," Gray said.

Claire groaned. "I'll be faster." Which was true—she could change a diaper in two minutes flat—but Tyler was wailing. It might take an hour to calm him down. She heaved herself up from the couch and shot him a look like a cold stake in his heart. "You wait here." She dropped the charm in his lap and scuffed her feet as she trudged down the hall.

Gray again reached for the phantom Scotch on the side table. He needed it to be real.

—

In the garage, Gray ripped the top from the Dewar's and tilted back the bottle, longing for the burn in his throat. But, thanks to his earlier drinks, he was too dehydrated and too numb, and now no amount of alcohol would bring back the buzz. He needed to escape, and the truth was that he only ever really lost himself while painting.

Recalling the passion that had surged through him on Saturday when he'd envisioned his painting of Charlie, he uncovered the canvas. The sketch hardly looked like Charlie at all. He looked sinister, silhouetted by sunlight from behind. Gray grimaced. No point in finishing the painting. The idea seemed meaningless now.

He removed the canvas from the easel and added it to his collection of unfinished works, which he kept hidden below the workbench, tucked behind some boxes.

Maybe if he painted the fortune-teller, he could grasp her reason for both giving him the charm and then insisting he destroy it. He recalled the way her tears had flowed into the deep crevices on her face. Perhaps she'd given it to him for his own good. After living for a day as Ashley York, he felt even more unsatisfied with his life than before.

He slapped a fresh canvas on the easel, selected a Vienna Taklon brush, and dabbed it in some black acrylic. As he blocked in the underpainting, the fortune-teller's face faded into darkness in his mind's eye. He fought to recall the way she'd looked in the candlelight, the backdrop of black curtains and the marigolds.

When he focused on the canvas again, he saw he'd painted a black, spiraling blotch of nothing. He tried again, and again, but still he painted only a sickening swirl of blackness, as if this was all he could paint now. How in the hell was he going to make it as an artist if he'd lost all control over his brush?

He'd lost control at Ashley's yesterday, too, but at least then he'd managed to paint a portrait: a man with a head like a boulder atop a mountain of trench coat. The amazing realism with which he'd painted this man, who he'd no recollection of ever seeing in real life, and who had seemed to appear on the canvas from some deep recess of his imagination, proved Gray could paint as well as he always knew he could. Painting was woven into the fabric of his soul. It was very core of his being.

Perhaps the fortune-teller was the problem. Maybe she was somehow impossible to paint? To test this new theory, Gray tried sketching the Dewar's bottle on the workbench... Another damn swirl. It was as if his hand could only draw a swirl now. What was wrong with him? Artist's block? Beside the Dewar's, the flattened head of the obsidian snake seemed to sneer.

He snatched up the charm and looked for a place to hide it. He wanted the thing as far from his paintings as possible. To reach the shelves on the opposite side of the garage, where he knew Claire never looked, he'd have to clear a path through the bins, boxes and junk they were too lazy to get rid of.

The kitchen doorknob rattled. Gray lunged to block the view of the easel.

The door swung open. She squinted in the fluorescent light, an empty Snapple in her hand. "What are you doing?"

What could he say? The cover was off the canvas, and the acrylics were out. "I'm just cleaning up."

Her face soured as she glared at the Dewar's on the workbench. Which was fine, for now. Better if she focused on the Scotch than on the sloppy spirals on the canvas behind him, which would undermine his case for quitting his job to become an artist. She would laugh in his face. *You and Mindy can open a gallery together.*

"I'll be there in a second," he said.

She dropped the Snapple in the recycle bin. "Whatever. Just don't interrupt my show."

They had said enough for one night, and they both knew it. She turned out the light and shut the door.

"I'm still in here," he said to the darkness.

He found his way the stool by the workbench, sat down, and slumped. The stone was still in his hand. He ran his finger over the pores.

What if, yesterday, his body wasn't on autopilot and someone else— Ashley?—had been driving it? What if she'd had sex with Claire? Would Ashley have wanted sex with Claire? While in Ashley's body, he'd only declined August Grant's attempt because August held no attraction for Gray.

He sighed. He could drive himself crazy trying to get the details out of Claire. When it came to answers she didn't want to give, he was better off asking a brick wall. Maybe next time she prodded about where he'd been going, he'd stonewall her, let her see what it was like. Because he knew how ridiculous it would sound if he said he was going to bars, not just for drinking —though he was drinking, probably more than he should—but to scope out some way to support her and the kids while at the same time supporting his art.

Art? She would laugh. And without any worthwhile pieces to prove his potential, he'd deserve it.

His thoughts were fuzzed from the Scotch. He should just go to sleep.

He found his way to the light and flicked it on. In his hand, the snake was still at the twelve. Mindy was safe now. He should just dial it back to the six.

He should.

He returned the canvas. Took a nip off the Scotch—just one more, to take the edge off the awful black swirl, to still the fear spinning through his head so he'd have some chance of falling asleep. This weekend, if he could just get a few hours to himself, he'd paint something spectacular.

But would he?

He slammed the stone down on the workbench, harder than he'd meant to, and instead of corking the Scotch, he decided to treat himself. He tilted the bottle back. *No time to get anywhere, and there never will be, will there?* All his life, he'd played it safe, and where had it gotten him? *Right here.* Boxed in. Drinking in a garage with an obsidian snake, its tongue out, mocking his sad attempt at a painting, his attempt to develop a skill with only two hours to paint every other weekend.

With his fingers, he smeared the paint across the canvas. "What did you expect?"

He tilted back the bottle. Gulped hard, and this time he felt the burn.

"Yeah, I know—no one ever gets anywhere by following the rules."

He wiped his hand on his jeans, yanked the phone from his pocket, opened Google Chat and started a new conversation.

Gray:
Dear Brad,
I quit.

He swirled his finger toward the little green icon for send. The message *swooshed* out of his phone and into the ether. *No taking it back, now.* Gray suddenly felt sick.

He leaned down and stared into the snake's eyes, which were really just gouges in the obsidian. "You happy now?"

But the obsidian snake had nothing to say.

As Gray tilted the bottle, he imagined Brad's panic as he read Gray's resignation. He slammed the bottle down and swallowed. He felt better. He felt free. Free for the first time since…since when? But he did feel free. He'd taken the first step, and the first step was the hardest. Now it was behind him. Now he was moving, gliding on the momentum from the change he'd set in motion. Keep flying or fall out of the sky.

He grabbed the bottle and tilted his head back, longing for the bite, the smoky liquid on his tongue, the burn from his throat down to his belly, the rush…

But got nothing.

The bottle was empty, and he had no memory of finishing it.

He reached toward the chiseled head of the snake. "It was you. You drank it. Didn't you?"

But the snake suddenly seemed, somehow, out of reach.

"What?" Gray tilted his head. The snake blurred. Now it was two snakes.

He rubbed his eyes and blinked the two snakes back into one.

And how are you going to support yourself? What about Mindy, Tyler, and Claire?

Gray stood, and the room spun. His pocket buzzed. The garage jolted into focus, the terrible black swirl on the canvas.

He knew it was Brad. He almost ripped his pocket yanking the phone out. He squinted at the screen.

Brad:
Thanks for the two weeks' notice.
Hope you don't need a recommendation.

Idiot, Gray thought. Like he cared about the opinion of a middle manager at a second-tier tech company. Brad's opinion was worthless now that Gray was an artist. But Ashley York, an endorsement from her—now that would count for something.

And Gray could get that, couldn't he? Maybe the fortune-teller had given him the charm for a reason. Maybe she'd sensed his desperation. Maybe she knew that by telling him not to turn the snake, he would.

Anyone would. Of course they would.

Gray had read in Evan York's biography how he'd clawed his way to the top by exploiting every opportunity he was given. All his decisions were made from the gut. Overthinking creates hesitation. Hesitation leads to failure. And right now, Gray's gut was saying, *Leave the snake at the twelve.*

Maybe nothing would happen, but what if? What if he woke up as Ashley York? Then, well, he could help himself.

He stumbled through the kitchen to the living room, which was filled with a jarring cacophony of light. The TV was muted, and Claire must have gone to bed. If he weren't so tired, he'd have turned the TV off, but fighting his way through the frenetic light to the button required more effort than he could muster. Besides, his sense of balance was lacking, and the remote was lost beneath Claire's magazine pile.

He half-stumbled, half-fell onto the couch, rolled onto his back, and tried to focus on the swirling people flashing on the screen. *What are they doing?*

He rubbed his temple. He felt hungover. If Claire thought he smelled like alcohol before, there was no way he could lie down next to her now.

On the screen was a close-up of a woman, blonde hair curtained across her face. She pulled it back—Laura. It's Laura. Her doe eyes and broad cheeks. Laura after their sophomore year when they went to Paris for the summer, when they thought they'd be together forever.

A roll of paper towels replaced the woman on the screen. She must not have been Laura. Of course not. Though now Gray pictured Laura perfectly in his mind. The tortured look in her eyes when she broke up with him. Living together, isolated in a foreign country, had strained their relationship. At the end, they had hardly gotten along.

Afterward, to stop himself from breaking down—to stop himself from begging her to come back—Gray had pursued other girls. Girls more mysterious than Laura. Girls like Claire. But, as he later came to learn, Laura's optimistic outlook outshone them all.

What if Gray could experience her life now, the older-but-still-smiling Laura who rarely posted on Facebook. Maybe, thanks to the charm, tomorrow he'd wake up in the body of her husband, who was probably even more miserable than Gray. He probably worked at some Midwestern insurance agency, adding weight as his hair thinned away.

Laura might have changed since college, but so had Gray. Her life might not be so different from his. Maybe if he just messaged her, he could stop thinking about her all the time. But he knew her reply—if she replied at all— would be some meaningless platitude, a half-sentence at most.

Pulsing light from the TV penetrated his eyelids. When had he closed them? The light made him nauseous. He rolled his head on the throw pillow.

Why Ashley York? If it weren't for Claire following Ashley's every action on Instagram, he'd hardly have known who she was when he woke up in her castle on the hill yesterday. Her isolated life had held a certain thrill. To be a woman, rich and young…

Drifting across the threshold of sleep, he was pulled back by a burning sensation in the skin between his thumb and forefinger where the charm had pricked him. He groaned. He should put something on it. But if he got up now, he'd never get back to sleep. His head throbbed. The Scotch had left him strung out, his mouth dry as sage in the sun. His brain shriveled in his skull.

Should have drunk water, not Scotch. He needed water now. But from the back of his mind, a whisper insisted, *Better to sleep… Everything shall all be better…once you sleep… Sleep…*

Sleeeeep.

From Out of the Fog

Startled from slumber, Saul's head knocked against the driver's side window. He glanced around.

Fog.

Across the street, the Wilsons' house was a dark blur in the fog.

Saul had followed Gray Wilson, who had left work early to go to a bar. If he had any idea that yesterday a maniac kidnapper and murderer had been following him, he showed no sign of concern.

Saul reviewed the facts again, trying to piece together the motive. Three people had claimed to be Wayob: First Saroyan, who murdered Luis Luna but who then, after provoking a fight in MDC that landed him in the hospital, denied all responsibility—despite admitting it had been his hands swinging the bat. Then Aleman, a guard at the MDC, who claimed to be Wayob while threatening to kill someone but later denied the whole thing. Last, Rydell, who claimed to be Wayob when he kidnapped and eventually killed Bob Jaggar. The question was, why?

Now that Rydell had killed himself, Saul feared he might never learn.

Fatigue burned in his eyes. He cracked open the window and rubbed them. If Hernandez were here, he wouldn't be dozing off. His heart fluttered whenever she was near. He could call her, but not this late at night.

Hernandez was not easily riled, but somehow Rydell had gotten under her skin. Maybe, once Saul solved this thing, it would bring them closer together. Maybe she'd forget all about how pathetic he looked in his tighty-whities. Once he was thin, it wouldn't matter what she'd seen before because that was a different person. He had to get thin.

His belly filled the space below the wheel. He sucked in and tightened his trench coat. *Get thin.*

The fog was thinning. Streeter, whose house Saul was parked outside, appeared in an upstairs window. He switched off the light and vanished in the shadow behind the glass. A minute later, the downstairs lights went out. By the front door, a curtain moved.

However, all remained still and quiet at the Wilsons'.

Saul's eyes began closing of their own accord. Only the vast hollowness in his stomach kept him from drifting off. He shook his head and started the car. Tomorrow morning he'd return to question Wilson.

As he drove up the hill, he pictured the steak at the Castle, a baked potato stuffed with cheddar, butter and bacon on the side. After the burger he'd eaten earlier, he shouldn't be hungry. But he was. And a starchy potato would help him sleep. Maybe, instead of the steak, he should just have a potato or fries—just a half order. The Castle didn't offer a half order, so he'd just eat half.

The fog thickened. The road narrowed and wound like a maze walled by darkened houses set close to the curb. No sign of an on-ramp. No sign of the 101 at all. He reached for his phone to check the map.

Hair stiffened on the back of his neck, like there was someone behind him.

He adjusted the mirror.

A cloud of solid gray closed in on his wake. Ahead, through the fog and the glare of his headlights, the blacktop faded away. He sped through the curves. At a random intersection, he turned right.

Saul knew his fear of being followed was irrational, but that did little to ebb his apprehension. This feeling he'd almost forgotten: the fear of a child.

In the headlights, fog swirled, made one last final barrage against the windshield, then abated. The road descended toward an intersection with a two-lane. A stoplight and a sign. Griffith Park Blvd.

Then he saw a girl, probably a teenager, standing in the road. Her hands swallowed in the sleeves of a plaid button-down. Black hair curtained the thin oval of her face.

He slammed the brakes. The asphalt was wet and oily. The descent, steep. And she just stood there in the street as the car skidded toward her, glaring at him. As if expecting him to mow her down.

Expecting *him*.

Andrea Won't Stay

Ashley stood in her driveway and watched Jonah seal himself in his cherry-red Maserati. He had made her repeat each line a hundred times, enunciating each word differently, until she had no idea how they should sound. And when she asked which way was right, all he said was "Whatever feels right to you."

Right. It all felt so forced and fake.

He extended his arm out the window and gave her a big thumbs-up, as if she'd actually learned something from all his classical training as an actor, as if he thought she actually had talent and might still think so without all the money she had paid him.

"I could *kill* him," she said to herself as he sped up her driveway and disappeared into the fog and the darkness. "I *could* kill him."

She felt even less confident now than before he had arrived. Tomorrow, at the screen test, Sean Penn was going to see she had no talent. No talent at all. She was going to embarrass herself. She had no idea how to *act*. The more she tried, the less she knew. And what for? She only wanted to be an actress because that was what the world seemed to expect. It was so hard to get anywhere. Rejection after rejection. Hard to get up in the morning and try again.

Maybe she'd feel more confident if Jonah hadn't made it all about himself, taking selfies of them together, fishing for quotes from her to put on his website. The way he kept name-dropping Jennifer Lawrence —*Jen* this and *Jen* that, all the spiff work they had done together. Like Jennifer Lawrence mattered more than anyone else.

And he kept wanting to rehearse the romantic scene with Ashley, saying she was *amazing*, like that would get him in her pants when he'd all but said the role was out of her league.

She returned to the house. She realized that, without Jonah's weird vibe to contend with, her fear was not all about the screen test. It was becoming harder and harder to pretend that yesterday—that feeling of appearing to be someone other than herself, being trapped and alone with no one believing who she is—was a dream.

Alone in the parlor, she watched the fog descend over the windows and snuff out her view of LA. She turned on the outside lights. The fog walled up the windows, solid white.

"Good night, Ms. Ashley."

Ashley jumped at the sound of Andrea's voice almost right behind her. She whirled around.

"Didn't mean to scare you." Andrea released her hair from the ponytail and draped it over her shoulders.

Ashley crossed her arms. "You're leaving?"

"Your dinner is in the kitchen. I'll wash the dishes tomorrow."

Ashley couldn't bear the thought of being alone in the house. Not tonight, not with Sammy, the only security guard she trusted, going off shift at eleven. And the portrait she couldn't explain shut up in the office. When Ashley told Andrea not to clean in there, Andrea had shrugged it off as though it made total sense to her, and now Ashley wasn't sure how to ask without sounding crazy.

"Ever get tired of the commute?" Ashley asked.

"I don't mind. Good night." Andrea turned to leave.

"Wait. Stay here."

Andrea turned back. "What?"

"I mean, you should move in here." Ashley couldn't believe what she was saying. Andrea did sloppy work, and now she was begging her to stay?

"I...don't know," Andrea said.

"It's silly for you to keep driving back and forth every day. You can have the guest studio. You clean it twice a week and no one ever stays up there." Ashley took both Andrea's hands in hers. "You don't have to pay rent or anything."

Andrea pulled her hands back. "Maybe. I'll sleep on it. Okay?"

"Sleep on it here." Ashley shrugged as if this were only some minor favor she was offering, as if she weren't afraid of being alone in her house. Because ordinarily she wasn't, and she didn't like the way Andrea called her *Ms. Ashley*, the way she always arranged things not quite the way Ashley had asked. But maybe the problem was that Andrea wasn't suited for a housekeeper. She didn't have any prior experience when Ashley offered her the gig. So maybe they could just be friends? From now on, Ashley only had room in her life for people who were genuine.

"I don't have any clothes for tomorrow," Andrea said.

"Okay." Ashley turned toward the kitchen. "Let's talk tomorrow."

Ashley's Assets

The Pacific Design Center was all lit up as August cruised past. The primary colors and rectangular shapes reminded him of the graphics in retro games. The colors were cool, though. Other buildings in LA should take note.

An Ariana Grande tune, "Dangerous Woman," sparked up on his phone. It was Raquel calling. She had totally played him. She had stepped out of her panties and led him into the dressing room, where he hiked her skirt up and pressed her against the wall. The things she did—*oh man*—too good to ask for. Then, afterward, she'd acted like she wanted more, but, of course, she knew he couldn't come two times in a row, which had made it a matter of pride for him. He'd had to force himself just to prove that he could.

Yeah, Raquel was good. Damn good. August wished that he *could* cast her, but the director, Sergei, wanted someone hotter and younger. Still, he'd call Sergei right in front of Raquel and beg him to cast her. Hopefully that would be enough to make her chill out. He had made an effort. No need to blackmail him.

He let the call go to voicemail, but if she figured out he was ghosting her, she might tell Ashley about the hook-up.

He turned left on Sunset, slammed his fist on the wheel, and called her back.

She answered right away. "Where you headed?" She must have heard the engine of his Porsche.

"Just driving around," August lied. He was headed to Ashley's, two dozen roses riding shotgun, which he hoped would patch things up.

"Want to stop by?" Raquel said lasciviously.

"Can't. I've got my insanity workout."

"At seven o'clock at night?"

"Uh, yeah, it gets me juiced up for the club."

"What club?"

"Don't know. Got to talk to the guys." In truth, it was up to him and he'd already decided. They were going to The Standard.

"The Standard?" Raquel guessed.

"Maybe."

"Ashley going to be there?"

"Probably." *Hopefully.*

Why the fuck did he tell Ashley he was too busy with *Quantum-Man*? Such an obvious lie.

It was just, no one had ever broken up with him before. So yesterday, when Ashley tried to break it off, he'd panicked and broke up with her first. No one breaks up with August.

Come on. As if Ashley really needed to focus on acting all of a sudden. *No way.* She was just overreacting because he'd wanted a BJ last night and then stormed out when she wasn't into it. It should have been a relief to him; he'd been exhausted from doing Raquel twice, and if he really wanted his dick sucked, he could have let Andrea go to town, like she'd tried to, with Ashley right there in the other room. He shouldn't have walked out on Ashley just because she wasn't into it.

The problem was that sex with Ashley no longer interested him, and he wasn't sure if it ever had. He'd only hooked up with her because the guys in his entourage all wished they could. And then he had to keep it going because dating was a prerequisite for marriage, and marriage was probably his only way to tap into her assets. He couldn't afford his lifestyle much longer. His accountant had taken to calling almost every day in a panic.

The main reason August had landed the starring role in *Quantum-Man* was his willingness to work for next to nothing. His agent, sworn to secrecy on the disheartening sum, had tried to negotiate based on the massive box office of similar releases, but the producers were hedging their bets. Who knew if it would be a success at all? What choice did August have? If they wanted to pay some big fee, they would hire a big-name actor. To them, acting was less important than fight scenes and explosions, and August was pretty face among many who would have signed on for even less than he had.

Yet, he was spending like a billionaire. You have to fake it until you make it, and August Grant was going to make it. He was on the way up, spending more on A-list parties than the richest actors in Hollywood. Plus, he was supporting his entourage, and the house in Malibu, which they hardly ever used, cost even more than his house in Beverly Hills.

So he had to get back together with Ashley. She was his ticket out of debt, and dating her had propelled his notoriety even higher.

"Hello?" Raquel said.

"Bad reception," he said. "I'm in the hills." He wasn't, but soon he would be. "See you later." He ended the call.

She was obviously going to show up at The Standard, whether he wanted her there or not, but so what? By then, Ashley would be back at his side. And if Raquel wanted any more favors from him, she'd keep her mouth shut.

In the Fog

Ashley ate dinner while watching the third season of *30 Rock*, a show that Raquel thought was uncool, which made Ashley enjoy it even more because she was done with Raquel. She no longer had room in her life for people who only gave a damn about what they could get from her. Aside from her dad, Sammy might be the only person in her life who truly cared about her. The way he smiled at her made her feel warm inside, which made her feel awkward for being his boss.

She turned up the volume on the TV. What she needed was a laugh.

Headlights raked the wall.

Probably August. Anyone else and Sammy would have called before opening the gate, but August made a sport out of sneaking into her house without any kind of a warning, as though he lived here too. She should have told Sammy they had broken up. And she should have been more forceful with August. Instead of saying she needed to focus on acting, she should have told him she simply didn't want to see him anymore.

She peeked out the front door. August's Porsche was in the driveway. As she stepped outside, he popped out of his car and flashed that charming smile of his that melted hearts around the world. But now she found it kind of creepy. He had brought her red roses. She loved roses. Clearly, she had been too soft. He wasn't taking her seriously.

"Nice touch," she said. "But I can't take those."

He held them out, his smile unbroken. "I'll just throw them away otherwise."

She took them. His fault for buying them. As she smelled them, he raised one eyebrow, his eyes smoldering in the floodlights. The fog behind him seemed to glow.

"Alright, well, I'll call you tomorrow." Now wasn't the time to have it out with him. She glanced over her shoulder toward the house, and when she looked back, he'd moved into her personal space.

"Let's take back what we said earlier," he said. "A relationship doesn't have to take a bunch of time, and we can help each other. Who's directing your screen test? I'll call him. No one says *no* to August Grant."

She shook her head. His oversized ego would only hurt her chances. Besides, she wanted to do this on her own.

"Nice speech." She clapped. "Too bad you hooked up with Raquel." His eyes widened. "She told you that? Fucking bitch."

"You're saying it's not true?"

He grimaced. "No."

Ashley dropped the roses in the driveway and turned toward the house.

"Wait," he yelled. "It meant nothing."

She whirled around. "What about with me? Was that nothing too?"

He raised his one eyebrow again, the other squinted down. "With you it was everything."

Behind him, the fog was like cotton in the floodlights. A dark figure marched toward them.

Without thinking, she took a step closer to August. Primeval instinct. Safety in numbers.

He pulled her into an embrace.

As she struggled free from his arms, she heard what the dark figure was whistling: the *Mission Impossible* theme song. Relief surged through her.

Sammy emerged from the cloud and flashed his Cheshire smile. "Everything cool?"

"All good, Sammy," August said.

Sammy ignored August. He was looking at her. In his hand was a leash, and beside him, the black dog he'd promised to get rid of.

"Why is the dog still here?" she asked.

Sammy's brows furrowed. "Yesterday, you said to keep her."

A chill ran down her neck. "Seriously?"

"You don't remember?" Sammy squatted down and stroked the dog's head. "You said if anyone could give her a good home, we could."

The portrait in the office was one thing. By avoiding it, she'd been able to get through the day, but now there was no denying it: someone else was in her body yesterday. "You okay?" Sammy asked. Near his hand, a wisp of fur floated in the air.

"It's going to shed all over everything," she said. "We don't even know where it came from. It might have some disease."

"Don't worry," Sammy said. "I got Shera a vet appointment tomorrow."

"You named her?" She meant to sound angry, but it was kind of cute.

"Way out of line," August said. "Not cool."

"It's time for you to go," Ashley said to August.

"Let's talk inside." He grabbed her arm. "Just for a minute."

Sammy abruptly stood and moved closer.

Ashley jerked her arm free. "Not tonight," she said to August. Then, to Sammy, "I'll pay for whatever Shera needs, okay? But find her a new home. Somewhere nice."

"You got it," Sammy said with his big white grin. He turned to August. "Later, man." He clicked his tongue against his teeth.

Shera growled and lunged at August, but Sammy held her at bay.

August slunk into his Porsche and made one last attempt with the brows and the smile before he finally drove away.

—

In Ashley's bedroom, fog pressed against the windows and the skylight like it might crush through, pour in, and drown her.

"It's just a cloud," she said to herself. Using the app on her phone, she closed the electric shades. *Out of sight, out of mind.*

But the room seemed too empty. Too big.

Too still.

She went to the window by the bed and peeked around the shade. Someone could be right below standing on the lawn, and they would be invisible in the fog.

She called the guard booth.

Sammy answered right away. "Ashley. What can I do for you?"

Her throat tightened. "Thanks." She swallowed. "That's all. I just wanted to say thanks."

"For what?"

"August." She wished she could talk to Sammy—really talk to him —and have him believe her that yesterday she'd been trapped in the body of this random guy, Gray. So whatever she'd said yesterday was really someone else—most likely Gray.

"That was my bad," Sammy said. "He fed me some bullshit about wanting to surprise you. Don't worry, I'll call ahead next time."

"Actually, next time, don't let him in."

"You got it," Sammy said. "I know it's none of my business, but did you two break up?"

Was that eagerness in his voice or just her own wishful thinking? "I'm not even sure we were together."

He laughed. "I know what you mean."

His easy laugh made her feel better, safer, just knowing he was here. She wished she could be more easy-going like him. "Actually, do you mind staying tonight instead of Franco?"

"You mean work a double?"

She chewed the knuckle on her thumb where the skin was raw from nibbling at it all day. She should ask Sammy to live in the guest studio instead of Andrea. She wanted him on site 24/7.

"I'll pay double."

"I'd better check with the wife," he said.

Wife. Ashley had almost forgotten she existed. What was she thinking?

"You know what?" he said. "I'll do it."

She sat on the bed. "Really?"

"Of course," he said without hesitation, like she could ask for a whole lot more, like maybe he wanted her to. In fact, she knew he did. The way he lingered around her, always smiling, his eyes searching.

"I owe you one," she said.

Hooking up with Sammy was a bad idea on so many levels. She pushed the thought from her mind, just like she was pushing away the question of how in the hell she'd ended up spending a day in someone else's body...because what could she do about it anyway? Right now, she needed to stay focused. If she could land the role tomorrow, it would be epic. She would almost certainly win an award.

"You don't owe me anything," Sammy said, and she knew that he meant it. He'd have stayed even if she didn't pay him.

After ending the call, tension clamped down on her shoulders.

She kneeled on the floor, stretched her arms into an extended puppy pose, and held it for a couple minutes.

She moved the throw pillows from the bed to the basket beside it, stacking them neatly, the corners aligned. She turned down the covers and went to the bathroom where she brushed her teeth and her hair.

Then, she turned off all the lights and climbed under her fluffy comforter.

And lay there, awake. On the nightstand, the pink glowing dials of the clock seemed stuck at twelve past eleven. She checked her phone. 11:12.

Her eyelids grew heavy with sleep. Although she wanted to be pissed the black dog was still here, it was sort of cute, and she liked the name Shera.

Her eyes popped open. Shera had slipped past Sammy. What if a person could, as well? What if someone had? What if someone was outside her house, right now?

And yesterday... What if it happened again?

She couldn't stay up for the rest of her life. But at least she could memorize a few phone numbers, starting with her own. She picked up her phone and opened her contact list. After committing her own number to memory, she memorized her dad's. Strange that he still hadn't called her back. Although it was sort of late, she tried calling him again anyway.

After several rings, she got his voicemail instead of Niles. She left a message for him to call her just in case Niles hadn't relayed her message from earlier.

As she scrolled through her contacts, she was struck by the lack of real friends in her life. Although she could count on Sammy and Don for some things, they hadn't believed her yesterday, so there was little hope they would believe her if it happened again. And forget about Raquel. Ashley had ended their relationship. Same with August, and after the creep-fest tonight, he was the last person she wanted to call. She climbed out of bed, plodded into the bathroom, and turned on the light. The medicine cabinet was jammed full of prescriptions from the shrink Raquel recommended. He'd scribbled them out before she'd even started talking, like he already knew everything she was going to say, like her feeling of isolation was due to a lack of pills.

She reached toward the Ambien, which would knock her out...but then waking up the next day always felt impossible. It left a fog in her head way worse than weed, which knocked her out just as well but also gave her amazing dreams. She left the Ambien on the shelf, took out a vape pen, and shoved in a cartridge.

She returned to bed and took a long hit. Stretched out her arms... and was floating, the bed a feathery ocean. She closed her eyes and drifted up into the sky through vast, multicolored clouds.

Wayob Versus Parker

Wayob wakes in a room of gray shapes. From a dim light outside the window, he can make out a desk, a chair covered with clothes, walls postered with pictures too dark to see. Beside him sleeps a man, a very young man who, beneath a tangle of sheets, appears to be naked. Disgusting.

What went wrong—way, way horribly wrong—with Wayob's plan? In order to escape the wrongful imprisonment Parker inflicted upon him, Wayob had to kill himself. Had to endure the agony of dying. He should have awakened in a new vessel, but instead he had been pulled back into the blackness, the torture of total nothingness, the Encanto. Helpless. How long had he been there? Days probably, not years. But too long—too long to endure. And yet he had had to. Thanks to Parker, he had suffered.

Alone in the darkness of the Encanto, a new thought had dawned on Wayob: he cannot end his own life. That priest, that fucking priest, had taken even this basic human right away from Wayob. Immortality is a curse when living is suffering, another curse Wayob must endure. Yet another unjust punishment inflicted by the wretched priest.

At least now Wayob is free. No thanks to that little girl, who shall suffer for refusing to free him. She shall learn the Encanto is no toy when Wayob kills her father, for her father is again the one who holds the Encanto. His mind is even easier than before for Wayob to reach out to, to tempt into acting on his desire to become someone better than himself. Yes, he who holds the Encanto must be in someone else's body now because Wayob is free. Wayob would rather not end his life.

But after all Wayob has suffered, does he not deserve freedom? Although Wayob's hand may do the killing, responsibility lies with the priest.

Wayob will not go back to the Encanto. Will not. Not. Not! So, he who has the Encanto *must* die.

Who is this boy-man asleep on the mattress beside Wayob? So far away from he who holds the Encanto. No end to this torture. Odious priest.

While distracted in thought, Wayob's host body, a girl-woman this time, starts putting on a pair of jeans. Habit is strong. A lower part of the mind—powerful.

Let her dress. Keep her distracted as he digs through her mind and masters it.

The first and most important question is, where is he who has the Encanto? The window looks out on a hillside of houses which descend into cheap stucco storefronts. Squeezed between the buildings, desert palms rise like pillars into the clouds snaking over the hill: Los Angeles again. Must be, for the only thing Wayob can count on is to awaken within some proximity of the one who holds the Encanto, whose location Wayob shall meditate to find.

Before leaving the house, there is *something*—a weapon. The body he now possesses, Sadie—her mind in a panic, muffled to a dull soundless scream by his own mind—she knows, and so now he knows: the gun her father keeps hidden in the back of the downstairs closet. She had found it one rainy day while her parents were out, wrapped there in an old rag, but she knows not how to use it. Nor does Wayob. But he shall. Soon, he shall.

He descends the stairs. In the closet, he finds a bag and throws in the gun.

He exits through the front door. Walks to the road. Feeling a sense of urgency, he runs down the hill.

Stops in the intersection, bewildered. Where is he? He must meditate. Find the mind of he who has the Encanto.

A car approaches, descending the steep grade. The lights blind him. The car is not braking—it is going to hit him. And for a moment, he hopes it will. If he concentrates as he dies, he will find a new vessel closer to the Encanto. The car stops. And over the headlights, Wayob can now see the driver, a wide, wide man filling up the front of the car. Parker.

Of course.

Parker had been on Wayob's mind when he committed suicide while in Rydell's body. It was Parker who had locked him there in that cell, Parker who ruined any chance Wayob had of finding peace in the darkness of the Encanto. So, Wayob had awakened near Parker.

Just like Guatemala City, when the chief of police hunted Wayob like a dog, and each time Wayob died, he would awaken in a new vessel close to the chief instead of close to he who held the Encanto. So the chief had to die.

How does this all work? How should Wayob know? That priest. That fucking priest. He had damned Wayob to eternal darkness with no explanation, thinking Wayob would never be free from the Encanto. Soon Wayob would show the long dead barbaric priest. Soon Wayob will free himself. Forever.

Wayob would be closer to the Encanto now, so much closer, if Parker had not invaded his thoughts. Wayob cannot—will not—stand for this. Parker shall not ruin what Wayob must do.

Wayob must stop Parker. Yes, Parker must pay.

Of course, Parker halts his car. He would not run down a defenseless girl. But Wayob is not defenseless. He reaches into the bag. Curls his fingers around the cold steel of the weapon.

—

As Saul slammed the car into park, the girl clutched her tote like a shield. From between long curtains of Asian hair, she stared back at him. Her expression changed from confusion to laughter, maniacal laughter, as though she found it hilarious that he nearly ran her over.

He climbed out. "Are you okay?"

She tossed her hair back over her shoulder and spread her feet as if daring him to fight her, despite that he was three hundred pounds—though hopefully less since he skipped lunch—and she was a waif in an oversized plaid flannel. Where had she come from? The houses lined along the street were all dark and closed. And it was too cold for the shirt to be unbuttoned.

"Parker," she snarled.

Saul frowned. Had he met her before? No, he hadn't. He was quite sure.

He moved toward her, extending his arm to usher her out of the street.

Her body tensed. She backed away. "Parker," she sang in a sinister tone that clawed into Saul's stomach with talons of ice and squeezed.

Impossible. It could not be...

"Parker-Parker-Parker-Parker," she said.

"Who are you?"

"You know who I am. Par-ker?"

He lunged and tried to grab her by the wrist, but she snatched her hand away.

"I'm a victim, like you, Parker."

She enunciated words the same way Wayob did. The impossibility angered Saul more than the threat. "I'm no victim."

"Not yet," she said.

"You don't know me."

"I'm sorry, Parker, to have to do this. I prefer to take revenge in equal measure. But you keep getting in my way, you see?"

The leather tote fell to the ground, revealing the pistol in her hand. A Smith and Wesson 45. A 1911, probably. Held loose in slender fingers, as if the weapon were a toy.

As she raised the gun, aiming at him, he stepped forward, grabbing for it. She jerked the barrel up toward his face. But too late—he gripped her arm below the wrist and, before she could pull the trigger, he twisted, aiming the barrel up and away from himself.

She was stronger than she should have been. Leveraging his momentum, she continued twisting her arm up, around, and down. He did not suspect she would turn the gun on herself, and by the time he realized what was happening, it was too late.

She laughed and pulled the trigger. The bullet entered her mouth, spraying blood and brain and bone behind her on the street.

Her body dropped. Leaving Saul holding her by one arm, like a limp doll of a girl he'd dragged into the street. The gun fell from her hand.

That final laugh had been a mask, he thought, and not enough to hide her fear—her pain. In that moment as she pulled the trigger, she'd clenched, a brief but intense hesitation before giving in. She hadn't wanted to die. She had done it, but it was not so easy for her as Wayob seemingly wanted Saul to believe.

Saul was sure Wayob was responsible—had never been more sure of anything in his life. Whatever sick form of hypnosis he was using could not be permitted to continue. Not on Saul's watch. Saul would find Wayob and Wayob would answer for forcing this innocent girl to turn the gun on herself—

He laid her body on the damp road.

No witnesses. He hated himself for thinking that, for considering that if he wanted to catch Wayob, his best option was to abandon this dead girl, leave her alone in the road, and avoid getting caught up in the inevitable investigation by Internal Affairs, who inevitably would put him on suspension.

But he couldn't leave her here. Not like this. Not with blood pooled around her head. Soaking her blouse, congealing in her hair. He had to shut her eyes at least, move her out of the street. But any evidence he left would cost him his badge, maybe worse. No, he had to call it in.

He called dispatch and ordered the parade: fire truck, ambulance, squad car—the minimum for a suicide. Neglected to mention his involvement.

He leaned into his car, turned on the strobes in his grill, and retrieved his coat. He wanted to lay it over her. *Screw the crime scene.* He would have, if he thought it would bring her any form of peace. Instead, he stood there holding his coat like a reluctant toreador, prepared to obscure her from any passersby.

The siren of the first responding officer approached from the south. As the patrol car sped through a red light and up the hill, blue lights spun across the night.

When it pulled up, the uniform cut the siren and leaped from the car. He was clean shaven with red cheeks, probably fresh out of the academy.

Saul marched toward him. "What's with the siren? This is code two."

"You've got shots fired and a body," said the uniform, J. Scott according to his name tag. "That's a code three. Figured you might need help."

"Get the scene cordoned off," Saul said. "And we'll need more uniforms."

Scott stared at the girl's body. She lay on her arm, her head at an unnatural angle.

"You get that?" Saul asked. "You woke the neighborhood. We need a perimeter."

Scott's gaze leaped to the blood on Saul's shirt. "What about the shooter?"

At this point, it was in Saul's best interest to say as little as possible. He grimaced. "She shot herself."

Yet it was not a suicide. This was a murder scene.

"Let me speak with my lieutenant before you report anything, okay? I'm thinking we'll handle the investigation."

When the ambo arrived, Saul moved his car down to the intersection. He ushered the firetruck to park diagonally, blocking access to the scene.

Levy didn't answer his call, so he left her a message explaining that although it would look like a suicide, the girl's death was a murder. However, afraid she might not buy that he'd just happened upon her at that moment, he didn't mention the connection to Wayob. He decided to save that for later.

He hiked back up to where the girl lay sprawled in the road, donned a pair of latex gloves, and checked her bag for ID. It was empty.

More uniforms arrived. As Saul returned to his car to call Hernandez, an unmarked cruiser backed up to his front bumper—Arcos and Carter from IA. They pinned him in, as if he needed their permission to leave. Technically, he probably did.

Saul would take anyone over Arcos and Carter. They seemed to have a fetish for blockading true detective work by pulling good officers out of action. They had arrived in record time, as if they had been circling, like vultures starved for fresh kill.

Although it was standard procedure for IA to investigate an officer involved shooting, he wondered who had called them: Scott or Levy?

He approached the passenger side of their car, where Carter sat looking down at his phone. He knocked on the window, smiled, and waved.

They leaped out in unison. Arcos's cranium was freshly shaved to match Carter's. Carter, the trendsetter as well as the alpha of the duo, had a mustache like a chunk of dark, wiry carpet. It twitched on his lip when he spoke. "We'll be needing your badge and your gun."

"If I'm suspended," Saul said, "that means you completed all paperwork and got it signed off without even bothering to learn the details. Good police work."

"It's just a matter of time."

"I'll take all the time I can get."

"Things will go a lot smoother for you if you play like we're on the same team."

"I'm on the team trying to stop a murderer," Saul said. "Don't know about you guys."

"Who's the girl?" Arcos asked.

Saul wondered if Arcos couldn't grow a mustache or if Carter had ordered him not to. He explained his theory that the girl, who was unidentified, may have been under hypnoses when she attempted to shoot him before committing suicide. He did not mention Wayob.

"Sounds like a load of bullshit," Carter said.

"Big steaming stinking pile," Arcos agreed.

Saul couldn't disagree, but they hadn't been there. They hadn't seen the conflicted look of fear on her face, the way she'd forced herself to laugh as she pulled the trigger.

"I'll start knocking on doors," Saul said. "She must have lived close by."

"You'll do no such thing," Carter said. "You're on the bench. This is our investigation."

An investigation they would surely botch by focusing on Saul and dismissing all other more relevant details. "I was there when she died. I should be the one to tell her family."

"Do we have to wake up command staff to get this into your fat head?"

Saul stomach constricted. The last thing he needed was the wrath of some commander pulled out of bed. The best he could do for now was to go. So he climbed into his plain wrap, ignoring their orders to the contrary, and sparked the ignition.

Arcos reached for his sidearm, and panic straightened Saul's spine. If he drew the Glock 22 in his shoulder holster, he might have to shoot it. But if Arcos drew on him first, then maybe Saul could have them both removed from the case. Drawing on a fellow officer came with consequences.

Carter grabbed Arcos's arm, and Arcos froze, his hand on the holster. He looked at Carter. With a shake of Carter's head, Arcos, the bulldog, was held at bay. Saul hoped to avoid ever encountering Arcos alone.

He hit reverse and worked his car out by backing up and pulling forward in short bursts until he was finally clear. Arcos and Carter just stood on the sidewalk, arms crossed, shaking their heads like synchronized puppets.

Go ahead, Saul thought as he drove away. *Report me for leaving the crime scene.*

Suspended

Later that night, in the Owl Bar at the Castle, Saul stirred a dry salad in the dim orange light. Behind him, the vacant grand piano played Chopin's Prelude in E Minor. A clever illusion. According to Castle legend it was the talented but invisible ghost of Irma playing the piano, and she appreciated real tips. The descending notes hit a chord in Saul's heart and pulled him down.

Pete, the bartender, was an average guy. Not tall or short. Not fat or thin. His nose was normal. His hair average brown. He was average in every way, with one exception: a continuous strip of hair ran across his brow, no discernible separation between left and right. Anyone else, especially in LA, would have shaved in a part above the nose, but not Pete. Saul suspected it was more irony than laziness that inspired Pete's unibrow, which he raised at Saul as he held up the bottle of blue cheese dressing.

Saul shrugged, like he might not smother his salad. Might not open the bottle at all.

Pete slid the bottle across the bar. Saul decided to live a little. After all he'd been through, he deserved more than just salad. Plus, he needed fuel to take down Wayob.

Saul loaded his fork with cheese. From above the bar, the stuffed owl seemed to glower. He added a piece of lettuce.

When Saul had called Scott to check on the scene, he'd learned the girl's name was Sadie Wu. She must have been sent by Wayob, but how? How could she possibly have known he'd be driving down that road at that time?

And then, after failing to kill him, why turn the gun on herself?

Wayob was growing more deadly by the day. Saul had to find him.

Pete planted a foot-high stalk of mint in a glass of ice and gin. Placed the glass on a napkin, and delivered it to the guy in a black suit at the end of the bar. He had a receding horseshoe of hair. He sipped his drink and summoned a flame from his hand.

Pete returned to Saul. "You performing tonight?"

Saul hadn't performed in over a year, but he appreciated Pete's persistence. "Someday, Pete. Someday."

"You're going to let me in on the Table of Death, right?"

"Next time I'm up."

"Just don't let me miss it." Pete, like Saul, liked to be in the know.

"I think I'll have those fries after all," Saul said. "A double order. And a slice of apple pie."

After the fries arrived, Saul covered them with salt and ketchup, and shoveled one after another into his mouth. As he glanced up the owl, he caught his reflection in the mirror. And was disgusted by what he saw. Then embarrassed. Here he was—cheeks so stuffed he could hardly chew—and Hernandez slid onto the stool beside him. Her raven hair, with the shock of white bangs combed back, flowed over her black leather jacket, the hair that in his dreams fanned out around her on the pillow as they made love, with him thin enough to lie on top and look into her eyes.

She sat erect, faced ahead, and said nothing. The silence was her way of pointing out that he'd screwed up again.

Yet, she was sitting so close they were practically touching, and she'd appeared so suddenly, so unexpectedly, like an illusion come to life. Saul felt hopeful, young, alive.

He swallowed.

The fries caught in his throat.

He reached for the water. Gulped it down. Turned toward her, her beauty, her intelligence. "Up late?" he asked. *Dumb question.*

Although she seemed determined not to look at him, the corners of her mouth seemed to soften. "Thanks to you."

If only he could tell her how much it meant to him having her here at the Castle. If only he could say all the things he'd rehearsed a thousand times in his mind. There was so much to tell her. But this was not the time, clearly.

"Let's grab a table," he said. The two-topper by Irma was open.

Hernandez squeezed his arm, the thick layer of fat above his elbow.

"I just came to make sure you're okay."

He sank into the stool. She patted his shoulder as if consoling a child, transforming the scene from a fantasy into a nightmare. She pitied him—and there was no path from pity to love.

His appetite had evaporated, yet he still yearned for the apple pie. He glanced at the ketchup. Fought his compulsion to cram all the fries in his mouth, to shred what little respect he had left.

Once he took down Wayob, maybe then she'd respect him. Hard to feel sorry for someone you respect.

"Thanks for coming," he said.

"Wish it was under better circumstances."

"What did they tell you?"

"A girl shot herself. IA is investigating your involvement."

"Sadie," Saul said. "Her name was Sadie Wu, and she was murdered."

Hernandez's eyes widened. "How?"

"I'm trying to figure that out." He told her how, after he prevented Sadie from shooting him, she turned the gun on herself.

"So, wait," Hernandez said, "how is that a murder?"

Parker-Parker-Parker.

Saul shoved the fries aside and squared Hernandez in the eye. "It was Wayob. He's hypnotizing them somehow. That's why Saroyan and Aleman can't remember. Probably why Rydell offed himself as well."

Hernandez blinked rapidly. "Hypnotizing someone to commit suicide? And murder? Is that even possible?"

Saul shrugged. "Susan Atkins claimed it was Charles Manson's 'hypnotic spell' that had compelled her to commit murder." *Not that it held up in court.*

Hernandez studied her hands. "I'm worried about you."

She didn't get it. If she could have heard the way Sadie was speaking, if she'd seen the fear behind the laughter as she was forced to eat the gun. "If you had been there—"

"Parker," Hernandez said harshly. Then started over, her voice thick with tenderness, like speaking to a child. "Saul, take it easy, okay? I'm just worried you're reading something into this that wasn't there. I know how obsessed you get."

This was the first time she'd ever used his first name. He'd always imagined that using first names would bring them closer together, but she'd said it in a way that actually increased the distance between them. He stared at the fries. More than anything, he wanted to stuff his face with fries and pie like the fatty he was.

She continued, "I believe you. It's just...it's a lot to take in right now."

"She knew me," he said. "She knew my name."

Hernandez smoothed back her shock of white, which hadn't fallen out of place. "This keeps getting crazier. Do you think she knew you'd be there?"

Saul inhaled deeply. Avoided staring at his food. "She couldn't have. To be honest, I was a little lost."

"Crazier and crazier," she said. "They must be tracking your phone."

It was possible. But how could *they* have predicted his route? Had they sent someone to intercept him at all possible routes? And why? This was more than a conspiracy.

If only Hernandez had seen Sadie's face. "She was hypnotized."

Hernandez raised her brows. *"It is a capital mistake to theorize before one has data."*

"Sherlock Holmes?"

"Arthur Conan Doyle, technically, but yeah."

"You're right," he said. "We need to know more. No assumptions."

"What did you tell Arcos and Carter?"

"Nothing."

"Well, they got you suspended."

"I figured."

Typically, an officer involved in a shooting went on paid administrative leave while the shooting was investigated, but Arcos and Carter had, of course, pushed for more punitive measures and succeeded because of Saul's history.

"I'm supposed to take your badge and your gun."

Saul's heart sank. So, she hadn't come here of her own accord. "Levy sent you?"

Hernandez nodded. "I nearly told her to fuck off but then I figured better me than someone else, right?"

"You can take my badge but there's no reason to believe Wayob's killing spree is over. I can't just sit on my hands." He didn't mean to sound bitter but what *did* she expect?

She winked. "Maybe I couldn't find you."

Although her wink was playful, Saul knew, she meant what she said. Stopping Wayob trumped LAPD protocol. He wanted to hug her.

Someone at the table behind them shouted at the empty bench

behind the piano, "Bewitched!" Irma jumped into the tune.

"Think Levy will buy it?" he asked.

"She has to. She's too chickenshit to do her own dirty work."

Saul laughed and nearly reached for her, despite that she might think it was inappropriate.

Then *she* hugged *him*. "Be careful, okay?" As she pulled back from the embrace, her hands remained on his upper arms. She looked him in the eye. "You have to be careful. If something else goes wrong..." She didn't have to say it—one more misstep and his badge was gone for good.

"Don't worry," he said.

Her eyes darted around the dining area. Was she concerned someone had seen her hug him? *What happens in the Castle stays in the Castle.* But if he said that out loud, it would be like admitting he thought she was embarrassed, which would garner pity.

"So, you came here to find me and tell me you're going to say you couldn't find me. I'm touched."

"That's not the only reason."

Saul's heart fluttered. She wouldn't come here at midnight out of pity. He studied her face.

A slight smile traced the corner of her mouth. "Wayob's not a common name," she said. "I'd never even heard it before."

His heart fell into the acid of his stomach, and he looked away. In the dining area, the guy with the horseshoe hairline was performing rope tricks, the Impossible Knot, for a couple drinking cocktails.

"I checked NCIC," he said. "If Wayob's a real name, he doesn't have a record."

"But he does on Facebook," Hernandez said. "I found a bartender at Versailles who says Wayob was an urban legend in Guatemala City. Twenty years ago, a string of murder-suicides were attributed to him."

A spike of energy surged through Saul's gut. "Suicides? What kind of suicides?"

"I don't know. Right now it's just a rumor, the bartender doesn't remember much because he was a kid when this all happened. This Wayob was never caught, and apparently no one even saw him in person."

"Seems like an obscure inspiration for a copycat in LA?"

"Maybe it's the same person. I'm going to make some calls to Guatemala City, see if I can find someone who was around back then."

"This could have something to do with what Mrs. Luna was hiding.

Were you able to get hold of them?"

"They're not answering my calls. I'll stop by their place tomorrow morning." Hernandez sighed and got to her feet.

"Hang out," Saul said. He nodded toward the guy with the horseshoe hairline. He had just turned a man's drink into a cup full of coins.

She pointed at Saul's chest. "Maybe some other night? I have to get up early if I'm going to drive to all the way to El Monte and question the Lunas before work."

As she left, making her way between the tables, her hips swayed against the hem of her jacket. Saul imagined those hips in his hands and sighed.

"Everything alright?" From behind the bar, Pete was leaning toward him.

"I do not know. But keep her on the guest list. Every night."

Saul reached for the pie. It was cold now and that was fine. He was only having one bite, one big bite, as much as would fit on his spoon.

He left the remaining fries along with a twenty-dollar tip for Pete and Irma.

He followed the hallway of dim chandeliers and plush carpet past the Parlor of Prestidigitation, past the homage to Die-Vernon and the signed posters of Harry Houdini. He grabbed hold of the dragon banister and heaved himself up the stairs. The stairs turned a corner, narrowed, and dead-ended into a shelf of ancient hardbacks. He twisted the candelabra on the wall. The bookcase slid open.

Outside, fog had closed in. The valet stand was unattended. Beyond it, the hill dropped into the mist, which reduced the streetlights below into white globs wavering in the grayness. The two blocks to Hollywood Boulevard seemed more like a million miles.

Saul wasn't paranoid, ordinarily, but what if *they* were tracking his phone? Going home would put his landlord Marla in danger. Besides, after all he'd been through, he deserved a peaceful night's sleep, and if she saw him, she'd rope him into whatever latest house project she'd dreamed up. Plus room service—pepperoni pizza (just a small or maybe a medium) folded like a taco and eaten in bed.

He decided to stay at the Roosevelt—good luck finding him there— and just to be safe, he parked next door at the Ace and left his phone in the car.

Ashley's Nightmare

That night, Ashley slept in fits and starts before finally drifting down far enough to dream…

She is a child again, locked in her room by Shayla, the mean nanny, who orders her to be quiet if she ever wants to get out. Then she hears Shayla moaning, the sounds coming from her dad's room down the hall. Is he home? What happened to Shayla?

Groans. It's her dad groaning loud and long. Shayla is hurting him. Ashley screams.

And keeps screaming. Her dad opens her door and hugs her to him, wipes the tears from her cheeks. "What's wrong?" He's smiling.

Unable to speak, she burrows into the folds of his flannel.

Later, Shayla serves dinner as if nothing happened, speaking all sweet to Ashley. So obviously fake, and her dad doesn't even notice. He's focused on the work papers he brought to the table.

"Guess what's for dessert," Shayla sings.

Ashley glares at her. Shayla winks.

Ashley won't stand for this. Shayla has got to go. Ashley will show her dad how bad Shayla is. He has to see. Ashley throws back her chair, but…Shayla's face has changed. She is not Shayla at all anymore… She's Ashley, her adult self.

Startled awake.

In the moonlight streaming through the window, someone leans over her in the bed… August.

The blade of his knife glints in the silvery light. He throws back his head and laughs. Hair unfurls over his shoulders—not his hair. Her hair. It's not August anymore. It is her. Her body anyway, but someone else inside it.

Like a snake striking, an arm streaks toward her. She opens her mouth to scream—but cannot. She gasps but cannot breathe. Her throat is sliced open.

She clutches her throat and leaps from the bed.

There is no blood. She must be awake now, for real. She stumbles for the bathroom, tripping over clothes on the floor.

In the bathroom, in the eerie moonlight pouring in, she checks the mirror. Gray's face looks back.

Ashley gasps. *No.* She is still dreaming. Has to be. She splashes cold water on her face.

She flips on the light…

Gray Wilson stares at her from the mirror.

No. It can't be. She shuts her eyes and squeezes them tight, rubs her hands frantically over the face that isn't hers. But it doesn't wipe away.

Now she remembers the clothes on the floor on the way to the bathroom; she never leaves her clothes on the floor. This bathroom that isn't hers at all. It's Gray's. She's back in his house. She is Gray. Again.

Claire appears in the doorway. "What's wrong?"

What's wrong? Ashley pushes past her.

In the bedroom, the nightstand is empty. There should be a phone. She wants to just curl up under the covers and close her eyes. This can't be happening. She's still in her house, in *her* bed. This is just a nightmare. All she needs to do is wake up.

It's useless. She knows what she has to do. She has to confront this thing head on.

She turns to find Claire almost right on top of her. "What are you doing?" Claire asks.

"Where's my phone?"

Claire rolls her eyes. "You lost it again?"

When Ashley tries to step around her, Claire blocks her. Ashley grabs her arms, moves her aside, and ignores her protests.

She goes to the living room and, by the silvery light coming through the sliding glass doors, she digs through the clutter on the coffee table. Amazingly, she manages to excavate Gray's iPhone.

Claire and Mindy emerge from the hallway. Mindy's wrinkled pink dress looks as though she slept in it. She holds out a drawing for Ashley with an eagerness that stirs Ashley's heart.

She squats and hugs Mindy, then stands again and pushes her way past Claire.

"What the hell?" Claire says.

Ashley locks herself in the bathroom and turns on the fan to muffle the call she's about to make. Good thing she took the time to memorize her number last night.

As it rings, she grinds her teeth and looks away from the mirror.

"Hel-lo?"

It's her voice. Her voice! But not at all the way she'd answer, if the mood actually struck her to pick up a call from an unknown number. But then again, this number might be familiar to the person who just answered.

"Gray?" she asks.

"Yes?"

"What the fuck are you doing in my body?" The anger leaps out of her. He must have been in her body on Sunday too, and he didn't even try to reach out.

"This is so weird," he says. "And, I know this is all kinds of messed up for both of us right now, but I need a favor from you before we talk about anything else. Wake Mindy and make sure she answers to her name. Ask her where we went on Friday night."

"You mean, like, you think she's not in her body either?"

"That's what I'm worried about."

"Unless she traded places with some other little girl who likes pink dresses and drawings, you don't need to worry about her right now. Where did you hide the artifact?"

"You mean the charm?"

"The stone thing with the snake on it. That's how we switch back, right?"

The line goes silent for a moment, then Gray swallows. "Did you sleep with Claire?"

Ashley inhales. She wants to pull out her hair, which would be Gray's hair—even better. "What's the big deal?" she says. "You stole my life."

"Not on purpose."

She exhales. *Is this happening randomly? Is he just as helpless as her?* In the mirror, somehow her frustration looks kinder on Gray's face than it ever would on hers. She speaks softer, sounding as nice as she can. "Please. Tell me where it is."

Silence.

Ashley looks at the phone. He's still on the line.

"I need the rest of the day," he says.

"Seriously? No." A sob wells in her throat, but she chokes it back. "I've got a screen test today. We have to change back now."

He inhales.

She has to convince him. That's all that matters now. "Look, I get it," she says. "Just tell me what you want. Just name it."

"How do I know you'll follow through?"

"I can give you the money, now. I'll tell you how to access my accounts."

"That sounds great and all, but you had sex with my wife."

"No!" If she tries to explain how this is the biggest opportunity she's ever had, she knows she'll start crying. "You can't fucking do this to me!"

Gray hangs up.

She calls back, but he doesn't answer.

Ashley tries her dad, who of course won't to answer an unknown number. His voicemail picks up.

"Dad. It's Ashley…" She falls back against the wall, slides to the floor, and now there's no stopping her tears.

He'll never believe it's her anyway. Or would he? What if he knows what the artifact does? It looks sort of like the cave painting he showed her on his phone of the one he's been searching for. The voicemail runs out of time.

She presses the pound button to re-record. "Mr. York, I'm calling on behalf of your daughter. Ashley needs your urgent help. Call me at this number, please. I've found an artifact. It's a black snake mounted on a round, white stone. It's what you've been looking for, and guess what happens when you turn it?"

"When Ashley was a little girl, she started a fire in her playhouse. I'm telling you this so you know I'm not just some random stranger. You really need to call me back. And call me, not her. Please. Ashley loves you."

She ends the recording, gets to her feet, and turns on the sink. It's Gray's stubbled face in the mirror, but the tears…the tears are her own. She washes them away.

Dad is the only one I can count on. Until he calls, she'll deal with this herself.

Sleepdriving

Saul woke up. He was behind the wheel of his plain wrap. Parked on unfamiliar street. But he'd gone to bed at the Roosevelt. How in the hell did he get here?

His legs ached, and his arm hurt. He slid back his sleeve. Scratches, four of them, gouged the skin from his wrist to his elbow. Thorns or fingernails?

He squeezed himself out of the car and looked around. The sidewalk was uneven and cracked by the roots of the olive trees that lined the street. He was on Berryman, in Mar Vista. But he had no reason to be here.

The three-story apartment building beside him triggered a dim sense of déjà vu. Above the entrance, faded cursive cutouts spelled *The Palms*. The *l* and *s* had fallen out, revealing a lighter shade of stucco outlined in dirt. The building appeared to rise into the line of sunlight along the top wall.

He rubbed his forehead and climbed back in the car. His phone was right where he had left it last night, in the glovebox. It was 7:15. If he hurried, he could make it to Silver Lake before Gray Wilson left for work.

Morning commuters had already clogged up the 10. Saul racked his brain but couldn't recall what happened the night before, aside from a vague dream perhaps of driving in darkness...fog and stoplights, and the low hum of his engine going slow.

He'd read about how Kenneth Parks drove fourteen miles in his sleep and then killed his mother-in-law. But Saul had never suffered from somnambulism. At least, not until today. Must be stress. The memory of Sadie Wu swallowing the gun mere inches from his face still haunted him.

It was almost eight thirty by the time he reached Silver Lake. As he turned onto Wilson's street, he noticed what he should have seen sooner: the unmarked Crown Vic trailing him. Behind the wheel, that unmistakable oblong head. Arcos.

Saul pulled to the curb a few houses down from Wilson's and on the opposite side of the street. Arcos parked three cars behind Saul. *Obvious.*

Saul considered ignoring him, letting him see how real detectives work. Maybe get inspired. But no, he and Carter would have Saul disciplined for continuing an investigation while on suspension, and, worse than that, they would get in his way.

So, what now? Until he could ditch Arcos, he'd have to back off on Wilson. And where was Carter? It made Saul nervous to see one and not the other, especially since Arcos was the worst of the two. At least Saul's sleepdriving to Mar Vista would give Arcos a nice little diversion to waste his time investigating.

Saul opened the glovebox, removed a bottle of NoDoz, shook out a couple pills and washed them down with the dregs of an old Mountain Dew. He unfolded himself from his plain wrap and took off his coat without looking around, as if he had no particular reason to be on this particular street. He folded his coat, tossed it in the backseat, climbed back in and started the car.

Across from Wilson's house, Streeter, who must have spied Saul from a window, emerged from his front door, impossibly gaunt. Today, in a gray suit.

Saul decided to use Streeter as a diversion for Arcos. He buzzed down the passenger window and waited.

Streeter hobbled across the lawn. As he leaned down to the window, he groaned and held his back. "Gray hasn't left yet."

"Good," Saul said, "but now we've got a problem."

Streeter's eyes widened. "What?"

"Yesterday you asked me about crazy officers, remember?"

Streeter glanced down. "I…" When he looked up, his brows twisted, all the lines on his face tightened. "I didn't mean to."

"It's okay," Saul chuckled. "It's just ironic that yesterday you warned me about the crazies, and now here today I've got one on my tail. Don't look."

Streeter looked. Then exhaled. His face relaxed. "That man is a crazy?"

"That's right. A crazy cop."

Streeter glanced around. He spoke in an almost whisper. "Do you know anyone who can help us?"

Saul shook his head. "No one we can trust. This guy is Internal Affairs. We're on our own here."

"I knew it."

Saul followed Streeter's gaze through the windshield. Wilson walked out of his driveway into the road. His brown hair tousled, his face darkened by two, maybe three, days' worth of stubble. He looked up and down the street.

Before Saul could stop him, Streeter yelled, "Gray!"

Wilson pretended not to hear it and hurried to his Camry.

Saul tapped a finger to his lips. "We can't let Arcos know I'm looking for Wilson."

Streeter glanced at Arcos again. He nodded slowly.

If Carter were here, no doubt Arcos would be out of the car confronting them.

"I have to go," Saul said. "Don't talk to anyone other than me."

Streeter scowled. "I don't talk to crazies."

"Smart. You've still got my card, right?"

Streeter nodded.

Wilson drove downhill in the opposite direction. If Saul made a U-turn, even Arcos might catch on that Saul was following Wilson, so he waved goodbye to Streeter, pulled out, and drove uphill instead.

Arcos followed. Saul made two rights and descended the hill. At the next block, he stopped at the sign. Looked left. Looked right. If Wilson was going to work, he should drive right by here, but there was no sign of him. Had he turned north? Saul would have to find him later, after he ditched Arcos.

Saul turned south, trying again to recall what had happened after he checked into the Roosevelt. He could recall ordering room service— unfortunately. He'd ordered a large sausage and pepperoni pizza, of which he'd eaten half and stashed the rest in the mini-fridge. And then he went back, slice after slice, until only two crusts remained. Which he ate. Then his memory went blank. Had he even undressed before falling asleep?

He wondered if Wayob's victims felt like this. If hypnosis was like sleepwalking. But no way had he been hypnotized. He would know, wouldn't he? Wayob would have to do that in person. What Saul needed was a solid description of Wayob. Saroyan had been useless, Aleman was worse, Rydell was dead and so was Sadie. Now it all came down to Wilson, if Wilson even knew anything about Wayob. Though probably better for him if he didn't.

And why was Saul sore? Yesterday, he'd only walked those few blocks in Hollywood, yet now it felt as though he'd hiked Mount Wilson. He should start exercising more. But exercise made him hungry and he needed to diet. How could he exercise more and eat less?

As he turned onto Sunset, he called Hernandez. He asked her to meet him at Langer's in thirty minutes. Not exactly romantic but if he suggested someplace upscale, she'd want to know why.

"Why?" she asked anyway. "What's going on?"

He could say he needed to ditch Arcos, but she'd know he could accomplish that on his own. The truth, which was so hard to say, was that he just wanted to see her. "Tell you there."

"Okay—"

"And don't park nearby."

Saul turned on Alvarado, and Arcos turned right behind him. *So obvious.* Levy must have said she had Saul's badge or Arcos would have confronted him by now.

He popped on the radio. Dione Warwick was singing *Do You Know the Way to San Jose.* He tapped the steering wheel to the beat, hummed along, and then sang.

Wayob Takes August

At the Skybar at Mondrian, August was checking Ashley's twitter feed for the fourth time when Jacob leaned over and glanced at the screen. "You got home pretty early last night. What's up?"

August had to be careful here. He needed to control the narrative, but what control did he have? At least he'd kept his cool last night when Ashley threw the roses down in her driveway. Although it had seemed like she was completely done with him at the time, she hadn't posted anything yet. And maybe that meant something. With no record of their breakup in social media, it didn't seem real. If he'd broken up with her, he sure as hell would have announced it right away. He was tempted to tweet a peremptory strike or have his entourage start some rumor about Ashley, but he had to hold back. He was broke and spending toward a cliff of insolvency and Ashley was his only hope.

He glanced around at his entourage: Jacob in his usual Dodgers cap. Sydney didn't seem to notice the glob of cheddar the color of his hair that had dripped onto his shirt. He was watching August. They were all watching him. He had taken too long to answer and now he had to say something.

Mark stroked his goatee.

August drained the Bloody Mary that he'd only ordered to maintain appearances, with no intention of actually drinking. Mark followed suit and finished his, as well. Jacob chugged the dregs of his third Bloody Mary and eyed the waitress. Sydney continued demolishing his grilled cheese.

"I broke up with Ashley," August said.

"What for?" Sydney asked the obvious question. His mouth still full.

"She wanted it to be exclusive. And you know me."

They snickered. "Oh yeah." Mark reached across and fist-bumped August.

"Open season, tonight," Jacob said. "Which clubs you want to hit?"

"I don't know about that. I mean, of course we're all going out tonight, but I still might get back with Ashley." August popped an olive in his mouth.

"She know you did her best friend?" Sydney asked.

Although August hadn't wanted to do Raquel—at least not the second time anyway—the look of envy on Sydney's face was worth it.

"And her housekeeper?" Jacob asked.

August motioned for them to lower their voices. "Guys! Not here."

"Chill man. It's cool," Jacob said. But he knew to shut up. After all, it was August's nonexistent money paying his tab.

"Yeah, well, let's not test it," August said. "People tweet everything."

"Hottie alert." Mark tilted his head toward the pair of bikinis reclining by the pool.

August straightened his shades.

The blond looked away. The brunette smiled lasciviously.

"Yeah," August said, "Ashley might just come around and see things my way. I'm good for her career."

"Oh yeah," Sydney said. "She knows what you're good for." He bulged his cheek with his tongue while pumping his fist toward his mouth.

"Another one?" The waitress's white shorts were practically right in August's face. Her muscular legs were well tanned.

The first Bloody Mary was mixing badly with his hangover from last night. He felt dizzy. "I have to be on *set*," he said.

The waitress bent over the table, further than necessary, to stack the empties on her tray.

"I'll have August's," Sydney said. "Haven't got shit to do today."

Jacob and Mark ordered another round as well.

The waitress propped her tray on her hip. "Three Bloody Marys. Anything else?"

Are the pig tails meant to suggest something about your sex life?

"Just your number," Jacob said.

She giggled, turned, and walked back to the bar slow enough for them to take notice.

"How hot is she?" Jacob said. He bumped fists with Mark.

August stood. "Back in a few."

"Where are you going?" Sydney asked.

"Got to take a deuce," he lied.

He made his way past the bar and the pool which looked out across Beverly Hills toward downtown, a low haze making it seem further away than it was.

He considered a room and a nap, but how long before one of the guys came looking for him?

In the bathroom, the handicap stall looked reasonably clean. He sat, leaned his head against the wall, and closed his eyes. Just a few minutes of quiet. To recharge.

If he wasn't fucked before Ashley broke it off, then for sure he was fucked now. Stupid to think he could have seduced her into a quick wedding, that he could tap into her fortune before his came crashing down.

He felt light-headed, disconnected from his body. Floating away. No, falling. No, pulled down toward unconsciousness. It was too late to stop it, nor did he want to. He welcomed the numbness.

When he tried to open his eyes, he could not. Something was tugging him down. Down, down, down, into his own subconscious.

—

Wayob awakens and laughs. Laughs at Parker, whose body Wayob could have remained in, but the trap Wayob laid is too good. The foul labyrinth of Parker's memories held pathetically little about the one who holds the Encanto. Parker was useless, his body so heavy it hardly moved. Wayob put it to sleep and found this new vessel, leaving Parker to suffer when he awakens, like Wayob suffered for killing someone when he had no choice—because the priest made Wayob like this. The fucking priest. And then Parker. Parker punished Wayob when Wayob had no choice.

"Saul Parker," Wayob laughs. "How does it feel? Treated like you treated me. All over for you soon. All over. Ha, ha."

"You alright in there?" a man asks from outside the stall where Wayob is sitting on a toilet.

Wayob must behave this time. He must blend in to find the Encanto. Though it is tempting to find Parker first. Watch him fall into Wayob's trap. Wayob longs to laugh in Parker's fat face, his revenge equal to the suffering Parker inflicted upon Wayob, and no more but certainly no less.

Wayob must focus on he who has the Encanto, Gray Wilson, the name Wayob gleaned from the mind of Saul Parker. Wayob must find this Gray and kill him. Perhaps he does not deserve death, but the atrocious priest left Wayob no other option, and Wayob has suffered so much that surely his freedom is worth more than the life of any one man. And Gray's little girl, the one who heard Wayob's whisper from within the Encanto and yet still refused to free him, she must be punished. She shall play a role in the death of her father. For it is her fault that her father must die.

Wayob fumbles with the latch of the stall door until it finally opens. At the sink, a man with dark skin and a red dot between his brows slicks his hair in the mirror.

"Fine sir," Wayob says. "Where are we at the moment?"

The man claps. "I had no idea that you were August Grant. Was that a new character you're rehearsing in there?"

Wayob has no idea what this man is talking about. (Why must awakening in a new vessel always be so confusing?) No matter. Wayob stands before the mirror, his reflection a young man with a round face and strong chin. He turns toward the door.

"Wait," the man says. "Can I get a selfie?"

The man extends his arm, his phone in his hand. A *selfie*? Why not? Why the hell not? Wayob stands beside the man and smiles.

The man's other arm snakes around Wayob's shoulder. Wayob jumps back and shoves the man away. "How dare you touch me."

The man looks scared, as he should. "Sorry, man."

Wayob does not wish to hurt this man, or anyone at all. "This shall not ruin our day."

Wayob exits the bathroom into a large interior space with low cushioned chairs clustered in circles, which turns out to be the lobby of a hotel. A man and two women, all in matching gray suits, idly stand behind a counter. Wayob finds the exit and pushes out.

Blinding sunlight. Wayob emerges onto a balcony. Below, the sun bounces on a pool. Wayob's eyes water as he squints into the glare. Tears ooze down his cheeks. After all the darkness he's endured, the sunlight fills him with ecstasy. "So beautiful."

Wayob descends a curved stairway toward the blue, blue water of the pool, which overlooks a vast city.

"August, where are you going?" asks a male voice.

Wayob turns toward it. Three young men, basically boys, recline in bed-like chairs with white cushions. A girl, her hair in pigtails, lifts aside a red velvet rope to the area where they sit.

Wayob steps in.

"Clogged pipes, eh?" says the big blond man.

From the table, the girl lifts a tray of dishes. Clear bottles of liquor catch the light of the sun.

"The hotties by the pool are checking us out," says the one with the large nose and the hat. "Let's invite them over."

Wayob considers if he can use these boys, who must believe he is the one they see before them, the one called August. Will they help with his hunt? Will they help him kill Gray Wilson?

The girl with the tray latches the rope behind her and walks away toward a bar.

The big blond one jabs Wayob with his finger. "Where did you go, man?"

Wayob grabs the outstretched finger and bends it backward. Something snaps.

The blond oaf screams. "Fucking asshole!"

The oaf should know better than to touch Wayob.

The people in the pool grow quiet and still. At the bar, heads turn toward the oaf and his friends and Wayob. Everyone watching. Music, from speakers all around them, grows louder.

The one with the hat laughs. "Damn, Sydney."

Wayob laughs as well. Then the other one, the one with the goatee and the sideburns tapered to a wiry cruft on his chin, laughs. "Might be a bit harder to get the chicks over now."

The one called Sydney holds his hurt finger to his stomach. "He broke it."

Wayob waves his hands. "I am quite sorry. But this you brought on yourself."

"Like hell."

"Not like hell at all. Trust me."

"Stop whining, Sydney," says the one with the hat. "He didn't mean to."

"Oh, but I did," Wayob says. A test. If the other two stand behind him on this, then perhaps they are useful after all.

"What the fuck?" Sydney says. "I was joking."

"Was I laughing?" Wayob looks to the other two boys. "Do either of you find it funny?"

Their smiles drop. "What's got into you, man?" asks the one with the hat.

"Something urgent," Wayob says. "Who is ready for a quest?"

"A quest?"

"Yes, an adventure. A mission—find Gray Wilson."

"Who the fuck is that?" says the one with the hat.

The man who holds the Encanto.

"A man of no importance. A man in my way. A man who meddled in something he should have left alone."

"Are you saying you want to hurt him?"

"I do not wish to. I do not wish to hurt anyone. But if this Gray Wilson is not stopped then I shall suffer a fate worse than death. A fate I have already endured for much longer than I imagine your young minds are able to comprehend. I assume you would wish to save your fair August from this torture, am I right?"

"He's gone mental," Sydney says. "Take me to the hospital."

"Go if you must. Permission granted." Wayob turns his attention from Sydney to the other two boys. "But we shall not be deterred. Let us depart."

The one with the goatee leans forward and extends a fist. "Okay. I'm in."

Wayob is unsure how to parse the gesture. Perhaps not an act of aggression. The boy holds his hand up as if waiting for Wayob to do something, but what?

Then the one with the goatee bumps his fist against Wayob's half-closed hand. "Khhhhh," he says.

Wayob stifles his urge to recoil at the touch and instead imitates. "Khhhhhhhhhh." He wiggles his fingers. He turns to the one with the hat. "And what about you?"

"This Gray guy really crossed the line, huh?"

"Yes. Crossed the line—good way to put it. He has crossed twice now. And we shall make this his last. We shall find him today."

"I'm with you, I guess. But, dude, quit acting so weird."

"Of course," Wayob says. *Higher dedication is required.*

"So where is he?" asks the one with the hat.

Wayob could, perhaps, have retrieved more from Saul Parker's mind than just Gray's name, but Wayob could not linger, could not risk Parker learning too much, like poor Edward Saroyan. Wayob smiles, thinking again of the trap he laid.

"I just need a quiet place to mediate," Wayob says, "and then I shall find Gray Wilson."

"Since when do you meditate?" asks the one with the hat.

"Come." Wayob steps over the velvet rope. "Let us retrieve our vehicle and begin pursuit."

Wayob waits, not sure where the vehicle is, but he does not wait long. The hat and the goatee both nod at Wayob and begin walking together toward the exit.

"Seriously, guys?" Sydney calls after them.

Only Wayob glances back at the oaf. Wayob smiles. Things are looking up.

As they exit the hotel, Wayob walks between his two loyal boys. "This shall be fun," he says. "I have never had a gang. My own posse."

"What are you talking about?" says the one with the goatee. "We've only done everything together since ninth grade."

"Not like this," Wayob says. "Not. Like. This."

Gray's plan

Gray throws open the door to Ashley's office at the bottom of the turret and is relieved to see his portrait of the large man still on the easel. He finds his paint supplies in the desk, replaces the portrait with a fresh canvas, and channels his frustration into each stroke of the brush.

An image materializes before him like a wave, washing all the ways he's imagined Ashley and Claire in bed together back into a dim recess of his mind. Although it's a landscape and not a portrait of the fortune-teller he'd planned on painting, he's happy just to be painting something other than a black blotch. Last night, he started to worry, so a landscape is fine with him. It strikes him how the view he's blocked in, across Beverly Hills to downtown, differs from what's out the window. It's from a lower elevation than Ashley's perch above the city, and from somewhere more to the east, a perspective he's never quite seen before, yet the haze, the angle of the light on the buildings, matches exactly what he's seeing outside right now. Weird. Still, it feels good to paint.

The problem is what to do next. He never told Claire that this year there would be no bonus, and now, with no way to catch up on the back payments, it was only a matter of time until the bank foreclosed on the house. They should have bought somewhere more affordable than Silver Lake. But the amount of money he needs is nothing to Ashley and her father. Paying off his mortgage and credit cards would be like grains of sand from the beach to Evan and Ashley York. And she'd even offered whatever he wanted. The problem is what she might say about it. Maybe no one would believe that he'd literally held her body hostage, but people might believe that he'd blackmailed her in some way. And a thing like that, even just a rumor, could ruin him as an artist. No one would buy his work.

He sets down his brush and pulls out her phone in its hot-pink case. He scrolls through the nudes he took before she called this morning. According to Dave at work, some guy sold a snapshot of Niran Lima half-disguised in a hat and sunglasses for sixty grand, so these could easily cover his debt and bankroll his new painting career, maybe even Mindy and Tyler's college.

When he gets to the photo of her touching herself, a sour taste rises in the back of his throat. He has to delete them all. He can't sell them any more than he could accept Ashley's money. There would be no way to explain the windfall to Claire, much less to Mindy.

He selects all the photos he took, but before moving them to the trash, he hesitates... Ashley is a wild card. He assumes she won't retaliate just because he needed a few hours to make sure he could paint something other than that horrible black blotch, but, just for the sake of insurance, he logs into his email and sends the nudes to himself before deleting the evidence from her phone. Once he gets back to his own body, once he gets his bar up and running and sorts things out with Claire, he'll delete the email. No one will ever know.

A deep voice booms from the hallway. "Ms. York?"

Gray trots down the hall to the living room. Standing near the door is a man built like a truck bulging beneath a black suit and tie. He has dark skin, a big, rounded head.

"Ready to go?"

"Go where?" Gray asks.

"Your screen test. You didn't get Don's message?"

"I'm not ready."

He looks Gray up and down. There's paint on his T-shirt and jeans.

"Just throw something on. They've got wardrobe and makeup for you." He wears what looks like an expression of practiced patience, like this isn't the first time he's come to get Ashley and found she isn't ready. Must be her driver. Andrea mentioned his name—what is it? Clarence?

"I've got a headache," Gray says. "Let's reschedule."

The man's brows come together, a big show of concern. "Sorry to hear that. I've got stuff in the car. Fix you right up."

"I need to make a phone call," Gray says. The screen test means a lot to Ashley. He has to at least let her know what's happening.

The man's eyes narrow. A look of determination. "You can call from the car."

As Gray starts toward the kitchen, the man starts after him. "I need to make a private call," Gray says. "If you can't accept that, talk to the hand." Gray has no idea how Ashley talks to her people but being bossy is sort of fun.

In the kitchen, Andrea is chopping a cantaloupe on the island counter. A lock of hair falls over her eye.

"I'm going outside," he says, heading for the door. As he walks, he taps the screen to wake up the phone—and trips over a ridge in the floor. As he reaches out to catch himself, he drops the phone.

"You okay, Ms. Ashley?"

He squints at the circular door in the floor, which he'd vaguely noticed before. Below the two half-circles of glass, framed by sleek steel, wooden stairs lead down into darkness. "What's down there?"

"You're making a joke, right?" Andrea flips a switch on side of the island.

Light floods the stairway. Hundreds of wine bottles line the wall.

"Of course," Gray says. "I have a wine cellar."

Andrea scrunches her brows together.

Gray picks up the phone, hurries outside, and shuts the door behind him. The phone still works but now it won't unlock without Ashley's passcode.

He stares at the screen. Without the passcode, now he can only call 911. It rings in his hand. The name *Don* appears on the caller ID.

Gray answers.

"Ashley, darling. What's the matter?"

"I've got a headache," Gray lies.

"A headache? Ashley. I've got a headache. We've all got headaches. Please, take something and get in the car."

"It's not going to help. I just need a few hours, okay?"

"You understand this *is* Sean Penn, right? And Charlie Kaufman? Just tell me what you need. I'll have it delivered to set."

"I just need some time… I'm not feeling like myself right now."

"Feeling? Doesn't matter how you feel; you're an actress, Ashley. Pretend. Make *them* feel. And I'm not just talking about the role. You need to sell Ashley York, the whole package, the smart charismatic beautiful woman who everyone wants to be around. They can't get enough of you. Of course, you know all this, right?"

"I guess so, but—"

"But you'll feel great once Shana works her magic. All you have to do is get in the car."

"Great, it's just..." But what can he say? The real Ashley will be pissed. More pissed. Who is Don anyway? Why should *Ashley York* have to do what anyone says? "Let's do it tomorrow."

"Ashley, baby." Don's voice sails up two octaves. "Would that I could. You have no idea what I went through to set this up *for you*. You've got to be there, or they'll go with someone else. You want to be an actress, right? That's why you hired me. That's why I'm working so hard for you. If you bail on this, you know how it is, how word gets around. You won't get another shot. This is Sean Penn, Ashley. Sean fucking Penn! So, what do you say?"

Clearly, canceling this one appointment would make things much worse for Ashley, and she could ruin his chances of making it as an artist. But maybe it doesn't have to be that way. Maybe in Ashley's body, he could pull off the screen test. He's come a long way since his eighth-grade acting fiasco in *12 Angry Men*. Maybe while he's still in her body he can get an audition for himself. Her recommendation might be more valuable than actual talent. If he can get into acting, maybe he *can* support his family, without the headache of running a bar. He could make time to paint between acting gigs.

And he would like to meet Sean Penn.

"Okay," he says.

"Great." Don pants into the phone. "You really had me worried there, Ashley girl. Thank you, thank you."

"Remind me where is it again?"

"Paramount, my queen. Just put your pretty self into that luxurious car of yours and relax. Clayton knows where to go."

After ending the call, Gray returns to the house and follows Clayton out the front door. Sunlight glistens on a pink Bentley Limo. Clayton opens the back passenger door. The seats are, of course, upholstered in pink leather.

"I need to borrow your phone," Gray says.

"In the car," Clayton says.

Gray frowns. He's beginning to dislike Clayton.

Clayton stares back. He blinks. "Sorry I called Don."

Gray shrugs and slides into the backseat.

The Bentley is not a full-length limo but spacious enough to sport a bar below the divider between the back and the front. The booze nestled into the dark polished wood is mostly schnapps and vodka, plus two bottles of gin. No Scotch. Not that he needs a drink. He wants one, but he's still trying to come down from Ashley's vape. After this screen test, he'll imbibe—after he meets Sean Penn. If he drinks before switching back into his own body, will he wake up sober?

Clayton folds himself into the front seat, starts the car, and adjusts the rearview. "Me," he says, "I think you'll get this one."

Should Gray be nervous? The whole situation seems so surreal. "I still need your phone. My battery's dead."

Clayton passes his phone back, an oversized Samsung in a rubber case. Gray inhales. He should have called Ashley back hours ago.

She doesn't answer. Is she still at his house? Instead of leaving a message on his own voicemail, he texts her.

Where are you? They roped me into your project. The show must go on, right? I'll do my best. Call me.

If she looks at the phone, she'll see the text. And if Claire happens to see it, she'll assume it's from one of his coworkers, hopefully.

At the top of Ashley's drive, the gate lifts. Clayton slows as he passes the booth and nods to the Black guard with a shaved head. The guard nods back, that knowing way of nodding, like some unspoken understanding between the two men.

Clayton accelerates smoothly down the winding road, past giant gates and hedges. As they round a curve where the road cuts into a mountain, LA sprawls below in a haze, and it hits him. What is he thinking? *I can't act.* The last time he even tried was eighth grade when he puked his lines out all over the stage.

Ashley and Andrea

Ashley enters the Whole Foods on Crescent and scans the shoppers: a man in flannel is smelling the coffee choices, a woman in yoga pants tows a little girl who insists on hopping from one tile to the next, and no one notices Ashley York, because the person they see is this random man.

The anonymity is sort of nice. No whispers, no pictures, no strangers introducing themselves. It would be hell for Raquel, who loves drawing attention to herself. Ashley had thought it was fun too, when they were younger, but now she's over it.

Andrea shops here on Tuesday mornings, regardless of how little Ashley needs her to buy, and sure enough Ashley had spotted her tango-red Audi in the lot below the store. The question is, will she listen? Will she believe that it's really Ashley in the body of this strange man? At least it's hard to hang up on someone's face.

In the aisle of health-food bars, Andrea's waif-thin figure is unmistakable, even from behind. Andrea removes an almond-chocolate bar from a box near the floor, but instead of the basket hooked over her arm, she slips it into her pocket. She looks around. When she notices Ashley, she smiles and shrugs. Then turns her back and walks away.

Ashley hurries after her. "Andrea," she says softly.

Andrea whirls around, gripping her basket with both hands like it's a shield. "I don't know you."

Down the aisle, a blonde with blue bangs glances up from the box of cereal she's studying.

"It's okay." Ashley offers her palms. Just blurting out that she was Ashley wasn't going to do any good. "Ashley sent me. Can we talk? Let get coffee."

Andrea's brows crinkle up. "How do you know Ashley?"

"That's what I want to talk about." Ashley glances toward the woman with the cereal, as if being overheard was her biggest concern.

"Okay. We can go to the café."

Andrea leads. They weave between the checkout line and a table offering free samples of cashew dip, which Andrea stops to try. Ashley realizes that for the first time in her life, she doesn't have to worry about calories. She marches to the coffee bar, where a barista with a large mole on her chin greets her, and orders a double large caramel macchiato, all for herself, and a café au lait for Andrea.

After the barista completes the coffees, Ashley pops the lid off her macchiato and savors the sweet, foamed milk, the three hundred and fifty calories that don't matter at all.

She finds Andrea at a small table, gazing out the window at the traffic on Wilshire. She pulls up a chair and launches into the speech she'd prepared. "What I'm going to tell you is unbelievable. I wouldn't believe it if it hadn't happened to me. I need you to hear me out."

"I don't even know who you are," Andrea says.

"We'll get to that. I know you've been working for Ashley York for almost a year. You came to LA from Spain on a student visa."

Andrea glances at the exit.

"I'm not a stalker or anything," Ashley says. "I just need you to listen. I know you met Ashley at a silly Samsung commercial while you were a waitress at Providence, working double shifts. But then Ashley hired you in order to give you more time for auditions. I know how she likes her clothes sorted by color and her magazines ordered by date. And last night, she invited you to live in her guest studio."

"She told you all this?" Andrea says.

Ashley shakes her head. "No, she didn't tell me. This is the part that's hard to believe but I swear to you is absolutely true: I am Ashley."

Andrea's dark eyes widen then narrow. Her brows plummet. Her head swivels slowly from side-to-side.

Ashley continues. "I'm trapped in this man's body, and he's in my body right now. If you saw Ashley York, he wouldn't know any of this information, if you asked."

Andrea studies her. The corner of her mouth twists upward. "If you're Ashley, then I guess you'll know what she—or you, or whoever—has hidden in the bottom drawer of her nightstand?"

Ashley inhales sharply. "You snooped through my stuff?"

Andrea shrugs. "I wasn't sure where to put the socks at first."

Ashley thinks of the stolen almond bar in Andrea's pocket. *You lie.* She takes a quick look around. At the table behind Andrea, a silver-haired man seems engrossed in his sushi and a hardback by Michael Connelly.

Ashley leans forward. "A vibrator. A big black one."

Andrea laughs. Then, a laughter wells up inside Ashley too, and the stress that has been building suddenly becomes too heavy to hold on to. They laugh together. And the laughter lifts Ashley up and away, as if this whole situation, somehow, is happening outside of herself.

Then, Andrea abruptly stops laughing and tilts her head. "What did you want in your smoothie yesterday?"

"Kale and carrots," Ashley says without hesitation.

"What about your magazines?"

"The issues of Vanity Fair on the coffee table in the parlor? I like them fanned out in chronological order with the most recent one on top."

Andrea's eyes widen. "But…how can this be possible?"

"I have no idea."

"I guess some things make more sense now," Andrea says. "This morning, you were—"

"He," Ashley says. "Gray. The man in my body is named Gray."

"Right. *He* was giving me the googly eyes."

"Probably would have made his wet dream if you'd come on to him."

Andrea snorts. "*He* found your weed."

"That's better than finding what's in the bottom drawer." She wants to laugh about the dildo again, but it isn't funny anymore. She tilts the paper cup back and shakes the dregs of her macchiato into her mouth. If not for Andrea watching, she'd lick the foam from the inside of the cup.

She stands. "Come on. I need you to get me past my own security."

Andrea glances out the window. Cars are collecting at the intersection. "What do you think would happen…"

"What?"

Andrea rises. "If this got out in the press?"

"No one would believe it."

She looks sort of disappointed. "Guess not."

Ashley collapses the cup in her hand as she skirts around the register to the exit. The automatic doors swoosh open. The underground garage is lit with harsh fluorescent tubes.

"Did you tell August?" Andrea asks from behind her. The sound of her heels on the concrete echoes off the walls.

Ashley tosses her cup in the trash bin by the carts and turns to face her. "What for? We broke up."

"You did? When?"

Ashley glances at Andrea. "Yesterday."

Andrea tilts her head, almost smiles. "For good?"

"Definitely. I'll follow you back to my place, okay?"

They pass Andrea's car, but she keeps walking. "So, what if…?"

Ashley stops. "What?"

Andrea looks around. She speaks softly. "You're totally done with August, right?"

Ashley nods. "He's a jerk." She squeezes herself sideways between a pair of SUVs. Gray's car is in the opposite row.

Andrea follows. "Did you know he came on to me?"

When Ashley glances back, Andrea's face reddens slightly under her dark complexion.

Now it all makes sense. Last week, when Ashley came home and August was there with that sheepish-stupid grin on his face... And why, after that, he only came over when Andrea wasn't around.

"Did you hook up?"

"No, but..."

"But you want to?"

Andrea nods and turns redder.

Ashley fumbles around for Gray's keys and unlocks the door. "Go ahead if you want. It's your funeral."

Andrea's reflection smiles in the window. Ashley opens the door and climbs into the car.

"You're awesome," Andrea says. "Thanks."

Ashley didn't feel awesome but what could she do? It was a free country. And she didn't want to jeopardize the connection she had made with Andrea. "Let's go. Just make sure Sammy lets me through."

"Okay. What are you going to do?"

"I'm going to get my body back."

Ashley shuts the door. She grabs Gray's phone from the cup holder, glances at the screen. There's a text from an unknown number, but it's obviously from Gray. He's planning to attempt the screen test as if he's her. "The show must go on?" *Bullshit.* A bad impression is worse than no impression at all. People never forget a bad performance. She calls the number...

No answer. She throws the phone down on the seat beside her, reverses out of the parking spot and steers around to Andrea.

"He's at my screen test," she shouts.

Andrea leans down and looks in through the window. "Yeah. He's pretending to be you."

"Not if I get there in time. Call Clayton and tell him there's an emergency. They have to wait for me at the gate. Tell him I'm Ashley's cousin."

"Is that going to work? Even if Clayton believes me, Gray will just say you don't have a cousin."

"He'll play along if he knows what's good for him. I'm heading over there. They've got a ten minute head start, but since I'm already out of the hills, I might be able to beat them. I'll text you Gray's number so you'll know to answer if I call."

Ashley speeds up the ramp toward the daylight, a pure white rectangle growing wider. Where the ramp meets the road, her tires squeal as she turns. Even if she gets her body back, she won't have time to rehearse. But that's fine. She rehearsed the hell out of yesterday.

She tries the number again that Gray texted from. Still no answer. Traffic slows to a standstill. A complete clog. She must wait. Wait an inordinate amount for each driver to slowly accelerate toward the intersection ahead. By the time she finally reaches the light, the maroon minivan in front of her insists on stopping at the yellow. He could have made it through.

She calls her own number. It goes straight to voicemail without even

ringing.
A text comes in from Andrea.

Andrea:
Clayton knows you don't have a cousin. I said to put you on the phone with Ashley but he won't do it because "she's already in makeup."

Ashley screams. The minivan moves forward and stops again. Although the light is green, traffic is backed up to the next light which is still red.

She opens apps on Gray's phone at random. His email—a bill from Verizon, American Express, and a recent message from Gray Wilson to Gray Wilson. She opens it and sees the photos attached. Explicit photos. Of her body. All of it. She scrolls through the *Playboy*-style poses. In the last photo, her legs are spread, exposing everything.

Behind her, a car honks. Traffic is moving. She glances again at the photos. Such awful lighting. And the expressions on her face!

She floors the gas, the phone still in her hand. She jabs at the trash icon until the email is deleted and gone. Then she opens the trash, finds the deleted email and deletes it again. After half a block, the minivan, of course, stops at the next yellow. She slams the brakes and swerves into the turn lane. As she passes the van, its driver, a woman with big curly hair, actually has the nerve to honk. Ashley buzzes down the passenger window to make sure the woman sees the middle finger thrust in her direction.

As soon as she gets back to her own body, she'll sic her lawyers on Gray. This is identity theft taken to a whole new level, and she won't stand for it. Even if the photos were just for jerk-off material, it's not okay.

Traffic stands still. She honks. "Fuck, fuck, fuck!"

Her life was great—well, maybe not great yet, but it was going to be. She was going to land this role. But not now. Now Gray is going to fuck it all up.

What does he think he's doing? He can't be serious. He hasn't starved and rehearsed and exercised and endured countless hours of torturous coaching.

Here it is, the day of the most important opportunity of her career—of her life so far—and thanks to some freak anomaly of the universe, all her preparation is wasted. Lost. Sean Penn will believe Gray's shitty attempt at acting is actually her. Even if Gray has some acting experience, this is a complex role, three roles, really. A schizophrenic with multiple personalities: one who loves a man, one who loves a woman, and one who hates them both. And she had worries, even before all this happened, that the role might be beyond her capabilities as an actor. The most positive review she has ever received described her as *melodramatic*. But if there's any way to reach Gray, to switch bodies back in time, she has to try. If she gets arrested for breaking into the studio, then that's on Gray. She has to give it all she's got. Because this movie could be amazing. It might change the way people see themselves in society.

She throws Gray's phone out the window. It clatters on the asphalt, bounces, and skids into the intersection where the tire of a Prius smashes it to pieces. She smiles and drives on with a new sense of freedom. The best she's felt since awakening in Gray's body. The best she's felt in years. Since before boarding this rollercoaster of fame she thought she wanted. Now, whatever happens, it's on Gray Wilson—and Gray is going down.

Denial

Saul arrived at Langer's before Hernandez. He sat in the usual corner booth by the window, his back to the wall. Outside the window, Arcos wandered around the intersection of seventh and Alvarado, as if he thought Saul wouldn't notice him among the pedestrians.

While Saul was waiting, he went ahead and ordered a salad.

She strode into the restaurant. Her raven hair with its streak of white stood in stark contrast to her gray blazer.

"Hi," she said, lingering by his side of the table. Waiting for him to get up because, after breaking the ice last night at the Castle, now they were huggers.

There was no way for Saul to slide out of the booth without thrusting his belly out practically right into her face, but this was a chance to get closer, like he'd always dreamed of, and if he hesitated for one more second, he'd blow it.

Just as he started to slide out, the waitress arrived and blocked his exit. She set his salad on the table.

Hernandez slid into the booth across from him. She ordered the pastrami sandwich, and the way she pronounced *pastrami* made his mouth water. He stirred the dry lettuce around in his bowl.

"You're not ordering lunch?" Hernandez asked, probably aware he had an appetite the size of the ocean and the salad was no more than a sponge.

"I'm not here to eat," he said.

Hernandez nodded. Her lips tightened as if restraining a smile.

"What?" he asked. Was she laughing at him?

"So," she said, "it turns out Wayob in Guatemala was more than a legend. There were actual murders. There was an investigation."

Saul's heart pounded against his chest. "Do tell."

"Not much to tell, unfortunately, because the chief of police, who was investigating the case himself, was shot by the Guatemalan army. They claimed he was attempting to assassinate the president."

Saul was startled by the empty mug plopped down in front of Hernandez. The waitress filled it with coffee. Then, refilled his.

A police chief attempting an assassination? Of the Guatemalan president? It sounded crazy. But…it also sounded like Wayob, his Wayob. Had he hypnotized the police chief into getting himself killed?

"What was the motive?"

"Don't know. I'm still trying to find someone else who was around back then. The chief's family seems to have disappeared."

Saul's stomach roiled. He swigged down the top third of his coffee.

"Should I go down there?" he asked with no desire to actually leave LA with Wayob around. But he couldn't expect Hernandez to go, not with her son in school, and all the slack she'd had to pick up while Saul was on suspension.

"You don't speak Spanish," she said. "Let me work the phones first and get a sense of what's down there. Might be nothing."

"Good idea." He poured cream in his coffee, refilling it back to the brim.

"I drove all the way to the Lunas' at seven this morning, and they weren't home. There was a flyer on their door from some kind of payday lender, so my guess is they were gone all night."

"Same thing Saturday," Saul said. "I slept in the lot outside their apartment."

It was odd, she agreed, but all they could do was keep checking.

"So, what's going on?" she asked, meaning it was time to reveal the big reason he'd insisted on lunch.

I wanted to see you, Saul thought to himself. "Check your eight."

She glanced over her left shoulder, out the window. Across the street, Arcos held his phone to his face. Hard to miss.

She combed back her shock of white. "You should have told me they're on your ass. Now I have to take your badge."

"You think Levy admitted she doesn't have it? Arcos has been on me all morning. Why didn't he take it?"

Hernandez frowned. Saul instinctively reached into the front pocket of his pants. His badge-wallet should be there. But it wasn't.

Something had felt off all day. The missing weight against his leg.

Last night, he'd had his wallet when he checked into the Roosevelt, and then what happened? He ate pizza and fell asleep. Then, somehow, he'd awakened in Mar Vista, with no memory of driving there. The bad feeling in his stomach rose to his throat. Where was his badge?

Hernandez laughed. "You're right. Levy's a chickenshit."

"Does she know you're here?"

Hernandez sighed. "No. She dropped a fresh kill on me, which now I have to investigate sans partner."

"Who's the vic?"

"Jenna Collins, a.k.a. Starla. She was a high-end escort with a website and a handler, but her body was discovered behind the Quality Inn on La Brea."

The remnant of a nightmare flickered out of reach in the back of Saul's mind. Déjà vu. He felt sweaty. His armpits were soaked.

"I could look over the murder book." Although he had no desire to see the body, he had to know what was bugging him. "If you think it would help."

"Levy would kill me. You can't go near the PAB."

Hernandez was right. Now that the case files had been digitized, it wasn't so easy for her to show him. He couldn't access the LAPD network while on suspension, and if he was caught looking at her screen, there would be consequences for both of them.

A glass shattered beside them, dropped by a busboy clearing the table. Clapping erupted from the kitchen and spread throughout the restaurant.

"You okay?" Hernandez asked. "You look like a wreck."

Saul swallowed. "Didn't sleep well."

She nodded. Her brows conveyed understanding; she knew how he felt about Sadie. But she had no idea he'd driven to Mar Vista in his sleep, and how could he tell her without sounding unstable?

She slid her hand across the table a few inches closer to his. "Want to talk about it?"

She was reaching out—maybe not to hold hands, but this was an invitation—and more than anything, he wanted to connect. So he told her again about Sadie. How, after he prevented her from shooting him, she'd smiled as she turned the gun on herself, like she was not dying so much as outsmarting Saul.

His chest tightened. "Her smile wasn't real." *It was like a mask.* "I think she was afraid."

The waitress delivered Hernandez's lunch on an oval plate. A three-inch stack of pastrami sandwiched with buttered toast, cut diagonally, sided with a pickle and curly fries. Saul's stomach rumbled.

"Sounds awful," Hernandez said. "For you and for her."

Saul swallowed. Hard to admit just how much it had affected him. Although he'd seen death before—he'd shot six men, including Brown—Sadie was innocent. The way she'd offed herself right in front of him was awful. The power Wayob had had over her.

The waitress refilled Saul's coffee. He poured in cream. The tan and white swirled so close to the rim he had to lean down to sip it without spilling any.

"Wilson could be the next victim," he said. "When he came out to his car this morning, he looked sort of confused."

"Like he was hypnotized?" Hernandez hefted a sandwich half with both hands. She had to compress it to take a bite.

Saul snagged a coil of fries from her plate. "Hard to say. I couldn't interview him with Arcos on my tail." He chomped the fries. *Needs ketchup.* He swallowed and told her about Wilson's detour to Beverly Hills yesterday.

It was strange, Hernandez agreed, but not quite suspicious. "What if Wilson is a dead end? Rydell was crazy. No telling if he was following Wilson or not."

But if Rydell had been hypnotized, maybe he wasn't crazy at all. Either way, it didn't imply that Wilson knew anything about Wayob.

"I'm going to stop by Sadie Wu's," Saul said. "Maybe she had a suspicious new friend. Maybe her parents met Wayob and can give us a description."

Hernandez dropped her unfinished sandwich-half. "You're on suspension." She wiped her hands with her napkin. "You can't talk to them."

"I was with their daughter when she died. They might *want* to talk to me."

"Arcos and Carter will find out. Maybe you don't care about your job, but I need my partner back."

Saul's stomach clenched. Arcos and Carter were the least of his worries. "If I don't stop Wayob, who will?"

"I get it," she said. "Let me talk to Levy. I'll tell her Sadie Wu is connected to Rydell—"

"She closed the case on Rydell."

"But we've got a new body now. She can't ignore that."

"Worth a try," he said, but they both knew Levy lacked the balls to interfere now that IA had taken charge of the investigation into Sadie's death.

Saul helped himself to another handful of fries.

"Just promise me you won't go over there," Hernandez said. "Maybe I can stop by after work, undercover, as a civilian. I don't stand out as much as you."

Saul glanced down at his belly. It filled the gap between him and the table. He gulped down the mouthful of fries.

"I mean that in the best possible way," she said. "I really do."

He glanced up at her. She smiled. It looked genuine. Saul had no right to feel hurt. She was right. He *did* stand out. Way, way out. And it was up to him to change that.

But for now, he could only change the subject. "I need to borrow your car."

She blinked. "My Mustang? You're kidding, right?"

"I need to ditch Arcos," he said. "We can use my car as a decoy."

She glanced over her shoulder. Arcos had disappeared for now, but almost certainly he was still lurking around.

"If he stops you," Saul said, "you can say you're returning my plain wrap to the motor pool while I'm on suspension."

Her shoulders slumped. "I just paid it off."

"I'll treat her like a princess," he said. "Don't worry."

She slid the key off her keyring. "If I find a scratch, you'll have a lot bigger problem than Wayob on your hands."

He waved his palms in the air in mock defense. "If you want to come with me and drive, I could use the help."

"I wish I could." She leaned forward. Her brows tensed. "But I've got this other case."

Saul nodded. All victims deserved justice. Hard to put any one above any other.

Outside the window, sunlight glared off Arcos's oily head as he strode past. He peered in at them, so obvious he might as well press his face to the glass.

Hernandez waved at him. Saul grinned.

Arcos quickly glanced the other way, as if something across the street had just caught his attention.

"So, where's Tweedle Dumb?" Hernandez asked.

"I'm wondering the same thing. Seeing Arcos alone makes me

nervous."

"Maybe he's acting as a decoy for Carter."

"You think they're that smart?"

She shook her head and laughed. The skin crinkled around her eyes. "Hell no. Where does IA find these guys?"

"I might admire their conviction—if they weren't after my badge."

"When a stupid man is doing something he is ashamed of, he always declares that it is his duty."

Saul chuckled. "Who said that?"

"George Bernard Shaw." She leaned forward. "I hear they live at Carter's. Arcos's apartment is just for appearances."

"Not surprised." Whether or not their relationship extended beyond work hardly seemed worth discussing. "I should go before he comes back." Saul pushed himself out of the booth. Felt around in his empty pocket. He checked his other pocket. It contained the keycard to his room at the Roosevelt. Nothing else. An arrow of panic shot through his gut. Where the heck was his wallet?

"Mind spotting me?"

"So, I do you a favor, and my reward is to buy you lunch? Something seems backward here."

"I'm buying; don't worry. I just forgot my wallet."

"Smart. Now no one can take your badge."

But he didn't feel smart. He felt off. "I owe you."

"That you do," she said with a slight smile. "And I intend to collect."

He made his way to the back of the restaurant, steered around the yellow "wet floor" cone by the restroom, and pushed out through the back exit and into the alley. To avoid Arcos, he detoured on Westlake to Wilshire, where Hernandez had parked her red Mustang.

He folded himself into the car. On the passenger seat beside him was a hardback translation of the *Tao Te Ching*. Hernandez had a lust for philosophy, a desire to expand her horizons. One of her many attributes he admired.

To make sure no one could track him, he powered down his phone. He rubbed his eyes. The coffee at Langer's had lacked a sorely needed jolt. He popped another NoDoz.

As he drove up to the light, he kept one eye on the rearview. No one behind him.

He merged onto the 101 north. Free and clear. For now.

—

Saul exited the 101 and tacked west on Hollywood Boulevard. Stopping by the Roosevelt was maybe not the smartest idea, but where else could he have left his badge? It was more valuable than his Glock. The badge was like a key to the city. When people saw it, they tended to open up.

Since his legs were still sore and he was in a hurry, he drove past the surprising amount of street parking and turned into the alley behind the Roosevelt, which contained the vehicle entrance. Ahead, the alley was cordoned off with yellow crime scene tape, behind which five or six uniforms were standing around.

Saul rolled up to the valet stand and heaved himself out from the Mustang. "What happened?"

The valet was a squat man with a block-shaped head. He glanced toward the alley and shrugged.

Saul had a bad feeling in the pit of his stomach.

He entered the back lobby and boarded the elevator along with a young couple and their stroller. The guy had a sparse, unkempt beard, like maybe he'd trimmed it once or twice in his life. He held his key card to the scanner and pressed three. Same floor as Saul.

The elevator ascended. The doors opened. Not wanting an audience for his wide load walking the narrow hall, he motioned for the couple to ahead of him.

The guy motioned to the stroller. "After you." He waited. So did his wife.

Stalemate. Saul hurried to his room.

At the door, he held his keycard to the electronic lock. No beep. The little light above the knob flashed red. He tried again.

"Excuse us," said the guy with the beard.

Saul turned and pressed against the door. The couple wheeled their stroller past. The baby inside was swaddled in a blue blanket, sound asleep. Saul examined the keycard. No room number, but he had a clear memory of the clerk printing "312" on the cardboard sleeve, which Saul must have left on the nightstand.

He blew on the card. Held it against the lock. The red light flashed.

Four doors down, the woman narrowed her eyes at Saul while her husband keyed open their door.

"Must have demagnetized," Saul said. Without his badge, the best he could offer to alleviate their suspicion was a sheepish smile.

She hurried the baby into their room.

Saul rode the elevator back down to the lobby. Maybe they had disabled the card after he missed checkout at ten? He marched to reception. "Did someone check me out?" He handed his card to a clerk, who had dark hair gelled to his scalp.

"I apologize for the inconvenience, sir." The clerk tapped Saul's card to a scanner and frowned. He typed into his computer. Frowned some more. Glanced furtively at Saul and scrolled and typed. He shook his head.

"Anything?" Saul asked. If housekeeping had turned over Saul's room, hopefully they had found his badge and handed it in.

"One moment." The clerk disappeared through a door embedded into the wood paneling behind the counter.

Saul turned and leaned his back against the counter. A half-flight of wide stairs descended to the marble floor of the lobby, which echoed every footfall of the people passing through, every whisper. Anyone could be Wayob or someone he'd hypnotized.

On one of the padded benches that flanked the lobby, a woman gazed up from her phone, looking directly at Saul. She wore a thin T-shirt over a black bra or bikini top and had wet hair. Did she recognize him? Or was it just his unusually large size?

Before Saul could react, she stood and marched to the front entrance. Pushed through the glass doors and out into the Hollywood sun.

"Officer Parker."

Saul turned. "It's detective."

The man standing by the clerk had a tense face. Same black pants and white shirt as the clerk, but no coat. He stood erect with an air of importance. "I'm Gary, the director of guest services. Please join me in my office." He motioned toward the door behind the counter.

Although the office was spacious, it looked out on a brick wall that blocked most of the light. Saul sank into the cushioned chair facing the oversized oak desk and the brick wall. A bad feeling twisted in his stomach.

Gary closed the door and hurried to the desk. He set down his phone and picked up a brown sandwich bag, which was folded closed. With his thumb and forefinger, Gary lifted it and held it away from his body. He carried it to Saul, dropped it in his lap, and returned quickly to the desk. He sat behind his computer and used his shirt sleeve to buff the spot where the bag had been.

Saul unfolded the bag and peered inside. It contained his badge-wallet. Nothing else.

"That's everything," Gary said. "Now we would greatly appreciate it if you left the premises quietly. You're no longer welcome here."

A feeling of panic expanded in Saul's chest. "What happened?"

Gary shook his head. "Nothing happened, okay?"

"Look. I didn't eat enough yesterday. My blood sugar was low. I think I might have been sleepwalking last night." Saul opened his wallet. "I'll gladly pay for any damages."

Gary looked down at his phone. "You didn't do anything."

Saul straightened. Maybe Gary had just noticed something on the screen, but to look down at that moment—it looked like he was lying.

If Saul had caused some kind of damage, they would just give him a bill. This was something worse. "So what's the problem?"

"No problem, detective. Bad things don't happen at the Roosevelt."

"I've been coming here for years." Saul heaved himself up from the chair. "You owe me an explanation. Please."

"Nothing happened. You were never here." Gary came around the desk. He kept his distance from Saul as he marched to the door where he performed a curt bow. "I've got another matter to attend to."

"Wait," Saul said.

But Gary, and the dark secret he refused to speak of, had disappeared through the door.

If Saul had done something, why hadn't he woken up? He couldn't have been hypnotized. He wasn't susceptible to hypnotic suggestion. He had failed the tests performed by stage hypnotists at the Castle. And Saul would remember if Wayob had tried to hypnotize him, wouldn't he? Could Wayob have blacked out Saul's memory? Was that even possible?

In his wake a pair of guards entered and stood against the back wall and waited for Saul to leave.

He got to his feet and faced them.

The younger guard glanced at his pal. The older, maybe thirty-five, narrowed his eyes. He wanted to fight. If he knew Saul was LAPD, he couldn't care less. Saul was tempted to indulge him, but there was nothing to learn here. The message was clear: there would be no cooperation, no questions answered.

At least he had his badge back. He whistled the Warwick tune as he strolled by the guards. They trailed close behind him all the way to the back exit.

While waiting for the valet to bring up the Mustang, Saul stepped into the alley and called Hernandez. He asked her to check the incident report for what had occurred in the alley.

"No need," she said. "That alley leads to La Brea, right? That's my scene: Jenna Collins. What are you doing there?"

Saul hesitated. He wanted to tell her but what could he say?

"I was on my way home to get my wallet. Just happened to drive by. What happened with Arcos?"

She snickered. "He pulled me over. Can you believe that? He actually pulled me over like he was making a traffic stop and asked for my paperwork. The balls on that guy."

"Yeah, brave but stupid. He still on you?"

"No, I'm back at the PAB."

As the valet pulled up from the garage, he rumbled the engine of Hernandez's Mustang. Saul covered his phone and turned away.

"Where are you now?" she asked.

"Stoplight. What about Carter?"

"I haven't seen him. When I asked Arcos, he changed the subject. It seemed to upset him."

"Strange."

Across the alley, a half-open dumpster reeked in the heat of the sun. Saul grimaced. If Carter was lurking around here somewhere, Saul would be easy to find. "I'd better go—"

"Wait, how's my baby?" Hernandez asked.

"I'll have her back by the end of the day, don't worry. She drives great."

"I'm not worried. I know you value your life."

Saul laughed.

"Just call me after you talk to Wilson, okay?"

Saul promised he would and ended the call. He tipped the valet a five. Folded himself into the Mustang and gunned it out of the alley. Away from the crime scene. Watching the rearview. No sign of Carter.

—

Before driving to Intrepid Solutions, Saul called to verify that Wilson was there. His voicemail picked up. Saul redialed and asked the receptionist for Wilson's supervisor.

The supervisor introduced himself as Brad Davies, and when Saul asked about Wilson, he laughed sarcastically. "Gray? He quit."

Saul felt a surge in his gut. "When did he give notice?"

"Give notice? You'd think, right? Common courtesy. But no, he just quit with a text message last night. His new job better be rock solid because he burned his bridge here."

This is not a coincidence. No way. "Do you have the number for his next of kin? He's not picking up on his cell."

"Hold on." Davies punched his keyboard.

Ahead of Saul, the light turned green, but the intersection was backed up from one light to the next. He was blocked.

"I've got his wife's number," Davies said, "but I can't give that it out, I'm afraid. Company policy." He sounded, perhaps, slightly remorseful.

"It's an emergency contact, right? This is an emergency."

"Not my employee. Not my responsibility."

Saul clenched the wheel. "This is a murder investigation."

"Is he involved?" Davies sounded hopeful.

"I don't know yet. It's LAPD policy not to release details of an ongoing investigation. But I'll tell you this anyway, because I'm worried. Wilson might be in danger. And he's not the only one."

"Sorry," Davies said. "Wish I could help you."

"I can get a warrant," Saul lied. "You're just slowing me down here. Don't be that guy."

"Hey, I'm just doing my job. I don't appreciate your tone of voice." Davies ended the call.

Saul punched the wheel. Wilson's resignation was starting to seem justified. Perhaps it had more to do with Davies than Wayob or anything else.

Gray

In the backseat of Ashley's pink Bentley, Gray tries to sketch the back of Clayton's head.

Instead of Clayton, the person he ends up drawing is Andrea. He starts with the profile of her oval face, then sketches a window around her head and shoulders. She's driving a car. If he'd planned on drawing her, he'd have visualized capturing her waifish beauty, the way she stood in the kitchen with the cantaloupe, the lock of hair across her eye. This time, the problem is not his hand working against him but his mind's eye. When he looks at the paper, he can only picture Andrea from the point of view of a car passing in the opposite direction, on the narrow part of Beverly Park Drive below Ashley's house. He draws the four interlocking rings of the Audi symbol. Déjà vu. He's never seen Andrea's car—he's sure—and yet he's positive it's an Audi. A red one. *Weird.*

"Here we are," Clayton says.

Gray looks up as they turn off Melrose and roll through the double arched gate of Paramount Studios. His pulse quickens. The screen test suddenly seems more real than it had before. They glide past the security booth. Beyond it, on the opposite side of a roundabout, a guard hurries to move the orange cones that block a side street leading further into the studio lot.

As they turn on the street, another guard, too scrawny for his security shirt, runs ahead, past a row of brownstones built to look like a street in New York City. Behind them, the familiar world wanes away beyond the gate.

The road narrows between large windowless buildings the color of sand, each labeled with a stage number. The guard motions for Clayton to park behind a black Lexus.

As Gray heaves the car door open, he catches a perplexed expression on Clayton's face reflected in the mirror.

Once he's out Clayton presses a button on the center console and the door shuts on its own. Now he remembers that the door had closed automatically after he got in the car. There must be some button to open it from the backseat as well.

He looks around. Bold capitals stenciled on the building declare it "STAGE 12."

"So, what am I supposed to do?"

Clayton shrugs. "Don't worry, you'll do fine."

The scrawny guard reappears in an electric golf cart. "I'll take you to wardrobe, Ms. York." His boyish cheeks blush bright red as he fails to make eye contact.

Clayton nods goodbye, leans against the driver's side door, and takes out his phone.

Gray climbs into the white cushioned seat behind the guard. The guard drives through the stage entrance, which is big enough for a four-ton truck to pass through. They pass lumber stacks and sheetrock, a living room set surrounded by cameras mounted on tracks and cranes, and people with clipboards and screenplays milling about.

Gray's heart beats hard. He has to pull this off for Ashley so she doesn't hold it against him that he's in her body. If he doesn't ruin her career, then maybe she won't ruin his.

They pull over near a queue of people waiting beside a table draped with white cloth and decked with baskets of muffins, bagels, fruit, juice bottles, and an urn of coffee.

Before Gray can disembark, a girl in a pink skirt with fake lashes hurries up the cart and beckons for him to follow her. "Shana's ready for you."

She leads Gray past long racks of clothes to a bright dressing room. Shana turns out to be a six-foot Black woman in a tube top with wavy blonde hair. She greets Gray with air kisses, one for each cheek, then ushers him into the swivel chair, where she wraps him in a blue barber cape.

"I need to practice my lines," Gray says.

"First, you need your hair done," Shana says, with a smile. When Gray doesn't smile back in the mirror, Shana adds, "You're going to blow them away, sweetie. Trust me."

As Shana brushes, spritzes and combs, she talks fast, her voice high with excitement. But Gray is too dehydrated to concentrate. He needs to drink something, preferably with caffeine, before the lightness in his dried-out brain becomes a full-on headache.

Shana whispers to her assistant, who snickers then attempts to cover it with a cough. Shana riffles through a pile of magazines on the counter below the mirror. Both seem to be watching Gray for a reaction.

Shana stops smiling. "You feeling okay?" she asks.

For the first time, Gray notices her Adam's apple. Not that it matters that she's transgender, and he feels pang of guilt that the revelation surprised him. He glances down.

"Ashley York. Such a privilege." A man with an Australian accent parades into the dressing room, his hair moussed up into spikes. Trailing behind him are a pair of waifs, one blonde and the other brunette.

"I'm Paul Davies, and I'll be your costume director today."

Shana moves aside as Paul squeezes Gray's shoulders, painfully, while issuing a fountain of compliments. He spins Gray's chair around to face the dressing room.

A lanky brunette emerges from the wardrobe holding up a clothes hanger with a ribbon of white fabric.

"I present to you your dress for today, Ms. York," Paul says with a slight bow, as if expecting a standing ovation.

"It's so beautiful." Shana clasps her hands to her neck.

Gray feels like he has drifted out into deep water. His stomach knots and rumbles, just like it did in eighth grade when he auditioned for a play—only to get close to Laura. When he came out on stage to say his line, what came out instead was half-digested macaroni, like little white worms stewed in stomach acid, all down the front of his shirt, his shoes, the floor. The audience had laughed at him as did the entire cast, especially Laura.

"Are you alright?" Shana asks.

"Guess I'm just a little nervous about the audition." More than a little. Much more.

"Ashley York is beyond an audition," Paul says. "This is a screen test."

Gray feels flushed. Sweat oozes from his armpits. His whole plan seems ridiculous now, to ace Ashley's screen test and put in a good word for himself. What was he thinking?

"Kimmy wore your dress for the lighting test." Paul reaches up to indicate the blonde waif standing behind his right shoulder, who is nearly a head taller than him. Seeming to realize he looks awkward, he withdraws his hand. "I promise you, it's a knockout."

But dress or no dress and despite Gray's disguise in the cute package of Ashley York, it's still going to be him standing up there, having no idea what he's doing—in front of Sean Penn.

But maybe if he's sick he can reschedule? And he has a feeling that if he's going to ask, he'd better ask the boss. "Where is Sean Penn?"

"Mr. Penn is on set with Zac," Paul says. "They'll be ready for you in twenty minutes, just enough time for Shana to finish your hair."

Shana nods.

"Who's Zac?" Gray asks and immediately regrets it from the way Paul's eyes widen and he exchanges a look with Shana.

"Zac Efron, sweetie," Shana says.

Paul raises both hands. "Your agent didn't tell you? That's ridiculous. You need better communication. I happen to have a friend who's an amazing agent—"

"No," Gray says. This is getting out of control. "I mean, he told me, but...before I get up there, I need to discuss character motivation." He'd heard the term "character motivation" in a movie once; it sounded important.

"You'll do fine." Paul moves behind Gray and begins kneading his shoulders again. "Look at you. I'll have my agent friend call you afterward. His name is Buckley. It doesn't hurt to talk, right? You two are going to hit it off. I just know it…"

Gray hardly hears what Paul is saying. He longs for the solitude of his garage, where he can paint without anyone watching him, where he can layer over his mistakes until his painting looks exactly like he intends. But at the screen test everyone will see all his mistakes, and how many takes will they give him? Two? Three? How can he pretend to know how to act when just the thought of public speaking makes him nauseous? Even the shitty software job he quit beats getting up on stage. Once Brad, his supervisor, decreed that they "reduce undocumented discussions," Gray hardly had to speak at all.

Shana shepherds Gray over to a folding screen, where Kimmy helps him change behind it. Because the dress leaves so much exposed, he has to strip out of his underwear and bra and squeeze into a bodysuit. In the front it forms a deep *V* of chest, exposing the sides of Ashley's breasts, and there's not much more fabric on the sides of the dress, just thin strips of fabric connecting the front to the back, exposing his hips and upper thighs. The bodysuit doesn't leave much to the imagination.

When he emerges from behind the divider, his cheeks are red in the mirror. *Ashley wouldn't blush*, he thinks. Goosebumps break out on his arms and legs. There's a chill in the air. Even the Kimmy's tank top has more fabric than his dress.

"You look a-mazing!" Shana says.

"I think we've got a winner." Paul throws an arm around Kimmy, the other around the brunette waif.

Gray crosses his arms, feeling uncomfortable.

Someone knocks lightly on the dressing-room door, a timid knock that seems distinctive given how everyone else just barges in. Shana exchanges another look with Paul and goes to check.

The scrawny guard who drove the golf cart edges in through the doorway and flattens himself against the wall as Clayton almost shoves him aside to enter.

"Some kook is claiming to be your cousin," Clayton says. "I told him to get lost, but he convinced me he's been to your house before. You look dope, by the way."

"What's his name?" Gray asks.

"Gray Wilson," the guard says. "He says it's an emergency. Sorry to bother you, but no one picked up." He points to the black office phone beside the magazines with a blinking red light. "My boss wanted to make sure he isn't legit before kicking him out or whatever."

Thank goodness, Gray thinks. Ashley got his message. Even if they can't switch back to their own bodies right away, she can at least tell him how to get off this train speeding toward a cliff.

Gray steps toward the guard. "Where is he?"

Shana grabs his arm and pulls him back. "We don't have time."

"You really have a cousin?" Clayton says, his beefy frame blocking the door.

Yep, Gray thinks, *I definitely don't like Clayton*. "He's a distant cousin. If you don't let me go talk to him this will just take a lot longer than it has to."

Clayton reluctantly moves aside.

The scrawny guard follows Gray out of the dressing room. Gray hops in the front of the golf cart, surprised to find he has more control than he thought. Clayton climbs in the back, glaring at him. The cart sinks under his weight.

As they accelerate through the soundstage, the guard casts near-constant sidelong glances at Gray's breasts. Gray pulls up on the straps, but there simply isn't enough fabric to actually cover them.

"Look out." Gray points at a stack of plywood. The guard swerves, narrowly missing it.

What would Ashley do? Gray smiles and arches his back.

Ahead, sunlight pours in through the stage door. They drive out into it and turn onto the narrow road between stages. They pass mock storefronts and a bank.

Gray twists around in his seat to face Clayton, who sits like a boulder in the back of the cart. "When we get there," Gray says, "I need to talk to him alone, okay?"

At the roundabout near the studio entrance, a tour group has gathered around a pair of young guides in studio T-shirts.

"Hold up," Clayton says. "Too many people."

The guard slows down.

"Doesn't matter," Gray says. "Just get me there."

They carry on toward security, steering a wide arc around the tour group at Clayton's insistence. The tour guides finish their spiel and lead the group in the same direction.

Parked by the security shack is Gray's car, and the person who hops out of it looks like his doppelgänger. She marches toward them, her gait less precise than his, toes twisted inwards, her face determined and desperate. There is something different about the way she pulls the corners of her mouth, too far down toward her chin. Not the way Gray would frown, but close.

A sunburned guard with a crew cut runs after her from the security shack, his shirt coming untucked. "Hey! Stop!"

The guard driving the cart slams the brakes a few yards away from Ashley.

"It's okay," Gray hears himself saying in Ashley's voice, as if from a distance or a dream. As he exits the cart, the people in the tour group train their cameras and cell phones on him, and Clayton is saying something, which Gray ignores. He's mesmerized by his own visage, inverted from what he sees in the mirror. *This is how others see me.*

"Is that what you're wearing?" Ashley says. "Seriously?"

Gray glances down at the dress as she pulls him aside.

"Ashley," Clayton shouts from close behind them.

Ashley in his body is taller than Gray in hers. She leans down and growls into his ear, "Found your photos."

He steps back, feeling exposed, as if it were his own body that had been stripped and posed in those photos, which he had no plans to use, but obviously there's no chance she's going to believe that now.

With one hand, she grabs a fistful of fabric below his right breast and pulls him closer. "You want to act? Act like this hurts a lot worse than it does. You're not going to do the screen test."

She draws back her hand, which is his hand—which looks naked without his wedding band, which he left by the bathroom sink, last night—and swings.

Her hand smacks his cheek. He feels the sting but is too stunned to move. His eyes water.

The crowd gasps and murmurs.

"Asshole!" She balls both hands into fists.

Gray steps back, gingerly rubbing his cheek where she slapped him. "I'm sorry."

Clayton grabs her arm and twists it behind her back. When she screams, it's Gray's voice, but higher pitched than he'd have screamed. "Sorry? You're sorry?"

Clayton twists her other arm back, forcing her to bend over.

"Let me go," she says, "or you will be sorry!"

The scrawny guard had jumped from the cart and is ripping the Taser from his belt, not noticing or pretending not to notice that the attacker is already subdued. He fires. "Take that, you bastard."

Her body jerks and goes limp.

Clayton lowers her to the ground. "You didn't have to do that, man."

Clayton nods toward the cameras and the phones. The guard seems to shrink two sizes smaller than he already is.

At the sight of his own body lying there on the slate pavers, Gray's throat tightens. He kneels beside Ashley and tries to hold up her head. She groans. The sunburned guard squats down with a pair of handcuffs and tries to roll her sideways to cuff her arms behind her back.

Gray shoves him away. She has every right to be angry. This is his fault.

Tears stream down Ashley's cheeks, so easily it seems. He always found it hard to cry.

Clayton comes around behind Gray and grips his shoulders firmly. "I'm sorry, Ashley girl. So who is this guy, really?"

The crowd circles in. A teenager dressed in black squeezes through a pair of fat guys in tan shorts, both with T-shirts tucked tight over their guts. All with phones, of course, pointed at him. What will Claire think?

Gray allows Clayton to lift him to his feet. How can he and Ashley switch back? He plants his legs wide to prevent Clayton from pulling him away. "I still need to talk to him," Gray says. "Is there like an office or something where we can take him?"

"No way," Clayton says. "I'm responsible for your safety."

The sunburned guard clicks the handcuffs on Ashley.

"Let's get you out of here, girl," Clayton says to Gray. "You're not thinking clearly." Then he raises his voice. "You could sue this studio into the ground." He tows Gray away by the arm, bulldozing a path through the crowd, who keeps filming despite the additional guards who have arrived and are shouting for everyone to move along.

Gray's head feels too heavy for his neck. He needs to sit. He needs to process seeing his own body outside of himself. But he can't abandon Ashley. He digs in his heels. "Get those handcuffs off him. We have to get him out of here. He's family."

Clayton puts one arm around him and uses his other hand to block Gray's face from the cameras. "I'll take care of it. But first I have to get you to a safe place." He nudges Gray forward with his massive arm that feels like an oak branch in a tailored suit.

Gray reluctantly starts walking. It will be good to get out of this crowd. With all the attention surrounding him, maybe it's better to stay away from Ashley for now. He'll call her and tell her how to use the charm. Hopefully it will set things back to normal.

"That guard overreacted," Gray says to Clayton. "I want him released before things get worse. Let me deal with him on my own."

"After we get you squared away." Clayton holds up his hand to a guard and whistles. "Bring the cart," he shouts. He motions Gray toward the double doors of the building nearby.

"No way I can do the screen test today," Gray says. "Not after all that."

Clayton chuckles low inside his chest. "I'll take care of it. Don't worry about a thing."

The doors lead to a circular lobby for a screening room. Gray sinks into a cushioned bench, his mouth too dry to swallow. Posters for various Paramount classics adorn the walls: *There Will Be Blood*, *The Virgin Suicides*, *Rear Window*.

Clayton keeps watch by the doors. "You'll feel better in the car. We'll get some ice on your cheek. It's going to be fine, by the way. Hardly red at all."

Gray pictures the bar in the back of Ashley's pink Bentley where soon he can get a drink—a real drink—and just the thought quenches the dryness in his mouth. His head feels lighter.

Wayob Gives Chase

Wayob's frustration grows into anger. They've been driving for hours, and his posse keeps jabbering. He cannot concentrate. The one called Mark, who insisted on sitting back here and crowding Wayob's personal space, points out one showy blonde after another. The one called Jacob, who drives the vehicle, stops again.

"Must you stop at every light?" Wayob asks.

"I do when she's next to us." Jacob honks and waves to the woman in the vehicle beside them: another blonde. A pale fleshy thing, insignificant compared to the beauty once held by Wayob's bride. Behind the glass of her vehicle, she smiles back, specifically at Wayob in August's body. She rubs her tongue over her lips. Disgusting, but not nearly so vile as Wayob's bride turned out to be.

Distracted again now, Wayob must concentrate. "Quiet!"

He closes his eyes, trying to ignore all the external sounds. Until, in his mind, he can make out the sound of he who has the Encanto, a feat which took Wayob hundreds of years to learn. Listening to Gray Wilson's mind in the darkness, he homes in on the direction.

"Dude." Mark interrupts Wayob's meditation again. "Are we getting close?"

Wayob slaps the empty seat in front of him. "How many times must I ask you for silence?"

"I was just asking, was all."

"*You were just asking.* You are of no use to anyone. Thanks to your incessant remarks about hotties in convertibles, we have traveled too far. We must go west now."

Mark looks out the window.

"Do you have an address?" Jacob asks. "I mean, your new meditation thing is really cool and all, but if I knew where we were going—"

"Go westward. Gray Wilson may also be traveling. I might know, if you could give me one moment of peace."

"What do you have against this Gray guy? You don't really mean to hurt him, right?"

"I have nothing against him," Wayob says. *But if I do not end his life, I shall suffer a fate worse than death.* "Now, please, I must concentrate."

"What are you talking about?" Jacob asks.

Wayob wants to scream. He wants to exit the vehicle, despite all the problems he encountered when he tried to hunt alone. At least alone, he has silence. Wayob inhales. Patience. He cannot tell these fools about the Encanto. They would want it for themselves.

"Just get me to him," Wayob says. "I will do what needs to be done." He squeezes his eyes shut. "Now be quiet. I am asking you as kindly as I can."

"We've got your back," Jacob says. "Just tell us what's going on."

"Do you understand the language of English?"

Jacob says nothing. Mark says nothing. They both seem to find something to focus on beyond the windows of the vehicle. Do they think he is joking? Wayob *must* kill Gray. Wayob does not joke. Except, as a part of his revenge, Wayob did sort of perform a joke on Saul Parker. Wayob laughs, which makes him lose his concentration. The trap he laid for Parker. "Parker," Wayob growls.

"Who's Parker?" Mark asks.

"I was merely thinking to myself. Now stay quiet."

The fucking priest died too soon for revenge, and the priest shall be the last to wrong Wayob and go unpunished. And who can blame Wayob for this? No one. Wayob only takes revenge in equal measure to the wrongs inflicted upon him.

Wayob watches the angle of sunlight change on the palm trees that pass outside the window. Jacob has yet again chosen a road that loops in the wrong direction. Now Wayob must begin his meditation all over again. He closes his eyes. Breathes in. Breathes out. Tunes out the sound of the engine. Retreats down inside himself. He tries to focus, tries to find the sound of Gray's mind. If he could find whoever is now in Gray's body, then he would have the Encanto, for Gray would have left the Encanto along with his true body. But Wayob can only hear the mind-sounds of he who holds the Encanto. It creates a marker on the holder's mind. Not that he understands at all how. Fucking priest explained nothing before banishing him to this existence.

If Wayob were to end the life of this vessel, if he were to endure the pain of dying once again, could he get closer to Gray? At least he could free himself from these vapid jabbering fools. However, this he can do without suffering through death, if he sees someone sleeping.

Wayob recalls the exhilaration when he first discovered his ability to transmigrate without dying. Back in Guatemala City, when the Policía imprisoned Wayob in a cell, Wayob left his vessel at the time and found his way through the iron bars they believed could contain Wayob and into an officer asleep at his desk outside the cell. If only Wayob could transmigrate from further away.

"Dude!" Mark says. "This who you're looking for?"

Wayob opens his eyes, ready to strangle the fool, as Mark shoves a phone device in Wayob's face. On the screen is an image of a man—the very man Wayob pursued in the vessel of Rydell—and he is attacking a young woman.

Wayob snatches the phone from Mark and pushes him back. "Personal space," Wayob says. "How many times must I tell you?"

"Damn," Mark says. "Don't take it out on me."

"What is it?" Jacob slows the vehicle and turns his head, straining to see.

"This dude just slapped the hell out of Ashley York." Mark smiles as he looks toward Jacob's reflection in the rearview mirror. When he glances back at Wayob, he seems to struggle to look serious. "It's the guy you're looking for, right? Gray Wilson? Guess your subconscious was telling you something after all. We were practically at Ashley's before you said we had to go east all of a sudden. Maybe he was with her."

"Perhaps," Wayob says. Though he was not merely *with* her; Gray must be in this Ashley woman's body, and she must be in his body. Wayob is sure of it. He practically heard it in the sound of Gray's mind. Wayob understands why she attacked him—oh, he knows—for he too has felt anger like hers but a thousand-fold stronger for the fucking priest who separated him from his body and imprisoned him inside the Encanto.

Wayob points at the screen. "Where is this?"

"Looks like the Paramount lot. Remember? When we considered that sidekick role for you in *Transformers*?"

"It is to the west of here, no? How far?"

"We'd be a lot closer," Jacob says, "if you had just said go to Paramount instead of '*go east, go west.*'"

"Go there now," Wayob says. "Go fast."

"Makes sense why you're after him now," Jacob says. "You think they've got something going on?"

"I'm not after him. Not anymore. We must find her." Wayob tilts the phone device toward Mark.

"Going to let Ashley have it, huh?" Mark says. "Guess you don't want to get with her again."

Wayob laughs. "This will be the last time we see each other." So, this vessel, August, has had relations—perhaps has even mated with—the girl whose body Gray now possesses. Perfection.

This morning, when Wayob discovered the distance between his new vessel and Gray Wilson, he fell into a state of furious despair. But now he shall have the upper hand, because in this vessel, Wayob can get close to Gray Wilson and the girl, Ashley, without suspicion. Very close indeed.

If Wayob had probed the mind of August, he could have discovered this sooner, would not have wasted so much time driving around with these vapid fools who seem in constant need of affirmation, always talking of nothing. But it is overwhelming to peer into the mind of a vessel—all the disgusting memories. Wayob had nearly lost himself under the avalanche of information in Saul Parker's mind, and nearly lost control. And by peering into a vessel's mind, Wayob exposes himself, for as he peers into the vessel, the vessel can see into Wayob. August must not learn of the Encanto, like Edward did. Foolish Edward Saroyan, who desired a body for himself with functional legs, and who wanted revenge on poor Wayob. Wayob knows all about revenge. Fucking priest. *No.* If August discovers what the Encanto can do, he will try to take it from Wayob, and then Wayob shall have to kill August, too.

"Is there no shortcut?" Wayob growls as Jacob stops at yet another intersection.

"This is a shortcut."

In the vehicle beside them, a fat girl waves. She shoves her saggy white arm out the window with her phone. Wayob jeers for the photo.

When the light turns green, Mark says, "We need to think about this. Ashley's got a shit-ton of fans. You don't want to be like the dude who slapped her."

"She's got no talent," Jacob says. "You've had girls twice as hot, and there are plenty more. Hell, they'll fuck us just for a chance at you."

"Ashley's got money, though," Mark says.

"August doesn't need money, numb-nuts. And it's Daddy's money, anyway. Not like she ever did anything. We earn ours. We'll be loaded after *Quantum-Man*."

Money. Wayob knows, from all the effort he spent whispering to Gray's subconscious, tickling Gray's desires to persuade him to use the Encanto, that Gray wants money. What he desires most of all is time for himself—time he believes can be purchased with money. And Ashley has lots of money. But Wayob knows better. Wayob knows. Eventually Gray will reflect upon his own pathetic life and succumb to a whim of nostalgia. He will dial back the Encanto. And trap Wayob once again inside the dark, dark nothing, alone.

"I don't care about her fucking fans," Wayob says. "But I do need to see her alone."

"That's what I'm sayin'," Mark says. "Let's go to her house."

"What if she does not go home? We can waste no time."

"Text her. She's your girlfriend, right?"

Wayob tosses Mark's phone back to him. "You do it. I have no patience for such communication."

"Better do it from your phone."

"Fine." Wayob finds the phone belonging to August in his pocket and tosses that one to Mark as well.

Mark fumbles it, dropping it on the floor between his feet. "Careful," he says as he retrieves it.

Jacob makes a U-turn and heads north into a neighborhood where each house is surrounded by expansive plots of green land. As they ascend a hill, each house seems larger than the one that came before it.

"She's not responding," Mark says. "But someone tweeted her pink limo leaving the studio. We can beat her home."

"Very good. Take me to the house that is Ashley's."

Once they near Ashley's, Wayob will proceed on foot. He must leave these fools. They cannot be allowed near the Encanto. If any one of them happened to hold it in such a way as to come to own it, it will transport Wayob back inside and trap him there.

As they drive up the same street where earlier they had turned eastward, silence—merciful silence—finally descends on the vehicle. They reach a gate. It opens. They follow the steep windy road up through a canyon, up a hillside of brown weeds, past rows of tended vines with autumn leaves of red. At the top of the mountain are vast palaces surrounded by fences and fields of green.

Near the summit, a row of trees with bark peeling from their trunks lines the road.

"This is it." Jacob slows as they approach a palace with its own road and a gate.

Wayob points toward trees to the right. "Let me out here. I shall go in on foot."

"We can't leave you stranded," Jacob says. "If you want privacy, we'll just hang by the pool with her hottie maid."

"The one in the Audi?" Mark says. "I could get with that."

"Yeah, Andrea."

"No!" Wayob hates contact, but he must. He must make his point. He leans forward, reaches across, slaps the back of Jacob's head. "I must go in alone, understand?"

"Whatever, dude." He adjusts his stupid hat and laughs, as if Wayob has made some joke.

Clearly, Wayob must try harder. These fools must obey. They cannot be allowed near Ashley's palace, or near Gray Wilson, or near the Encanto. Wayob has suffered too long alone in the dark nothingness to risk going back. Wayob balls his fist and, with all his might, strikes Mark in the ear. Mark's head impacts the window with a satisfying thud.

"Jesus," Jacob says.

Mark raises his arms defensively. Makes no effort to strike back. "What the fuck?"

Wayob wipes his hands on his shirt. Wayob is still the alpha. "My orders are to be obeyed. I shall go in alone."

"Whatever," Mark says. "You're the boss."

Jacob stops the vehicle by the thicket near Ashley's gate. As Wayob gets out, Mark informs him, as if Wayob cares, that they'll go pick up Sydney from the hospital. "Then we'll have some ladies over. So don't expect us to come get you."

"I wouldn't dream of it." Wayob swings the door closed.

As the fools drive off, Wayob enters the thicket. He climbs up a fence. On the other side, a vast field of green grass surrounds the palace that is Ashley's, and beyond her palace, the city of Los Angeles lies sprawled out in the sun, full of promises. Wayob deserves it all.

Who Knew Sadie Wu?

In front of Sadie's home, Saul parked the Mustang and stared at the rust-colored stain on the asphalt. A Prius drove over it. Saul scowled at the driver as she descended the hill and turned left.

By being here, Saul was breaking his promise to Hernandez, but Wilson was AWOL, and idling the investigation would be worse than breaking his promise, worse than facing the Wu family. Wayob was out there somewhere, and Saul had to find him.

The front door was lacquered black, closed tight against the bright afternoon. As he approached, he watched where he put his feet on the uneven slate walkway.

The door unlocked and opened, and Saul looked up. The man standing there was unmistakably Sadie's father. Same square chin. Same high prominent cheeks. Same wiry way of holding himself like a tree in the wind. The resemblance brought Saul back to Sadie's death, and he relived it all over again, her mask of laughter as she ate the gun.

Wu stood there, his mouth turned down, squinting against the sun and the tragedy and the waste. He was a short man, maybe shorter than Sadie, and thin. Which gave Saul an idea of what to search for, perhaps a connection to her death.

Saul clasped his hands. "Mr. Wu, I am very sorry for your loss." He introduced himself and reached to shake Wu's hand, to maybe pat him on the back or hug him, but Wu didn't lean in.

Instead, he shook his head. Inhaled a deep ragged breath. "It was you... I saw your picture." He stepped out of the house and tried to push Saul back from the doorway.

Saul dropped his arms and stood his ground.

Wu balled his hands and pounded Saul in the chest with the side of his fists. First one hand and then the other. Again and again, as he moaned one long mournful note.

Saul accepted it. Because he'd failed to save Sadie's life. Because she'd had her whole life ahead of her. He should have let her shoot him, let her live instead of him.

As Wu's rage dissolved into exhaustion, Mrs. Wu appeared in the doorway, a head taller than Mr. Wu, pale and blonde with dark bags below her eyes. Saul felt like collapsing, or like retreating to the car and driving away.

She put an arm around her husband. "Let him in, Hiromi."

He turned toward her, leaned his head into her chest, and sobbed. Saul's throat tightened. He wanted to cry too. But he had to stay calm. He had to get answers.

She ushered Mr. Wu inside and gestured for Saul to follow. She led him to the living room, where Mr. Wu withdrew and collapsed on the couch. Mrs. Wu whirled around to face Saul. Fixed him with a cold stare.

Saul inhaled. "I don't know what the other detectives may have told you—"

"They didn't tell us shit," Mrs. Wu said, her face cold. "But they sure had a lot of good questions about you. Like why would you be meeting our daughter in the middle of the night?"

"Last night was the first time I ever saw her. I thought it was a chance encounter at first."

"Is that so?" She tried to sound sarcastic, but as her pitch raised, her voice cracked. "Then why would they seem to think you had something against her?"

"I'm under investigation by Internal Affairs," Saul said. "It's a matter of protocol when there is a shooting. They have to cover all the bases. But I was there. Your daughter... Sadie, she turned the gun on herself. I was trying to stop her."

"No. She would never do anything like that. Whatever you think you saw, you're mistaken. Sadie did not kill herself. If you're here to ask more questions, like if she was unhappy at school or at home, then get out now."

"Do you mind if we sit down?" Saul tried to sound soothing.

Mrs. Wu stared at him.

"I'm here to get to the bottom of this," Saul said. "It won't bring your daughter back, I know. But she wasn't acting on her own." Saul seated himself on the recliner and waited.

On the couch across from him, Mr. Wu seemed to collect himself, nodding slowly as if coming to some kind of acceptance.

Mrs. Wu remained standing. "What does that mean? You make it sound like she committed a crime."

"Nothing like that," Saul said. "Sadie was the victim."

"You've got that right."

"I'm trying to find out what really happened. Why was she in the middle of the road with a gun?"

Mr. Wu swallowed. "Sadie was a straight-A student. She would never do anything like this. She was my little girl."

"I understand," Saul said.

Mrs. Wu stepped toward Saul and clenched her fists. "You understand? What do you understand? You don't know anything about our daughter."

Saul kept his voice calm. "Tell me about her."

"They always say the parents must be out of touch," Mr. Wu said. "But that's not us. We knew our daughter."

Each man is an island onto itself, Saul thought. Hernandez would know whoever said that. Saul shifted forward in the recliner. An eerie silence drifted in the dim light filtered through the curtains, which covered the two windows in the room, one behind Mr. Wu and the other beside him. "I believe...someone manipulated her. She may have been hypnotized."

"Who would do that?" Mrs. Wu asked.

"Did she have any new or unusual friends?"

"No," Mr. Wu said. "She spends all her time with Bethany and Isabella. They've been inseparable since middle school."

Mrs. Wu went to the window beside her husband and peeked through the curtain. An oblique bar of light divided the room.

"No boys?" Saul asked. "Or men?"

Mr. Wu shook his head. He glanced up toward his wife. She closed the curtain. "Not outside of school."

"Anything unusual happen recently? Anything out of the ordinary at all?"

"No," Mrs. Wu said without turning around. "Nothing."

Above Mr. Wu hung a thirty-inch framed photo of a steep hillside above the ocean. From the hillside, an oak tree arched toward the sky. When he noticed Saul looking, Mr. Wu turned toward it. "That's one of Sadie's photos from Big Sur," he said. "She was going to be a photographer."

Saul rubbed his hands over his face. Sadie was an innocent teenager who'd had so much to live for. "Where did she get the gun?"

Mrs. Wu turned from the window and fixed her husband with a stare. "We don't know."

Mr. Wu pressed his lips together.

Saul said nothing. He'd hoped that the gun Sadie used would trace back to Wayob, but now it was clear the gun belonged to Hiromi Wu.

"You want to see her room?" Wu stood, brows knotted, almost pleading. "Some of her best work is up there."

"Love to," Saul said. He needed to search her bedroom anyway.

As he heaved himself up from the chair, Mrs. Wu marched past. "I have to clean the kitchen." She wiped her eyes and disappeared down a hallway.

Mr. Wu led Saul to the stairway by the front door. He lunged up the steps. Saul followed, the stair planks creaking under his weight. By the time he hit the third step, Wu was already at the top. Saul's legs were incapable of moving any faster. *Exercise. Need to exercise.*

"Did the Internal Affairs detectives check upstairs?"

"Carter did."

"Carter?" Saul stopped midway up the stairs to catch his breath. It surprised him that Carter had searched beyond the forensics at the murder scene, or that he'd done anything at all without Arcos following at his heels.

"He's the one with the mustache, right?" Wu asked. "While I was out this morning, he came back to see her bedroom. Laura let him in."

In Sadie's bedroom, light poured through a window above her desk. Outside the window was the twisted limb of an oak. Below it was a flat roof where the first floor extended out beyond the second. Photos lined the walls, fog and ferns and Big Sur redwoods. Mr. and Mrs. Wu on a rocky beach. A portrait series of two girls about Sadie's age, one Anglo, the other Latina, posing on lifeguard towers. A candid shot of the same two girls and Sadie, their arms intertwined and feet buried in the sand.

"That's Bethany and Isabella," Mr. Wu said.

"Cute girls."

The bedroom got to Saul. All her photos and the corkboard of selfies with her two friends, the three of them always laughing. The pile of stuffed animals arranged in the cubby under her window. Saul knew why Wu had wanted him to see her room, this cocoon of a teenager excited about life, and about her future—as if seeing her eat the gun was not enough for Saul to put everything he had into stopping the bastard who somehow invaded her head.

He approached the bifold doors opposite the bed. "Mind if I look?"

"I guess not."

As Saul opened the closet, Wu peered in behind him. The dresses and shirts were small enough to be children's clothing, except the style was too chic. Saul found only one flannel, a baby-blue and white plaid. He pulled it out.

"Are you looking for something in particular?" Wu asked.

"Did you notice what she was wearing when you identified the body?"

Wu rubbed his face and looked down. "No."

"That's normal," Saul said. When identifying a deceased loved one, the shock could be overwhelming. A parent should never have to see their child's body. Saul returned the shirt to its hanger. "She had on a men's flannel shirt. It came down to her knees. A large tall, or maybe an extra large."

"That doesn't make sense," Wu said.

Saul nodded. "Do you or your wife have anything like that?"

"No." Wu looked down at himself. "I'm a small."

"You might want to wait downstairs," Saul said. "I need to search her room. Is everything how you found it?"

Wu planted himself in the chair at the desk. "I made her bed. That's about it."

The bed was a double, two pillows, white sheets, and a thick pink comforter. Saul went over and pulled back the covers. The sheets looked clean. He kneeled down and examined them. Three long, dark hairs clung to the pillow. Sadie's hair. And also, a gray hair—two and a half, maybe three inches long. Saul clutched it carefully between his thumb and forefinger. Held it up to the light. Wu's hair was solid black. And this gray hair seemed too thin to be Asian. Probably not Latino, either. It was the wrong color and length to be Mrs. Wu's or Bethany's or Isabella's. And certainly, it wasn't Sadie's.

"What is it?" Wu's voice climbed an octave.

"Just a hair," Saul said. "Probably nothing."

Wu inhaled through his nose. "Maybe I *should* wait downstairs," he said but remained slumped in the chair.

Saul pulled a plastic evidence bag from his coat pocket and dropped in the hair. *Could be everything.*

Ashley's Pony

Ashley awakens on the ground with a pair of studio guards standing over her and surrounded by a crowd of tourists taking photos of her agony with their phones, probably video as well. A glance at her hands reveals she's still in Gray's body.

The shrimpy guard, who looks too young to work here, helps her to her feet, while the meathead who Tasered her grumbles an apology. "Look, I know you're Ashley York's cousin and all, but this isn't the place to air your dirty laundry. We've got policies and procedures we have to follow to keep everyone safe."

At least Gray had the brains not to press charges.

She drives to a strip mall on Sunset and enters a store called *Phones* with strobes in the window and bad house music. Using Gray's card, she buys a disposable smartphone and checks her twitter feed.

The photos of the confrontation are no surprise, but the comments like, *'Ashley York gets what's coming #RichBitch,'* are disheartening. As badly as she wants her body back, sometimes she's sick of being Ashley York.

She crosses the parking lot to escape the noise of *Phones* and calls Gray.

He answers hesitantly. "Hello?"

"Is the screen test rescheduled?"

"Um," Gray swallows. "Clayton said he'd handle it."

Clayton will call Don, who will be anxious for her to get right back in the saddle. But Ashley knows the best way to delay Don is to avoid him. He'll make up an excuse for her rather than admit he's out of touch. And if anyone can persuade Sean Penn to give her another shot, it's Don.

"When Don calls, don't answer. No matter what."

"No problem," Gray says. "And for what it's worth, I wasn't planning to do anything with those pictures."

"Then why take them?"

He sighs. "I didn't think it was a big deal. Look at what's already on the web."

Ashley wants to scream. She wishes she'd *punched* him in the face, even if it was her face. She calms herself before responding. He's not worth it. "You don't know anything about me," she says. "Why did you even go to the screen test? I told you how important it was."

"Don and Clayton practically forced me into it," he says. "I thought it might help you if I went."

"You wanted to help me? Then why switch bodies in the first place?"

"Look. I'm sorry." His apology rings hollow, as if he knows it's not okay.

"I don't want your apology. I want my life back."

"I'm with you there," Gray says. "At least, I want to be me again. The charm is in the garage on my workbench, I think."

The sidewalk is almost as noisy as *Phones*. Traffic barrels up through the intersection toward the Sunset Strip. She turns back toward the lot, toward Gray's car. "Where did it come from?"

"A fortune-teller," he says. "At the Day of the Dead festival, downtown."

Holding the phone to her ear, Ashley unlocks Gray's car and sinks into the driver's seat. "So how does it work?"

"I'm not sure, exactly. She doesn't speak English, and when I accepted it, I never expected I'd wake up the next day as you."

"But you knew the second time, right?"

"No. I sort of had someone else in mind. I wasn't sure anything would happen at all."

"So why me?" Ashley says. "This whole damn thing is like a nightmare."

"Look for a round stone with a snake," Gray says. "You have to turn the snake. If nothing happens, try sleeping, and I'll go to sleep too. Oh, and don't hold the stone in your hand when you turn the snake. It stabbed the hell out of my hand."

Ashley closes her eyes. "Assuming this actually gets us back to normal, what's next?"

"I don't know…" Gray says. "I'm making some changes in my life. I need to figure some things out—"

"Uh, no. I'm talking about the charm. No offense, but I don't want to be you again."

Gray laughs. It sounds forced. "It's that bad?"

"Bad timing," she says. In truth, if not for the screen test, it might have been interesting to experience life in his body.

"I guess I'll destroy it," he says.

"Promise me."

"Promise."

She ends the call and checks Instagram. It's just as bad as twitter. Her anger mounts as she scrolls through her feed. It was bad luck that the tour group happened to be there to photograph the whole incident, the slap and Taser—but still, it was Gray's fault. He was the one who had used the charm twice. Even if she could forgive him the first time, the second time was deliberate. He doesn't get it. This is *her* life he's fucking with.

He deserves a little gift, she decides, to commemorate their time together: his own image that can never be erased. Beside *Phones* is the Sunset Tattoo Studio.

Inside, the walls of the narrow space are lipstick-red and lined with framed posters of tattoos. There's a black leather couch and a black lacquered counter, and behind the counter, a stocky woman in a wife-beater shirt, no bra, her arms tattooed from wrists to shoulders in busy black ink.

Ashley approaches. "I want a tattoo on my butt."

The woman's expression remains blank. "You have a design?"

"I think so." Ashley glances at the photos behind the woman. Most people she knows wouldn't be caught dead with a Harry Potter tattoo, but that's not embarrassing enough for Gray. "You have other examples, right?"

The woman opens an iPad and hands it to Ashley. Pictures of tattoos are organized into albums. Ashley scrolls past tribal, Japanese, realism, and dives into the kitsch album where she swipes past Bambi, cartoon cats, and a baby mermaid riding a seahorse. She pauses on a doe-eyed My Little Pony surrounded by butterflies and hearts and stars. The pony is pink with baby-blue wings and a long flowing mane of blue hair.

"This is the one," Ashley says.

The woman tilts the iPad, and the image rotates one-eighty, such that it's upside down for Ashley and right side up to the woman. She studies the image. "How big you want it?"

"How big can you make it in an hour?"

She zooms out. "I could do a three-inch version without the stuff around it in an hour and a half. But we don't have to do it all in one session, if you want bigger."

"Three inches should be big enough."

"Take some time and think about it. This is a permanent piece of body art, and you need to be sure. I'll be here when you're ready."

"I've thought about it." Ashley says more forcefully than she intended. "I know I don't look like the kind of guy who would want this tat, but I've got my reasons, trust me."

"Hey, I don't judge. I just want you to be happy is all."

She leads Ashley to a back room and begins gathering her tools from the candy-red metal cabinet. Ashley undresses and lays face down on a cot lined with white paper.

The tattoo artist spreads her tools and inks on the nearby table and pulls up a stool.

Ashley laughs. Gray deserves worse. What if Don can't delay the screen test? What if Sean Penn already has someone else he wants to cast, some other actress with more experience. She tries to force herself to feel angry instead of relieved at the thought of a missed opportunity.

As the tattoo artist begins, Ashley feels the scratching sensation on her butt cheek, which seems to spread to the back of her mind—is she taking things too far by getting this tattoo? Honestly, how much does she care about the screen test? It's not just that the role is out of her league; it's the months and months of commitment. Is a movie really worth so much time? What else could she do with her life?

Kids. She knows for sure now, from her time spent as Gray. A boy and a girl, just like Tyler and Mindy, would be amazing. It would be hard to provide a stable home environment as an actress, with all the traveling and long days and late nights. Sure, she could hire all kinds of help—that's what her dad did—but Ashley wants to raise her kids herself. And preferably not alone.

It must be hard to stay together for so long. She wonders if Claire still cares about Gray in some tangled, twisted way, because clearly she's checked out. Maybe all relationships become like that over time —like hating the person you love. Ashley has never stuck around long enough to find out. Is it even possible for two people to stay in love long enough to raise a child?

Her butt cheek starts to burn. Like the time she fell off her scooter, trying to ride it down the stairs, and scraped her knee. That was right before her mother died, when Ashley was five, when the adults in her life seemed to answer every question with the word '*cancer*,' as if cancer actually said something about who her mother was.

The memory of the hospital—its long quiet hallways and serious nurses, everyone whispering high over her head— makes Ashley shiver. She remembers how Michelle, her first nanny, shoved her into a room with the harsh smell of antiseptic and a frail, shriveled woman propped up on a bed.

"Ashley, it's so good to see you," the woman had said, trying to smile. She sounded like Ashley's mother, but her mother had hair, thick blonde hair.

Ashley had tried to squeeze back out through the door, but Michelle picked her up and carried her in. "Say hello to your mother."

She plopped Ashley on the bed by the woman, who Ashley refused to believe was her mother. The woman wrapped Ashley in her twig-like arms that snaked with all kinds of wires and tubes. They both cried. Eventually, after Ashley managed to squirm off the bed, Michelle took her home. She should have stayed at the hospital. If she ever got a do-over, she'd go back to that moment and hug her mother back.

After the funeral, after all the strangers patted her on the head and said '*cancer*' and '*sorry*' and not much else, and then her dad drove them back to their home to Bel Air. That night, Michelle moved into his room.

In the weeks following, her dad took a break from work, and they stayed out at the house in Malibu. Those few weeks were the happiest of her childhood. They *were* her childhood: playing on the beach with her dad and Michelle. On her sixth birthday, her dad gave her a golden puppy, who she named Rexi.

But a few days later, her dad returned to work and Ashley was sent off to a summer camp in Idyllwild where Rexi wasn't allowed, and where Ashley cried herself to sleep every night.

When she finally returned from camp, Michelle was gone, and Shayla was the new nanny and she made Rexi stay outside in a pen that had been built around Ashley's playhouse. It dawns on Ashley now, as the tattoo artist attacks her butt cheek, how much Raquel, with her D-cups and Brazilian blow-out, looks like Shayla, who must have been in her early twenties when she was hired. The same age as Raquel is now.

It feels like a cat dragging its claws over and over on the same patch of skin. Ashley wants it to stop, but she grits her teeth and bears it, like she did when Shayla levered herself between Ashley and her dad.

It started one of times when Dad slept at work because of some big deadline, but Shayla told Ashley it was because Ashley bothered him. So, when he came home, Ashley kept to herself. Meanwhile, Shayla threw decadent adults-only parties where she acted all bubbly and fake while she sat with him at the head of the table, touching his arm and laughing at everything he said while Ashley had to eat in the kitchen.

The fire was the breaking point. Shayla used it to force Ashley out of the house. It had been cold outside, and Ashley had only meant to warm her playhouse with just a small fire, but the little curtains caught fire, and they made so much smoke that she couldn't see the flames well enough to stop them. The smoke burned in her lungs and her eyes. She and Rexi almost choked to death before they escaped. The fire department came with hoses and put out the fire, which by then had turned her playhouse and the nearby hedge into ashes.

That night, Ashley listened at her dad's door while Shayla—who had moved into his room by that point—went on and on in her shrill voice about how Ashley was too much to handle, a delinquent who deserved to be committed for her own safety, and for theirs. Ashley wanted to apologize to her dad for the fire, but Shayla was always hovering around, always talking over Ashley when she tried to say something.

The next week, Ashley got packed off to the Oakhurst Academy for troubled girls in Santa Barbara. She went without a fight because she thought it would be the end of Shayla, who was hired to be Ashley's nanny. Instead, somehow, Shayla persuaded her dad to get married again.

They let her out of school for the wedding, which was held on a private island in the Caribbean, but by then it was too late. There was no way to stop him from walking down the aisle.

The marriage ended after a few months, followed by an intense year of legal battles during which her dad became more distant than ever. He let her move home, at least, but Shayla had gotten rid of Rexi by then and the house was empty without him.

After the divorce was finalized, her dad gradually came out of the fog. He became more attentive to her. And she forgave him for the neglect, because although he dated occasionally, the women never moved in, and he'd never even brought one home. If Ashley's plans for the two of them ever collided with a date, he'd quietly cancel on whatever woman he was seeing. As he often said, Ashley was the most important girl in his life. Even when he'd thrown himself deep into his work, if Ashley called him, he always made time for her.

He still does. Whenever she goes a few days without calling him, he calls her. So, it's strange that he still hasn't returned her call after the message she left this morning.

The artist puts down her tools and hands Ashley a mirror. "I finished the outline. Check it out." She angles another mirror toward Ashley's butt so Ashley can see the pony prancing on Gray's left cheek surrounded by pink, irritated skin. It looks like a drawing by a pre-teen girl. No need to fill it in. It's more than Gray deserves already.

"I'll come back and get the rest later," Ashley says.

"You don't like it?"

"No, it's good," Ashley says, but she doesn't feel good.

As the artist bandages her butt, Ashley notices her hands are trembling.

So Close

Outside Sadie's, Saul folded himself into Hernandez's Mustang. To get the hair sample analyzed, he'd have to ask her for another favor. He pulled out his phone, powered it on, and saw she'd already texted, asking him to call her.

He dialed and started the car. In front of him, a Mercedes SUV had parked too close for him to maneuver around it. Hernandez answered and filled him in on her news as Saul eased the car backward. She described how Wilson had attacked Ashley York and was Tasered by studio security, and how Ashley then, surprisingly, fawned over him.

A rim grated against the curb. Saul slammed on the brakes.

She stopped talking. "What was that?"

"Nothing," he said.

He had to go forward. No other option now. He turned the wheel, clenched his teeth, and pressed the gas…ever so gently.

The rim grated against the concrete, even louder than before. The vibration reverberated through the car, from the wheel to his shoulder, which held the phone pressed against one ear.

He spoke over it. "Do me a favor and look up Ashley York's address. Dollars to donuts she lives in Beverly Hills, in a gated neighborhood north of Sunset."

As he rolled away from the curb and past the Mercedes, the clacks of Hernandez typing came through the phone.

"Beverly Park," she said. "How did you know?"

"That's where I followed Wilson yesterday. He watched her gate for an hour."

"Weird," she said. "You think they had some kind of fling?"

"I don't see it. Wilson's not plugged into Hollywood. It must be something else. Can't be a coincidence that Rydell was following Wilson and now this. Maybe Wilson is Wayob, although I don't think so. He might be the next victim, though. Or maybe Ashley."

"You really think their confrontation has something to do with Wayob?"

"That's what I intend to find out," Saul said. "Can you find a number for Wilson's next of kin? He's not picking up on his cell."

"I'm slammed with the Collins case right now. It might be faster if you stop by his house."

"I'll try again, but I'm going to hit Ashley's first."

"Seriously? You think she'll see you?"

"If she cares about her safety."

"Ooh. Get me her autograph while you're there."

"Ha."

"Call me afterward?"

Saul agreed and tapped off. Ashley York and Wilson took priority over the hair. He'd give it to Hernandez later.

—

As Saul approached Beverly Hills, the sunlight grew softer, filtered through haze. He turned north on San Ysidro and drove past where Wilson had parked yesterday and up to the gate. He badged to the guard, and the guard nodded and opened the gate.

Saul rolled through. After the guardhouse and garden area, the road narrowed and rose. It banked up a dry hill and turned, and after a couple of miles seemed more like remote desert wilderness than the middle of LA. Then the road parted around a manicured median and leveled out, revealing a sparse row of mansions with manicured lawns.

Ashley York had her own guard stationed in a four-foot-wide booth in the middle of her driveway with an arched gate on either side, one for coming, one for going. The iron bars of the gates were bent and twisted into geometric shapes and freshly painted with black paint— probably painted once a year. The gates were mounted on stone pillars connected to a wooden fence. As Saul rolled up to the booth, he could see through the gate. The driveway cut a lazy arc through a vast expanse of tended lawn bathed in warm light, punctuated by long shadows of palms. Below the lawn, the house featured a stone turret on the eastern side.

The guard slid open the window to the booth. He was a muscular

Black man, his head shaved bald.

Saul flashed his badge. "Ashley home?"

"I'm afraid I can't answer that, Officer Parker."

Beside the guard, a black dog leaped up and clamped its big paws on the windowsill. It tilted its head, cocked its ears, and sniffed the air.

The guard pulled her back by the collar. "Down, Shera."

"It's Detective." Saul smiled.

The guard's arm jerked as Shera squirmed against it. He winked. "Lot of detectives drive a Mustang, do they?"

"Some do," Saul said, though Hernandez was the only one he was aware of who drove a personal ride on the job. "Mind opening the gate?"

"You got a warrant?"

"Not exactly."

"Then I can't exactly let you in."

"What's your name?"

The guard scratched Shera's head. "Sammy."

"Sammy who?"

He hesitated. "Johnson. I'm just doing my job here. You understand, right?"

"Of course." Saul nodded. "So, call your boss and let's get this settled."

"I'm afraid I can't do that."

"I believe you will."

Johnson crossed his arms. "And why is that?"

"Your job is to protect Ashley York, am I right?"

Johnson nodded.

"Well, she's in danger. And if anything happens, I'll tell the world that I came here today to warn Ashley, and Sammy Johnson refused to even call her."

Johnson frowns, shuts the window, and picks up a phone.

To Be Mindy's Hero

Gray rolls over in Ashley's guest bed, which feels less obtrusive than sleeping among the personal things in her bedroom. He's almost certain he must sleep for Ashley to return to her own body, but sleep will not come. He's too drained to really sleep, thanks to the Scotch he sucked down in her limo, in a useless attempt to forget that most of his time here had been wasted. He wasn't about to make any demands on Ashley when there might be consequences later on, but if she was still feeling generous after they switched back to their own bodies he might just have to accept.

He imagines the portrait he started of Charlie silhouetted in the doorway, the way he wanted to paint the sunlight streaming in from around him. And even more than Charlie, the person who Gray truly wants to paint is the fortune-teller, the way she looked in the candlelight, pain etched into every line on her face, shadows almost as dark as that horrible black blotch.

His eyelids pop open, and sunlight pours in through the expansive windows of Ashley's guest room. He's still in her body. Exhausted and, at the same time, wide awake. Is this what it's like for Claire?

He sits up in bed, grabs a notebook from the bedside table, and starts doodling. The lines converge into a city skyline, LA, with buildings sprawling from downtown to the Santa Monica Bay. A bank of low clouds roils over the Pacific. In the foreground, he sketches grass and the lawn below Ashley's house. Although Gray hasn't seen it from this point of view, he's quite sure this is exactly how it looks. *Weird.*

On the bedside table, Ashley's phone riffs a pop tune he doesn't recognize. '*Front Gate*,' according to caller ID. He answers.

"There's a Detective Parker here to see you," says Sammy. "He thinks you're in danger, but I told him everything's cool while I'm around."

"In danger from who?"

Sammy chuckles. "The dude who attacked you today, or someone he knows. Some shit."

Gray smiles. "Oh. I don't think we need to worry about him."

"That's for sure," Sammy says. "He won't get near you again. Not while I'm around. No way. Hold on…" Sammy muffles the phone.

Gray lies back on the bed. Will the police go to his house? Have they already? Doesn't seem like they can do anything since he, as Ashley, isn't pressing charges. The detective is probably just here to try and change Gray's mind. As if that will happen. Maybe he doesn't have to worry about the police, but Claire will be freaking out. She must have heard all about the slap by now.

Sammy continues. "He's saying other people are in danger too. He wants to talk to you in person."

But Gray is more worried about causing more trouble if the detective asks a question that he can't answer in the same way Ashley would. "I'm kind of busy right now. Tell him Gray Wilson is completely harmless. I'm not at all worried about him, and he shouldn't be either."

Sammy agrees and ends the call.

Gray sets the phone aside and lies back on the bed. He closes his eyes. The sooner he goes to sleep, the sooner things can return to normal.

Thud.

The sound came from downstairs. Like a sack of potatoes dropped on the floor.

"Andrea?" Gray calls out.

Silence.

If he goes to check it out, he can forget about falling asleep. A familiar headache from the Scotch leaving his system is building behind his temple.

He reaches for Ashley's phone, but he's still locked out of the device, of course, and there's no point in calling her. By now, she must have turned the obsidian snake, hopefully.

The windows cast rectangles of orange on the wall, which shiver as a cloud passes over the sun. Gray wraps himself in the comforter. Ashley is right about the pictures he took, about him holding her body hostage. Deliberate or not, he has no right to be here.

Was it only yesterday that Mindy drew him riding a tiger? It seems like so long ago. He longs to be her hero again, to hold Tyler in his arms. He even almost looks forward to the inevitable questions Claire will ask once he's back in his own body. He has to tell her he's quit his job. It's time to face life head-on.

Saul Takes a Hike

At the booth, Johnson hung up and shook his head. Saul considered charging the gate. A formidable work of iron, for sure, but only as strong as its weakest link. The hinges would yield to the two tons of Crown Vic at his disposal. But if he smashed through the gate, Johnson would call 911. That was a given. And then he could forget about Ashley's cooperation, the whole point in coming here.

Saul glanced around and nodded, as though he appreciated what he saw. "I can see you keep it tight around here, but what about before your shift? Not everyone is as diligent as you."

Johnson tapped an iPad. "We keep a log of everyone who comes and goes. Including you, although you're only going."

"Who else is down there, besides Ashley?"

"Just the maid and gardener," Johnson said, "and my orders are to keep it that way."

Saul pulled a card from his wallet and passed it out the window to Johnson. "Call me if Wilson shows up."

"Sure thing." Johnson chuckled. "After I kick his ass."

Saul backed up the drive and into the road. He drove up the hill until he was beyond Johnson's line of sight from the guard booth and pulled over. Took out his phone and zoomed in to his location on the map. Wayob wouldn't give up, Saul knew, and so nor would he.

He drove up to Mulholland and turned right. Wound his way through the curves. Past the million-dollar views of the San Fernando Valley and the mountains behind it, burned by recent fires and now sunshine as the day downshifted from afternoon into evening. At the light where Mulholland crossed Coldwater, Saul turned onto a narrow road which led down into Franklin Canyon. A couple of miles below the gate, he parked at a dirt turnout and glared up at the daunting climb to Ashley's property. Yes, he was going to hike. He was that desperate.

He shoved Hernandez's small binoculars in his pocket, unfolded himself from the Mustang, and pulled off the new coat and tie. He tossed them back inside. What did Ashley know? Did she even know anything?

He started up a narrow trail, which snaked its way up the canyon, and was almost instantly out of breath. The trail steepened to the point where he had to scramble on hands and knees, half-sliding and wading through loose dirt and gravel, half of which seemed to lodge in his shoes. He had to remind himself of the urgency, that it was only a matter of time before Wayob claimed his next victim.

He passed rocks the color of dark mustard, radiating heat from the sun like an oven. He removed his button-up, tied it around his waist, and stretched up his T-shirt to mop the sweat and the dust from his face. At least tomorrow when he woke up sore, he'd know why. He pressed on.

The trail seemed to end near a rock outcropping. Saul swatted his way through a thicket of sage and walked out onto the rock. It was like emerging into a different world. A moist wind blew cool and constant. Mansions peppered the opposite rim of Franklin Canyon, beyond which the LA basin stretched from downtown to the Pacific. Miles and miles of pavement and cars. Slow streams of red and white light moved through the long shadows cast by the buildings, most of them stucco but some made of glass, which mirrored the sky. Beyond downtown, the San Gabriels rose up like sentinels in the haze.

He eased himself down. Dangled his legs from the side. Too exhausted to care that the sandstone might crumble under his weight. He wiped his face again and noticed his right pant cuff was shredded. The cost of new pants plus the Roosevelt would consume most of his paycheck for the week. Not that money mattered, not compared to stopping Wayob.

Saul removed his shoes and emptied the dust and gravel into the wind. Shook out his socks and laid them on a rock to dry. Maybe that oversized flannel shirt Sadie wore belonged to a secret boyfriend. Could be a lot of reasons for her having it. But if she kept it from her parents, then no telling how far her secret life went.

"Parker-Parker-Parker-Parker," she'd sung. Sadie with Wayob's musical, mocking cadence. She had laughed as she raised the gun, like it was a toy.

From out over the ocean, a shifting cloak of clouds spread toward the city. Saul shivered. He put his shoes on, heaved himself to his feet, and took out the binoculars. He scanned down the hillside to Ashley's immense lawn, which seemed almost alien against the dry scrub that surrounded it. Her house was built from large stones. The main part of the house had three balconies, a deck, and an immense wall of windows. The roof was tiled with terra cotta and sloped steeply upward. Above the peak was the turret. It was the house of a princess, an LA princess. But smaller than he'd expected, maybe three thousand square feet, certainly less than four. And it seemed all alone up there surrounded by so much land. Alone and masked by the glare of the sunset on the windows.

Scattered about her lawn, a dozen brown rabbits nibbled peacefully on the grass. The lawn rolled down to a dull fence of sun-faded wood that made an arc along the cliff. Two rows of crossbeams connected by posts at uneven intervals, with the top row no more than three feet above the lawn. Easy to climb over *if* he could get up there.

He pocketed the binoculars and started back across the boulder. The outcropping seemed to shrink in the growing shadow of the cliff. The wall of the canyon rose up at a near vertical, all loose rocks and dust. He was going to have to scramble on hands and knees if he had any hope of reaching her property at all. Near his foot, a white rabbit leaped into the sage. If there was any such thing as real magic, he could count on the rabbit to help him up the cliff.

Watch Him Sleep

It is late in the afternoon when Wayob sits in the sun in the cut grass field that is the garden of Ashley York and overlooks the city and the ocean. Wayob, in the vessel of August Grant, folds his lower legs toward his body, interlocks his fingers in his lap, closes his eyes, and focuses all his energy on the desperate sound of the mind of Gray Wilson. Wayob inhales. He breathes out...

Deep within, inside the blackness, Wayob finds Gray's mind. Coming closer. *Come to me, Gray.* Wayob shall have his freedom soon. Soon indeed.

Wayob hears an engine approach the opposite side of the palace from where he sits. He waits. A door closes. The engine drives away. He keeps his eyes closed and his mind focused on the sound of Gray's mind. And from the resonance of the low hum, Wayob knows Gray is close. He is in the house.

Wayob stands.

Below Ashley's palace, clouds of gray have enveloped the ocean and the west side of the city.

Wayob enters Ashley's palace through a garden doorway, which turns out to lead into a kitchen. Inside is the skinny woman who, many hours ago when they passed her vehicle, Jacob had called "the hottie maid." Her hair is tied back and her skin is the color of copper, several shades lighter than Wayob's once was, back before the odious priest imprisoned him inside the Encanto.

She is putting dishes into a cabinet, and for a brief moment, Wayob considers backing out the door and trying some other entrance to the palace, but it is too late. She turns toward him. An annoying grin spreads across her face.

Inconvenient, Wayob thinks.

"You'll never believe what happened to Ashley." She approaches Wayob. This woman has no respect for Wayob's personal space.

Wayob steps back. "I know far more than you. Where *is* Ashley?"

"That's what I'm trying to tell you. The guy that slapped her. He might be in Ashley's body. It sounds crazy, I know, but—"

"Yes, yes." Wayob tries to sound calm. "So you know of the Encanto?" If she knows, then she will want to take it for herself. Wayob shall have to stop her.

The woman steps closer. "So, wait, you believe me? She told you too?"

"Yes, that is what happened," Wayob says. "She told me." His skin crawls. She is so close, he can feel heat coming off her. Wayob wants to create more space between them, but now he cannot afford the luxury. Not yet.

"What's the En-cant-o?" She puckers her plump lips and presses herself into Wayob.

Wayob laughs. Of course. Why would Gray tell anyone about the Encanto? He wants it for himself. "It is nothing. Forget it." Wayob is grateful that he does not have to kill this woman, but still, she needs to get out of his way. The sickening sweet smell of her soap oozes off her face. Wayob backs away. He bumps into the refrigerator.

"What's wrong?" she says. "Ashley doesn't care if we hook up."

Wayob tries to resist his urge to push her back. Wayob must be smart. Use the influence that August holds over her to his advantage. But now she presses her lips into his—in the same manner that his young bride once did—and shoves her tongue into his mouth. It feels slimy, like a fat worm that tastes of mint and overripe fruit.

It is all Wayob can do not to retch. He shoves her back. "Not here," Wayob says, his voice strained almost to a whisper. "Go to your house and I will meet you there."

"My apartment? Think you can wait that long?" She flutters her dark lashes. She turns and saunters to the counter, swaying every curve she can. She hops up and sits on the counter facing Wayob. She slides the strip of cloth she wears as an undergarment down her thighs, over her knees.

"Stop it," Wayob says. "Get down from there."

"Why don't you come get me…down?"

Her voice sounds just like his bride's did, somehow, even though the language is different. Fear and anger transfix Wayob where he stands.

She raises her feet, points them at Wayob, then kicks off her panties toward him. She opens her legs and reaches down to grip the counter between them. A lascivious smile. She slides forward, spreads her legs, her crotch pressed against the back of her wrists. She laughs, and now she looks like his bride as she jumps from the counter and comes toward him.

No, Wayob thinks. *Not here. Not now.* His young bride died centuries ago. This palace that Wayob is in is where Ashley York lives. This woman, yanking at his belt, she is not his bride.

Wayob's voice fails him. He can only manage to hiss, "Stop it."

His hands clamp her neck. She moans, her voice high and thick with pleasure. She tears apart his belt, zips down his pants, reaches in, and gropes around. Then, understanding seems to dawn in her eyes. She claws at his arms. But he cannot stop now. He saw her with the fucking priest. She gave him no choice.

With all his strength, Wayob squeezes. He squeezes and throttles until her body goes limp. Until she is no longer his young bride but just some flaccid doll of a skinny woman who would have screamed if Wayob had let her have even a sip of air. And her scream would have alerted Gray. He would have dialed back the Encanto, and then Wayob would have been trapped alone in the deep terrible darkness, disembodied.

Was she lying about the Encanto? Probably. Almost definitely.

He releases her body. It collapses at his feet, and her head knocks like a drum on the hatch embedded in the floor. Wayob regrets having to kill her. If only she could have understood all that Wayob has been through. If she had suffered even a fraction of the centuries that Wayob spent alone in the Encanto, she would have done the same as Wayob. No one would blame Wayob for killing her, not if they knew.

He listens. The house is silent. He drags her body aside and opens the hatch in the floor. Wooden stairs descend below ground. Wayob lifts the woman and carries her sideways down the stairs. Her feet rake the many bottles of wine in racks along the wall.

He drops her at the bottom and returns to the kitchen.

Wayob grimaces at the disgusting panties on the floor. They had nearly hit him in the face. Beside the sink is a rag. Though the cloth is dirty, it is still a million times more agreeable than the foul panties.

Careful not to touch them, Wayob rolls them into the rag. He holds it away from himself as he stands, and throws the rag with the panties into the dark open door of the cellar.

In the living room, Wayob's every footfall on the wooden floor seems to echo. He moves slowly past the two-story windows, quiet as he can. Will Gray fear August? He should be wary of anyone sneaking into the house.

Beyond the living room is a large parlor which contains a grand piano and a white sofa. Never before has Wayob seen a house so vast and uncluttered, so immaculately clean—you miss such marvels, spending your life in utter darkness. Does anyone live here besides Ashley? This is wonderful, just walking alone in the quiet.

After finding no one on the first level, Wayob creeps up the stairs. In the bedroom to the right, he finds the young Ashley York, who must still be Gray, otherwise Wayob would have returned to the Encanto and been trapped inside.

Gray is stretched out under plush white covers, dozing like royalty in Ashley's body. It would be so easy to strangle him before he wakes, but Wayob is smarter than that. Wayob killed the last holder of the Encanto, who was in the body of Luis Luna at the time, and what good did it do? Before Wayob could destroy the Encanto, Abuela had given it to Gray.

Wayob has spent far too much time tortured and alone in darkness to take such a risk again. The next holder of the Encanto might never set Wayob free.

Wayob searches as fast as he can without making any noise, afraid that Gray will awaken at merely the stirring of the air. There is a phone on the nightstand, but the drawers are all empty. Wayob kneels on the floor and looks under the bed. Nothing.

But Wayob has an idea. Can he make Gray his next vessel? Is it possible with Gray in Ashley's body? Barbaric priest. Should have told Wayob how this works.

But since Gray is sleeping, Wayob could try to transmigrate into Ashley's body. If it works, he should be able to probe Gray's mind to find out where he hid the Encanto. Then, Wayob shall destroy it and kill Ashley in Gray's body. And then he will be free to live Ashley's luxurious life. Wayob deserves this much. After all he has suffered, he deserves more.

As Wayob sinks into the cushioned chair beside the bed, he must swallow his laugh. Gray does not stir. Wayob leans back and closes his eyes. He concentrates on the darkness. Finds the sound of Gray's mind, closer now than ever before—definitely still in Ashley's body.

Wayob imagines himself lifting up into the ether. His mind, descending down upon Gray. Dominating him under the weight of all that is Wayob. Wayob imagines how peaceful life will be in Ashley's palace above the city, alone. He drifts off…

Rosa and Abuela

Rosa knew something was truly wrong when Abuela refused to have her hair brushed that morning. Abuela had been breathing raggedly for weeks, maybe months, yet she refused to see a doctor. She stirred the quinoa around in her bowl, as if spreading it against the sides made it look like she'd eaten some, and insisted that Rosa go to school. Rosa shouldn't have, but she went anyway, for there was no denying the will of Abuela.

It was great that Abuela cared so much about education, but what was the point? What was she going to do with a degree and no documentation? And USC was too expensive. They couldn't afford it, even before her father's murder, and now without his income there was no way she could possibly pay. Yet Abuela insisted it would work out and tuition would be covered somehow, like the sum was just going to fall from the sky. Maybe Rosa could cover tuition for somewhere less expensive, if she had a green card, or a visa. Then she wouldn't have to wash dishes in a Thai restaurant that only paid in tips shared from waitresses, many of whom were skimming. And what could Rosa do about it? Nothing. She might even be fired tonight for missing her shift. But there was no way she could have gone to work after she spoke to Abuela, after class, and she sounded so far away that Rosa had rushed back home to their small apartment.

Abuela lay on her back in bed, gasping. It sounded more like drowning than breathing, as if her lungs were filled with fluid, and Rosa didn't want to think about that.

She climbed in beside Abuela. There was hardly room in the narrow twin bed. She held her tight, just like Abuela had been holding Rosa her whole life. She nuzzled her white tresses and inhaled, but instead of the gardenia perfume that Abuela always wore, there was only the smell of stale skin and lotion. She smelled almost like a stranger.

The bedroom seemed smaller now than it ever had. On the wall near the door was a carving of the Virgen de Guadalupe, her red dress faded from all the years of Abuela's hands running over it every time she left the room. When Abuela lost her eyesight, she didn't go blind. She saw with her hands.

Abuela's lips quivered. She restrained a cough. Outside the one narrow window, the sun was sinking.

"Deja que una pobre vieja muera en paz," Abuela said.

Rosa sat up. *Let her die?* She was only sick. Abuela could not die. Not yet. Rosa would not let that happen. "No te estás muriendo. Los médicos te ayudarán."

Abuela coughed spasmodically. She tried to cover her mouth with the handkerchief balled up in her hand, and it unfurled. The fabric was stiff and specked with brown. Dried blood.

Rosa's tears came on suddenly. All the time she'd wasted denying Abuela's decline, she should have been doing something. She could not lose Abuela too. She just couldn't. Her shoulders shook convulsively.

No, she needed to be strong, like Abuela. Rosa wiped her face on her sleeve and reached for her phone. Abuela's hand came down on Rosa's arm, the thin bones of her fingers loosely covered with skin.

Abuela could practically read minds, just from the slightest action or the tone of a person's voice. That's why, at Rosa's insistence, she'd started telling fortunes as a way to make extra money.

"Es la hora," Abuela said. She insisted Rosa let her go, let her die at home in peace, here with Rosa. All these years, it was Abuela who had made all the decisions, but not this time.

Rosa wasn't ready to be alone. Not even a week had passed since she had lost her father. She would give anything just to have one more day with Abuela. *Just one more day.* She dialed 911 and requested an ambulance.

"No," Abuela said. "Estoy lista para unirme a Miguelito."

Rosa was a kid the last time she'd heard Abuela refer to her late husband by his nickname. The Guatemalan army had shot him, but Abuela had been vague about the circumstances, which Rosa suspected were the reason that they had fled Guatemala when she was two. After crossing into Mexico, they were robbed—Rosa knew that much—and something had happened to her mother, something so horrible that Abuela and her father didn't want to tell her. *When you're older*, they'd promised. But now her father was dead, and Abuela was so sick she could hardly speak.

Rosa remembered the endless walking, how cold it was after they crossed the US border, her father commanding her to lie still as spotlights swept over them, as trucks plowed through the sand inches from their hiding place, as militiamen with their guns and their loudspeakers boomed their hatred across the desert in the night.

She was glad they came, though. Despite the many hardships, Rosa loved it here in LA.

Abuela coughed into the handkerchief for what seemed like hours. She wiped her mouth. Fresh blood smeared on her chin. Rosa should have called 911 sooner. She should have listened when Abuela started beginning sentences with *When I'm gone...*

But she hadn't been this bad until after the funeral. Now Rosa doubted if Abuela could even get out of bed on her own.

"Todavía está con nosotros," Abuela said. "Tu padre. Mi Luis."

Rosa understood the feeling. Her father had been such a huge part of her life that it was hard to let go. And she never saw the body, because Abuela had had it cremated, so there was no sense of closure.

In the weeks before his death, he'd become sullen and hardly spoke. Rosa had assumed it was his job, that he might be losing it. But now she realized he must have known about Abuela, how sick she was. He must have been desperate to help her. Of course he was.

What had he done?

"¿Qué hizo?" Rosa asked. "Dime, Abuela. ¡Por favor!"

"Todavía está con nosotros," Abuela sputtered out between ragged breaths.

Why did she keep saying that? And how could he still be with us? Did she think he was trapped in some kind of limbo?

Between fits of coughing, Abuela ordered Rosa to forgive him. He was only trying to help. It was Abuela who had sinned, she said, for she was the one who had kept the Encanto all these years and she didn't tell them what it was. She kept the secret to protect them, but in so doing, she'd doomed her only son. For if he'd known about Wayob, the evil spirit trapped inside the Encanto, he would never have freed him.

And then giving away the Encanto was the only way to stop the spirit, Abuela insisted. The only way to trap him back inside. Her eyes squeezed shut. "Debería haberlo destruido cuando tuve la oportunidad." Tears streamed through the crevices on her cheeks. Her mouth twisted into a grimace.

Rosa frowned. She wasn't sure what Abuela was talking about but it was frightening to see so much strain on her face, which typically radiated so much kindness. Rosa smoothed her hair against her head. "No tenías otra opción."

Abuela's eyelids flicked open. But she seemed utterly lost behind the clouds in her eyes. "Antes de que. Debería haberlo destruido en Guatemala. Pero tenía miedo. Como el mono. No podía dejarlo ir. Yo no..." Her lids fluttered closed. Her breathing slowed. She seemed to have fallen asleep.

It made no sense. No sense at all. Why would she smuggle a thing she knew to be evil on the arduous journey from Guatemala and then keep it here where she lived with her son and Rosa? But she must have had a reason. Rosa trusted her completely.

Where the hell is the ambulance? She dialed 911 again, but they were on the way. Nothing more could be done.

She went to the bathroom and got a towel, which she used to wipe the smeared blood from Abuela's chin. The tension in the lines around her mouth seemed to ease. Rosa got back in bed and held her, her grandmother, who had loved her like a mother as well.

The sun dropped away to the west. It bounced off cars on the freeway and through a slim path between the warehouses, through the window, a bright slit of pulsing light on the wall. For a moment, the whole room glowed. Dust sparkled in the arm of light as it moved toward the worn Virgen de Guadalupe. Then it was gone. Leaving the room cold and dull, echoing with wind from the freeway and the dry sound of tires.

Nightfall

As dusk descended, wind whipped through Franklin Canyon and chilled the sweat on Saul's skin. He was thirty feet from Ashley York's fence, but the terrain was almost vertical, the soil loose and dry. With each step up, he slid back down.

The sound of someone whistling carried on the wind. The *Mission Impossible* theme song.

At the top of the cliff, Sammy Johnson leaned over the fence. "I'd give up if I were you."

Saul grimaced. "Don't think I can make it?"

"I've seen idiots half your size fail. But go ahead, try. If you get close, I'll come back and Tase you."

"I'm trying to protect her."

"You're welcome to apply for the job," Johnson said. "But for now, she's hired me." He turned and disappeared beyond the rim of the cliff. Resumed whistling. The melody fading into the twilight.

"Damn it," Saul said aloud to no one. *Must be hidden cameras in the fence.* How long had Johnson watched his struggle? He was right though. There was no way Saul could climb any higher.

Saul reluctantly turned and began to retreat. He had to crab-walk downslope. His butt dragged in the dirt. He was thirsty and had nothing to drink, and he was so hungry he felt light-headed.

He lumbered back out onto the boulder outcrop, his chest heaving for air. Clouds had carpeted the city. All but the tallest buildings. Their spires pierced the roiling mass. Beacons of light above a glowing sea. Then they too were swallowed by the clouds. Wayob was down there, somewhere beneath it all. Saul had to find him. But how? The lives Wayob had taken seemed to have nothing in common. No parallel thread.

By the time Saul caught his breath, the fog had slid into the canyon. Vapor rolled over the boulder and submerged him too in the whiteout.

Beneath the boulder, he found the trail. By a very faint glow in the mist, he navigated his way down the switchbacks. The fog seemed to muffle his footsteps. The blur drifted around him. A face came to Saul, a dream-fragment conjured from the gloom. A woman. Her smile, coy. And as she sauntered toward him, Saul realized they were in the hallway at the Roosevelt. But that was all he could remember before the memory faded into the mist.

He stopped. Closed his eyes and focused. In the blackness, instead of the woman, he imagined the face of Saroyan—cowering. Eyes wide. What could it mean?

He snapped his eyes open and shivered. Saroyan had admitted to killing Luna. He'd said that his body had acted against his will, and now Saul believed him—Wayob was responsible. He should question Saroyan again.

He reached the road and trudged toward the vague outline of the Mustang. His legs heavy as stumps. Behind the Mustang, a shadow loomed. A truck. As he neared, the driver's door creaked open and a light popped on inside the cab. A dark figure hopped down. The light circled on the pavement. Toward Saul.

Saul crouched low, drew his gun, and scrambled toward the Mustang. The figure with the flashlight came around the car and leaned over the windshield, his light on an envelope. As he slid the envelope under the wiper, light bounced off the glass and illuminated a uniform. A park ranger. He had a dark brown beard, a solid two inches thick.

Saul holstered his gun. "Wait."

The beam swung into Saul's face. Saul pulled his badge and waved the light away. "Do you mind?"

The ranger lowered the flashlight. "You're out of your jurisdiction."

Saul motioned around him. "This is the middle of LA!" he said, though he knew this was a national park. "I've got a right to pursue a felon."

"I didn't get a call about that."

"I didn't have time for the courtesy," Saul said. "I've got lives at stake here. How about a break on that ticket?"

The ranger shook his head. Tapped the little printer clipped to his belt. "You're in the system now. It's out of my hands. Easiest just to pay before the late fees."

"I'll file a report," Saul said. "This will come back on you."

"Good luck with that." The ranger climbed back into his service truck and reversed.

As the headlights swept over Saul, he snatched the envelope from Hernandez's wiper. $256 for parking after dark. He crumpled the ticket and shoved it into his pocket.

The truck rolled unhurried down the hill. High above the canyon, the beam of a helicopter swept the fog.

Saul folded himself into the Mustang. Retrieved the NoDoz from his coat. Shook the bottle. Nothing. He tapped it against his palm, but it was empty. He needed something. He was tired and famished, the night was slipping away, and he was getting nowhere.

He fired up the Mustang and rolled down through the canyon toward the city. Saroyan was recovering downtown in the Good Samaritan ICU, and Silver Lake was on the way there. Maybe Wilson had come home.

—

Gray snaps into semi-consciousness. His head throbs. This always happens after he drinks. He blacks out and then wakes up an hour later unable to fall back to sleep.

Before opening his eyes, he knows from the tone of the silence that this is not his house, and he is not alone. He struggles to focus and rolls over. He's still in Ashley's guest bed, but he should be back in his body by now, shouldn't he?

A faint light filters in through the windows. The white chair by the bed sort of glows, and draped over the chair, dark as a shadow, the figure of a man leans to one side.

Gray's heart pounds in his throat. The man's chest rises and falls. As Gray sits up slowly, he can just make out the round face and gelled hair. It's August Grant, and he is sleeping.

Why is he here?

Last time Gray was in Ashley's body, when August just showed up at her house uninvited, it seemed weird, but watching her sleep is a whole new dimension of creepiness.

Gray shuffles to the opposite side of the bed, gets to his feet, and sneaks barefoot out of the bedroom and down the hall. He glances over his shoulder. Darkness folds in from the hallway and blankets the bedroom door. Had he dreamed August there?

He descends the stairs. A wall of fog presses hard against the windows. In the living room, the blurred outlines of furniture lurk below the light streaming out from the kitchen. He moves toward the kitchen door. He bangs his shin into a shadow that turned out to be the coffee table. It groans against the floor. Gray stands there frozen for a long moment.

He forces himself to turn, to look back up the stairs. They darken and disappear. For a moment, it seems that August is up there, a shadow within a shadow peering down upon Gray. But there is only silence. Gray sees only his own fear projected up into the darkness.

He exhales and hurries to the kitchen. Beside the fridge, the trap door to the cellar stands open at a right angle. He peers down the unfinished stairs, along rows and rows of wine into the darkness. He's afraid to look away from the darkness. Afraid to approach.

"Andrea? You down there?"

Perhaps the light has burned out. But then why doesn't she answer?

Almost right behind him, August practically sings, "Andrea has departed early."

Gray tenses. He turns. August is standing almost right on top of him. Gray stumbles backward. Though he's a head taller than August, he's dwarfed by August's intensity. August stands rigid, every muscle tensed, his face tight and unfriendly. Irises like dark swirls of ink. And he doesn't seem to realize that his nose is running.

"What are you doing here?" Gray asks.

"I could ask you the same thing, couldn't I, Gray?" His tone makes Gray's skin crawl. It's pure malevolence.

He knows. But how? Unless…Ashley told him.

"Look," Gray says. "I apologized to Ashley. We're trying to switch back."

August's brows furrow, and his voice trembles as he speaks. "Unfortunately, I cannot allow that to happen."

"What?" He struggles to imagine what August could mean.

"Don't play coy with me, Gray." Spit sprays from August's mouth. His breath reeks of onions. "You thought you could fool poor Wayob, but now I know why *she* was angry with you. You had me following Ashley, with her in your body, because I knew you held the Encanto. I should have expected it, but you're the first one who after switching into the body of another went back and retrieved the wretched device. Clever, very clever."

"Who's Wayob?"

"I am Wayob."

Gray wishes he had let the detective in. He glances around for a phone but there isn't one. "You need to leave." If he runs, will August follow? He sounds crazy, calling himself Wayob. He turns toward the door. If he makes it outside, maybe he can outrun August and make it around the house, up the driveway to the guard booth.

August edges sideways, putting himself between Gray and the door. Gray steps back along the opening to the cellar. He'll go around August's other side. If he tries anything, Gray will shove him down the stairs.

"I hate doing this," August snarls.

Gray charges past, zeroing in on the door. The fog presses in against the window.

August dives into him and knocks him forward.

Gray's knees slam into the tile. He catches himself with his hands. "Help! Andrea!" Gray crawls toward the door.

August jams his elbow between Gray's shoulder blades. "You're making this worse for yourself." He grabs him by the hair and yanks him back. All Gray can focus on is the pain.

"Give me the Encanto and you may live."

August knees him in the spine, and his legs collapse under the weight. He needs to turn around and fight head on, but August has him pinned flat on his belly. He can't reach him. Can't push him off. August's hands slide around his neck, cold and bony. Gray squirms and accomplishes nothing. The hands tighten like a vise.

"If you will not give me the Encanto, then you must die," August says. "This is not my fault, you understand; I'll be tortured if I don't kill you. In the reverse situation, you would not hesitate to kill me."

"Wait." Gray chokes. Unsure if he's said anything at all.

August loosens his hands. "What?"

Gray gasps for air. "You're talking about the charm, right? The stone thing with the obsidian snake."

"Yes, the Encanto. If you only understood how much I have suffered, you would surrender it gladly."

"I will," Gray says. "It's caused me nothing but trouble."

August releases Gray's neck. "I knew you had it here. Where is it?"

Still pinned to the floor, Gray wrenches his head to the side, but he can only see white tile and the stairs leading down into darkness. If he could get something to use as a weapon… "I left it in the car," he says, glad that August can't see his face. "Let me up and I'll show you."

August eases off his back but grips Gray's elbow as he gets to his feet. He stands back with his arm extended, as if he'd rather not be near Gray at all.

Gray glances over August's shoulder at the door that leads out to the garage. "It's in the garage."

August releases his arm and moves aside. "If you're lying, I will kill you."

"How do I know you won't kill me after I give it to you?"

"You will have to take that risk."

Gray walks toward the garage. Not inclined to try anything with August so close behind him. He pulls the door open.

"It's right there in the white Mercedes. On the passenger seat." He steps aside, motioning for August to go see for himself.

August, his face eager and mouth slightly open, edges past him and approaches the Mercedes in the dark garage.

Gray whirls, shoves the door closed, and opens drawers at random in search of a knife but the best he can find is a drawer full of flatware. He hears August wrench the door back open behind him. He grabs a fork and leaps around the island. Avoiding the opening to the cellar, he turns and spreads his feet, ready to defend himself. August is already nearly upon him. Gray swipes the fork at August.

August steps back and laughs, his laughter like a mask that Gray has no desire to see behind. His eyes seem to reflect Gray's fear back at him. The pinpoints of August's pupils are not just on him, but *in* him

The thought of harming another human being almost freezes Gray, but August seems to have no qualms about killing, and Gray cannot let him near his house. *Must protect my family.*

August grabs for the fork. Gray withdraws. Then rams his head into August's stomach. August falls backward, hitting his head on the base of the island as he comes down hard on the tile. Gray loses his balance and drops the fork in order to catch himself on August's chest.

He grabs August's feet and twists him around. His hands scramble for purchase. Gray kicks him backward, headfirst into the cellar. He screams as he falls into the blackness. His body thumps into the stairs.

Gray hops around the opening and pushes the door. It doesn't budge.

Just a few feet below, August snarls in a strange language as he struggles to get upright. Gray drops to his knees and examines the hinge. It's latched into a groove to prevent it from moving. He yanks the hinge from the groove and the door starts to close, but the hinge is hydraulic, designed to slow the door's movement. He shoves all his weight against it, and slowly, ever so slowly…the door closes.

But there's probably a way to open it from below.

Gray leaps up. With adrenaline surging through his body, he shoulders the steel refrigerator, rocking it back on its wheels. Ignoring the strain in his back, he rolls it across the floor. The plug jerks from the wall. Just as August starts to push the door open, Gray manages to roll the fridge on top. August bangs and shoves from below, and the fridge rocks a little but remains in place.

"You think this will stop me?" he screams.

Gray slumps against the kitchen island. All the energy drains out of him. Maybe the little man screaming in the cellar isn't really August. Gray is sitting here in Ashley's body, so it's no more crazy to believe that someone else could be in August's body. Someone insane. With each passing moment, Gray becomes more convinced that it might not be August down there. He called himself Wayob because that's who he is.

Wayob stops fighting against the trap door. "I only have to kill one of you," he says. "You can live out your life as Ashley. Her beautiful body shall be yours."

"That's not going to happen," Gray says.

"You think I want to hurt her?" Wayob says. "I do not wish to harm anyone. I wish only to be left alone, but I have no choice, you see? If I do not kill her, then when you return to your own body, I will be trapped inside the Encanto, trapped in darkness a million-fold worse than this cellar. This is no fault of yours, Gray; Abuela gave you the Encanto, so it will be her killing Ashley. It's Abuela's fault. Her and the fucking priest who cursed me into this miserable existence. You and me, Gray. We are innocent."

Does he expect Gray to believe all this? After nearly strangling him? Even if he's telling the truth, Gray will not trade Ashley's life for his.

"You're not killing anyone," Gray says.

The refrigerator resumes rocking. Glass bottles clatter inside.

"You cannot keep me trapped in here," Wayob says. "I will find you, Gray Wilson. I will find you. No matter where you go. I can be anyone. You hear me? I am offering you a better life. Give me the Encanto, and I shall give you your dreams."

Gray closes his eyes, rubs his hands over his face that is Ashley's. Dreams? How can he think about dreams? All he wants is to get back to normal.

Claire's New Husband

Claire struggles to see through the fog of insomnia. Her life is so far away, unreal. How can Gray just stroll into the living room, all nonchalant, like everything's normal? Like just another normal night with plain old Gray?

She clicks off her phone and stares at him. "Nice time at work?"

He looks around the room as if taking it in for the first time. "I guess so."

You guess so? Like she's clueless. Does he think she might have missed the video of him that's blowing up on Instagram? He knows she follows Ashley York. She tries her best to quell the accusation from her voice. "Why didn't you call me back?"

"I didn't get the message."

Yeah, right. "I only called you like a thousand times."

Mindy bursts from her bedroom, dashes toward Gray, and hugs him around the legs. Gray leans down and hugs her back, ignoring Claire as if she doesn't exist at all.

Claire unlocks her phone, and there he is: her husband slapping Ashley York in the face. And with a surprising number of likes.

Claire launches off the couch and holds out her phone. "Mind explaining this?"

His brows flicker only for an instant. "Later." He plops down on the floor, crosses his legs, and turns his attention to the coloring book Mindy hands him.

Claire kneels down and shoves her phone in his face. As she plays the video, his lips tighten. Of course he's not surprised, because, after all, he was there.

"Why the fuck would you do that?" Claire says. "Explain."

Gray's eyes widen. Mindy looks down at her drawings, but yeah, she heard. So what if she heard her mom cuss? Does he really think she's going to go her whole life and never hear a bad word?

"You wouldn't understand," he says.

"Damn right. How would you even know where to find Ashley York?"

Gray pretends not to hear her and focuses on the drawing Mindy has shoved into his lap. "Who's the elephant?"

"His name is Paul," Mindy says. She points to the scribbly man riding him. "And this is you."

Claire throws up her hands. "You can't just ignore me."

Gray stares back at her. "I don't want to talk about it now."

Claire stands, feeling like she's the only adult in the room. "Well, too bad. Man up."

"We'll talk tomorrow, okay?"

Claire is speechless. Mindy holds a new drawing in Gray's face, imitating how Claire held her phone, mocking her anger and insistence.

Gray takes the drawing and thanks Mindy. He hugs her, squeezing his eyes closed.

Claire feels like she's watching a movie where she missed the beginning as he carries Mindy's drawing into the garage.

Fine. If Gray wants to make a fool of himself, then why should she care? The consequences are his responsibility. Claire sits on the couch and scrolls through Instagram, though she's unable to focus on the images.

She gives Mindy the thirty-minutes-to-bedtime warning and goes to check on Tyler. He's fast asleep in his crib.

From the hallway, she hears their bedroom door close. Is Gray seriously going to bed right now? Doesn't he know she needs help?

She throws open the door and finds him lying on the bed. His eyes are closed. On his chest is the stone thingy with the black snake he got at the Day of the Dead.

She snatches it off his chest. "What is the deal with this thing?"

He jolts upright. "Don't touch it!" He reaches for her hand but she steps back.

"Fine." She throws it down and stomps on the hideous black snake with the ball of her slipper. It makes a satisfying snap.

Gray gasps. He falls to his knees and snatches the stone from the carpet. It's basically fine, except that the snake has broken off. He tries to shove it back on the stone, tries to hold it in place, but it won't stay. "No, no, no." He runs his hands through the carpet searching for more pieces. "Do you have any idea what you've done?"

This is insane, Claire thinks. "Do you?"

Gray gets up and pulls a phone from his pocket, but it's not his phone.

"Where is your phone?" Claire asks. Did he drop it again? Maybe he really had missed her calls.

He dials and holds the phone to his ear, turning his back on her. Who is he calling? There is something truly different about the way he's been lately. And he's built a wall around the change, a big, gray stone wall. And Claire is on the opposite side.

She wants to feel angry. If she could get angry, then they could fight. And if they could fight, they could get through this—whatever this is. But she can't feel anything other than tired, because last night she woke up at three a.m. again and couldn't go back to sleep.

A truly insane thought dawns on Claire: what if Gray slapped Ashley because of her? Could he be *that* jealous of how much time she spends scrolling Ashley gossip? It's just a way to amuse herself. It's not like she's obsessed with it, not the way he's obsessed with his painting.

Gray paces back and forth, making one call after another and getting no answer, acting like she doesn't exist at all. Her pulse races. For some reason, she's drawn to his obstinance. She can see now that even if she'd slept, this change in Gray makes no sense. No sense at all.

—

Ashley keeps calling Gray but can't get through, and now Claire is standing very close, staring with those her electric blue eyes of hers. She takes the phone from Ashley's hand.

"I don't care about Ashley," Claire says. "I just wanted to know what's going on."

Ashley has to look away from the intensity in Claire's eyes, because a part of her wants the release, to give in, to let go like she did the first time when Gray's body was more like a dream. But how can she now when she might be trapped here forever?

What Ashley needs is to get back to her own body, her own house. But now Claire has broken the charm and Gray is— Why won't he answer? How could a stone cause them to change bodies anyway? *Can't think.* If the house wasn't such a disaster, maybe she could think.

Ashley shoves past Claire, lifts a pile of clothes from the stained carpet, drops them on the bed and begins folding.

"What are you doing?" Claire says. "Some of those are mine."

"Then help me."

"Chill out. I'll clean up some, okay?"

Realizing there's no chance she can calm herself with Claire in her face, Ashley leaves the bedroom. She needs to do something.

In the kitchen, she attacks the dirty dishes in the sink. There are so many she has to move them onto the counter to make enough room to wash them. She feels Claire's eyes boring into her back.

Ashley turns just as Mindy parades past Claire with a cute look of intent. "Can I help?"

Something surges deep in Ashley's heart. "How about I wash and you dry?"

Mindy nods with enthusiasm. Claire, with a lot of head shaking and sighing, helps Mindy find a towel and a little stool to stand on.

After the dishes are washed and dried, she begins putting them away. She doesn't feel like asking Claire where things go, so she opens random cabinets, looking for a place to stack the plates. She finds a cupboard containing four shelves of spices in such disarray that it makes her skin crawl. She begins moving them from the cabinet to the counter. Three bottles of thyme, two half-empty. Two full bottles of cayenne pepper. Oregano, bay leaves, turmeric. A box of ground black pepper, which looks like it hasn't been used in years.

"What are you doing?" Claire asks.

"Sorting." Ashley glances at her. "Height or alphabetical?"

Claire stares at her in amazement. "Why do you care all of a sudden? It's been like this for five years."

"Alphabetical is better." Ashley places the basil on the left and wasabi on the right, leaving a lot of space between them.

Tyler whines through the baby monitor by the stove. Ashley and Claire lock eyes. His sobs ramp up to a wail.

"Way to go," Claire says. "You woke up Tyler." She storms out.

Mindy drags over her little stool, and, at her request, Ashley dishes out little samples of some of the milder spices for her to taste. Beneath all the canisters and the dust, Ashley discovers the shelves are lined with floral contact paper that has faded to brown. She cleans it and begins replacing the spices in neat rows. Having order, even just in this small part of this small kitchen, calms her.

Switching bodies, she thinks, can't be as simple as twisting the charm Claire broke. That would be…magic. What if Gray has no idea what he's talking about?

When Mindy leaves to get changed into her PJs, Ashley goes into the hallway bathroom to check out her tattoo. It doesn't hurt so bad now, thanks to the Advil she took. She peels off the bandages, cleans the three-inch outline of the prancing pony with a damp towel, and smears on the greasy ointment she bought at the tattoo shop. She buckles her jeans and splashes cold water on her face.

Is Gray's life really so bad? It sure seems more fulfilling than hers, her never-ending quest for a meaningful role. If she had a little girl like Mindy, then maybe her wealth would be worth something. She could stay home with her. Every day, they would play in the pool. Ashley would give her a puppy. And Tyler: he's so cute. But these aren't her children. None of this is hers. Crazy to even think like it could be.

—

Claire stands outside the bathroom, listening to the sound of water running in the sink. Something's not right. What's Gray doing in there? Without knocking, she opens the door. And he's just standing there in front of the mirror. Mesmerized by his own reflection.

"Why are you looking at yourself so much lately?"

"I'm not," he says.

"Ha-ha." Claire laughs with the highest level of sarcasm she can muster, because he's been in here the whole time she was putting Tyler to sleep. And this morning, he shut himself in the bathroom for hours. Maybe not yesterday, but the day before, he was certainly checking himself out every chance he could. Hard to believe this is the same man who often just wets his hair before heading to work so it looks like he took a shower.

So what's changed?

This is the insomnia. That's why everything feels strange and nothing makes sense. If she could just close her eyes, just for a minute… Claire leaves Gray alone without saying another word and drags herself to the living room couch. Before she can lie down, she notices something move outside on the deck. Outside the window, where there should be only darkness, there is a hand pressed against the glass. Someone standing out there, peering in.

Claire screams. Then, realizing who it is, she screams again. *"No. Way."*

Ashley York steps back from the window into the darkness, too late not to be noticed. Claire runs across the room, flips on the outside lights, and shoves open the door. It really and truly is Ashley York, standing on their deck, and she's holding a giant stuffed bear.

Ashley waves sheepishly.

Claire, incredulous, turns toward Gray, who has come up behind her, and somehow he appears not to be surprised at all. She blinks and swivels back to Ashley, who lets herself in and shuts the door behind her. She's wearing white tank top and jeans, which are, of course, form-fitting. The stuffed bear might weigh more than Ashley does.

Claire never imagined what she'd do if she actually met Ashley. It always seemed like she lived in some other separate LA, a world apart from Claire. It seemed impossible that she could be standing here in Claire's living room. *But here she is.* It occurs to Claire to take a selfie, but all she can manage to say is, "No way. You are not here."

"What's with the bear...Ashley?" Gray has his arms crossed when he should be groveling for Ashley's forgiveness after what he did.

Ashley holds the bear in one arm and moves toward him. She doesn't seem mad at all. "It's for Mindy," she says.

Claire grips her phone. Something is not right. "How do you know our daughter?"

Ashley fixes Gray with an intense look. A look that says a lot.

He turns to Claire with an almost imperceptible shake of his head. "I wanted to surprise you. I have a friend at work whose niece works for Ashley."

Claire stares at him. *That* is the best he can come up with? "You don't have friends at work."

Mindy appears in her PJs. Obviously, she has been listening. She glances from Claire to Gray. "For me?" She reaches hesitantly for the bear.

"Absolutely." Ashley kneels and gives it to Mindy. The bear has curly brown fur, a white muzzle, and black beady eyes spaced too far apart. Mindy hugs it and it engulfs her. Ashley picks up Mindy and the bear, its head craning over her shoulder. She lifts her above her head and spins her, almost exactly the way Gray does when he wants to make her laugh, and that's exactly what happens. By the time Ashley sets her down, Mindy is giggling uncontrollably.

She falls on the bear. "Do it again!"

"I need to talk to your father. Alone." Ashley glances from Gray to Claire and then turns toward the kitchen.

"What's going on here?" Claire says.

"I want to see his paintings," Ashley says. "They're in the garage, right?"

Gray shrugs slightly and follows her.

Claire lunges after them. "Paintings? Seriously?"

The doorbell rings. Ashley's head swivels toward the front door. "Don't answer it."

Like Claire would bother with whoever's at the front door while Ashley York is standing right here at the entrance to her kitchen. She puts her hands on her hips. "How do you know he paints?"

The doorbell rings again, followed by hard rapping.

"Gray, get that, please," Claire says. Maybe Ashley will make more sense without Gray here to lie for her. *Office-friend's-niece? Pl-ease.* Just because she's exhausted doesn't make her an idiot. She wonders how much time they've spent together, and why Ashley would have anything to do with Gray?

"Don't." Ashley holds out a hand. "Turn out the lights."

The knocking grows louder, but Gray just stands there.

Ashley approaches the row of switches on the wall, but she's living in a dream world if she thinks turning out the lights will stop whoever is knocking so insistently.

"We have a sleeping ten-month-old," Claire whispers.

"Don't answer it," Ashley says. "It might not be safe."

Claire has to stop herself from laughing. Ashley must think that anyone who lives outside her Richie Rich neighborhood is besieged by crime. "Don't worry. I'll get rid of them. If they're looking for you, you're not here."

As Claire starts toward the door, Ashley whispers frantically to Gray.

Claire cracks the door and peers out. And sees nothing. Only darkness and fog.

She flips on the porch light, undoes the latch, and opens it up all the way. Fog rests over the neighborhood like a blanket. The air is still, heavy, silent. Nothing stirs. Nothing at all.

The chaos is inside, behind her, where Ashley's whispering has moved to the kitchen. It's not really even whispering; it's more of a squeaking, like a chipmunk chattering.

Claire closes the door and locks it. As she turns, Gray hurries out of the kitchen and down the hallway. "Where are you going?" she asks.

He ignores her. *Fine.* Now maybe she can get some answers out of Ashley.

In the kitchen, she watches in amazement as Ashley squats down and hugs Mindy with a weird familiarity, as if she and Mindy go way back.

"Okay," Claire says. "What's the deal?"

"She was thanking me." Ashley gets to her feet. "Isn't that right, sweetie?"

Mindy nods. "I ready for my story now."

Claire reaches down and gives Mindy a gentle pat on the back. "Go find your father. I think he's in our bedroom." Claire stares at Ashley, who looks sort of wistful as Mindy hurries out.

"What I'm asking," Claire continues, "is why you're really at my house? The way my husband attacked you, I was expecting to hear from the cops or your lawyers, not you in person—here, on our back deck."

Ashley glances away. She fiddles with the alphabet magnets on the fridge. When she finally speaks, the words come out slowly. "Gray was upset that I showed his painting to an art-dealer friend of mine, because it's a work in progress. But Gray is a brilliant artist." She grabs the doorknob to the garage, like she owns the place, and glances back at Claire. "He told me to go ahead and look at his stuff."

"Wait." Claire moves to follow her. Gray never shows his unfinished work, not even to her, and now he gave a stranger permission to dig through it?

"Alone," Ashley says. "I look at art alone."

Mindy's footsteps return to the kitchen, but Claire keeps her eyes on Ashley *Alone?* With anyone other than Ashley, Claire would call bullshit. But what else could explain Ashley's presence? Claire is too tired to think.

Mindy pulls on Claire's shirt. "Daddy said you wanted to read to me, Mommy."

Wow. This must be serious if Gray turned down a chance to read Mindy's bedtime story. "Fine," she says to Ashley. "But he doesn't finish anything. You'll see."

If this wasn't Ashley York, no way Claire would let her dig around in the garage alone. She lifts Mindy, and her new giant bear, and carries them to her little bed. Sure, Gray has talent, but why would Ashley care? No way they're having an affair. Not even a friendship makes sense, but what does? She liked Ashley better back when she'd existed in a glitzy version of LA that was completely apart from Claire's world. Once she gets Mindy to bed, the three of them are going to have a long and no doubt unpleasant talk. And, probably, she'll stop following Ashley on social media.

As she tucks Mindy in, hurried footsteps brush the carpet in the hallway. "Gray?"

She gets up and peers out in time to hear the door to the garage open and close.

Claire says good night to Mindy and turns out the light.

"What about my story?"

"If you're still awake when your father comes to check on you, he'll read to you."

She shuts the door. Mindy knows better than to protest. That might work on Gray, but not her.

She considers changing clothes, like she would for any visitor, but now it would be too obvious. Instead, she grabs the hoodie she left on the couch, which will at least cover her faded T-shirt.

As she pulls the hoodie over her head, she feels a creepy stare and glances out toward the deck. There's a man standing there, almost exactly where Ashley stood, peering in the window. A big man in a suit with disheveled gray hair and a look of determination. He looks oddly familiar.

Claire fixes him with a fierce look. "I'm calling the police."

He presses a police badge against the window.

Charlie Lost It

Charlie peeks through the curtains at the crazy on his front doorstep. It's the crazy with the bald pate smooth as putty that was almost arrogantly oiled, the one Detective Parker warned him about. The crazy knocks again. But anyone with even a lick of sense knows better than to open up for a crazy.

Across the street, outside the Wilsons' window where the crazy woman with the giant stuffed animal was spying in on them, a giant bird of paradise casts strange shadows through the fog. No sign of her now. If Charlie had their number, he could warn them. His daughter, whose house he's living in for three months while she's out of the country, didn't even have a phone book. Good thing he stayed inside. If he'd gone to warn the Wilsons in person, he'd have run into the bald crazy who is now on his doorstep. Crazies are everywhere, and now there is no chance of sleep tonight. Not without the Oxycontin, which he stopped taking.

The crazy holds up a badge, not toward the door but toward the window. The crazy looks right at Charlie. *Can he see me?*

Charlie snaps the curtain shut and steps back. He nearly trips into the wingback chair. He turns out the lights and creeps to the door.

He looks through the peephole. And there's the badge again, as if a badge makes the crazy officer any less crazy. After all, it was an officer who clubbed the bum, and who scared him into the street. Charlie should have told Detective Parker all about it, the way the crazy officer's eyes were out of focus, the mucus running into his mustache. Charlie shouldn't have driven away, but what else could he have done? He wanted to confess, but then Detective Parker didn't give him a chance. What if all these crazy officers are in cahoots?

"I know you're in there," the crazy says. "I need to ask you about Saul Parker. He's under investigation. I'm with Internal Affairs."

"Detective Parker thought you would say that."

The crazy knocks again. "Come on. Open up. Have you seen him since this morning? I saw you talking to him."

The crazy looms forward. His bloodshot eye fills the lens of the peephole.

Charlie falls back against the wall. "I'm calling Detective Parker right now," he shouts. "I'll be sure to tell him you're here."

"You do that. Tell him I need to see him."

In the kitchen, Charlie spreads his stack of papers across the table. Anyone who knows anything about anything knows to keep things organized so they're easy to find. But Parker's card isn't here where it should be, and with the crazy shouting outside, Charlie can't concentrate.

Yesterday, he scrapped a bunch of junk mail. Parker's card must have gotten mixed into the junk mail somehow by mistake. Charlie turns over the trash can and empties the contents onto the kitchen floor. He kneels and smears his hands through the papers, which are torn and shredded and wet with god knows what. Coffee grounds, eggshells, brown banana peels, expired cheese. Smeared across the floor is everything he's thrown out since last week. Except, of course, for Detective Parker's card. It's not here.

He remembers, distinctly, how Detective Parker had plucked it right out of thin air. At the time, Charlie thought there would never be any need to call him. After all, Parker was only interested in Gray Wilson, who's just a dolt. Charlie knows crazies and Gray is not a crazy; he's just a slouchy dolt who refused to listen when Charlie warned him about the crazies. He was too preoccupied with whatever drove him outside in his underwear. Some problem with his wife, Charlie assumed at the time, but what if that wasn't it? What if Gray *is* crazy?

Anyone with even a lick of sense knows that when you lose something, you have to think back to the last time you saw it and go from there. Charlie recalls how after making the card appear out of thin air, Parker placed it on the side table next to his Oxycontin. Only a half-dose so far today, but now his back is killing him worse than ever —he needs a double.

He struggles to his feet, wipes his hands on his pants, and grabs his phone. When he pushes through the kitchen door to the living room, a blast of cold cuts through his thin shirt. Lights are on. The front door is open. The crazy is standing there in his cheap suit. Holding Detective Parker's card like a carrot.

"Looking for this?"

The crazy's jacket hangs open. Inside is a shoulder holster. If Charlie wants to live, he'd better placate this crazy or he'll meet the same fate as the bum that other crazy officer shoved practically right out in front of Charlie's car.

"I have to take my pill," Charlie says. He begins crossing the room, slowly. No sudden movements.

The crazy's eyes spark. He rips the card in half, and half again, until it's shredded to confetti, which he showers on the floor.

"From now on," he says. "You talk to me."

Charlie sets the phone on the side table and eases into the wingback. If the crazy intends to end his life, then Charlie should first at least ease his own suffering. He'll just take a half, better to keep his wits about him. But a half isn't much better than none at all, not with his tolerance. To ease the pain even a little, he needs a whole, minimum. He opens the bottle of round blue pills that he's been dreaming about all day and shakes one out in his palm. He salivates. His hand trembles. He lifts it to his lips. The pill has two flavors: first the vague sweetness when it touches his tongue, and then the distinct acidic taste as he crunches it with his right molars.

He swallows. When he focuses again. The crazy is standing right over him.

"You want to call Parker?" the crazy says. "Fine." He takes Charlie's phone and dials the number by heart. He straightens his shoulders and looks up with his mouth slightly open. For a moment, the crazy looks almost hopeful. Then, desperate.

"Straight to voicemail." He drops the phone in Charlie's lap. Drops his shoulders. His face sours.

Charlie looks down at the plastic phone. A tinny voice suggests he leave a message. Maybe Detective Parker won't get it in time, but anyone with half a lick of sense knows you have to take every chance. "This is Charlie Streeter. The crazy you warned me about just broke into my house and—"

The crazy snatches the phone. "I didn't break in. I was concerned for the old guy's wellbeing...when he couldn't open the door. But, it turns out, you spooked him. You better explain yourself. You hear me,

Parker? I know you had something to do with Carter." He hangs up but does not return Charlie's phone.

Instead, he pulls out his own phone and shows Charlie a photo of a cop on a beach. His uniform is pressed and creased, and the hat has gold trim. His mustache looks just like Tom Selleck's. "Have you seen this guy?"

"Never," Charlie tries to say, but his dry mouth bumbles the word.

"That's Carter," the crazy says. "He's dead now. And your pal, Parker, had something to do with it."

Charlie reaches for the pills, but the crazy snatches the bottle. He sits on the loveseat. In one hand he has both phones, and in the other, he studies the Oxycontin. "Jonesing, huh?"

"It's a prescription," Charlie says. "For my back."

"Tell me what's going on, and you can have all you want." He shakes the pills.

Charlie's mouth waters. No point in fighting an armed man half his age. Anyone who knows anything knows that it's better to live to fight another day. The crazies are all in cahoots, all of them. They must have seen Charlie watching. They must suspect Charlie knows, and if Charlie admits it, this crazy will tear him apart like he scrapped Parker's card.

So, Charlie says nothing. He sits there and pretends to listen while the crazy goes on and on about what a good man Carter was. How he was too young to die. If there is one thing Charlie can do, it's sit. He'll sit all night if he has to. He leans back, wishing he could sleep, but the air practically buzzes with the current coming off the crazy.

"What do you think about that, old man? Huh? Don't fall asleep. Help me nail Parker."

Charlie feels emboldened. Maybe because of the pill he already took or maybe it's his need for more, but he's not afraid of dying, he realizes. This crazy, what can he do? "I think you're crazy, is what I think," Charlie says. "You blame Detective Parker for your crazy partner's death? But what did he do? I bet he had it coming."

"Fuck you," the crazy says. He empties the Oxycontin onto the floor: Charlie's last eleven pills. With his black leather boot, he grinds the pills into the carpet until they're nothing but chalky-blue dust.

Charlie stands up. It's not the medicine; it's the gesture. It feels like Charlie's life crushed by the crazy's boot.

The crazy rises from the loveseat. "Sit down."

But if Charlie doesn't stand up for himself, then who will? "You're going to pay for that."

"What did Parker tell you?"

Charlie curls his fingers into a fist. "You're crazy, is what he said. And I should have listened harder."

"Come on. Parker didn't drive all the way here just to warn you about me. He knew I was following him. Tell me something else. Something I don't know."

Charlie snorts. Fishing is what the crazy is doing, trying to scare Charlie into admitting something. This crazy standing over him, nostrils flaring, has no idea about the car in the garage with the dented fender and the shot-out rear window. And Charlie is not about to tell him. He's not going to say anything about Wilson either. Whatever reason Detective Parker had for asking about him, he wanted to keep it a secret. And if Charlie knows how to do anything, it's how to keep a secret.

He'll find someone to replace the glass, someone discreet. No one will ever know. The crazy officer who shoved the bum is probably so far gone he doesn't even remember.

Charlie stares at the blue smear in the carpet. The Oxycontin will still work fine, if he can figure out how to get it up from the carpet. It's just a little dirty, that's all. A little dirt never hurt anyone. Then he sees how out of control he has become. He must fight the urge to get down and lick the blue powder like a dog. He can almost feel the carpet on his tongue—he can taste it. He needs to stop. This is it. Cold turkey. No more.

"You still want it, huh? I bet you'd lick it up from the floor."

Charlie glances up at the crazy's big arrogant face and imagines it with a black eye. He swings.

But the crazy's arm lashes out fast as a snake. He grabs Charlie's fist, nearly crushing it with his meaty hand. He spins Charlie around and twists his arm behind him.

"My back," Charlie screams.

"Your back, huh?" The crazy wrenches Charlie's arm up until he's forced to bend over. "How about now? Does that hurt?"

The pain is excruciating. Charlie hasn't bent over this far in years, maybe a decade. He might never stand up straight again. "Fucking crazy..." He can hardly breathe as the crazy twists him around and pushes him toward the loveseat.

"On your knees."

Charlie tries to carefully lower himself. The crazy shoves him down.

Forces his face into the carpet and the blue powder.

"Go ahead, old man. Take your medicine."

Charlie tries not to breathe, tries to hold his mouth closed. But his jaw opens all on its own. Pretty soon, carpet covers his tongue. Fibers lodge between his teeth. His throat goes numb. Disgust replaces the pain in his back. How can he fight a crazy? He can't even fight his own addiction.

Touch

While waiting in the garage for Ashley to fetch the charm, Gray removes the canvas with the awful black swirl from the easel and leans it against the workbench. He shoves aside the boxes that hide his collection of unfinished paintings and digs out the portrait of Charlie he'd started before all this happened. He places it on the easel. It's hardly more than a sketch, and Charlie looks cruel, not at all the way Gray remembers him in the doorway Saturday morning with the sunlight streaming in around him. But everyone looks sinister in silhouette. If he cheats the angle of the sun, the light will capture Charlie's kindness in contrast with the deep grooves that line his face.

Ashley still hasn't returned, so he squeezes a dab of black paint on his palette and selects a small brush. As his brush connects with the canvas, his feels a pull in his hand. Then he sees it in his mind. Another terrible black blur is what he's going to paint. Not Charlie.

He tosses the brush on the workbench.

But there was more than just blackness this time. There was light there too. Light streaming in. A dark angular object. A dim hint of stairs. As if he were looking at Ashley's cellar from Wayob's point of view, assuming he was still there in August's body, looking up through the glass door blocked by the refrigerator.

Something rattles, and Gray starts.

It's the knob on the kitchen door as Ashley swings it open and steps out. "It's totally broken." She holds up two objects: the obsidian snake and the white stone. The door closes behind her. The sight of her in his body still dizzies him.

"So what are we going to do now?" she asks.

He struggles to focus. "Maybe we can fix it?"

"Yeah, I tried that." She shows him how Claire broke the snake off from the stone.

"Well, we have to do something. Our lives are in danger. August tried to kill me."

"Whoa. Okay, what?"

"It wasn't August, exactly. Someone else was in his body. He said his name was Wayob and that he can become anyone."

"Seriously? And you believed him?"

"Not at first, but— If you could have seen his face. Why would he make that up?" He explains how desperately Wayob wanted the charm, or *the Encanto* as he called it, and how he locked him in her cellar.

"So, we're safe for now?"

"I don't know. If Wayob can just become anyone, I don't know how long this will stop him."

"Well, you got us into this, so I hope you have another idea."

He swallowed. They could try finding the fortune-teller. But Olvera would be empty this late on a Tuesday.

"Wow." She proceeds to the workbench, sets down the two pieces of the Encanto, and studies his sketch. "Starting a new one?"

"Sort of." He picks up the porous white stone and the snake and tries to force them back together.

Ashley kneels and reaches toward his stack of canvases, below the workbench.

"Those are rejects," he says.

She doesn't seem to hear him. She pulls out the landscape of Malibu Lagoon with the burning bush, which he'd discarded before starting the portrait of Charlie.

His heart pounds. He feels naked, more exposed than just skin— here all his hopes, his dreams are spread bare before her in this harsh fluorescent light.

"This is amazing," she says. "The flames are so emotional."

Something surges in his chest. Maybe the painting is better than he thought? She reaches for another one. He should put the landscape away before she gets a better look, before Claire comes out here and makes another negative comment. He can paint better than that now; he knows he can.

But first he inspects the narrow hole in the stone where a spindle anchored the snake like a dial. It must have connected to some internal mechanism that drove the quill to stab his hand.

"We're missing the shaft," he says, squatting beside her and pointing at the hole.

"I ran my fingers through every inch of carpet," she says. "Here, let me see." She reaches for the stone and obsidian snake. As he passes it to her, her fingertips graze his palm—her skin feels like sparks.

Time slows down.

What he could only describe as energy—though it's so much more—consumes him, overcomes his whole body, overrides his vision. First there is pure white energy, then nothing. It's like floating. And though he can't see Ashley, he knows they're together. In this warm, dark place.

They transcend into what seems like some other dimension. They leave their corporeal forms—his body, like a weight, drops away—leaving all of Earth like a memory fogged by time, half-forgotten. It doesn't matter; there is so much newness to explore. He and Ashley could know every atom in the universe and beyond. A childlike excitement bubbles up within him.

Someone screams. Someone here with Gray and Ashley in this non-place. The scream sounds like August.

No, not August. Wayob.

Wayob is here with them. Screaming. As though dying a thousand deaths. The scream goes on and on at an impossible volume that grows from everywhere. The scream swallows Ashley, and then she becomes the scream, and then Gray's own mind drowns in the sound and the scream is all there is.

He's Not Here

Most people would have been wary of an officer at their back door, but not the woman with the curtain of mocha hair that fell across her face as she shoved open the slider.

"What do you want?" She sounded curt, approaching annoyed. And something about her was familiar.

Her skin was pale, almost translucent, the veins in her cheeks visible by the light on the deck. It was her eyes, the color of steel, that were unmistakable. Now Saul recalled their brief encounter on Olvera Street when he was searching for Aleman, who must have been under Wayob's influence at the time. If Wilson was there too, it removed what little doubt remained. It went beyond the realm of coincidence—this was a convergence.

Saul returned his badge to his pocket. "Mrs. Wilson?"

She tucked her hair back behind her ear. "Good work. You solved the mystery of the millennium."

"Do you remember me? From Saturday?"

She squinted at him and shrugged as if Saturday might have been more like three years ago instead of three days.

"At the Day of the Dead, I helped you get your stroller through the crowd." Saul remembered how her little girl, in a pink dress, had smiled up at him.

Mrs. Wilson gripped the handle on the slider. "So, you're stalking us now?"

"No. But I'm afraid someone is."

"Seriously?" She glanced doubtfully behind her. "Who?"

Saul pulled out his phone, which was still off. As he pressed the button to boot it up, his stomach roiled again with an uneasiness. It was more than just worry that Arcos might use it to track him. The home screen came up. He flipped on airplane mode. As he opened the photo roll a sense of dread overwhelmed him, and his eyes squeezed shut. He scrolled with his thumb. Forced his eyes open. It was the mugshot of Rydell. He swiped to the picture he'd saved of Aleman from the MDC's staff directory.

"Have you seen this man?"

She glanced at the phone and shook her head. "No. Why would he be stalking us?"

"That's what I'm trying to find out." He swiped forward to Rydell. "What about him?"

Mrs. Wilson studied the mugshot. "I've never seen him in real life, but his photo was all over the place."

"Mind if I come in? I need to talk to your husband."

She glanced over her shoulder. "Now's not a good time."

Behind her, the room was empty and in the same disarray he'd seen yesterday, except for the additional laundry basket of spilled towels by the couch. The flat-screen was on but muted and showed a news anchor in front of an alley cordoned off with crime scene tape. Then an exterior shot of a Quality Inn—Hernandez's new case.

"It will only take a minute."

"He's not here." She grabbed the door handle. "Thanks for stopping by."

As she tried to close the door, he blocked it with his foot and tried to look casual. As though his shoe just happened to be there in the way.

"His Camry is on the street."

She centered herself doorway, her feet apart. "He took a Lyft."

Saul frowned. If he forced his way into the Wilsons' house, he could forget about their cooperation. However, he'd learned from experience that people who were scared usually opened up. "As you may know, this man was involved in a carjacking and fatal shooting. What hasn't been released yet is that immediately afterward he was seen following your husband through Hollywood."

"But Gray was at work on Sunday," she said. "He was nowhere near Hollywood."

"You know that for a fact?"

She folded her arms across her stomach. A hardness crept into her face. "Is he a suspect?"

"Not at all," Saul said. "But it is suspicious."

"He doesn't know shit, trust me. *If* he was there, then it was just a coincidence."

"I don't believe in coincidences," Saul said. "There's a connection between this man and the man I was tailing when I ran into you at the Day of the Dead."

"What kind of connection?"

What could he say? The fact that they had both acted like someone else on separate occasions would do little to convince her. "All I can tell you is that the man behind all of this is looking for your husband."

"Whatever." She gripped the door. "I'm tired of secrets. Please step back."

Somehow, he had to convince her to help him. So he took a deep breath. "Listen...a young woman is dead, and I believe she was coerced, possibly hypnotized, into taking her own life. Talking to your husband may help me find the man responsible. I have to stop him before anyone else dies."

"I hope you do," she said. "But you're wasting your time here."

"Have you noticed anything unusual about your husband?"

Cold light glinted in her eyes. "Unusual is a crime now?"

"Not typically."

"Ashley York's not pressing charges, so don't worry about it."

"That's the least of my worries," Saul said, although he assumed it was related. "Think about it. What if this killer who can coerce people got to your husband as well?" He shifted forward, his whole body in the doorway.

But Mrs. Wilson held her ground. Apparently, she did not care to keep the usual distance from Saul's girth. She straightened up and faced him.

"I need to come in," he said. "Let's do this the easy way."

She exhaled hot air into his face. "You got a warrant?"

"Don't need one. It doesn't work like TV."

"If you don't leave, I'll call 911 and find out how it works." She held up her phone.

She had called his bluff. All he really had was some odd behavior and a hunch. Not probable cause to enter the premises, even if he weren't on suspension. Using force wouldn't work either. If he plowed his way in, Gray Wilson would clam up for sure. Saul had to lure him out somehow. Make him want to talk.

"We got off on the wrong foot. I apologize. It's no excuse, but I had a rough night last night. Let's talk when you're ready." He stepped back, snapped his fingers, and produced a card.

"Cute." She took the card. Somewhere back in the house, a baby cried. Mrs. Wilson sighed, rolled the slider closed, and locked it. Then she drew the curtains.

Saul descended the steps from the deck to the side yard, where he was plunged into darkness. She had turned out the lights.

He used his phone as a flashlight to find the latch on their gate and let himself out.

Ashley Felt It, Too

Ashley fell back from the warm, dark place—fell down into her body. Into cool dry air, on the floor of the garage. The bleak fluorescent light shone above her.

She had been kneeling when she reached for the Encanto, when her fingers grazed Gray's hand. He had felt electrified. Like a circuit connected between them that snapped them into a darkness. They had floated, weightless, like a plane dropping through an air pocket. An entirely different existence. She'd felt herself drifting through Gray's consciousness while, at the same time, he was inside her. The two of them were just thoughts, intertwined, and floating. She had felt who Gray was, completely, and all at once.

Then, that horrible screaming was everywhere.

Now she was lying on the floor with no idea how much time had passed—an hour or a second or a day—and her head on Gray's chest. *His* chest.

She bolted upright. Felt her face, her breasts, her hips. *Mine.* My *body.* "Do you have a mirror?"

Gray opened his eyes and blinked at her. He stood groggily and offered his hand. She reached for it—remembered the electricity—and shrank back. "I think I'll, uh…"

"Yeah." He nodded and looked around, as if he couldn't believe where he was.

She grabbed onto the workbench and pulled herself up.

"You don't need a mirror," he said. "You're Ashley York. What about me?" He gazed at her with intensity.

No one else could understand the impossible experience they had shared. "You're you," she said.

She looked at her slender hand and felt like laughing. She touched her chin, soft and hairless, and inhaled deeply. Even her insides felt younger somehow—more like *her*. Then she did laugh. Giggled like she was six again.

"How did you do that?" he asked.

Did he think *she* had pulled them through each other's consciousness and back into their own bodies? "I thought it was you."

"Did you hear Wayob's scream?" He studied her.

Hear it? She had felt it, deep inside herself, even when she'd had no self at all. "Wayob is the guy in August's body?"

"Yes. I'm pretty sure it was him." He picked up the stone from the floor, where it had fallen. Then, with thumb and forefinger, he gingerly picked up the shiny black snake.

"So, what do we do now?" she asked.

"Get back to our lives, I guess." He slapped the button by the kitchen door. The garage door growled into action.

Ashley felt uncertain. Her life—what was it? Outside the door was fog and the dim, orange ambience of LA. Gray was right, she realized. What else could they do?

"I'm getting rid of this." He held up the stone and snake. "Claire was right to throw it away." He marched out into the moist air.

She followed him. Between the house and a big leafy bush was an overfilled garbage bin, its lid propped half-open. Gray shoved the stone between a pair of slimy white bags. He forced the lid down. But when he let go, it popped back open.

He turned to face her. "I'm so sorry. If I had known..."

Ashley was sorry too, though she couldn't quite say what for. She felt hardened by the experience. The life she'd been so desperate to get back to didn't seem to matter so much anymore. She might even miss seeing his jade eyes in the mirror, the way the bristles on his chin felt in her hand.

Gray squinted up the hill into the fog, as if considering what to say. Traffic hissed in the distance. He shoved a hand in his back pocket and scratched the tattoo he had no idea he had on his butt.

By the side of the house, a man appeared. He wore the same cheap trench coat from the portrait that she'd found in her office—which she now recognized as Gray's from the bold strokes that captured the man so exactly—the same giant shoulders and thinning hair, the same penetrating eyes staring back at her. He paused for a moment behind the trash bin and then hurried past it and around the bush toward the driveway.

"Run," Ashley screamed.

Gray glanced around. "What?"

The man cleared the bush and huffed toward them. His pant cuffs were ripped and basically solid dirt up to the knees. At least his shirt was tucked in. His hair was matted down and moist, gray at the temples.

"Gray Wilson," he said between breaths, "you're a hard man to find."

"Hold it right there, Parker," another man yelled from across the street in the fog.

Parker tensed his big shoulders and turned slowly.

The second man crossed the street. He held a gun aimed at Parker, she hoped, and not them. Streetlight glared on his sweaty shaved scalp.

Ashley and Gray exchanged glances.

"Dammit, Arcos," Parker said, "put your gun away."

Arcos's face twisted with raw anger. But when he glanced at her, his expression changed. "Oh my god. You're Ashley York!"

She shrugged.

"This man's harassing you, isn't he?"

"I'm not sure what he was about to do."

Parker reached toward his coat. "I'm a detective—"

"Not anymore." Arcos waved his gun. "Step aside."

Parker stepped back, his shoes scuffing the pavement. Arcos kept his gun trained on Parker and showed them a badge.

"We were only taking out the trash," Gray said.

Arcos seemed puzzled. "Spill it, Parker. Why are you here?"

Parker half shrugged. "I wanted an autograph."

"Not going to happen." Arcos motioned Parker toward the street, then fixed his gaze on Ashley and Gray. "You want to file a report?"

Ashley glanced at Gray. Whatever he knew about Parker, he wasn't saying anything in front of Arcos, which made sense because where would they start? *August is locked in my cellar*. Talk about publicity.

"What's to report?" she asked Arcos.

"Don't worry. Parker won't bother you again." He handed her his card. "Need anything else, you call me. Got it?"

Arcos waved his gun and ushered Parker across the street.

"I'll walk you to your car," Gray said to Ashley.

As they walked up the hill, she glanced back. Parker was standing in the road, his hands held up in surrender. He was arguing with Arcos but seemed to be watching her.

"So, who is he?" she asked.

"I have no idea."

"But you drew him."

"I thought I made him up, like a character. I didn't know what to believe when he showed up in real life."

"I thought he was Wayob."

"Yeah, that's what I was afraid of," Gray said, "but I don't think he is. At least he wasn't acting like it. Wayob was out of control."

"Weird." Ashley glanced back at the two men. Arcos was shouting at Parker, but if he was under arrest then where were the handcuffs?

Her white Mercedes stood out from the line of dark cars along the curb. She discovered her key fob in the front pocket of her jeans, where she would never have put it.

"I should come help you with August," Gray said.

A part of her wanted Gray to come, but what could he really do? Assuming Wayob was gone, then it would just be August locked in her cellar. She was so done with August and his creepy flowers and fake smile.

"I'll let Sammy take care of it," she said.

She wondered if Gray had felt it too—the way they had drifted together on another plane of existence, inside each other's consciousness.

She followed his gaze down the hill. Beyond the two angry cops, fog blurred the road into white nothing.

"I should probably go." She wanted to hug Gray, but she was afraid of the sparks, all that electricity that charged into her when they touched. "Your kids are amazing, you know."

"I know." Gray stood in the road, his hands in his pockets as she unlocked the car and got in.

She rolled down the window and waved.

He nodded, his lips pressed tight together. Was he hoping they would meet again?

Ashley pulled out and drove away without looking back. She imagined him waving goodbye as he faded into the fog behind her. That was how she wanted to remember him.

Saul Versus Arcos

Saul was sick of obstacles, and as far as obstacles went, Arcos was insubstantial.

Arcos seemed to have no idea why Saul was here outside the Wilsons', didn't ask who Wilson was, and didn't even seem curious about Ashley York, here at night in a neighborhood so far below the stature of her net worth. All his anger seemed focused on Saul.

And it was better this way. Better to confront him as far as possible from anyone else, because Arcos was coming unhinged. So, while Wilson and Ashley disappeared up the hill and into the fog, Saul let Arcos march him down the street at gunpoint.

Arcos's plain wrap was parked under a massive eucalyptus whose roots had wrecked the curb. He ordered Saul to get in, but getting in would be a full surrender. From the backseat, it would be almost impossible to gain the upper hand. So Saul turned to face him. "How did you find me?"

The gun shook in Arcos's hand. He stepped into Saul's face, his breath stale. "What happened to Carter?"

Saul had wondered the same thing. Ordinarily, Arcos and Carter were joined at the hip. "Shouldn't you know?"

Arcos frowned, and his already sagging shoulders slumped. All his usual smugness drained away, leaving him looking defeated and ten years older. "Look, Parker, level with me."

"About what?"

Arcos looked at his shoes and back up at Saul. "About whatever you're up to."

"You think I'm up to something?" What he needed to do was to create a distraction so he could disarm him.

"I talked to the old guy." Arcos pointed his thumb toward Streeter's house.

"And?" Saul shoved his hands into his pockets and felt around.

"Hands where I can see them."

Saul slowly withdrew his hands, and in the process palmed a deck of cards and a receipt into his left sleeve. In his right hand, he grabbed a crumpled piece of paper, probably another receipt, and a tin of Altoids. He held them up. "Mint?"

Arcos shook his head. "You're not going to open that."

"They're just mints." Saul shook the tin as if that proved it. Then with a flick of his wrist he made them disappear into his right sleeve, along with the crumpled paper. "I guess you knew I was tailing you this morning," Arcos said.

"You were? Why would you do that?"

"The old man doesn't know shit. He was a decoy, right?"

"A decoy for what?" he asked.

"You tell me." Arcos's voice, which was already high, shot up in pitch. "Why would Carter go nuts?"

Saul paused. Up the hill, the fog had thinned a bit. Wilson and Ashley were standing by a white Mercedes. "What did he do?"

Arcos stared at Saul. "Don't pretend you haven't heard."

If Carter had done something, Hernandez would have been dying to tell Saul, but he'd turned his phone off because he was afraid of being tracked. "My phone died."

Arcos glanced down at the road. His voice cracked. "You threatened us."

"The man I'm investigating is extremely dangerous. I told you to back off, for your own protection."

"You have no investigation, Parker. You're on suspension."

"You want to spout IA bullshit? I've got lives at stake here—maybe even Carter's life."

"Carter's dead."

Saul inhaled sharply. He waited for Arcos to continue, but he said nothing further. His eyes went watery in the streetlight.

Arcos without Carter; it seemed impossible. For a moment, Saul tried to let go of the animosity between him and Arcos. He asked as gently as he could, "How?"

"He was shot. A witness claimed Carter was stealing a car, but he'd never do that. Straight up no way." Arcos looked away. "If I had just given him a ride."

Saul could think of one reason for Carter to steal a car—Wayob made him—but he wasn't about to share this with Arcos, who was still aiming his gun vaguely in Saul's direction. Saul would be hard to miss.

"Carter said he saw inside you." As Arcos turned back to Saul, shadows from the eucalyptus in the streetlight swam across his face. "What the fuck does that mean?"

Hair prickled on Saul's neck. The fog was closing in. "Tell me exactly what he said."

"He pulled a gun on me," Arcos said, "and the thing is, to even think that he'd do that is ridiculous. There's just no way."

Saul said nothing.

Arcos swallowed. He squared Saul in the eye. "You and Carter. Were you… Were you getting together, after hours?"

The hesitation, the naked concern on his face. So, the rumors were true. Arcos and Carter had something going.

"No." Saul almost felt sorry for him. "Of course not."

"Then why would he say that?"

"When did he say it?"

"Last night. Outside that shithole you visited in Mar Vista. He said you were trapped. And he laughed, like you two had some inside joke going."

Saul blinked. A figment of a dream came back to him. And in this dream, he was inside an apartment—it was Saroyan's apartment—in the darkened bedroom. Standing in the shadows by the bed where Saroyan slept under a blanket.

It was just a dream—*had* to be a dream. He hoped. And yet his heart hammered against his ribs. A vise tightened on his gut.

He needed to know. "I have to go."

Arcos waved the gun. "I don't think so. You have to help me clear Carter's name."

Saul glanced down the hill to where he'd parked the Mustang two houses from the Wilsons'. It was hard to feel like helping a man who made his demands from behind the barrel of a gun.

With a wave of his hand, he made the crumpled paper appear, as if out of thin air, between his fingers. He flattened it out. "This might clear him." He held the receipt up sideways so that Arcos couldn't read it.

As he slowly turned it, Arcos drew closer to see, the gun only inches from Saul's chest.

Saul flicked the receipt and made it disappear while simultaneously popping the other one out in his outstretched left hand. "Oops. Here it is."

Arcos turned his head to look. Saul grabbed the gun, wrenched it sideways, and tore it from his grip.

As Arcos reached for it, Saul stepped back and turned sideways. In one fluid motion, out of Arcos's view, he dropped the gun in his pocket and threw the tin of Altoids over Arcos's head. It gleamed briefly in the streetlight as it sailed into a cluster of bushes.

"Asshole!" Arcos chased after it.

Saul yanked open the driver's side door of the plain wrap, squatted, and opened the fuse box below the steering wheel. He pulled the fuse for the ignition and several others, tossed them in the backseat, then closed the door and started down the hill.

Arcos was still thrashing around in the bushes. "Where's my gun, Parker?" he screamed.

Saul fired up the Mustang. He stowed the gun in the glovebox and steered around Arcos, who ran into the road, shaking Saul's tin.

Saul buzzed down the window.

"Hand over my gun, now," Arcos said. "Or I'll take your badge with it."

"Go ahead and try. I'd like to see how you justify drawing your weapon."

"I'll bury you with my report. You're done."

Saul laughed. "Be sure to include how I disarmed you. Look, I'll call you tomorrow, okay? Right now, I've got to get to my gig at the Castle."

As Saul rolled up the hill, he heard the insubstantial clunk of the tin as it bounced off the rear window. Then it clattered behind him in the road. Ahead, the white Mercedes along with Ashley York and Wilson had slipped away in the fog.

Homecoming

After leaving Gray's, Ashley found the 101 easy enough. She shivered as she plowed up the Cahuenga Pass and into the white vapor. She should slow down, but then she'd lose sight of the taillights of the only other car ahead of her, and she'd be alone.

"But I am alone," she said to her own eyes reflected in the rearview mirror, to the empty space behind her in the backseat. She was the only car that exited on Mulholland and drove up out of the fog into the moonless night. Through Gray's eyes, everything in the distance had seemed sort of blurry, but now the rooftops and the tree limbs along the ridgeline stood out, distinct against the void above.

Mulholland snaked north. It swerved toward the overlook perched high over the San Fernando Valley where the grid of streetlights and cars stretched out for miles and miles. She drove past cliff-top mansions, bougainvillea, past weathered oaks and dry grass. As Mulholland twisted toward Laurel Canyon, a pair of headlights came on fast. She dreaded dealing with August. But at least Sammy would be there to help her, and at least she had her body back.

The hillside dropped away to the south where an ocean of white cloud engulfed the LA basin. The three tallest downtown skyscrapers stabbed up through the white vapor and shone brightly for a moment before they too went under. Above Hollywood the clouds gave way to the hills. Lights glowed through the mist that snaked up the canyons and cast an eeriness into the otherwise stark night.

At the gate, her guard booth was empty. Sammy must have gone on his rounds. She used the gate-clicker and cruised down the drive.

Andrea's car was parked by the house. Gray hadn't mentioned seeing her, and normally she'd have left by now anyway, but maybe she'd decided to stay after all Ashley had revealed this morning?

Inside, the house was filled with a vast silence.

"Andrea?" Ashley's voice echoed in the kitchen.

"Ashley!" It was August, his voice muffled from below the refrigerator parked on top of the cellar door. Now she understood the soreness in her back.

"Is that really you down there?"

"Of course it's me. What the fuck happened?"

But how could she be sure? "Where's my mole?"

"Get me out of here." He choked and started crying. "Hurry, please."

"Not until you answer me."

"What are you talking about? How did I get down here?"

"I have a mole no one knows about, but you've seen it."

"The one on your hip?"

"Which hip?"

"Your right hip." Before she could correct him, he added, "I mean my right, your left."

"What's our status?"

"What do you mean?"

"The status of our relationship."

"I don't know. We broke up. Is that what you want to hear?"

"Yeah, but who broke up with who?" This, she knew, would be hard for him to admit.

"Why does it matter?"

"It doesn't matter if you want to stay in the cellar. Fine with me."

"You said you wanted to focus on your career. But you didn't have to break it off."

"Okay. I'll call Sammy." Although she couldn't think of a good explanation to explain to Sammy why August was trapped in the cellar, she knew she could count on him. In fact, he was just about the only person she could count on.

"Don't call Sammy," August whined. "*Please*, just let me out."

Sammy to the Rescue

Sammy set his Red Bull by the window of the booth an answered as calmly as he could. Mr. Mellow. Mr. Smooth. "Ashley. What can I do for you?" He mentally kicked himself for missing her return.

"I need your help," she said. "Mind coming down here?"

The way her voice wavered told him that maybe he could do something—maybe this was his chance to finally prove himself to her. She had never invited him inside this late at night. This was it. By the time he reached the house, he'd convinced himself that maybe Ashley didn't need his help at all, that she'd called him down there under false pretenses, and maybe, just maybe, her intentions were romantic. Maybe things were about to get hot and heavy like he had fantasized.

He threw open the front door and called her name.

"August is trapped in the cellar," she shouted from the kitchen.

Sammy jogged to her. Her explanation—as if she needed to justify herself—was that August had attacked her. She stated it matter-of-factly, as though throwing August in the cellar was self-defense 101.

Sammy was disappointed that this was why she had called him down here but at the same time amused. "I'm fine if we just keep him where he is."

Ashley shook her head. "I want him out of my house."

"Understood." Sammy rocked the fridge leaned back on its wheels. Almost the instant he rolled it off the cellar door, August burst out, threatening to sue for pain and suffering.

Sammy took him by the shoulders and steered him toward the door. "Ashley should sue you, little man. You're not even supposed to be here."

Ashley screamed, "What have you done?" She bolted down the cellar stairs.

Sammy resisted the urge to run after her because he couldn't leave August here unguarded.

August stared at his hands. "It wasn't me."

"Uh huh." Sammy wasn't even going to validate him by asking what it was. Instead, he clamped an arm around August's neck and dragged him toward the cellar.

Ashley wailed from below.

"I'm going, okay?" August said. "Let go."

Sammy eased up on the pressure and August started walking on his own. Sammy released him, pushed him forward, and followed him down the narrow steps.

At the foot of the stairs, Ashley was crouched over Andrea's body, pumping her chest.

"There's nothing you can do," August said. "She's been dead a long time."

Sammy shoved August aside and pulled Ashley off her. He lifted her into the air and tried to hug her. She balled his shirt in her fists and cried.

In the light streaming down from the kitchen, Andrea's skin was pale. Her head lay twisted and lifeless on the concrete floor, one leg bent under her.

Ashley threw off Sammy's arm and whirled on August, slapping him and punching him. "You evil asshole fucking bastard!"

He just stood there in a daze, his eyes out of focus. "It wasn't me." His voice shot up an octave, as if even he doubted even his own denial.

Sammy had been dying to smack that arrogant I-own-the-world smile off August's face, but watching Ashley do it was even better. He only pulled Ashley back because he knew she'd regret it later.

Ashley pulled out her phone, tears streaming down her cheeks.

"Hold on," August said.

Ashley held her phone up over her head in search of service.

"We have to figure things out," August said, "before we call."

Sammy leaned in real close to August and stared down into his dark narrow eyes. "What's to figure out? Why you killed her?"

"I didn't touch her." August raised his voice as Ashley started up the stairs. "If you call the police, you're going to have to answer a lot of questions. And once the media finds out, they'll never let it go. It'll ruin your life. You can think what you want, but you can't prove I had anything to do with it."

Sammy hated to admit that he might be right. Once the media got wind of a dead body at Ashley's house, a shitstorm would rain down on all of them. August, Ashley, and Sammy, too.

He followed Ashley up the stairs, a little nervous to turn his back on August. He glanced over his shoulder. August was following wearily behind, as though dragging himself up the stairs.

In the kitchen, Ashley had set her phone on the counter. She rubbed her hands over her face and through her hair. "We'll say it was an accident. That's what it was."

It was hard to imagine that an accident caused the bruises on Andrea's neck, but Sammy bit his tongue.

He scowled at August as he emerged from the cellar and stepped back from the door. He looked terrified. And it wasn't Ashley or even Sammy that he was afraid of—it was something else. Something else entirely.

"What about the little psychopath? We can't just let him go."

"What else can we do?" Ashley said. "We can't lock him in the cellar and throw away the key."

But reporting Andrea's death as an accident might even be worse for Ashley than if August confessed to killing her. Ashley was probably here when it happened. And nothing could change the fact that Andrea was dead. It was terrible, but Sammy couldn't let her death ruin Ashley's life. He had to think about the future, his future and hers.

"We can't say anything. I'll take care of this for you."

Her eyes widened.

"How?" August asked.

"None of your damn business," Sammy said. "You just keep your mouth shut. And stay away from Ashley from now on. You got that?"

August blinked rapidly.

"What do you think's going to happen if the cops find your fingerprints are all over the cellar, and I bet they'd find your DNA on Andrea, too. Wouldn't they?"

"Doesn't mean I killed her."

"You want to roll the dice? My brother got fifteen years in San Quentin just because he ran when the cops came out shooting."

"So what do you want me to do then? Just go home?"

"For a start. If we need anything else, you'd better deliver or it's your ass, not mine." He glanced at Ashley. She was staring at her phone, but she wasn't reaching for it.

"I'll call my driver," August said.

"What did I just say? You're not calling anyone. You weren't here tonight."

"So you'll give me a ride home?"

"No. Hell no. But I'll help you up the driveway."

Sammy ushered August out to the road and watched him walk downhill into the fog as if his feet weighed one hundred pounds each.

Arcos and the Castle

"Damn fucking mother-jacker," Arcos said as he replaced the fuses Parker had removed.

Across the street, there was a trundling sound. Arcos looked up. The dude Ashley York had been hanging with was rolling a trash can down his driveway to the curb.

Since Parker had been dumb enough to say where he was going, Arcos decided he had time to question the dude, so he crossed the street and introduced himself to the man. He apologized for his earlier curtness and got the dude's name: Gray Wilson.

Gray looked around wildly, seemingly unable to focus on any one thing. "What happened to Parker?"

"Parker?" Arcos glanced back toward his Crown Vic, where Parker should have been handcuffed in the backseat but wasn't. "He's gone."

"You let him get away?"

Arcos balled his hand into a fist. Who did Wilson think he was? Arcos didn't have to explain himself to Wilson. If Carter were here, he wouldn't take any lip, but he wouldn't lose his cool either. Without Carter, Arcos was finding it harder and harder to keep his anger in check. But thinking of him helped Arcos focus. The most important thing was to clear Carter's name. This was all that mattered. Maybe he didn't have to explain anything to Wilson, but it was a good opportunity to rehearse what to put in his report. "Turns out Parker had an accomplice. I didn't get a good look at him because of the fog and my back was turned, but I got in a pretty good kick. I would have taken him out, too, but Parker got the drop on me. It was two against one."

"Why was he here?" Wilson asked.

"I was wondering that myself. I don't buy it that he wanted an autograph. How do you know Ashley York?" The fact that she had been here was more than a little suspicious.

"It's a long story," Wilson said. "You'd never believe it."

"You'd be surprised what I'll believe, after today."

Wilson took a shallow breath. He glanced around again, and then proceeded to unload the biggest pile of bullshit Arcos had ever heard, which started with a body-switch between Wilson and Ashley York, thanks to a magic charm. When Wilson got to the part about August Grant trying to kill him, Arcos clapped. "Bravo. Great performance."

"I knew you wouldn't believe me," Wilson said.

"Can you prove anything you just said?"

Wilson shook his head no.

"What about the what-did-you-call-it?"

"The Encanto. It's broken. We threw it away."

Arcos followed Wilson's gaze to the trash bin. "So it's in there?"

Wilson's eyes widened. "Along with my son's dirty diapers. Take my word for it: it's broken."

But it seemed like it was more than just diapers he was afraid of. Was he hiding something? Probably Parker hadn't set him up with a prop to back up his outlandish story. "You're going to have to show me."

Wilson glanced around but didn't move.

Arcos marched to the bin and threw open the lid. The stench assaulted him. Wilson wasn't lying about the diapers. He appeared beside Arcos, gingerly moved aside a bag, and reached slowly toward a round, white stone...but then pulled back.

"The bag leaked. Probably better not to touch it."

"Ever heard of soap?" Arcos snatched it up and shook it.

Nothing happened.

"Did Parker give this to you, or is this some old knickknack you just happened to throw out?"

"I got it from a fortune-teller."

"Which fortune-teller?"

Wilson swallowed. "I don't know her name."

Arcos shook his head. *Nice move, Parker.* He wanted to press Wilson harder to make him admit this was a diversion, and probably would have if he weren't already feeling a little guilty for taking things too far with Streeter. Besides, he knew where to find Parker. Parker was at the Magic Castle. Parker had said he was going there because he thought Arcos wouldn't believe him. An obvious fake-out.

"Tell Parker to try harder next time." Arcos threw the stone in the bin and kicked it. It scraped along the gutter. A crumpled milk carton spilled out. He kicked the carton into the road and started toward his car.

If it had been the other way around and Arcos had been shot while supposedly jacking a car, then nothing would have stopped Carter from finding the truth. So Arcos owed it to him. He had to find Parker and make him talk this time. Whatever it took.

By the time he reached the Magic Castle, it was nearly ten. He rolled down his window and badged the valet. "Is Parker still here?"

The Latino with slicked-back hair opened Arcos's door and tried to hand him a ticket. "Yes, Officer. I take good care of it don't you worry."

Arcos shook his head. "¿Está el Detective Parker aquí? Muy gordo." He motioned to his belly.

The valet stared at Arcos as if he'd spoken Latin instead of Spanish. But Arcos was fluent. The valet understood, and they both knew it.

"Fine." Arcos took the ticket and got out.

He stepped over the velvet ropes and passed the insubstantial man with a clipboard, heading for the front door.

"Excuse me, sir. Are you on the list?"

He ignored the man and entered a small room that looked like a vintage furniture shop with a velvet couch and shelves of faded hardbacks, never to be read again. Flames flickered behind a tacky gold-colored screen in a fireplace framed by dark carved wood. On the mantel was a vase of dried flowers.

Arcos turned to find the guy with the clipboard had followed him in. His tux was clean, pressed, and decades past its prime, just like the guy wearing it. "You must be Arcos."

Arcos straightened.

"Saul put you on the list."

Arcos didn't know what to say to that. Old guy had his wires crossed thinking he was on the guest list when Parker had no doubt asked for him to be banned.

"He's in the Parlor of Prestidigitation," the guy said.

"How do I get there?"

The old guy waved toward the bookshelf. "Say the magic word."

Arcos wanted to wring the guy's arrogant white neck. "Please."

The old guy raised his eyebrows. "Getting warmer."

"How about you take me to Parker or we have ourselves a problem."

"Try *abracadabra*." He winked.

Arcos slid a hand into his coat to show he meant business. The old guy didn't know his holster was empty, and lucky for him that it was. "You try."

The old guy stepped back and waved his hand. "Abracadabra." The bookshelf slid open to reveal a narrow staircase.

Before Arcos could react, a knot caught in his throat. *Carter would have loved this.* Arcos turned away and hurried down the plush carpeted stairs as the bookcase slid closed behind him.

The stairs emptied into a sitting room with chandeliers, dark varnished walls, and gaudy, gold-framed portraits of men in formal wear. Arcos and Carter had teased Parker for moonlighting at the Castle, but now he wondered if Carter might have been jealous. He had a love for geek stuff which he kept well guarded. If Arcos hadn't happened to glance through the browser history or Carter's phone, he'd never have learned that Carter spoke Klingon.

Beyond the sitting room was a dim bar and a dining area with small round tables where couples sat seemingly entranced by the theme song of some old TV show, which Carter would no doubt have recognized, stroked out of a grand piano seemingly all on its own. *Yeah, right.*

Arcos intercepted a blonde in a tight black dress on her way to the tip jar by the piano and asked her where the Parlor of Presti-whatever was. She told him it was downstairs.

But the stairs weren't so easy to find. The Castle was a labyrinth of narrow hallways that snaked at odd angles between bars, theaters, a restaurant, and more bars.

When Arcos finally found his way down the stairs, a tall man, double-wide, appeared in the narrow hallway ahead of him. *Parker.* His back was turned, but his size was unmistakable in that awful brown suit. Who wore brown? If Carter was right about anything it was that brown suit wearers should be shot on sight.

Parker walked down the corridor as if in a hurry, unaware of Arcos. Although the carpet went out of style a century ago, at least it absorbed the sound of his shoes.

Twenty yards ahead, Parker turned a corner. By the time Arcos caught up, Parker had disappeared into a short side-hall, which led to a door beside a bust of Houdini. The door was locked. Beside it, a lit sign said "Houdini Séance."

Arcos banged on the door.

No answer.

"Parker!"

"Sir," a man's voice boomed behind him.

Arcos turned.

A pair of men in dark suits wedged themselves into the side-hall, blocking the way out and trapping Arcos into the narrow space in front of the door. The white guy was tall, too solid to call wiry yet too slight to be heavy. The Latino had the broad shoulders and chest of a bodybuilder and held his arms as if ready to pounce. If it came down to blows, Arcos could take one of them, he figured. Probably the tall guy, but not both.

"When the sign's lit," the tall guy said, "we require silence."

Arcos pulled his badge. "Look buddy, I don't mean to interrupt, but either Parker comes out or I go in."

The tall guy waved the beefy dude away. "I've got this."

The beefy dude grunted with annoyance and plodded off down the hall.

The tall guy held a finger to his lips until the beefy dude was well out of earshot then whispered, "I can get you in for fifty."

He must have known Arcos couldn't do shit without a warrant. So Arcos paid him forty, plus another empty threat.

Tall guy took the bills, folded them, and smirked. He slid them into his front pocket then brushed past Arcos and knocked softly on the door. Three long knocks, two short.

"They'll let you in once they've contacted the medium."

"How long will that take?"

The guy motioned a flattened palm toward the floor. "Keep it down. If I have to come back, you'll be leaving."

He seemed pretty confident as he walked away, as if he knew Arcos was powerless to do anything besides stand there like a dumbass beside the bust and a golden statue of a half-naked angel with her arms raised, practically mocking him.

It was as though Parker had the whole city in on his scheme to rob him from learning what really happened to Carter. And just learning wasn't going to cut it, Arcos realized. *No sir. No siree.* What did he think would happen when he cleared Carter's name? No one cared about Carter except Arcos. Arcos and no one else. Carter was the only man he'd ever loved, the only one he ever would.

Arcos inhaled through his nose in short, ragged breaths. His anger ticked up with each passing second. Damn it all. He should break down the door and make Parker pay. All that mattered now was avenging Carter's death.

Overs

Gray stood at his easel and considered the underdrawing he'd started of Charlie. Living Ashley's life had given him the distance he needed to realize something: the unspoken elephant in his marriage was him standing in his own way. He had to let Claire in on his dream of being an artist. But how?

He decided to paint Charlie in front of his house with all the Halloween decorations. The painting would be like American Gothic meets Edgar Allen Poe. Crows everywhere. Charlie's coat trailing off behind him, blending into the witches on the walkway. Gray's pulse quickened and something rose inside his chest. He felt lighter as he imagined how to paint the lines around Charlie's mouth and eyes, every detail on his haggard face.

Claire burst into the garage with an ah-ha expression on her face as if she'd caught Gray with his pants down, which she might as well have, because that's how he felt with his half-finished sketch out in plain sight.

He moved to block her view of the easel, wishing he could throw a drop cloth over it without drawing her attention.

"Where's Ashley?" she asked.

"She left."

"So what's going on?"

What could he say? The truth? He had tried that already on Detective Arcos, who, of course, believed none of it, and neither would Claire. When Gray had tried to explain to the detective how he and Ashley had switched bodies, and then how Wayob had tried to kill him because of the Encanto, it had only made him angry. Arcos only cared about Parker, who up until tonight Gray thought he'd invented in his painting.

"Did you hear me?" she asked.

"Just cleaning up."

"Looks to me like you're staring at a scribble."

This is it, Gray thought. *Now or never.* He leaned on the workbench, his fingers curled around the handle of a brush.

"What did he want with you?" Claire asked.

"Who?"

"Who? I could hear that detective yelling from inside."

"Sorry. Did it wake up Tyler?"

"Don't apologize," she said. "The guy was a jerk. He tried to bully his way into the house."

Gray wondered when, but he didn't want to get diverted from what he needed to share with her. "Listen, Claire, we need to talk, okay?"

"Damn right we do."

Gray stepped toward her. "Let's go inside."

She stiffened in the kitchen doorway. "What did Ashley want? And don't lie. She didn't come all the way over here for your painting." She wasn't budging without answers.

Had Claire ever faced such a dilemma where the truth seemed unbelievable? Maybe she thought he'd never believe wherever she went after that big argument in college, so she just said she was driving around "all night."

But the truth was, that was in the past, and the past was over and done. He could only change the future, and the first step was to tell Claire what he wanted.

"I quit." Relief flooded through him. There it was. He had finally said it out loud. The first step was the hardest and now he'd taken it.

Claire blinked rapidly. "You quit? Quit what?"

"My job. I quit my job."

"Because of Ashley? When were you going to tell me?"

"This has nothing to do with Ashley. I didn't tell you because I wanted to get my plan together first. I...I'm going to open a bar."

She glared over his shoulder at the Scotch on the workbench.

Just two bottles. He hoped she didn't know about his stash underneath the workbench, and then there was all the booze in the kitchen. Why did he have so much booze?

"Seriously?"

"It's just the start. The bar is so I can paint. I'm going to set up a studio in the back room."

"Okay, yeah. That sounds smart. Maybe I'll open my own consulting firm with a nursery in the back so I can spend more time with the kids."

It did sound a little ridiculous when she said it like that. But there was no point in explaining; he could tell she was too charged up to listen right now.

"You paint all the time," Claire said. "Even after everything that happened tonight, you were painting. You don't care about anything else."

"That's not true." He never had enough time to finish anything. She didn't get it. She didn't understand how much uninterrupted time he needed to focus on his craft, if he had any chance of improving, any chance of achieving anything at all.

"It costs a lot of money to open a bar," she said. "What about the mortgage and day care?"

"I did the math. We've got enough for five, maybe six months." In truth, it was more like four months, and they would have to take out a second mortgage for the down payment on the bar.

"That's our savings. Our safety net."

"And who do you think put the money in savings?"

Her jaw clenched. She inhaled sharply through her nose. "Fuck. You."

"Let's go inside. We need to sit down and be calm about this." Gray put his hand on her shoulder.

She shoved it away. "I don't want to calm down. You insisted I quit my job for the kids. You think I wanted to quit?"

"I—"

"You said it was a new phase of our marriage."

She was the one who had insisted her job was so much worse than his that he'd had to concede the point because, after all, he didn't come home with stink in his clothes. "I thought you wanted this."

"You think I like changing diapers? Stuck here all day with no adult interaction. Work was easy compared to this."

"Are you saying you want to get back into sewage treatment? Your salary wouldn't cover the mortgage, much less daycare." He regretted saying it like that, but it was true.

Her jaw twitched. The acetylene sparked in her eyes. He had crossed the line.

She leaned toward him as she spoke, her breath hot in his face. "If you don't care about us, then think about the career you're throwing away." The flame in her eyes was too intense to look at, but he had to. If he couldn't hold her gaze, then he knew she'd never listen.

He swallowed. "I care about Mindy and Tyler and you, but my career was a carrot on a string, dangled out of reach. You don't know how it felt, going in there every day."

She shook her head. "Get another job then. Why not try that first?"

"I can't think about other jobs right now." Jobs were like prison. He needed to paint. If he could just create one piece he was happy with—his masterpiece—he could endure anything. He could tolerate a shit job to support his children, and it would be worth it. He loved Mindy and Tyler, and he loved Claire too, but he needed to make a mark on the world—his mark—even if no one ever saw it like he did. And if not now, then when?

"I have to do this." Gray examined the brush in his hand, having no recollection of picking it up. A Princeton Select Black Taklon, with a blue handle and nickel ferrule.

"You don't know a thing about running a bar," she said.

"So, I'll learn. It's not about the bar anyway. I told you—"

"You've never finished a painting."

"Yes, I have. How would you know?"

"Where?" She glanced toward the workbench, as if she knew about the unfinished paintings he'd hidden beneath it, the paintings he could have finished if he'd wanted to, but what was the point? When a painting failed to achieve his vision, he moved on.

"They're not good enough," he said.

"Not good enough." She nodded once, like those three words summed up his whole life.

A stone rose up in his throat. He tried to swallow it back. What if his art was an invented obsession? A way to avoid accepting his shortcomings?

He glanced at his feet. "I need some time alone. To figure things out."

Claire clenched her fists. "You mean with Ashley. You want to hook up with her."

"No. Of course not."

"Go ahead and try it. I dare you. You're a fool if you think you stand a chance." Claire opened the door to the kitchen.

"Ashley has nothing to do with this." Gray snapped the brush in half. "None of this would have happened if you weren't so obsessed with her." He had twisted the snake, true, but he never would have even thought of Ashley if it weren't for Claire.

"So now you're jealous of who I follow on Instagram?" Claire turned her back to him and marched inside.

He tossed the broken brush on the workbench and followed her. They had gone off track. He had let his anger distract him. He'd rather lose a limb than give up painting. He felt selfish for that, but money was a distraction. Money, and the job, and not dealing with Claire despite how bad they both knew things were.

Claire was at the sink, the water running. He spoke to her back. "I'll never see Ashley again. This is about me. I have to do this for myself."

She shut off the water and turned to face him. In the soft light, her face looked calm, her eyes an unfathomable blue. She ran her fingers through her hair and stepped forward.

"Why did you want to have Tyler and Mindy?" she asked, "if you're going to go off and leave?"

There it was again. He was the one who had wanted kids, and she hadn't. A fact she threw back at him every chance she could. He had hoped a child would change things, would bring them together. Claire had resisted so fiercely for two years that when she finally agreed, he'd thought maybe a part of her wanted a child too.

But when Mindy came—as much as they both loved her—she couldn't bring them any closer. No closer at all. It was a mistake to put expectations on a child.

"I'm not leaving," he said.

"Maybe you should. You're exhausting. Everything's all about you."

She had a point. Maybe he'd been ignoring her needs, like she'd been ignoring him. Belittling his art. They needed to work this out together. "Let's sit down. Let's talk."

"I can't," she said. "I'm too tired. I'm done." She turned abruptly and marched out of the kitchen, leaving a silence in her wake so cold that it froze him in place.

"Claire?" He trudged after her.

But she had locked the bedroom door. He knocked softly, so as not to wake Tyler. "Claire?"

She didn't respond.

He returned to the kitchen, opened the pantry, and took out a bottle of Scotch. For the first time in his life, the scent did not entreat him. It smelled like industrial cleaning solution. His eyes watered. He tilted the bottle up and took a long pull of the brown liquid, forcing it back and finding no comfort from the burn in his throat.

In the living room, he navigated around the magazines and towels on the floor. He stood at the back door looking out at the fog that had settled over the yard, choking the crickets into silence. It creeped him out.

He shivered. He turned off the outside lights, and the fog was replaced by his reflection. Split by the frame of the door. He locked it.

He scratched his left butt cheek, which he realized had been bothering him for hours, and felt some sort of plastic beneath his jeans. He unbuckled, dropped trou' and turned his backside toward the mirror.

The lights suddenly brightened.

"What the hell are you doing?" Claire had appeared from the hallway. "What the hell is that?"

It was a clear plastic bandage, and beneath it was the outline of a unicorn.

She marched toward him. "You got a tattoo? Are you kidding me?"

"It's temporary," he said, although from the burning sensation he could tell it wasn't. "I thought Mindy would like it." As the words came out, he heard how dumb they sounded.

"You want Mindy to look at your butt? What the hell?"

"I..." *Dammit, Ashley.*

"You got it for Ashley, didn't you? Don't lie."

"No. She—"

"That thing's not sleeping in the bed with me. When I wake up, you'd better be gone." She turned off the lights and left the room, furious...and yet, he thought he'd caught a slight smile tracing her lips. The tattoo was just so ridiculous she didn't know how to respond. In the morning, they would talk.

He lay on the couch and closed his eyes, and as he tried to focus on what he could say, the more obvious it became that their marriage was failing. Maybe they needed some space. Maybe if they lived apart for a while they could come back together and start over.

Sometimes the only way up was all the way down. Even Monet had tried to drown himself. A sinking feeling washed over Gray, pulling his heart down like *Ophelia Drowning* by Paul Steck. He reveled in it. He wanted to feel like this forever, to live in the stillness far below the waves where the sunlight was dim and impossibly far.

With no job, there was no way he could afford his own place plus continue to support them all. Would he even be able to get a loan for a bar? Just the thought of running a bar made his head hurt. The amount of work it would take to fund his art. How could he abandon his whole life just to be an artist? What was most important?

Mindy and Tyler.

He would have to beg for his job back, and even then, Brad would only hire him if he absolutely needed him to meet all the deadlines. Meanwhile, Gray would rent whatever cheapest place he could find close to Mindy and Tyler. Anything was fine, so long as he could see the sky—just a tiny slice of blue from a basement window would be enough—and a corner where he could paint.

Where's Parker

At the kitchen counter, Hernandez scrolled through the gruesome photos on her laptop, feeling more and more defeated with each passing minute. The likelihood of solving a murder dropped exponentially after the first day, and now twenty hours had passed since the murder of Jenna Collins, and still there were no leads.

She knew Parker would have a hunch of some kind, but where was he? It had been hours since he went to Ashley York's, and still his phone was going straight to voice mail.

It was a custodian, at the Quality Inn on La Brea, who had discovered Collins's body discarded in a back-alley dumpster. Collins had been a high-end escort with a website and handler. She was leagues above the Quality Inn, and Hernandez doubted she'd been killed there. Still, Hernandez had to be thorough. So, she'd spent all day eliminating the staff and the guests, except for a retired couple, from Ohio, who had checked out before the discovery of the body. Unlikely they hired a prostitute for a three-way and then murdered her, but Hernandez asked the local police to keep an eye on them, anyway, because of Ruiz's Third Agreement—*Don't Make Assumptions.*

The Four Agreements was one of the many books she'd discovered in her philosophy course, at USC Extension, that had expanded her world. In order to stay positive and to make sense of the terrible things she saw, she studied a few pages every night.

"Whoa," Rumi said, from behind her.

Hernandez slammed the laptop shut and turned toward her teenage son. "Why are you still up?"

"I was thirsty." His wavy hair held the imprint the headphones he wore while playing video games in his room.

"I've told you how bad all that violence is before bed."

"Like you can talk." He pointed at the laptop. "She looks like a zombie."

Hernandez hated when her job affected her personal life, and tonight it was her fault that Rumi had seen the shot of Collins laid on a bed of black trash bags, her arms sticking straight up in the air.

The medical examiner had determined that Collins died on her stomach with her arms and head hanging below her body, while her blood cooled and coagulated for hours and rigor mortis stretched her muscles into tight bands. Why wait so long to move the body? Had the sick bastard actually slept beside her? Only the Hulk could have carried her after rigor mortis set in. Yet her corpse showed no sign that it was dragged, no post death trauma at all.

"I'm sorry you saw that," Hernandez said.

"No big deal," Rumi said. "She was a hooker, right?"

"She was a person. She had right to live her life."

Rumi shrugged. He scuffed back to his bedroom, and no doubt continued his video game.

She wanted him to understand why she cared so much about Collins, a victim who could no longer help herself, but was he ready? Was he willing? Even when he listened he never seemed to hear her. He was at an age, now, where she'd to let him learn on his own.

Parker she could count on to understand that Collins deserved justice, to help in spite of his suspension, except that he was already consumed with Wayob, who she'd learned more about and she was dying to tell Parker what she'd discovered. Dying to talk to him, in general. Just to hear his voice. Except, when he made jokes about himself. There was no reason for him to be insecure, to say he was on a diet when she asked him over for dinner. Couldn't he see how attracted she was to that big brilliant brain of his? To the playful man who emerged when he practiced magic?

She texted again, then called. "Pick up. Pick up. Pick up."

But it was only his voicemail that answered. "Don't disappear on me, Parker."

Where the hell are you?

She carried her laptop to her bedroom, where tonight her king size bed seemed too much mattress for just her, alone. It practically filled the room. A ridiculous amount of bed, and she wasn't tired at all. And she knew where to find Parker. Sooner or later he'd show up at the Castle.

She knocked softly on her mom's door and when she didn't answer left a note that she was going out.

Déjà Vu

Saul parked in the lot under the Good Samaritan Hospital and took the elevator to the fifth floor.

When the doors opened, he charged out.

Tonight, the nurse at the station was a heavyset white woman. Her mouth tightened into a thin line and her shoulders tensed forward as Saul approached.

"I know it's late," he said. "But I need to see Saroyan."

"He's discharged. You forget?"

If Saul had been notified, he'd have missed it because he'd turned off his phone. "Discharged where?"

The nurse, Dana Atkins according to the name tag clipped to her collar, squinted at him. "You really don't remember? He made bail. He went home."

Saul's stomach sank. "What's his address?"

She sighed heavily. "How about you write it down this time?"

As she searched in her computer, Saul realized he already knew. Saroyan lived in Mar Vista—the stucco building—where Saul had awakened behind the wheel of his car.

He returned to Mar Vista and parked on Berryman by Saroyan's apartment, next to the same olive tree from that morning.

He lingered around at the entrance and turned off airplane mode on his phone. Scrolled through the texts. All from Hernandez. He wanted to tell her that he'd driven here, last night, in his sleep. He should tell her. If he told her that he'd dreamed of entering Saroyan's bedroom—*if* it was a dream—would she believe that it was a glimpse of his real room? First, he needed to see for himself, see if it looked anything at all like his dream. He told himself again that it would be totally different. And he knew it was a lie.

A man wearing earbuds, in his midtwenties, pushed out through the door and past Saul. Saul grabbed the handle and swung it wide.

Inside, he found Saroyan's apartment: 112. He knocked and waited…

No answer.

He knocked again. "Mr. Saroyan? It's Detective Parker, LAPD."

He carried a set of picks in his coat, but he first pulled out a handkerchief, wrapped it over the knob, and turned. It was unlocked.

Inside, the cramped room that served as a living room and kitchen was bathed by a dim fluorescent near the entrance. Saul waited for a reaction. His feeling of déjà vu, triggered when Arcos had mentioned the apartment, now morphed into dread.

"Saroyan?"

No response.

Using the handkerchief, he closed the door. Suddenly certain his fingerprints were already on the knob. He wiped it down.

The couch was angled toward a flat-screen and buried beneath a mountain of newspapers and yellowed junk mail. Between the couch and a side table stacked with cups was an empty space the size of a wheelchair. A glass slider opened to a small patio surrounded by a wall.

There was only one other room, and Saul's stomach lurched at the thought of going in there. *Don't.* But he had to.

He used the handkerchief to push through the door—and was assaulted by the stench. On the bed, lying on his back, was Saroyan. He was not breathing, and his arms were frozen by his head as if his last living act had been to raise them in defense. Against who, Saul would rather not guess. And certainly, he did not care to read the torn paper in Saroyan's hand. The note, which Saul now realized he'd already known was here. The single sentence scrawled in black ink as if penned by a child.

He stood paralyzed at the foot of the bed. It had been him—and yet not him. But…his own hands. This morning, when he'd convinced himself that he'd driven here in his sleep, that was denial. It was worse than somnambulism. Worse than Kenneth Parks, who had driven fourteen miles to murder his mother-in-law and then to a police station before he woke up. Parks had not left a note. Sleepwalkers never left a note. This was murder.

The dream-like images drifting back to Saul were memories. He had been more than asleep. Somehow, Wayob had gained control of Saul's actions, induced Saul's muscles. Forced Saul's hands to suffocate Saroyan with a pillow, left carelessly on the floor by the bed. Impossible.

Yet here Saul was. Standing by the corpse of a man murdered by his own hands. Murdered by Wayob.

Wayob had used Saul like a puppet. But how? Saul was not susceptible to hypnosis. This was worse than hypnosis.

From his pocket, Saul pulled out a latex glove. Size XL, but it barely squeezed onto his right hand. He lifted the torn piece of paper.

If you're reading this note, then Saul Parker murdered me.

His stomach dropped. His head throbbed. The large, black letters etched into the paper were familiar. The text arced unevenly down.

Perhaps, at one point, before he believed Wayob was real, Saul might have thought that Saroyan deserved to die. But not now. Now he knew the man was a victim, like Rydell. And Sadie.

On the back of the note was the Ford logo and a copyright notice in small font. Saul sealed the note in a plastic bag.

He thoroughly searched Saroyan's apartment. The bureau contained starched shirts folded tight, pants and underwear. When he opened the top drawer, a mound of crumpled receipts toppled out. The closet was filled with dirty clothes and more old newspapers. The note was the only thing Saul found related to the murder, aside from the body, which might remain undiscovered for days if Saul left without reporting it.

That way, he could also buy himself some much needed time to investigate on his own. But what if time wasn't enough? What if thorough forensics uncovered some clue that he'd missed? Some way to find Wayob? Saul would not take such a risk.

So he inhaled deeply, and swallowed, and called Hernandez. He needed her here first. She still had his plain wrap, which he feared contained the origin of the note.

When she answered, he heard a piano playing in the background.

"Tell me you're not at the Castle," he said.

"I was looking for you. What's the problem?"

"Arcos is there."

"So what? You don't think I can lose Arcos?"
"The problem is Wayob framed me and I need your help."
"Framed you how?"
"Saroyan's dead."
"You mean…murdered?"
"Most likely."
"Shit, Parker."
"Exactly." He gave her the address.

Sammy and Ashley

Sammy slowed as he approached the exit gate and smiled too big at Edwardo in the guard house. He'd meant to play it cool, but he'd messed it up already, because usually he only nodded to Edwardo, who ordinarily ignored him. There was too much animosity between the security employed by the Beverly Park Homeowners Association and the additional private guards, such as Sammy, hired by some residents. But Edwardo hardly glanced up as the gate arm raised. If he noticed Sammy's smile, he didn't acknowledge it or that Sammy was driving Andrea's car.

What am I doing? Security guards don't hide bodies; mobsters do. And Sammy certainly didn't. Yet here he was, turning out of Ashley's neighborhood and onto Mulholland with Andrea's body in the trunk. For his own sake as much as Ashley's, he'd kept her out of the plan. She had had nothing to do with Andrea's death. She simply couldn't be responsible for the massive bruises on Andrea's neck. Hard to believe that even August Grant could have caused them. Sammy had always hated August and would have turned him in to the police if there were any way to do so without igniting a long bitter trial by the press that would harm Ashley and everyone involved.

The problem was that there was no *right thing* to do. Not anymore. There was no reason Andrea's death should ruin Ashley and therefore Sammy's life. Maybe Ashley could hire better lawyers than his brother, CJ, had, but lawyers weren't shit when it came down to the media lowlifes who hovered around her like vultures. Andrea's death would create a frenzy. Even if Ashley were proved innocent, she might end up like OJ, her life ruined. And if the shit came down on Ashley, it would come down on Sammy too. So, he had to hide her body. It was the only way.

After this, he hoped, she'd finally see him as more than just an employee. He would take a bullet for her if he had to.

Low fog crept north across Mulholland and thinned out over the valley lights below. He slowed around a turn, pulled out his phone, and called Greta.

"Just wanted to let you know I'm going to be late."

"Yeah, I noticed," she said.

"It's going to be a couple more hours." He tried the soft sell. It was going to take a lot longer than that by the time he buried Andrea's body and stashed her car at LAX. "I've got to help Ashley."

"What are you, her only staff?" Greta asked.

"I gotta do this. I thought you wanted me to get ahead."

"You'd better make sure she appreciates it is all I'm saying. You're having a child, Sammy; your child needs a future."

At Coldwater, Sammy stopped at the light. "You're not even pregnant."

"Maybe if you weren't at Ashley's all the time, I would be. Here I put my career on hold, which was going somewhere by the way, to have your baby, and you can't even come home and give it to me."

"I've got to go," he said.

"Well, I'm not done talking. Did you get rid of that dog?"

Sammy regretted telling her about Shera, who he'd hoped to adopt, but fat chance Greta would ever agree to that. "Working on it."

"What do you mean *working* on it? Are you keeping it in the booth? What, do you think it's your secret little pet?"

The light turned green, and Sammy sat there. "It's a she, by the way. I'm just keeping her until I find her a home."

"That's not your job, Sammy. This is what I keep telling you. You're not focused. You need Ashley to see your drive and ambition, not some dog she told you to get rid of. You'll never be shit, the way you're acting. You're going to get yourself fired again."

Headlights raked across his car. He looked suspicious just sitting there while the light was green. He turned right onto Franklin Canyon.

"Don't worry about it. I've got this."

"Don't worry about it? What about the other guards? Huh? They'll dime you out. Is that why you're staying late? You'd rather spend time with a dog than—" Her voice cracked and cut out.

"I've got to go." He hung up before she could ask where he was that he was losing reception.

The road snaked down past a cluster of houses to a steel gate that barred the entrance to Franklin Canyon Park. It closed at dusk. Sammy shifted the car to park and hopped out. A hundred yards up, the concrete house built on the cliff might have a view of the gate, but with all the lights on, anyone inside would be oblivious. He popped the trunk. Inside, Andrea's body had shifted to the right. She was curled in the fetal position, facing away. He pulled the bolt cutters from beneath her legs, carried them to the gate, and cut the padlock that secured the chain. The gate swung open.

He drove through, closed the gate, and secured the chain with the padlock at an angle that required close inspection to see the damage.

He drove down into the fog, past a pond and a reservoir surrounded by redwoods. The road narrowed.

He backed into a dirt turnout, killed the engine, and clicked off the headlights. Darkness filled the canyon. From somewhere high above, a pack of coyotes barked and howled.

He got out. On the ridge of the canyon, the lights of Ashley's house glowed indistinctly. So close, yet a world apart from the wilderness where he stood.

He popped the trunk and killed the light but could still make out the shape of Andrea's body. The engine ticked in the stillness. He slumped her over his shoulder, grabbed the shovel, and stepped into the fog that shrouded the trail.

After a few hundred yards, the trail tapered into brush that tugged at his pant cuffs as he ascended the hillside. He whistled as he climbed, trying to ward off the feeling of being watched.

At the foot of an oak, he carefully lowered Andrea's body to the ground. He glanced around and listened hard. From one of the limbs above him, an owl hooted twice. Then another owl resounded in the distance, as if to say they were out there in the darkness, watching.

Sammy stood there for a long moment. Doubting himself. What was he doing? He reimagined his goal, working at Ashley's side with a big new title and a suit. He was done with security. It had merely been a means to get his foot in the door, and now that door had finally opened.

He dug and chopped into the dusty ground, hacking through tangles of shallow roots woven like nets into the hillside and wrapped around stones as if to squeeze out water. The shovel threw sparks as it scraped rocks. He tried in three places, but the rocks were everywhere.

He pulled off his shirt, used it to wipe sweat from his face, and then tossed it over a bush to continue digging. Andrea deserved better than this, but it was too late to stop now. He felt like an archaeologist excavating the big irregular stones by digging around them, then using the shovel as a lever to pry them from the earth. One boulder refused to be dislodged and nearly cracked the handle. So, he dug under it and left it jutting into the hole.

An eerie pinkish hue diffused through the fog. He needed to hurry. When it got brighter, he'd be easy to spot, and a Black man with a shovel had no business in Franklin Canyon.

He carried Andrea to the hole, but with the boulder in the way, he could only prop her inside it partway. He climbed down on the opposite side of the rock, grabbed her legs from underneath, and pulled. In order to gain enough leverage, he had to sit in the dirt with his back against the side of the hole and his legs braced in front of him.

The hole should have been larger, but he managed to get her body fully in and under the rock, her head propped forward with her chin on her chest. Her blue dress appeared almost silver in the dim filtered light.

He had gone too far. This was the wrong choice. If there was a way back to the point before his involvement, he'd have let Ashley call the cops, regardless of the consequences. But too late now. Now he'd look guilty. They both would.

He climbed out. The fog lingered in the canyon as if waiting for Sammy to say something. He tried to speak. "Andrea." What else could he say? She was sarcastic, sure, but he would miss her energy. Without her there would be a void in Ashley's house, a void filled with guilt.

He tried not to think about her panties, which he had found balled up in a rag beside her body in the cellar, and what that might mean.

He couldn't stand seeing her body contorted under the boulder, in that hole not fit for a grave. With the back of his hand, he wiped his eyes. He began shoveling dirt on top of her, regretting that he couldn't do better for her, and that her body was too stiff to lay in a more comfortable pose.

Dawn lit the sky but the canyon remained in shadow. As the sunlight tracked down the cliff toward Sammy, he regretted many things. More than burying a Spanish woman in the sagebrush, he regretted letting Greta push him to this point. Making him promise to try harder, day after day, making him push and push until Ashley made him some kind of big shot. He regretted that Greta's ambition was his. He'd tried to make her dream his own, but in so doing it had grown to include Ashley, and now Ashley was all he cared about.

If Greta knew about Andrea's murder, she'd insist that Sammy use it as some kind of leverage over Ashley. Which might work, if he cared about anything other than Ashley. But he wouldn't blackmail Ashley. And Greta wasn't going to say shit, because he wasn't going to tell her.

Diversion

Arcos was fed up with standing here like a turd stuck in the bowels of the Magic Castle. He didn't give a shit about whatever was happening in the séance room. And, for that matter, why did Parker care? What did he think? The spirit realm would help his unsanctioned investigation? *Ha.*

Arcos backed up three paces, ran forward, planted his heel into the door. It swung open so easily that he lost his balance—it wasn't even latched anymore—and he caught himself on his hands. The door sprang back and hit his leg.

He got up and found himself not in the séance room but another hallway. About forty yards long and dark. It led to another door.

Arcos ran down the hall and twisted the knob. The door opened. He stepped through. Inside, six upholstered accent chairs were arranged around a desk which faced a poster of *Thurston the World-Famous Magician* framed with ornate, tarnished metal. Thurston's cheeks were rouged. His lips the same bright red as the little pair of devils who sat one on each shoulder, the left one whispering in his ear as he seemed to be peering out from the poster, looking directly at Arcos.

Beethoven's Ninth pumped through speakers hidden somewhere in the ceiling. Arcos had thought he hated classical music before he met Carter, but then Carter awakened something inside him, some hidden part of himself that he never knew existed and never would have known if not for Carter and the way they had lain together and let the music wash over them.

Across the room was another door. Arcos twisted the knob. It was locked. Behind him, the door he came through closed. He ran back and tried to open it, but now it was locked as well. He was trapped here in this strange room, with Beethoven's Ninth, and Thurston, the World-Famous Magician, with his little devils and lips red as blood.

Arcos kicked the door. It hardly budged. Solid oak. "Parker!"

He sat in a chair and faced the poster. The World-Famous Magician's eyes seemed focused to the side with a look of intense determination, the way Wilson had looked away as he spouted all that bullshit about switching bodies.

Arcos sat up a little straighter. He'd assumed that Wilson had been glancing at the trash bin because Parker *hadn't* set him up with a prop to back up the ridiculous story. But the stone was there. Wilson had started to reach for it, and then pulled back, as if drawn to it yet afraid and determined to resist, and Arcos had been too pigheaded to realize it at the time. But obviously, Wilson believed it was truly powerful. He tried to recall if he'd noticed anything unusual about the stone. Maybe it had been a little lighter than a regular stone would have been. Could that mean something?

Arcos glanced down at his hands. What would Carter have believed if he heard Wilson's story? He'd probably have come up with some kind of theory, like dark energy or something, from one of those crazy podcasts he listened to at the gym.

Arcos's scalp prickled. Someone was watching him.

He glanced around, and then up at the poster. Had Thurston's eyes just moved?

Arcos marched to the poster and grabbed the metal frame with both hands, but it was mounted solidly to the wall. Behind the glass, the poster appeared to be just a cheap painting. Yet the eyes *had* moved. Arcos was sure Thurston had been looking to the side before, and now he was looking down. Down at Arcos.

He stepped back, clenched his fists, and fought back the urge to punch Thurston's goddamn, red mouth, because Carter wouldn't have bothered wasting his time with this. He would have found out why the hell Wilson was afraid of the allegedly broken Encanto.

Did Parker know?

He knew something, alright. Could be why he'd gone to Wilson's, and why he'd tricked Arcos into following him here. Arcos had fallen for yet another diversion. Yet again, he was playing the chump. Clearly, Parker wanted him out of his way. What if it was because there was some element of truth to Wilson's fairytale? Smart move making it sound so preposterous that Arcos had dismissed it. It could be related to Parker's unsanctioned investigation, which might be related to Carter's killer.

He had to get back to Wilson's.

The locks on the doors had the sort of ancient slot below the knob that required a skeleton key. He rummaged through the desk, but all he found was a deck of cards, a calligraphy pen, and three dice with sixes on all sides. Since he joined IA right out of the academy, he'd never picked a lock before, but he'd seen it plenty of times on TV. It looked easy enough.

He grabbed the pen and approached the door opposite the one he'd entered through. He shoved the tip of the pen into the keyhole and wiggled it around. Nothing gave. Nothing budged. He pried the pen against what he imagined must be the tumbler. The pen broke. Ink sprayed out onto the doorknob and all over his hand. He flung the broken pen at Thurston, the World-Famous Magician. It bounced off the wall below the poster where it left an unsatisfying black smear.

Since both doors opened inward, he could forget about kicking them in. He picked up the nearest chair. It was heavier than he'd thought. He turned it over, arched his back against the weight, and with a running start slammed it into the door. It made a satisfying thud, with an echo from beyond the door. Although the door refused to budge, he hoped the Castle bastards would respond to the noise. The overdressed customers would, no doubt, complain about the banging.

Arcos took a break. Caught his breath. Untucked his shirt and wiped his hand on the T-shirt underneath. Then lifted the chair, charged across the room, and slammed the chair into the door through which he'd entered. He tried again and again until his arms gave out. He dropped the chair and slouched against the door, catching his breath.

The opposite door was now ajar.

Arcos shouted as he ran toward it. "Hey!"

Outside the door, stairs led down into darkness, and the sound of hard soles pounded on wood. Arcos yelled again.

At the bottom of the stairs, someone pushed through a door. Dim light spilled in and flung their shadow into an emergency exit on the opposite side of the landing. Then the door swung closed, and they were gone.

Were they expecting him to follow? If so, then he wasn't going to fall for it. He wasn't going to step willingly into another trap. As he felt his way down the stairs, he wondered if the emergency exit was even real.

He couldn't trust anything here. If it was real, it might be hard to get back inside the Magic Castle, but did that matter?

He found a horizontal push handle on the door and shoved it open. An alarm blared. He stepped out into moist, night air.

He was in the alley behind the Castle facing a brushy hillside. Above, a car slowed around a bend. Its headlights swept the fog and lit up the back wall of the Castle.

He hustled along the side of the building, and the alarm ceased.

As he rounded the corner, he caught sight of Detective Hernandez exiting the building.

"Hold up," Arcos yelled.

She ignored him, as though she had no idea who he was. She handed some cash to the valet and strode toward her unmarked cruiser parked near the entrance.

"Halt right there and that's an order," he said.

She turned toward Arcos, combed back her bangs, and cupped her hand to her ear, as if she couldn't hear him. She ought to know better than to fuck with IA.

"If you get in that car, I'll cite you for impeding an investigation."

She shook her head and tapped her watch. Before he could reach her, she slid into her cruiser and sparked the engine. He slapped his fist against the trunk but she put it in gear and rolled down the hill toward the exit. *Fine. Just fine.* Like he needed her to find Parker anyway. He knew what Parker was looking for, and once Arcos had the goddamn Encanto, Parker would come to him.

The valet with the slicked-back hair resumed his perch on the stool by the little stand. He gazed off into the night, as if completely unaware that anything had happened.

"I need my keys," Arcos said. "I'll fetch my car myself."

The valet held out his hand for the ticket. Arcos reached into his pocket. The ticket was gone. He'd definitely put it in his left side pocket—he was sure of it. The fucking tall guy. He must have lifted the ticket when he brushed past Arcos. Lucky for him, Arcos was in a hurry.

"Lost my ticket." Arcos smiled. He repeated in Spanish and showed his badge again.

The valet shrugged and shook his head.

"¿Hablas español?" Arcos asked.

"No, señor."

"What about English? Do you speak English?"

"No. Sorry."

"What *do* you speak?" Arcos glanced at the entrance. The front door of the Castle was unmanned.

"I don't."

Arcos wanted to punch the valet in his pockmarked face. He reached past him to the lock box with the keys, which, of course, was locked. "Key." He twisted the air.

"Sir." The valet motioned him back.

"You remember me. I know you remember me. My key is in there. My car is property of the LAPD." Arcos held out his badge again and pointed to it. "You don't want to mess with the police."

The valet blinked and shook his head.

Arcos slid back his sleeves. Time for the valet to learn respect.

The valet whistled, loud and shrill.

The broad-shouldered bodybuilder stepped out from the shadows by the entrance. "There a problem?"

"Yeah," Arcos said. "Your buddy lifted my ticket."

"We can't give you a key without a ticket."

"I'm a cop. You're obstructing my investigation."

"You'll have to talk to the manager about that."

Arcos started toward the entrance.

"He gets in at ten tomorrow."

Arcos stopped and stared at the bodybuilder.

He stared back and shrugged slightly, as if punching Arcos to a pulp would be all in a night's work. "How about I call you a cab?"

"You'll regret this when I come back tomorrow with a few of my fellow officers. We're going to question everyone and scour this dump top to bottom. Might take all day."

"Looking forward to it." The guy stepped toward Arcos.

Arcos turned and started down the drive. He should have called a uniform right then. He would, except he had no way to explain losing his car *and* his gun without becoming the laughingstock of the department. He summoned an Uber with his phone.

While waiting on the sidewalk in the fog, he considered the part of Wilson's story where August Grant became possessed and bent on killing Wilson. If there was any truth to it, then maybe August Grant had been trying to scare Wilson into giving him the Encanto. Well, he didn't scare Arcos. And if Parker and Hernandez weren't at Wilson's, then no one would be around to see him raid the man's trash. Not this late at night. He'd grab it quick and get out.

At 1:12 a.m., a black Prius with the Uber logo in the windshield rolled to the curb. The driver had pasty skin and a hipster beard. His belly sagged over the lap-belt. He mumbled a greeting as Arcos situated himself in the back.

As the Prius accelerated, Arcos leaned his head back. All the energy drained out of him. He tried not to think about the miserable look on Streeter's face when Arcos shoved it into the carpet. He should apologize. He had gone too far. Maybe with Parker too. Parker didn't kill Sadie Wu, and after everything that had happened, Arcos couldn't even recall anymore why he and Carter had been so determined to turn the screws on him. Now, Parker hardly seemed to matter.

Carter was dead. And Arcos had made it worse by lashing out.

As he drifted off, his wrongs washed over him. So many wrongs. He needed to escape. The ride to Silver Lake would take twenty minutes, at least, and twenty minutes of sleep would be a relief after the all-nighter and the worst day of his life.

Saul and Hernandez

While waiting in the Mustang outside Saroyan's apartment, Saul texted Pete at the Castle.

Saul:
I need you to hold Arcos for a few more hours.

Pete:
I was just about to text you. He's in the wind.

Saul's stomach churned uneasily. Arcos had been here this morning, and if he showed up now it would seal Saul's fate.

Saul:
When did he leave?

Pete:
A few minutes ago. We held his car at valet, but he called an Uber. When you said he was a jerk, you weren't kidding. It nearly got violent.

Saul:
Impressive you were able to hold him as long as you did. Thank Barney for being me.

Fog drifted between the streetlights. His eyelids grew heavy in spite of his fears of Arcos showing up here. Even worse was the thought that Wayob might regain control. What if he only let Saul live because was planning to force him to commit another murder?

Saul had no intention of sleeping until he learned exactly how Wayob had done it. From what he'd read about the human brain, he knew its functions were triggered by simple impulses transmitted by electrochemical signals. Science was always advancing. Who could say with any certainty that a brain, at least the motor cortex, couldn't be controlled? Not Saul.

He startled awake, surprised to find his eyes had closed. He powered the seat upright. Buzzed down the window. Tore open a new bottle of NoDoz and downed a double dose.

Headlights approached from behind and flashed in the rearview. Hernandez. *Thank god.*

She slowed as she passed in his plain wrap and parked in front of him. Saul swallowed and finally made the call to dispatch he'd been procrastinating. For the second time in twenty-four hours, he reported a murder. But he only admitted to finding the body.

Saul climbed out of the Mustang and met Hernandez. As she emerged from the car, the shock of white falling across her forehead, his heart fluttered. He engulfed her in his arms with no forethought whatsoever.

She pulled back.

His gut. He had practically pushed her back with his big stomach.

Last night at the Castle—when *she* had hugged *him*—he was leaning over such that there was a gap and his belly didn't press into her. He kept it hidden in the trench coat so she'd no idea how immense he was. Until now. He felt naked before her.

She eyed him up and down. "Looks like you waded through a dust storm."

Was she just mentioning the dirt on his pants to cover her disgust of his belly? He probably didn't smell great either. "I made the mistake of trying to hike to Ashley York's from Franklin Canyon."

"Surprised you didn't badge your way in. She wouldn't know you're on suspension."

"She has a guard who's all full of himself." Saul tossed her the Mustang key. "Thanks for the wheels."

She pocketed the key and glanced around at the stillness, the fog, the arching limbs of the olive tree above them. "Can't believe I beat the circus."

She was right. By now, emergency response vehicles should have clotted the street. Except that he'd deliberately delayed calling in order to buy time.

He opened the door to his plain wrap and lowered himself into the driver's seat, dreading what he'd find.

"You're not leaving?" she said.

"I just need to check something," he said over his shoulder. "Call the L-T. Tell her you're on this case."

"Never going to happen," Hernandez said. "You found the body while you're on suspension. We'll be lucky if IA doesn't get involved."

"You're first on the scene," Saul said. This gave them temporary control, and if Levy had any say at all, she'd keep this out of IA, if not for Saul's sake then for her own, because they should have had an officer watching Saroyan's apartment.

Hernandez crossed her arms. "This is the part where you tell me what the hell is going on."

He searched his pocket for a glove. "One second."

"We've been partners for how long?" she asked.

"Two and a half years." He found one.

"Three in January."

"I thought you started in July?" As he stretched the glove over his fat hand, the latex ripped.

"No," she said. "You always forget. It was January when I got the transfer to Homicide Special. Remember how cold it was?"

He tossed the glove into the floor well. Maybe he didn't remember the month, exactly, but he remembered the first time he saw her. It was cemented in his mind. The way she strode into Homicide Special. Tight leather jacket, broad hips, and not-entirely-white-yet bangs, which she had brushed back from over her right eye before shaking his hand. His hand already sweating as she shook it.

"I thought it was hot," he said.

She sighed. "I bet you're always hot in that coat. My point is, I've always had your back, haven't I?"

Saul found another glove and inched it onto his hand. "I'm not holding out on you. I'm just still trying to figure this out myself." He leaned across the center console and opened the glovebox. Removed the manual.

He turned it over.

Déjà vu.

He opened the back cover. The next to last page was half missing.

Now he knew for sure.

From his pocket, he retrieved the plastic bag containing the note and held it against the manual for her to see. "Perfect match." He handed her the note.

She smoothed the plastic over it and angled it to the streetlight. "Shit, Parker."

"You need to get this to forensics tonight," Saul said. "Compare it to my handwriting."

Her eyes grew wide. Her brows ratcheted down, creating furrows across her nose. She held the note further from her face. "You didn't write this."

But Saul knew now that he had, or rather, his hand had. He heaved himself out of the car and shut the door. "Wayob's framing me. That's how I wrote when I was a kid."

"So why not copy Saroyan's handwriting?"

"That's his mistake. And I hope it's enough. Check for fingerprints."

"Fingerprints won't clear you." She patted his gloved hand. "I wish they could."

"I know. I'm afraid the prints you'll find are mine."

"Wait. What are you saying?"

"I think…somehow…Wayob got control of my body while I was sleeping."

"Whoa. You think Wayob hypnotized *you* into killing Saroyan?"

Saul shook his head. "Worse. I read all about hypnosis. You can't compel someone to act against their belief system."

Hernandez stepped back. "You mean…like a demon?"

"It seems impossible, I know. But if I wrote that note—"

"I'm getting worried about you, Parker. You look like a wreck. You could use some sleep."

"I can't sleep. Not until I stop Wayob."

Hernandez shook her head slowly.

From the distance, the sound of sirens approached. Saul had said this wasn't a code three, but of course they hadn't listened. He had three, maybe four, minutes to convince her. "Listen…" As he stepped toward her, she stepped back.

If she was freaked out, he couldn't blame her. But at this point, all he had was the truth. So he gave her some space. He leaned against the car and told her everything. How he'd woken up here this morning with no memory of driving here, the flashes of dream fragments that turned out to be memories— of his hands shoving the pillow over Saroyan's face, of Saroyan slapping and clawing. Then falling still.

As he rambled on with no explanation for how what he described could have happened, Hernandez stood there in the mist. Behind her a firetruck careened onto the street. She turned and hurried toward it, as if relieved by its arrival.

The firetruck's red strobes flashed, out of sync with the blue from a squad car behind it, creating a chaos of frantic lights slashing the fog.

Hernandez motioned for the firetruck to pull aside and marched toward the squad car. Saul followed. He rubbed his sleeve over the scratches on his forearm—the scratches he'd been avoiding all day. They were from Saroyan.

A pair of uniforms leaped out from the squad car. Young and fresh, hungry for action. Saul ordered them to cordon off Saroyan's apartment. They rushed toward the building, unaware of his suspension.

"You want to see the body?" Saul asked Hernandez.

She gazed down the street. More blue strobes approached through the mist. "We better steer clear until we know who's in charge." She whirled to face him so suddenly he almost gasped. "Occam's Razor. Saroyan wasn't a young guy. He probably died from a stroke or a heart attack or something."

"I wish," Saul said. "But the evidence will show foul play. The obvious explanation is that I killed him. But think about it. Why would I leave a note lying around like that?"

Hernandez bit her lip. "You weren't there."

Saul appreciated her willingness to believe that he hadn't been involved, but the theory didn't work. "The note alone would fry me. So, why make it look like I wrote it?"

Hernandez shrugged. "It doesn't make sense. But regardless of who wrote the note, it's a setup. No other explanation."

The note was a setup, she was right about that, but there *was* one other explanation. One she was not ready to believe. Saul wondered if his own belief was influenced by his conviction that Sadie did not commit suicide. If Wayob could control someone's body, it explained Saroyan's change from Friday night to Saturday. It explained almost everything.

But how was Wayob doing it? Until he could explain how, no one would believe it. It seemed impossible to him too, except that it *had* happened. He had experienced it himself.

The second squad car rolled up, followed by a plain wrap driven by Garcia, another detective in Homicide Special except he reported to Lieutenant Delrawn instead of Levy.

He parked and unfolded himself from the car. His suit was wrinkled and his gray hair tousled like he'd climbed out of bed and left in a hurry. He nodded gruffly to Hernandez, turned to the squad car, and spoke to the officers through the window.

"Shit," Hernandez said. "This might be worse than IA."

"At least he's a real detective." Saul hoped he'd remain impartial. Saul's freedom might depend on it.

As the squad car reversed back to Washington to block the intersection, Garcia approached Saul and Hernandez.

"So, Parker, what brought you here in the middle of the night?"

"The victim was our suspect," Saul said. "We'll take the case if you don't want it."

"Wish you could," Garcia said. "But from what I understand, you're on suspension."

"Hernandez isn't."

"I suggested that, too, but Delrawn says it's out of her league."

Saul crossed his arms. "Yeah? Levy might say the same thing about you."

Garcia shrugged. "But not to my face though, right?"

Saul exchanged a glance with Hernandez. She mouthed, *Chickenshit.* Garcia was right about Levy.

Garcia motioned toward his plain wrap. "Mind stepping into my office?"

"We're good standing," Hernandez said.

Saul's knees were tired of holding his weight and he *did* feel like sitting, just not with Garcia. He glanced toward his own plain wrap, which he shouldn't be driving on suspension.

"Who found the body?" Garcia asked.

"That would be me." Saul described the scene, without mentioning the note or Wayob or his fear that Wayob had used his hands to do the killing.

"What makes you think it was murder?" Garcia asked.

Hernandez looked away, and Saul followed her gaze. Above the street, a turbulence spiraled through the fog. An eerie texture to the darkness between the intervals of light.

"Check for yourself," he said.

"Your suspects have an unusually high mortality rate, don't they?"

Saul squared him in the eye, but before he could speak, Hernandez said, "Saroyan bludgeoned a guy to death in plain daylight. No one's going to mourn the bastard."

Garcia grumbled. "Why are you even here, Detective Hernandez?"

"I called her," Saul said. "Saroyan was ours, like I said."

"*Was*," Garcia said. "So, I'll ask again, what brought you here tonight? Don't expect me to believe you just came to check on his wellbeing."

No way Saul could tell Garcia his theory about Wayob. "I found out that Arcos and Carter had followed me here, and I had a bad feeling. You ever get a feeling in your gut?"

Garcia frowned. "I've got one right now. You think this is related to Carter's death?"

Saul shrugged. "Arcos sure seemed panicked. Something was off." If Garcia found evidence that Carter had entered Saroyan's apartment, he might tie Saroyan's murder to Carter. Which would buy Saul some much needed time to find out how Wayob did this.

Garcia turned to Hernandez. "What do you think?"

"About Arcos and Carter?"

"Who else?"

"Hard to say." She glanced at Saul. "*The heart of another is a dark forest.*"

Not exactly backing his diversion, but at least she wasn't contradicting him. And she wasn't mentioning the note. And for this, he owed her. Big time. She had put her career on the line.

Garcia turned toward the apartment. One of the uniforms Saul had sent to cordon it off had stationed himself by the entrance. "Alright, I'm going in for a look." He glanced back at Saul. "Stick around where I can find you."

Saul held his palms up defensively.

Garcia cut across the lawn toward the building.

"Thanks," Saul said to Hernandez.

She tilted her head toward the Mustang. "Get in. You have to hear what I learned about Wayob."

She slid behind the wheel, and he eased himself into the passenger seat. His weight sunk the car. As he closed the door, it scraped the curb.

He grimaced and pretended to focus out the window. Garcia was at the entrance to the apartment speaking with a uniform, who nodded and scowled toward the car where Saul sat.

"Saul!" Hernandez slid her seat forward and levered it straight up.

"The curb is too high," he said. "I'll call Public Works."

"Forget it," she said. But he knew how much she cared about the car.

She swiped her phone and showed him a black-and-white photo of a familiar-looking Latino in a dark uniform. Saul had seen this photo before. No doubt about it. Same proud nose. Same cleft chin. Same sun-shaped insignia on his lapels.

"His name was Miguel Arredondo Sosa," Hernandez said. "He was the chief of police for Guatemala City back in the nineties. And he was investigating Wayob himself."

"Luis Luna's father?" Saul felt a charge in his gut.

"Exactly. How did you know?"

"She has the same photo in her apartment. How did he die?"

"Shot by the Guatemalan army for attempting to assassinate their president, allegedly."

"It was Wayob," Saul said. "Wayob forced him to do it. Don't ask me how."

"It is suspicious. I'll give you that. The chief of police, who is investigating Wayob, suddenly tries to kill the president, and with seemingly no motive? I'm wondering if Wayob is a CIA codename. The CIA orchestrated the Guatemalan coup in the 1950s. Who says they stopped there? Maybe they brainwashed Sosa into the assassination, like in *the Manchurian Candidate*."

"Wayob confessed to killing an officer decades ago. Dollars to donuts it was Sosa."

"That confession was over the phone, right?"

"Right. It was Aleman's voice, but he was channeling Wayob. I just don't get why he'd confess at all?"

"Maybe it was to throw you off course," Hernandez said. "The CIA could have faked the whole phone call with some kind of voice-matching software. That's why Aleman denied it. He never actually called you."

But she hadn't seen the conflicted emotions that played across Aleman's face when Saul questioned him, the way his throat constricted and turned red. Probably recalling dream-like memories of whatever Wayob made him do the night he walked off his shift at the MDC.

Saul buzzed down the window and inhaled. He felt light-headed, like the fog had choked all the oxygen from the night air.

If Sosa had been the fall guy for a conspiracy, then why involve Aleman? The theory was too complicated. Plus, Saul had experienced Wayob's ability firsthand. Wayob had forced him to murder Saroyan.

"What happened to the president?" Saul asked. "Did he die?"

Hernandez shook her head. "A year later, his own Minister of Defense overthrew him in a coup. He spent the rest of his life in prison awaiting trial for crimes against humanity."

"That certainly supports your conspiracy theory," Saul said, "but then why wait so long to off Luis Luna?"

She combed back her shock of white. "I don't know. Maybe the two deaths are unrelated."

But Saul couldn't stomach the coincidence. "The son of the man who was killed while investigating Wayob is himself killed by a man who, at the time, claimed to be Wayob. These two events must be related."

She pressed her lips together. "So maybe it took them this long to find him?"

"Why bother? After so much time, how could he be a threat?"

"I don't know. But Rosa's grandmother went back to her maiden name when they came to the US. Her real name is Gloria Sosa, and the army claimed she robbed the National Palace. So, maybe she *did* take something. That's why she had to leave Guatemala. An article I read actually blamed the army for her murder."

Saul rubbed his forehead. He recalled Gloria Luna's warning, spoken in measured English: *Leave it alone.* Her milky eyes had glanced down and to the right. What was she hiding? Maybe now, with this information about her husband, they could pry it out of her. "We should talk to her again. She might be the key to this whole thing."

Hernandez held up a finger. "On this, we agree."

"Want to drive?"

"We can't go now. It's the middle of the night. Plus, you're on suspension."

"Hasn't stopped me so far."

Hernandez shook her head. "We have to be careful. If Wayob's CIA or something, we might stir up a nest of hornets and still never get close to the truth. I'm wondering if we should leave it alone."

A chill shot through Saul's stomach. Leaving it alone was not an option. Not now, not for him. "Let Wayob go free? Is that what you want?"

"No, but..." She gazed at him intently. "I'm worried about you, Parker, from the bottom of my heart."

"I appreciate that. I do. But we can't afford to wait." He wanted to reach across and turn the key himself. While they were sitting here talking, Wayob could be claiming his next victim. "Remember at the death notification, how Mrs. Luna said it was her fault?"

Hernandez nodded. "That was weird. She said it three times. But Saroyan killed her son. We've got video."

"That's how it appeared. Wayob deceived us with our very own eyes. He used Saroyan to kill Luis Luna, and I think Mrs. Luna knew. You saw how she acted. She was hiding something."

Hernandez's eyes widened. "So now you believe Saroyan's *confession?*"

Saul's fingerprints were almost certainly on the note, and the note was in his handwriting. He needed Hernandez to believe what he knew in his gut to be true: Wayob had written the note with Saul's hand, probably after it had killed Saroyan.

"Most of it," he said. "Let's see what Mrs. Luna says." Maybe if Hernandez heard it from the elderly Luna, she'd believe.

"She's sick and blind, and you're too wound up. You'll spook her. Let's just go in the morning."

Saul said nothing. With or without Hernandez, he had to go, and he had to go now. He had to learn what Gloria Luna knew.

From his coat, he removed the plastic bag with the hair. If Hernandez wasn't going with him, at least she could get it analyzed discreetly. "I found this in Sadie's bed. We need a DNA test."

Hernandez shone her phone on the bag. She puffed her cheeks and exhaled.

"How about a little quid pro quo?"

He didn't have time, but what could he say? Every victim deserved justice. "Sure thing."

She swiped to an image on her phone and handed it to Saul. "That's how we found her."

Saul stared at the screen frozen with disbelief.

Impossible.

He blinked but the image remained.

He held the phone closer... The girl. It was the girl from his nightmare. Except with all the color drained from her face. Her dark hair dull and tangled. She was on her back on a bed of black plastic bags at the bottom of a dumpster. Arms above her torso, sticking straight up.

Saul should have told Hernandez, right then and there, how in his dream, in the hallway at the Roosevelt, Jenna Collins had smiled as she approached him. How she'd whispered in his ear. The words. What had she said? All he could recall was the way her breath tickled his ear lobe, the way her lips brushed his neck.

His stomach twisted.

Had his body been used by Wayob to murder Collins as well?

Saul hoped not. He hoped with every fiber of his being.

Hernandez was staring at him, her mouth half-open.

His mind was reeling. He had to say something, but what? He stated the obvious. "Looks like she was moved after rigor mortis set in."

A frown flickered briefly across her face and was gone. "She wasn't robbed, and there was no recent sexual activity. So, what's the motive?"

"How was she killed?"

"Strangled. There is some minor bruising on her neck, but besides that, there's not a mark on her. Want to take a look at the murder book?"

He had wanted to, at Langer's, earlier. But now...he felt nauseous. He stared out the windshield at the flashing lights in the fog. "Can't imagine I'll find anything you missed."

"I'd consider it a favor."

Saul was torn. He was curious, yet at the same time he wished to block Collins out of his mind. The less he knew, the better. "Levy will freak," he said, which was what Hernandez had said when he asked at lunch.

"She'll never know. I have it on my laptop, at home."

Saul blinked. He tried to focus on the fog. But the strobes, the discordant chaos of light.

"You can sleep over," Hernandez was saying. "Save yourself a trip to Hollywood and back. We'll go to the Lunas' first thing in the morning."

Saul stared at her. Was she really inviting him over? After he'd fantasized for so long.

But, not like this. Not while he was a bloated whale. Not when he might lose control of his own body.

"I'll keep an eye on you," she said, "if you're worried about becoming

Wayob or whatever."

She means her bed. How could he say no? He swallowed. "Not a good idea."

She crossed her arms. "I can handle myself. If it'll make you feel better, I'll cuff you to the bed." Her lips twitched.

She had smiled, almost. Or had he imagined it? Was she joking or was she flirting with him? "Oh, I know you can handle yourself," he said. "That's what I'm afraid of. Might set a bad example for Rumi, though, if he finds out you've got a crazed fatso cuffed to your headboard." He forced himself to laugh.

Hernandez closed her eyes and pressed her lips together. It wasn't funny. "Nothing's going to happen," she said. "Don't worry."

He felt his ears flush. What was he thinking? Presuming *her* bed?

"I should stick around. Might be dawn before Garcia's done with me." But they both knew Garcia would order Saul to vacate the scene as soon as he got a handle on it.

Hernandez nodded. She pressed a hand to his arm. "Want me to stay?"

"Nothing you can do here." He cracked the door and tried to wedge himself out through the gap without scraping the door on the curb again. And failed.

Hernandez glanced away from the harsh grating of the metal on concrete as if she hadn't heard it. She might not be so kind when she discovered the scratches on her rims.

Before closing the door, he leaned down and waved goodbye.

"Parker." She leaned toward him across the seat. "Promise me you won't harass the Lunas in the middle of the night."

"You got it." He glanced right. The roots of the olive tree had shattered the sidewalk. Without Hernandez, communicating with the elderly Luna was going to be difficult, but what choice did he have? Lives were at stake.

He shut the door, and Hernandez looked up at him through the window, her brows rippled with sorrow. Her mouth opened and closed. As she brushed back her shock of white, her face went blank. And Saul wasn't sure if he'd seen anything at all.

He straightened, knocked twice on the roof, and stepped back onto the sidewalk.

She looked straight ahead, clenching the wheel with both hands. She k-turned, eased around the squad car at the end of the block, and turned right. Her taillights faded away, drowned by the strobes of the firetruck, ambulance, and squad cars. Drowned by the fog. And the night.

More than any other moment in his life, Saul wished he could change the one he had just lived. Let someone else worry about Wayob. Go home with Hernandez—to *her* bed—wrap her in his arms, close his eyes, and just feel. The warmth of her body against his.

He crammed himself into the plain wrap. Downed a double of NoDoz. Checked his face in the mirror. His eyes were bloodshot from the combination of sleep deprivation and caffeine. His hair was solid gray. No more pretending that in dim light it looked brown. He pulled back the wattle under his chin and flattened his cheeks.

He looked ridiculous.

He angled the mirror away from his face toward the VW van parked behind him, and the blue lights spinning through the fog.

He sparked the ignition and yawned. Across the street, limbs reached into the mist that drifted in the streetlight. In spite of the NoDoz, he felt drowsy, and he needed his mind sharp now more than ever.

Ashley in the Mirror

Ashley curled into a ball on her bed and tried not to think about where Sammy was and what he was doing. She turned the lights up as bright as they would go, but it wasn't enough to ward off the awful image of Andrea at the bottom of the stairs, one leg twisted under her body at an impossible angle, the purple bruises on her neck, the wrong paleness of her skin, eyes glazed over and bulging as if in disbelief.

Ashley was going to go crazy if she didn't talk to someone. Where the hell was her phone? It wasn't in the bedroom. She wandered out to the stairs and looked down into an impossible darkness. *Maybe check the guest room first.*

And that's where she found it. Right there on the nightstand. *Weird.* Gray must have been sleeping in the guest bed.

There were like twenty texts from Don, which she ignored. She unlocked her phone and called her dad. It was the middle of the night, but he always answered her.

Not this time.

She left a message saying to forget the message Gray had left this morning. He should just call her at her number as soon as he could, no matter how late.

She played the voicemail from Don. He was basically yelling at her for leaving the screen test. Apparently, because of all the drama, they had cast someone else into what would have been the breakout role of her career, and now the opportunity was dead, as dead as Andrea at the bottom of the stairs.

Don's texts were a blur. As she blinked away her tears, she saw the one from August.

August:
You home? We're coming over.

August would have known he wasn't welcome, so why announce he was coming? Unless he was Wayob, and Wayob was crazy, but then who was *we*?

She gazed out the window. Beyond the fence at the edge her lawn, fog roiled in the canyon. It glowed from all the lights of LA. Somewhere out there in the fog, Sammy was hiding Andrea's body.

She shivered and stepped back from the window. How had it come to this? Sammy had nothing to do with Andrea's death. She should have kept him out of it somehow. She had tried to, but he'd taken charge, as if she wasn't thinking clearly. And she hadn't been at the time—he was right about that—but now he'd implicated himself in a crime. Why would he do that?

She returned to her bedroom, locked the door, and changed into her softest PJs, the ones covered with stars and moons. They reminded her of Mindy's bedroom in the nightlight. Ashley lay on her bed with the lights still on and closed her eyes.

She had felt something special with Mindy. Of course, to Mindy she would have seemed like her father, but Ashley still felt the connection —a real human connection. That's what was missing in her life. Connection. She wanted someone who truly cared about her. Someone like...Sammy.

The idea struck her so suddenly that her whole body shook. He obviously cared about her more than she had realized before, and maybe it went deeper than work. It wasn't just that she felt safer with him on duty, she felt comfortable around him. And the way his white shirts clung to his muscles made her drool. She'd always had the feeling that it would be so yummy to get physical with him, and now she wondered if maybe they could be something more.

With each passing minute, she grew more awake. And she had the feeling that someone was watching her, that Wayob was peering down through the walls of her house, and that she might wake up with him here in the room with her.

She sat up. The room was empty. And she knew in her rational mind that her house was empty too, but she'd never stop worrying until she talked to someone.

Why wasn't her dad responding? Strange that she hadn't heard from him since Friday.

She had no idea what Sammy would believe, and she wasn't ready to go there with him. Not yet. *One step at a time.* So, the only person left she could talk to about this was the last one she wanted to call. Maybe Gray had traded bodies with her by accident the first time, but not the second. Yet she kept right on talking to him in her mind, so fuck it.

She'd smashed his phone while in his body, so she dialed the number of the disposable smartphone she'd bought. It rang and rang. *He's not going to answer.* But then just when she was on the verge of breaking down, he answered.

"Thanks for the tattoo," he whispered. "If Claire finds out I'm talking to you—"

"Andrea's dead," she blurted out. "Wayob killed her."

Gray went quiet. And she could almost feel the weight of the news sinking into him.

When he finally spoke, his voice trembled. "Maybe if I had called 911—"

"No. Wayob probably killed her before he came at you. Her body was in the cellar. There was nothing you could have done."

"So, what did you tell the police?" Gray asked.

"Nothing. Sammy's hiding the body."

"Oh my god." Gray sounded panicked.

Shouldn't have told him. "We had no choice. Like you said, it was Wayob in August's body. He's a jerk, okay, but not a murderer. If you had seen the body…" Her throat tightened. She couldn't speak.

"I'm so sorry," Gray said. "I guess no one would believe the truth. August is *August* now though, right?"

Ashley recalled how August had lost all his usual self-confidence. He wasn't sure what had happened and was obviously freaked out. She almost wished that he had been responsible. At least then she wouldn't have to worry about who Wayob was now, and they could have called the police instead of going down this dark, dark road from which there was no coming back.

"Yeah." Ashley lay back on the bed and twisted her hair through her fingers. "It's him, alright. He threatened to sue."

"For what?"

"Locking him in the cellar."

Gray groaned.

"What if he's still out there?"

Gray sighed heavily. "You mean Wayob? He's trapped in the Encanto, I think."

"You think?"

"That's what he was afraid of. Getting trapped in there when we switched back to our own bodies."

A chill ran down her spine. "But you don't know for sure?"

"He was trying to kill me," Gray said. "I didn't exactly have time to ask questions."

"I don't know why I thought you'd know anyway. It's been a rough day."

"Yeah. Claire and I are splitting up."

"Oh man." Ashley got out of bed and went to the mirror. "Because of me?"

"No. It's been a long time coming."

"Did you tell her we switched bodies?"

"How could I?"

"Good point."

"Let's get some sleep, okay?" he said. "Tomorrow I'll come help you."

"I don't need your help. I just want to make sure we're safe from Wayob."

"Me too. I think the fortuneteller who gave me the Encanto knew about Wayob. I'll go talk to her tomorrow. She had a girl with her who speaks English."

Ashley glanced at the window. The solid gray mass of fog pressed against the other side looked about ready to burst through. The image of Andrea's contorted body at the bottom of the cellar stairs flashed in her mind, and her throat tightened again.

"Promise?" was about all she could say without crying.

"I promise," Gray said.

Ashley ended the call, fell back on her bed, and gave in to the tears. Andrea was dead. Nothing Ashley could do would change that, still the tears came anyway. Andrea had been more than an employee—maybe not a friend, yet—but they were getting there.

After the tears stopped, Ashley wiped her face with the sleeve of her nightshirt and tried texting Sammy again...

Her texts still refused to go through. Nothing else she could do. Things would be better in the morning.

She turned out the lights, climbed under the covers, and closed her eyes. She tried to focus on something else, anything else. The breakout role she'd lost in the Kaufman-Penn project. She should be furious about missing her chance—she totally could have played the crazy girlfriend—so why did she feel relieved?

She had wasted so much time rehearsing, trying to overcome the queasiness in her stomach that always built up to the point of vomiting. And for what? So she could pour her heart out for the critics and the haters to shit on? She felt nauseous thinking about all the lunches, the schmoozing, and the screen tests, which, in the best case, would only lead to a long road of tedious rehearsals and publicity.

Acting just didn't seem worth all that. If she tried something else, the haters would no doubt say she failed, but who cares? Why waste her life worrying about their opinions? How had pretending to be someone else become the basis for her self-esteem when she could be helping others, when her money could do so much good? She could open a charity to provide support for victims of violence, and she could name it after Andrea... Not that it would make up for her tragic death, but it would be a start.

—

At 3:13 a.m., Ashley was no closer to sleep and still had no word from Sammy. She got out of bed. Dim light oozed through the blinds she'd left open. She found the glass of water on the dresser.

As she drank, something tickled her lip—one of her hairs must have fallen in. *Gross.* But she was too thirsty to fish it out in the dark. As she gulped, a whole clump brushed her lip and wiggled.

She turned on the lights. In her glass, an upside-down brown spider was struggling not to drown. She dropped the glass, which shattered on the floor, throwing water everywhere.

She stared at the shards of glass around her feet. No sign of the spider. It would be hard to spot against the wood grain, unless it moved.

She stepped carefully back from the spill, stripped off her shirt. She picked up the larger shards of glass and used her shirt to mop up the water, the smaller pieces of glass, and hopefully the dead spider. Gingerly, she carried the glass and the wet ball to the bathroom and threw them away.

In the mirror, her hair was tangled, her eyes bloodshot and dry. Her skin looked blank and unlived in. After all the treatments for eczema, all her struggles to banish the blackheads, the pimples, the deep pores and imperfections, she had lost sight of her life.

Behind her, a creepy shadow stood in the shower. She marched to the line of switches and banished the shadow and all its brethren. The lights were too bright for this hour, but she needed to rid herself of this eerie feeling that someone or something was watching her, that her big, empty house wasn't quite as empty as it should be, and for this she needed a little help.

From the medicine cabinet she snatched the big bottle of quick-release Ambien, which she opened on her way back to the bedroom. She took two, closed the electric blinds, and checked the alarm. No doors or windows had been opened since Sammy left with Andrea's body at 11:38.

Sammy was going way out on a limb, and she knew August had nothing to do with it—he was doing it for her. How could she ever repay him? He was far too charismatic to be wasting his days in her security booth. He deserved better.

Leaving the lights on, she climbed under the covers. Her pillowy bed seemed too big for just one person. She flopped around until finally she felt the dulling effect of the Ambien pulling her to sleep, and, gladly, she gave in to it.

Charlie Goes Down

Lying in bed, Charlie's aching back refuses to let him sleep. It feels like Vietnam. Like he's still humping the boonies outside the wire, with the M79 and extra grenades in his pack and all his false bravado as his squad eggs him on: *Hulk, Hulk, Hulk!*

Despite all the Oxycontin that the crazy degraded Charlie into licking from the carpet, his thoughts return again to the after-midnight pharmacy—the one he heard about in Glendale where they have an on-site doctor who writes prescriptions no questions asked, and they supposedly take Medicare.

Like all the beds and the sofa here in his daughter's house, the mattress sags and pinches his spine. No better than a pile of bricks. He counts to a hundred, and then to a thousand, as a dim line of moonlight flickers along the wall.

He hears a noise outside. The sound of glass bottles stirred together. What kind of crazy recycles this late at night? One more interruption, and that's it: he'll go to the pharmacy.

Something smacks. Bottles rattle. He groans as he sits up.

He gingerly gets to his feet and shuffles to the window. He cracks the curtains and peers out. Across the street, some kind of crazy—blurred by the fog washing over the hill—is rummaging through the Wilsons' bin. Doesn't he know removing items from the trash is against the law? Can he not read the clear English spelled out in not one but two places on the bin?

Charlie works his way downstairs using the banister for support. He checks out the front window. The crazy is still there, digging through the trash. Don't the Wilsons know that if you allow even one crazy in the neighborhood, you might as well invite the whole horde? Do they want crazies clogging the street with their dilapidated carts full of junk? Of course not, but they'd rather lie in bed and let someone else take responsibility. Like Charlie has nothing better to do. He ought to let it happen, see how the neighborhood likes it once they have the crazies camped up and down the street using their lawns as toilets.

The crazy has emptied the garbage bin into the street and is studying some object he's found. It's more than Charlie can stand. It really is. No one gives a damn about anything anymore. They probably won't even care when their street becomes another Skid Row.

"That's how it is," he says to himself. "Yet again, all up to Charlie."

He hurries out the front door, not quite running but shuffling quickly. Fast as a man his age can be expected to move.

The crazy is on his knees, peering into a pile of scattered trash with his face close like a dog about to devour it.

"Hey," he yells, "you can't do that!"

The crazy snatches up some small object and presses it against whatever he has in his hand.

Charlie shuffles across the lawn, the grass cold and wet on his bare feet. It soaks his pajama bottoms. The crazy is wearing a suit and has a bald pate that Charlie would recognize anywhere. The crazy is not just some vagabond; Arcos is back.

Arcos stands, his face twisted with deranged anger. Whatever regrets he'd mumbled earlier when he left Charlie's house are all gone now. His eyes seem out of focus, like they don't see Charlie at all. And there's something familiar about them. Something in his eyes that wasn't there before. If he wasn't completely and utterly crazy then, he is now.

He screams and drops whatever he was holding: a baseball-sized stone, and something smaller. They land on a half-opened plastic bag.

"It stabbed me," Arcos says.

"Serves you right." Charlie balls his hands into fists, still high on the Oxycontin—he's fearless.

He swings.

Arcos ducks. "Don't touch me!" He reels back, slips on a dirty diaper, and falls backward.

Charlie forces his aching back to bend enough for him to pick up what the crazy had been holding: the white stone and a small black snake.

"Clean this mess up and get out of here," Charlie says.

Arcos struggles to his feet, his arms rigid. Ready to strike. His fierce eyes bore into Charlie as if gazing straight through to his soul.

"Give it back to me, and you may live."

Mucus runs from Arcos's nose. He does not wipe it away. Just like the officer who bludgeoned the bum on Halloween and scared him out in front of Charlie's car.

"I know you, old man," Arcos says.

Terror seizes Charlie. *It cannot be.* Yet somehow…this is no longer just Arcos.

Behind his crazy, out-of-focus eyes, Charlie also sees the crazy officer.

Charlie's muscles refuse to act, as if the crazy's stare has reached in and frozen his blood all the way down to his heart. Very slowly, Charlie offers the round, white stone. The crazy reaches for it with trembling hands, stubby fingers stained with dirt. Just before they reach the stone, Charlie tosses it into the road.

Anyone who knows anything about anything knows better than to give to a crazy, or the crazy will take and take until you have nothing left.

The stone clacks on the pavement and rolls down the hill under Gray's car, with the crazy chasing after it. He crouches down by the rear tire, then springs to his feet and bolts to the next car down the hill, where he falls to his knees and reaches under it.

Charlie scurries toward the house. Not that he's running away; Charlie never runs from a fight and he's not about to start now. He's not afraid of some trash thief who can't even wipe his runny nose, but Charlie means to have the upper hand. He means to have some sort of weapon by the time the crazy realizes that Charlie still has the snake in his fist.

Despite the flood of adrenaline, Charlie can't move any faster. The pavement chafes the brittle skin of his feet. The wet grass will be a relief, he thinks, but when he steps over the curb, his feet nearly slide out from under him.

"Where is it?" The crazy growls.

Charlie glances back. The crazy is squatting down in the dim streetlight over the trash. He examines a diaper and the plastic bag that the stone fell on. Then, he places them back in the bin.

"Ha," Charlie chuckles to himself. *Cleaning up, just like I asked. The Wilsons should thank me.* Too bad they'll never know.

As the crazy runs his hands chaotically over the pavement, Charlie realizes that he doesn't have time to take the safer route up the street to the front walk. So, spreading his arms for balance, he makes his way diagonally across the wet lawn to the front door.

"You took it," the crazy says, much closer behind Charlie than he expected.

Charlie focuses on the front door, which he left half-open. His feet smack the steps. If he could just make it inside…

He crosses the threshold, and he shoves the door shut behind him. But instead of the satisfying latch click he longs to hear, the door smacks the crazy's fingers. The crazy howls.

Charlie doubles down on his luck and throws all of his one hundred and thirty pounds against the door. It crunches the crazy's fingers against the frame. This time, he retracts his hand and screams.

Charlie shuts the door and locks it. "That'll teach you," he says. "Now get out of here."

But Charlie knows better than to expect the crazy trash digger to give up so easily. As he hurries through the parlor, his chafed feet streak the carpet with blood.

In the kitchen, Charlie yanks the largest knife from the wood block. Its steel blade tapers to a deadly point. He grips the oak handle firmly in his palm and swipes the air. "This will teach him."

Glass shatters and breaks, and a heavy object crashes through the living room window. Charlie reconsiders his plan. Anyone who knows anything knows it's better to live to fight another day.

Hurrying into the garage, he ignores the pain as the concrete floor scuffs his feet. He throws open his car door, tosses the knife onto the passenger seat, and falls in behind the wheel. He turns the key. As the engine starts, he glances in the mirror. He was in such a hurry that he forgot to open the garage door, and the door opener is…right where it belongs, of course: clipped to the visor of his son-in-law's car, which Charlie moved to the street in order to hide his own dented car.

Charlie climbs out of the car. Before he can make it to the button by the kitchen door, the crazy bursts through, shoving him back. Charlie falls on his butt. A bone snaps. Sharp pain in his hip.

The crazy stands over him. "I remember you."

If Charlie could get to the knife on the passenger seat… He scoots backward. Hits his head on the driver's side door.

"I looked a bit different." The crazy steps forward and leans over him. He stinks like baby shit. "This is the same car, isn't it?" He runs his hand over the dent in the fender. "I had to finish him off, thanks to you. A mercy kill, you understand?"

Charlie is mesmerized by the crazy's eyes, by the stream of mucus running from his nose. It takes all Charlie's effort to turn away. Coughing on exhaust, he clutches the door handle to pull himself up, ignoring the pain in his hip, the dizziness. If he could just get up higher, get better air.

"I believe you have taken a piece of the Encanto."

Charlie glances through the window to the knife on the passenger seat.

The crazy grabs him by the shirt and shoves him down. He hits Charlie in the face, then slams him against the fender, right below the dent where he hit the bum.

Charlie slumps down against the tire, light-headed and sick. Blood oozes from his nose into his mouth. Charlie spits, but more fills his mouth, and all he can do is watch the crazy lean into the car where the knife is sitting right there in plain sight.

Now the crazy is standing over him. Charlie realizes that he must have blacked out.

"Thanks for this." The crazy wields the knife. "Now, I expect you'll cooperate."

"I'd rather die," Charlie hears himself say.

"Is that so?" As the crazy leans down, he sways, seeming to lose his balance.

Charlie tries to scoot away, but the crazy's hand slams into Charlie's chest, pinning him against the tire.

The crazy leans forward and presses the razor-sharp knife against Charlie's throat. But giving in now would be like giving in to all the crazies who ever were. If Charlie hands over the little snake this crazy seems obsessed with, he'd be no better than a crazy himself. If he gives in now, then it might as well have been Charlie bludgeoned by the officer and mowed down in the road.

Clutching the snake in his palm, he hides his hand in his pocket. He inhales. The pressure of the knife blade against his skin perhaps weakens, ever so slightly.

"I'd rather not hurt you, but I will." The crazy stares at him, his breathing deep and irregular. The intensity of his eyes, still malicious but fading, as if he's unable to maintain his evil train of thought.

The exhaust, Charlie realizes. The car is poisoning the air. Charlie laughs, or he tries to. At least if he's going out, he's taking the crazy down with him.

Charlie can no longer move. Even without the blade against his throat and the reeking crazy pressing against his chest, he couldn't get up now.

The knife pressure lessens, this time for sure, and the crazy's eyelids flutter half-closed. He's saying something, speaking in gibberish, or at least that's how Charlie hears it.

He drops the knife and slaps himself lethargically, his face now purple and swollen. His mouth hangs open and drool slimes down his chin.

He slumps sideways. His head lolls against Charlie's chest. The white stone rolls out into Charlie's lap.

Charlie pulls his hand from his pocket, but it falls uselessly to the floor. He can no longer feel the shape of the snake in his palm.

He turns his head toward the kitchen. He could still survive, maybe, if he could get out from under the crazy...but he can't even see to the door. Beyond the dented fender, everything blurs and swims.

Charlie never should have abandoned that bum on Halloween, leaving him behind like roadkill. He should have stopped. He should have called for help. He should have plowed his car into the crazy officer, who is somehow now here, in Arcos's body, pinning Charlie against the fender just below the dent left by the bum's body.

Charlie's eyes are closing, and he knows the last thing he sees will be that dented fender. He cannot bear it. He tries to scream, but the sound is trapped in his throat. He summons all his will. And more. And manages, just barely, to tilt his gaze. Miles away, on the floor beside him, the black snake, which he had to go and get himself killed for, slithers into shadow in the palm of his hand. He tries to focus on the white stone in his lap. On the roundness...

It fades to black.

Driving To A Dead End

At three in the morning, Saul was speeding east from downtown on the 10, Hernandez's words reverberating in his head: *Nothing's going to happen.* He slapped the steering wheel. That was the problem. Nothing would ever happen. He grabbed hold of a fat roll and squeezed. Not with this belly.

He should have told her that he recognized Collins from his nightmare, but what if she didn't believe that it was just a dream? And...what if it wasn't?

He had to tell her. But first he'd question Mrs. Luna. Maybe now, with what they had learned about her past, now that he was prepared to believe, she'd tell him whatever it was she was hiding. And it would help him make some kind of sense out of all this. It would explain how Wayob had forced Saul's own hands to end Saroyan's life. And possibly Collins's.

Hungry.

Nothing to eat. No time to stop. He listened to a podcast about weight loss through meditation. A soothing British voice instructed Saul to concentrate on his breathing, which he did, for eight minutes, while keeping his eyes on the road.

When the voice returned, Saul did feel less famished. But now his chest hurt, and his heart hammered against it. Now he realized what he'd been avoiding: the true reason he'd shut down his phone. It wasn't that Arcos and Carter might track him; it was the awful image. The photo on his phone that he'd unconsciously avoided when he showed Claire Wilson the photo of Aleman.

Behind him, a car honked. It took him a moment to realize that it was at him, that his foot had slipped off the accelerator.

He had to delete the photo. Which meant acknowledging its existence. But there was no denying it now. He held up his phone so he could glance at the screen and still see the road. He opened the photos app… His stomach lurched. It was worse than he feared. He tapped the trash can icon, but the image remained. He pressed harder. His phone seemed to insist that he take it all in: Jenna Collins, on a gold bedspread that matched the one in his room at the Roosevelt. Her eyes open. Seeing nothing. Lifeless. His badge on her chest. Bruises on her neck. From his hands.

Saul had, of course, fought against it desperately. This much he remembered clearly now—like he was in a free fall trying to rise against gravity, being forced to not only witness her murder but to feel her body go limp.

Finally, the awful image vanished, replaced by a photo he'd taken at the Castle, of the Disappearing Woman trick.

He blacked the screen and tried to think of something else. The elderly Luna. He prayed she was home. He prayed she wouldn't hold back. Prayed she'd know how to prove his innocence. How to stop Wayob.

His phone buzzed in the cup holder. It was Hernandez. She would know if he ignored her.

He swallowed. Had to answer.

"You're in the car," she said. Not a question, an accusation, and her assumption was correct: he was breaking his promise to her by going to the Lunas.

"Put yourself in my shoes."

"Not possible," she said with a harshness in her voice that jolted his head back in the seat. Through the phone, he heard the sound of keys, a door closing. Footsteps on stairs. "Forget the Lunas," she said. "Meet me at the PAB. We've got some new evidence you're going to want to see for yourself."

His stomach twisted. He wasn't allowed at the PAB while on suspension, and they both knew it. "Evidence on who?"

Through the phone, he heard the door chime of her car, then a guitar chord ripped in his ear and abruptly went silent. Her engine turned over. "You were at the Roosevelt last night, right?"

"For a few hours," he said.

"You didn't spend the night?"

"I went to bed after I checked in. But evidently, at some point, I went to Saroyan's."

"You don't know when?"

If Collins's murder had occurred at the Roosevelt the way Saul now recalled it, then why did Wayob move the body?

"I'm almost at the Lunas," he said. "I'll call you afterward."

"No, wait for me. You'll need help translating."

Time was running out. He had to prove what had happened before Hernandez arrived, and he had a bad feeling about this new evidence. Almost certainly, it implicated him in the crime.

"Promise me," she said, "you'll wait outside."

"Sure thing," he lied.

A cloud slithered across the moon.

He ended the call and exited onto Loma Avenue. He sped between shadowy warehouses, their fences topped with razor wire.

The road dead-ended into the lot for the Lunas' building. A faded red Civic with a dented bumper and a patch of rust by the plate was parked beside a brand-new-black Tesla sports car with dealer tags. It was probably worth more than the whole building.

Saul parked by the Tesla. He unfolded himself from his car. Above the lot, tires hissed along the freeway. The clouds had thickened up and all but erased the moon.

As he climbed the stairs to the second floor, they shook under his weight, and the rusted rail offered little support. The whole upper porch sloped away from the building.

He knocked on the Lunas' faded-blue door.

No response.

He knocked again.

"Not a good time," said a voice behind the door. A man's voice.

Saul held his badge to the peephole. "It's urgent. I need to speak with Gloria Luna."

The door cracked an inch. A sliver of face peeked through the slit. An eye, a cheek, and a chin—a white man, familiar, his silver hair moussed up and trimmed neat.

"Abuela passed."

Saul Goes Down

As the door opened wider, Saul staggered back a half step. Light flickered behind the man in the doorway. His tailored suit fit snug on his broad shoulders. Spry energy seemed coiled in his posture. His lip twitched.

Saul steadied himself. "When?"

"Yesterday," the man said.

"How?"

"Cancer."

"May I come in?"

"Now's not a good time."

"I need to speak with Rosa. It's urgent."

"It's almost four in the morning."

"Could be a matter of life and death."

"Let him in," Rosa said from behind the half-open door, her voice flat and defeated.

The man looked toward her. He held the door firmly and pleaded with her in fluent Spanish.

Rosa, who had lost her father and now her grandmother, both in less than a week, raised her voice to the older white man who had answered her door like he owned the place.

Saul stuck his foot in the doorway and leaned closer.

The man stepped back. Rosa pulled the door open. She wore a long black dress. Her eyes were bloodshot and teary.

"I'm so sorry for your loss," Saul said.

She pressed her lips together and nodded, then abruptly turned and led them into the apartment.

Candlelight trembled on the ceiling and walls from a host of prayer candles on the kitchen counter and on the shelf by the window. There, a photo of Gloria Luna had been added beside the one of her son. Only one ceramic owl remained of the collection that had been on the shelf beside the couch. Strewn about the floor were a half dozen half-packed boxes.

Saul navigated through the boxes and faced the man. "I didn't catch your name."

"Evan." His voice shot up an octave, as if trying out how his name sounded. "York."

Impossible. But it was him. Saul recognized him now from the news, and from googling Ashley York.

Evan York stood there fidgeting like his hands felt wrong. No sign of his characteristic charisma. If anything, this man with a billion-dollar net worth looked almost ashamed.

The odds of encountering both Ashley York and her father on the same night in separate locations were slim, but possible. But the odds of finding him here, at the Lunas, were implausibly low. Wayob must have something to do with his presence, though Saul couldn't fathom what the connection could be.

He tried to sound calm as he asked, "So, how do you two know each other?"

She looked at York as she carried a wooden chair from the table and planted it beside her grandmother's empty recliner.

"I help people out," Evan York said.

"A philanthropist," Saul said. "Very kind." It sounded fishy, although he wished it was true. York's limitless resources could provide a bright future for Rosa.

Rosa sat in the wooden chair and motioned Saul to the sofa.

He took a step toward it and paused. There were thousands in Rosa's situation or worse just in LA alone. And why come here in person? Was it something Evan York couldn't trust to any one of the countless people in his employment?

He glanced at York. "Why Rosa?"

"I help a lot of—" Evan York's brow roached. "Many people."

Saul held his gaze. "That's great. Really great. Surprised I haven't read about it. You must have reporters lining up for an exclusive."

York studied his empty palm as if it suddenly contained something important to consider. "I keep a low profile. For security reasons."

Saul nodded. "I would have pegged you for the generous donation sort of man, but why the personal touch?"

"It's, uh, like family. The people I help." York looked down and to his right. "It's rewarding, you know?"

Saul nodded, keeping his face neutral.

Rosa, in her little chair, had gazed off toward the shrine by the window, where the marigolds and candles surrounded her grandmother's photo now instead of her father's.

Saul sank into the cushion across from her and leaned forward. "Can we speak alone?"

"I need him here," she said.

Behind her, the narrow hallway led to a bedroom illuminated by a floor lamp. On the bed was a suitcase and a modest stack of clothes.

"Are you moving?" Saul asked.

Yet again, Evan York answered for her. "She needs to be closer to school." He took the last ceramic owl from the shelf and crossed the room. "She has to take a bus and two trains from here, twice a day." He stood behind Rosa, clutching the owl to his chest with one hand while gripping her chair with the other.

Rosa flicked her eyes up at him. "It's not that bad."

"It's too much. I'm so glad you're moving."

Saul's phone buzzed in his pocket. He reached in and squeezed the button on the side to silence the call. Hernandez, probably. She would be here soon.

Evan York kneeled, tore some bubble wrap beside one of the boxes, and began wrapping the owl. An unsavory scent hung in the air.

Saul placed his hands on his knees and focused on Rosa. "Have you heard of a man who calls himself Wayob?"

Rosa glanced at York, who seemed consumed with fitting the owl into a box.

"Your grandmother might have known him," Saul said, "or known about him."

Rosa pulled her hair over her shoulder and smoothed it through her hands. "He hurt someone." Not a question. A statement.

"Who is he?"

Rosa lowered her voice. "Wayob is an evil spirit."

Saul shook his head slowly. A spirit was like no explanation at all. Spirits and ghosts were illusions he'd seen conjured from backstage by actors and projected onto smoke. Houdini had made a career of debunking spiritualists, and Saul agreed: they were a hoax. Although he did not understand Wayob's ability—so far—Wayob was still a man. Had to be. No other option.

A logical explanation had to exist, Saul was quite certain. Like the ghost of Irma at the Castle, who had to be a person in another room playing the piano remotely through some secret mechanism Saul had not yet discovered.

"Wayob is more than a spirit," he said. "He's responsible for multiple homicides. Including your father."

Rosa's eyes darted to Evan York. He sat back and froze.

"How do I find him?" Saul asked.

"Find the man who has the Encanto," Rosa said. "Wayob will kill him, if he hasn't already."

"What's the Encanto?"

"It's like a compass made from white stone, and the dial is carved black glass in the shape of an evil-looking snake. It traps Wayob." Rosa's eyes seemed to stare past Saul.

On the floor beside the armchair, York gazed up at Rosa, his brows bunched up forlornly.

"How does it work?" Saul asked.

"I have no idea," she said. "Abuela told the man to destroy it."

"What man?"

"She had to give it to him. We were in danger—"

A burst of knocks rattled the door. "Policía. Parker, open up."

He couldn't let Hernandez in. Not yet. Not until he understood the truth behind this fairytale, enough to convince her of his innocence.

"That's just my partner," he said. "Before we let her in, you have to tell me how the Encanto traps Wayob."

Rosa glanced toward the doorway. Sat forward. "I don't know."

"Why give it away?"

"Abuela knew somehow that Wayob was coming to kill us. By gifting the Encanto, she drew Wayob's spirit inside, somehow, and trapped him there. If Wayob is free, then that man did not destroy it. He must have used it."

"For what?"

Rosa inhaled. "To switch bodies."

Saul would have laughed—he wanted to laugh—except Rosa appeared dead serious. She believed this. York's face went pale, his lips tightened to a grim line.

"Mrs. Luna," Hernandez knocked again. "I need you to let me in. Parker is dangerous."

Evan York leaped to his feet and looked from Saul to the door. "How about you go stall her while I talk to Rosa," Saul said. "I'm not leaving you alone with her. No way." Saul held up his palms. "Wayob's got me in a real tight spot here. He's framing me. What I'm giving you is a chance to explain yourself. It's more than a little suspicious finding you here with Rosa the night after her grandmother died. I'm trying to reserve judgment, but my partner is not going to like it. She'll find this inappropriate."

The doorknob rattled. "At the count of ten, I'm going to break down the door."

York sat straighter and tensed his shoulders. His head swiveled from Rosa to the door to Saul. Stalling was a sign of guilt.

Maybe Hernandez would believe Saul's innocence if she listened to Rosa. At this point, it was the best he could do. He heaved himself up off the couch. "When I let her in, you have to tell her what you know, both of you. Tell us everything."

He shouted toward the door. "Stand down. I'm coming."

What could he say? He had rushed here seeking answers, but so far he had none. Maybe if she saw the sincerity in Rosa's eyes, that would be enough for Hernandez to at least question the evidence that she must have found that linked Saul to Collins. And Evan York, whatever his reason for being here, seemed to agree with Rosa's story.

Saul opened the door and motioned her in. "You have to hear this for yourself."

Hernandez stood there, her chin tilted up, her chest puffed. "*He who fights with monsters should see to it that he himself does not become a monster.*"

"Nietzsche, right? What's the part about the abyss?"

She combed back her shock of white. "*When you gaze long into the abyss, the abyss gazes also into you.*"

"That's about the size of it."

"Hands behind your head," she said. "You know the drill."

"Please, you have to listen to Rosa. And get this, Evan York is here. Evan-fucking-York!"

Her eyes hardened. She stepped back to the porch rail. Hand to her weapon.

"Cuff me if you want, but just listen for ten minutes. Please, Rhonda."

"This isn't a negotiation, *Barker*." She had flattened the P. He was back to Barker now. "You're under arrest."

He held her gaze. Stepped out onto the porch. Did not ask what for or who. Could be Saroyan or Collins or both. Both dead by his hands. By Wayob using Saul's body.

"I need your weapon. Nice and steady."

He held his coat open and slowly pulled his pistol from the shoulder holster. He passed her his pistol, the barrel pointed toward his chest.

She checked the safety and slid it into her pocket. "I need your phone too."

"Why?" Saul asked but he knew why. She had found out, somehow, about that awful image, which, thank goodness, he'd deleted.

She stood legs apart, gripped the Glock holstered to her hip. "That's an order."

She wouldn't shoot him. Would she? If he was going to make a move, now was the time to do it. But what could he do? Without Hernandez he had nothing. He had to appeal to her sense of reason. He had to convince her that he wasn't responsible, but how?

Very slowly, he slid his phone from his pocket and held it out toward her.

She refused to take it. "Unlock it."

He didn't have to. The Fifth Amendment protected him, but if he refused, she'd assume the worst. He pressed his thumb to the screen and handed it over.

She scrolled through the photos.

Saul's legs felt like giving out. "What are you looking for?" He tried to sound innocent, but his voice cracked and he couldn't quite meet her eyes.

The tension in her cheeks was almost unbearable.

She frowned. Tapped. Swiped. Tapped and swiped. Her eyes widened. She stepped back as if he'd struck her, and he felt like he had. She nearly dropped the phone but recovered it with her other hand. She gripped it gingerly at the edges, fingers extended, as though it were scalding hot, and turned the screen toward him.

It was the photo. Collins. Her lifeless eyes boring into him.

Saul looked away. His vision blurred. He couldn't speak.

"Just because you deleted it," Hernandez said, "doesn't mean it's gone."

Did he know that? He should have.

"You disgust me," she said. "I trusted you."

It took all his strength just to stay on his feet. He reached toward her. "Hernandez—"

"Hands on your head." She shoved his phone into her pocket and reached for her weapon.

He wanted to fall on his knees and beg her to believe him, but begging wasn't going to get him anywhere. "Think about it. Why would I have a photo like that?"

"I have thought about it. I thought about it the whole way here. How I had a partner who was holding back, keeping me out of the loop. Your reaction when I showed you a photo of her corpse. And now I get it." She drew her gun. "I said hands on your head!"

He complied. "I didn't remember. Not at first. It just came back in a haze, like a dream. That's what I thought it was, just a dream. I sound crazy—I know I do—but there is an explanation. Maybe it was my hands, but Wayob did the killing."

"Sounds like you've got a real good defense. I was willing to believe that you were framed for Saroyan, but I don't buy that you were possessed. People kill people. Not demons." She snapped the cuffs off her belt. "You know the drill."

If he didn't cooperate now, she'd never listen to him again. He held out his arms. "Wayob framed me. If you won't believe me, listen to Rosa. Wayob is still out there. We need to stop him before he kills again."

She shook her head and snapped the cuffs tight on his wrists. As she marched him down the rickety stairs, she kept a safe distance behind him.

"How did you know about the photo?" he asked.

"Anonymous call."

"Nine times out of ten, anonymous tips with real information come from the perp."

"Guess this is one of those rare times, then, unless you called in the tip on yourself?"

"That would make about as much sense as staging that photo with someone watching."

"Well, I doubt you told anyone about it. Ergo, he saw you do Collins. We found fibers under her nails that match for the carpet at the Roosevelt."

"You talk to the staff?"

"They didn't see shit, and there's nothing on the security footage. If you're suggesting a conspiracy, then what's the motive? Collins has no connection to Guatemala or the Lunas. It's too complicated. Plus, the way she was murdered—it was personal. What did she do? Laugh at you?"

Saul shook his head. "I don't know what triggered Wayob. When time did the call come in?"

"This morning, but you know how many phony tips we have to sift through on something like this."

"Collins's murder wasn't reported until noon."

"Exactly—he saw you. Occam's Razor."

Nice play, Wayob. He took two more steps down and turned to face her. She raised her gun. For the millionth time, he wished he'd accepted her invitation. If he'd slept at her place instead of coming here, she probably wouldn't have stayed up working the Collins case. Wouldn't have reviewed the tip log or the forensics. But all that could have been was no good to him now.

"Were you able to confirm his story?" he asked.

"We're working on it." She waved her gun barrel toward the lot. Her Mustang was parked behind his plain wrap, blocking him in.

At the bottom of the stairs, Saul paused again. "How about I drive to the PAB? Save the man hours on the boot who'll have to fetch my car. You can follow me the whole way."

Hernandez snorted and opened the rear door of her Mustang, her weapon stiff by her side.

Saul obeyed her unspoken order. He tried to make eye contact, but she refused to look up at his face. He eased himself into the backseat. The shocks groaned from his weight.

"Think about it," he said. "Evan York here, in the middle of the night, with a girl less than half his age. A young girl who just lost her whole family."

Hernandez slammed the door in his face. Threw open the driver's door. Sat decisively and jammed her key in the ignition.

He thought about what Rosa had said.

He watched Hernandez's reflection in the rearview. When she finally glanced up at him, he asked, "Do you believe in ghosts?"

Hernandez and Rosa

Hernandez gazed up through the windshield of her Mustang. Concrete pillars towered up into the gray mass of low clouds that had descended over the 10 freeway and blurred the traffic into red and white arcs through the fog. The clouds had sealed in the city with a layer of cold air below them.

On the existence of ghosts, she was undecided. But people killed people. She was sure of that. And two days ago, Parker would have agreed. He was a non-believer. Yet now he blamed Wayob, who was nothing more than a legend, a scapegoat for a string of unsolved murders in Guatemala. Claiming that Wayob had forced Parker's hands to strangle Jenna Collins was like saying *the devil made me do it*.

She sparked the engine and glanced in the rearview.

In the backseat, Parker held her gaze. Such intensity. The air between them seemed to spark.

How could she have been so wrong about him? That she'd invited him into her home, where her family lived—to spend the night in *her* bed—it made her nauseous. He might as well have shot her in the heart.

"You betrayed me," she said.

"No." He held up his fists, the cuffs on his wrists. "I'm the one betrayed."

"How can you say that? You let me chase dead ends on Collins. Meanwhile, the whole time, you had that photo of her corpse on your phone."

"I didn't know it was there."

"Then why delete it?"

"I panicked."

A pained laugh escaped her throat. "I'm thinking you killed Saroyan as well. Turns out it *was* your handwriting on the note."

"Think about it," he said. "Why would I frame myself?"

"Because it was the perfect cover, almost. The way you came forward with the note blaming you for Saroyan's murder basically guaranteed I'd think you'd been framed. I assumed it was Carter." The overzealous IA detective and his partner, Arcos, had been trying to get Parker fired from the LAPD. "But he had nothing to do with it, did he?"

Parker shrank in his seat. "I should have told you it wasn't Carter. I was just struggling with the truth myself. I wanted to believe it was a nightmare. It was so awful. Wayob forced *my* hands against my will. He forced me to hold a pillow over Saroyan's head. And hold it there until he stopped breathing."

A horrible taste rose in the back of her throat. "I thought I knew you."

"I wish you did. Then you'd know I didn't kill anyone."

She stared at him in the mirror.

He stared back, his face obscured by shadow, his heart a dark forest.

But he did have a point. Without the note, Saroyan's death would have seemed natural. And the anonymous call that tipped her off about the photo of Collins's corpse on his phone was a little too convenient, and weird. Still, the carpet fibers placed Collins solidly in The Roosevelt, where Parker claimed to have been sleeping at the time of her death.

"Talk to Rosa," he said. "Please."

"What do you think she's going to say? Nothing can override the evidence against you."

"Do it for her sake. Evan York is in her apartment, right now. Why would he be there? Think about it."

Evan York was just the sort of smooth-talker who would prey on a girl like Rosa, who might not be thinking clearly after losing both her father and grandmother. She was all alone in the world, her options were limited, and she was probably too young to realize if someone was using her.

The idea gnawed at Hernandez. Evan York in Rosa's apartment was almost too preposterous for Parker to invent. And parked right in front of her, beside Parker's plain wrap, was a jet-black Tesla Roadster still sporting dealer tags. It didn't belong here outside an apartment building with a blue tarp on the roof, in a lot with a landscaper's truck and a faded red Civic with a dented bumper.

Hernandez killed the engine. A slight smile traced Parker's lips. She had relented. No choice.

"Stay put." She opened the door and double checked the child locks were engaged. She had cuffed his hands in front to provide a little extra comfort, which they both knew she'd never have offered any other perp. Still, there was no chance he could climb over the seat.

A security light tacked onto the building bathed the stairs in harsh orange light. Beside the stairs, chalky cracks webbed the stucco.

She knocked on the Lunas' apartment door.

Rosa opened it.

Inside, standing behind a stack of boxes and a suitcase, was Evan York. He wore a black tailored suit and his white hair was coifed up like he was about to showboat for the press, which was the only way Hernandez had ever seen him.

He drew up his broad shoulders and slid his hands into his pockets. The posture reminded her of how Armondo, the older man she'd dated when she was twenty-four, had acted when she introduced him to her mother, which should have been her first clue that Armondo was lying about all the money he claimed was coming his way. Not that she'd have cared at that point. What she'd fallen for was his freedom and his souped-up Challenger. By the time she finally saw through all his machismo bullshit, she was six months pregnant. Unable to raise Rumi on her own, she'd doomed herself to another fifteen years living with her mother.

Rosa was younger than Hernandez had been at the time, and, unlike Armondo, Evan York actually had money—change-your-life money.

Rosa spun toward the living room where Evan York was standing. Hernandez marched past her and stabbed him in the chest with her index finger. "I know what you're up to."

Incense saturated the air. "I'm just helping her," he said, hardly a trace of his British accent. No sign of his trademark confidence either. He kneeled over a box as if it suddenly required his attention.

"By moving her into a love nest?"

"No, into an apartment near campus."

Rosa motioned Hernandez to the couch beside the window. On the little shelf with the marigolds and the prayer candles that flickered on the framed photo of Luis Luna, a photo of his mother had been added.

Rosa was staring at the floor. Hernandez had to duck down to catch her eyes. "We need to talk alone."

Rosa glanced at York, who opened his mouth to speak.

Hernandez held up a hand. "Spare me." She had no tolerance for some rich dude lurking around Rosa at three in the morning.

Rosa led Hernandez to her room. Beside the bed, which was stripped to the mattress, was a red suitcase and two packed boxes. Jammed between the bed and the wall was an Ikea desk. Above it, a poster for *Il Volo*. Three boys with moussed-up hair posed in outlandish suits.

"A boy band?" Hernandez asked as she closed the door.

Rosa nodded, slightly.

"They're cute."

Rosa sat on the edge of the bed.

Hernandez sat beside her. "In a lifetime long, long ago, I shacked up with an older man just because of his car. Can you believe that?"

Rosa scooted back, brought her legs up on the bed, crisscrossed them and leaned against the wall. "There's nothing going on like that." She ran her fingers through the tress of dark hair flung over her right shoulder. "He's just helping me is all."

"Other people can help you, Rosa. Let me help you. When I got involved with an older man, it changed the whole course of my life. It feels like I'm just now getting back on my feet."

"You have a kind heart," Rosa said. "But he's paying for my college."

Hernandez combed her bangs off her forehead. Maybe tuition was nothing to a guy like Evan York, but still, he could pay it from Bel Air. Only one reason for an older white man to be here at this hour, and Rosa wasn't getting it.

Hernandez slid off her shoes, folded her legs onto the bed, and turned to face Rosa.

"Has he ever said or done anything that made you feel uncomfortable?"

Rosa scrunched her nose. "Don't worry. It's not like that."

"Maybe not yet," Hernandez said. "But if something happens, call me, and I'll kick his shriveled balls so far up in his body they'll never come back out."

Rosa laughed—the first time Hernandez had seen her smile—and for a moment she looked like a normal girl with normal problems, like boys and exams, instead of an undocumented immigrant who had just lost her whole family and had some creepy billionaire lurking around.

Rosa sucked in a breath, and the gravity returned to her face. "What happened to your partner?"

"I had to arrest him." Hernandez tried to swallow back the lump that swelled in her throat. She was here now. Might as well ask. "What do you know about Wayob?"

Rosa's eyes widened. "Not much."

But not much was more than nothing. Mrs. Luna must have said something to Rosa about whatever had happened all those years ago in Guatemala.

In the hopes that Rosa would open up, Hernandez decided to unveil her own vulnerability. "My *former* partner, Parker, committed two murders, and I never even suspected…" The lump in her throat was the size of an orange. She could hardly breathe. There must have been signs about Parker. She must have missed them. Some kind of a detective she was. "He claims Wayob forced him, somehow. Can you believe that?"

Rosa nodded. She looked pale. "Wayob is an evil spirit."

Hernandez crossed her arms and tightened her fists on the fabric of her coat. People killed people, not spirits. She smoothed back her hair. "Is that what your grandmother told you?"

Rosa blinked rapidly. "You would believe her, if she were here."

"I'm sure I would."

"Wayob was responsible for my abuelo's death."

"How was that?" Hernandez regretted the trace of sarcasm in her voice. The old woman's intentions were probably good: blaming her husband's attempted assassination of the Guatemalan president on an evil spirit allowed his granddaughter to remember him as a good man.

"He was trying to stop Wayob," Rosa said. "So, Wayob took revenge. I think the president wanted the Encanto for something horrible. That's why Abuela stole it. She was a hero, and so was my abuelo—and we never knew until last week." She sighed.

"What's the Encanto?"

"The stone that traps Wayob."

Hernandez struggled to keep her face neutral. This was getting weirder and weirder. "Where is it?"

"It's gone. Abuela gave it away."

"Why would she do that?"

"For me." Rosa leaned her face into her hands. "She was trying to help me."

451

Hernandez admired Rosa's desire to find good in her grandmother. "I'm not sure I understand, but your abuela sounds like an amazing woman."

"She told the man to destroy it—but he let Wayob out."

Hernandez flattened the emotion from her voice. "Why not destroy it herself? If she had this Wayob spirit trapped in a stone, why keep him around her son and her granddaughter, who she obviously loved very much?"

"I don't know." Rosa turned and dropped her feet to the floor. She slid her hands into the pockets of her dress. "She said she was afraid."

Afraid? Gloria Luna, who had escaped Guatemala with her son and Rosa, and who must have ridden *La Bestia,* also known as the train of death. Those who survived the horrible journey up through Mexico were often robbed or raped, or both. It was hard to imagine such a woman spooked by the legend of some spirit in a stone. Yet, at the death notification, the old woman's hands *had* trembled when she spoke.

"She seemed like a real special lady. I can only imagine how much you miss her."

Hernandez put an arm around her, and Rosa stiffened.

Hernandez dropped her arm, waited for a moment, then asked. "Do you understand why she said her heart was in a prison?"

"She felt responsible for my father's death—but that wasn't her fault. She kept so much to herself that I never knew what she was thinking."

According to Atticus Finch, you never really understand a person until you climb into his skin and walk around. But the idea was a paradox. Even in someone else's skin, you were still you; you could never really know *them.* To Hernandez, Willa Cather had stated the fact more plainly: "The heart of another is a dark forest, always, no matter how close it has been to one's own," she quoted.

"I guess that's true," Rosa said. "But you can know someone's nature. Like your partner. Maybe you don't know exactly what's in his heart, but in *your* heart, you know if he'd kill someone. Right?"

Hernandez was ashamed to admit that deep in her heart, her feelings for Parker had not been entirely annihilated by the picture of Collins's corpse on his phone, which the anonymous caller had described with uncanny detail before saying he was concerned about what Parker might do to Rumi. Hernandez shuddered to think what might have happened if Parker had spent the night—but then, how did the caller know her son's name? *Suspicious.* And why block his caller ID? She needed to listen to the message again.

Find the caller. Follow the evidence. Evidence told no lies. People did.

Hernandez wasn't interested in hearing much more about spirits but because she was a detective, she had to ask. "So, *if* Wayob is a spirit, how can you stop him?"

"You have to destroy the stone with Wayob inside it. Abuela told the man to destroy it. Maybe he finally did."

Seems too easy, Hernandez thought as she stood to leave. "I'd better book Parker before IA takes the case out of my hands."

"But what if he's innocent?"

"Then we have to find a way to prove it. No one's going to believe a spirit made him do it."

Rosa looked up at her. "What do you believe?" Her eyes dark yet luminous. While looking into them, it was hard for Hernandez to say.

"Maybe I'll talk to this Encanto guy. What's his name?"

"Abuela wouldn't tell me."

"Do you know anything about him?"

"Only that he's a white guy with, like, blue-green eyes."

"You saw him?"

Rosa nodded.

"If I find a sketch artist, would you be willing to describe him in more detail?"

"Okay, but do I have to come to the police station?"

"We'll come to you." Although it wasn't standard procedure, Hernandez wanted the excuse. She was concerned about Evan York and his good intentions more than Wayob. "On my way out, how about I remove Mr. York from the premises?"

Rosa laughed. "He stays." She hopped to her feet and squeezed Hernandez.

Hernandez hugged her back. "You still have my card, right? Call me if anything comes up. I mean anything. I'm here to help. I want to help."

Ashley Rides the Nightmare

A figure stands over Ashley's bed. In the moonlight streaming through the window, the blade gleams. It's Andrea, and she's laughing, laughing at Ashley, all her teeth showing, her lips pulled wide. She brandishes the knife, but she's not Andrea anymore—it's her corpse, her skin pale, almost blue, and writhing. The bruise on her neck tears open. Worms spew out. Her throat disgorges a horde of roaches. A writhing mass of bugs and worms wriggle up the bedcovers toward Ashley. Andrea's corpse lunges. Ashley opens her mouth to scream—but she can't.

Her throat is cut.

She leaps out of bed, clutching her throat, gasping for air. It was just a dream.

She stumbles into the bathroom, where moonlight glimmers cold silver on the tiles and mirrors. She closes her eyes as she reaches the sink and braces herself to look in the mirror.

She opens her eyes. Her reflection is a corpse: her own decomposing face staring back at her. Ashley squeezes her lids shut, trying to unsee the worms in her cheeks.

She needs to wake up. *Wake up.* A rumbling—a machine—vibrates the floor, the cold tile of the sink in her hands.

She opens her eyes—it's August. He glowers back at her from the mirror, his face covered in blood. She screams and lunges for the light switch.

—

Ashley wakes up. Still in her bed, warm and cozy. The machine she heard is a garbage truck, rumbling closer. Its brakes squeak. Its hydraulic lift whines into action, empties a trashcan into the truck, thumps it back down on the street. Its lid bangs against it. The truck sounds closer than usual, closer than the street beyond the hedge above her front lawn. Did it come down the driveway?

She struggles to sit upright, groggy from the Ambien she took last night. She rubs her eyes. Her fingers brush against bristle on her cheeks, the bristle of a three-day beard.

She bolts to her feet, heart pounding. She's in Gray's living room. In Gray's body. Not impossible, she knows now, but she'd hoped it would never happen again. The body-switch-disaster was supposed to be over and done with. Then it dawns on her—the trash! Gray threw away the broken Encanto.

She tears open the front door and runs out into the street, barefoot. She's only wearing boxers and a T-shirt. The garbage truck continues obstinately up the hill and away.

Beside the curb, the battered, brown bin in which they'd disposed of the Encanto last night is now empty. Its lid open. She looks inside but sees only a pool of dark, rancid liquid at the bottom. A surprising amount of spilled trash litters the road beside the bin. She kicks dirty diapers, wilted lettuce, and paper towels soaked with god-knows-what slimy substance.

"What the hell are you doing?" Claire yells from the doorway, her hair tangled. She's wearing the same faded soccer shirt as yesterday.

Ashley has no idea what to say to Claire, who is the least of her worries. She shoves past her into the house.

"You don't have to leave this morning," Claire says.

She searches frantically for Gray's keys while trying to calm herself. *One step at a time.* She finds them on the side table by the couch.

Claire is still in the doorway, her mouth open but speechless, her hands up as if to say, *what the hell?* As Ashley hurries past her again, Claire finds her voice. "You're not even dressed. You can't leave like that."

Ashley considers Claire's minivan in the driveway but then spots Gray's Camry, which at least she has practiced driving, a half-block up the hill where she parked it. She runs, despite the rough pavement on her bare feet.

She narrowly avoids a brown sedan as she peels away, and speeds for half a block to the sanitation vehicle, which she almost rams from behind before slamming to a stop. She jumps out.

The driver eyes her warily in the side-view mirror. She approaches his door and motions for him to open up. He looks down at her through the window, unmoving, and she motions again.

Seeing that she's not giving up, he finally lowers the window. "If you've got a complaint, the number is right there on the side of the truck."

"I need my trash back."

"Lemme guess, grandma's ashes? Wedding ring?"

"If you don't want to help me, I'll climb back there myself."

"You don't want to do that. Trust me."

"I don't have a choice."

"Sorry, Bub. Once it goes on the truck, it's city property."

"You don't understand," she says, "this is life or death."

He shrugs. "I dump off at the transfer station on Washington. Feel free to try there." Which, judging from the level of sarcasm in his voice, will be impossible.

"Please." Her voice cracks.

He pulls off his gloves. Unwraps a stick of gum. "Feel free to call customer service." He slaps the side of the truck. "That's the number."

She balls her hands into fists.

He eyes her warily. "Don't make me call the cops," he says. "They'll get here faster than you think." He powers up his window and eases forward.

Even if she managed to climb into the truck bed before he can stop her, what good will it do? The Encanto is broken. Or did Gray fix it somehow?

She returns to the Camry. Time to find Gray. Last night, in order to return to their own bodies, it seemed like all they had to do was touch each other. What worked once would hopefully work again.

—

Ashley grits her teeth as she turns off Sunset. If she has to, she'll smash Gray's car through the gate. But it turns out the gate to her neighborhood is wide open. The guard waves her right on through without looking up from his phone and completely misses the obvious red flag of a guy driving an old Camry while wearing nothing but underwear.

On the street beside her house, she parks some distance back from her driveway. The security cameras should catch her, but it's doubtful Franco, who's on duty today, will be paying attention. Good thing she hasn't gotten around to replacing him.

She should have given Sammy more than just a day off after burying Andrea's body, but he'd insisted on working. She'd agreed to it, not just for her safety nor because of how buff he looks in his white security shirt (though that was part of it); the truth is she feels good around him. There's chemistry. Even without touching, she can feel it. And last night he wasn't wearing his ring, so even if he's still married, that makes him fair game, right?

The wooden fence around her property stands a good foot and a half taller than her, even in Gray's body, but the wooden slats are easy to grab onto. She pulls herself up and climbs over. She half falls into the thicket of oleander and regrets not taking the time to get dressed. Shame she has to endure the scratches when it's not even her skin.

She strides across the lawn. Last night, she'd believed Gray wanted to get back to his own body maybe even more than she wanted to get back to hers; he was clearly afraid. But what if he had changed his mind? What if he only promised all that about finding the fortune-teller just so she'd chill out and get off the phone, and then he snuck back to the trash and retrieved the not-so-broken Encanto? What if this time he'd intentionally triggered the switch? Does he really think she would lie back and let him be her from now on?

In the garden, she plucks a fist-sized rock from a bed of blue flowers and hurls it at the patio door. The glass shatters with a satisfying crash. The alarm blares. Carefully, she reaches through the shattered hole and unlocks the door. Once inside, she enters the code on the alarm panel to disable it. Franco had better come check this out or he's double fired. A half-dressed stranger should never make it onto her property, much less into her house.

Gray and Ashley

Gray drifts into a half-conscious state of dreaming where it seems like he can become Ashley again just as easily as he lifts his arms. He runs across her lawn and soars off the ground and up over Los Angeles. He drifts above downtown, over the scaffolding of a half-constructed skyscraper, and drifts out over the Palisades.

And he's not alone.

A face emerges from the shadow of the cloud beside him. It's August. He pulls Gray down. Down to where August waits beside Ashley's pool, where the concrete has weathered and cracked and the water drained away. Only a green sludge remains at the bottom.

"We have to finish this," August says.

"This is not my dream." He tries to regain control of his dream by raising his arms to fly up into the sky again.

But August grabs him before he can lift off. "You started this."

Gray faces him, struggling to free himself from his tightening vise-like grip. The flesh of August's hands turns spongy as it falls from his fingers. The bones sharpen to points. His face morphs into a decomposing corpse. A long, white worm writhes from the oozing red hole in his cheek. He laughs, his breath the smell of death.

An alarm sounds. Gray glances around for the source, but dense fog has swallowed Ashley's house, and it's getting dark. When he looks back, August has vanished. The pool is widening into a deep earthy pit.

He turns to run, but the ground falls away beneath his feet. He tumbles into a web of dark tendrils, vines growing out of nowhere.

They wrap around him. He tries to grab hold of them but they're wet and slippery. Constricting. Can't move.

Darkness overcomes him.

A heavy rumble. Stone grating on stone. A dim light appears. A great stone door rolls aside to reveal a passage. The light at the end of the long dark tunnel—it's sunlight—streaming in behind the figure approaching like a shadow. Like Death coming toward Gray, intent clear in each footfall.

Gray struggles, hopelessly tangled in dark tendrils. The figure exhales a dark fog into the narrowing space between them. Total blackness. Gray can only hear the figure approaching.

He wrenches himself awake. Finding himself in tangle of sweaty sheets, he thrashes free and jumps out of bed, the sound of August's raspy laughter still echoing in his ears. No—not August—it was Wayob. Wayob in August's body.

The alarm from his dream is still ringing, drowning out his memory of the laughter. He looks around. Sunlight streams in through cracked blinds. Not his blinds. Not his house. He's in Ashley's bedroom.

The alarm stops. The phone rings. Maybe it has been ringing the whole time.

Gray answers.

"Ms. York, guess the alarm went off by accident?"

He exhales and squeezes the bare skin on his hip, which is Ashley's hip. He's wearing blue pajama bottoms and no top.

The last thing he recalls after Ashley called last night was trying to force himself to fall asleep on the couch in his living room, which wasn't long enough for his legs—and then the nightmare. And now... here he is again in Ashley's body. How?

"Want me to come down there?" the guy on the phone, who must be Sammy, asks in a flat tenor.

"No," Gray says. "Thanks, Sammy."

"It's Franco. Sammy's off today."

Gray hangs up, tosses the phone on the bed, and flips on a light. As he approaches the mirror, he hears feet piston the hardwood outside the bedroom door.

He dives onto the bed for the phone to call Franco for help. As he tries to unlock it, the door swings open. His own body launches into the room, scratched up and still wearing the briefs and T-shirt from last night.

"Ashley?"

She jumps on top of him. "What the fuck did you do?" She sits on his stomach, pinning his arms under her knees.

"Take it easy. These are your arms, remember?"

"Explain."

"I can't," he says. "I just woke up like this. Same as you, I guess."

In his nightmare, he became Ashley simply by willing it. Is that all it took?

"What about the Encanto?" she asked. "Did you fish it out of the trash?"

"Of course not."

"So, what did you do?"

"Nothing. I don't know. If you'd seen what August was like, you'd know I didn't want this."

"I saw Andrea's body. It was horrible." She climbs off him and starts toward the dressing room.

"How did you leave things with Claire and the kids?"

Last night, when he'd told her he needed some time to figure things out, she'd ordered him to leave. Did she really mean to end their marriage? Did he?

When Ashley doesn't answer, Gray goes after her. "You just ran out?"

"I had to." Ashley turns to face him. "The garbage truck emptied your trash, and I had to try to get the Encanto back, because obviously it still works somehow." She motions to her body, which is his body.

"You couldn't find it?"

"No. I couldn't get close. The driver was all sketched out. Not that I really wanted to dig through the garbage, but we've got to get it back, right?" She turns her attention to a rack of clothes and slides the hangers from side to side.

Then, suddenly, she spins back to him and takes his hand. "This worked last night."

He looks up into her hope-filled eyes that are his green eyes, and the urge to kiss her—to kiss his own lips with hers, to lose himself in a kiss and forget everything that has happened—consumes him for a moment.

Her brows furrow. She releases his hand, and he realizes that kissing her would have been just about the worst thing he could have done.

"I think," he says, "we have to be touching the Encanto, too. At least that's how it worked last night."

"I was afraid of that." She hands him a tank top with the Guess logo.

"The garbage truck for your neighborhood dumps at a transfer station on Washington."

"So, it's gone." He pulls the shirt over his head.

"Maybe not." She chooses a pair of jeans from a neatly folded stack and hands them to him.

As he struggles into the jeans, she explains her plan to hire an army of workers to comb through the transfer station until they find the Encanto.

He follows Ashley from the dressing room. "That could take a while. Let's go to my house while we wait. You need to help me convince Claire that I didn't just walk out."

"Later. First we go to your fortune-teller." Ashley grabs her phone from the bed and starts toward the door.

But Mindy needs to know that Gray isn't leaving her, that he loves her more than anything. He can forget about salvaging things with Claire—and he's not sure he wants to try—if she thinks he walked out with nothing and no goodbyes, not even to Mindy. All he has is the truth, and the only hope of convincing Claire is if he and Ashley deliver it together.

He follows Ashley into the hallway. It's like she's holding his body hostage right when he needs it the most. "You need to put some clothes on. You can't go like that."

"We'll stop by a store," she says without looking back.

"Claire could help us. She used to work for the sanitation department."

"Let's try the direct approach first. One step at a time."

"But—"

Ashley turns to face him at the top of the stairs. "In case you didn't notice, Gray, we switched bodies again. So Wayob or August, or whoever he is, will come after us."

"We don't know that for sure."

"That was your theory last night. Do you really want to put your kids in danger?"

Gray recalls his nightmare, August's rotting face and Wayob's laughter. "I guess not."

The truth is, Wayob aside, going to his house won't be quick, or easy. He doesn't know what to say to Claire or how to say it.

As the bottom of the stairs, Ashley stares into her phone, then shoves it in Gray's face to unlock it.

As much as he wants her help explaining to Claire, he realizes that it would be a cop out. He should handle his life on his own.

By the time they reach her car, Ashley is already on hold with the Bureau of Sanitation. She transfers the call to the car speakers, and they are subjected to bad-saxophone Beatles covers as she drives down the windy road from her neighborhood.

She tells Gray to get the iPad out of the glovebox and see if he can find anything on the internet about what happens to trash after collection. He searches, but he finds no specific information.

They turn east on Sunset. After ten minutes of *Yesterday*, a customer-service representative, Yolanda, finally comes on the line. Gray gives her his address, and she looks up the transfer station where the truck dumps his trash, which, of course, is closed to the public.

"Not even for a fee or donation or something?" Ashley asks.

"I wish I could, but this is LA Sanitation."

"Where does the garbage go from the transfer station?" Gray asks.

"It's incinerated, sweetheart. Then it goes to a landfill. What did you lose anyway?"

"It's a family heirloom," Ashley says.

"Is it valuable?"

"Only to us. We can't replace it."

"I'm sorry, my hands are tied."

"Please transfer us to your supervisor."

"We don't do that here. If you have a complaint, there's a form online."

Ashley ends the call. "Okay, let's try Claire."

"I doubt she can really do anything," Gray says. "She worked for Wastewater Treatment, a whole different division."

As Ashley turns on Fairfax, she hands Gray the phone. "Put her number in. You wanted me to talk to her, now's your chance."

"I wanted to explain to her what's really going on, but she'll never believe it over the phone."

"I'll FaceTime her."

Gray groans. Even if he still wanted Ashley's help, it wouldn't be so simple. A FaceTime would surely exacerbate the situation. "Maybe it's better, for now, if she doesn't know I'm with you. Just pretend to be me. Say I'm at work and see if you can get Mindy on the phone. Tell her I love her and that I'll see her soon."

After Claire answers, Ashley says, "It's Gray."

"Gray! We need to talk."

Talk? Hadn't Claire said it all last night?

Ashley seems distracted by the traffic slowing for a red light. Gray motions for her to say something. She needs to drive the conversation, like they planned.

"Come back," Claire says.

"I can't right now," Ashley says.

"You don't have to stay. I just want to talk."

"I want to, too. But there's something I have to do first."

"You mean paint? You'd rather paint than deal with me."

"No…" Ashley looks to Gray for help. He and Claire have had this argument a hundred times and there's no way to respond without escalating. He shakes his head.

"I'm in danger," Ashley says. "Safer if I don't come home for now."

"Seriously? What danger?"

"I can't talk about it now. I just— I need our trash from last night. It's at this transfer station on Washington? Do you know someone who can help?"

"What for?"

"I threw something away I shouldn't have."

"Your wedding ring?"

Gray rubs his temple. His head feels like it's spinning in a vortex spiraling down the drain.

Ashley taps her ring finger, which should be his. Below the tuft of hair on the knuckle, his ring is missing. He must have taken it off last night after he opened the Scotch. Probably it's on the workbench in the garage.

"Nothing like that," Ashley says. "It's a long story."

"Why would I know anyone in Solid Waste? I was just an engineer in Water Reclamation."

"Fine." Ashley exhales. "Put Mindy on."

"You know how much garbage you'd have to go through? You need to get your head out of the clouds, Gray. I'm worried about you."

"I'd like to talk to Mindy."

"She's at daycare. Did you think I wouldn't take her?"

Gray's life is so upside down that he'd completely forgotten what day it was.

"I told her you had to go to work early," Claire continues. "Be glad she didn't see you run out of here in your underwear."

"Thanks," Ashley says, turning into the massive parking structure at the Grove. She needs clothes, sure, but the fanciest mall in LA?

"So, you're coming over?" Claire asks.

Ashley glances at Gray, who shakes his head.

"I have to go," Ashley says.

"I'll tell you where I went that night."

This is bait Gray can't ignore. After asking Claire so many times, and her always dismissing the question or denying it, he had tried to believe her. He wanted to believe her, but his mind kept going back there, kept dwelling on where she might have gone. He had made the mystery into a blight on their marriage.

"Gray? I should have told you a long time ago. Do you remember what you said when you proposed?"

Gray feels a little uncomfortable about Ashley hearing all this, but he has to know. He can't miss his chance.

Ashley slows at the turn for valet parking. Her attention wavers.

Gray leans across the seat and whispers to Ashley, "I said the past doesn't matter—"

"Who's that whispering? Whose number is this, anyway?"

They should have muted the mic.

As Ashley drives up the ramp to the next level, she glances at him for what to say. What can they say?

"This is my new phone," she says.

Behind them, a car honks. Ashley continues driving.

"Who's with you?"

"No one."

"Tell them to say something. I need to hear their voice."

Maybe they can convince Claire, after all. She deserves to know the truth. He snatches the phone from the mount. "I told you I didn't care about the past, only the future—our future."

"Ashley? Excuse me but what the fuck are you doing with Gray?"

"It's hard to believe, I know—"

"I can't believe Gray told you that."

"I've never told anyone. You're the only one who knows, Claire. It's me."

"Put Gray on the phone."

"Ask me anything. The other night Mindy pricked her hand on the Encanto—that charm thing I got at the Day of the Dead. Remember you broke it? That's what I threw away, and we need it back. We need to fix this. Now."

Claire says nothing.

Gray continues, "That was me who showed up last night with the bear. Ashley and I switched bodies somehow, because of the Encanto, and it's happened again."

Claire hangs up.

He stares at the phone. Was Claire really going to finally say where she went that night? The idea seems even more surreal than being in Ashley's body.

"I can't believe you told her," Ashley says.

Gray notices, now, that they've parked. On the right is a stairway and to the left, at the far end of the garage, the area around the elevators has been dressed up like a hotel lobby with maroon carpet, chandeliers, and upholstered chairs.

"What are we doing? We're in danger." Why didn't the fortune-teller explain about Wayob?

Ashley shivers, still wearing only his briefs. She hands him her wallet. "Go to Topman. Get me some jeans and a decent shirt."

"No, I mean afterwards. Even if we find the fortune-teller, I'm not sure she'll help us."

"One step at a time." Ashley swipes through the contacts on her phone. Her finger hovers over the one labeled 'Dad,' which reminds Gray of the brief call from Evan York last night.

"I guess you told your father what happened?"

"He called you?" Ashley almost shouts. "Why didn't you tell me?"

"I just now got a chance."

"What did he say?"

"Not much. He wanted to know if I still had the Encanto. I assume you told him to call the number of that phone you got?" Last night, he'd been surprised to find a phone that wasn't his in the pocket of his jeans.

"Did he ask about me?"

No. Which seemed odd to Gray, but then what does he know about the relationship between Ashley and her father? "He was glad to hear you were back in your normal body and that the Encanto was out of commission."

Ashley squeezes her eyes shut like she's bracing herself against a punch in the face. She presses the phone to her ear.

"Speaking of which," he said, "what happened to my phone? I couldn't find it last night." Not that he'd really looked after his marriage started to unravel.

"Just hurry up and get the clothes, okay? I'll explain while we're driving."

Gray climbs out of the car.

The metal door to the stairway is so heavy he has to shove it open. It groans on its hinges. Shadows shift in the concrete stairwell. The light is out on this floor, but dim illumination trickles up from below.

As he begins to descend, the stench of urine masked by some vaguely citrus antiseptic makes his eyes water. The door groans shut behind him.

Ashley and Gray

Ashley calls her dad again, and again the call goes to voicemail. No point in leaving a message with Gray's voice, so she texts him again, and waits. And waits.

Did he call Gray before or after she sent all those texts asking him to call her on her phone? Either way, it's strange. He usually responds within a few hours, no matter how busy he is, no matter how late.

If he believed the message she left him yesterday from Gray's phone, he'd want to make sure she was okay. And if he knew that she'd actually switched bodies with some random guy, he'd be dying to hear about it.

She hears footsteps. Hard-soled shoes on the pavement. She leans her seat back and hunches down. What if it's Wayob? She can't call the police—Sammy is right about that.

The footsteps meld into the indistinct warble of the jazz music pumped throughout the Grove, including through the speakers by the elevators.

Ordinarily, when she gets in a jam, she turns to Don, but this situation is way beyond his realm of expertise, not that this would stop him from getting involved (if he actually believed her). He involved himself with *everything* in her life, when really he was just her agent. Her fault for letting him control her life. But, no more. The whole idea of becoming an actress almost seems ridiculous now, especially after seeing Andrea's corpse at the bottom of the stairs, her lifeless eyes staring up—as if in disbelief of death itself.

She'd told him about the death, but if Gray had seen Andrea's corpse, he wouldn't have dared to use the Encanto again. Then again, he'd nearly been killed by Wayob in August's body. Was he really such an idiot as to risk his life again, just to be her?

He wasn't. So why *had* they switched bodies this time?

This fortune-teller damn sure better explain it. If she knows what the Encanto does—which she must—why give it to Gray?

Footsteps. This time running up the stairway beside the car. Ashley racks her brain for a reasonable explanation, a reason for someone not to call the cops on this grown man, sitting in the car in only his underwear.

But it's Gray who emerges from the stairway.

She exhales. Relief washes over her. The sight his smile on her own face gives her a warm feeling in her chest. She unlocks the car.

He climbs in with a bag from Nordstrom's.

"I said Topman," she says.

"I couldn't handle the DJ in there, and anyway I don't know my size of *skinny jean*."

The Levis he got are serviceable, but the hoodie has hideous, oversized pockets. If not for the fact that their lives are in danger, she'd go buy something better. In the right shirt, Gray's physique might actually look good.

—

It's noon by the time they find parking near Olvera Street. As they cross the plaza, Ashley shields her eyes from the blinding sunlight. *What I'd give for a pair of shades.*

The entrance to Olvera is marked by a giant wooden cross on a brick pedestal. Low awnings with terracotta tiles hang over the narrow street. Merciful shade. The bricks are uneven, and she has to watch her feet so as not to trip as they weave between kiosks and store displays overflowing into the walkway. The clutter, color, and narrowness of the market feel foreign to her. The market is a relic, Gray explains, from when California belonged to Mexico. The handmade pottery and blankets are quite the contrast from the fashion and fountains at the Grove. Still, Olvera seems more quaint than crazy, and Gray seems to agree. "It was different on Saturday…" He starts to explain then runs down a half-flight of stairs.

Ashley follows after him into an alley. He stops in front of the Olvera Candle Shop and looks all around, as if bewildered.

"She's not here," he says. "Nothing's here."

The alley funnels to the bathrooms at the end. It's a small place. The only other storefront, across from the candle shop and below a stairway leading to the second floor, is papered over and has a *For Rent* sign on the door.

"This is the place?" she asks.

Gray waves his arms around the nook below the stairway as if he could make the fortune-teller reappear. "Her booth was right here on Saturday night."

If this is the right place, then the booth must have been smaller than he'd described it with all the candles and flowers and rooms walled with curtains. "It actually fit down here?"

"It looks bigger at night," he says.

The candle shop is closed, so they head upstairs to ask at the restaurant.

The hostess is young, maybe twenty, and decked out in a traditional Mexican dress with white ruffles. Her eyes lock on Gray, in Ashley's body, and her mouth falls open. Her face lights up.

"Were you working Saturday night?" Gray asks.

She nods.

"Do you know the fortune-teller?" He points toward the stairs.

She shakes her head and grabs a pair of menus, her eyes unwavering from Gray.

"We're not eating here," Ashley says. "There's no time."

The hostess slumps. A look of devastation crosses her face.

"Maybe someone else here knows something," Gray says. "Besides, I'm starving."

All morning, Ashley has been ignoring the emptiness building in her belly. Maybe if she eats something, she'll figure out who to call. Besides, where do they have to go, anyway, now that Gray's fortune-teller has vanished?

"Fine," she says.

The hostess skip-walks their menus to a table on the balcony.

Their waiter appears, his hair slicked back and a smile behind his mustache. Gray asks if he was working Saturday night. He was, but he did not notice any fortune-teller. He trumpets the made-fresh margaritas.

Since she doesn't have to worry about her figure, Ashley goes ahead and orders the burrito special. Gray orders tacos and "just a coffee," but he keeps the drinks menu and studies it as the waiter bows and hurries off.

The hostess returns with a friend from the kitchen. "I'm sorry for asking," she says. "And we totally, completely understand if—"

"Will you take a selfie?" her friend asks.

Gray looks at Ashley for permission. She shrugs, glad to let him deal with the attention while she sits here, anonymous. The hostess and her friend lean in on either side of him, and he smiles as the waiter takes photos with each of their phones. The friend says she doesn't know anything about the fortune-teller, either.

The food comes out steaming. Ashley slices into the burrito covered in sauce, and takes a huge bite of tortilla, carnitas, and Mexican rice. It tastes amazing. *How can this be only eight dollars?*

Gray reaches for her phone. "You mind? There must be a record of who rented the space."

She slides it to him. He begins swiping intensely. She takes another bite. If they manage to return to their own bodies, what will he do?

"So, you want to get back together with Claire?"

Gray glances up, barely making eye contact before gazing down into the alley. "I don't know. I guess right now, I don't feel like I can be with anyone until I feel good about myself."

"I totally get that. Maybe it's good to give her this space, whatever you decide."

"I don't want Mindy to think I walked out. Or Claire."

"So blame it on me. I could say I hired you, or lured you away, or something."

Gray laughs but not with his eyes. "That would be a shit storm."

He glances down at the phone.

"Shit."

He shows her the text.

Sammy:
Psycho coming for you.
I'll stop him if I can.

She snatches the phone and calls Sammy. Gray gulps down his taco. The phone rings and rings. Finally, Sammy's voicemail picks up.

Gray points over her shoulder. "Maybe he's just talking about paparazzi?"

Ashley turns and looks down. A man with a scruffy beard is crossing the street with a camera attached to his face, his long lens trained on Gray.

"We have to go," she says. "They're like flies." She leaves a hundred on the table and hands Gray her clutch.

"We need to ask around more," he says. "I couldn't find anything online."

"There isn't time."

He doesn't get it: the effect on her life—on her career—that just the two of them being seen together will have. As they descend the stairs, he seems oblivious to all the cameras. A woman with a microphone lunges toward them.

"Ignore them," Ashley says. "Walk fast."

"Ashley!" The woman gets in Gray's face, twisting her vicious smile to the cameras. "Is this your new boyfriend? What happened to August Grant?"

Finally seeming to grasp the situation, Gray backs away. He grabs Ashley's hand and practically drags her around a kiosk. She ducks under the low awning.

Meanwhile, the woman with the mike pursues with her cameramen. "Ms. York. Are sleeping with both men? Are you carrying his baby?"

Gray and Ashley run through the parking lot.

"Is this what it's like every time you go somewhere?" Gray asks.

Ashley starts the car. Hard to believe that she once craved this attention, that she and Raquel would get all dressed up to go out and be seen, and if the paparazzi didn't arrive fast enough, they would *leak* their own location. A different life. She's done living like this. "This is the monster I created."

As they speed past the clot of paparazzi and reporters amassed at the exit of the lot, Gray gives them the middle finger.

"Great," Ashley says, "now I'm going to look like a bitch." But she smiles because really she doesn't care. Not anymore.

Gray slides her iPad out from under the seat as she turns toward the hills, toward home. Is her house even safe? She'd given Sammy the day off, so unless he just happened to see some tweet about her being downtown, he'd expect her to be home—and so would this *psycho*.

Her phone vibrates in the cup holder, and the call rings through the speakers. The navigator screen reads, "Incoming Call: Don Kaufmann."

Ashley hesitates. Maybe she should use Don this one last time. He would, of course, claim to know just the right person to find this fortune-teller, at her expense. But Gray will have to talk for her. She clips her phone into the dash mount. On the screen, along with Don's profile pic, his hey-I'm-such-a-good-guy-so-now-do-what-I-say smile, is a text message, which he must have sent a second before calling.

Don K:
I'm worried about the choices you're making.

Ashley declines the call. What can Don do anyway that she can't do herself? What has he ever done? Everything Don did, he did for himself.

"Check Facebook," Ashley says. "You said the fortune-teller was at Dia de Los Muertos, right? There has to be a page. Maybe someone tagged her."

The car in front of her has stopped. She hits the brakes. Beside them, a woman in yoga pants struggles sideways up the sidewalk, arms stretched between a little boy lagging behind and a black lab tugging ahead at the end of its leash. The dog sort of looks like a lean cousin of the dog Sammy wanted to keep, *Shera*. Ashley sort of regrets that she told Sammy to get rid her. Shera deserves a home. Sammy was right.

"Found her," Gray says. "You were right. Three people tagged her. She goes by 'Abuela Luna,' and she has a website. Not much on it, but her domain name is registered to her apartment."

Gray programs the El Monte address into the navigator, and it directs Ashley toward the freeway.

Nowhere To Run

As they speed from the 101 onto the 10, Gray feels all hope of redemption with Claire stretching back like an invisible cord that tightens and breaks.

He can't blame her for hanging up on him. If the situation were reversed, he wouldn't believe her either. But he'd have listened. He wonders what she thinks is going on, because she is perceptive. Maybe she's too exhausted to see that something is truly wrong: that regardless of the fact that she told him to leave, *he* would never just run out in his underwear without even saying goodbye to Mindy and Tyler.

He needs her to know he's not running out on her, only leaving the marriage, which she had effectively left long ago with the distance she'd built around herself, the storm always brewing in her eyes whenever she looked at him.

When they first met, her eyes were the color of a deep blue dawn after a long rainy night—he was found. Her eyes shone as though she saw through to his core self, and she truly believed that someday he'd accomplish something great.

When he met Claire, he was still reeling from his breakup with Laura. He can't remember her specific reason for breaking it off, but he remembers the arguing, and that it was in Paris, of all places. It had been Laura's idea to go to Paris for the summer, their *summer of love*. He had expected to spend the summer in a dreamlike state of inspiration, not in the isolation they both felt living in a foreign country with only each other to talk to. They could have worked through it, or at least he'd thought so, but by the time Laura broke up with him he was so frustrated that he actually felt relieved. Relieved and looking forward to the new possibilities, mysterious girls who maybe weren't so prone to state how they felt so firmly that there wasn't room for his own opinion. It was years before he realized how much he missed her positive outlook, how much he missed her.

Claire is too insightful to be an optimist, and too smart. Last year, when Gray thought his promotion was in the bag because Brad was nitpicking every line of Manny's code while approving Gray's sight unseen, it was Claire who predicted that Manny would get the bump, and she was right. She sees through the false colors of the world, while often Gray cannot.

Yet she slept with Gray, seemingly with no idea that it was Ashley in his body, which raises an ugly question, a question to which he'd rather not know the answer, but it comes alive inside him. He can feel the claws digging their way out.

Traffic slows. He turns to Ashley. "Was it more than once?"

Ashley's eyes dart from him to the brake lights ahead. She grips the wheel with both hands as she slows to a stop.

"What?"

"When you slept with Claire."

"I had no idea what was going on. I mean— I knew, but… I didn't think it was real."

"I know what you mean; I sort of thought it was a dream at first too. But I bet Claire thought you were acting weird. It was a Sunday, and you were gone all day, right?"

Cars pass on the left. Ashley hits the turn indicator. "I was trying to get my life back. I was overwhelmed. Claire was a total stranger at the time."

A subtle redness seeps into her cheeks, which Gray only notices because he knows his own face. "How did it start?"

"It just sort of happened. I almost felt like I had to, you know?"

But Gray doesn't know. He can't imagine anything just happening between him and Claire. He wants to reconstruct their sexual encounter in his mind, to know every sordid detail and destroy himself with the images. He has to let it go. He and Claire are over.

Ashley merges left and accelerates. The lane slams to a standstill. They sit there while the middle lane starts moving beside them. Maybe it was easier for Ashley because she'd nothing to lose with Claire, and maybe Claire sensed it—maybe, on some subconscious level, she'd sensed someone else in Gray's body, and this was her way of escaping, her first step toward ending their relationship. Maybe her softening the next day, following him out of the house—that kiss—was only guilt.

But, being honest with himself, Gray's desire to know the details isn't about Claire, not entirely. There is something about Ashley, something about the way she looks in his body that he doesn't want to think about, or can't. The thought slips behind the fog that has accumulated in his mind after all that has happened. *Is* happening.

A BMW with a freshly smashed front bumper blocks the right lane. The driver is talking on her phone, held against the dark hair that cascades across her face, as if to shield her from the glowering looks of the motorists slowing as they pass. Why won't she move to the shoulder like the van she obviously rear ended?

"Anyway," Ashley says, "it was you she was into, so no need to be jealous or anything."

After they pass the BMW, traffic accelerates. The sun beats down on the freeway and the squat warehouses beside it. Gray squints at the faded lettering. Hard to imagine Claire attracted to him now.

The navigator signals their exit in a mile.

"Do you have an agent?" Ashley asks.

Although it sounds to him like a lame attempt to change the subject, she looks serious.

"An agent?" he asks.

"Your paintings should be in a gallery. You've really got something."

Gray's pulse accelerates. Other than Charlie, the old guy staying across the street from Gray's house, Ashley is the first person to appreciate his art, to imagine it worthy of professional representation. In all his daydreaming about becoming an artist, the thought of an agent had never occurred to him. It would be nice to have someone in his corner.

"I need to finish a painting first. At least one good painting."

Ashley points to the navigator as she turns right onto a narrow road between warehouses. "Are you sure this is right?"

Gray checks the address. It's correct, but it doesn't look like any kind of place to live. If Abuela Luna's website is registered to a fake address, he's all out of ideas.

—

They turn again. The road loops back toward the freeway. Beyond the last warehouse, Gray spots the apartment, the address outlined on the sun-bleached stucco where the missing numbers left rusty holes. Three signs label the lot beside the building for "TENANT PARKING ONLY." They park in the alley.

As they approach, Gray has to watch his feet in order to avoid tripping on the broken asphalt. The sound of the freeway washes through the alley, amplified in the narrow gap between the warehouse and the apartments.

Beside the building, Ashley pauses to consider a brand-new black Tesla Roadster. "My dad has one like this."

It does seem out of place, Gray thinks as he starts up the stairs.

The upstairs porch runs in front of five faded blue doors, all closed tight. He knocks on 2B.

No one answers.

He knocks again.

"¿Quién es?" asks a female voice from behind the door.

"Is your grandmother there?" Gray asks. "I came to your booth on Olvera."

The door parts, stopped by a chain. Peering out through the crack is the girl who refused even to touch the Encanto when Gray tried to return it.

Her eyes go wide. She obviously recognizes him as Ashley York. She slams the door and shouts in succinct Spanish to someone else who must be inside. Then she unlatches the chain and opens back up.

"You're Ashley York, right?" she says a little louder than necessary.

Gray nods as she steps onto out onto the porch and closes the door behind her.

That's when she notices Ashley, in Gray's body, who is standing off to the side. The girl's face drops. "I thought you destroyed it."

"Who told you that?" Ashley asks.

The girl blinks fast. She glances from Gray to Ashley. "What happened?"

"We were hoping you could tell us," Ashley says. "Somehow, we switched bodies without even touching it."

The girl pulls at her dress, twisting the fabric around her fingers. "Where is it?"

"We threw it away," Gray says.

Her mouth falls open.

"We thought it was broken," he says. "Is your grandmother here?"

She inhales deeply and makes the sign of the cross. "Abuela has passed on."

A knot tightens in Gray's throat. Fear replaces his sympathy, because without the fortune-teller, what hope do he and Ashley have?

"Oh…" Ashley reaches for the girl, as if to put an arm around her, but the girl backs away. She bumps into the door behind her.

Gray and Ashley glance at each other.

The girl introduces herself as Rosa, motions them in, and then double-locks the door behind them, as if the flimsy wood could do anything to stop Wayob if he found them here. "You are in great danger," the girl says.

She leads them past a stack of boxes and two suitcases to the living room and gestures for them to sit on an old, brown couch.

Ashley brushes the cushion and takes a seat. The room is dark aside from a slice of sunlight pouring in through a narrow, slit-shaped window. The light hits a shelf where three marigolds lay withering in the heat.

The couch faces a dim hallway with three closed doors. Rosa drags a wooden chair over from the dining table and sits in front of the hall facing Gray and Ashley. She wipes her eyes with the back of her hand, and begins to explain how her grandmother had cancer but refused treatment, and eventually died from it. "Abuela wanted to die in her own bed," she finishes. "With dignity."

"I'm so sorry," Ashley says. "Are you sure you don't need a hug?"

Something thumps in a back bedroom.

Rosa glances over her shoulder. "That's the neighbors."

But it's not the neighbors. Gray gets to his feet and glances toward the exit, feeling a bit trapped in Ashley's body with the threat of Wayob hanging over them and Rosa clearly scared of something.

For the first time today, Ashley seems to be looking at him to make the next move.

"When you said we are in danger," he says, "did you mean Wayob or something else?"

"What do you know?"

"I know he tried to kill me last night. Do you understand any of this?"

"Only what Abuela told me. She said Wayob is an evil spirit who wishes to remain free in the human world, and that he can become anyone. Even me if he wanted."

"We're not trying to stand in his way," Gray says. "Why can't we just stay out of it?"

"When you switched spirits, you set him free; and when you return to your own bodies, his spirit will be returned to the Encanto."

"Even though it's broken?"

Rosa pulls her hair over her shoulder and runs it through her fingers. "I don't know. How badly broken is it?"

"We don't even have it anymore," Ashley says. "Can we switch back without it?"

Rosa hesitates. "I think so."

Gray sits back on the couch. "How?"

Rosa gazes toward the window where the light seems to wane. "By letting go."

"Letting go?" Ashley plops down beside Gray. "Let go of what?"

Ashley could let go of a lot, Gray thinks, but all he has is Mindy and Tyler now that he's already let Claire go, and he's not going to let them go, even if it means he has to stay Ashley for the rest of his life, however short that may be.

"Maybe everything," Rosa says. "In the village where Abuela grew up, men used to hollow pits in Ziricote trees. Then, they made a big show of pouring nuts into the holes for any monkeys watching from the jungle. After the men left, a monkey would come down to investigate. He would peek in and see his favorite nuts. Then reach through the opening and grab a fistful.

"But the hole was too small. His hand wouldn't fit back out with so many nuts in it. So, he was trapped, you see? All he had to do was to drop the nuts, but he just couldn't let go... That was the last thing Abuela said to me, before she... She said she was like the monkey; she could not let go."

Silence fills the room.

"So," Ashley asks after a long moment, "what happened to the monkey?"

"He was traded to other tribes. Sometimes, I think, they ate him. Abuela said the trap worked every time. Monkeys would throw tantrums and struggle as the men returned and easily captured them. But they would never let go."

Outside the window, clouds have blotted out the sky and seem to be sinking. The room feels smaller. Stuffy. *It must be crazy*, Gray thinks, *to ruin your life for something you can never have.* But people do it all the time. *Am I doing this by pursuing my dream to be an artist?* If so, then by letting go, Rosa means giving up, and he'd like to think there's a difference.

He looks at his hands—Ashley's manicured hands, which might be his from now on. Then he looks beside him at the hands that are

Ashley's now, which she's clenching and unclenching with a curious fluttering motion of her fingers, as if to dispel what she has heard. The knuckles are lined with wrinkles. When did that happen? Gray rubs his temple. He can almost feel the fortune-teller's leathery hands reaching out from the grave to clamp down on his soul.

He pictures Mindy's face and feels like crying. "I'm sorry, Rosa— and I'm sorry about Abuela—but I still don't see what we're supposed to do."

"I wish I could answer that for you."

Gray has an urge to grab hold of Rosa's shoulders and shake her, but he can see it's useless. She's already squeezing her knees so hard her fingers are turning white.

"So why didn't you tell me Saturday night? If I had known what would happen, I would never have touched the damn thing."

"I didn't know at the time," she says. "Abuela kept the Encanto hidden in her bottom drawer. Before I even knew it existed, I was drawn to it, somehow. The day I found it—I must have been about seven or eight—I knew it was wrong even before I pulled it out and unwrapped it from the blue cloth Abuela had tied around it. Just holding it in my hand felt awful.

"I lost all track of time. The next thing I knew, Abuela had returned from the market and she was screaming at me. She snatched the Encanto away and started kissing my face all over. I told her I hadn't done anything, but she was crying so hard I don't think she heard me. She rushed out of the apartment and did not return for several hours.

"When she came back, she told me she had buried the Encanto, and I should never try and find it. I almost forgot about it, until she gave it to you. She was sorry, believe me."

Gray shakes his head. "Your grandmother should have warned me then; she could have told us both. I didn't think it would do anything. Who would?"

Rosa presses her palms together as if in prayer. "She said it was better not to know—easier to destroy it that way."

The truth is, she *had* warned him. When he'd started to twist the black-snake dial, she had clamped her cold, leathery hands down on his with such force that there could be no mistaking her intention.

"Was there some reason she couldn't destroy it herself?"

"Wayob had been freed and was coming to kill us. By giving the Encanto to you, she trapped him back inside. She had no choice."

Gray could see the truth in this. When the fortune-teller spoke to him, her voice had trembled, every line on her face tightened with distress.

"So, she cursed me to save herself."

"No. Not herself." Rosa glances over her shoulder. She looks down at the floor. "She was already dying."

Her coughing had sounded bad, but Gray hadn't realized... "She was protecting you. It was her dying wish, and I failed her."

"Maybe it's not too late. Abuela had faith that if anyone could stop Wayob once and for all, it would be you. She said you had a gift to see Wayob, maybe better than she could. She saw something good in you."

A lump swells in Gray's throat. How could the fortune-teller see anything in him at all? She was blind. "I'm just a guy. And I'm struggling here."

Ashley rubs the bristle on her cheeks, bunching the skin up below her eyes. "We can't be stuck like this."

"You're not stuck," Rosa says as she stands. "You have to let go."

"Let go of what?" Gray asks. "And how? How can it make a difference?"

"I wish I had some idea, but I've told you all I know, honest. Wayob will find you here. You should go."

Gray slowly rises, feeling as though he has awakened to find his life is a dream. He wishes it could be a dream. Dreams are easy.

"Where did the Encanto come from? Maybe there's another one."

"Abuela brought it with her from Guatemala. She said many people died because of it, and that's the most she ever said about the past. I think she was trying to protect us, though I don't understand how. A detective was here who seemed to know more about my family than Abuela ever told us. I could call her, but she arrested her own partner for crimes committed by Wayob. She doesn't believe."

"No police," Ashley says. "I mean, I have my own security. Safer not to involve strangers, right? Let's try on our own, first."

"That would be wise," Rosa says. "With Wayob out there, trust no one."

"Come with us," Ashley says. "You might be the only one who believes any of this. You can move into my guest house for as long as you like. I'll send someone for your stuff." Ashley motions toward the boxes and the suitcases, already packed.

Rosa glances toward the back hallway. Gray is curious what's back there. A cat? Hardly matters: Rosa wouldn't lie about her grandmother.

He wonders how safe they'll be at Ashley's house, and for how long? At least it's isolated; they'll see Wayob coming. A thought arises that he can't quite grasp on to. He feels the urge to draw, as if by drawing he could reach the idea. At the same time, he wants to get out of there, to run. He's caught between conflicting urges, trapped in a tightening spiral.

"Bring whoever you want," Ashley is saying to Rosa. "I've got plenty of room."

Rosa shakes her head. "Until your spirits return to your proper bodies, everyone near you is in danger."

"But, if Wayob was going to pop into your body, he'd have done it by now, right?"

"Not while I'm awake. Abuela thought his spirit can only reach us while we're sleeping. I haven't slept since she passed on yesterday."

As Rosa returns her chair to the table, her shoulders slide like rails beneath her dress. Gray regrets that they pressed her so hard so soon after her grandmother's death, when probably she is all alone now. That's why Ashley asked Rosa to stay at her place. Gray wishes he could offer something more.

"Do not worry about me," Rosa says as if she could read Gray's mind. "It is you who are in danger. Nowhere is safe from Wayob."

They follow Rosa to the door. Ashley gives Rosa her number. "Call me if there's anything I can do."

"Good luck," Rosa says, "and I am sorry."

When she hugs Gray, the tightness returns to his throat. "Me too." He chokes. "I should never have asked for my fortune."

"No, it was destiny. Regret is useless."

Outside, on the porch, Gray turns back to Rosa to ask her… what? He knows there's something, but the words linger just out of reach.

She crosses herself, gazing up at the stormy sky, and closes the door.

Warning

Ashley collapses into the passenger seat and watches Gray start the car, seemingly caught up in his own dark cloud of silence. His shoulders, which are her shoulders, hunch forward. She wishes she could help him. Better not to tell him she's afraid to go to her house, because where else can they go? Where else could be safer?

As they pass the Roadster that looks like her dad's, she feels almost grateful, in a way, that he never called back. She has no idea what she'd have told him, but he'd have come to help her, which would have put his life in jeopardy—all because of her.

She closes her eyes, exhausted and too scared to sleep.

Shortly after Gray merges onto the freeway, her phone goes off in her hand like an electric jolt. It's Sammy, finally calling back. She almost accepts the call before realizing how crazy it would be to answer with Gray's voice.

"Ask him if the psycho is Wayob," Ashley says to Gray. Then, she accepts the call.

Gray changes to the left lane without looking over his shoulder. "Sammy, what's going on?"

"Where are you?" Sammy's voice booms though the sound system.

"Driving. Listen, were you talking about Wayob?"

"Wayob?"

"The psycho you warned us about. How did you know?"

"I warned you," Sammy says.

Gray squints at Ashley. She shrugs. Maybe it sounds weird to Gray, but not to her. Sammy likes to be thanked. He'll keep mentioning stuff until he hears the praise.

"Where is he?" Gray asks.

"No, don't worry," Sammy says. "Nothing to worry about. Just some harmless fan of yours who found my number. I overreacted."

Excellent. Best news she's heard today. She mutes the call. "Ask him to meet us at my place. Be sure to say how much you appreciate him coming in on his day off."

"I don't know. You heard what Rosa said. We should hole up and do our own research. We know the Encanto came from Guatemala now. Maybe that helps?"

"Someone has to watch the security cameras and stuff to know we're safe. I know Sammy well enough to know if he's... himself." After the way he'd stepped up for her last night—even though hiding Andrea's body was a bad call—she trusts him more than almost anyone now. Certainly, she'll feel better with Sammy there than with her and Gray alone at night on her vast property.

Gray looks at her, blinking rapidly. "You're sure? You know him that well?"

"Yes," Ashley says with more certainty than she feels. "He doesn't have to come in the house with us."

"Are you still with me?" Sammy asks. "This psycho is probably nothing, but I would feel better by your side, just in case."

Gray breathes out heavily as Ashley unmutes the call. "I'm on my way home. Want to meet me there?"

A loud clack emanates from the speakers. Then nothing.

The call ends.

Ashley tries calling Sammy back, but of course, it goes to voicemail. Maybe he dropped his phone? "Hope he heard you."

Gray runs his fingers through his hair that was once hers.

Nowhere To Hide

It was the same cheap mahogany table. Same thick shiny lacquer. Same warped ceiling tile with the brown water stain. Except this time, *Saul* was in the box, squinting into the can lights, sitting in the broken chair that sloped down. In order keep himself from sliding off, he had to prop his leg out and hold the table. The chair plus the lights plus the glare from the table put perps at a disadvantage when the questions came. Now it was Saul's turn.

They were making him wait. He had only vaguely noticed the hum of the lights before, but now it filled the room, which was hot as a sauna. Sweat soaked the pits of his shirt down to his waist.

A great cloud of helplessness sank over him. He felt terrible about Collins, and Sadie was worse. He had been awake when she died, but now he doubted his own memory. Had she really turned the gun toward her face? Did she really pull the trigger?

Or did he?

As the hours ticked by, Saul tried to harden himself. He redoubled his resolve to stop Wayob, regardless of the consequences. But how? He couldn't stop a spirit.

Rosa seemed to believe that the Encanto contained some kind of real magic, but he knew magic—slight-of-hand and misdirection—only culminated in the appearance of the impossible. Magic, as a supernatural power over natural forces, did not exist. Still, the Encanto, whatever it was, might be the key to this whole thing. Rosa might be right about that.

His leg twitched, threatening to give out under the strain of bracing himself in the chair. He stood. Despite the heat, he considered putting his coat back on to hide the sweat stains on his shirt.

Hernandez pushed through the door.

She glanced at Saul, shook her head once, and looked away. In each hand she gripped a cup like a grenade.

Lieutenant Levy slunk in behind Hernandez. She wore a white button-down with suspenders. Dark hair framed her face. Her mouth tightened into a line. Her eyes narrowed. The crow's feet at the corner of her eye twitched.

Saul forgot what he'd hoped to say.

Hernandez set the cups of water on the table, closer to her than to him, and sat down. Saul sat across from her, reached for a cup and downed it in two gulps.

"Both for you," she said.

Saul tilted his head and tried to catch her eye, imagining they were anywhere other than here in this stuffy room with Levy and the two-way mirror, with the camera behind it no doubt recording everything he said, but she looked at her lap.

He couldn't let that stop him from saying what he had to say to her. "You know I would never have relations with a prostitute, right? Much less murder one."

She looked up at him again. Said nothing.

Levy tossed a plastic bag on the table. It had a fresh printed label and contained a single hair. She leaned against the wall beside the mirror and crossed her arms. Despite the heat, her face remained snow-white. Her gaze chilled the sweat on Saul's skin.

"Mind telling us why you asked for a DNA test? It's your hair."

Saul had asked Hernandez to keep the test private. He swallowed. *Wayob.* "The sample from Sadie's bed?"

Levy glanced at Hernandez.

Hernandez sloughed off her coat and combed back her shock of white. "Or so you told me."

Levy, who ordinarily avoided confrontation, dropped the next bomb. She flung the note on the table. The one he'd found at Saroyan's. "Your fingerprints are all over it, and the handwriting's a match. That's three murders, Parker. Then there's Rydell, who you basically killed by leaving in a holding cell. How do you think it's going to look when it comes out that the highest-ranking female in Homicide Special had a killer working right under her nose all this time?"

"I didn't kill anyone," he said.

"What about Brown?"

"The shooting was justified. And it's ancient history."

"You think that will stand after the press catches on to Saroyan? They'll dig Brown up all over again and compare him to Saroyan— another murderer put down by Saul Parker, judge and jury, they'll say. All these years, I've given you the benefit of the doubt and you've made me into a fool."

Saul said nothing.

"And Saroyan is nothing compared to Collins. She did what? Overcharge for a BJ?"

He couldn't tell if Levy really thought he'd hired Collins or not, but clearly, in her mind, he was the worst of the worst—a bad cop.

"The Collins case will go nuclear," Levy continued. "The fallout will end my career for sure, and Hernandez, if she still has a job after this, will be writing parking tickets in Van Nuys."

"The sooner I get out of here, the sooner I clear this up," he said.

"Are you kidding me?"

"When's my bail hearing?"

"You think you're going to bond out? Do you not comprehend the shitstorm about to rain down on your head?"

Saul looked her square in the eye. "I get it."

"Then explain." Levy snatched up the note. "Without this, Garcia is running blind on Saroyan. Give me one reason not to hand it over."

Saul gathered what little he knew in his mind. If could at least persuade Hernandez…

"At lunch yesterday, remember my badge was missing?"

"I remember you stuck me with the bill," Hernandez said.

"After Langer's, I stopped by The Roosevelt. The manager returned my badge and barred me from the establishment."

"So someone saw you with Collins," Levy said. "And they knew she was a prostitute."

"If that were the case, then why not say so? He was hiding something." Saul leaned forward. "Let's review the timeline: In the photo of Collins on my phone, which I swear I didn't take, she's lying with her arms by her side. But when you found the body, her arms were sticking up. So shortly after the photo, someone rolled her face-down on the bed, or somewhere, such that her arms hung free for several hours while rigor mortis set in." He glanced from Hernandez to Levy.

She shrugged. No argument.

"But a couple hours later," Saul continued, "I'm supposedly suffocating Saroyan. Arcos can place me outside Saroyan's at five in the morning, and he stayed on me until I met Hernandez at Langer's."

"So what are you saying?" Levy said. "You had an accomplice?"

"It's a hole that needs to be plugged."

Levy snorted. "Tell that to the DA."

She wasn't listening to what he said. Hernandez still refused make eye contact. Saul felt the ground shifting out from under him. "Do I need a lawyer?"

"You want your lawyer? Is that where this is going?"

"No. I want to stop the man responsible."

"And who would that be?" Levy smirked.

Saul tried to imagine a more plausible explanation. He wanted to put his weight behind something tangible. But anything he invented would almost certainly collapse when, eventually, they found some evidence proving his hands had done the killing. The truth was all he had. He had told Hernandez already, but, if she'd heard him at all, she hadn't seemed to consider it as a possibility.

"I thought it was a nightmare at first, and a coincidence, when Hernandez showed me a photo of Collins. But there are no coincidences. The truth is—and I know it's hard to believe—a man who calls himself Wayob got control of my body. He killed Collins and Saroyan with my hands."

"No." Levy shoved the table into Saul's stomach. The remaining water spilled. The cup rolled off the table onto the floor. "I don't want a horror story. I need something we can use."

Saul slid back as water spilled into his lap. Hernandez's face darkened behind the lights and the glare on the table. Shame reeked from his pores. Levy's nostrils twitched as if his stench had ruined the air.

How many times had Saul sat across this table, listening to all the lies and blame and justifications? He had heard it all. And now here he was trying to convince Hernandez and Levy that, somehow, Wayob had gained control of his body and used it to commit murder. And he had no idea how.

But he'd heard of unexplained phenomena, like dark energy. "Science, as we know it, is blind..." He sounded ridiculous. How could he be telling them to take Wayob on faith when, as Hernandez well knew, Saul always required an explanation? He stood the cup upright. *Except for love.* He believed in love. He did, and he hoped

Hernandez did too. He believed that someday they would be in love, somehow. And their love would defy explanation.

He gazed toward her shadow behind the lights. "Think of all the things you cannot see which you know to be true..."

"Sleepwalking," she said. "There's a precedent. Albert Tirrell nearly decapitated a prostitute in his sleep, and he was acquitted."

"I wish this was simply a case of somnambulism," he said, "but I'm afraid Wayob is real. He's out there."

"Look, Saul, think carefully," Levy said. "We don't believe you killed Sadie Wu. But then there's Collins and Saroyan, and for him at least your motive was clear. You had means, and now you say Arcos will place you at the scene of the crime."

"What motive? You think this is like Brown? Saroyan was innocent. Wayob forced him to commit murder. Just like me."

"And who's going to believe that?"

"Who would believe I left a note accusing myself?"

Levy leaned on the table, exhaling in his face as she spoke. "If Wayob is real, I'm looking at him right now. I'm thinking we'll find a criminologist to testify that the note fits with the photograph of Collins you took as a morbid trophy." She stood back. "I feel nauseous." She knocked twice on the door.

"Please—" Saul's voice faltered. "I have to get back out there."

"Nope. We follow procedure here."

The door opened, and Levy marched out into the hallway. Saul got to his feet and wiped the sweat off his brow. What else could he say?

Hernandez came around the table. "You know the drill."

He turned his back and she cuffed him.

She marched him to the elevator. As they rode down, she stood behind him, silent. When the doors opened, she shoved him out into the parking garage and over to her car.

She stuffed him behind the driver's seat, same as the ride downtown, only this time she left his hands cuffed behind him. They went numb from lack of circulation as Hernandez drove out of the PAB.

Light ricocheted off the glass buildings, glared off the concrete. Came in at Saul from all angles. Hernandez slipped on her shades. Saul squinted and looked down.

"Better enjoy it," she said. "Might be your last daylight for a long time."

Saul said nothing.

"Wilson and Ashley York seem to have patched things up."

Saul tried to find her eyes in the mirror. "How's that?"

Her eyes flicked up and met his for a millisecond then darted ahead. "They had a romantic lunch at El Pueblo. I saw an article on Facebook. Apparently, no one knows who Wilson is. How much you think the gossip mags would pay for his name?"

"She was at Wilson's last night. I saw her there. Whatever was going on seemed serious. Did it really look like an affair?"

"Sort of."

"I don't buy it."

"It's hard to believe, I'll give you that. But nothing compared to your Wayob tale. That's for sure."

She parked at the MDC, got out, and opened Saul's door.

"Listen," he said, "I want to say, first and foremost, that I'm sorry, but please—"

She looked away. "Just get out."

With his hands cuffed behind him, he had to bend over and awkwardly rock his weight out of the car.

As she marched him into booking, Vasquez, the officer in charge, a squat man with a bowling ball hanging over his belt, did a mock double-take. "Ho-ly shit. What the hell did Detective Parker do?"

"We're working out the charges," Hernandez said.

Vasquez rubbed his mustache. "Ho-ly shit."

Saul shrugged. Offered no explanation. He had delivered dozens, maybe a hundred criminals, to Vasquez for booking, and now here he was—unable to convince his own partner of the truth. No point in trying with Vasquez. Under Vasquez's supervision, Saroyan had been beaten within an inch of his life. Saul had complained, and because of that complaint, Vasquez might have been disciplined—lectured at the very least.

"Just put him in custody," Hernandez said. "Can you manage that?"

"Skip the portraits and the prints. Go directly to jail. Do not pass go."

Hernandez left without looking back. Her boots tapped out an ominous tempo on the marble floor of the hallway as Vasquez marched him in the opposite direction, while guarding him from behind.

Ahead, a door opened and the man who stepped into the hall was Victor Aleman, who was perhaps the one person in the world who might believe Saul. As they approached, Saul looked down into his terribly narrow eyes, the features of his face shoved together. "I know what happened to you, now," Saul said. "Same thing happened to me."

"Shut up." Aleman, unfortunately, was a violent little man, who expressed only anger and fear.

"It could happen again. You're not safe." Although he doubted Wayob would bother with Aleman again, it was technically possible. According to Wayob, he could take anyone as his 'vessel.' "You have to call Hernandez. Tell her what happened to you Saturday night. If you help me get out of here, I can protect you."

"What's he talking about?" Vasquez asked Aleman.

"A bunch of bullshit." Aleman came around behind Saul and shoved him forward.

In their eyes, Saul was no different from any other prisoner protesting his innocence. In fact, he was worse. He was a bad cop.

They escorted Saul to the showers, where they ordered him to undress and surrender his personal effects, which they took their time bagging and tagging while Saul waited in his underwear, in the cold concrete room.

"Don't worry," Aleman said, "we'll get you a classy orange getup after your cavity search."

"We're on the same team here, guys. Take it easy."

"Sorry, Parker," Vasquez said. "But you know how it is. We've got to follow procedure." He muttered something to Aleman, who replied too low for Saul to hear.

Vasquez laughed, and as he did so, the bowling ball shook over his belt. He tossed Saul the soap. It felt like steel wool on his skin and smelled like industrial cleaner. It made his eyes sting, even when they were closed.

Aleman ordered him to scrub his armpits. Between his legs. Bellybutton. Ears. Belly. "Man boobs," which garnered another chuckle from Vasquez.

As Saul shivered in the torrential cold stream, he realized that he hadn't been charged with a crime. Levy was stalling. Probably to keep the story quiet while she figured out a way to salvage her career; once she did, Saul would be thrown to the hounds.

He rubbed the soap from his eyes. Stepped out from the water. "I'm clean, okay, guys?"

Vasquez looked away. His laugh became a cough.

"You made me lose track," Aleman said. "Now we have to start all over. There's a whole procedure we have to follow."

"Vasquez?" Saul said. "You're going to stand by for this?"

Vasquez glanced down. "We're just doing our job."

"One minute to comply," Aleman said. "Your choice. If you play tough-guy, I'll have to scrub for you. We'll have to get more guards to hold you down, and I'd prefer not to get close to all that." He made a big circular motion with his hands. "Easier to do it yourself, trust me."

Once Saul had finally humiliated himself enough to satisfy Aleman, they gave him a ten-count to dry off.

Aleman barked for him to bend over and grip the rail bolted waist-high on the wall. He parted Saul's whale-blubber thighs. "Believe me, this is less fun for me than it is for you," he said. "But I have to go deep. Them's the rules."

After Saul donned the orange scrubs, gave blood, and submitted to the nurse's exam, Aleman shoved him into a cell with fifty or so other inmates.

"Enjoy your stay, Detective Parker," Aleman shouted loud enough for them all to hear.

The electric door slid closed and locked, with Saul inside. He extended his wrists through the hatch in the iron door for Aleman to unlock the cuffs. Hair prickled on the back of Saul's neck. Men loomed behind him.

Aleman whistled as he fumbled the key in the lock, taking his sweet time. He dropped his keys twice. Finally, Saul's hands were freed, and he turned to face the approaching men. Big white men crowded between the bunks. Sharply drawn muscles inked with tattoos. Tattoos on foreheads and necks. Latinos, arms crossed, brows narrowed. Huge, bald Black men. No shirts. Arms like steel coils wound up and ready to strike. And wiry men, bunching up behind the big alphas, craning to get their hateful eyes on Saul.

Gangs of men with one thing in common: they all hated cops.

Fog Rising

Onlookers gawking at an accident on the opposite side of the 10 had backed up traffic, which adds an extra forty-five minutes to the trek back to Ashley's house. As they roll up to the gate, Ashley is disappointed to see Franco's profile in the darkened booth, his face shadowed by a cap. She had really hoped Sammy would be here by now. Franco opens the gate and waves them absently through.

She groans. "Hold on," she says to Gray.

Franco reacts slowly, as if he forgot how to slide open the window, and when he finally does, the sound of a Dodger's game escapes. She wishes he'd turn on the light, at least, but if she asks Gray to tell him to, she knows he would just switch it off again after they drive out of sight. He only turns halfway toward them, as if unable to tear his eyes from the game on the little TV below the desk.

From the passenger seat, she leans across Gray and asks the question to which she already knows the answer, "Is Sammy here?"

Franco snorts as he turns down the volume. He directs his answer to Gray, who he sees as Ashley. "Didn't even call in. I stayed on past the end of my shift so you wouldn't be stuck up here with some new guy."

Gray thanks Franco. But Ashley would have preferred the new guy. This morning, it had been far too easy to break into her house. They need vigilance now more than ever, not Franco.

"No one gets through," she says. "Doesn't matter who, okay?"

Franco glances toward 'Ashley' to confirm the order. Then shuts the window.

As Gray eases through the gate, Ashley calls Sammy for the

thirteenth time since leaving El Monte. And again, his voicemail picks up without even a single ring. She stares at the phone and re-reads his messages from before they lost contact. *"Psycho coming for you. Get out of there."*

The metallic clack they heard when they lost contact gives her a bad feeling, and she regrets that she's never even asked him where he lives, while he cares so much about her that he'd moved Andrea's body just to keep her out of trouble. What if she let herself feel for him? Would she feel as much for him as he does for her?

As the garage door slides up, she slouches in her seat feeling small and helpless, like when she was sent to the Oakhurst Academy for troubled girls, back when her only trouble was Shayla seducing her dad for his money.

"Is anyone here besides Franco?" Gray asks.

"Shouldn't be."

Her big empty house doesn't seem so safe here in the semi-dark haze. For all she knows, Wayob is inside. They should just drive away. How far could Wayob chase them? Across the world?

"We should check," Gray says. "Want to call him down?"

"His search would be worthless. He might stare Wayob right in the face and not notice. Let's just keep him on the gate."

Gray pulls into the garage. "Do you have a gun?"

Ashley feels uncomfortable around guns. She hates it when bodyguards insist on carrying. "There're knives in the kitchen. That's about it."

Her mind jumps to the cellar, to Andrea's lifeless body, and then to the look on August's face when he saw it. The look said so much. It was more than fear—he'd been hiding something. Maybe Wayob never left him.

She grabs Gray's arm. "It must be August. That psycho Sammy texted about. He didn't want to tell me for some reason, but he never trusted August. August was psycho even before all this."

"He was Wayob last night. No doubt about that."

As the garage door closes behind them, Gray stares warily at the kitchen entrance. He makes no move to get out.

"If Sammy went to August's..." Ashley tries not to consider why he might have done that. He would only end up causing more trouble. "I'd better call Clayton to check."

"Your driver?"

"He's a bodyguard too."

Calling Clayton is awkward, because of course she has to whisper for Gray to tell Clayton that Sammy might be over at August's, and she needs him back here, now.

Clayton asks the obvious question. "You can't call him yourself?"

"He's not answering his phone," Gray says.

"Tell him August isn't right in the head," she whispers.

"You should call Don," Clayton says.

It was Don who had hired Clayton for her. But what can Don do? She already knows from his texts that Don's pants are all in a wad over the photos of her and Gray at Olvera, as if that matters at all.

"So, you'll call Don?" Clayton asks for the fourth time.

Like she'd call Don just because Clayton says so. She's the one paying him—paying him and Don both. "Forget Don," Ashley says. "I'll handle Don. Just get your butt over to August's, and be careful."

"Who is that?"

Shit.

"That's my friend," Gray says. "You should get to August's, like he said."

"Don't worry," Clayton says. "If Sammy's there, I'll find him."

—

They begin their search in the kitchen, which only reminds Ashley of Andrea. Just the day before yesterday, she was chopping onions on the island so fast her hands were a blur, all while laughing about her little brother back in Spain.

It's so wrong. She deserved better than having her body hidden somewhere. Maybe the bald cop who arrested the big man, Parker, last night could help. If Parker is or was Wayob, then maybe the cop would believe that it was Wayob, not August, who murdered Andrea.

Unlikely.

Still, Ashley cannot let her just disappear without a trace. Not to keep out of trouble, and certainly not for August. Andrea deserved better. She deserves a memorial.

Ashley pulls a butcher's knife from the knife block and walks around the island, sees the cellar door in the floor, and shivers. She squeezes tighter on the cold steel handle. "Let's start upstairs."

As they cross the living room, Ashley uses her phone to activate the alarm. Except she has to disable the patio door, because of the window she smashed that morning. The alarm should still sound if someone opens the door but, either way, she feels uneasy about the hole in her security. Even if the alarm goes off, it won't matter much if Franco can't be bothered to leave the booth.

Still no reply from Sammy, and the thing is… if he meant August was the psycho, then why not just text his name? Was he trying to distance her from August by calling him that? As if she still had feelings for him. She now realizes that she never did. She was only fooling herself because it seemed like she was supposed to like him.

Gray pauses in front of the windows. Outside, below her property, LA basks in the orange haze of last light. A boiling mass of low clouds shrouds the ocean, moving in on the beach.

"Looks like fog," he says.

"It stays down there, usually." But last night it came up the mountain. Same with the night before.

She follows Gray up the stairs.

He halts and whispers, "You hear that?"

She stands very still, detecting what might be a slight disturbance in the air. Maybe. Something vague. It could be nothing at all, or, it could someone creeping around in her bedroom.

"Wait here," he says.

When she tries to hand him the knife, he waves her away and tiptoes into the bedroom. It's been a long time, maybe never, since someone not on her payroll went out of his way to help her, and she could get used to this feeling.

After waiting a while, he still hasn't returned, so she makes her way, slowly, toward the gloomy light from the half-open door to her bedroom.

"Gray?"

Slam.

She drops the knife and it clatters on the hardwood inches from her foot. She lunges into the bedroom and collides with Gray and he's striding toward her. He throws his arms around her. Holds her with her own body.

"I closed the window was all."

She laughs at herself.

When Gray releases her, she pulls him closer, comforted by the closeness of her own body. She looks into her own eyes, but they seem not like hers at all anymore. A distant sadness pools inside them, a sadness that probably has nothing to do with Wayob or being in her body. It seems as though he has lived with this melancholy for a long time, and she wishes she could wipe it from his eyes.

She could so easily change his fortune—if they ever untangle themselves from this mess—but the biggest, hardest changes, he'll have to make himself.

"How come the alarm didn't go off when I shut the window?" he asked.

"I think it's just on the first floor."

As she heads out of the room, Gray follows. She retrieves the knife, straightens her shoulders, and marches into the bathroom as if she wasn't scared at all. *Fake it to make it.*

She flips on the lights.

Nothing there. In the mirror, she glimpses Gray's face, mouth parted and eyes wide, and it's just too funny. A great laughter wells up from inside her, as if spurred on by her jangled nerves

"What?" Gray studies her, totally confused. "What's so funny?"

She points the knife at her reflection. "There's a strange man in my bathroom."

Gray's Drawing

When Ashley collapses into laughter, Gray realizes she is delirious with fear. That's why she doesn't want to let go, like she is trying to squeeze herself back into her own body.

They search the rest of the house, and he notices she has this way of presenting each room with a wave of her hands that seems more like she's searching for approval than an intruder. In almost every room, there's a photo of her father—seated in an immense office, stepping from a plane, standing on a beach or a yacht or arm-in-arm with Ashley, both of them impeccably dressed and styled. Gray's favorite photo is the young Ashley on the mantel. She grins from her perch on a palomino horse.

After they have searched everywhere except the cellar, Gray pauses in the living room and stares out at the layer of low clouds that has crawled across LA. At first, he found it comforting—a clean white carpet instead of the congested city below—but now the fog seems to be creeping up the mountain, creeping toward him, immense and unstoppable.

But all they can do now is wait for Sammy to get here or for Clayton to call back. Hopefully both.

They search online, but the only mention they find of a "Wayob" is on an archived website of a defunct Spanish-language newspaper. Someone left a comment tagged Verdad34 that blamed Wayob for a string of unsolved murders in Guatemala City. The main article quoted the chief of police, Miguel Arredondo Sosa, saying the president deserved to die. Then, apparently only hours after he made the comment, the army killed him for attempting to make good on his threat. Even through Google Translate, Sosa's quotes sound like Wayob. But Gray doesn't see how it helps now, and he can't find anything about the Encanto.

On the distant horizon, the sun lowers and reddens, the color of a wound. Mist reaches up to swallow it. Gray thinks that maybe if he loses himself in a drawing, he'll be able to relax, and perhaps something will come to him, some angle they haven't considered.

He nods to Ashley, who has collapsed on the white sofa, and proceeds to the office at the bottom of the turret. In the doorway, he pauses, almost paralyzed by the darkness. He clears his throat and lunges for the light switch.

The lights come up bright in the sparse, round room. Beside the desk stands the portrait of Parker, shoulders bulging against the seams of his trench coat, which Gray somehow painted without ever laying eyes on the big man—until last night when he appeared at Gray's house as if he'd materialized from the canvas. Was Parker now Wayob? He'd certainly escaped Detective Arcos without any problem.

Gray's art supplies have been cleared from the desk. As he opens the drawers, every movement seems to echo in the stillness. He hates being alone in Ashley's house. In the bottom drawer he finds the Michaels bag. He removes the sketch pad and hurries back to the living room.

Ashley's eyes are closed, but he doubts she's sleeping. He sits by her feet at the end of the couch and starts sketching. It's automatic. He's spent so many hours drawing and painting that it's like his hand can draw on its own.

His mind drifts.

Outside the windows, fog has filled the canyon. A solid white void. As daylight diminishes into darkness, tendrils of cloud spill up onto the lawn and devour the hedge.

Without planning to, he sketches Franco right down to a mole on his nose, which, if he has a mole, Gray hadn't noticed. Definitely he hasn't seen Franco smile. Gray would remember such a mean little smile. When they drove in, a baseball cap obscured Franco's head, but now Gray drew him with a receding hairline and a buzz cut.

Ashley sits up beside Gray and looks at his drawing. "That looks exactly like him."

Weird, he thinks. It's like his mind's eye can see details he has never actually seen. Like the portrait of Parker he painted, which turned out to be dead on. How is he doing this?

Ashley bites her lip as she rearranges her already neatly arranged magazines. "We have to check the cellar. Just to be sure."

"How about we just slide the fridge back over it?"

Something smacks the window. The clack reverberates in the vast room.

On the other side of the glass, dead even with Gray's face, a dark blur struggles and flaps, a flurry of feathers that fall out of sight.

The alarm starts beeping. Faster and faster, on a countdown to high alert.

"What was that?" Ashley asks.

He wants to say it's just a bird. There were feathers, at least, but it seemed to hit the window deliberately, like a threat. "We'd better check it out, I guess."

After Ashley disables the alarm, they cautiously step out onto the patio.

Everything's a shadow, and darker than shadow is the crow thrashing on the stones. Gray approaches. It beats its wings, jumps, looking around frantically. It squawks as if swearing revenge for the wrong that has befallen it.

Gray squats a few feet from the ebony bird, his hands outstretched.

The bird quiets, cocks its head and glares at Gray with one black beady eye and then the other, jerking its head from side to side, as if daring Gray to... do what?

"Did it break a wing?" Ashley is standing behind him.

But the crow remains focused on Gray. Peering into him.

His chest tightens and sinks. He has a bad feeling—a very bad feeling—about this bird. This crow so dark it seems to cast a shadow on itself, almost disappearing into the dim evening and the oncoming fog.

"Shoo!" Gray says.

The crow only stares.

Gray stands and stomps near the pitch-black bird.

But the bird does not budge. It glowers at Gray as he slams his foot down on the stone.

"Shoo!"

The crow hops toward Gray. A hop more like a leap, a lunge, a dare —do not cross this line. Gray steps back, and the crow wrenches its head to the right, its eye boring into Gray, a black demented bead.

An eruption echoes up through the fog. Screaming, howling,

yelping. From somewhere down in the gray that fills the canyon.

"Coyotes," Ashley says. "Fresh kill."

"Coyotes," Gray repeats. A big pack. Their cries echo up through the canyon as if approaching, as if summoned forth by the crow—or by Wayob.

"They almost sound human, don't they?" Ashley says.

Gray gazes into the fog creeping toward them across the lawn. It has swallowed all of Hollywood and, in the far distance, a last cluster of skyscrapers strains up through the clouds and shimmers for one last breath before drowning.

Fog erases the half moon.

When Gray looks down, the crow is closer. Close enough to slash him with its sharp black beak. He steps back. His heel plants on Ashley's foot.

She grabs his waist. "Watch out."

He does not dare look away from the crow, its eyes like a demon dreaming, like Wayob. *I can be anyone.*

Gray shivers. "Let's go inside and check that cellar."

Although he's not keen on searching the cellar, he'll feel safer down there than out here with the crow and the coyotes and the fog coming up to choke out the house.

The Cellar

Ashley hesitates at the staircase. It leads down into a dank blackness so thick she can taste it.

"No one's down here." She raises her voice into the void. "Anyone would be stupid to hide in the cellar."

She shoves her phone in her pocket and, wielding the knife, takes the first step. The first is the hardest. She takes the next and the next, then reaches forward and forces herself to feel along the bottles for the switch. Why didn't she install a light switch for the cellar in the kitchen?

She rakes her palm across the switch and braces herself for the sight of something horrible.

Warm light floods up the stairs, bathing the landing where they'd found Andrea's corpse with her head twisted, purple bruises on her neck.

The step behind her creaks. She lunges down three steps before she realizes it's just Gray. She whirls around unsteadily, tightening her grip on the knife in her right hand but keeping it lowered.

Gray is standing above her on the stairs, a look of concern on his face. "Did I scare you?"

She places her free hand on her chest and inhales. "No. I'm just a little jumpy is all."

She continues down to the landing where she presses herself against the wall to avoid stepping on the spot where Andrea's body lay. Shelves racked with wine extend into the far shadows of the cellar.

"I've never seen so much wine in one house," Gray says as he approaches. "How about you take the left and I'll take the right? We'll meet in the middle."

She steps off the landing onto the concrete floor. How is he so calm? Before she can suggest that they search together, he launches off between the racks, and the coil of her heart winds tighter and tighter, like it might burst at any second. Losing sight of him is like losing sight of land on an angry sea. She fights the urge to run back up the stairs and out of the cellar.

They should have just blocked the door with the fridge, like Gray did last night. She steels herself forward with mock confidence—fake it to make it. Gray is brave; she will be braver.

One foot forward. Then the next.

The smell of mold clogs her sinuses. This is the last time she'll come down here, the last time anyone will, because—damn the expense—she is going to have the cellar filled in as soon as possible. Filled in and sealed over with white tile like the rest of the kitchen. She doesn't even drink wine.

She freezes. Something lies on the floor ahead of her. Something organic and wet. All the air escapes her lungs as she forces herself to move closer.

It's a pile of wet rags, twisted and abandoned at the end of the aisle, and soaked with a dark red liquid. Wine or blood? She squats for a closer look.

The lights go out.

"Gray?"

No answer.

"Gray!"

"Coming." His voice echoes in the concrete tomb.

"Where are you?" She strains to see but it's too dark.

She pulls out her phone and enables the flashlight.

Beside her, a wet squishing sound.

She shines her phone light on the rags: there's a foot on top, pressing out the dark liquid.

A cold hand grabs her shoulder. She screams, clenching the knife.

"It's just me!" Gray says.

Wayob can become anyone.

No, she reminds herself. Rosa said Wayob could only reach people who are sleeping. Besides, when she raises the light, the serious expression on her own face is clearly Gray. She can't help but laugh at the two of them down here in the cellar afraid of the dark.

He laughs too and leads her past the wine racks toward the landing. They round the last rack, and now she can see the trickle of light from the kitchen spilling meekly down the stairs. Then it's not funny anymore. Only the cellar light is out.

She hesitates, but up is the only way out. Maybe it just burned out on its own?

The stairs seem steeper. The kitchen at the top seems to stretch up and away. Light bathes the last few steps. She lunges toward it, like swimming up through dark, cold water.

The phone she's still clutching like a lifeline blares out, "*Daddy calling you*," her dad's ringtone. The distinguished smile of his profile pic fills the screen, styled silver hair and three-day beard. As her head emerges into the kitchen, something glints above her, and she glances up.

It's August, standing by the island and he's holding a cleaver. He turns it over in his hand like it's no big deal, like he's making no threat at all.

August Gets Wise

Wednesday Afternoon

Even the Swedish hotties splashing around in the pool weren't enough to distract August's mind off what went down last night. All day he'd been waiting for the police to arrive. All the evidence probably pointed to him, despite his innocence. Ashley and Sammy would say that August was in the cellar with Andrea's body, and that alone would make him look guilty. And the truth was, he had no idea how he'd ended up down there. He had been brunching with his entourage at Skybar at the Mondrian and then he'd awakened in Ashley's cellar, sitting on the stairs, his head on a wine rack, and there had been no way to account for the time in between.

As he sat there brooding in a recliner by the pool, a shadow slipped over the water, and cold air pouring down from the hills sank into his bones. Yet the girls continued right on splashing around in their skimpy bikinis, seemingly oblivious to the declining temperature. Maybe they were real Swedes.

August glanced at Mark in the recliner beside him. "So where's Sydney?"

Mark looked toward the pool, where Jacob was pushing a bowl-sized margarita on the Swedes. "He needed some alone time."

Something was off. Sydney hated being alone. They all did, but Sydney even more than the other two. He would want to get in on this.

Jacob, seeming to sense the tension, turned to look at them. "What?"

"August was asking about Sydney," Mark said. "I said he needed some alone time."

"Right," Jacob nodded. "He's doing a cleanse, I think."

"He's not inside?"

An image floated up from August's subconscious—Sydney with a broken finger. A dream? After being locked in the cellar with Andrea's corpse, he hadn't been able to sleep at all, so when could he have dreamed such a thing?

And there was this feeling that there was something else, something more, in the back of his mind that he was only now starting to allow himself to believe, because he had to, because he had no other way to account for yesterday.

Things that had happened were coming back to him. Things he'd watched himself doing as if from some great distance. With a will that wasn't his own.

He couldn't shake this vision of Andrea, his hands around her neck as she gasped for air, her face going blue. It felt like a dream, a waking nightmare.

He'd been trying to break it off with her, yet he let it go on long past the point where it should have ended, afraid she'd publicly shame him with a #metoo. She hadn't threatened him directly, but she had implied it.

But he hadn't killed her...

His hands, maybe, but not him.

If he pleaded temporary insanity, maybe the right lawyer could get him off, but afterwards? The world would be done with August Grant. Perhaps he'd get a movie deal for his story, but no one was going to cast him to play himself. Plus, he was already living way beyond his means, and now all his plans to tap into Ashley's fortune had gone to shit, when the money he needed was nothing to her.

"So," Mark said, "you find that dude you were looking for?"

"The dude?" August doesn't remember a dude.

"Ashley's new man. Was he there? At her place?"

Mark must be talking about this new dork who Ashley was flitting all around town with. Was she dating him?

"No," August said. "I don't give a shit about him."

"Why didn't you want us there? We would totally have had your back, whatever it was."

"Was I a jerk?"

"Nah," Mark said. "Forget about it. Did you at least get some?"

August smiled as though he had. Mark, of course, believed that August was the one who had broken it off with Ashley and that she wanted to get back together, because that's what August had told him.

On the table beside him, his phone buzzed. He glanced at the screen, saw it was Ramon calling, and picked up. "Yo."

"You're going to want to see this, boss." The excitement in Ramon's voice piqued August's curiosity.

"What is it?"

"Not what but who. Can you come out front?" Ordinarily, Ramon escorted intruders off the premises without bothering August, so whoever it was was someone special.

August went through the house and exchanged his swimwear for dark jeans and a hoodie.

Out front by the turnout, a Black man built like a wrestler sat on one of the benches—Clayton, Ashley's driver and bodyguard. He was dressed in a suit and, as August approached, he relaxed back into the bench, as if he were free to leave whenever the mood struck him, only right then he just happened to prefer to sit there and admire August's nice property, as if Ramon standing over him was no bother at all.

Ramon straightened. "I got him coming over the fence, boss." Ramon's arm came up as if to salute, but instead he pointed down the drive. "His BMW's outside the gate."

Clayton was bigger than Ramon, much bigger, but Ramon carried a gun. If Clayton was packing, Ramon would have disarmed him by now.

"Good work," August said, then crossed his arms and smiled at Clayton. "So, the tables have turned."

Clayton shrugged and said nothing.

"Are you at a loss for words? Star-struck?"

"Guess that's it."

"I tend to have that effect. Usually with the ladies though."

"Where's Sammy?" Clayton asked.

"How the hell would I know?" August looked to Ramon. "Ashley send all her guys to spy on me?"

Ramon shook his head slowly. "No way, boss. My perimeter is tight."

Clayton gazed off toward the long shadows of the palms on the driveway. August knew they wouldn't get anything out of him no matter how hard they pressed. Still, just the fact that Ashley sent him here said a lot.

If the tables were turned and he'd discovered the corpse at his house, he would have called the police and pointed his finger at whoever had anything to do with it. So why hadn't she? Not only did Ashley let him go, she'd covered it up. There was nothing online about Andrea's death. And now Ashley had waited too long. Now August had leverage. Sending Clayton showed just how worried she was.

August turned to Ramon. "Get the car ready. We're going to pay Ashley York a little visit."

"What about him?" Ramon frowned at Clayton.

"He stays until we get back. Do you have someone to watch him?"

"Sure thing, boss. I'll call Yakim. We can keep him in the garden hut."

"You have no right to detain me," Clayton said.

"Think of it as entertainment." Ramon cracked his knuckles. "Everyone wants to be entertained, am I right?"

—

August sat behind Ramon in the big Escalade for the ride up to Ashley's. It would have been better not to involve Ramon, but if Sammy was on duty, he might need to apply a bit of force to get past the gate, and Ramon's military training could come in handy.

August couldn't allow himself to become broke, again. He just simply could not. He should have taken matters into his own hands sooner.

What did he have to fear? He was August Grant.

As traffic stalled on Sunset, he grew restless. "Isn't there some better way?"

"It's rush hour, boss," Ramon said as if August couldn't tell.

How could all these people in all these cars be so content to sit here in total gridlock? August couldn't stand to see them. He leaned back and closed his eyes.

He didn't want to take advantage of Ashley—but he had to. Besides, being trapped in her cellar with Andrea's dead body had profoundly affected him. Lawyers would line up for the chance to sue Ashley York for the pain and suffering he'd endured at her estate... and without implicating him in any crime.

And Ashley owed him because she knew. She knew the truth, and she was shutting him out.

Now he remembered. A man—a ghost? A demon?—who had been with him there in the cellar, not just *with* him but in August's own body... and his name was Wayob. Wayob had killed Andrea, not August.

"Fuck." August rubbed his eyes.

He had been possessed. Was that even possible? He would have thought no, but... it had happened.

"What's up, boss?" Ramon asked.

"Nothing." August gazed out at the lush entrance to the Beverly Hills Hotel. The light changed, and they rolled through the intersection.

These dreamlike memories coming back to August, they were not all his own. He had seen the darkness where Wayob had spent most of his life—inside something called the Encanto. He wasn't sure what it was exactly, but it held some sort of power over Wayob. Wayob had, for some reason August did not understand, vowed to kill Ashley and the dork, whose name was Gray Wilson. But the most interesting thing, the amazing thing, was that Ashley and Gray had somehow switched bodies.

As crazy as it was to believe, it made sense. Now he understood: it had been the dork in Ashley's body who broke up with August, not Ashley.

And this, this power, was something August could really use. Could he too become Ashley? If so, he could access her funds. But why stop there? She wasn't as rich as her father. If August could become anyone... perhaps he could also become Evan York, and he could hand himself billions.

———

By the time they turned into the hills, darkness was falling. As they snaked up the road leading to Ashley's, fog rose up the mountainside behind them.

Ramon rolled to a stop at Ashley's guard booth, and Franco turned his body toward them, keeping his eyes fixed on the flickering blue light of a TV.

August lowered his window, and Franco fumbled for the volume.

"I'll handle this," August said to Ramon, and then louder: "What's happening, Franco?"

"Just checking the score real quick."

"Who's winning?"

"Lakers, thirty-six to four. I'll let Ashley know you're here."

"Thing is," August said, considering his words, "it's a surprise."

"Sorry, Mr. Grant. She gave strict orders not to let anyone through. I could lose my job. You understand."

"I sure do." August handed a hundred in through the window.

"I can't accept this." Franco took it and folded it in half.

"Late birthday present. I've been meaning to give it to you for a while."

Franco slid the bill into his shirt pocket and buttoned it shut.

"It's so hard sometimes, you know?" August continued. "Last week, she wanted me to surprise her, and now here you have orders not to let me."

"Hard to please." Franco sighed.

"You don't know the half of it."

The gate began to open. "You snuck in," Franco said. "I was in the bathroom." He turned back to the game.

Ramon pulled through the gate and eased down the drive. The headlights swept over a half dozen rabbits that peppered the lawn. A few of them hopped once or twice then continued grazing. The fog made Ashley's mansion look like an ominous dark ship blurred by light from the windows.

August told Ramon to park by the garage and wait in the car. First he'd threaten Ashley with the lawsuit and then, if she still insisted on hoarding the Encanto for herself, he'd test Ramon's eagerness to use force.

"I'll call if I need you." August climbed out of the car and shivered in the uncommonly cold blast of clouds spilling up from the canyon.

The path to the front door stretched out in the fog. He walked slowly, already regretting his decision to approach Ashley alone. He sure hoped Wayob was trapped in the Encanto.

Something sputtered, low to the ground, startling him. He froze mid-step and listened.

Sprinklers hissed into action. He shook his head at himself.

The stoop was silhouetted by light blasting through the windows. Out of character for Ashley. She always insisted on moodily dim lights.

He tried the door, but it was locked tight. If he knocked, would she open it? Probably not for him. She'd been screening his calls. Besides, what if she had the dork in there? August decided to find out what she was up to before making himself known.

He rounded the side of the house. The fog thickened. In the mist beyond the garden, the pool was a blue blur.

If anything, Ashley had the back rooms of the house cranked up brighter than the front.

Through the windows, he saw no sign of her. No sign of anyone.

Someone had shattered the patio door right beside the knob, but it was locked.

509

A crack broke the stillness: a gunshot somewhere uphill around the house. Then, only the dulling sound of fog, like a blanket thrown over the night. He texted Ramon.

August:
You hear that?

Ramon:
On it

August's heart pounded. Crouching, he made his way back through the fog and the garden.

Ahead in the grayness, the Escalade loomed, untouched by the light from the house. The driver's side door hung open. No interior light.

August stood in the fog before the car and listened.

"Ramon?" he whispered.

A gunshot rang out in answer. Close. Then four more in rapid succession.

If Ramon had just shot someone...

He tried calling Ramon on his phone. No answer.

His inclination was to hide and wait, but instead he forced himself toward the sound. The driveway lights were off. An eerie luminescence diffused through the fog, from the moon perhaps, or the city below. His hoodie, which was light gray, practically glowed, making him a walking target. He took it off. Luckily, his T-shirt underneath was black. Safety beat warmth.

He crept up the drive, away from the house, toward where he'd heard the shots. After a few hundred yards, the fog cleared somewhat. He came upon a shadow, stark against the concrete, stretched out in the shape of a man. August approached cautiously...

It was Ramon, his legs sprawled, one arm clutching his chest.

"Ramon?" August whispered. When he got no answer, he repeated it louder.

August gingerly touched his chest. His hand came away sticky with blood. Without thinking, he backed away and crouched on the lawn. The echo of his heartbeat hammered in his head. And the fog seemed to be lifting, thinning out. Exposing him.

August remained there, paralyzed by fear, until his legs shook from the strain. He had to move. He needed Ramon's gun. He wiped his hands on the wet grass and dried them on his pants. He forced himself to stand, to go back to Ramon.

The gun was still in Ramon's hand, his arm outstretched. As he took it, Ramon's fingers fell limply from the weapon. Ramon was dead. He should call the police. This was out of control. Ramon was a professional, a trained soldier; he should have had the drop on whoever had killed him—but Ramon was dead. What if Wayob was the killer? He might kill August too.

His heart kicked like a boot in his chest as he headed back for the Escalade, his legs pumping. Ashley's house glowed behind it like a beacon. He should just drive out of here, but he had Ramon's gun. It brought him a sense of control, and if he was ever going to dig himself out of this hole he was in, this might be his one and only chance.

Ashley's front door was now wide open, beckoning him forward.

As he approached it, he slowed. He saw no sign of her, or anyone, in the doorway. He crept inside and shut the door behind him. With the gun held out stiffly in both hands, he swept the living room, just as he had when he played Officer Pell in *Bosch*. Across the room, he had a direct line of sight to the kitchen. The cellar door in the floor was wide open. If anyone was down there, the advantage was his.

As he approached the kitchen, the island flooded by overhead lights, something moved in the corner of the living room.

August swung the gun toward the shadow emerging from the curtain. It was a man: a man with a gun aimed at August.

Sammy.

"Don't shoot."

"Likewise," Sammy said in a singsong voice.

August realized what a stupid line it was, *Don't shoot.* How many times had he said it on screen?

The gun in August's hand trembled against his will. Sammy held his weapon out steady as rock. A grin crept onto his face. August knew Sammy had never liked him, but Sammy he could handle. It was Wayob he feared the most.

"Who are you?" August asked.

"You don't know me, August?"

They stood twenty feet apart, at least. August had never fired a real gun in his life. He would almost certainly miss. "I know who you look like."

"Interesting. So you learned about the Encanto?"

"Yeah, I know about it. How do you know?"

"Your girlfriend told me."

His mocking tone got under August's skin. "I broke up with her, okay?"

"So then, why are you here?"

Assuming he was Sammy, it was time to make his play. "Look. How would you like to be rich?"

"Go on." Sammy's lips spread. His white teeth made his grin look maniacal.

"I need to know I can trust you."

Sammy held the gun out for a moment, his grin growing impossibly wider. Then he shoved the gun into his belt. "That better?" His smile remained.

Sammy probably knew August couldn't shoot. Would Wayob know? "Where is the Encanto?" August asked.

"How would I know?"

"What did Ashley tell you?"

Sammy seemed to consider the question. "She didn't tell me; I overheard. She and her new boyfriend switched bodies."

"You believe that?" August believed it.

"Why would they lie?" Sammy shrugged. "You're wasting time standing here like this. If you're not going to shoot me, put the gun down."

"It's not just Ashley and Gray who switched bodies. I didn't kill Andrea; it was someone named Wayob."

"Wayob?" Sammy's smirk faded. "Yes, you and Wayob did spend some time together down in the cellar." Then he sneered. "The guy who stole your woman also stole the Encanto: Gray Wilson. We must kill him."

"Why? Did he kill Ramon?"

"Oh, yes. I witnessed it. He would have killed me too, but I was sneaky, you see?"

"But I thought... you said he and Ashley switched bodies." In fact, August knew that they had, from Wayob.

"That was before. Now Wayob has taken Gray for his vessel. He intends to end the life of your woman."

"She's not— I told you, I broke up with her."

"Then we're both glad your relations have ceased."

Sammy's crush on Ashley had always been obvious. Made sense he wanted to protect her. Regardless of whether Gray was now Wayob or not, Sammy would want the dork out of the picture so he could have Ashley all to himself, as if that would ever happen.

At least Sammy was easier to understand than some crazy ancient ghost. Why would Wayob care about Gray and Ashley, anyway? August didn't entirely trust Sammy, but seeing no other way forward, he lowered the gun.

Sammy started toward the kitchen, turning his back toward August seemingly without concern.

August's confidence rose. He still needed to come out of this with the Encanto. If Sammy knew about it, then he almost certainly wanted it for himself too. "Where are you going?"

"They're obviously in the cellar."

August couldn't let Sammy go down there alone, and yet there was no way he was going back in the cellar. He hurried after Sammy.

"Have you ever been down there? There's no line of sight until you reach the landing, and Gray's obviously armed, if he killed Ramon. Up here we've got the drop. Better to wait up here. I'll distract them while you cover them from behind."

Sammy stopped by the cellar and turned back to face August with that sarcastic smirk that seemed to be his new default expression. "So how long do we wait?"

"If you're in such a hurry, then turn out the lights. That'll get them up here."

"You think you have it figured, little man?"

"Damn right I do. The switch is a few steps down, in case you didn't know. Better hurry."

As Sammy climbed down to switch off the cellar lights, August went around the island to the knife block, pulled out a cleaver, and returned to wait by the island near the top of the stairs.

When Sammy emerged from the cellar and saw the blade, a hand shot to his belt.

"Relax," August said, "this is just to scare them."

"Your plan had better work." Sammy moved back by the patio door, his boots crunching the broken glass from the busted pane into the tile.

A man screamed.

"That him?" August asked.

Sammy nodded and smirked.

August transferred the cleaver to his left hand and pulled his shirt down over his belt to hide the gun. He might be able to gain their trust by surrendering the cleaver while keeping Ramon's gun for backup.

The problem was going to be Sammy. Outgunning him seemed unlikely, but maybe disarming him wouldn't be so hard. All August had to do was take Ashley hostage, and Sammy would have to surrender.

"You must kill him before he kills you," Sammy said.

"I get it," August said. But he knew more about Wayob, and he didn't want blood on his hands—Andrea was bad enough. No one had to die, or so he hoped.

The Gray-dork came up first, clutching Ashley's phone in its pink case, which he dropped when he saw August. While Gray scurried back down after the phone, Ashley grabbed a bottle of wine and slammed it into the rail, but it didn't break.

August stifled a laugh, and she glowered up at him.

He sat on a stool beside the island, acting calm yet concerned. "Relax. I just want to talk."

She turned the lights back on and grabbed another bottle. "How did you get in?"

August shrugged. "Front door was wide open." He twisted his brows to look concerned. "Of course I knocked, but I was worried about you."

She locked eyes with him and said nothing. At least she wasn't throwing the wine bottles. August imagined they could do some serious damage.

Sammy remained in the shadows by the door.

Gray appeared again, on the stairs behind Ashley. He followed Ashley out of the cellar and stood beside her, wielding a knife.

"I just want to talk," August says. "No need to get testy."

"You want to talk," Gray says. "Put down the knife."

August shrugs, sets the cleaver on the counter and slides it away, according to plan. *Next step: confirm Gray is Wayob.*

"What did Ramon do to you?" August asked Gray. "I just want to know."

Whether he was Gray or Wayob, he played it coy. "Ramon's here?" he asked like he really had no idea. However, his casual use of Ramon's name surprised August. Hard to imagine Ramon introducing himself in a gun fight. Gray wouldn't know Ramon, but if that was Ashley in Gray's body, then the question made more sense, as did his look when he dropped the phone, like he'd lost his whole world.

Regardless, it was time to drop the headline. "Ramon's dead."

Whoever was in Gray's body frowned and brought the knife up. "You killed him."

"Whoa," August said. "Why would I kill Ramon?"

"Because you're Wayob."

So, they think I'm Wayob. He could waste a bunch of time convincing them otherwise, but what if he rolled with it? If they were afraid of Wayob, this could play out to his advantage.

Gray's eyes darted from August to the cleaver.

August stepped theatrically away from it with a flourish of his arms, a harmless reasonable guy. "Look, I don't want to hurt anyone. Give me the Encanto, and I'll be out of here."

"No!" Sammy stepped out from the shadows. The skin of his face stretched tight over muscle and bone. He went for his gun.

"Sammy!" Gray cried, and now August knew it was Ashley in there.

But Sammy, obviously threatened by the middle-aged man approaching, shoved her so hard she tripped sideways and stumbled into the cellar. She barely managed to catch herself on the side, scrambling her feet for purchase on the stairs. The wine bottles clattered as they fell and rolled down the stairs, thumping and breaking open.

August took advantage of the distraction and pulled his gun. Sammy knelt beside 'Gray', apologizing, but he avoided touching him, letting 'Ashley' do the work of pulling him up from the cellar.

August was done with the charade. Time for someone to give him the Encanto. He locked his elbow and aimed at 'Ashley.' "Hold up."

She turned toward August and froze. Her pupils dilated.

As Sammy got to his feet, his lips pressed into a tight smile. Here August was with a gun on the girl Sammy must have spent countless hours lusting over in his little booth, yet he was smiling as he positioned himself behind 'Gray' like it was nothing if August pulled the trigger.

"Drop your gun," August said. "Or I'll shoot her."

But Sammy drew his gun. His eyes constricted into tiny black dots as he wrapped a massive arm around 'Gray' and pulled him against his chest.

That was when August realized his mistake. Hope had convinced him that this was Sammy. With Sammy, he had options. Not with Wayob. Wayob wanted what August wanted, only more.

And now Wayob had a gun trained on August. "I don't want to hurt you, little man. But I will."

August swung his gun toward Wayob.

There would be consequences if he missed and shot 'Gray', but what choice did he have?

Wayob ducked behind Gray's body, looking over his shoulder. August aimed at the top of Wayob's head. The five feet between the gun and Wayob seemed to yawn apart like a canyon.

He tried to hold steady.

He pulled the trigger.

Wayob Takes Sammy

Wayob is grateful for each passing moment outside the stone prison of darkness. Thankful. Thankful he had not been pulled into the Encanto after the old man poisoned him. Instead, he drifted into a new vessel where he is still too weak to gain control.

Wayob chances a peek into the mind of the sleeping man whose body they share. The man calls himself Sammy. They are in a place known as Inglewood. Is Gray Wilson nearby? Does he still hold the Encanto? Wayob has to know. He must risk that Sammy might notice him and dive deeper into Sammy's memories. The memories are like a vast hallway of moving images, where any one of them could mesmerize Wayob for hours watching it turn and reform. As he scans past the recent ones, a feeling of vertigo overtakes him. He tries not to panic. None of the memories answer his questions. Sammy does not know of the Encanto or of Gray Wilson, nor does he know who holds it.

Wayob stops looking into Sammy, having risked too much already. Still too weak to listen for the sound of Gray Wilson's mind, Wayob rests, growing stronger while Sammy remains sleeping for some time.

Last night, in the roadway near the house of Gray Wilson, Wayob held the Encanto—the horrible relic, so beautiful in his palm. He felt the porous stone between his fingers. The snake carved from black glass was broken off from the stone, but he had found it. It was his. All his dreams there in his hand. Wayob should have destroyed it. He would be safe, now, if he had, free. But the fucking old man had meddled.

Wayob opens his eyes. The room around him is dark and small. A slash of light seeps past a cloth that blocks the one window. As he sits up, he fears there is someone in the space beside him in the bed.

It is empty.

He finds his way outside. A fence encloses a small area of grass. Wayob sits down, crosses his legs, and closes his eyes. With his arms across his knees, palms upward, he presses thumbs to forefingers. He concentrates. He is still weak from the poisoned air which came upon him so suddenly in the garage where he battled the old man.

He breathes in. Out. He pictures the altar where the priest, the fucking priest, imprisoned him in the Encanto, now crumbling and covered in vines. The whole temple sinking into the rain-soaked forest, where mist rises into a sudden wind above the treetops, up through glens. The steep face of a volcano forcing the moisture up into the atmosphere where it cools into clouds, drifts out to sea. Sweeps north, to where California juts into the Pacific and desperate, dry mountains draw the air inland. There, the mist falls, becoming fog. It flows through the city, past cars and buildings, to Wayob. He inhales the sweet air denied him for so long. And grows stronger.

Wayob finds the low hum of Gray's mind: a distant echo that he might not hear at all if he was not already tuned to Gray.

Why has Wayob awakened so far away? Always before, if not concentrating on someone specific, Wayob could count on awakening in a vessel close to he who holds the Encanto. But now, with the Encanto broken, apparently Wayob can no longer count on even this. Do all his centuries of struggling and testing the rules of his existence now add up to nothing? Wayob can almost hear the black-hearted priest laughing at him from the past. After all Wayob has suffered.

Yelling. A woman shouting for Sammy.

Wayob must concentrate—must find Gray—before Gray returns to his own body, returning Wayob to the tiny stone prison. Before Gray discovers him coming.

He cannot concentrate with all this yelling. This woman, who must be Sammy's mate, refuses to allow Wayob any peace.

Wayob opens his eyes. He stands as the woman approaches. She has dark skin, though lighter than Wayob's new vessel. Her body, compact and erect, is defiant, despite his superior physique towering over her.

"I need silence, woman. Go inside."

She comes closer, straining upward, jutting her jaw at his face. "You do not tell me when to shut up, Sammy Johnson. What the hell's got into you? Sitting in the yard like you're Buddha or some shit."

The force of her will almost shoves him. Wayob steps back. Back centuries. Back to when his young bride made her will known. This woman, Sammy's mate, is much older than his bride had been at the time. More than old enough to understand a man's need for peace.

"I will not explain myself to you," he says.

"Yes you will; you sure as hell will. You need to call that white bitch is what you need to do. You tell her stop keeping you so late and make good on her promises, or you quit. What the hell did she have you doing last night? Coming home at dawn all dirty and smelly. You're not her gardener, Sammy. You'd better know that."

Wayob balls his hands into fists. "Go back inside."

"Don't you talk to me like that. You don't own me. You forget we're a team? Here I am, the one with a career, and where are you? Hanging out in Beverly Hills. Like you're worth something. When you're not, Sammy. You ain't worth shit."

"I do not want to hurt you."

"You're a joke!" she laughs. "Here I am supposed to sacrifice everything to have your baby for you, and you can't even get up off your ass and give it to me."

Instead of Sammy's mate, Wayob now sees his bride standing there, begging for deplorable acts of carnality. His hands clasp her neck. He must choke the vile from her face, the depravity from her mind. His bride. She refused to accept purity. Betrayed him. With the priest no less, the repugnant priest and his rotting teeth. And when Wayob found her at the temple, she lacked even the decency of shame, her hair tied back behind her shoulders as if to display her face as she took the manhood of the rebarbative priest in her mouth, looking up at his misshapen eyes bulging with delight when she should have been gagging, like she chokes now.

And him, the odious, fucking priest at the top of the temple, looking out over the jungle and holding her head like some sacred offering to the gods, as if not for himself, as he guided her up and down on his pleasure.

In his hands, Wayob feels her weight shift. Looks down as her knee comes up at his manhood. He twists and blocks it with his leg.

He tightens his hands on her neck. And instead of a baby, he gives her a knee to the belly.

She breathes in his face. Stale warm air. He lifts her off the ground, the tendons of her neck breaking one at a time. Without effort, he carries her, her feet kicking and dragging. As he shoves her against the house, his hands feel like stone on the hot flesh of her neck.

He watches, as if from a higher place, this statue of a man and a woman by the altar of a temple above rain-soaked forest. Her eyes flutter, and hair falls half over her face. Her fingers clutch at his wrists. Her nails pierce his flesh, her sound an ugly wet ripping, the way she should have sounded with the priest's swollen manhood in her throat.

"I am a joke... so laugh. Laugh like when I found you with the fucking priest!"

He lifts her and shakes her again and again, her head jerking and bobbing. No end to his strength or how long he throttles her.

Her hands fall away. Silence.

The daylight seems to brighten, stark and white hot on his face. Her limp body, her huge breasts harnessed up in tight layers of cloth, now looks nothing at all like his bride. His bride was lithe. She bore her breasts uncovered.

What if he had submitted to her perversion? Would she have gone to the vile priest? Wayob feels sick to his stomach, impotent, like when the priest's minions pinned him on the cold slab of the altar and held him there, helpless, as the priest, with his foul breath and his tiny chin, placed the Encanto on Wayob's head. He recited a ritual, damning Wayob. The Encanto stabbed into his skull, burning his scalp. It drew Wayob out from his body and into the stone prison.

The pain in his skull disappeared. All feeling gone.

He became physically nonexistent, there in the Encanto, yet his mind continued on, immersed in darkness and silence for a thousand years. All because of his bride and her egregious act with the wicked priest. The priest made Wayob kill his bride, and now Sammy's mate. And all the others. Just like it will be the heinous, hateful priest who kills Gray. Wayob has no choice. Anyone who suffers like Wayob suffers would kill any number of people, a thousand times more than Wayob, to be free from the hell of the Encanto.

As he steps back from Sammy's mate, she slumps down against the wall; her torso leans forward. Her head bows to Wayob—a brief show of respect—before her body tilts sideways and topples into the strip of bare dirt between the house and the grass.

Wayob wants to swallow. His mouth too dry. Sammy's anguish rings in his head as if he is screaming up from the depths of Wayob's subconscious.

"I know your pain, but she made you suffer, has she not?"

Blood pumps in his ears. Wayob imagines that if he cared to look in Sammy's mind, he'd find the usual story, their history like his own, with Sammy disgusted by his mate's vulgar desires. Wayob has freed Sammy; now he can love her like Wayob came to love his own bride after her death. Sammy will see that deep down, he has loved her the whole time.

If Wayob could speak with Sammy, he would explain that this was an accident. Wayob had not meant to kill Sammy's mate any more than he had meant to harm his own young bride, who he had loved more than life itself. And the priest. The ghastly, detestable, barbaric, cruel priest should have just ended Wayob's life, or even allowed Wayob to end it. Surely the priest saw that Wayob had suffered more than his bride. Why doom Wayob into eternal solitary darkness? For a mere accident, which never would have happened if not for her sins, and the sins of the fucking priest.

Wayob drags Sammy's dead mate by the arm. He wonders what happened to his own body. If the priest had any respect at all, he would have placed maize in Wayob's mouth and buried his body facing west. But instead, Wayob is almost certain, the priest cut out Wayob's heart and had his body thrown on the excrement heap behind the temple, so that if Wayob ever dies, he will never reach Xibalba.

Wayob knows he should hide her body, but the access door at the base of the house refuses to open. He punches the latch, tearing his skin on the hard bolt of metal before it finally opens. He drags her by the hair. Shoves her head and upper torso into the dark crawlspace below the house. No disrespect intended. He has an understandable distaste for enclosed places. No one would expect Wayob to crouch down and carry her entire body in. Backing up, he turns her over so she's face-down in the dirt. Lifts her legs and plows her ahead of him through the access door. The dust stirred up in the air causes Wayob to cough. He kicks the door shut and latches her inside.

Now where was I?

Gray. Wayob faces the direction from where he heard Gray's mind before Sammy's mate interrupted. The morning sun warms the right side of his face. Gray is north, somewhere. Too far by foot.

Inside the house, on a small dark table, a wooden bowl contains fruits from distant lands. Wayob takes one, and from beside the bowl he takes Sammy's keys, wallet, and phone.

After finding the front exit, he surveys the cars along the street. Too many to guess which might be Sammy's. Of course, Wayob could find it by looking through Sammy's memories, but doing so would allow Sammy to see what Wayob knows; he could discover the Encanto. Wayob cannot allow this. Cannot afford for Sammy to become an opponent when Wayob moves to a new vessel.

He was careless with Edward Saroyan, the hapless paraplegic, and Wayob can hardly blame himself, for he had little choice at the time, after Parker stuffed him in the prison. But probing Edward's mind bore nothing useful, leaving Wayob yet again with violence as the only way out. But that wasn't the worst part. The worst part was, of course —for Wayob knows no way to blind a vessel while looking into them —that Edward learned of the Encanto. And, of course, Edward wanted a new body. He wanted legs that worked. And he wanted revenge on poor Wayob, when Wayob had no choice. He had to do what he did, and it was not like he had chosen Edward as a vessel. So, it was Edward's own fault that Wayob had to end his life. A mercy killing, really.

But Sammy is young and strong, and Wayob wants to hurt no one. Wayob just wants a peaceful life, or two or three. So Wayob must try the cars one by one, starting with the faded brown one directly in front of the house. The second key slides into the lock. Wayob nearly shouts, *What luck!* But the lock refuses to turn. Of the seven keys, two more seem to fit, but none work.

Behind the brown car, a shiny black one sits low to the ground, its windows darkened. Upon his first attempt, the car begins emanating a horrible, harsh pulsing. People emerge from the row of connected houses across the street. He tries another key; the screeching refuses to cease.

"Hey man." A man as big as Wayob, perhaps bigger, runs toward him. "What do you think you're doing to my car?"

More men, young and mean-looking, approach Wayob. Coming at him all at once, and each one seemingly bigger than the other. Wayob must run. Leaving the keys in the lock, he must stay focused on the goal, his freedom.

He dashes a half-block and chances a look back. The men are slowing.

"Yeah that's what I thought, fool." The first man points a finger.

Wayob hurries on, past squat houses and apartments, iron bars in the windows, iron gates on the doors. At an intersection, where the houses give way to a tire shop and a garage, the sign reads "Crenshaw

Boulevard."

He turns north and continues, walking block after block in the stark sunlight. No foliage, no shadows. Making only minuscule progress toward Gray through the sprawling city. Wayob again regrets that he must kill Gray in order to ensure his freedom, for Gray is likely as innocent as Wayob once was. But death is nothing compared to what Wayob faces. He would die a thousand times before spending eternity isolated in the darkness of the Encanto. A life is the blink of an eye. Wayob must harden himself; if he could tear out his own heart, it would be easier. Easier not to care.

Although... Wayob could just destroy the Encanto, if he can find it again. Then he would be guaranteed the remaining life in Sammy's body. Sammy makes a fine vessel and is fairly young, it seems. Would it suffice? How long before someone like Parker pursues Wayob with the mistaken notion that he should answer for the death of Sammy's mate? Wayob could hide. Could cross the southern border of this country. Return to his homeland, now known as Guatemala.

But why run? If he merely ends the life of Gray, he will be free from the wicked hold of the Encanto. Then, once he finds it again, he can use it for himself. But last time it did not work for him. Was it because the snake of black glass was no longer attached, or because the old man snatched it away too soon?

Once Wayob holds the Encanto and comes to truly possess it, Wayob will find a new vessel. A clean vessel without the shadow of crime hanging over him. After all he has endured, Wayob deserves this. He deserves this and more. He will have a much better life here in Los Angeles, better than his wildest dreams from his early days in the miserable jungle. With so many people to use as vessels, he can avoid disgusting rituals like eating and shitting, all the needless touching.

He stops and wipes his sweating brow. He finds a place to sit on the dirty sidewalk beside a laundromat where a sad cluster of stores bakes in the sun. He crosses his legs and closes his eyes and tries to ignore the passing cars.

He finds the sound of Gray's mind. Faint. Further away. Still north, but he has moved east. Too far away, almost, for Wayob to hear his mind. But Wayob does hear it. He listens. And from the tenor of the sound, he comes to know that Gray is, once again, in the body of Ashley.

If Wayob kills himself, and if he concentrates as he dies, he will awaken in a vessel near Gray. Like he should have this morning. Why had he not? The Encanto—something is wrong with it. It is broken. The snake, which the old man swiped last night, is the key to operating the Encanto. What if Wayob endures the agony of dying only to awaken in a vessel even further away? Or trapped back inside the wretched device?

No. One way or another, he must appropriate a vehicle.

Crash

Wayob enters an establishment called Smith's Army Surplus and strides past the odd assortment of caps, backpacks, pouches, portable stoves and military memorabilia. At the back of the store, a young man with a thin scraggly beard sits behind a counter, entranced by his phone. Behind him, a television blares through an open door.

As Wayob approaches, the young man glances up and stiffens. "We don't sell guns."

"That is fine," Wayob says. "All I need is a vehicle."

The man sets his phone on the counter and motions toward the dusty shelves in the store. "What does this look like to you?"

"A museum?"

"Fuck you."

Wayob restrains an impulse to strike this belligerent fool. He is smarter than that. He ratchets up his smile. "I did not mean to offend you, sir."

The young man laughs but his eyes remain cold. "Nah. I get it. This crap has been here since I was a kid. No one ever buys anything, and Pop won't get rid of it."

The volume of the television decreases, and an older man with stooped shoulders appears in the doorway. "Want to see the merch?" He motions Wayob around the counter toward the back room.

"I've got this, Pop. Go back to your show."

"He's not here for a gun?"

"No pop. We don't sell guns, remember?"

"The hell we don't." The old man glowers at the young man, and the young man stares back.

"I do not need to procure a weapon," Wayob says. "What I need is a ride."

The old man scowls. "A ride?"

Wayob clenches his fist but remains calm. He shrugs and smiles. "Or a vehicle would suffice."

The old man throws up his hands. "Buddy, you're in the wrong place."

"That's what I told him, Pop."

"So stop wasting time."

His pop retreats into the back room, leaving the door partially open, and the young man's face reddens behind his scraggly beard. The volume of the television ramps up.

"Time to go, buddy."

Wayob leans closer, but not too close (Wayob can only tolerate so much). "I can see you are much smarter than your pop. Let me hire you to give me a ride."

The young man snorts. "I'm not driving you anywhere, man. But for fifty bucks I'll tell you how to find a ride."

Wayob extracts three twenties from Sammy's wallet and slaps them down on the counter.

The young man snatches the bills. "Take an Uber."

"What is Uber?"

"You're kidding right?"

"I do not kid," Wayob says. Does this young fool need a demonstration of just how serious Wayob is?

The fool rolls his eyes. "It's like a cab. Hand me your phone and I'll show you."

Is he trying to trick Wayob? Not that it matters. Wayob pulls the phone from his pocket. It wants a passcode. He sighs. But then the device recognizes his face and the screen unlocks.

The fool reaches across to take the phone, and the stench of his body odor assaults Wayob. It is all Wayob can do to stand there and not retch.

The fool motions him closer. "You want to see this or not?"

Wayob swallows back the revulsion welling up in his throat and reminds himself that he must find Gray. He leans across the counter and tries not to inhale.

"The app is already on here," the young man says, showing him the screen. "Guess your wife set it up for you?"

Wayob stares at him, realizing that of course he means Sammy's wife and not Wayob's bride. The fool has no idea, and he also has no idea that Wayob can now see into the open drawer behind the counter. It contains a pistol. Does this fool intend to draw it on Wayob?

The fool stares back from beneath his droopy lids. "What's the address?"

"I do not recall the address. I need to go north and east from here."

The fool sighs. "You need an exact address for Uber, but a cab'll drive you around, so long as you're paying."

Wayob has a brilliant idea: since Gray is the body of Ashley York, Wayob knows almost certainly where to find him. "I am going to the palace of Ashley York. Please find for me her address."

"You're shitting me. Come on, buddy. Ashley York, really?"

Wayob stares at him. This fool is wasting time. Perhaps Wayob is being too gentle, too congenial. Perhaps it is time to impress upon this fool that Wayob's very freedom is at stake.

"Fine," the fool says and does something else on the device. "But Ashley's near downtown right now. It's blowing up on Twitter."

A picture of Ashley York appears on the screen, scantily clad in a white undergarments, lounging near a pool. The fool draws the phone closer to his face. "Holy shit. You have her number? Is this for real?"

Wayob snatches the phone and studies the screen. Indeed, he does have her phone number and also her address. "The Encanto still works!" *There is sense in the madness after all!* And to think he had wasted all morning wandering around when this vessel knows everything he needs. Wayob looks up at the ceiling and laughs.

"Whoa, buddy," the fool says. "Glad you got it all figured out."

"I am called Wayob. Not Buddy."

"Well, nice doing business with you, Wayob."

"Our business has not concluded."

"That's what you think."

"You do not want more money?"

"I'm not going to step in your shit. You're stalking her, aren't you? I should call the police."

Wayob smiles and shakes his head. "That would be unwise. I know her, and I am desperate to reach her. Seems like a smart guy, like you, would take advantage of the situation. So, what is the problem?"

"The problem is I want you out of my store." The fool glances down at the drawer. Whether he intends to grab the weapon or not, it hardly matters, because Wayob has endured all he can take. Words are getting him nowhere. He has already wasted too much time.

He springs over the counter and throws his body down on the fool, who somehow manages to grab the weapon as he falls.

Wayob lands on top of him and lunges for the gun, but the fool is quick, and the gun barrel is already swinging toward Wayob.

"Zack!" a voice yells from behind them.

It distracts Wayob for only a split second before the gun fires.

A ringing sound assaults his ears. Am I shot? Did the fool actually manage to shoot me?

Above the ringing, Wayob hears the fool yell, "Pop!"

He turns to see the old man clutch his hand against his chest, blood already soaking his gray flannel. His other hand grapples for support on the door frame as he slides to the floor.

"Pop!" The fool crawls over and presses his hands on top of the wound. "Call an ambulance," he shouts toward Wayob.

Wayob leaps to his feet and grabs the pistol from where the fool dropped it on the floor. While the fool keeps one hand pressed to his pop's chest, he pulls out his phone with the other.

Wayob levels the gun. "Drop the phone."

"Pop needs an ambulance!"

"Drop the phone or I shall kill him now."

The fool drops the phone.

Wayob breathes in. *At last.* "I merely want a ride. You may call help once we are away from here in your vehicle."

The old man grabs his son by the collar. "Don't worry about me, Zack," he whispers hoarsely. "Understand?" His hand falls to the floor and strains to reach his leg.

"We go *now*, Zack," Wayob says.

The fool ignores him and leans over his pop, as if to hug him, but instead he reaches down and slides up the cuff of the old man's pants, as if Wayob cannot see the weapon strapped to the old man's ankle.

It leaves Wayob no choice. A gun seems so much easier than using his hands to inflict death. Not that he takes it lightly. He never does. Ending the life of another is a terrible thing to have to do, but no one will blame Wayob for defending himself.

He steps forward and pulls the trigger. The gun cracks. It kicks back so hard that it nearly sprains Wayob's wrist. But it has the intended effect. The old man's head practically explodes. Blood sprays everywhere and probably on Wayob, but he cannot worry about that now, because Zack seems undeterred by Wayob's demonstration.

His scream roars above the ringing in Wayob's ears. As he rips the tiny gun from his pop's leg, Wayob steps forward and shoves the barrel of the pistol into Zack's skull.

Zack freezes with the gun in his hand still pointed toward the floor.

"I do not wish to kill you," Wayob says, "but no one will blame me if I must."

Zack turns his head slightly and looks up at Wayob from the corner of his eye. "Fuck you, you motherfucking piece of shit."

Wayob pokes the barrel harder into his skull.

Finally, Zack drops his little gun and raises his hands.

"His death is on your hands," Wayob says calmly. The whole situation is so sad, so unnecessary. "I ended his suffering. Wayob did for you a favor—for both of you. He would have died soon. I know; you must believe me. I gave him mercy. Now you shall focus."

Wayob gestures with the gun, and Zack stands up slowly, keeping his hands in the air.

"Lead me to your vehicle."

Zack complies. After unlocking the car, Zack sinks into the driver's seat and reluctantly gives Wayob the keys. Wayob hurries around to the passenger side, gets in, leans across and shoves the key in the ignition.

"Okay, start driving."

"To where?"

"Ashley York's, of course."

Zack just sits there. "I forgot my phone."

"You have no need for the device."

Zack stares down at the blood splattered on his shirt. "I need directions."

Wayob unlocks Sammy's phone, hands it to Zack and trains the gun on him. "If you go the wrong way, I will know."

Zack looks at the phone a moment. "I have to install Waze."

"What is Waze?"

"It's just an app. It'll take a few minutes, unless you want me to get my phone?"

"No." Wayob plants the gun on the armrest, eight inches from Zack's side. "Do what must be done to find Ashley York." *But can he trust Zack's directions? No, he cannot.* But he can verify the general direction, by meditating, which requires surrendering control—a daunting predicament—but Zack does not need to know.

Wayob leans his head back on the seat. "I will close my eyes for a moment." He tightens his finger on the trigger. "Then you begin driving."

The sound of Gray's mind is faint, and before Wayob can home in on its direction, a buzzing sound interrupts him. He flicks his eyes open and glowers at the fool, who is still toying with the phone.

"Sorry," Zack says. "I'll set it to silent."

Wayob closes his eyes and starts all over again, and again he finds the sound of Gray's mind. This time he manages to zero in on the direction they must travel: northeast.

He opens his eyes. "Give me the phone," he says to Zack. "And start driving."

"I need to see the map while I'm driving." Zack snaps the phone into a clamp on the dash and shows Wayob the route to Ashley's supposed location. *We shall see...*

They drive in silence. As they merge from one freeway to the next, they rise to a sweeping view of mountains and the city, and to miles of roadway jammed with cars.

Wayob scowls. "Is there no other way?"

"No," the fool says. "We have to wait it out." He swats away some text that appears on the phone's screen and returns to the map.

As they exit the highway north of downtown, Wayob meditates again on the sound of Gray's mind... it is nowhere nearby. Wayob's anger boils, and he nearly pulls the trigger, nearly ends the life of Zack —damn the consequences if the car crashes—but no... No. Wayob calms himself. As he opens the eyes, Zack passes a familiar-looking street made of brick, turns into a parking lot, and hands some bills out the window to the attendant. Gray may have been in the area, before. If only they had arrived sooner.

"She is not here," Wayob says. "We must go east."

"I just paid for parking," the fool says as he turns into a space between two other cars.

Wayob levels the gun to his skull. "East."

The fool glances all around before slowly backing out. Wayob lowers the gun as they pass the parking attendant.

"Which way do I go?" Zack asks.

"East." Wayob props the gun on the armrest. "Take the highway."

The first turn Zack makes is in the wrong direction, but Wayob remains patient. He knows how some roads serpent around. But when Zack turns west, Wayob jams the gun in his ribs, and then all of a sudden Zack manages to find the eastbound highway.

Once they are moving at a reasonable speed, Wayob pulls the gun back to the armrest. "Find for me the new location of Ashley York."

"I thought you knew where she was," Zack says.

"Not the address."

"Well, I have no idea how to find her."

"Before you found her on this device." Wayob points at the phone. Its screen has turned black. He wakes it up and unlocks it. "So do so again now."

Zack taps an icon which brings up a bunch of text and photos of Ashley York. He scrolls to the one at the bottom in which she—though it is probably Gray Wilson in her body—is fleeing a bunch of men with cameras and a woman with a microphone. They're on a brick street. And Wayob has been there before.

"That's where we parked," Zack says, "but you didn't even want to get out of the car."

"She left that place. So where is she now?"

"Hold on. I have to keep my eyes on the road." Zack removes the phone from the dash and holds it against the steering wheel. He performs some fast motions on the screen while driving. He shakes his head. "No one has tweeted anything about where she went next. It's not like she makes a PSA every time she goes somewhere."

Wayob tells himself to calm down as he stares out at all the concrete baking in the afternoon sun. *This shall be a challenge.*

"So do you want me to exit somewhere," Zack asks, "or just keep driving until we run out of gas?"

"Keep driving and be quiet. I require silence." As they approach at such speed, Wayob must concentrate, must meditate constantly, on the sound of the mind of the one who has the Encanto, Gray Wilson. Yet Wayob must also direct Zack as they draw near. What if the streets tangle like vines? What if Wayob cannot find his way to Gray without a proper address on a map?

And Zack. Should Zack grow so bold as to take the gun, Wayob can do little, so deep in trance, to stop him.

But Wayob has resources. This vessel, Sammy, knows Ashley York. Wayob should not have doubted the power of the Encanto when he awakened in this body, for Gray is in Ashley's body, and she and Sammy seem to have some kind of relationship. Wayob's lip curls at the thought. But wearing Sammy like a suit of skin and bone is the perfect disguise for Wayob.

Wayob decides to peruse Sammy's mind after all. No one would blame Wayob for learning what he can, what may help ensure his freedom. If, as Wayob sifts through Sammy's memories, Sammy chooses to look into Wayob's mind and learn of the Encanto, then it will be Sammy's own choice to die. Who would blame Wayob for ending the life of someone who wishes him to suffer an eternity of darkness? And what life could Sammy hope to live with his mate dead, and now the murder of Zack's father and soon Ashley York on his hands? If Parker refused to believe that Saroyan was innocent, the same will go for Sammy. Plus, he deserves to die; he cheated on his mate.

Sammy's core memories are layered all over each other like moving tapestries of light. Wayob doesn't have to venture far to see how much time he spends at the palace of Ashley York, almost all of it out in the little hut at her gate, wearing his uniform. He is her security lackey, or one of them, but he wants to be more. So much more. Too bad for Sammy.

Wayob opens his eyes. Zack has moved into the right lane and slowed. Other travelers zip past them. Fine. Wayob decides to allow the fool to distract himself with his little game to slow their progress. It will accomplish nothing. They are close now, oh so close. Wayob snatches the phone from the dash.

Zack asks what Wayob is doing. He ignores the question and finds the contact for Ashley York just as simple as he had seen it in Sammy's memory.

A female voice answers, and Wayob smiles at the undisguised tension and the fear.

"Sammy, what's going on?" It's Gray, pretending to be Ashley. *He has no idea.*

"Where are you?" Wayob asks.

"Driving," Gray says. "Listen, were you talking about Wayob?"

"Wayob?" The question surprises Wayob. Gray may know about Wayob, fine, but he has no idea Wayob is inside Sammy, in full control. *Careful. Careful.*

"The psycho you warned me about," Gray says in Ashley's voice. "How did you know?"

Psycho? The fucking priest who made Wayob suffer like this, he was a psycho. What is this warning?

Wayob turns to Zack, asking the fool and Gray at the same time. "I warned you?"

Zack's jaw clenches. He accelerates. So much for his plan to slow things down. Wayob wants to laugh. He would laugh, if he was not so furious. Whatever the fool has done, this warning, it makes no difference.

"Where is he?" Gray asks.

"No, don't worry," Wayob says. "Nothing to worry about. Just some harmless fan of yours who found my number. I overreacted."

The car careens up a hill. The land slopes away as the highway rises above drab rooftops that sprawl in all directions. Zack has betrayed Wayob. Betrayed Wayob without considering his predicament. Without even caring to ask. If Wayob ends the fool's life now, no one will blame him.

Gray is still quiet. "Are you still with me? This psycho is probably nothing, but … I would feel better by your side, just in case."

A wall, suddenly coming straight at Wayob. Without warning, Zack has swerved into the concrete wall beside the highway. It crunches the car like a bug. All over in an instant. No time to scream.

Such a fool, Zack.

—

Darkness.

How long has Wayob been here?

Trapped again inside the Encanto?

Panic overcomes him. Then pain. Physical pain.

Pain he shall endure—not only endure but be grateful for, because pain does not exist inside the Encanto. He is still free. Still in the vessel of Sammy. Before opening his eyes, Wayob listens in the darkness of his semiconscious state. Searching for the off-key whine of Gray's mind.

It is no easy feat with so much pain throbbing through him. It almost drowns out the sound of Gray's mind. But then he realizes that the dim sound of Gray's mind is caused by distance. Gray is far away now and moving further, and for this Zack will pay.

Wayob considers his mission. Must stay calm. Time for a new vessel…

He listens. Hears no one. No one sleeping within range. Of course not. Without dying, his range for finding a new vessel is hardly more than a few paces. Why did the repugnant priest and his rotting teeth curse Wayob so?

Wayob opens his eyes and swats away the white bag that inflated from the dash and slammed his chest, though it did protect him in the crash. Beside Wayob, Zack has slumped into his own bag of air. He lies still with no sign of breathing.

Wayob shakes Zack. His head lolls to the side. Blood stains Zack's shirt and pools in the seat beside his jeans.

It appears Wayob shot him. Wayob vaguely recalls squeezing the weapon in his hand, and now remembers the sound of the shot almost smothered by the crunching metal and shattering glass.

Sirens wail in the distance. Best be gone before they arrive.

The door resists opening. He jams his shoulder into it. Falls out onto the highway, landing near the wheels of a truck that has stopped nearby, mere inches from his arm. Zack's car now faces the wrong way.

Someone shouts. Demands to know if Wayob is *alright*. Of course he is not *alright*, but he does not care to explain that this is one more thing on the long list of grievances Wayob must endure thanks to the odious, fucking priest.

Wayob struggles to his feet. Looks down at his body.

Legs fine. He gingerly touches his chest. Sore, but fine. All fine. He is just disoriented. That is all.

A man with a phone pressed to his ear hops down from the truck and moves toward Wayob. "You shouldn't be moving around. Wait for the ambulance."

Wayob finds the gun in his pocket and clutches it as he makes his way around the car to the side of the highway. He feels trapped on this walled platform of pavement. Cars slow as they pass him. People gawk out their windows at him with stupefied eyes, their jaws hanging open. He breaks into a run.

After some distance, he looks back. The shrill wail of the sirens grows slowly closer, but the emergency vehicles are probably impeded by all the other vehicles slowing to stare at the crash. Below the wall of the freeway, dull, windowless warehouses reflect heat from the sun. Wayob has seen these structures before. The faded lettering on the sides… he has been there, on the street below the freeway, once before.

It was before Abuela gave the Encanto to Gray. It was nighttime then, and Wayob was in the vessel of Victor Aleman. He had walked that stretch of street beside the broken curb, hunting Abuela. So, Gray has gone to Abuela's.

Of course. Where else?

Wayob should have guessed. He forces his legs to move, faster and faster. Wayob recalls her address from Parker's memory. Smart of Wayob to peek into Parker's mind after forcing his body to smother Saroyan. Parker had met her in Apartment 2B on Loma Avenue, the same place where Wayob suffered through untold years in the Encanto with Abuela refusing to free him.

All the energy he'd wasted whispering to Abuela in her sleep. Yet still—*still*—she refused to use the Encanto, or even to destroy it when Wayob whispered, as if perhaps it was her own suggestion that destroying the Encanto would end Wayob's life.

If Wayob kills her now, no one will blame him. Not after all the time he suffered, imprisoned, disembodied in the dark nothingness of the Encanto.

Wayob laughs as he runs. How ironic that it was Abuela's own son, living under the same shabby roof, who finally freed Wayob.

Wayob Takes Rosa

After her father helped her pack up the small apartment where they had lived with Abuela, she told him to go on without her because she needed one last look at the place, alone, and he reluctantly complied. She wanted the black-and-white photo he'd slipped into the pile of trash they'd left stacked in the apartment when he thought she wasn't looking, the photo of the abuelo she'd never met. Abuela would have wanted her to keep it. Whenever she spoke of him, her whole face shone, but she only ever spoke of their courtship and the early days of their marriage, never the circumstances surrounding his death, as if silence could erase them. He had died in Guatemala, Rosa knew that much, but who killed him and why? These questions had always seemed to baffle Abuela into losing her train of thought. And Rosa's father preferred to pretend that his own father had never existed. The first thing he'd done after Abuela died was throw out the one photo they had.

Someday, Rosa hoped, he would come to terms with whatever emotions caused him to shut down at the sight of his own father. Maybe he'd even thank her for preserving this small piece of their history.

Without Abuela, the apartment was just three rooms, three small, empty rooms, not a place where she had lived.

She began sifting through the pile of discarded bills and Braille books that they'd left in the corner. They hadn't bothered carrying the trash down to the dumpster because the landlord would charge a cleaning fee, regardless. And she didn't care about the money; she just wanted to move on.

It was eerily quiet. Usually by this time in the afternoon, she could hear the neighbors stomping around, slamming doors, arguing through the thin walls. The only sound was someone whistling outside. What was that tune?

Mission Impossible.

Rosa felt terrible about Ashley York—and about Gray too, but Ashley had looked so distraught in Gray's body when they came here desperate for answers. And what had Rosa told them? Nothing useful. She didn't know anything useful about the Encanto or Wayob. She had told them what little she had learned from Abuela.

But…

Ashley had the right to know what had happened to her father, Evan York. Rosa should not have been intimidated into silence by the presence of her own father eavesdropping from the back room.

He meant well, of course—and she'd always love him, no matter what—but he should have known better. He had come unmoored after losing Abuela.

In the trash pile, beneath a tax return, she found the photo of her abuelo that had been on the wall since she was a little girl. He stood proud in his uniform. Same dimple in his chin as her father's. Same nose. They had looked so much alike.

She opened the door and took one last look over her shoulder before stepping out of the apartment that had been her home for so many years. She crashed into someone standing right outside.

"Stay back."

She screamed. Then saw it was startled a security guard and closed the door before he could get a good look at all the abandoned junk inside. "Excuse me. I live here. I'm just leaving."

He smirked. "Where is Ashley York?"

Rosa's heart pounded in her throat. The guard's half-tucked shirt clung like a second skin over his bulging muscles. His nose was swollen and running, and she feared the condition of whoever had dared to hit him.

And he did not belong here. This was not the sort of high-end apartment that sprang for private security.

She squinted at the man, who stood like a shadow in full sunlight, except for the whites of his eyes—they almost glowed—and then she knew. This was him, the one who Abuela had lived in fear of for most of her life.

Wayob.

No way she could slide past to the stairs. She backed up slowly and opened the door. "Wait here."

She stepped inside, but when she tried to shut the door, his arm stuck into it like a log. He shoved the door into her.

She staggered backward and dropped the photo. It hit the floor. The glass shattered as she caught her balance, turned and sprinted.

"Where is Gray Wilson?" he shouted from the doorway as she ran to Abuela's room. "Tell me, and you may go free."

She slammed the door, the only one in the apartment with a working lock, and hit the button in the knob. He could probably punch right through the door, but maybe it would slow him down.

She dumped her purse, snatched up her phone, and texted her father a warning.

The door burst open. One kick was all it took, and then Wayob stood there. He had a gun. He aimed it at her.

"Drop the phone."

Rosa dropped it and balled her hands into fists. "It's too late. I told them how to stop you."

Wayob stepped into the room. Dim light spilled through the bars on the window. "Where are they?"

"Long gone."

"What did Abuela tell you?"

"Enough."

"Did she even mention how long I suffered inside the Encanto?" Wayob sounded miserable. And sincere.

But it was hard to imagine Wayob as a victim after what Abuela had told her. Rosa looked at the double bed where Abuela had died and tried to imagine her sleeping there peacefully instead of having Wayob in the room, trapping her in this nightmare.

"She's the one who suffered."

"Is that what she told you?"

"She didn't have to tell me." If Abuela had caused Wayob to suffer, then he deserved every second.

It suddenly dawned on her what Abuela had tried to tell her before she died. "You killed my grandfather."

Wayob's lip twitched. "Abuela's mate? He was killed by the army."

"Then you caused his death."

"I just wanted to be free. They had me killed. You don't understand. *They* were the greedy ones. They were using the Encanto for gain."

"And how many lives does your freedom cost?"

"Just one. Maybe two. You would do the same if you were forced to live for centuries in total darkness."

He glanced down at the contents she had dumped from her purse while looking for her phone, kicked aside her tampons, wallet and brush, and kicked her keys toward her.

"Pick them up."

She felt like refusing. Let him shoot her and see how much cooperation he got from her dead body. But little good that would do. There were four keys on her chain and only three cars in the lot.

Staring into his pin-sized pupils, trying to look like she wasn't afraid, she knelt and picked up the keys.

He snatched them away from her and marched her out the door, his gun in the small of her back. As they passed by the kitchen, she glanced at the knives by the sink, hopelessly out of reach.

She stepped around the broken photo of the abuelo she never knew. Behind her, Wayob's boot crunched the shattered glass, grinding it into the photo.

Rosa should have smashed the Encanto when she had had the chance, but at the time she had no idea about Wayob. She recalled Gray's naked fear, and how childlike and innocent the emotion had looked on Ashley's face. Did Abuela really think he would destroy the Encanto when she could not? Rosa would have destroyed it. She had no interest in becoming someone else, not even for a green card... And if she'd known that anyone's life was in danger, she'd never have let Gray walk away with it. She understood that Abuela had only meant to protect her—and Rosa loved her for this—but if Abuela had just included her, had given her the Encanto instead, then maybe now Rosa wouldn't be marching down the stairs with Wayob's gun at her back.

"Look, I do not want to harm you," Wayob said as they reached the lot. "Anyone else would hold you accountable for the years your abuela tortured me, but your father released me from the Encanto, and I feel bad about ending his life. However, I had no choice. You have to know this."

Rosa took a step back, wondering how much he really knew.

"You look just like her, you know? When she was young." He threw the keys at her. They bounced off her chest and landed on the cracked asphalt.

"Get in the trunk. Or I will shoot you. Your choice. I shall count to ten, and if you are still standing here like an imbecile then it will be you killing yourself. Not me."

Rosa picked up the keys and unlocked the trunk. She unpacked the trunk at gunpoint, as slowly as she could get away with, in order to give Gray and Ashley more of a head start. She had to abandon the suitcase with all of her clothes, the photos of her father and Abuela and all the happier times they had together, and Abuela's blanket. She resisted the urge to cloak it around her, as if it could somehow protect her from Wayob.

Once there was barely enough room for Rosa to curl into the trunk, Wayob told her to stop. "Cause me no problems and I will release you soon."

But why would he lock her up just to let her go? She clenched her fists and stood her ground.

He leveled the gun, the barrel aimed right between her eyes. "Do not be a fool."

She closed her eyes. She thought of Abuela, her father, and the path to her degree now paved with Evan York's money and the guilt of how her father came to have it. She didn't need things done for her.

He coiled his big arms around her, lifted her off the ground as though she were insubstantial. He made a guttural-choking sound as if he had tasted spoiled milk. "This is worse for me than for you."

"Okay," she said. "I'll get in."

He instantly released her, and she fell to the ground, hitting her head on the bumper. Her vision swam. She forced herself up and climbed into the trunk. The last thing she saw was Wayob's dark grimace silhouetted against a stark blue sky. The trunk lid slammed her down into darkness.

Stars swam through the darkness. A knot swelled on the back of her head.

As the engine started and the car reversed, she felt around her surroundings. A box barricaded her from the pass-through to the backseat.

By folding her knees against her chest, she was able to roll onto her back, and that was it. Her old Honda lacked a lever to open the trunk from the inside. She should have accepted the Tesla from her father instead of worrying about showing up at her new place looking like some fresa.

The car swerved. She slid against the box and the insulated walls of her coffin. With her dying breath, Abuela had begged Rosa to forgive her father for using the Encanto—a wrong thing he did for the right reasons—and to forgive his spirit for surviving in Evan York, after Wayob had killed his body.

After Abuela's funeral, when he told Rosa that she was all he cared about now, that she was his whole world, she had repaid the sentiment by pulling away when he tried to hug her. And now she regretted it.

Because he was her whole world too, and she might never have another chance to say so. She regretted all the time she had wasted resenting his choices when she'd have done the same herself, if she had known Abuela was dying. Rosa had made choices too: she had let Gray take the wicked stone. She had known there was something wrong with it that Abuela wasn't telling her at the time, or him. He believed it was nothing, and she had watched him carry it off into the night. Her only thought at the time was that she and Abuela would be better off.

Wayob Takes August

The brakes squeal as Wayob plows across the double yellow lines on Mulholland. Such a ridiculous rule. Surely people do not follow these lines. Wayob does not have time to slow down for curves; he must find Gray Wilson. From the general direction of the sound of his mind, Wayob assumes he is hiding out at Ashley's palace. That's where Wayob found him yesterday.

Security might be a problem. Wayob is smart enough to know that Rosa's rusty car would raise suspicion at Ashley's palace. *Where is Sammy Johnson's car?* they will ask. And if Rosa screams from the trunk, will they hear her?

So, Wayob pulls off the road and parks at a dirt turnout that overlooks the valley to the north, where a vast grid of lights wink on in the twilight. Millions of people in their cars and their houses, unaware. So many vessels at Wayob's disposal. So easy to disappear.

He knocks on the trunk. "Back soon."

Hearing no response, he half-considers opening it. Is she sleeping? She's lucky to have that option. In the Encanto, Wayob had to endure endless centuries without sleep. So, he cannot feel bad for Rosa. If she suffers inside the trunk, it is for Abuela's sins. She gave the Encanto to Gray Wilson. If she had just left Wayob alone and free, he would never have come to this immense city. It was Abuela who brought him here and kept him trapped in the Encanto for decade after decade. So it was Abuela who locked Rosa in the trunk of her car, leaving her here by the side of the road. Wayob has no choice.

As he strides along Mulholland Drive, the gun in his pocket slams his leg with every step. After all the centuries Wayob endured trapped in darkness, surely Rosa can endure a mere few hours. She should thank Wayob. He spared her life. Unlike Sammy's mate, she kept her distance, respectful. Still, he cannot trust Rosa's silence. Sammy makes too good a vessel to risk having his disguise ruined. His access to Ashley York's palace is even better with Sammy than it was with August Grant. Wayob will walk right in. It shall be no problem to end the life of Gray Wilson.

Lights spiral the trees surrounding the entrance pavilion to Beverly Park. It looks like a festival, except no people are outside. As Wayob walks into the light, the twilight seems to recede into the surrounding darkness.

He strolls up to the little stone house with the sole purpose of restricting access to the neighborhood containing Ashley's palace. "Good evening, Edwardo."

The pudgy guard stares blankly out at Wayob. His eyes flick to the road, as if hoping Wayob might disappear back the way he came.

But no. Wayob stands, waits. He smiles when Edwardo finally gets up and slides the glass door a fraction wider than his oblong head. He leans out and looks all around.

"My car has ceased to function," Wayob says.

"You call a truck?"

"I need to get to Ashley's. Late for work."

"Where's your keycard?"

"Left it in the car." This was true. The gate card of Sammy's was in Sammy's car. In Inglewood. To think how much time Wayob wasted by not looking in Sammy's mind from the start. Wayob tenses his hand around the gun in his pocket.

"You got a ride back up? I can't let a truck through."

"This shall not be a problem for me."

Edwardo shrugs, closes the door and returns to his seat.

Wayob strolls past the entrance pavilion and through the big iron gate, which Edwardo has so graciously opened.

Wayob rubs his arms and shivers. It seems colder now in the darkness. Inside the Encanto, there is no cold or hot. There is nothing. Is misery worse than nothing? For now, he shall endure the cold and this wind, just as he endured the isolation of the Encanto; it cannot last as long.

The road curves. Clouds sweep up the mountain from the south, stretching out like a vast cold sea in the moonlight, spotted with warm orange blotches from the city below the mist.

As he nears the private gate to Ashley's palace, Wayob descends into the fog. Headlights coming up the hill sweep over him. His thin, useless shirt reflects like a beacon. He should remove it and let his dark skin blend into the night, except the shirt serves his disguise. Gray, in Ashley's body, will expect normal old Sammy to have his standard white security shirt.

Wayob stands like a stone as the large, black vehicle turns into Ashley's personal road, apparently not noticing Wayob. When people expect darkness, it is darkness they see.

Something seems familiar about the vehicle as it stops at her gate and the rear window comes down. Wayob ducks low and approaches from behind.

By the time Wayob can hear them talking, the gate opens. Enough delays. Wayob hurries but does not quite run. Do not look suspicious.

The car drives through. In the small structure, in a flickering blue light, sits pudgy Franco. Is Sammy the only guard who does not gorge himself? Franco, so consumed by his television, does not see Wayob.

Not until a miserable dog begins barking in the house halfway down the road to Ashley's palace. Wayob considers bolting; he could make it through the gate. Except, Franco might warn Gray. Wayob cannot allow this.

"Sammy, what the hell?"

"My car has ceased working," Wayob says.

"Well, I already got your shift. Sorry, man. And you need get that dog out of the guest house before Ashley finds it."

"I shall do so." Wayob takes a step toward the gate.

"Just don't interrupt Ashley. She's otherwise engaged at the moment."

"What do you mean by this?" Stay calm. Raise your brows with concern.

"August Grant's here. Said he had a *surprise* for her."

But Wayob knows that after last's night's fiasco in the cellar, Gray wants nothing to do with August. So, it must be as Wayob feared. August came here for one reason, one thing only: the Encanto.

Standing just outside the window, Wayob speaks very softly. "I need to ask you something."

"I can't give you a ride, man." Franco's eyes remain on the TV. "I've got to stay on the booth."

Wayob notices the panic button on the little desk, easily within

Franco's reach. He does not wish to harm Franco, but what else can he do? Time is of the essence. He grips the gun by his side.

"Something else," he whispers.

"What?" Franco turns toward Wayob.

Wayob feels himself smiling, not because of what he must do, of course, but because sometimes it is just too easy. He raises the gun. Jams it into Franco's cheek. Pulls the trigger.

The recoil flings his arm back so hard he drops the gun. His hand hurts, and again the ringing assaults his ears, this time almost to the point of bleeding.

But, at least the gun did its job. Franco slumps against the window frame, blood draining from a fractured hole below his dull, lifeless eye.

Wayob reaches into the window and slaps the button, which opens the arched gate of twisted black metal. He retrieves the weapon from the ground and walks through the gate and down Ashley's drive.

The fog thickens, obscuring Ashley's palace, as if trying to prevent his progress. As if Wayob needs another obstacle after Franco, who he had no choice but to kill but, with no way to restrain him, he had to prevent him from warning Gray. And with August here—for the Encanto, Wayob just knows it—he must hurry. Probing August's mind last night in the cellar might now cost Wayob his freedom. Such a waste. He runs.

Wayob hears growling. As he slows, it erupts into a barking. Wayob stifles the urge to bark back. The animal should respect him. He can just discern the outline of the small house beside Ashley's roadway where the miserable animal must be trapped. It cannot harm Wayob. Still, he should silence the beast for alerting others to his presence. He would, if not for the recoil and the noise it would cause. The ringing in his ears has only now started to subside.

After some distance, the lights of Ashley's palace pierce the fog. *Gray Wilson, let us do this thing which must be done.*

A click.

Wayob stops. Was it two clicks or one? How near? Someone trying to be quiet.

He steps off the drive and crouches, trying to blend into the mist and shadows cast from the palace of Ashley York.

And just in time, too. The dark form of a man stalks past, going up the drive toward Franco's corpse. If he sees it, he will surely sound the alarm.

Wayob raises the gun. He follows the man, trying to walk softly, but the wet grass swishes under foot. He steps onto the driveway, and Sammy's bulky boot scuffs against the pavement.

The man, only a short distance ahead, reels to a stop. In the dim, filtered light, Wayob can barely discern that this man is not August Grant. His skin is a deep brown, the color Wayob's was before the fucking priest forced Wayob from the body of his birth. And this man has a gun of his own. Wayob must shoot this man; he cannot afford the delay of dying and making his way back here all over again in whatever new vessel he happens to awaken. If Gray gives the Encanto to August, or returns to his own body, Wayob will be trapped inside it again. He could be trapped forever this time, in darkness and isolation.

Wayob feels sorry for this man for whom dying is real. The stench of his fear ruins the night air as he turns, raising his gun to *kill*.

Wayob pulls the trigger. This time not dropping the gun when it kicks his arm back.

But he misses. Ten feet away, the man seems unaffected, his gun still rising toward Wayob, his body lowering to a crouch.

Wayob fires three more times, hitting the man's chest at least once. The man clutches his heart as he falls. Wayob wants to scream above the ringing in his ears—at this man he had to shoot in *self-defense*.

Wayob runs the rest of the way to Ashley's palace, where he uses Sammy's key and the alarm code he found in Sammy's mind. Inside the front door, light fills the space.

No one in sight.

He moves slowly through the parlor and living room, then climbs the stairs. He is unsure of the upper floor for which Sammy has no memory, though there are many memories gazing up at the stairs toward it, probably pathetically yearning for Ashley to invite him up.

In the giant bathing room, Wayob stands before the mirror. His nose, which has been hurting since the airbag slammed into it, is quite swollen. He touches it gingerly. Nothing he can do now. He wipes his oily head on a clean, white towel, smooths his shirt, and tucks it into his pants just like Sammy would. Sammy does not carry a gun, but Wayob can say it is to protect Ashley from August Grant. Gray will appreciate that.

Ashley's immense white bedroom is empty, boring. Wayob sneaks to a half-open door, only to find a room full of clothes.

He creeps back down the stairs. Voices emanate from somewhere in the kitchen. Wayob tries to blend into the meager shadows as he moves through the living room, stepping carefully to keep silent his heavy black boots.

But all Wayob's effort is ruined by August plodding across the room. He has a gun of his own, and Wayob has nowhere to hide—so he pretends to be Sammy.

———

Once they are all together in the kitchen, and Ashley and Gray have emerged from the cellar in each other's bodies, Wayob must restrain his laughter. He must not reveal himself to Ashley and Gray, who remain unaware of him standing here in the shadows. *This is too good.* They do not have a gun, but August does. *Now just shoot Gray and be done.*

But no, August ruins everything. "Look, I don't want to hurt anyone," he says. "Give me the Encanto and I'll be out of here."

Wayob's pulse races. "No!" If they hand the Encanto to August, Wayob could be plunged back into utter darkness. He starts around the cellar.

Ashley, in Gray's body, lunges toward him, her arms out for an embrace—she, of course, thinks he is Sammy, her hero. Wayob thwarts her vile need for physical contact by pushing her back with his free hand. As she stumbles back, her mouth comes open, a look of shock on her face. Sammy would have behaved differently—but too bad. Even Wayob has his limits.

She falls into the cellar hole but catches herself on the side, and Gray moves to help her up. Wayob kneels beside them as if he might help too but does not. Will they still believe he is Sammy?

"Sorry, *he* came at me," Wayob says. "I saw the knife, and…"

As Ashley climbs out of the cellar, Gray seems to freeze. He follows Gray's gaze to August, who has his gun aimed at Gray.

August's hand trembles. His eyes bulge with fear.

Wayob must restrain his smile. *Go ahead and shoot, little man.* If he would just shoot Gray, then Wayob can kill August in turn, and then he will be Sammy the hero in Ashley's eyes.

"Drop your gun," August says. "Or I'll shoot her."

Surely Ashley knows where the Encanto is. He wonders if they switched into each other's bodies before or after Wayob battled the old man. Once she tells Wayob where to find it, she too must die, for he now realizes that Ashley will never be satisfied to live out her remaining years in Gray's life.

All of a sudden, August swings his gun toward Wayob. How? How does he know? Wayob must grit his teeth and pull Ashley-in-Gray's-body close, using her as a shield.

"August," Ashley says. "Drop the gun."

Does she no longer believe August is Wayob?

Wayob cannot focus with her against his body. It makes his skin crawl. He loosens his grip, steps back slightly. Wayob reaches his arm out over Ashley's shoulder, aiming the gun at August's head.

"I do not want to hurt you, little man," Wayob says truthfully. Merely hurting August will not suffice. "But I will."

August pulls the trigger. Wayob jerks to the side—but the gun is silent.

What happened? Even Wayob has learned to check the safety and the load of the weapon. He has two bullets left in this gun, one each for Gray and Ashley, but now he must waste one. He re-aims and braces against the recoil.

It is August's own fault that the bullet rips through his neck. He drops, slumping against the kitchen island, clutching his throat with both hands. Blood pulses through his fingers. He chokes, trying to speak, a jumble of wet raspy syllables.

"He was going to shoot you, Ashley," Wayob says. He wishes there was some other way, but that's just how it is. Except, wait, did he just say Ashley?

Gray-in-Ashley's-body looks to the real Ashley. Did he catch Wayob's mistake? Is he suspicious?

"We need to call an ambulance," Gray says, and Wayob hopes he is too distracted by August bleeding out on the floor to have noticed Wayob's little slip of the tongue.

"My phone broke," Ashley-in-Gray's-body says. "Sammy?"

Sammy. Wayob wants to clap at his own performance. Hopefully he can keep them both believing that Sammy is here to save the day. Maybe they will even hand over the Encanto to Sammy the hero.

Wayob uses the wall phone to call 911. He knows the drill. It reminds him of the anonymous call he made yesterday, reporting Saul Parker for murdering the whore. Wayob cannot wait to find out if Parker has been arrested. Not that Parker could have stopped him today. Wayob is on a roll.

"911. What's the address of your emergency?"

He recites Ashley's address, which he'd found in Sammy's memories. "There has been a shooting at Ashley York's palace," he says. "I saved her life."

"Okay, stay on the line with me. I'm getting help sent to you. What's your name?"

"My name is Sammy. Sammy Johnson." They are sending 'help'? Help will surely get in Wayob's way. Besides, this ruse is taking too much time.

"Are you or anyone else in danger?"

"Not anymore. I shot the little man who was going to kill us."

"Is he dead?"

"He is bleeding badly."

"Okay, we do have help on the way. Are you—"

Wayob ends the call and repeats to Ashley and Gray. "They are sending help."

Ashley tilts her head, as if trying to decide something. She still holds the knife. "Where were you today?"

Hunting Gray Wilson. But if they want him to believe that she is really Gray, then she should not be the one asking the question. "Why do you care?"

"We couldn't get in touch with you," she says, as though unconcerned with maintaining the pretense.

But it could play to Wayob's advantage if they think he is unaware, and the beautiful thing is that he can answer her honestly, because the phone of Sammy Johnson was lost when Zack crashed the car. "I dropped my phone." Wayob turns his head toward Gray-in-Ashley's body, as though he believes it really is her. "Plus, I was tired, you know? After all that digging last night."

Gray glances at Ashley, who now has nothing to say. So Wayob fills the silence with the one and only question that matters. "Where is the Encanto?"

Her eyes widen. "How do you know about the Encanto?"

Of course, there could be an answer—Sammy could have learned of it, somehow—but the fact that she is asking suggests she lacks an understanding of its power. Wayob shakes the gun at August. "Death only slows Wayob down. He will find another vessel. Give me the Encanto, and I shall stop him. Hurry!"

"Sammy… how do you know?"

A Light in the Fog

Gray can tell from the edge in Ashley's voice that she didn't reveal anything about the Encanto to Sammy.

Sammy hesitates before answering. "Franco. Franco told me, before he died."

"He's dead?" Gray glances at Ashley.

Her eyes go wide, and the knife comes up slow and steady.

"Wayob shot him," Sammy says. "I saw the whole thing."

"You mean August?" Ashley asks.

"Yes." Sammy looks down. "August is Wayob, but not for much longer. When he dies, Wayob will take a new vessel."

August coughs and gasps. His eyes dart around, as if unable to grasp onto anything. He tries to shove his slumped body upright against the island, but his hand falls away from the wound. He coughs again, and blood drains from the corners of his mouth. His head lolls, his face white.

"We have to apply pressure," Gray says, and starts toward August. It's clearly too late for him, but Gray wants his gun.

Sammy practically leaps in front him. "Stay back!" The gun is held tense by his side. "It is not safe to go near Wayob."

Gray stares at him, at the anger on his face, the trembling corners of his mouth curling into a Grinch-like grin, as obvious as Mindy's face when she lies. Gray sees now that this is Wayob: his grin is not even in the ballpark of Sammy's smile.

Ashley grabs Gray's hand. "We'll go get the Encanto," she says to Wayob. "You stay here with August."

"No." Wayob points the gun at her. "We all go."

Gray steps between her and the gun. *"Run."* To Wayob, he says, "You'll never find the Encanto."

"Then you are useless."

Gray thinks of Mindy in her pink pajamas. At least he'll die knowing his family is safe. Wayob pulls the trigger, and he braces for the pain. Feels his body jerk backward. The gun cracks.

He falls to the floor.

But the only pain is in his tailbone from the impact on the tile. Ashley had pulled him down before Wayob fired.

"Come on." She pulls at his elbow.

Too late, he thinks. Now Wayob will shoot them both.

But instead, Wayob snarls, showing all his teeth, and hurls the gun at Gray. It slams into his chest like a rock. Gray falls back, astonished, as it clatters on the tile beside him. *Empty?* Wayob lunges for August's gun as Gray and Ashley scramble for the side door, fog pressing against its window like a solid white wall.

"Stop!" Wayob shouts. "You need not both die."

Ashley throws open the door and fog pours into the house as the gunshot sounds. Shards of wood from the doorframe pelt Gray's face. They flee out into the fog and Ashley disappears ahead of him in the gloom.

As he jogs after her, everything blurs into a gray-white stew.

Somewhere nearby, she shrieks.

Gray stops. "Ashley?" He listens. Hears nothing. Moisture swirls in the floodlights. He's afraid to look back toward the house where Wayob is. Afraid to speak, afraid to venture further into the roiling cloud.

"Ashley?" he whispers.

A hand reaches out of the gloom below and grabs his leg. He nearly falls, nearly screams, but he knows that hand: it's his own. He kneels and finds Ashley sitting against a hedge, legs stretched out before her.

"I think I twisted my ankle," she whispers.

"Can you walk?"

"Maybe. Not well."

An eerie whistle materializes near the house and drifts closer... The theme song to *Mission Impossible*. The tempo slows.

Gray ducks down between Ashley and a bush, clutching its scabby trunk.

She cups a hand to his ear to whisper, "After he passes, we sneak back to the garage."

The wet grass soaks through the knees of his jeans. Despite the fog, Gray feels exposed.

Dark shadows sweep through the mist. Wayob's legs, close enough to touch. "I know you're there," he says. "Let's be reasonable about this. Ashley, surely you must be furious with Gray, for this is all his fault. Think about it. Gray took your body, put you in danger. Help me end his life, and I shall leave you in peace."

Down the hill, a dim light appears in the fog. It approaches.

"Good," Wayob says. "Come to me."

Gray wants to call out to whoever is out there, to warn them away, but Wayob is just a few feet away. He looks toward Ashley. Another security guy?

As the light grows closer, maybe twenty feet from the end of Wayob's shadow projected by the floodlights through the fog, a voice calls out hesitantly, "Gray?"

It's Claire.

What the hell is she doing here on Ashley's lawn?

"Claire." Gray stands. "Claire, he's got a gun!"

Claire just stands there, her phone lit up like a target, as the muzzle flashes.

Claire's Turn

Wednesday Afternoon
Hernandez leans forward in the wooden armchair that Claire hates because of its uncomfortable back. "You entered Mr. Streeter's house through the front door, correct?"

Claire slouches down on the couch. "I knocked first." They'd been over this three times, already, and she needs to find Gray. She's got her own questions that need answering. She promises herself that as soon as Belinda shows up to watch Mindy and Tyler, she's out of here.

"What prompted your visit?" Hernandez asks again.

At the time, the photos of Ashley and Gray dining in some Mexican dive had just hit Instagram. It seemed ridiculous that they were having an affair but there was sure as hell something going on, and she did not want her children to witness their mother punch that skinny blonde bitch in her perfect nose and then beat their father to a pulp.

So Claire had the brilliant idea to take Charlie up on his many offers to babysit. She had thought he was weird, yes, but harmless. But now that she has learned about the pills and whatever caused him and the cop to suffocate in his garage, she knows it would have been irresponsible to let him watch her children. She's embarrassed and a little alarmed by her lapse in judgment. If she weren't so sleep deprived, she would have known better.

"I was just stopping by," Claire says, yet again. "Like I said."

Hernandez scribbles in her notebook, writing much more than what Claire had said, especially since she'd just repeated the same lie. Hadn't she?

"When was the last time you saw him alive?"

God, how is she supposed to remember that? She's so tired she can hardly remember this morning. "The day before Halloween, I think."

"That would be... Thursday?"

"I think so. He was decorating his front yard. I'm sorry, I just— I don't sleep well."

"Sorry to hear that. How come?"

Claire points at the baby monitor on the side table. But Tyler isn't the problem. He sleeps through the night, most nights, now.

"How old?"

"Ten months. It's not just Tyler. It's..." How can she explain? How could anyone understand what it's like to lie in bed with a tornado of thoughts swirling through your head, trying to figure out if you had even slept at all in the last few hours, hoping that you will sleep if you can chant the Kirtan Kriya enough times in your mind. How did they even get on this subject? "It's just... insomnia," she says, as if insomnia isn't the worst thing in the world. And then, to make matters worse, she had basically ordered Gray out of the house.

"He say anything strange or unusual?" Hernandez asks.

"Who?" Gray said a lot of strange, unusual things—like about switching bodies. What the heck was up with that? But Claire isn't going there with Hernandez.

"Streeter, when you saw him on Thursday?"

"He warned me about the crazies. But he thought everyone was crazy, everyone but him at least. Probably thought I was too. Guess the crazies finally got him, huh?" Claire has a sinking feeling that whatever happened in Charlie's garage has something to do with Gray, and possibly Ashley too. He is in trouble. Serious trouble.

A coo erupts from the monitor. Claire snatches it and twists the volume down before Tyler's own amplified voice wakes him up. On the screen, he shifts in the crib, but his eyes remained closed. She shoves herself up from the couch. "He's waking up, so if you'll excuse me..."

Hernandez claws back the gray clump of bangs from her forehead and stands, practically blocking Claire's path to the hallway. "I don't mind talking while you change him or whatever."

"Have any experience with children? I've actually got to go out. Maybe you can cover until my sitter gets here?"

Hernandez presses her lips and shakes her head. "Just a couple more questions."

Claire pretends to stare at the monitor. "Looks like he's going back to sleep," she says, as if he wasn't sleeping the whole time. She plops back on the couch. *Where the heck is Belinda?* The instant she gets here, Claire will hit the road, regardless of Hernandez's "couple more questions."

"Where is your husband?" Hernandez asks without looking up from her notebook. Could she really be the one person in the world who hasn't seen the photos of Gray with Ashley York?

"Should be at work."

Hernandez clicks her tongue as she jots this down. "What's his number?"

"His phone is broken." At least that's what Claire convinced herself this morning after her call went straight to voicemail. If he dropped his iPhone again it might explain the burner he had last night.

She shouldn't have hung up when he called just because she heard Ashley in the background. If he'd just come back. Underneath her exhaustion, she still loves him, still feels it, despite all the talk of ending their marriage.

That's all it was. Talk. If she had stayed on the line, he could have explained. *Switching bodies?* She should have at least heard him out. Judging from the look on his face when he and Ashley fled Olvera, this clearly isn't an affair. It's something else entirely. When he ran out of the house in his underwear, she should have realized that something was terribly wrong. She would have, if she hadn't been too tired to think.

He'd been acting weird ever since Halloween. He said it was about his job, and maybe that's a part of it, but not all. If anything, it's just the tip of the iceberg. This is more than some sort of early midlife crisis, more than some cheap affair. Gray needs her help.

Hernandez clears her throat. "He doesn't have a phone at his desk?"

It takes Claire a moment to process the question. She looks up Gray's work number and gives it to Hernandez. He'll probably never even check the message.

"Do you know when he last saw Mr. Streeter?"

"Halloween." Claire scratches behind her ear. "When he took our daughter trick-or-treating." But he must have seen Charlie more recently. He'd started a painting of Charlie.

And the stone thingy that he got at the Day of the Dead—what did he call it? The Encanto? She had found the stone in Charlie's lap, and in his palm was the black snake. How did Charlie come to have it?

Ashley said they had thrown it away, but then she also said she was Gray, so it would be easy just to ignore everything she said if not for the Elmo's receipt from the terrible Halloween-night dinner. It had been stuck to the pants cuff of the other dead guy, who Hernandez said was a cop. So he, and maybe Charlie too, had been in their trash... Maybe Gray did throw the Encanto away and not his wedding ring after all. She recalled how he'd freaked out when she broke it. What if whatever the hell is going on is her fault?

Hernandez asks again if Charlie's door was unlocked.

"I told you," Claire says. "It wasn't even all the way closed."

"I appreciate your indulgence. People sometimes remember things differently the second time through. Any extra details you can recall could be helpful."

Claire sighs. She can't be sure what she said before, thanks to this damn insomnia fogging her mind. What if Hernandez thinks she's lying? What if she becomes a suspect?

Stick to the truth, she thinks. *It's not a lie if I don't say it.*

"I knocked," she says. "But I was worried, so when no one answered, I went in."

"Understandable," Hernandez says. "So you entered the house with your two children?"

"I had no idea anything was wrong at the time."

"Of course not." Hernandez again scribbles in her notebook. "Just trying to get the facts straight. So, you entered the house with Tyler and your four-year-old—"

"Mindy's five."

"Right, five. After you entered the house, where did you go?"

"I followed the tracks to the garage. There was blood. I thought he might be hurt or something."

"Did you enter the garage?"

Claire recalls the burst of flies when she opened the door. When Mindy lies she always fidgets with her clothing, so Claire sits very still, stares Hernandez straight in the eye and says, "No, I couldn't let Mindy see the dead guys. I shut the door and herded her back out the front. Then I called you, or your partner anyway."

Hernandez pauses with her pen on her notebook and stares at Claire, her eyes dark and unblinking.

But Claire's statement is basically true. She just skipped over the part where she left Mindy on the front steps holding Tyler—Mindy is very good at holding Tyler—and took twenty seconds to jog back to the garage and retrieve the stone from Charlie's lap and the snake from his hand, which was outstretched, as if his last dying wish was for her to have it.

And she isn't the only one holding back. When she called Detective Parker, it was Hernandez who answered, who said that he was "no longer available," and that she was taking over his cases.

"What did you say happened to Parker?"

"We'll get to that," Hernandez says. "Did he say why he came here?"

"You don't know? I thought you were partners."

Hernandez reaches up to claw her bangs again, but they're still combed back in her hair. "We were... I thought." She inhales. "I'd like to hear it from you."

Parker's questions about Gray acting strange make a lot more sense now than they did last night. "He said someone was following my husband."

Hernandez slides to the edge of her chair. "Who?"

"The guy who shot Bob Jaggar, but he's dead now, right?"

"Right." Hernandez exhales. "I don't think you need to worry. So, did you open the door from the kitchen to the garage?"

"Huh? Detective Parker was on the back deck." Hadn't she said that?

"At Streeter's." Hernandez glances at her notebook. "You followed the tracks to the garage..."

"Oh." Claire closes her eyes and tries to reorient to the sudden change of subject. "Right. It was open."

"What about the outside garage door?"

"Closed."

"How would you describe the scene?"

"Two dead guys," she says. "I turned around as soon as I saw. The engine was still running, and I was concerned about the exhaust and my children." And now she is even more concerned about Gray. He's in trouble. She has to do something. She glances at her phone. What's taking Belinda so long? And how long can these questions go on?

"Mind elaborating?" Hernandez seems to have all day. "How were their bodies positioned?"

Claire takes a deep breath. She explains how the bald guy, the cop, was lying practically right in Charlie's lap, exactly how they must have been when Hernandez arrived. But Hernandez writes it all down in her little notebook anyway.

"Did you go anywhere else in the house?"

"Hell no."

Hernandez's phone buzzes on her belt clip and, as she glances down to see who is calling, she looks puzzled. "Excuse me." She answers the call on her way out the front door, speaking angrily. "You're wasting your time calling me."

Claire sits forward on the couch and texts Belinda.

Claire:

Where are you?

Belinda:

Almost there. Ten min.

She searches for Ashley York's address, but of course it's not readily available. Then she finds an article on the real estate holding company created by Ashley's accountants to purchase a property in Beverly Park. It lists the address.

Claire is looking up the directions when Hernandez returns, her dark complexion turning deep burgundy. She's smiling slightly with a far-off look in her eyes. As she approaches, her brows twist. "I... have to go," she says. "Here's my card. We're not done."

Claire stuffs the card in the pocket of her sweatpants. She can throw it away later.

"One last question," Hernandez says. "If you didn't enter the garage, how did you know Streeter and Arcos were dead?"

"The flies." Claire grimaces at the memory, the drone of a thousand flies buzzing all around her in the hot, stale air. But even the stench wasn't enough to stop her from going in, from prying the black snake from Charlie's stiff hand.

—

Claire swings open the front door. In the fading light, Belinda's squat figure stands below her on the front step, with a bothered expression on her pink, slabby face. "This is the fastest I could get here on such short notice, and then I couldn't find anywhere to park on your street."

Claire motions her inside. "We could have switched cars. I'm leaving."

Belinda rushes into the living room, looking around wildly as if expecting to find Ashley York standing there.

"Guess you saw Instagram."

"And Facebook and Twitter." Her small eyes widen to their full extent. "So, what's going on? Where's Gray? Is he really— Is she really?"

"No. It's just gossip. There's nothing going on."

"I mean, I know you two have problems, but I never would have guessed..."

Problems? Where did she get that? Certainly, Claire had never said anything, and it was hard to imagine Gray saying anything more than the absolute minimum.

"Well, what is going on?" Belinda asks again.

Good question. Claire wishes she knew. "That's between me and him. I have to get ready." She hands the baby monitor to Belinda.

"Where are you going?"

"You're just a big ball of questions, aren't you?" Claire says more harshly than she intended. The clog of exhaustion left in her mind by the insomnia almost causes her to try the truth, to pour her heart out in spite of how she feels about Belinda. But the words catch in her throat, and she needs to get moving.

Belinda cowers back a step. "Sorry. I just..." She straightens. "My *boyfriend's* coming over to my place later." Belinda emphasizes *boyfriend* so strongly that it's obviously a lie or at best a Tinder hookup. "I just need to know what time you'll be back."

"Nine," Claire says. Four hours should be enough time to get to Ashley's and... do what? "Ten at the latest."

"Okay, but I've got a hard out at ten."

Claire shuts herself in the bedroom. The faded T-shirt and the sweatpants she's been wearing all week won't cut it. She jerks on a pair of stiff jeans and throws off the T-shirt. Ordinarily, she sort of likes her sagging mommy breasts, but the thought of Ashley's perky little tanned tits sparks her to grab a bra from the floor and pull it on.

From the back of the closet, she digs out the purse containing the pistol that Gray doesn't know about. Her father gave it to her when she was living alone. She digs through a pile of clothes to find a never-yet-worn shirtdress that matches the purse.

On her way to the nursery, she rakes her tangled hair back into a ponytail. Tyler is on his back in the crib, his eyes shut tight. He breathes heavy. She wants to kiss his chubby little cheeks, but it's better not to wake him.

In Mindy's room, Belinda is sitting on the floor surrounded by drawings as Mindy digs more out from the chest at the foot of her bed.

"That's how you get on her good side," Claire says.

Belinda smiles. "It's a privilege to see all these. Mindy's got talent."

When Claire tries to hug Mindy, she struggles free. "I'm trying to do something, Mom."

"I can see that." Claire kisses her on the head. "I'm counting on you to go to bed when Belinda says. It will be late when we come home."

We, Claire thinks. *Get real.* What if Gray refuses to come back with her?

Outside, it's dark except for the dim echo of sunlight held in the thin layer of fog sliding over the neighborhood. She clicks "unlock" on her keychain, and the minivan's lights wink on. She climbs in. Pops up the directions on her phone, clicks it into the mount, and starts driving.

The only night she can remember sleeping in the past weeks, maybe months, was Sunday, after she and Gray had sex. The intensity had been like making love to a stranger, and it left her wanting more the next day, but he'd acted as if nothing happened. She had wanted to get closer to him, at least until he ruined it by talking. That's how it had been for their whole marriage: him wanting to talk. To understand her. To needle his way in, when there was nothing to know. Someday, he'd realize she has nothing inside but blood and guts and bone. So why hide herself? He would either love her or he wouldn't.

All her withdrawing had only stretched out the inevitable. And what if her reluctance to engage exacerbated her own insomnia? How can she expect to receive love when she can't give it?

Gray's vivid inner life, the way he's always imagining what he's going to paint when she can only get through the day, intimidates her. If she tried to paint, it would come out drab. He makes ordinary things so colorful. *But I shouldn't compare myself to him.* She should be curious. All the things she could have asked him about but didn't. What does he think about politics or art, or her? Is his dissatisfaction only with his job? The answer to this question scares her. She's seen that look on his face, and she would love to know what it feels like. When she was working, she felt a sense of accomplishment but was never able to get into a flow like Gray seems able to.

Maybe he would have finished a painting if she could have just told him how beautiful they were. And why couldn't she? Why did she have to sneak into the garage while he was sleeping to look at his paintings? Because she really couldn't handle his questions? Was it really so hard just to say what it meant to her? It shouldn't be. But she's just so exhausted all the time. No wonder Gray has lost all respect for her. She's hardly functional, wearing the same sweatpants day after day, barely a mother and not much of a wife at all, when she wants to be so much more.

She can't blame Gray for not telling her about his crazy idea to open a bar because he had tried to tell her, hadn't he? And what had she said? She had acted just like her mother, who could never be bothered when she was watching her show. Her *show*. The marathon of soap operas her mother watched when Claire was a kid might as well have all been the same show. It wasn't just TV, either; her mother always seemed too busy, regardless of whether she was cleaning or eating or just sitting there. "I'm thinking," she'd say.

Despite drowning in this fog of insomnia, despite how hard it is to think, much less form her thoughts into words, it's no excuse. She needs to tell Gray that he should just forget about the bar and focus on painting. That's his true passion. What is the bar? A distraction. Another headache they don't need.

She feels bad about giving him a hard time for not finishing a painting. When had he ever had more than an hour here or there? That's not enough time to focus, to concentrate. To really master something takes ten thousand hours, they say. It took more than that for her to become an engineer, and now she can give Gray a chance.

Though it was irresponsible of him to just quit his job without even telling her—he can be such an idiot sometimes—the truth is, what she should have told him instead going off the deep end was that she felt thrilled. This is her chance. She can go back to work. She can finally get out of the house. She could be the breadwinner for a change. So, why not tell him the truth? Because she's afraid?

Thanks to Gray's strange request about the transfer station, she had called her old boss, Kwesi. She knew he couldn't grant her access but she asked anyway as an excuse to get in touch, and good thing she did. In the years since she'd left, the turnover rate had gone from bad to worse. Kwesi had been covering three positions because he can't find qualified candidates. He not only begged her to come back but promised a promotion to senior wastewater collection manager.

She accelerates up the 101 on-ramp. She can't wait to tell Gray her solution to their problem. The lights on the freeway are blurred by her insomnia. She blinks and squints them into focus. Traffic is crawling. She slams the brakes just short of ramming a car stopped ahead of her in the merge lane.

It was sheer luck that Claire ended up at Public Works after college, because if anyone else had offered her a job at the time, she would have taken it instead. All the newbies were assigned to Wastewater, which her coworkers saw as a steppingstone to somewhere better. But Claire discovered she liked working among the pipes, the pumps, and sediment pools. No one bothered her there because of the stink, which she could only smell for the first few minutes and then it was gone. During the green energy boom, when her coworkers flocked to the private sector, one after the other, Claire never even bothered to update her résumé.

Why had she let Gray convince her to stay home with Mindy? Because she wasn't sleeping well, even back then, and she had this naive hope that without the get-up-and-go and the commute, maybe she could get some rest. But of course, there was no sleeping with a newborn. Even after Mindy had started sleeping through the night, Claire still couldn't.

The second time she got pregnant, Claire meant to tell Gray she was going back to work, regardless of whether daycare cost more than her paycheck. But having won the argument over the worst job, she just couldn't capitulate to Gray. She loves her children, she does, but she's overwhelmed by their constant need for attention. She misses the water, the effluent and the biosolids, the peacefulness and the structure.

She exits onto Sunset and waits at the light. Her biggest regret is that she let her own bitterness, and the insomnia, blind her from considering what *Gray* might be going through. He was disappointed, clearly, possibly depressed, and she had let it come between them. Why? He is such a beautiful man who cares about them so much... she feels selfish for just now realizing his level of despair.

Traffic crawls along Sunset, as if no one can drive at a normal speed just because of some fog. By the time she finally reaches Beverly Hills, she is ready to scream.

The road into Beverly Park is blocked by a gate and guarded by a security station built like a little house. She steels herself to sound like she belongs here, but what can she say? *I'm married to Ashley's latest fling?* No. Ashley's cousin? Will the guard know that Ashley doesn't have a cousin?

Claire slows to the gate and tries to look relaxed, like she belongs here. A guard in the security station waves her through without even bothering to open his window.

Weird, she thinks as she waves thanks but the guard has already looked away. She's not complaining but it seems like they'd be a little more thorough in a gated community with high-profile celebrities. She drives through the gate and up into the hills, where the estates are set back from the road. They're a class or two, or more like three classes, above the mansions she drove through to get here.

She rounds a curve, and her high beams catch on Gray's eight-year-old Camry parked beside a hedge. On the other side is Ashley's house, according to the icon on Claire's phone. Something sinks in her chest. A part of her—deep down—was hoping she wouldn't find him here, even though she knew she would.

Is it too late, now? Too late to know him, to love him, to really love him?

Can't be.

She kills the headlights. The street plunges into darkness. She marches along the road to the driveway. The light from a little booth glows through the fog like gauze: another gate with a guard. Claire throws back her shoulders. She's Ashley's cousin. Maybe a second cousin. Her car broke down and she took a Lyft. Ashley's guard can't know Ashley's whole extended family, can he?

As Claire approaches, the figure in the booth remains static, a silhouette slumped against the glass. Asleep on the job? The gate is wide open.

When she reaches the booth, her breath catches in her chest. The guard's cheek is punctured. Fissured skin, rust-red, surrounds the hole. He's dead.

Her pulse races. The world suddenly seems more tangible, more real. It's like she's finally coming back into herself, back from the insomnia, which had made her life like an out-of-body experience.

Her pulse feels like ice in her veins. Who shot this guy? And why? And what if he has killed Gray? Maybe she can still help. Maybe there's time.

She draws the gun from her purse and jogs through the gate and into the fog. She follows the driveway down toward an array of floodlights, which carve the mist around what must be Ashley's house.

She passes a smaller, plantation-style house that's still bigger than her and Gray's Craftsman. Its windows are all dark, but inside, a dog barks. Claire's adrenaline surges. She sprints toward Ashley's mansion. When a darkened SUV looms out of the fog, she slows. The driver's door hangs open. No one inside.

A gunshot rings out.

She falls to a crouch and strains to discern the source of the sound. Behind the mansion?

Through the stillness, a scream echoes, high and shrill—that's Gray, definitely, and it definitely came from behind the mansion, behind the wall of darkness and fog.

Claire hurries toward the scream. Gray could be hurt. Shot. She strains to listen but only hears the sound of her boots on the driveway. She reaches a fence and pauses, afraid to call out to her husband.

The darkness seems to have swallowed him.

Using the flashlight on her phone, she edges around the fence and into a garden which leads to a pool, still as glass and glowing blue from eerie lights below the surface. Steam rises into the fog. A deck surrounding the pool juts from the hillside. Claire skirts back around the fence, around the pool, and down the hill below it. Her boots swish through wet grass.

After rounding the pool, she doubles back up the hill through the fog toward the blurred lights of Ashley's mansion. Gray must be nearby.

A voice bellows out of the mist, "Come to me."

Claire lowers the phone. "Gray?"

But she knows it's not him even before she sees the silhouette of a hulking dark man emerge from the fog, wearing a white shirt and an almost luminescent grin.

"Claire," Ashley shouts. "Claire, he's got a gun!"

The muzzle flashes. Claire dives to the ground. A swoosh of air tickles her ear as the gunshot claps out in the night.

Not wanting to be a target, she tosses her glowing phone.

"Get up." The man speaks with a singsong cadence. "I do not wish to hurt anyone… else, but I shall if you make me. Come out, come out, come out."

Tightening her purse over her shoulder, she crab-crawls toward the shooter, wishing she had some sort of gun training other than Xbox and cop shows. She finds the safety and flicks it off.

From somewhere behind the man, Ashley asks, "What are you doing here?"

Claire knows she should stay silent, but already she feels delirium clouding into the great rush of clarity from the adrenaline. She didn't come here to hide.

She cups her mouth and shouts to the side. "I'm helping you, you selfish assholes!"

The gun rings out again, but this time she is well hidden in her dark clothing and the fog.

"Missed me, hot shot." She rolls in the opposite direction from which she spoke, crawls a little way, and then marches up behind the muscular man. He turns as she approaches. Too late. She shoves the barrel to his head. "Drop it or you're dead."

He snarls, his teeth practically phosphorescent in the filtered light from the floodlights.

"No!" Ashley leaps from the shadows. Behind her, Gray tries to hold her back. Why the hell isn't Gray the one leaping toward her? But Claire has to stay focused on this guy; he's not dropping the gun.

"Claire!" Ashley shouts.

Sweet that Ashley cares so much, but she should have stayed hidden.

The guy actually grins at Ashley, like he doesn't even care about the gun shoved to his temple.

"I said drop it, asshole." Claire has to do something.

She has to shoot him.

His gun fires—she hadn't seen him raise the muzzle—and heat rips through her insides. She tries to pull the trigger on her own gun, but her hands refuse to obey. The gun falls, and she clutches at the blaze in her stomach. She's falling into darkness...

For a moment, she yearns for the relief of unconsciousness.

But, of course, she can't sleep.

The singsong voice of the man who shot her reaches down from somewhere far above. "She gave me no choice."

Someone screams—either Ashley or Gray. Claire can't be sure anymore.

A shot booms, and then all that remains is a high-pitched ringing in her head.

If Claire was shot again, she can't feel it. She can't feel anything.

As the ringing subsides, a sound like a sack of meat smacks the ground beside her.

Gray! Claire forces her eyes open and finds the man has fallen and Gray is on his chest pinning him down.

Someone takes Claire's hand—it's Ashley, leaning over her.

Claire shivers. *So cold.* She tries to say something, but her words come out garbled, as though her mouth is full of gauze.

"Shhh," Ashley whispers.

Claire's eyes close. A moment later, she feels Gray there too, his fingers caressing her cheek in the gentle way he always does. His fingers touch so lightly they almost tickle. She has to tell him, has to show him the stone and the broken-off black snake are in her purse. And— Wait... wasn't it ... Ashley leaning over her?

She wrenches her eyes open.

It's still Ashley leaning over her.

"Claire? You have to stay awake." She emphasizes "*aire*," just like the way Gray says her name. And she's holding her hand like they're old friends even though they only met last night.

"It's in my purse," she manages to croak. "Tell Gray."

Ashley stares at her blankly. "What?"

Claire tries to answer.

The gun fires again. The two men are struggling on the ground beside them. Ashley reaches an arm out, as if to shield Claire from any more bullets.

Her ears ringing, Claire slides her hands weakly through the grass, trying to find her gun.

It's not there.

She tries to push herself up... cannot. Her eyes crash shut again, and this time they refuse to open.

It would be a relief—like the spark of freedom when she threw her phone away, watching it sail off in an arc of light—to let go, to drift down into the blackness... sleep.

But everything unfinished claws at her mind. Gray and Mindy and Tyler.

Am I dying? Am I fucking dying? She can't die. She did not come all the way here to fucking die! Not when she needs to tell Gray how grateful she is that he stuck by her, that she knows how hard it must be to live with her insomnia—maybe almost as hard for him as for her, and how from now on she's going to live in the here and now. She needs to tell him that she loves him. They have to stay together.

He moans, long and sad and far, far away. It sounds as though he's underwater. Maybe they both are... drowning. Drowning together.

Kill or Die

Ashley screams as she charges through the fog toward Wayob in Sammy's body. She shoves the blade between his ribs.

Wayob turns toward her. She twists the knife.

He coughs and smiles, his teeth slicked with blood, and raises the gun.

She ducks, throws her weight against his chest as she reaches down, grabs his leg behind the knee and lifts just as he fires, sending the shot wide. He topples backward, and Ashley falls on top of him.

She lunges for his gun, but Wayob snatches it away from her, holding it out of reach. She pins her knees on his chest and turns sideways so she can reach further, but he twists to roll her off. The knife sticking out of his side smashes into the ground. He groans and goes limp.

She rips the gun from his grip. He rocks forward, grabs her head with his other huge hand and shoves it down.

She recalls the smirk when he shot August. This is Wayob, not Sammy. He killed Andrea and left her body discarded like garbage at the bottom of the cellar stairs—and he will kill her too.

He pushes her head into the ground beside him and struggles, lifting his torso despite the knife in his side and her knees planted on his chest. She breathes in. Shoves the gun back between her knees. When the barrel hits his flesh, she pulls the trigger.

Crack! The recoil slams her hand back, and his arm goes limp. It falls off her.

She slides from his chest and turns. The acidic smell of the gunpowder, sort of like spent fireworks, tickles her nose. A dull ringing, from everywhere all at once, fills her ears.

As she kneels over him, Sammy's facial muscles relax. The fear and the anger, and Wayob's sardonic smirk, sink into a sadness that seems to reach so deep perhaps Sammy can feel it too.

She runs her fingers through his coarse hair. His lids flutter, struggling to stay open. "Ashley?"

She tightens her grip on the gun.

He grunts and coughs up blood. "He made me... kill them."

Is this really Sammy now? Had he been in there the whole time? And does he know she just shot him? She drops the gun, lifts his shirt, and presses her hand over the bullet wound, trying to staunch the blood. This can't be happening. The blood gushing between her fingers is like a nightmare. A nightmare of her own doing. Sammy can't die. He just can't.

Sammy reaches out for Gray, in Ashley's body, who is leaning over Claire nearby. He touches his leg, and Gray whirls, nostrils flaring. His eyes dart to the gun.

Ashley snatches up the gun and hurls it away. "He's Sammy now."

Gray stares at her. Says nothing.

"Where's 911?" she says. "Call them again, while I keep pressure on his wound. Tell them to just drive through the yard."

"I don't have a phone, either," Gray says. "And I can't leave her." He turns back to Claire. Her face is placid and grimly pale.

"Ashley," Sammy says.

She looks down at him, and his eyes widen.

"It's you!" he says. "How?"

"Rest," she says. "We're going to get help for you."

"It's too late," he says. "Tell them I didn't do it..." Tears stream down his cheeks. "My wife. It was like, my hands—I didn't have control. I would never hurt her. You know that, right?"

"I know," Ashley sobs. "Sammy, I know." Blood oozes through her fingers.

He groans, reaches out toward her. "Ashley, I'm so sorry."

Sammy coughs and grimaces. "It was the only way." He gazes up, ˹as if not quite seeing Ashley, his eyes intense. His brows crinkle. "I love you, you know that?"

"I know," she sobs. "I know."

"My love will never die." He tries to smile, his lips trembling, straining, smearing blood across his stark-white teeth. His pupils dilate.

Sammy exhales one last rasping breath. The life flows from his face and then it freezes. A mask of fear.

She searches his neck for a pulse, tears falling from her cheek to his, and finds nothing. She moans. She killed Sammy.

When she tries to wipe her tears from his cheek, she accidentally smears blood across his face. She unbuttons his shirt and stretches the collar up to clean the blood. Then she wipes the crimson from her hands on his shirt tail and dries her face.

As she gets to her feet, she recalls Rosa's warning: *Wayob will find you*. She shivers.

Gray has curled himself over Claire's limp body, holding her as if to squeeze her life back in.

Ashley places a hand on his shoulder. "Is she breathing?"

He presses his ear to Claire's mouth, her face placid and grimly pale, then begins pumping her chest with both hands.

Ashley lets him try for a while before pulling him back. "She's gone. We're in danger here. Wayob will find us."

He collapses on the ground beside his wife. He stares up at Ashley, his eyes glistening green. "I can't believe it."

She squats down, takes his hand in hers and looks him square him in the eye. "We have to go."

She attempts to pull him to his feet but he pulls away. He blinks, then snatches up Claire's purse and begins digging through it. He drops it as he stands, holding the round, white stone and the snake they'd thought was lost forever. He presses the snake onto the stone.

"Wow," is all she can say as he reaches for her hand.

Her hope buoys, anticipating the tingly feeling of being transported, of escaping all the death around them if only for a moment, floating weightless, intertwining with Gray's thoughts. The last time they had done this, she'd felt sparks, like a sort of circuit connected between them. Was it a dream that they had floated in some other plane of existence? Something special had happened before they'd landed back in their own bodies. She had felt Gray's consciousness.

But nothing happens. Just his sweaty fingers on her hand, which still have his hairy knuckles. She pulls away. She's still in his body.

And Wayob is coming. *He can be anyone.* By calling 911 he had basically assured himself a whole selection of new people all their way to 'help', and no telling which one he'll become.

"We don't have time to mess around," she says. "We have to get somewhere safe."

She heads for the house, and Gray reluctantly trudges along behind her. He's in shock, she thinks. They both are.

Entering the kitchen, her shock becomes horror at the sight of August's body, still slumped on the floor against the island counter. She looks away from his glazed, lifeless eyes.

"Look out." Gray tries to pull her back, but he's too late.

Without paying attention, she has stepped in a pool of blood on the white tile. She lifts her Doc Marten, peers at the coagulating blood in the treads. She wants to rip the shoe from her foot, to hurl it away—but of course, she has nothing else that will fit Gray's feet.

She steels herself and marches around the body and blood to the garage. She hits the button, and the electric door sparks into action. She slides into the driver's seat of her Mercedes and checks the rearview mirror as Gray plops into the seat beside her. Mist drifts in from outside, and something else…

The pear-shaped man—the one who had appeared in real life last night, just as Gray had painted him—has appeared again from the mist. Parker. He's wearing that same awful, khaki trench coat.

She shouldn't be surprised. At this point, nothing should surprise her. They expected Wayob and now here he is.

"Wayob!" Gray states the obvious. "Go!"

Wayob raises his gun.

Too late, she thinks.

But they can't just give up. Not now, not after Sammy, and Andrea, and even August—who didn't deserve to die. She'll kill Wayob again and again if she has to, until they stop the evil bastard once and for all.

His giant frame, surrounded by fog, looms in the mirror. She slams the shifter into reverse. Over her shoulder, he raises the hand without the gun, palm flattened, and shouts for her to stop.

You wish.

A car can't outrun a bullet but, she hopes, he'll have no time to aim. She grits her teeth and floors the gas.

For Ashley

Last Friday

Evan awakens to find Niles timidly shaking his shoulder. Niles was supposed to wake up Luis, not him.

"What happened?"

"You fell asleep," Niles says in a low voice. "As I'm sure Mr. York explained, the grogginess will fade in a few minutes. Can I get you anything? Water? Coffee?"

"Just a few minutes alone." Evan rubs his eyes.

In the bed beside him, the person sleeping—just as he'd hoped but not dared to believe—is him... his body. Lying there, eyes closed, chest rising and falling.

His pulse races. *Is this a dream?*

He lifts his hands. Brown, leathery, creased—these trembling hands are not his. They are Luis Luna's hands. The Encanto works!

Evan leaps from the bed and looks around. No mirror. He grabs Luis's phone. Holds the blacked screen in front of his face and studies the reflection. Chiseled nose, cleft chin, dark eyes. It's Luis, definitely. Evan feels the face with his hands.

This is happening. He *is* in Luis's body! It feels too real to be a dream, but he pinches himself anyway. The pain feels normal, in the same way that everything looks normal, except for himself.

Presumably, he can return to his proper body by simply turning the snake-dial back on the Encanto, which remains right where he left it, on the bed beside his own sleeping body, which must be Luis now.

But what's the hurry?

He might be the one living human being ever to experience transmigration. He should enjoy the amazing experience, explore a little.

His legs feel strange, perhaps lighter than his own, and more than a little unsteady. He wobbles like a kid fresh off a carnival ride. As he paces the examination room, he discovers that the less he thinks about the mechanics of walking, the smoother the movement. It's as though the Encanto transferred only his conscious mind and connected it, somehow, to Luna's subconscious, automatic ability to walk. Amazing!

He wonders about the other senses, how coffee will taste on Luis's tongue. Now he can finally go to Starbucks—like a normal person.

But what if Luis awakens? If he freaks out, Niles might not take the passphrase so seriously. Best he remains sleeping.

Evan considers using the spray, but applying it to Luis's skin might awaken him, plus it only induces a natural sleep from which it's easy to awaken. Evan did. He needs something stronger, guaranteed.

In the cabinet, he finds a vial of propofol and a box of syringes. He stabs a syringe into the vial and pulls back the plunger. But what's the dosage? He can't ask Amelia. She'll think he's Luis.

He pulls out Luis's phone and thumb-types in the search bar, before being distracted again by the surreal sight of standing outside his own sleeping body.

Luis's eyes flick open.

No time. Evan strides to the bed as Luis looks around wildly, through Evan's own eyes. They land on Evan and widen with recognition.

Evan puts a hand on his shoulder, prepared to hold him down if he has to, if he can, but Luis just stares back. "What the hell?"

"Just a bad dream," Evan says as he jabs the syringe into Luis's arm and shoves in the plunger.

"What the hell!" Luis tries to sit up.

Evan holds him down with both hands. Luis clutches Evan's wrists, tries to pull them away, but already the propofol has weakened his grip. He mutters. His eyes swim around and finally roll back in his head. His lids close. His body goes slack.

Evan waits a beat before removing his hands. He places twinned fingers to the skin below his ear to check his pulse… tapping along just fine.

When he opens the door, a man's hulking back fills the frame. Pressed white shirt, neck bulging against the collar. Dimitri. Dimitri steps aside. Across the hall, Niles rises from a blue lounger that hadn't been there before. No sign of Ernesto, and that's a good thing. Ernesto might speak to Luis in Spanish, which Evan wouldn't understand, and then Niles would realize something is wrong.

"Is Mr. York awake?" Niles asks.

"No." Evan shuts the door before they can peer in. "I think he used too much of that spray. He said not to disturb him until I get back from Starbucks."

Niles groans. "I keep telling him we stock better coffee in the office."

Dimitri snorts. "Put it in a Starbucks cup. He'll never know."

"I bet he will," Evan says.

"Hundred bucks." Dimitri holds out a hand.

Evan shakes it. "Two hundred says he'll know just by smell, but you guys can try later, okay? I'm sticking to the plan. Want anything?"

"I only drink real coffee," Niles says.

"I'll probably take a walk as well," Evan says. "He said he needed a solid hour at least."

"Guess it's catching up with him. Can you believe he only sleeps four hours a night?"

"I get it," Evan says. "Sometimes a day is just not enough."

—

There's a line in Starbucks. Evan hasn't had to wait for anything in decades, and he wouldn't mind waiting now, except that it's torture to stand here and smell the coffee, his mouth watering. The heavyset woman with mousy hair in front of him, after fifteen minutes in line, only now looks at the menu. The barista at the register maintains her smile and adjusts her green apron while she waits. The dozen people waiting behind him somehow manage to distract themselves in their devices.

He wishes he could call Ashley, now… but what would she think if she heard him speaking with Luis Luna's voice? This is far too big of a shock to drop over the phone.

Finally, the woman sets her big blue purse on the counter and orders a tall medium roast. *That's it?*

"Grande macchiato," Evan blurts out.

The barista, at the pre-made tank of medium, still has her back turned.

She hands the heavy woman her coffee and turns to Evan with a smile. "Anything else?"

"Sorry. You know what? Make it a venti. Might as well treat myself."

Luis's wallet contains only twenty-one dollars. *Add it to the tab,* Evan thinks. Now it's six hundred thousand and ten dollars. He drops a five in the tip jar.

"Have an extraordinary day," the barista says.

"I already am."

"Then make it a double."

"Not possible," he says. What could be more incredible than experiencing the world in someone else's body?

While waiting by the pick-up counter, Evan salivates at the sound of the grinder, the slur of the frother, the milk foaming in the stainless-steel pitcher. The espresso seems to smell stronger through Luis's nose. More earthy, less acidic.

"Macchiato, Evan," the barista shouts as though she forgot him. She sets his venti on the counter. He had given his true first name without even thinking. If he'd used his surname too, she would have remembered.

Outside, he sips his venti and strolls along the sidewalk, invigorated. He passes Checks Cashed and a pink van advertising *"Topless Maids $99."* There's extra bounce in his step, a sort of springiness in his ankles, which he's not sure he ever felt in his own body.

Excitement surges up through him. Reverse-engineering the Encanto might not even take all that long. Sometimes all you have to do is show enough smart people a thing is possible, and they will figure out how. How hard can it be?

A human mind is basically just biological circuits and data, massive amounts of data. And data can be transferred. Given how rapidly bandwidth is improving, a thousand percent in the last decade alone, it's no stretch to imagine a technology capable of transferring data between brains. Maybe he can make a backup of his mind just in case something happens. Could the data be partitioned into memories?

Practically lifted off the ground by the possibilities, Evan doesn't notice the man in a wheelchair rolling out of the carwash by Checks Cashed, baseball bat in his lap.

Like always, Evan is thinking ahead. This could be so much more than just a jaunt into someone else's perspective. There's an ethics quagmire that might be tricky to avoid. Wealthy customers will find donors willing to surrender their healthy young bodies, willing to sign any kind of waiver, desperate to trade the long hard years ahead for an abbreviated life on easy street. The backlash from society for allowing people to sell their remaining lives will have to be directed towards the wealthy who buy them, who choose to live lifetime after lifetime, moving like hermit crabs from one body to the next. For InGenetic, avoiding this backlash should just be a matter of marketing. (And a top-tier legal team.)

But in the long run, it's a bad idea to throw your best paying customers under the bus. And it may not have to go there at all. At InGenetic, they can already grow a functioning liver, and they know how to make brain cells from stem cells. How much brain tissue is required to contain a person? What if, from a person's own DNA, they could clone a younger version of their body? People could transmigrate into a younger version of themselves. A return to youth.

To most people it might sound like science fiction, but he *has* the resources. The hard stuff has been developed; it's just a matter of linking it all together.

He *will* change the world.

Behind him, something rattles. A rolling sound. Hard plastic on the gritty pavement. A scuff.

He goes to turn but— Something slams into the small of his back. His teeth crash together, and he falls face-down on the sidewalk. Pulse racing in his head.

His vision dims and tunnels on the sidewalk. His Starbucks cup lies a few feet ahead, the lid partway open. Macchiato oozes out onto the pavement. He reaches for it.

His back throbs as if broken in two. Something heavy shifts on his calves. A man yells.

Evan manages to roll onto his back, despite finding that his legs are trapped under a toppled wheelchair. A man with disheveled hair and sagging jowls uses a baseball bat to lever himself up onto the side of the chair, thin legs dragging limply below his potbelly. He perches above Evan and says, "I'm sorry, I must kill you. You would do the same if you were me." A massive shelf of brow shadows the dark hollows of his eyes.

Evan's throat clots with the metallic taste of adrenaline. He shoves himself back, tries to force his legs out from under the chair. But, too late. This man—is he a man or is he the spirit who killed Luis's father? —swings the bat down, all his weight behind it.

Evan twists to the side and slams his eyes shut. He hears more than feels the solid smack of wood against bone.

When his eyes blink open—sunlight flashes on the cement, cerulean sky above the carwash—his vision blurs.

Everything goes black. He cannot feel his body, Luis's body, or anything… at all.

The bat slams his head into the pavement again, and he thinks of Ashley. She will inherit countless companies and assets, controlling interest of InGenetic—all nothing compared to the *Encanto*. She has no idea.

When he told her all she'd inherit (though, at the time, he meant decades in the future), she'd only feigned interest. All his plans to change the world. All the time striving for the future. Was it worth it? Out of all the products he launched into the market, now he can't recall a single one. Only that he was doing it all for Ashley.

But is that true? No. He was doing it for himself, he realizes now, but he wanted to share it all, and not just the money, with her. She is the only woman he ever really loved.

As the bat splits his skull, it demolishes his ambition, spews his talent, his dreams, and soon all his love out onto the Venice sidewalk in the sun.

But for now, for the first time in his life, he makes time. He goes back to Ashley's sixth birthday, and this time he plays tag with her on the beach. He holds her new golden puppy, lets it lick him in the face.

Maybe it's just his memory, but to him the puppy and Ashley have the same golden curls—they seem one and the same. All movement. All gold. A blur, bouncing and waving. As gold as the sand on the shoreline. And the clouds, too, are blonde.

A golden storm rains down. And the rain is not wet. Not water at all. It's light—golden light. It's softness and warmth. Breathing, sleepily, all around him.

Closing In

On Wednesday afternoon, in the Metropolitan Detention Center, inmates circled Saul's dirty mattress like sharks. So far, the rivalry between gangs had stalled them from attacking. There was a dispute over who got first go. But it was only a matter of time. He was a cop. They all hated cops.

A wave of horror crashed over him. The image of his hands on Jenna Collins's neck, in his room at the Roosevelt—though it had been Wayob in control of him at the time. Wayob had been in him, somehow, hadn't he? Or was this some kind of defense mechanism, his subconscious fooling him to save him from suffering the awful guilt of what he had done?

As a detective, he was well aware that memories are fallible. That's why he'd learned early in his career to take detailed notes. But no one was ever going to believe that Wayob had used him like a puppet.

Unless he proved how.

And he had to prove it to Hernandez more than anyone else. She thought he was the worst of the worst because, in her eyes, not only had he murdered Collins but he'd also betrayed her trust. Now the way she looked at him was like a dagger in his heart.

He closed his eyes. Thought hard. Set aside his assumptions. If he took Rosa at her word, that meant Wayob wanted to kill the person who had the Encanto. And if the Encanto actually allowed a person to switch bodies with someone else, like Rosa said, that explained Gray Wilson's strange behavior: the way he'd slapped Ashley York, her presence at his house, the uncomfortable looks on their faces last night. Wilson had been operating Ashley York's body. And it made sense that he would choose her. She was young, beautiful, rich.

Nearby, inmates argued. Feet scuffed the floor. Time was running out. He had to get out.

Trying to ignore the voices around him, he counted backward from a hundred. Concentrated on each number. From the blackness at the back of his mind, a memory of Wilson emerged: Wilson yelling from his car, at the gate of a mansion.

But Saul hadn't been there. He couldn't have seen this.

Now he recalled Wilson reversing from the gate and speeding up the street, then the carjacking. The kidnapping of Bob Jaggar. His murder. The memory must be Wayob's.

Saul's eyes snapped open. The abyss might have gazed back into him (Hernandez was right about that) but in so doing, Saul had seen into the abyss. He had glimpsed Wayob's memories.

He concentrated again, and the memory of a muddy river rose in his mind. A rainforest. A stone temple. Wayob's life before he became whatever he was now, which Saul supposed you might call a ghost. Wayob's body must have died long ago, and yet his mind lived on. How? Apparently, it had something to do with the Encanto.

There was nothing unique in the universe—not even the universe itself—so how many more like Wayob were out there? Saul shuddered. It was a daunting thought. But for now, he could only focus on Wayob.

Wayob intended to murder Gray Wilson to ensure his freedom from the Encanto, and he might have learned from Saul's mind where to find him. Saul had to stop him. Thanks to what he'd just learned, he now had a good chance of getting released from the MDC, if he could just get Hernandez on the phone. He regretted all the hours that she must have doubted him. That he'd put her in a position of doubt. He'd rather die than go on living with her believing he'd betrayed her, and now he knew how to convince her that Wayob was responsible.

He climbed off the bed. Angled his massive belly through a narrow aisle of bunks. Men glowered at him as he passed. Saul avoided eye contact.

A gaunt man, *ARYAN BROTHERHOOD* tattooed across his chest in blue capitals, stepped in front of Saul. "Where ya think you're goin'?"

He looked familiar, but Saul couldn't place where from. He ignored the question and walked around him, toward the ancient pay phone mounted on the rear wall, its frayed cord partially wrapped in aluminum. As the man fell in behind him, Saul realized that he'd seen him in Wayob's memory. Friday night, Wayob—in Saroyan's body—had provoked a fight in this very same cell, and this Aryan, with his ribs jutting from his skin, had escalated the confrontation, which led to Wayob's escape.

As Saul neared the phone, the Aryan behind him whistled. "There's a toll."

From the nearby bunks, voices murmured. Shoes scuffed the floor, men getting to their feet.

Saul made a show of considering the idle handset, the surrounding graffiti, then turned. "So, who do I pay?"

The man puffed his ribcage. "Two smokes."

"That sounds reasonable. I'll have to owe you."

"Credit's no good."

Saul approached the Aryan. "That's all I've got right now."

The little man straightened his back and raised his shoulders, an almost comical display for a man who weighed one-twenty at the most. "I ain't alone here, bub."

It seemed a fight was unavoidable, but it didn't have to be here and now. If he could just get them away from the phone and stall them a few minutes somewhere while he doubled back. "Neither am I," Saul lied. "You going to run to Daddy? Little baby run to Bruce? Bruce got beat down by a cripple, and look at me. I'm bigger than Bruce."

The little Aryan twitched. Bruce was the barrel-chested Aryan with "SIN" tattooed across his forehead, who this little man had riled into confronting Wayob. And then Wayob, in Saroyan's body, had managed to knock Bruce unconscious and transmigrate into his body instead.

The little man jutted his chin. He wasn't leaving, so Saul shoved him aside and took off.

"You're going to be sorry for that," he shouted after Saul. "Ain't nowhere to run."

"You sure?" Saul ran.

When he glanced over his shoulder, the little man was striding along leisurely, an evil grin spread across his face. Saul jerked a bunk out to block the path behind him and continued on, his prison-issue cruisers slapping the floor. A group of Black men gathered solemnly in the aisle to watch him flop by, as though the little man and his fellow Aryans had dibs on kicking Saul's ass. There were two dozen in this dorm, at least, each one bigger than the next, but no one was behind him.

Heaving to catch his breath, Saul turned down a random aisle and headed for a cluster of beds that seemed deserted for the moment. He swung a bunk out into the aisle, its metal legs scraping the concrete. He snatched the saggy mattresses off the top bunk, dumped the sheet and pillow, and repeated the procedure for the bottom mattress. Then he leaned them upright, side-by-side, against the bed frame. From another bunk, he grabbed two more mattresses and arranged them in the same way on the opposite side of the frame. A mattress for the front, and one more for the back. Now, the entire bed was enclosed.

"Hey you!" A trans woman with long hair and fleshy lips, shirt tied above her midriff, sauntered toward Saul. "That's my bed!"

Saul pointed in the direction from which he'd come. "I need you to stall the Brotherhood for me."

She swung a hip to the side and propped a hand on it. "You shittin' me?"

"I can help you," he whispered. "When are you up for parole?"

"You really a cop?"

He held out a hand. "Detective Parker."

She glanced around before shaking it with just her fingers, no palm. "I don't care who you are. I'm not lying to the Brotherhood."

"I'm not asking you to. Just let them make the wrong assumption."

"Don't tell me you're going to hide in those mattresses. That's about the dumbest idea I've ever heard."

"Let me worry about that." These men weren't geniuses to begin with, and now they were hyped up on adrenaline, in addition to whatever contraband was in their system. Their amygdala would spur them into action before processing what they saw.

"How you going to get me parole if you're dead?"

"I'll be out of here today," Saul said, "if you help me. What's your name?"

"At the hearing, I'll be Lester Jones."

Saul nodded. "Got it, and what's your true name?"

"Leslie."

"Okay, Leslie. Hurry." Saul pushed the mattress aside like a sliding door and climbed into the bunk behind it.

"I hope you know what you're doing," she said as she sauntered off down the aisle.

He knew better than to try and hide in plain sight. As soon as she was gone, he scooted off the bed and into a crouch. He glanced around, seeing no one.

In the distance, men shouted. Leslie yelled, "I'm trying to tell you what I saw."

Keeping his head below the bunks, Saul made his way to the far wall of the dorm. His little mattress diversion might not buy much time, but every second counted.

He reached the back wall and turned toward the phone, walking quickly without making noise.

He called Hernandez collect.

"I was going to decline the charge," she said on answering, "but I wanted to tell you about the porters myself."

Saul's stomach sank, and the hotel director's words echoed in his head. *Bad things don't happen at the Roosevelt.*

"It doesn't matter now," he said. "Listen—"

"It doesn't matter? Are you serious? They confessed to moving Collins's body from *your* room to the dumpster, and you think that doesn't matter? You're toast."

He'd wondered how Wayob, in Saul's body, could have moved her on his own—and why he couldn't remember it, despite having memories of the murder.

Shouting erupted down the aisle. Saul's diversion had been uncovered.

"Wayob said that you reminded him of his 'young bride,'" Saul said.

"What are you talking about?" she snarled.

"He was in Rydell's body. When you drove Rydell to the PAB, he asked if you enjoyed carnal acts of perversion."

"He told you that?"

"I saw his memory."

Silence over the line.

He had never known Hernandez to blush, but he remembered how, when Wayob suggested she might enjoy said acts with Saul, her ears had reddened.

Angry voices, bellowing, approached.

Saul turned toward the wall and focused on Hernandez, trying to recall exactly what he'd seen in Wayob's mind. "You turned off the stereo," he said, "but you were listening to M. Ward. Do you think Wayob knew that? You think he knew the song? It was 'Chinese Translation,' and you were singing along in that faraway voice of yours—I bet you didn't even realize you were singing out loud. You were on the 101, almost downtown, when you hit the chorus and combed your hair back in that way you always do. You had the window cracked, and your bangs kept blowing in your face. That's when he started ranting about his bride—"

The line went dead. A hand lay on the receiver, attached to a skinny arm tattooed with swords and a swastika on a shield. The little Aryan.

Saul reeled back and punched his tiny stomach.

The Aryan went down.

Before Saul could turn to see who else had followed him, someone shoved him from behind. *Big guy*, he thought, as his head slammed into the metal box of the pay phone.

Fireflies swirled into his vision as the space behind them darkened.

—

Someone was shaking him awake. He blinked his eyes open and tried to focus on the blurry figure standing over him.

"Nap time's over," a man said. A man in uniform—a guard. The frayed mustache and sallow skin came into focus. A terribly narrow brow on a face too small for his head. Victor Aleman.

In a flash, Saul recalled Wayob's memory: on Saturday night, Wayob had transferred his consciousness from Saroyan to Bruce to Aleman, and once in Aleman's body, he was free to walk out of the MDC in pursuit of Gloria Luna and the Encanto. Saul could only hope he did not yet possess it.

Aleman leaned over him. "Can you walk?"

Saul's head hurt. His knees hurt. He was strapped to a gurney in a hallway, which, from the looks of the drab cinderblocks and the bars blocking the passage, was somewhere in the MDC. He wasn't sure if he could even get up.

"I'll tell your visitor to come back tomorrow." Aleman turned away.

Saul struggled to focus. Had Hernandez come to see him? Special permission was required to visit an injured inmate.

"I can walk," Saul said. "If you'll let me."

Aleman returned. "You better not be wasting my time." He unstrapped Saul's torso with the same harshness with which he'd humiliated him in the shower.

Saul had to slide his handcuffs along the rails of the gurney in order to sit up. "Guess you had to break up the fight?"

"Not really."

"How's the other guy?" he asked in hopes of humanizing himself.

The scowl remained on Aleman's face. "You slipped and fell. That's what goes in the report. Got it?"

Saul nodded. No point in arguing and giving him any excuse to prevent him from seeing his visitor.

Aleman released Saul's hands one at a time, chained them to his sides, and unstrapped his feet. He stood back, crossed his arms.

Saul ignored the tingling pulsing through his legs. He wriggled off the gurney and unsteadily onto his feet.

Aleman shoved Saul along through a series of locked corridors to a narrow visitor's room. Inside, a table and three chairs were bolted to the floor. Across the room, Hernandez stood in the sunlight streaming through the slot-shaped window, gazing out at the afternoon haze.

As Saul entered, the chains rattled on his wrists, and she turned.

"Un-cuff him, please," she said, a slight smile on her face. "He's free to go."

Saul stopped. Even if the memory he'd seen had convinced her, it wouldn't hold sway with Levy. There was more to this. Had to be. And Saul was dying to hear it.

He turned toward Aleman so he could unlock the cuffs.

"Not according to the system," Aleman said. "I checked."

"Call the warden," she said. "There are no charges, and there never will be."

"The warden calls us. We don't call him."

"Well, I've got an issue with that."

"Take it up with the warden."

Hernandez pulled her phone and started texting. Aleman muttered under his breath and shoved Saul into a chair. The plastic bowed from Saul's weight as he situated himself, hands still chained to his sides.

Hernandez returned the phone to her belt. "Lieutenant Levy wants him out ASAP."

"Whatever." Aleman unlocked the cuffs. "Your ass if he turns out to have a concussion or something." He stomped to the door. "I'll be right outside."

Hernandez stepped out of the sunlight and approached the table. "Politics."

Because of the rivalry between the Sheriff's Department and the LAPD, Saul could count on his release being delayed at every step along the chain of command.

"Was it what I said, or did you find some new evidence?" he asked.

She sat across from him and leaned toward him. "What happened to your face?"

Saul felt the bruise where his temple had been slammed into the pay phone. "You should see the other guy."

She combed back her shock of white bangs. "They shouldn't have put you in with violent offenders."

Saul shrugged. It didn't matter now. It was just so good to see her, to have her sitting here with him, and without a trace of contempt on her face. "What did you find?"

"You booked *him* for murder, and now *you're* here." Her eyes were dark yet luminous, as if they held a light of their own. He wanted to lose himself inside her eyes.

"You're talking about Wayob?"

"Rydell, or whoever the hell he was," she said. "He made a big point about revenge. *No more and certainly no less*, he said, like I was giving him no choice. But all I did was drive him downtown; you're the one who locked him in the holding cell."

Saul gestured at the stark room, the bars on the window. "Guess I should have taken him more seriously." He'd only made the mistake of discounting Wayob's threats because he'd assumed Rydell was merely *acting* like Wayob. The truth was much worse.

"We traced the call to the tip line," Hernandez said. "It originated at eight fourteen a.m. yesterday at a tower near Sawtelle."

"That's pretty far from the Roosevelt." He'd assumed that Wayob had reported him shortly after the murder, while still in Saul's body, but Saul had already awakened by eight. At that time, he was probably driving toward Wilson's.

"The number was blocked," Hernandez said, "so it took time to get the warrant." She placed her hands on the table and leaned forward. "Do you know whose phone it was?"

"Almost definitely," he said. "Whose?"

"Carter's." She leaned back and looked at him.

Saul exhaled. He had wondered last night, when Arcos said Carter died trying to hijack a car, if Wayob had gotten to him. "When did he die?"

"Shortly after the call. He was found a block away."

"So, if Carter supposedly saw me murder Collins, why not just arrest me? He must have waited hours before calling the tip line." The answer was obvious to Saul, but he was curious if she'd drawn the same conclusion.

"That's the question I've been asking myself. At first, I thought someone else used his phone."

"Could you recognize the voice?"

"Forensics matched the audio. It was Carter's voice. And the thing is, he'd have known better than to use his own phone." She glanced out the window. Behind the MTA building, the sky had faded from orange to dull gray. "I'm starting to believe that… Just the idea that you would photograph a victim"—anger swelled in her voice—"like some sort of demented memento…" She searched his eyes.

He wanted to give her more than just another denial, but it seemed beyond words he could say.

"It seemed so…"

"Contrived?" he said.

"Absurd."

Saul wanted to clap. But she hadn't said why he was free to go. "What about the porters?"

"They didn't see the murder; they only moved the body. And there's no physical evidence to back up their statement. Your room was cleaned so well, we can't even place you in there, much less Collins."

Saul looked at his hands. Would she still release him if she knew that Collins *had* been in his room? Had died there? His own fingers had squeezed her neck. Wayob had been in control, but Saul remembered the look in her eyes, the shock and disbelief as she gasped and gasped and got no air.

Hernandez took Saul's hands—the same hands which had strangled Collins —and squeezed them tight in hers. "You're off the hook, Saul Parker."

He hated to say anything, hated to jeopardize the kindness in her eyes, but... "What about Saroyan?"

"He died of cardiac arrest."

"No sign of violence?"

"Just the blows he sustained Friday night. Nothing close to the time of death. They're dropping the homicide. You just happened to find the body, and that's it."

"What about the note? It was my handwriting and my fingerprints on the page."

She shook her head slowly. "The note's gone." Her brows twisted, eyes imploring him to ask nothing more. She had destroyed the evidence. Committed a felony. For him.

He regretted putting her in this position. He should have destroyed the note when he found it, but at the time he wasn't positive that Wayob had written it with Saul's hand, and he'd needed to know.

"What about Levy?"

"She's decided that Arcos and Carter were framing you to make her department look bad. And now that they're both dead, everyone's ready to move on."

"What happened to Arcos?"

"He died from carbon monoxide in the house across from Wilson's. Crazy, right? Wilson's wife found the bodies."

Saul's stomach dropped. "Bodies?"

"There were two of them. The other guy was an elderly relative of the homeowner."

Saul whistled. "Charlie Streeter?"

"You knew him?"

"I questioned him about Wilson. This is quite a coincidence." He was almost positive that Wayob had killed them, but why? He waited to hear what Hernandez believed.

"Coincidences are shitty detective work," she said. "You taught me that. Do you know why Arcos would have been there?"

Saul nodded. "I sent him on a wild goose chase. He must have thought I had returned to Wilson's."

"He and Streeter died during a struggle in the garage. Could have been an accident, unless... Did Streeter seem suicidal to you?"

"He definitely seemed paranoid, and he was taking pills, so who knows?"

"Mrs. Wilson might know something. When I spoke with her, I got the impression she was holding back. She's a piece of work."

"Who shot Carter?"

"We'll probably never know now that IA took the case. I did all the legwork, and now I'm supposed to hand it over to Grimes and Feldman, like they have any experience with homicide."

With Grimes poking around, things could only get worse. Arcos and Carter had been idiots; Grimes was an accomplished asshole. And his partner, Feldman, backed him like a soldier. "I guess Arcos and Carter were *their* guys though, huh?"

Hernandez nodded. "Cobb put in a call to Chief Decker, and now that's that."

According to the rumors, Cobb, the commander of IA, had some kind of dirt on Chief Decker. "What did you tell them?" he asked.

"I'm not telling them shit. Wayob is ours."

Saul nodded. He liked the sound of that. Him and Hernandez taking down Wayob, together. "But Saroyan *was* murdered. We can't let it go down as a natural death."

"You want to get out of here, you keep that to yourself. Not much good you can do behind bars. Plenty of other murders to put on Wayob. He'll get the juice for sure, and I need your help catching him."

She pulled her phone, started playing a video, and placed it on the table before him.

It was a wide-angle security-camera shot of some kind of surplus store. A man in a dark T-shirt stood behind the register with his back to the camera. Across the counter was a Black man in a security uniform. Shaved head and hulking, broad shoulders. Ashley York's guard, Sammy Johnson. No doubt about it.

"My name is Wayob," Johnson said, but his lilting cadence was unmistakable.

"When was this?" Saul asked.

"The video was uploaded at one oh eight," Hernandez said. "What's your take?"

"The way this guy speaks is like Sadie, Rydell, and Saroyan. Wayob's got another puppet."

On the screen, Johnson leaped over the counter and attacked the man in the T-shirt.

"And he's murdered another victim too."

"Where was this?"

"Inglewood." She stopped the video and locked the screen. "That's my next stop. Want to come with? Unofficially, of course. You're still on suspension."

"Do you have any leads on where to find Wayob now?"

"That's the problem with this bastard. We don't know his motive."

"What did Rosa tell you?"

"Not much. But you were right about Evan York. There's no way he was just there to help her pack in the middle of the night—that was bullshit."

Saul nodded. "She told me about a device called the Encanto that her abuela gave to Wilson."

Hernandez's eyebrows shot up. "Wilson's the Encanto guy? Why in the hell did he let Wayob out?"

"I don't think Gloria Luna told him about Wayob."

"I guess if she did, he wouldn't have believed her anyway."

"Did Rosa tell you what the Encanto can do?"

"She said it traps Wayob."

"Right, and she also told me that it can be used by a person to switch bodies with someone else."

From the way her eyebrows shot up, Saul could tell the idea was news to her. He debated whether he should tell her his theory, and decided to go for it. His intuition was too heavy to deny; it had the weight of fact. Plus, she loved logical thinking, and if he couldn't tell her, then who could he tell?

"I know this sounds crazy," he said, "but I believe Gray Wilson used the Encanto to switch bodies with Ashley York."

Hernandez blinked. Said nothing.

"And Wayob's after them," he continued. "We find Wilson, we find Wayob."

She sighed. "Look, I'm not saying I don't believe you. We've got one crazy guy after another claiming to be Wayob. And the things you said over the phone, it was like you read his mind. No way he told you all those details."

"I didn't read his mind. I saw the memory."

"Okay." She nodded. "You wouldn't kill an unarmed civilian. I know that now—I knew the whole time, deep down. That's why I'm accepting your explanation." She glanced toward the window. "And what you're saying has a certain logic... especially with the way Gray Wilson and Ashley York have been acting, but... Levy will never buy it. We need evidence. There's a psychopath on the loose, and I need a connection to pursue."

He should tell her, he knew, that the man in the video was not just any security guard but Sammy Johnson. He wanted to tell her, but she would be obligated to follow procedure and try to arrest Wayob, but they had already arrested Wayob—twice—yet the killing continued. Repeating the same mistake and expecting a different result was the definition of insanity. Better if she didn't know what measures might be required to stop Wayob. As much as he wanted to work the case with her, she had a bright future with the department, and he didn't want to ruin it.

The door opened. "The warden called," Aleman said. "Guess you've got friends in high places."

As Saul stood, he tried to suck in his gut and twisted it away from Hernandez.

"It's about time," she said.

Aleman shut the door behind him. "Hold up. The cuffs go back on until we process you out."

"Seriously?" she said. "I'll take responsibility."

"Can't let you do that. It would mean my job."

She rolled her eyes.

Aleman secured Saul's hands to the chain around his waist and ushered him through the door.

In the corridor, Hernandez walked along beside them.

"Thanks for believing me," Saul said to her. "I'd hate to think…"

"You want to thank me, help me stop this bastard. I've got a bad feeling."

"Me too."

After returning through the gauntlet of locked doors, they reached the gurney where Saul had awakened, cuffed to the rails.

"Take a left at the T-junction," Aleman said.

Saul slowed. "Exit's the other way."

"You have to wait in holding."

"That's ridiculous," Hernandez said.

"Look, he's not the first in line, okay? The warden said to stick to the program, and until I hear otherwise, that's what I'm doing."

"He's a cop. We've got lives at risk out there."

"Yeah, well, you'd best wait in the lobby, Wonder Woman. Could be a while."

Saul studied Aleman. His narrow brow was slack with indifference. There was nothing they could do. If Levy called the warden again, Aleman would only drag his feet even more.

"You should go ahead," Saul said to Hernandez. "I'm not going to Inglewood."

Her eyes searched his face. "Why not?"

Because if Wayob had left any evidence, it would be useless. They were behind him, but they needed to get ahead. "I want to keep an eye on Wilson. Like you said, we don't have enough to officially protect him."

"The uniforms are still at Streeter's place. I'll have them stick around a little longer."

But Wilson was in Ashley's body, and Wayob was in the body of her guard, which meant Wilson was a sitting duck. Saul had to get to Ashley's before anyone else got hurt.

"Good idea," he said, "but I want to talk to him myself."

"If you two want to keep talking," Aleman said, "I have to take you back to the interview room instead of processing out guys in line ahead of you. I'm off at six either way. Your choice."

"You act like you're the only one who works here," Hernandez said. "Where's Vasquez?"

Aleman shrugged. "We're understaffed. He's off for the day."

Hernandez sighed. She squeezed Saul's shoulder. "Call me. Don't go cowboy, okay? Promise me."

"Don't worry." Saul wished his hands weren't chained to his sides, wished he could do something other than stand there looking fat in the orange scrubs.

She launched down the hall and turned right at the T-junction as Aleman ushered Saul through a locked door. They passed a long row of cells. Inmates leered at Saul as he jiggled by.

When they reached a corridor, Saul turned to Aleman. "I want you to know I'm going to get the guy who took you down Saturday night."

Aleman pointed to the bruise on Saul's forehead. "Looks to me like he got you."

"I'm talking about the guy behind Bruce," Saul said. "I'm talking about Wayob. He put the frame on me. One *cop* to another, I could really use your help."

Aleman responded with a bitter edge in his voice. "I'm not a cop."

Saul restrained a smile. Most guards—at least the honest ones, and some of the ones who weren't—aspired to be cops. "But you could be. A good word from a detective grade three goes a long way."

Aleman glanced down and to the right. "Happy where I am."

Threatening Aleman was the one play he had left. "Okay. Fine. But if you want to keep it between us what happened in the shower, I need a phone, and I need to get out of here ASAP, or you're not going to like the calls I make when I get out later."

Aleman said nothing.

"Don't take it the wrong way. It's nothing personal."

Aleman nudged him forward, his brow blank as the concrete wall of the corridor.

They reached a solitary cell with a solid steel door. Aleman unlocked it. "Park it here, Parker."

Saul obeyed.

"There is not a single thing I can do to expedite your release," he said, releasing Saul from the cuffs and the chains. "We have procedures, you understand?"

Saul shrugged.

Aleman removed a phone from a cargo pocket. He placed it face down on the cot. "You'll be out of here in half an hour."

"What's the passcode?" Saul wondered what this would end up costing him.

"No passcode. It's a burner I confiscated from a prisoner. You owe me big time. Don't forget."

After the door clanged shut and the bolt thrown, Saul sat on the cot and powered on the phone. According to the logo it was a ZTC, some sort of cheap Android model, probably with limited number of prepaid minutes. But it had two bars of service. Now that he was almost out of jail, he could focus on his next challenge: gaining access to Ashley's compound.

Saul opened the web browser, searched for the number he was looking for, and called it. A soft-spoken woman answered the phone: an assistant. After he identified himself as a detective with the LAPD, she transferred him to a personal voicemail.

He left a message. Five words. Guaranteed reaction. Followed by the address of the PAB.

—

Less than an hour later, Saul was released from the MDC. His badge and gun were not—no surprise. It might take months to get his badge reinstated, if ever, given the evidence linking him to two murders. He didn't complain when Aleman returned his wallet with all the cash missing. His keys were more important. In particular, the key to his plain wrap. Although he couldn't drive it while on suspension, he could at least let himself in and retrieve his Beretta Nano from the trunk, assuming the vehicle had been returned to the motor pool.

He huffed up Temple Street, passing through the long shadow of City Hall, to the PAB. It looked like a glass ship anchored there among the skyscrapers, reflecting the fading light and the oncoming clouds.

As he entered the lobby, the desk sergeant shot to his feet. "Whoa, Parker. I heard you went down for murder one?"

He held up his hands. "Don't believe everything you hear."

"I never do." He winked.

Saul took the elevator down to parking and searched for his plain wrap. On P2, he found it. He glanced around and saw no one. Hoping that no one was watching through the camera at the end of the aisle, he opened the trunk, lifted the spare tire, and retrieved the Beretta. He hurried back to the elevator.

Outside the lobby, parked on Spring as instructed, was Evan York's Tesla. Saul glanced back. A woman in a pants suit rushed for the crosswalk before the light changed. None of the pedestrians appeared to be cops or to pay him any attention as he opened the passenger door and climbed in.

Evan York was behind the wheel, looking a little stiff despite the crewneck and black jeans. "Where is Rosa?" He rolled his *R* into a soft *O*.

Last night, Saul had been too overwhelmed to key into his accent: it wasn't British at all, but Latino. And his brow was all beetled up with an uncharacteristic look of concern. Energy surged through him. It was as he suspected. This was not Evan York. He was Luis Luna, just as Saul had said in the message.

"You know the way to Ashley York's?"

"You said you could help. That's why I came, homes. We find Rosa, or you can get out of my car."

"Your car? I don't know about that. I'm thinking this car belongs to Ashley York. Evan York is dead."

Luna looked down. A shadow flashed across his face. "How do you know?"

"You guys used the Encanto to switch bodies, right? Rosa told the truth about what it could do. If you're Luis Luna, then Evan York must have died in your body."

Luna sighed. "So how did you know... I'm me?"

"Who else would I expect to find with Rosa the night after her abuela died? And who else would move her out of that shithole the second he could afford it?"

Luna nodded. His brows tightened almost to the point of breaking. "So now it's my fault that... Wayob took her."

Saul inhaled. If Wayob took her, then most likely she was dead, but there was no reason to say that until they knew for sure. "Wayob is on his way to Ashley's."

"Why didn't you say so?" He pulled out into traffic. "I thought you were arrested?"

"Wayob framed me. And he's going down for it. I don't care what it takes."

At Fourth, Luna swerved into a turn and cut off a Land Rover. The Rover barreled toward them, collision imminent. "Watch it," Saul shouted.

The torque of the electric engine flung Saul back in his seat as they fishtailed. Narrowly skated past. Saul clutched the grab handle. "We can't help her if you kill us on the way there."

"Relax." Luna regained control and sped toward the on-ramp. "You'd be amazed what this car is capable of."

Saul asked, "When did you last see her?"

"Last night. We were leaving the apartment, and she insisted I go ahead without her. And she had that look in her eye. You know the look, right?" Luna raised his left brow at Saul and his right one went down. Probably not the look he intended to convey. "No arguing with the look," he said. "So, I took off. She said she needed one last look on her own. My mother basically raised Rosa, you know? We called her 'Abuela,' but it should have been 'Madre.'

"But I should have waited for Rosa, and I should have followed her to her new place."

Luna swerved as he reached for his phone. He swiped the screen and showed it to Saul.

Rosa:
Wayob found me. He's a security guard. Black guy. Ripped. Help Gray and Ashley.

A tightness gripped Saul in his gut. They had to get to Ashley York's as fast as possible.

"My mother gave the Encanto away," Luna said. "So what does Wayob want with Rosa?"

Saul wondered if there was any kind of motive to Wayob's madness. If Gray Wilson returned to his own body, Wayob would be trapped inside the Encanto, which gave Wayob a clear motive for trying to kill Wilson as long as he was in possession of the device. But why kill Collins? Why kill Saroyan and Wu? Maybe it was out of some sick sense of revenge against Saul, like Hernandez thought.

But Rosa had nothing to do with Saul.

He closed his eyes and considered what he'd seen in Wayob's memories. The only person who stood out with any clarity was a dark-haired girl who existed in some other place and time. Wayob had claimed he was a thousand years old, so Saul could not guess when she was from. Did Rosa remind Wayob of this girl? They seemed about the same height, though her skin was darker and her hair longer and duller than Rosa's. She was thinner too, with an indented breastbone, and she had a rounder face with flat cheeks. Her skin glowed in a way that made it seem as if Wayob revered her.

But in the memory, when she motioned for Wayob to come closer, he held back. She took his hand, placed it on her bare breast, and held it there—and Wayob jerked it away. With tears in her eyes, she tried to kiss him, but he pulled back again and fell to the ground on the leafy bank of a brown river. He bowed at her feet, which were bare, dirty and small.

She kneeled before him, tried to raise his chin, but again he shrank back.

And Wayob remained there, watching her heels as she walked away along the path beside the water.

Saul was thrown forward against the seatbelt as Luna slammed to a stop behind a black SUV.

"Did you call the police?" he asked Luna.

"You are the police, homes. When you said I had to come meet you if I cared about Rosa, I thought… I don't know what I thought, but I hoped—"

"We'll find her," Saul said.

Luna studied Saul, not seeming to notice as the SUV inched forward. A car honked behind them. "Maybe I should call 911."

"Keep driving." Saul needed Evan York's face to get through Ashley York's gate. Besides, diverting to file a missing person's report would cost hours. "I'll call if you want, but are you ready for the hard questions? They might think Rosa had some reason to disappear."

"Like she faked it?" Luna's shoulders hunched over the steering wheel. His brow beetled up so tight it looked painful.

"I'm just playing devil's advocate," Saul said. "No one is going to believe you're Rosa's father. They're going to ask why Evan York cares so much."

Luna was silent for a long time. Traffic accelerated and then slowed again as they neared the split between the 110 and the 101.

Luna blew out a long breath. "I get it."

"Any signs of foul play at the apartment?"

"Her purse was emptied on the floor. Including her phone. She would never leave her phone." Luna swallowed.

Saul placed a hand on his shoulder and waited for him to continue.

Luna blinked tears from his eyes. "It was the photo. She went back for the photo of my father—she must have seen me throw it away. I never explained to her how it was his fault we had to flee Guatemala."

He fell silent. The electric engine whirred, less than a whisper beneath the wind and the sound of the tires on the road as they rolled through Echo Park.

"How did it happen with you and Evan York?" Saul asked. "I doubt he stopped by and asked to use your Encanto."

"My mother had cancer…"

"I was very sorry to hear that." Saul waited another long moment.

"We didn't have money for the doctors. I had to do something. But… it was too late…"

"Why didn't your mother switch bodies with him? She could have had a healthier body as well as his fortune."

"She was too good for that. And I didn't intend to take his body—she didn't tell me the Encanto did that—I was just going to sell the Encanto to him." He pressed his palms against the steering wheel and stretched out his fingers. The skin bunched and wrinkled on his knuckles, and he stared, as if losing himself in the strangeness of Evan York's hands, which were now his. "I didn't mean for anything to happen. To Evan York or anyone…"

Trying to save his mother had cost Luna his body and now probably the life of his daughter. Saul almost felt sorry for him. "So, Evan York knew about the Encanto? He knew what it could do?"

"He knew more than I did. That's for sure. When I heard about how he was collecting Mayan artifacts, I checked the website, which showed off his collection as well as items he was looking for. One was a photograph of a primitive drawing of a snake with a monster head that looked sort of like the snake on the Encanto, which I knew my mother had stashed in a drawer. So I figured, nothing to lose, right? I sent a picture of it." Luna shrugged. "I couldn't believe it when he called me himself."

Hernandez had mentioned something about Evan York's obsession with ancient artifacts. Saul's mind suddenly flashed on an image from Wayob's nightmare-like memory: a shriveled man with skin like leather, probably the priest Wayob hated so much, holding a round stone with the S-shaped black snake mounted on top. The priest spun the snake like a dial and held it high above an altar. He placed the stone on Wayob's forehead, and then abruptly the memory seemed to end.

"I think I know how Wayob ended up in the Encanto," Saul said. "But I don't know how it keeps his spirit, if that's what you want to call it, trapped inside, or how it transfers a mind to another body."

"Beats me. I guess it's magic."

Saul shook his head. Magic was an art form, a performance of that which appeared to be manifestly impossible, but it was not an explanation for the unknown, and it was lazy to think so.

"If it's magic," Saul said, "then there's a logical explanation. Magic is just about concealing the method."

"I bet Evan York would have agreed with that." Luna laughed to himself. "*Five hundred grand.* He was going to pay me five hundred grand and I wasn't even suspicious… until I woke up to see my own body standing over me. Before I could even react, he drugged me to sleep. Cold as ice."

Saul imagined what the Encanto might be worth to a man like Evan York.

A younger body, more life. Probably he was just using Luna to test-drive the device, because his fortune could no doubt provide him with any number of much younger volunteers desperate to trade half their life for a fee.

"*Artifact collection,*" Luna said. "Ha. Guess he didn't believe me about Wayob. I guess I didn't believe it either. Not really. I mean, I knew my mother believed; I just hoped she was wrong, you know what I'm sayin'? I thought it was just a story." He glanced at Saul and back at the road. "I was an idiot."

"I wouldn't have believed it either," Saul said. "Not without proof. Do you know how to use the Encanto?"

"You just turn the snake-dial and go to sleep. Not much to it."

"So, you turn this dial, go to sleep… and then, abracadabra, you wake up in someone else's body?"

Luna shrugged. "That's what happened to me."

"Can you control who?"

"I don't know. Evan York had a pair of beds set up for us in the back room of his shady clinic, and that's about all the equipment I saw."

"What about Wayob? Rosa said that when you switch bodies, he is released from the Encanto."

"That's exactly what happened. And he killed my body with Evan York inside it."

"And his motive was that if York returned to his own body, he would have been trapped again?"

Luna nodded. "Right."

"Do you know how to switch back?"

"According to my mother, the same action also reverses the switch, but she didn't seem too sure about that, and I never got to try it. Evan York was dead."

"So, you just turn back the dial, take a nap, and then problem solved? Wayob's out of commission?"

"If he doesn't kill you first."

In the opposite lanes, headlights winked on in the twilight. Ahead, the Hollywood Hills were obscured by low clouds sweeping in from the west. Saul shifted in his seat. "We have to warn Ashley York."

"She's been trying to call me," Luna said.

Saul grabbed the phone from the dash mount and thumb-typed a text.

Evan York:
Stay away from Sammy Johnson. I'm on my way. See you soon.

Luna merged right, floored it past an eighteen-wheeler toward a slow-moving car ahead, and swerved inches from its bumper back into the left lane, into a narrow gap between the truck and a Land Rover. But the Land Rover wasn't moving any faster. Luna hit the brakes and sighed.

They inched past the Hollywood Tower, a faux French-Normandy–style apartment building that towered above the east side of the freeway like an aging sentinel, standing strong in the face of all the new construction.

"What do you know about Gray Wilson?" Saul asked.

"Never heard of him."

"I'm pretty sure your mother gave him the Encanto."

Luna's face tightened. "I wasn't there."

"Seems kind of harsh to give it to a stranger."

Even if she had warned him about Wayob, who would have believed her?

"She had no choice." Luna practically shouted. He glanced at Saul then back at the traffic. "Giving it away resets the thing and forces Wayob back inside, somehow."

Spotlights from the Hollywood Bowl swept across the ceiling of clouds lowering on LA.

"But you had it after Evan York died, right?"

"Yeah."

"So why not give it to your mother instead of Wilson?"

"I did," Luna said. "She insisted I give it to her, but then nothing happened. She knew Wayob was free, somehow, and she could see him coming. It was like she had like a third eye, or I guess since she was blind it was her only eye. Pretty crazy, huh?"

Saul had come this far, so he might as well suspend his disbelief. "No crazier than a ghost trapped in a stone. The idea that she could see Wayob coming does have a certain sense of cosmic justice."

Luna nodded. "My mother thought she might have built up some sort of tolerance to the Encanto over the years, so we had to give it to somebody else. I suggested Rosa—that way we could make sure she destroyed it—but my mother refused. Once she had her mind set, there was no changing it." Luna sighed. "I was afraid of the Encanto, but you get that I didn't really understand what it does until after I lost my body, right? I never would have touched that damn thing if she'd told me everything."

"I hear you," Saul said, but Luna's claim didn't ring true; after all, he'd gone behind his mother's back to try and sell it. "Did she say what happened after she gave it away?"

"I guess it sucked Wayob inside like some kind of spirit magnet, and just in time too. Wayob had almost reached her fortune booth. Rosa was there with her."

"Sounds like a close call. When was this?"

"Saturday night."

Saul clenched his jaw. "You waited more than twenty-four hours after you released Wayob?"

"I know," Luna said. "I know. But she thought I might die when she gave it away, which I would have deserved, but I had to do something for Rosa first, set her up with a little piece of Evan York's fortune, you know? Nothing anyone would miss. Besides, she wouldn't give it to just anyone. She thought she could find the right person at the Day of the Dead, where she told fortunes for extra cash."

A chill gripped Saul's spine. "On Olvera Street?"

"How did you know?"

"I was following Wayob. He was in the body of Victor Aleman, a prison guard."

"Crazy."

Saul inhaled. "If the Encanto worked, it didn't hold. The next day, Wayob was out again."

"She really thought Wilson would destroy it. That was her problem: she always believed people were better than they were. And it got worse as she got older. You saw the shithole we lived in, right? She had stopped locking the door."

Saul nodded. "It's a common thing, unfortunately. That's why so many scams target the elderly."

Luna blew out a long breath. "Probably didn't help her judgment that she pulled an all-nighter Friday. She wouldn't let any of us sleep because apparently Wayob can move from one body to the next while people are sleeping."

"What are his limits?"

"What do you mean, 'limits'?"

"Wayob freed himself from the Metropolitan Detention Center by transmigrating from one body to the next, but when I put him in a holding cell alone, he freaked out and killed himself. Must have been the only way he could escape."

"Sounds like you know more than me, homes. She didn't say anything about suicide."

Traffic thinned somewhat as they summited the Cahuenga Pass and descended toward Universal City and the 134-170 interchange.

Luna hunched over the wheel. Saul was about to repeat the directions displayed on the console screen when the car began drifting toward the lanes for the 101. Saul glanced over his shoulder to make sure they weren't cutting someone off and wished he was driving.

"It was all the stress," Luna said. "That's what killed her. If I had just left the Encanto alone, I bet she would have pulled through."

"Sounds like a Catch-22," Saul said. "If she'd told you everything about the Encanto, would you have believed her?"

"Guess not."

"It sounds like she tried to scare you and Rosa off with a vague story, but the real question is why she kept the Encanto at all. She had decades to get rid of it, right?"

"That was her biggest regret."

"Pay attention." Saul pointed ahead at the slowing traffic where the 134 joined the 101. "Take Coldwater."

As Luna struggled to cut across five lanes of traffic in less than a mile, Saul glanced south at the clouds roiling along the ridgeline of the Santa Monica

Mountains, as if impatient for the oncoming darkness.

He recalled the intensity on Luna's mother's face when he and Hernandez delivered the death notification, the pain mapped into the deep furrows around her mouth. Now that he understood what she meant when she said Saroyan was innocent, now that he knew what questions to ask, it was too late. Now Wayob might be the one person—if you could still call him a person—who knew how the Encanto worked. Was there a way to make him talk?

"So, what will happen to me?" Luna asked.

"You're going to help me put Wayob back where he belongs. Then whatever Evan York does is up to you."

"I do want to help. Ashley York didn't deserve to lose a father."

"No, she didn't. And Evan York might have been an asshole, but he didn't deserve to die."

Luna nodded meekly and exited the freeway.

At the bottom of the ramp, they waited at a red light. On the corner by the overpass, a girl in a hoodie held a torn piece of cardboard that said, "anything will help." Behind her was a sleeping bag, a red backpack, and a Rottweiler.

The light changed, and Luna and Saul rolled under the freeway. They waited again at Ventura as the clouds poured over the ridgeline toward them.

"You say it was her biggest regret," Saul said, "but why couldn't she just destroy it?"

"She wanted to, but I guess it's not so easy."

"A sledgehammer won't do it?"

"A sledgehammer sounds perfect to me. After we find Rosa, I say we take the Encanto from this Wilson guy and smash it—and Wayob—into dust. My mother, I think she got confused. Last weekend she confessed she'd been having nightmares about Wayob for years. I think she was tempted by the Encanto, but of course she would never have actually used it."

As Coldwater snaked up into the fog, the fact that the elderly Luna had so many years to destroy the Encanto and yet did not twisted in the pit of Saul's stomach. She hadn't seemed like the sort of woman to be easily stalled by temptation, or doubt.

Luna turned right on Mulholland and glanced at Saul. "You think Rosa's alive?"

Saul stared ahead at the fog sliding across the road. "No reason to assume otherwise at this point." *Aside from all the bodies in Wayob's wake.* "The best we can do is stop Wayob before he hurts anyone else. We'll make him tell us what he did with her."

Luna nodded and said nothing. Even in the darkness, the worry on his brow was unmistakable. He leaned forward and squinted into the fog, which seemed to thicken in the headlights, obscuring the parallel yellow lines of the two-lane.

They slowed through a hairpin turn beside a dirt turnout that edged to a cliff drop-off. Parked at the end was a Honda Civic with a dented bumper and a patch of rust by the plate. Saul had seen it before, but where?

Fog spilled over the cliff. Down in the valley, cars' lights blurred into red and white streams.

Saul was dying to tell Hernandez that all this time, Luna had been Evan York. He really should have told her that the man in the video, whose body Wayob now possessed, was Ashley's guard. But in case things went sideways at Ashley's, it was best to keep her out of it.

Saul instructed Luna to turn into the manicured oasis surrounding the Beverly Park entrance.

"What do I say to security?"

"As little as possible. You're Evan York. Remember you belong here."

Luna buzzed down his window as he rolled up to the gate, and Saul tapped on the interior light.

The guard glanced at Luna. He did a double take. "Go right ahead."

They passed through the gate.

The road narrowed, descending the hill. Luna swerved over the divider line, then over corrected. He seemed unable to anticipate the turns in the fog. Saul clutched the grab handle.

Ahead of Ashley's drive, the road widened. Luna turned in and rolled up to Ashley's personal security booth. An arm hung limply out the window.

Luna hit the brakes. "What the fuck?"

The arm belonged to a heavy-set body slumped against the glass—not Johnson. Saul reached across and killed the headlights. The booth blurred into a gloomy mass of shadow and light. Fog sifted up over the windshield.

"Back it up," Saul said. "Nice and slow."

Luna reversed all the way out of the driveway and parked on the road in front of a Camry, probably Wilson's. Behind the Camry was a minivan, which looked equally out of place in this neighborhood.

Saul deactivated the interior lights before opening the door. "Wait here," he said. "That's an order."

He moved close to the hedge and drew his Beretta as he approached the drive. At the last bush, he peeked around. Fifty yards ahead, an orange halo radiated out of the booth into the fog.

He listened hard. Heard nothing.

Behind him, the fog had swallowed York's car.

He approached the booth.

Lolled against the window frame was the guard's head, his white shirt stained with dried blood. A bullet wound in his left cheek.

It's my fault, Saul thought.

Although arresting Wayob was useless in the long run, it still could have saved this man's life.

Standing in the circle of light surrounding the booth, Saul felt exposed. He took a step toward the open gate. Beyond it, fog surged up the hillside and into the sky, which gave the illusion that he and the dead man were sinking. Saul actually felt it in the pit of his stomach.

He pulled his phone. At this point, he had to report the murder, and the first person he wanted to tell was Hernandez. He wanted her here with him.

She answered immediately. "Where are you?"

Saul spoke low, in case he wasn't alone out here in the fog. "Ashley York's."

"So much for calling me. You said you were going to Wilson's."

Technically, he'd said he was going to keep an eye on Wilson, who happened to be in Ashley's body, but no point in explaining that he'd basically let her make the wrong assumption.

"We've got a body," he said, stepping away from the light. "Black male, maybe thirty. One of Ashley's security guards."

"Shit. Is Ashley okay?"

"Don't know. I've only made it to her driveway."

"I'll be there in thirty, an hour max."

"Better call in the parade."

"I'm on it. Don't go in alone, okay?"

"Rodger dodger."

"Promise me, Parker."

He promised. When she arrived, he'd explain that Wayob was Johnson, and that Ashley was in imminent danger, and that going inside was basically procedure, except for the fact that he was on suspension, but still, he couldn't wait for backup.

He hung up the call and started down through the gate, toward Ashley's house. The fog thickened. Billowed cold against his face. Thirty yards ahead, the driveway faded into nothing. No telling how much further it was to the house.

He heard something. A whimper, maybe? He paused and listened but heard only an absence of sound. An acoustic dulling. As if the fog had muffled sound as well as sight.

He glanced back up the hill. The drifting cloud had muted the booth down to a wavering smudge of dim light.

His heavy soles clacked on the concrete. Each step resonated in the silence. He moved off the concrete onto the wet grass. It soaked through his pant cuffs and his socks, whispering his progress step by step. He aimed his Beretta ahead, into the darkness.

Faint lights appeared through the mist. Growing brighter as he approached, drifting into focus. Floodlights. The shadow of a roofline, a turret.

Her house blocked the fog as it rose up the mountain, forcing it higher, and he emerged in the clearing it created, exposed. The mist drifted overhead for a ways before finding its weight up the hill behind him.

In the turnout behind the garage was a Land Rover parked at an angle to the house. The driver's side door was open. Saul crept toward it.

An electric growl erupted. Saul froze. His heart hammered in his chest as the garage door eased upward and light spilled out from below it. He ran the last few yards to the Rover. Crouched behind it and peered around.

Inside the garage, a white Mercedes sedan sparked its ignition. The engine revved. Through the rear window, he saw Wilson at the wheel and Ashley in the passenger seat.

He hurried toward them. "Stop!"

The reverse lights came on, and Wilson gunned the Mercedes. The rear of the white sedan swerved toward him. Ashley—or was it Wilson in Ashley's body?—looked over her shoulder at Saul, eyes wide with panic.

He stumbled back, but the car was reversing too fast—they were going to hit him. His only hope was to reduce the impact by leaping onto the trunk. He jumped, but his feet had hardly left the ground before the bumper clipped his knee. His belly smashed into the trunk. Metal crumpled and bent. Despite all his padding, pain shot through his ribs.

In his struggle to hold on, he accidentally fired the Beretta, which he had forgotten was still in his hand. It had a trigger safety—no safety at all in a situation like this.

His ears rang from the discharge.

The Mercedes slammed to a stop, rocked back on its shocks, and threw him onto the pavement just short of the Rover. The gun clattered beside him.

Go

Ashley expects blood when she looks down after hearing the shot, but there is none. She's fine. She looks Gray over. He doesn't appear wounded either, and none of the windows are broken. Relief floods through her.

"You okay?" She's almost getting used to seeing him in her body, but not quite.

"We're blocked in." He flings his door open.

They get out and find Parker sprawled on the concrete between her back bumper and August's Land Rover and beside the Land Rover is a gun.

"His gun!" Gray dives across Parker's vast torso.

But Parker reaches for it first. "LAPD," he says. "I'm not Wayob."

Of course Wayob would say he's not Wayob.

Parker's fingers almost reach the gun as Gray grabs his arm. Ashley leaps over it and kicks the gun away, and it clatters off under the Land Rover. Then she kicks him in the side. "You tried to kill us!"

"Accidental discharge," he groans through clenched teeth. "Here to help."

"Then do something," Gray shouts in his face. "He killed Claire."

"Leave him. Let's go."

Parker gulps for air. "Call Detective Hernandez at Homicide Special. She'll tell you. They're on the way."

Ashley drags Gray off him. Even if Parker isn't Wayob, the police can't help them and they both know it. *Wayob can be anyone.* They can't be here. They have to get away, go somewhere Wayob can't find them.

Gray gets to his feet and steadies himself, staring out into the fog as if in a trance. She takes his hand and leads him around the Land Rover, ignoring Parker's pleas for them to wait.

Of course, the keys aren't in the ignition, and she's not about to go search August's corpse. She can't recall him ever driving it himself.

"Do you have the keys to my car?" Gray asks.

"They're in the ignition. Hopefully it's still parked on the road."

They hurry up the driveway, but the fog is so thick it seems to slow their progress. As they pass the cottage, something scratches at the glass door. A black shadow.

"What was that?" Gray asks.

It must be Shera, the stray she'd told Sammy to get rid of. "Just a dog." She tries to laugh at her fear, but she can't.

"What's it doing in there?"

Sammy had kept her, despite her order, and he was right: she needs a home. "I'm going to adopt her," she says.

Shera growls so deeply that Ashley feels it in her bones. She shivers. Shera launches into the window, falls back from the glass, and barks and barks.

Ashley starts jogging toward the cottage. "Something's wrong with her."

Gray grabs her arm and pulls her back. "She might be Wayob."

"But what if she's not? We can't just leave her trapped in there."

"We have to. Just for now."

She can see that he's right, but if Shera is Wayob, that means she kicked a cop after hitting him with her car. Unless Wayob had already jumped from Parker to Shera. Was that possible? *If he can move that fast, how can we ever escape?* The thought spurs her legs into motion.

As they ascend the driveway toward the blurred halo of light emanating from the security booth, she listens for the sound of Franco's TV, but the fog is like gauze in her ears, soaking up all the sounds of the night into a silence so alive it almost rings.

"Franco?" He must have heard Shera's bark.

As they near, Franco's arm comes into focus, hanging lifelessly out the window, his body leaning against the frame, head tilted at an odd angle.

They stop. Fog thickens around them, as if it could erase Franco's dead body, the gory hole in his cheek, and the whole horrible night.

Behind them, a crash—glass shattering. She wheels around and strains to make out the vague blur of the cottage. If they were lucky, it was just Shera jumping through the front window and not Wayob.

"Ashley!" Gray breaks into a run.

She pumps her legs as fast as she can. Gray's legs still feel awkward when she runs.

She tries to focus on Gray, his long blonde hair—her hair—flowing back in the wind. But she stumbles.

The piercing howl that emanates from close behind them leaves little doubt that it's Wayob in Shera's body. Ashley catches herself and continues running, not daring to look back. Can't slow down.

As they sprint past the palm trees at the top her driveway, she begins to doubt herself. Did she really leave the keys in Gray's car?

Fog seems to clot around the security lamps where her driveway meets the road. As they clear the hedge, she sees a Tesla Roadster parked on the street a few yards away—and in the driver's seat is her dad.

After all her texts and calls, how can he be just sitting there?

In the dim light, he looks gaunt, pale, like he's aged years in the month since she last saw him. His eyes dart around in a panic, completely devoid of his characteristic confidence. And since when does he leave the house without styling his hair? It's twirled around all crazy.

"Dad?"

Ashley yanks at the passenger door. It's locked. Behind the glass, he mouths something... *Sorry*? He's sorry?

She slaps the window. "Dad, it's me." She's in Gray's body, but still. She points at Gray, who is hurrying toward his own car behind the Tesla. "Look."

But he shakes his head *no* and refuses to look. He faces forward, eyes wide, hands tight on the steering wheel.

Ashley raises her hands. "What the hell?"

"Ashley! Come on!" Gray leaps into his car.

Down the mountain a chaotic stream of flashing blue lights cuts through the fog, coming up fast.

The Tesla rolls forward with hardly a whisper from the electric engine.

"Where are you going?" She runs out in front of him. If he thinks he's leaving with no explanation, he's going to have to run over her.

He frantically motions her aside. That's when she hears the claws pattering on the pavement, and before she can so much as turn, paws hit her back, shoving her forward.

She falls to the ground. As she rolls over, a blur of black fur leaps onto her chest, baring its teeth, stale breath in her face.

"Here, doggie," Gray says. "Wayob want the Encanto?"

The dog turns toward Gray, who stands a few paces down the road, holding the white stone. "Yeah, you want this, don't you?"

The animal leaps off.

"No," her dad says, and all of a sudden he's out of the car. "You must not let Wayob have the Encanto!"

What the hell? Ashley scrambles to her feet.

Gray reels his arm back as if to throw the stone and pretends to let it loose. Wayob launches across the road in the direction of Gray's fake throw.

Gray stands there a moment, as if he can't believe that worked.

Wayob skids to a stop. The black head swivels back to Gray, gaze locked on the stone still in his hand. Gray backs toward his car. No way he'll make it.

"Throw it to me," her father yells, running toward the driveway. "Let me take care of Wayob. This is my fault. Go somewhere safe."

Ashley glances from her dad to Wayob, who is crouching, muscles tensed, as he creeps toward Gray. She marches forward and before Wayob can leap, she grabs his collar. He thrashes and snarls, pure muscle. She widens her stance, holding his collar with both hands. His whole body turns, head twisting up to slash teeth at her arm. Nothing she can do now to stop him; she holds on through the pain. He growls and writhes and jerks his collar free from her grip.

The black blur whirls toward Gray, who runs backward and—just before

Wayob reaches him—throws the Encanto for real.

Her dad, who has made it to the driveway, catches the stone with both hands. And fumbles. The stone smacks the pavement.

Ashley moves to grab Wayob as he charges for the Encanto. Oily fur slides through her fingers, but she manages to grab his tail and yanks it back. Wayob lands on his muzzle but quickly recovers, jerking free of her grip. But she did buy a second for her dad, maybe two. He has the stone now, and he's running.

Gray's feet slap the pavement as he sprints for his car. "Get in!" he shouts at her.

As she slides in, he guns the engine. The accceleration throws her door closed.

She braces for the right turn, but he banks in the opposite direction, away from her driveway where her dad is sprinting toward the guard booth.

"Where are you going?" she says. "We have to help him."

"Like he helped us?"

She pulls the handbrake. "He did help us."

She throws open the door in time to see her dad reach the booth, slip inside, and shut the door in Wayob's face. Parker has made it to the gate. Sirens wail through the canyon and blue lights are closing in.

"Even if Parker believes us," Gray says, "they'll hold us for hours. We'll be sitting ducks. I have to think about my kids. Claire's dead."

Gray's right. They have to go. She pulls the door closed.

As they plow up the road and into the fog, mist droplets gather on the windshield. Gray flicks on the wipers.

———

By the time Saul reached the gate, a numbness had crept into his arms. Not good. At the booth, he stumbled and nearly grabbed the dead guard's arm for support.

"Careful," Luna said from inside. "That dog is Wayob."

Saul staggered a few steps, and then his legs gave out. He slumped against the booth. Wiped cold sweat from his forehead. Too dizzy to move.

But he had to…

Wayob growled. His claws scratched uselessly on the door.

Luna struggled to get the window closed, the arm of the dead guard still in the way.

Wayob landed beside Saul, turned, and then leaped and sailed through the open window. Luna screamed.

As the fog twisted over Saul, he heard snarling followed by a wet ripping sound, and a meaty thud as something heavy fell against a hard surface.

Then a yelp. A clack of stone on pavement.

He found the strength to turn his head—just in time to see the Encanto rolling onto the driveway. The window slammed shut. Luna moaned and began gasping.

Saul forced himself to his knees. The booth swayed before him. He felt nauseous. No chance of helping Luna, whether Wayob was killing him or merely trying to take his body.

The ground turned sideways and crashed into Saul. More barks and howls echoed out from the booth. He had to reach the Encanto before Wayob emerged.

Covered in a fresh layer of sweat, he dragged himself in the direction the stone had rolled, around the corner of the booth. It had almost reached the gate before stopping in the grass.

The few yards between him and the Encanto stretched out like a vast yawning canyon. If he could just stay conscious... Where was Hernandez? He must look pathetic floundering in the driveway, but it was all he could do.

He rested on his belly, struggling to catch his breath. The back of his neck prickled.

Someone was watching.

He gulped air. Forced himself to roll over.

As the fog swam above him, he clenched his eyes shut against the nausea. He leaned on his elbows, trying not to think about the numbness in his arms, and opened his eyes. He was only ten feet from the booth. In the window, the dead guard had been replaced by two paws against the glass. The dog's burning black eyes seemed to reach down into Saul and shake his soul.

His heart pumped wildly. In those glassy eyes he saw his own pathetic reflection. And he saw the fog. The fog which had fallen over everything he thought he knew and understood. And in this fog, logic held no sway, magic had no explanation.

And he had allowed it to blind him from the awful truth—the hopelessness of ever holding Hernandez's heart.

Saul lay sideways and held Wayob's gaze. Clutching his chest so hard his fingers pierced the skin.

He held that horrible stare until it seemed he was looking into himself. And then he had to look away. Look away or die right here with Wayob watching the strength drain out of him.

He rolled onto his belly and continued crawling. The ache in his chest sharpened. His arms were nothing more than fat slabs of meat strangely connected to his torso. He flung them ahead and rocked himself forward like a seal blubbering onto a beach.

He gulped and wheezed and failed to get enough air into his lungs. His vision dimmed.

An overwhelming fear paralyzed him. What had happened to Wilson and Ashley York in the fog above the driveway?

Maybe he could have saved them all, if only he had just eaten a piece of broccoli every once in a while, if only he'd done an occasional push-up instead of all the sitting and eating saturated fats.

Luna's horrible choking sounds had died out. He had sacrificed himself to prevent Wayob from reaching the Encanto.

I can't die, Saul thought. Not now, not with so much unfinished business, so much mystery left in the world to uncover. Must reach the Encanto. He flopped himself forward.

He actually felt Wayob's eyes boring into his back. The sirens grew louder. *No one goes near the dog,* he'd have to tell them. For their own safety. But how to make them heed his warning? And the dog must be held in isolation to prevent Wayob from escaping it. Could dogs commit suicide? Wayob would have to be restrained such that he couldn't gnaw through some vital artery.

Saul needed to close his eyes for just a minute. Must rest. But if he stopped now, he knew the pain in his chest would overtake him. He would never start again.

He managed to flounder across the driveway, to within a few feet of the Encanto. He reached out with numb fingers but couldn't quite grasp it. He tapped it toward him. It rolled closer. He pawed open the side pocket of his coat and raked the white stone in with his fist.

He struggled onto his back, intending to sit up, but... the fog drifting over him made him dizzy. He felt like slipping away...

Darkness surrounded him.

Above, at some great distance away, a needle of light pierced the sky.

Which burst all at once. Light cracked the clouds with such a force that it resounded like a double bass drum in his head. Some unseen weight crushed his chest. He tried to call out but couldn't. No air in his lungs. He could not move. He felt his life shrinking inward. And then he felt nothing. No pain. It was as if he had no body at all. He was just a head now, a brain. That was all anyone ever was, really.

His vision dimmed at the edges. The clouds melted away. He lay there, gazing up into the shimmering stars. If he could just get through this, he'd eat right, he'd exercise.

Between the stars, the darkness flickered. Not like night at all. And the stars were winking and sparking. Spinning. Flashing.

—

Gray drives uphill and away from Ashley's, away from the sirens and the flashing lights and the only woman he ever loved—dead and abandoned on the lawn. But what choice did they have?

Ashley grimaces, holding the gash in her forearm as blood oozes between her fingers.

"How deep is it?"

"I can barely move my hand."

While keeping his eye on the road, he reaches back and feels around for the drool bib on Tyler's car seat.

"Sorry, this is all I have."

"Seriously?" She turns on the interior light and studies it. "I can't even tell what these stains are."

"They're from before it was washed," Gray says, though he has no idea. It's not like their shirts are any better. "You have to stop the bleeding."

"It's your arm, I guess." She groans as she wraps the bib around it.

They pass the outer guard gate and reach Mulholland. Gray glances at the phone mount clipped to his vent. Without his phone he feels lost. How long has it been since he found his way without a phone?

"Left," Ashley says. "We'll go to Malibu. That's probably what Dad had in mind when he said to go somewhere safe. He wouldn't have wanted to say it in front of Wayob; our Malibu house is kind of a secret."

Gray turns right, presumably toward the 101 and Silver Lake. "We have to take my kids." For now, at least, he knew Wayob was the dog, but how long would that last? "What do you think your dad meant when he said he could take care of Wayob?"

"He always does what he says." Ashley sighs. "But I don't see how. I don't even understand what just happened. How did he know about Wayob? It could have been some rabid dog chasing us."

"That was my next question. Listen, I understand if you don't want to go with me, and I have no idea what to tell Mindy about Claire, or how to even attempt it in your body, but I can't just disappear on them."

Ashley slumps back. "I get it." Her eyes close.

He rounds a curve, passing an overlook where an abandoned Civic with a dented bumper is parked in the fog spilling over the cliff, where it dissolves into the warmer air rising from the valley. Far below, the lights keep right on shimmering in the night, indifferent to his terrible loss.

The tires hit uneven pavement and thump off the road. He jerks the wheel and swerves back into his lane.

"Slow down," Ashley says.

But he's afraid to slow down, afraid she'll demand he go back for her father, and he will lose his own resolve—he left Claire back there. How can he protect Mindy and Tyler?

He watches the odometer turn the miles. Each revolution seems to take five minutes, even though he's hit fifty-five.

Mindy and Tyler are all he has now. More important than even his own life. He'll feel better once he's with them—so long as he's not putting them in danger.

The one thing that seemed to distract Wayob was the Encanto, and Gray still had a piece of it. He recalled the intensity with which Wayob had launched himself after Evan York, not even seeming to notice Ashley and Gray leaving, or Parker approaching up the driveway. Parker, who Gray had painted *before* seeing him in real life. Maybe Parker isn't as big as in the portrait, but still, it was Parker he had drawn—no doubt about it.

If Parker had been trying to stop Wayob, then Wayob had seen him first. What if Wayob had been looking at Parker when Gray drew him?

What if that's what Rosa's grandmother meant when she told him that he has an eye? Maybe that was why she gave him the Encanto: because he can see through Wayob. He has been drawing what Wayob sees, Wayob's point of view.

That must be how he drew Franco with that mean smile, which he'd certainly never seen in real life... and yet Ashley told him it looked exactly like Franco. Like he must have looked just before Wayob shot him.

And when Gray drew the dark swirl, he was in his own body; therefore, Wayob must have been in the Encanto at that time.

What had Wayob said about the darkness?

It makes sense, he thinks. If Wayob can find Gray, like he claims, then why can't it work both ways? The idea is no crazier than anything else that's happened in the past few days. When he draws, he sees what Wayob sees, so if Wayob comes after them, Gray will know; he can draw Wayob's approach. And if he draws the black swirl again, then he'll know they're safe from Wayob.

"So," Ashley says, "after we get Mindy and Tyler, we'll go to Malibu. Okay? We'll figure this out together."

Gray likes the idea of the ocean, as if the salt water could somehow cleanse away all the death, and the evil, wash everything back to the way it was, to Saturday night before Rosa's grandmother gave him the damn Encanto.

"Okay," Gray says. "Mindy and Tyler will think you're their father." He's going to need her help.

Ashley shrugs and cracks her window. Air blows in, thick with the scent of desert sage. She crosses her arms and hunches, gazing out into the night.

Gray slides a hand into his pocket, running his finger over the feathered ridges of the obsidian snake, the broken dial from the Encanto. Is this how it is now? Is he doomed to live outside of his own life gazing in?

A sour taste wells up from his throat. He swallows and rests his hand on the center console, next to Ashley's leg that was his leg. The closeness, somehow, helps him feel a little more like himself.

Hernandez Turns Toward Saul

Hernandez leaned into the turn. Blue and red strobes swept the fog ahead of her. Parker had obviously ignored her order and entered the premises on his own, and now he wasn't answering his phone. *Damn it, Parker.* Her mind jumped from one horrible scenario to the next.

She spun into Ashley York's driveway, her tires squealing as she plowed through the yellow tape and nearly clipped the uniform unrolling it as she steered off into the grass to avoid hitting him. That's when she saw the ambulance backed up to the security booth.

She leaped out of her Mustang. A beam of light from a chopper cut through the mist and narrowed on the lawn by Ashley's mansion.

"This is a crime scene!" the uni yelled over the chop. With his smooth skin and rosy cheeks, he looked nineteen, though he had to be older.

She flashed her badge. "Where's Parker?"

"Who?"

"Who's in the ambo?"

"I don't know but he's a goner."

She sprinted toward the ambulance, ignoring the uni's shouts.

Behind the ambulance, a hulk-sized body overflowed a gurney as if it were a toy. Parker.

He wasn't moving. His eyes were closed.

Her vision blurred as she rushed toward him, her arms reaching. She would have thrown herself across his vast torso except she feared the sheet covered a bullet wound, so instead she cradled his big, beautiful, block-shaped face. His cheeks were cold.

Something tore in her chest. If she'd kept him in the MDC, he'd have lived.

Her tears fell into the furrows of his forehead. At least he'd died knowing she believed him, and she had needed to believe this big, beautiful man.

She ran her fingers through his graying hair. It was softer than she expected. "No. You can't be dead."

It wasn't fair. She never got to tell him how she felt.

A kid in an EMT uniform jumped down from the ambulance. He had a pale, shiny face and bloodshot eyes. Twenty-five, at the most. Was anyone here over thirty?

With practiced speed, he hung a bag of fluid above the gurney and attached the IV.

Her mouth fell open and it took a moment for her to find the words, to ask the only question that mattered: "He's alive?"

The kid nodded. "I gave him an ampule of epinephrine, but his pulse is still thready."

She glanced down at Saul. His chest rose. His massive jaw quaked. He was alive. If she weren't worried about injuring him further, she'd have climbed onto the gurney right then and there.

"What are you waiting for?" she said to the kid. "Let's get him to the hospital."

"My partner will be back in a minute. He's helping out with the airlift for the other patient."

Hernandez moved to lift one end of the gurney. "Your partner can ride in the chopper."

The kid just stood there.

"Get moving or I'll report you for negligence," she said.

That got him moving. As he strapped Saul to the gurney, her legs turned to jelly. She clutched the gurney's rail for support.

"She's going to faint," someone yelled from behind her. The other EMT, a trauma bag slung over his shoulder, jogged through the gate.

"I'm fine," she lied. "Fire this monkey up."

The EMTs rolled the gurney into the back of the ambulance while she held on to the door. Saul's massive form bulged against the straps. The feeling came back in her legs.

She climbed in and managed to sit upright on the metal bench. Cold through her slacks.

The big engine fired up, as did a faint beeping from the bio monitor the kid had attached. Hernandez's own heart pounded in her throat.

The kid locked the gurney in place, shut the doors, and strapped himself into the seat beside her. The ambulance started rolling.

She leaned forward and traced the grooves on Saul's forehead. Last night, when she offered to watch him sleep, he didn't get what she meant. Maybe she herself hadn't understood, then—but she knew now. She wanted to do a lot more than just watch him sleep.

What they could have together seemed more meaningful than the LAPD policy on relationships between partners. Life was too short to waste on bullshit. *Live as if you were to die tomorrow*, Gandhi had said.

Fuck protocol.

Saul's eyelids flickered.

"Saul," she said.

He blinked his eyes open. Looked around wildly. His heartbeat accelerated. The kid's hands moved swiftly on the equipment.

"Thank god!" She fumbled for his hand. "Stay with me. Saul, you have to stay with me."

"Hernandez." He pushed against the restraints.

"Call me Rhonda." Tears streamed down her cheeks.

"Rhon-da. I could get used to that."

"Unstrap him," she said.

"Not while we're moving," the kid said. "I gave him a sedative. He'll be out soon."

Saul turned toward the kid. "Where are you taking me?"

"Cedars."

As the ambulance rounded a curve, Hernandez grabbed the straps beside her. His mouth opened and closed.

"You're going to be fine," she said. If only saying so made it true. She leaned over him and brushed a wisp of hair from his forehead.

His eyes fluttered to stay open. "I scratched your... rims."

She gulped back the lump in her throat. "I know." Her Mustang didn't matter. It was just a thing. "What happened?"

Saul's brows knotted. "I was going to tell you on the phone and... I got distracted—"

"Forget the rims. I mean, what happened at Ashley's?"

Saul swallowed. "How many bodies?"

"Five. Plus one more that's critical."

Saul's eyes widened. "You think... it was me?"

"Of course not. Were they dead when you arrived?"

Saul grimaced. "Not Luna. We arrived together."

"Which Luna?"

"Luis Luna."

Were the meds affecting his memory? "Luis Luna was murdered on Friday. Remember? He was bludgeoned to death on Lincoln."

"That was Evan York. He and Luna switched bodies."

Hernandez pushed the hair back from her forehead. It was a lot to take in. But Saul was hard to convince, so if he believed it then she believed him.

He squirmed against the straps. "You have to get me out of here. I have to take care of Wayob."

"You just had a heart attack. You almost died."

"Wayob took Rosa."

"What do you mean *took* her?" If Wayob had dared to so much as look at Rosa...

"She's gone. Luna thought she might still be alive. Wayob is trapped in Ashley York's guard booth, in the body of a dog. No one goes near him until I get there."

"I'll take care of it. You just get better. You hear me? We'll take care of Wayob."

"Guess I'm still suspended." He tried to smile, but his lips trembled. A look of fear came into his eyes.

"Fuck suspended," she said. "We're partners."

Saul made a guttural noise in his throat, which could have been a laugh or a groan. He squeezed her hand. His lids lost the battle against whatever the EMT had given him.

Partners. She should have said what she really meant, but with the kid right there it seemed like the wrong place to say it.

And now he was out cold, but still she held his hand all the way to Cedars, watching him breathe as the bio monitor echoed his heartbeat. Carpe. Carpe. Carpe. Diem.

To Malibu

As they speed down the 101, Ashley leans her head against the window, exhausted. Gray is hunched over the wheel, staring ahead at the road in what looks like a semi-catatonic state, probably broken up about Claire. She opens her mouth to say something, but only air comes out. Her thoughts are so scrambled from all that has happened she doesn't know where to begin. He just lost his wife; nothing she can say will comfort him.

She lets her eyes close because she knows there's no chance of sleep. She may never sleep again, because behind her eyelids is Sammy's face, dying again and again—by her hand. *You had no choice*, she reminds herself, but after killing another human being, a man she cared about...life will never be the same.

And her last words to him—after Sammy declared his love for her—had been "I know." She knew? She could have said she loved him too. It didn't have to mean I-want-you-babe.

The truth was, she was attracted to him, though maybe she'd never have acted on it. All those times lying out in a G-string, hoping he'd notice. All those times she'd touched his arm and lingered. He must have felt the chemistry. Had she led him on? He'd buried Andrea's body to protect her. If not for her, he'd still be alive.

And seeing her dad had only made her feel worse: the way he looked at her like she was the last person he wanted to see, the way he just sat there in his Tesla—the only man in the world who could break her heart—just shaking his head as Wayob chased her.

She'd seen that look before. Maybe not since she was eight, when InGenetic was releasing some weight-loss drug that so excited the older girls at Oakhurst Academy that they watched the press conference on the lounge TV. When her dad started speaking, Shayla—this was during the divorce—yelled out from the crowd that he was a fraud. He stuttered, his smile vanished, and for a moment he lost his train of thought as security surrounded

Shayla and escorted her out. He'd had that same stunned expression on his face then.

She knew that if Gray hadn't come to her rescue, she might have been killed; her dad had sprung into action only when Gray held up the Encanto, as though that accursed stone mattered more to him than her. It wasn't like him. Once she gets to a phone that works, he'll have a lot of explaining to do.

Although the bleeding has stopped, her arm is still throbbing, and the scab has glued the dirty rag to the wound. She decides to have her doctor visit them at Gray's, and not just for the arm; once they get through this, she'll need some help sleeping.

As they approach Gray's house, he sighs. "Belinda's here." He points out a cherry-red Kia sporting a green bumper sticker with the slogan, *I Think, Therefore I'm Vegan.* "You have to go in on your own or we'll never get out of here."

"What do I say?"

"As little as possible. Just say Claire..." His eyebrows scrunch together. He gazes at the house. "Say you haven't seen Claire. I don't know. She's going to ask all kinds of questions. Give her an extra fifty bucks and say you need some sleep."

"What fifty bucks?" Aside from Gray's clothes, she has nothing.

Gray pats his pockets, which she knows are empty, and shakes his head. "Unless someone moved it, my wallet should be on the table beside the couch."

Ashley holds up her throbbing arm. "What about this?"

Gray leans his head back on the headrest, his face pale in the light reflecting off the house. "You fell?" His eyes are bloodshot and dark bags are forming under them. She hopes they'll return to normal if she, somehow, gets back to her body and gets some rest.

As she opens the door to get out, Gray starts the engine. She hesitates. "Wait, where are you going?"

"To park down the street. I don't want her to see me— Uh, see you, I mean."

As Ashley approaches the front door, it swings open. A frizzy brunette in tight jeans with a muffin top peers out.

"Where's she going?" Belinda asks.

Ashley glances over her shoulder. Maybe she thinks that's Claire in Gray's car?

"She had to run an errand. It's been a long night. Let's get you paid so you can get out of here."

In the living room, Ashley sits on the couch and sifts through the mess on the coffee table. She finds no sign of Gray's wallet in the disorganized pile of magazines and papers there.

"Claire promised she'd be home by nine." Belinda makes a big show of studying her phone. "Which is two hours ago. What happened?"

"Sorry about that." Ashley finds the *Vogue* magazine with her cover shot but not Gray's wallet, nor does it appear to be on the floor in the disarray of kids' stuff and clothes.

"I called her like five times," Belinda continues. "I told her I couldn't stay late."

"I'll be right back."

"Seriously?" Belinda crosses her arms as Ashley hurries by. "What happened to your arm?"

In the bedroom, Ashley finds Gray's wallet on the dresser next to the disposable phone she bought after smashing his.

"Holy shit!" Belinda's voice reverberates down the hall.

Ashley hurries back in the living room, where Gray stands near the doorway, motioning with his palms for Belinda to chill.

Belinda's head swivels to Ashley and back to Gray, who she thinks is Ashley. "That was you in Gray's car, wasn't it? Does Claire know?"

"I'm here to surprise her," Gray says. "So, if you don't mind."

"Oh, yeah. Of course." She slings a milk-white arm around Gray and holds out her phone. "I really thought those photos of you and Gray were fake."

"Actually"—Ashley reaches to block the camera—"no selfies."

But Belinda has already snapped the picture. She shoves the phone into the tight pocket of her jeans before Ashley can grab it. She backs away toward the door. "I'm not going to post it or anything. I don't do Facebook. I just want to show my boyfriend."

"Great." Ashley advances on her. She doubts the photo can really do any more damage once the news breaks about the massacre at her house. "But still…"

Belinda opens the door and backs through. "Okay, I've really got to get going."

Gray grabs the knob, preventing Belinda from pulling the door closed after her. "Should I stop her?"

Ashley shrugs. "Not worth it. At least we got rid of her."

From the driveway, Belinda snaps another shot of Gray in Ashley's body. Behind him, Ashley tries to pull him back from the door.

"Don't worry," Belinda says, "I'll send these to Claire. She'll never believe this."

Gray turns to Ashley. "If she doesn't post it herself, no doubt she'll share it with someone who will."

"It's okay."

"Really?" Gray shuts the door. "I should have waited in the car, but it was taking so long—"

"It's really okay. I'm done with social media."

"Wow."

She remains in the foyer while he goes to check on Mindy and Tyler. Claire's absence seems to hang in the air. Ashley crosses her arms, hugging herself. She's ready to get to Malibu.

From the hallway closet, she borrows one of Gray's coats and pulls it on.

He emerges from Mindy's room and hurries to the living room, where he rummages through the mess on the floor, digs out a box of colored pencils and some paper, and shoves aside the magazines on the coffee table.

"Seriously? We need to get going. You can draw later."

"You saw my portrait of Parker."

"Yeah, it was amazing, but—"

"I didn't even know he was a real person when I painted him."

Ashley has a vague recollection of him saying this before. "How is that possible?"

"I don't know how, but remember my drawing of Franco? He never smiled once when I saw him, but while I was drawing him, I kept visualizing him with that expression, and it was so vivid."

"So, you're saying you had some kind of vision?"

"No. I'm pretty sure I was seeing Franco through Wayob's eyes, probably right before Wayob killed him."

"Okay." She can hardly claim it's impossible while she's stuck here in his body. And she saw him paint the uncanny resemblance—he had nailed Franco's fake smile. This theory did help explain it. "How long have you suspected this?"

"I just figured it out. If I'd known sooner, we could have saved Claire."

He hunches over the page, looking somehow more strung out and exhausted than her, if that's even possible. How's he going to deal with his kids?

"How about I get started packing up Mindy and Tyler?"

"Good idea," he says without looking up. "There's formula in the fridge, and they'll need some clothes and diapers and stuff."

It's only a start, and she wishes she could do more. Something that would really help him. As she starts toward the kitchen, something moves in her peripheral vision...

She whirls to the side. It's only her reflection of Gray's body in the glass doors to the deck. Behind it, someone could be right outside yet completely hidden in the darkness.

———

Gray begins sketching, but he finds it hard to focus in the eerie stillness that remains in the room. He wants to help pack Tyler and Mindy's things—he knows better than Ashley what they'll need—but more important right now is to make sure they're safe.

Maybe focusing isn't how this thing works. Maybe he has to let his mind wander. That's how it happened before. He surveys the pile of towels that has been there on the floor for days, the magazines and the coloring books. The constant mess pervading the house no longer seems like some unspoken mountain of ruin between him and Claire; it's just stuff, just insignificant stuff. That's all. What couple lasts a decade without at least some kind of stupid crap coming between them? If only he and Claire hadn't let it pile up. That's where they went wrong; they never resolved anything.

He glances at his drawing, almost surprised by the mesh of lines that has appeared on the page. It looks like a cage or a fence. Does this represent the Encanto imprisoning Wayob?

As he gains a sense of the image, he sketches faster. It is a cage, and the cage is in the back of a car. He outlines the rear window. Outside, police tape crisscrosses the familiar line of palms that flank Ashley's driveway. An officer, visible from the neck down, approaches with his hand on his belt.

Someone knocks.

Not on the car window; it's the front door—an insistent rapping. Gray's heart sinks. It's probably the police. They've found Claire's body. And if so, then they've also found all kinds of evidence linking him to her death, and perhaps to Sammy's death as well. Ashley killed him in self-defense, but they'd never believe it. She had been right about needing to go somewhere no one could find them, but he had hoped they'd have time.

He's not ready to deal with what happened, with Claire's loss. He just wants to be normal again. As he steels himself to answer the door, Ashley bursts out of the nursery carrying Tyler's diaper tote and the burner phone Gray had found in his pocket last night. What happened to his phone?

"He got here fast," she whispers.

"Who?"

"My doctor. I called him to treat your arm, technically, so pretend you're me and thank him profusely."

The relief that washes through Gray makes it hard to feel angry that she told someone where they are.

He opens the door for a clean-shaven man in his thirties cloaked in a black hoodie and points toward Ashley. When he learns he was summoned here to treat some random guy, he grumbles under his breath as he unpacks medical supplies from a gym bag.

Gray leaves him there with Ashley and tiptoes into Mindy's room to gather some clothes and books for her. Something snaps softly under the ball of his foot. He raises his leg. It's a pink crayon smashed into the beige carpet. As he bends down to pick it up, he recalls how oblivious Claire was to the mess, and a sob catches in the back of his throat. He leaves the crayon where it is.

"Who's here, Daddy?" Sleep slurs Mindy's voice.

Daddy. Gray glances at the nightlight, tempted to lunge across the room and shut it off, but it's too late: she is already sitting up.

"Ashley!" She leaps out of bed and throws her arms around his legs.

He squats and wraps his arms around her, the warmth of her little body thawing the ache in his chest. Anywhere is home so long as he has Mindy in his arms.

"You sounded like my dad." Mindy looks down at her feet. "But he left."

"No. He would never leave you." His voice cracks. "We're all going to the beach together. Pick out some stuffed buddies to bring with us."

Mindy gazes up at him with her big innocent eyes. "Mommy too?"

He swallows. "She's… She can't."

If this registers with Mindy, it doesn't show. She spins out of his arms, practically leaping to the foot of her bed, where the giant bear he gave her last night is resting.

"I don't think the big guy'll fit in my car. Got someone smaller wants to come?"

"How big is your car?"

"Your dad's car, I mean."

"He's here?"

She rushes out before he can tell her—he's not even sure what he could have said: *Your father might be acting a bit strange because it's really Ashley in his body?* No way.

He follows her to the living room, where she dives into Ashley's lap. Ashley hugs Mindy with her good arm while trying to keep the other one still as the doctor wraps it in gauze. It's not quite the big hug Gray wishes he could give her with his own arms. Mindy closes her eyes and smiles, seemingly accepting Ashley as him.

Ashley explains that she hurt her arm falling down, and Mindy sits back in her lap and watches the doctor work.

By the time Gray finishes packing Tyler's stuff, Mindy has already returned to her bedroom and crammed her backpack full of stuffed animals.

"I need you to pack some clothes too," Gray says, "okay?"

Mindy glances back at her bed. "My hand hurts."

Gray falls to his knees and snatches her arm harder than he meant to. He rips the Band-Aid from her palm and examines the wound where the Encanto stabbed her. It's almost healed, just a pink dot of new skin, which he has to hold himself back from kissing because Mindy hardly knows Ashley. He touches it gingerly. "Does that hurt?"

Mindy shakes her head.

"How about a new Band-Aid? I bet that'll make it feel better."

Mindy nods.

Gray goes to fetch the Band-Aids. When he returns, Mindy is sitting on her bed clutching her stuffed unicorn against her chest.

"Can I help you pick out some clothes?" he asks as he finishes applying the Band-Aid.

Mindy shakes her head. She hops down and shuffles toward her closet.

While Mindy is packing, Gray returns to the living room where Ashley is standing by the doctor near the foyer. The doctor fishes a handful of pill samples from his gym bag, hands some to Ashley and some to Gray, then looks at Gray with an expectant expression, like a valet waiting for a tip.

"Can you send me the bill?" Gray asks.

His brow furrows.

"Her phone's broken," Ashley says. "You usually pay from your phone, right?"

Gray nods.

"Just pay me later." The doctor starts toward the door. He pauses in the foyer and looks back at Gray again, his brows down.

Ashley whispers in Gray's ear, "Cheek kiss."

But Gray has never cheek kissed before. She nudges him forward. Fortunately, the doctor leaves before Gray can make the situation any more awkward by attempting the kiss.

He turns toward Ashley. "Do you think he was offended?"

She shrugs. "He's always like that."

———

As they barrel down the 10, Gray sketches on an envelope he found in the glovebox. Judging from the illustration, Wayob is still in the cage, and his agony is evident from the aggressive lines Gray finds himself sketching.

Gray turns in his seat to check on Mindy and Tyler, both fast asleep.

They speed through the McClure tunnel and out onto the PCH. Low clouds blockade the sky, casting an unending gloom over the ocean and the Santa Monica Pier. He wishes for rain. He wishes it would pour down and wash away the horror, but he knows it won't.

It had taken him a few years to adjust to the stoic skies of Southern California. During his junior year at UCLA it didn't rain at all. He'd met Claire that fall while he was wandering the quad, reeling from his breakup with Laura. He probably passed her three times before she looked up from her book and shielded her eyes from the golden light of that late afternoon. "You're wearing me out with all your walking," she said, and when she smiled, gazing up at him like she'd been waiting specifically for him to show up there and sit down beside her, he felt warm inside. When she lowered her hand, the sunlight caught in her irises like the horizon of some faraway sea, and he wanted to gaze into them forever.

Whatever either of them said next, he cannot remember now, but somehow she had agreed to go out with him. He'd hoped it was more than just curiosity on her part, because those eyes of hers... they seemed to see right through to his core and all that he could be.

At the beginning of their relationship, she didn't mind that he was an average student, because he had a head full of dreams, and she believed in his dreams, maybe even more than he did, and she was right to believe.

They had made it a month, maybe two, before everything changed. They had an argument over something so stupid he can't even remember what it was now, but he remembers how she shut down and walked away. Instead of letting it go like he should have, he'd gone looking for her. After finding her car missing from the lot, he'd waited on the steps outside her dorm, letting his legs go numb on the cold granite, staring into the shadows cast by a pine in the dull orange lights along the walkway.

Hours passed like days. When the steel light of dawn finally crept into the sky and faded the shadows of night, she appeared there below the steps, a storm brewing in her eyes—unreachable. She climbed past him and shoved through the heavy door to her dorm.

He remained there on the steps, lost, paralyzed.

Hours later she emerged, and the warmth had returned to her eyes. It was as though nothing had happened at all. She had just been out driving, she said, but she couldn't remember where. She just needed some air; that was all.

And when she smiled, he felt warm inside, like he was found, maybe even rescued, and he knew in that moment that without her, he would drown. He proposed right then and there.

She beamed brighter than the sunlight shining down on them, and without a flicker of indecision, she threw her arms around him and they fell back on the steps. He has no memory of the stairs being painful or hard, only of the way she kissed him when he told her he didn't care about the past, only the future —their future—together.

He had meant it, he really had, but... the fact that she refused to say where she had gone that night dwelled in the back of his mind where it undermined his confidence in their relationship.

He couldn't stop himself from asking, maybe a dozen more times, where had she gone? And each time she gave the same answer, more and more sternly: she had just driven around to get some air.

And now he'll never know. The answer died with her.

Ashley stops at a light. Below the bluff, dark waves crash against the rocks. Gray can see now how he was the problem, how he was on a treadmill expecting to get somewhere, when if he'd just stopped running, maybe things would have been fine. Maybe he should have just packed the car one morning and driven them all down here to the beach. Claire might have enjoyed it, if he'd somehow made her leave her phone behind. She always talked about wanting to go out for the day. How could he have left her—the woman of his dreams—lying face up in the grass, her body not even cold yet.

At a narrow strand of houses crammed between the shoreline and the PCH, Ashley merges into the turn lane. Headlights from an oncoming car flood the windshield. Ashley waits for it to pass then parks behind a box-like house constructed from concrete and framed with wood that almost touches the neighbors' houses. It's a letdown compared to the sort of place he had imagined.

Ashley bites her lip and gets out of the car. Gray follows her to a panel by the garage where she punches in a code. The garage door buzzes into action.

A Latina emerges from a Prius parked next door, her curly hair and hoop earrings bouncing as she waves with a star-struck smile.

"We've got company," Gray says.

"I hired a nanny." She waves at the Latina.

"Were you going to tell me?" The question comes out more sarcastic than intended; he is so exhausted.

"Should I tell her to leave?"

"No, I could use the help."

Ashley ducks down, peeking under the door as it raises. Her shoulders slump.

"What?" he asks, peering in. The garage is completely empty. Not even a trace of oil on the concrete.

She scans the street and frowns. "He had plenty of time to get here."

"Who?"

"My dad and I always planned that if anything happened and we couldn't get in touch, we would meet here."

The nanny squeezes between the car and the house, her smile growing impossibly wider with each step. "Hey, I'm Marta, and I'm a huge fan! Guess I parked at the wrong house; should I move my car?"

"Do you mind parking across the street?" Ashley says. "We're keeping the garage open for my dad."

Marta glances at Gray, who nods confirmation, and then she hurries off to park.

When Gray begins unstrapping Tyler from his car seat, she appears back beside him, out of breath. "Let me do that."

If anyone can get Tyler out without waking him, Gray can, but if he's going to trust Marta with his son, he might as well start now. He backs out to give her some room.

"Ordinarily I don't respond this late at night," she said, "but your text really pulled at my heart strings."

Wondering what she said, Gray glances toward Ashley, who is lifting Mindy from the other side of the car. Mindy's arms drape around her neck.

They follow Ashley into the garage. Mindy squints from the light and buries her face in Ashley's shirt.

Marta coos to Tyler that he's the cutest baby in the world as she cradles him to her chest.

"Thanks for coming on such short notice," Ashley whispers to her.

"Of course," Marta says. "How are you holding up?"

"Still in shock, I think."

Whether Ashley was answering for herself or him, he does indeed feel like he's still in shock, and he grimaces. Mindy may seem half asleep, but she takes everything in, and sooner or later, she'll ask, and he will have to tell her that her mother is dead. The reality of it seems distant, shrouded in haze, almost like a dream he can still wake up from.

He opens the door to the kitchen and holds it for Ashley and Marta. Inside, the kitchen steps down to a vast living room with a wall of glass that looks out over the expanse of black water. Ashley flicks on the lights, and the dark water is replaced with a reflection of the interior.

She leads them downstairs to a den, which she says they can use as a nursery. Long slats of reclaimed wood run lengthwise along the walls, and the white pile carpet looks like a fresh install. At the far end of the room, glass doors open to a deck that seems to hang out over the ocean.

Mindy struggles free of Ashley's arms and runs to look out. Across the bay, the lights of Santa Monica glisten on the waves.

Ashley and Gray retrieve the supplies from the car and carry them downstairs. Mindy is on the couch, next to Marta, looking at a magazine.

Tyler wakes in Marta's arms and she rocks him gently. "Does this handsome man have a favorite lullaby?"

"Twinkle, Twinkle, Little Star," Gray says.

Marta scrunches her brows. The question had been directed at Ashley, but she recovers without missing a beat. "My favorite too."

"How are you on sleep?" Ashley asks her.

"Don't worry about me. I'm on for as long as you need me. A day, a week, whatever. You two rest." She glances from Ashley to Gray. "I'll take care of everything."

Gray kneels beside Mindy and strokes her hair. "Let's get you into a bed."

As he tries to lift her, she wiggles out of his arms and runs behind Ashley, where she peers out from behind the legs that should be his—*are his*, from her point of view. She smiles her shy smile, and it lifts his spirits more than he could have hoped.

He pretends to pout. She's okay, or she will be once he figures out how to explain this situation, which he still hasn't accepted himself. Given time, she'll rebound.

"I guess you want your dad to tuck you in, huh?" Ashley says, and winks at him.

Mindy nods up at her.

She takes Mindy's hand and leads her to a bedroom by the stairs.

Marta leans toward Gray and whispers, "I know it's none of my business, but isn't that the man who attacked you yesterday?"

"It was more like a misunderstanding," he says.

"Oh." Her eyes go wide and she makes big sweeping nods. "I see."

But she doesn't see, not even close. He transfers Tyler's formula from the cooler to the minifridge at the wet bar, then digs a sketchpad out of his backpack.

As he doodles, he lets his mind drift until the lines start to resemble something and the image materializes in his head. He's getting the hang of drawing what Wayob sees. Wayob has been moved to a bigger cage, probably a kennel, because the cage now faces another cage which contains a German shepherd. Above it is a sign that says, *To Protect and Serve.*

Ashley emerges from the bedroom and shuts the door carefully behind her. She puts a finger to her lips and motions for Gray to follow her.

She leads him up two flights of stairs to a vast white bedroom. "You can sleep in here, if you want."

He nods his thanks and crashes gratefully onto the bed, lies on his side and looks out at the dark, oily shimmer of distant boat lights flickering on the waves.

He's surprised when Ashley's weight sinks into the mattress behind him. But, if she wants to lay on her own bed, at this point what does he care?

"What did you tell Marta in your text?"

"I said you lost your wife. Not much else I could say."

He inhales. He'll have to claim Claire's body from the police, if they don't arrest him for murder first. The longer he and Ashley hide out here, the more guilty they'll seem.

But he's so tired. The burden is so heavy. If only he could just let it all go, just for a few minutes...

Surf crashes beneath the house and retreats. He closes his eyes, letting the waves carry him away.

Artificial Sleep

Claire awakened, but she did not open her eyes. She had only a vague sense of her body, as if it were drifting, and by letting it drift she'd return to sleep, glorious sleep. A chemical haze blurred the edge of her consciousness, but it was nothing compared to the delirium of insomnia she'd finally slept her way out of. How long had she been out? Hours? Days?

Her last memory seemed more like a nightmare. She had gone to Ashley York's to save Gray from whatever he'd managed to get himself into, but before she found out what was going on, Ashley's crazy guard, with his maniacal grin and his perfect white teeth, had shot her. She must have passed out, because next she found herself on the ground with Ashley leaning over her, then Gray, then Ashley—her memory flickers between their two faces, but only one of them could have been real. She must have been drifting in and out of consciousness.

It must have been Gray touching her cheek the whole time. It made no sense the other way. She must have dreamed that Ashley yelled her name the way Gray says it. Or perhaps it was the blood loss combined with her insomnia that had distorted her perception? Gray had been there, right? She hadn't dreamed him holding her.

She had only blinked, it seemed, and then he was prying her eyelids apart, practically burning her retina with a light, except it wasn't Gray anymore but an EMT with slicked hair parted perfectly at the side.

"Don't go to sleep," he said.

Like that's an option, she tried to say but couldn't.

He poked and prodded and told her to wiggle her fingers and ankles, and then a female EMT, who Claire never got a good look at, joined him. They must have lifted her body, for she had a dim awareness of movement, more bright lights. A plastic mask with a tube came over her face, then blackness.

A long sleep.

She still had that feeling of floating, but now time had slowed back to normal. She opened her eyes… saw metal rails on the side of her bed. Her body had all kinds of wires and tubes jammed into it. She was in a hospital, but where? And what time was it?

There was no clock she could see. The small table was jammed between her bed and a beige curtain and the chair beside it was empty. Where was Gray? If he hadn't made it home, Belinda would have stayed with Tyler and Mindy, wouldn't she? She couldn't have just left.

Claire rolled her head. Beyond the foot of her bed, through the vertical window on a door, harsh white light flooded in. When she tried to sit up, the wound in her gut caught fire. She could hardly move her arms with all the tubes and wires attached, but if she yanked them out, it might summon a bunch of doctors and nurses to swarm all over her.

The harsh light coming in from the hallway brightened as the door opened and someone approached her bed. A cop.

Claire closed her eyes. He blocked the light, at least, but she could feel him standing over her.

He cleared his throat. "Mrs. Wilson? I'm sorry. I just need to ask you a few questions. I'm Officer Blake."

He waited for her to respond, then reached into his uniform and came out with a notebook.

"Where's my husband?" she asked.

"I was hoping you could tell me." He clicked his pen.

"What about my kids?"

"We believe they're with your husband."

"So he's okay?"

"How about we start with what happened?"

"What did happen?" She tried to lift her arms for emphasis, forgetting they were practically tied down.

"Exactly."

"I got shot is what happened."

"I'm very sorry. We want to know about the events leading up to that." He stood there, with his little notebook and a placid look of patience pasted on his face.

"I'm not saying shit until I see my husband and kids." She and Gray needed to get their story straight together. Did he know she was here? She looked around and saw no sign of her stuff. How would she call him? He had come home with that cheap phone she didn't know the number to.

Blake crossed his arms, looking stoic, like he could stand there forever. "I'll wait until you're ready."

"I might never be ready. Maybe you should wait at home."

"Wish I could. My orders are to take your statement. If you could just give me something to tell the detectives, I'll get out of your hair."

Great, Claire thought. Detectives would no doubt scrutinize every little detail, asking their endless questions. Maybe better to give him some form of appeasement. "I went to Ashley York's. Check social media if you want to know why. That's my husband she's been hanging out with."

But the buzz on Instagram and Twitter hardly mattered to Claire. What alarmed her was the phone call. When she'd promised to finally answer the one question he'd been asking their entire marriage—to finally tell him where she went the night before he proposed—he still refused to come home. And he'd put her on speakerphone with Ashley right there butting into the conversation. It must have been Ashley's number he called from. Claire would find it in the call history.

Officer Blake scribbled in his notebook, like she'd said something he didn't already know. "Was your husband involved in the incident at Ashley York's house?"

Involved? He would have been a victim if she hadn't shown up when she did. "Did you see him there?"

"That's what I'm asking you."

"When can I get out of here?"

"You'll have to speak with the doctors about that."

"Fair enough." She pressed the red call button on the side of the bed.

"Mrs. Wilson, you need to tell me how your husband was involved."

"All I know is that Ashley York's security dude went apeshit and shot me. He would have killed us all, if not for Ashley." She pressed it again. "She only had a knife, but she came at him like a banshee."

"So, you're saying that Ashley York stabbed Johnson?"

"Johnson's the security guard?"

A nurse rushed in: a squat, all-business brunette with a scowl on her face for Blake. "She's not ready for visitors. I thought I made that clear."

"Sorry, but this is a murder investigation. Mrs. Wilson doesn't mind answering a few questions. Isn't that right?"

The nurse shook her head and went to the machinery behind Claire's bed.

"I can't sit up," Claire said.

"Don't try to move," said a man in a white coat who had appeared in the doorway. He glanced at the nurse. "Maxine, please clear the room."

He brushed past Officer Blake without acknowledging him and glanced at the screen behind Claire's bed.

"I'm Dr. Epstein," he said as Maxine ushered Blake into the hallway and closed the door behind them.

Dr. Epstein held up his pen and asked Claire to follow it with her eyes as he moved it side to side. "Are you feeling any pain?"

"My guts are on fire."

He raised his bushy eyebrows, the left one higher than the right. "We'll titrate your drip. You need to rest on your back for seventy-two hours, just like you are now. Even rolling onto your side could damage the healing process."

She was glad to get some sleep, but three days? She couldn't lie around that long. "When can I get out of here?"

"That depends on several things." He spoke slowly. "The bullet punctured your small intestine. I think we got it in time to prevent septic peritonitis, but there's always a chance of infection, so we need to monitor too." His brows lowered. "The bullet also shattered your eleventh thoracic vertebrae. The good news is we got Dr. Rhee up from San Diego for your operation. He's one of the best spinal surgeons in the country."

Anything that required a special surgeon did not sound like good news to her at all. "But bones heal, right?"

"That's right. We've stabilized your spine with titanium rods while the bone heals, but the nerve damage is likely permanent, I'm afraid."

"What *nerve damage*? What does that mean?"

He placed a hand on her shoulder. "You need time to heal before we can test the extent of the injury."

"But..." She swallowed. He was holding back. "How bad do you think it is?"

"It's too early to say. The outcomes range from paralysis to full rehabilitation. The most important thing right now is for you to rest."

She shook her head. "Is that why my legs are numb?"

"Yes."

"I'm paralyzed?"

"Generally, spinal injuries such as yours result in paraplegia."

She couldn't believe this was happening to her. Paraplegia? No way. Maybe she misunderstood? "Will I walk again or not?"

"We don't know for sure yet." Again, he placed a hand on her shoulder. "But you should prepare to make some adjustments in your life..."

Adjustments. She wanted to adjust his face. She jerked the sheet aside. Her legs looked like they always had, pale, with dark stubble from not shaving in weeks. But from the lack of feeling, she knew the truth. They were useless now, nothing more than dead logs anchoring her to the bed. Her whole body felt heavy. The fire drained out of her. She felt numb.

A wheelchair. Darkness crept into her vision. She lay back and closed her eyes, ignoring whatever he said next. How in the hell was she supposed to look after Mindy and Tyler from a wheelchair?

"Where's my husband? Can you find my phone?"

Letting Go

When Gray opens his eyes, he finds himself lying beside an aquamarine pool lit up at night, his head in Claire's lap. The pool shimmers in the night. It's Professor Reinhart's pool, which Claire and Gray have made into their own special place while he's off on sabbatical.

Claire caresses Gray's cheek. He turns to face her, the young Claire, the Claire with carefree eyes, shining deeper than the pool: the Claire he fell in love with. He closes his eyes, relaxes to her touch.

A wave crashes into the shore and sighs over the sand.

And then another wave, reality washing over him.

He opens his eyes. It's him—or rather, his body with Ashley in it—touching his cheek with a vague smile, lying beside him in her big white bedroom. The mirror behind her reflects the windswept waves, and clouds breaking apart beneath a pale sky growing brighter in spite of everything that has happened.

———

Ashley studies her face. It doesn't quite look like her anymore. The tightness in the brows is all Gray, his thoughts shining through as though her body is entirely his now—him. As she touches his cheek, it feels like she has known him forever. His eyelids flutter and he looks at the ocean.

Pink-orange streaks bloom across the horizon with each new moment, until Point Dume rises from the shadows as the sun clears the mountains and blazes hot yellow against the cliffs, burning the murky grayness from the Pacific into an endless sapphire.

"Ashley, I'm so sorry."

"Shhhh." She presses a finger to his lips. "Don't blame yourself."

"But I'm the one who used the Encanto."

It's true, but he almost seems innocent now. Gray hadn't had any idea what he was doing.

"You heard my dad say 'this' was his fault, right? I'm wondering if, like, he knows we switched bodies?" She remembers the look on his face as he sat there and watched Wayob attack her.

"Yeah, that was weird, but last night was the first time I've seen him in real life. Rosa's grandmother told me to destroy the Encanto, but... instead..."

Ashley finds she has it in her to forgive, and forgiving is the best feeling. "I don't blame you. I don't blame you or my dad. I really don't."

—

Gray gazes up at Ashley as she leans over him, and in that moment, he surrenders all hope of returning to his own body. Maybe it's the angle, but somehow her chin looks better on her than on him, more chiseled.

She leans close enough that her nose touches his. Her lips hover. Like she might kiss him. And he might want her to. But... they shouldn't. A magnetic charge diminishes the sliver of space between his lips and hers. He yearns to feel something, anything, besides the heartbreak, besides all the death surrounding him. Her breath smells like mint. His lips prickle with anticipation.

And when she finally does kiss him—is this wrong? It seems right, so right —it feels like the easiest thing in the world, to close his eyes and let go.

—

Ashley only intends a quick comforting kiss, not even on the lips, but then she remembers the moment in Gray's garage, how they had seemed to share a single consciousness, and she wants to be that close again, wants to let go of all the badness and just feel. Needs to.

Feeling her soft lips that are his now, and Gray there behind them... the kiss lingers. Long and slow. She is curious, and then something else. More. The kiss opens up inside her, inside her whole body. And it is not enough. She wants to dive into Gray. Needs to. She pulls back from his arms to unbuckle her jeans.

—

Gray wants more—more of the intense rawness from Ashley's coarse shave on his lips. He pulls her toward him, needing her in the warmth between his thighs. She breaks out of his arms and tears off her clothes with an impatience that reminds him of Claire back in college, when they had only precious minutes alone before her roommate returned.

Seeing his nude body before him doesn't feel strange. It's familiar: the same graying hair on his chest, the same mole below his belly button, but it's Ashley York in there, like she is a part of him, and they have already connected in a more intimate way than he ever can with anyone else.

As he tugs his shirt over his head, she pulls off his jeans. If she wants to get this physically close, despite everything, then maybe, with time, he can forgive himself. And the only way to ease his guilt, to stop thinking about Claire, is to let himself go, to be in the moment. To be here, out here with Ashley and not in his head.

—

Ashley pushes him gently against the pillows and climbs on top of him, her hand on his ribs. She slides it up. Her hands on the breasts she was once so proud of. They're part of Gray now, like a gift she is giving him.

His eyes catch the light, sea-green and wavering. And she can see all the way down into him. As though he is a universe she has uncovered.

He reaches behind her neck, and this time she opens her mouth. They kiss so hard their teeth knock together. *Don't think about Dad,* she thinks. *Or Sammy or Wayob. Just be. Just be here, now.* She kisses his eyes, his nose, his neck. She lowers herself on top of him.

The ocean roars against the shore. A wave crashes, and this moment is all there is. Far away. An island. Together.

Ashley inhales sharply as she slides into Gray and closes her eyes. She moves slowly. The way she'd want Gray to move in her if they each had their own bodies. He grabs her butt and holds her inside him and sighs. It's a sad sigh.

She moves, forgiving him again with each movement, letting go of all her animosity, all the fake worthless things she thought she wanted in her life. Now she wants nothing. She wants whatever Gray wants.

"Tell me what you want," she says.

He gazes up at her, while at the same time he seems to travel somewhere inside himself.

And she glides, her body moving all on its own. As they move together, feeling all of each other all at once, they become one body, moving faster, faster. Too fast to maintain, and yet an immense need to keep moving grows inside her.

They fall into a spin there in the bed. Arms and legs, lips and hips folding into each other. Like falling upward to a crescendo. She can't stop, and she wants more, wants to know Gray feels what she feels.

"I want to hear you," she says.

Gray moans with her voice, lifting her onto a plateau where her life drops away. And she can only focus on the moment. Not even. Not anything.

She sighs, and feels her sigh with his voice deep inside herself, and Gray moans with her as he tightens. Tight together and slicked with sweat, she plunges. She lets go.

———

A wave crashes, tumbling with the incoming tide. It washes up against them.

Gray shuts his eyes and lets the glide carry him away.

The ocean exhales as it slides from the shore.

———

The car sloshes through a turn, throwing Wayob against the side of the cage. The wound in his neck throbs. He feels sick.

"Oops." The uniformed man laughs as he drives, reeking of stale sweat and roast beef.

Wayob has never before used a creature for a vessel, and it is so much worse than he expected. At least in a human body he would not be assaulted by smells several feet away. The law officer's awful digestion practically roars in Wayob's ears, and then, as if that is not torture enough, he flatulates, drowning Wayob in the wretched smell of dung.

Wayob cannot concentrate on finding an unconscious vessel within range to transmigrate into, thanks to the detestable officer who muzzled Wayob before locking him in this cage, leaving him trapped in this foul furry body with no means even of taking his life. Such agony. Wayob whines.

"Smelly, huh?" The officer chuckles. "Shouldn't have had beans for lunch."

Wayob turns his head away and considers how to punish this officer for the sick joy he receives from making Wayob suffer. Palm trees slide past the back window as the sky above them washes from gold to pale blue, down through all the layers, deep and infinitely wide. If Wayob could just get free of this foul creature, some small piece of this world could be his.

Finally, the car stops. The officer grunts as he gets out. He shakes hands with a dark-skinned man, also in uniform, who speaks with a deep voice. "I don't see why you had to bring her here."

"I just do what I'm told. She should be put down, but it's Ashley York's dog, so you know how that goes."

"If she was just trying to defend herself, she shouldn't be put down regardless of who owns her."

The stench of both men reaches Wayob, the new man stinking only slightly less than the one who drove.

The new man approaches the back door of the vehicle where Wayob lies with his muzzled head on his paws, trying to block out the scent of the men and the sound of gravel under each footfall. It sounds as if the stones are grinding together inside Wayob's skull.

The door groans open.

The new officer kneels and speaks to Wayob through the cage, his voice going up two octaves: "Sounds like you've had a rough night, haven't you, girl?"

According to the tag on his shirt, this man goes by Shy. He reaches out to torture Wayob with the flowery scent of antiseptic on his hand. It ricochets around in Wayob's nose until he sneezes, practically choking when the muzzle prevents his mouth from opening.

Shy chuckles, opens the cage. "Oh man, he got you pretty good, didn't he?" He reaches in toward Wayob.

Wayob growls and backs up as far as he can in what little space he has.

"You don't like being touched, do you, girl?" he asks, as if Wayob could answer while trapped in this primitive creature incapable of speech, as if anyone would want to be touched by someone so disgusting.

Unable to retreat any further, Wayob can only sit as Shy inspects the wound on his neck. "Looks like you're one lucky dog." He attaches a rope to his collar, which he then uses to drag Wayob mercilessly to a building.

Inside a windowless room, a woman in a white coat approaches and stabs his neck with a syringe. Wayob jerks away and then the pain begins to ebb, not just from the shot but from the wound. A feeling of gratitude rises from deep within this primitive creature Wayob inhabits. He must struggle not to succumb. As the woman holds him down and doctors his wound, Wayob finds that he hardly cares.

Then Wayob is led into a long hallway of cages and imprisoned dogs. Some welcome him. Some warn him. Wayob ignores them all.

After leading him into an empty cage, Shy removes the muzzle and the leash.

Again, that feeling of gratitude swells in Wayob's chest. And for what? Shy is merely releasing him into another cage, though granted it is bigger than the car. Wayob retreats to the back of his cell, as far as he can get. He lies on the cold concrete and closes his eyes.

He concentrates on the mind of he who holds the Encanto. It's still Gray. Wayob finds his mind almost instantly. The amplified senses of this dog-vessel allow Wayob to hear the sound of Gray's thoughts much louder, much clearer than ever before, even though he's farther away.

Perhaps it was foolish for Wayob to tell Gray he must kill him, but Gray is greedy. He must wish to remain in Ashley's body. Of course he does. He probably considers himself safe from Wayob, thanks to Luna's clever trap of locking Wayob in the small hut.

Wayob would have preferred to let Luna live, since he was the one who released Wayob from the Encanto for the first time in decades, but then the man had thrown the Encanto through the window of the hut and stood in Wayob's way, leaving Wayob no choice. Did he think it was pleasant for Wayob? Biting Luna's throat had caused Wayob to vomit up the half-digested filth that this wretched animal had eaten.

Just thinking of the blood in his mouth makes him gag. Wayob must focus. Wayob will get to Gray. He will get the Encanto, and he shall be free. In order to transmigrate out of here, he must concentrate on someone other than Gray and the idiot canines around him. He must ignore the smells and his own anger boiling in his veins. He closes his eyes and listens, but the only mind within reach is an ignorant mongrel sleeping in the cage across from him.

Wayob snaps his eyes open as boots approach down the hallway. The smell of eggs and tomatoes precedes yet another officer, who appears at Wayob's cage.

"Hey, girl, how about a walk?"

Wayob wants nothing to do with this officer, whose breakfast oozes from his pores. The smell causes Wayob to salivate in spite of his revulsion.

The officer takes a leash from the rack on the wall. This gives Wayob an idea. He stands and wags his tail.

The officer opens the door, wraps a new collar around Wayob's neck, and affixes the leash. "How you like this training collar, girl?" He shows Wayob the device in his hand and presses the button.

A horrible pulse rips through Wayob's neck. He whimpers and tries to retreat, but the man is too strong.

"Now, be a good dog or you'll get a lot worse." The officer releases the button and finally the torture ceases. No, Wayob has no choice. If the officer gets injured, it's his own fault.

Wayob lowers his head in submission and allows the officer to lead him out of the cage and down the hallway. When they reach the door, Wayob darts around the officer's legs, wrapping the rope around his knees, and as the pulse hammers through Wayob's neck, he musters all his will to overcome this animal's instinct to lie down and give up. He jerks forward instead. The officer shouts and topples, slamming his head into the doorframe.

A better outcome than Wayob had imagined.

The rope goes slack, and the button falls from the officer's hand. Wayob leaps onto the man's chest. His eyes are open. He is alert, trying to push Wayob off.

Having no other option, Wayob goes for the throat. The officer tries to shove Wayob's head away, but he's too late. Wayob's lips curl with disgust at the salty skin between his teeth, but he forces his jaw to clamp down, careful not to break the officer's tender skin, not wanting to taste his filthy blood— plus killing him is worthless—if he can just cut the officer's air supply long enough for him to fall asleep and remain unconscious long enough for Wayob to transmigrate from this vile creature and into his body.

But no, of course not. Wayob smells the odious antiseptic of Shy just before the rope tightens and yanks him away from his would-be vessel.

Back in the cage, Wayob realizes his only option to escape this canine vessel is to end his life. He must again suffer the pain of dying. But how? There's nothing here besides a bowl of water and steel bars, which would inflict only pain if he slammed his head into them. He lies on the hard floor and inspects this foul, furry body as best he can. The most vulnerable place he can reach with his jaws appears to be the hairless patch of skin on his abdomen. Tearing through the flesh of Luna's throat was torturous enough, yet now he must gnaw out his own gut? When will it end?

No choice. He bites himself, whimpering with the pain. But he inflicts almost no damage, because already the canine occupant of this vessel he possesses fights with a will to live that is stronger, so much stronger, than anything Wayob has encountered.

And something is happening. Wayob sniffs the air... Nothing. He listens... The sound he hears is not nearby—it is not even a sound at all—it is the pull of the Encanto. What is Gray doing? What has he done?

No.

No-no-no-no. No!

The Encanto overrides Wayob's will, rips his consciousness from the primitive mind of the vile canine, and pulls him out of the cage and into a dark stream of magnetism toward the terrible prison of stone. The overpowering force of the Encanto drowns out the sound of Gray's mind. Wayob reaches out to Gray's mind, but the Encanto overpowers him. Wayob expends all his will, all his energy, into fighting the current.

Somehow, to his own surprise, Wayob finds himself moving against the Encanto—perhaps because it is broken? Or has he always had a choice?

Last time, trapped in that cellar with the corpse of the deplorable woman who forced Wayob to kill her, he had been so desperate to escape the vile body of August that he practically welcomed the pull of the Encanto. Perhaps, if he were not so overwhelmed, he would have noticed the Encanto was merely pulling him, not *forcing* him into its impenetrable dark isolation.

He focuses on Gray's mind and wills himself through the dark energy that connects everything to everything else, traveling past millions of souls unaware of his passing, covering an unknown distance, past the Encanto itself, wherever it may be. If Wayob reaches Gray, he shall take Ashley's body this time. He shall never return to the immense blackness of the stone prison.

Although Wayob had failed the last time he tried to transmigrate into Ashley's body, Gray had occupied it then. Now, with the Encanto activated, Gray and Ashley must be in the process of returning each to their own body, leaving Ashley wide open for Wayob to claim her as his vessel. A window of opportunity—Ashley has so many years left to live, and Wayob deserves them. He deserves to live in her big, isolated house after all he has suffered.

The Encanto puts forth only a token effort, a gentle tug now, almost pleasant. It is so far away and growing farther, and Gray is close, so close. Wayob's fingers can practically reach his mind.

Just as Wayob suspected, he finds Gray with Ashley. She moans. What is he doing to her?

Repulsed by what the moaning might mean, Wayob loses focus. He slips. He finds himself falling…

He reaches for Gray's consciousness, but it is too far… It rockets away as Wayob plummets, falling… into Ashley's body. Which is fine. Great, actually. Wayob has ended up right where he intended, right where he deserves to be. *Goodbye, Gray*, Wayob thinks, wishing Gray could hear the thought in his subconscious.

As Wayob reaches to take control of Ashley's body, instead of the vacuum of control he expected, it is Ashley—plunging like a comet back into her body, moving with blinding speed, force, and vitality. She crushes Wayob down into some dark recess of her mind. He cannot stop her. Nothing he can do. And now he cannot leave. Wayob is trapped here. Helpless. As helpless as he was in the Encanto, but worse—much, much worse—because here Wayob feels what Ashley feels: Gray's disgusting body all over and inside him.

—

Gray awoke, but he kept his eyes closed. He had dreamed, but the dream was already receding into darkness, and he couldn't reach back to grasp it. He lay there for a long time trying to bring it back. But it was gone.

When he opened his eyes, the bedroom seemed to sway in the light bouncing in off the tide. Light from all angles. Nothing hidden.

Yet, despite the brightness, he could only see Ashley as herself now, her hair like a golden storm across his chest. As he inhaled, he felt the tickle of her eyelashes against his skin. He combed a lock of hair behind her ear.

It was his hand. *His* hand.

He eased her head off his chest and sat up, reluctant to break the closeness of the moment.

But he had to check...

His knees were his knees. His groin was his groin. He was himself!

The ocean crashed and sighed back. Sunlight blasted off the waves into the room and danced around. He felt his cheeks, his brow, his hair—oily; it needed washing—but it was his. He tested his voice. "We're back."

After all that had happened, it was hard to feel solid in his body, but here he was.

———

Ashley had been listening to Gray's heartbeat when he lifted her head from his chest to the pillow, and she drifted back down into a warm slumber.

Waves rolled over rocks.

Gray said something, his voice far up above, but she was down deep somewhere, falling deeper.

Something clawed inside her.

She bolted awake, brushing at her face, expecting to find a spider. But there was nothing. It must have been a dream. Had to be. It had felt as though something was somehow *inside* her skin, trying to claw its way out.

But her nose... She touched it again, feeling its shape between her thumb and forefinger. It was... her nose. Her face.

Then she noticed Gray standing at the mirror—Gray, in his actual body.

She sprang from the bed, looking down at her feet, her own feet, and her breasts. She traced her hips, feeling like a girl suddenly awakened as a woman. She rushed to the mirror beside Gray.

"When we made love," he said, "it was like..."

"Literally," she said.

Seeing him in his own body was sort of disorienting now, after seeing him for so long in hers. She threw her arms over his shoulders, pressing her body —her own body—into his.

He lifted her up and spun her around. She forced herself to laugh, to hide how shy she felt, naked in her own body against his, self-aware. It was as if they had lost some part of the closeness they'd just shared.

He set her down and she stepped back. A shard of light flitting across his face caught his eyes, changing them from green to blue, glistening with tears. His face darkened. He looked down and turned toward the bed. He had lost Claire. Although Ashley knew their relationship was rocky, she also knew that he loved his wife.

He bent down to grab his pants, giving her a clear view of the half-finished unicorn tattooed on his butt. She snickered.

"What?"

"Nothing."

Then she laughed, because she needed to laugh; they both did. "Just glad to be back."

Was it over? Really over? If having sex had returned each of them to their own bodies, then what might happen if they got together again?

While Gray went downstairs to check on Mindy and Tyler, Ashley dressed and then sat on the bed, feeling the loss of Sammy, Andrea, and even August crushing down on her. No one had deserved to die. She lay down on her side and gazed out across the water, deep and cold, indifferent. Allowing the horror to consume her wouldn't change anything. As bad as it was it couldn't touch the pain she had felt when her mother died. White arcs of sunlight skated on the waves.

She Believes

Saul knew he was still alive because he was hungry. Starving, actually. The vast hollowness in his stomach far exceeded the soreness in his chest. When he opened his eyes, Hernandez was sitting by his bedside shuffling a deck of cards. It reminded him of Saturday morning when he'd waited by Saroyan's hospital bed with a head full of questions, except now Hernandez was waiting for him.

"Can I still call you Rhonda?"

She smiled, but there was a tightness in the lines around her mouth, and the smile quickly faded. "Depends on when you knew Ashley's guard was our guy in the video."

"I should have told you." He had tried in the ambulance, but he should have told her right when he knew, when she showed him the video of the murder performed by Wayob, in Johnson's body.

"Damn right."

She stacked the cards and slid the deck back into its box, which had a familiar red drawing of the Castle and a torn flap. His cards. From the inside pocket of his coat. He'd stashed the Encanto in the side pocket, he was pretty sure, but she might have found it while searching for the cards. What if she'd activated it? Wayob could be after *her* now.

"Where's my coat?"

Hernandez glared at Saul. "You wanted him for yourself, huh? Judge and jury."

"Johnson's dead?" Dumb question. When Wayob showed up in the dog, Saul should have realized—*would* have realized, if he hadn't been crippled by the pain in his chest—that Wayob had gotten himself killed in his former host-body.

"Him and four others." What she didn't say was that the deaths could have been prevented if Saul had just told her where Johnson was headed instead of going to Ashley York's on his own.

She let his guilt linger. A stench in the air.

How could he make her see that arresting Wayob would have been useless, because he'd have just taken some other vessel? Saul reached toward the wound in his chest. His finger found a bandage there, and below it a cord taped to his skin. His arm was surprisingly sore.

The wrinkles softened around her eyes. "Should I get the doctor?"

"No." Tentatively, he touched the gauze, felt the sutures below. He was afraid to ask about the incision.

"They installed a pacemaker," she said.

Saul's stomach dropped. He had a machine in his heart. He had nothing against prosthetics himself, but he couldn't help but worry that even if he got thin, it might be too late for Hernandez to see him without this new pity welling in her eyes.

She stood. "I'll get the doctor."

"No, wait." Maybe he could show her that the pacemaker wasn't going to slow him down at all. He was still going to stop Wayob. "Johnson was Wayob. I can prove it," he said, but there wasn't any more proof than Wayob's terrible singsong cadence in the video. But if Wayob was still in the dog, if he was still acting insane, maybe once she saw how desperate he was for the Encanto, she'd start to understand what they were up against.

"Where's my coat?" As he tried to sit up, pain bloomed in his chest.

She pressed her hand against his shoulder. "Slow down, Saul. I believe you."

He stuttered. He had not expected this. "You don't need proof?"

"Some things in this world you have to accept." She took his hand.

He didn't want to argue—she believed him now, and that was the important thing—but he needed an explanation. In order to stop Wayob, he had to learn everything he could.

"I know," she said. "You can't accept anything without an explanation, and I admire that about you, even though it would drive me crazy. Most of us enjoy magic because we want to be amazed, to see something that seems impossible actually happen. The not knowing is what makes it fun."

"There's nothing fun about Wayob."

She nodded. "Okay, bad analogy, but my point is that some questions might never be answered, like the meaning of life—I just have to accept it and be grateful. The problem right now is that we need a reason for your presence at the scene of multiple homicides. You're on suspension, and this was hours after you were released from jail."

"Don't cover for me. I went on my own."

"I'm not worried about me; I'm worried about you. August Grant was one of the victims, and people are demanding answers. I think Delrawn wants to make you the scapegoat."

"Why isn't Levy in charge of the case?"

"Captain Malone formed a task force."

Of course. Malone always formed a task force for investigations he wanted to control without offending the lieutenants below him.

"Are you on it?"

"I am. But he partnered me with Garcia, who reports to Delrawn."

"Garcia's a straight shooter," Saul said. "Look, whatever comes down, it's on me, okay? I'm culpable. I should have told you about Johnson. I didn't think you'd believe me, but I should have tried."

"No, you were right. Last night, I wasn't ready to believe. I would have arrested Wayob again, and it wouldn't have stopped him any more than before."

"It's too late for me to escape this unscathed, but you've still got a long career ahead of you, if you avoid the political fallout."

Hernandez sat down and combed back her shock of white bangs. "It wouldn't be enough. This isn't about your badge; this is about your freedom."

Saul appreciated her point of view. If she was in trouble, he would damn sure do everything he could. "So, we follow the case. We stop Wayob. Maybe it will make a difference to the top brass, maybe not. We let the cards fall where they may." Though, he had every intention of dealing the high cards to Hernandez. The highest ones he could get. She was a good detective, and she had a son to support.

"There's no *we* here," she said. "I mean, not in regard to going after Wayob. I thought I lost you last night. You need to recover. Okay?"

"Right," he said. But there was no way to fully recover. He'd have a pacemaker for the rest of his life.

Her eyes darted around without focusing on any one thing. He tried to catch them. "What?"

"I'm wondering about Luna. You said that was him last night, in York's body?"

"No doubt about it." He wanted to tell her how Luna had sacrificed himself by luring Wayob into the guard booth, but right now it seemed more urgent to make sure the Encanto was still safe. "So do the nurses have my coat?"

"Are you cold?"

"No."

"Don't get any ideas about sneaking out of here. I told them you're a flight risk."

"Thanks for that."

She smiled briefly, but then her expression darkened. "I was wondering if Luna had been in contact with Rosa. She hung up on 911 yesterday, and she missed her psych class this morning."

Saul's stomach churned. He sat up. "She texted Luna to say that Wayob had found her."

Hernandez clenched her jaw. "LAPD doesn't declare a death without a body, and nor do I."

"It's worth investigating," he said. But kidnapping was not Wayob's MO, and they both knew it.

"Not officially. No one has reported her missing."

"Luna reported her."

"But that was after he officially died on Friday," she said. "So we can't accept the report, whether that was him in Evan York's body or not."

And now that he had actually died, Rosa had no one left. "An official report won't help anyway. I'm going to make that Wayob bastard tell me what he knows."

"How are we going to do that?" she asked.

"Where's the dog?"

"At the KOK, but you're riding the bed. I mentioned the pacemaker, right?"

"You might have mentioned it." The K-9 Officers Kennel was in Atwater Village. If he had a car, he could be there in thirty minutes. He couldn't risk Hernandez going near Wayob. "Just make sure they keep him isolated and muzzled, okay? Wayob might try to kill himself in order to take another body. We can't let that happen."

"I gave them the order, already, but I'll check in on him, don't worry. How do I make a dog tell us about Rosa?"

"No idea. We don't even know for sure that Wayob is the dog. The next step is to find Wilson. If he's still alive, Wayob will be looking to change that." Although, assuming the Encanto was in Saul's coat, Wayob was probably after him now.

"Wilson and Ashley have been MIA since last night," she said. "Any idea where to look?"

"I assume his wife wasn't helpful."

"She's unconscious, but as soon as she can talk, I'll question her."

Saul was almost afraid to ask. "What happened to her?"

"Johnson shot her."

He exhaled. "But she'll live?"

Hernandez nodded. "She'll live, but she might not walk again. And you'd better not blame yourself. If anything, I'm as much to blame as you, but I don't blame myself either; I blame Wayob. He's the one who shot her."

"But if we'd gotten there sooner—"

"Next time," she said. "Next time, promise you'll tell me what you're up to and we'll handle it together. You scared the hell out of me, Saul." Her eyebrows drew together. "I was afraid I'd lost you…" She sniffed.

"What doesn't kill you makes you stronger," he said, but he felt weaker. His chest ached and his body was begging him to just lie back down.

"Nietzsche," she said.

"I've been thinking about him and what you said about gazing into the abyss."

She pinched the bridge of her nose and closed her eyes. "I never should have said that." She opened her eyes again and emotion poured out of them. "I could never think of you as a monster, no matter what." She inhaled. "Anyway, I like Joseph Campbell's quote better. *It's by going down into the abyss that we recover the treasures of life.*"

She reached her arms around him and squeezed, though only lightly, as though he might break.

His heart pounded at her touch, though it wasn't all his own heart; there was the machine in his chest beating it for him. He put his arms around her, and when her shock of white bangs fell over her eyes he reached up and combed it back.

She sighed. "I should go."

"Thanks, Hernandez."

"For what?"

"For being here."

"Call me Rhonda."

"*Rhonda.* I could get used to that." Saul had a sense of déjà vu. Had they said this before?

"What's your address? I'll bring you some clothes tomorrow."

"Don't worry about it. I was going to buy a new suit, anyway." The last thing he wanted was for her to see how he lived, or to meet his landlord. Marla would ask all kinds of nosy questions.

"It's really no problem."

"My clothes are all packed up. It's too hard to tell you where to find them." She frowned. Obviously, she didn't believe it. "Suit yourself."

"Exactly."

She chuckled.

"I really am moving," he said, and this time he meant it. Now that he had a pacemaker, he couldn't keep helping Marla with all the chores she tended to rope him into. The discount on rent wasn't worth it.

"Any idea where to?" Hernandez asked. A slight smile on her lips.

"Working on it." He decided not to explain that right now he had bigger concerns. Let her assume he was staying put, if she wanted.

She kissed his cheek, and her lips lingered for a moment. She grabbed her purse and disappeared into the hallway.

He crossed his arms, unmoored by all that had happened. He closed his eyes and counted upward, his worries like cards scattered in the wind. He just had to pick them up, examine each one: Was the Encanto still in his coat? Had Wayob escaped from the dog? He returned each card to the imaginary deck in his mind. He would find Wayob and find a way to stop him. But the *how* was just out of reach, hidden in the darkness of his fear.

Picturing his uneasiness like a switch, he imagined turning it off.

But it didn't work. It wouldn't work until he knew the Encanto was safe. In order to give Hernandez time to clear the floor, he counted down from fifty, then opened his eyes.

He gingerly peeled off the tape that attached the heart monitor to his chest. The little machine whined and then bleeped in alarm. He slid off the bed, the marble cold on his bare feet, and stepped into the hallway. His powder-blue gown bloused up around him as he walked. He reached back and held the flaps closed across his butt as best he could. Two doors down, he ducked into a room, closed the door, and pressed his ear against it.

"Who are you?" a raspy voice demanded from the bed behind him. He didn't turn to look.

Footsteps in the hallway—rubber soles on the marble floor—ran past. Would there be more? It would take only a few seconds to see that his room was empty. He counted to ten.

"I'm calling the nurse."

He turned toward the woman in the bed. "Please, don't. I was never here." He flung open the door.

As he rushed down the hall, he glanced back at his room. A nurse stood in the doorway, her back turned, speaking urgently into her phone.

The nurse's station was deserted. Behind it, a door opened to an alcove filled with shelves of plastic bins. He entered and began opening them at random. The blue ones, he learned, contained medical supplies. The white bins by the door contained personal items in plastic bags labeled with last names and alphabetized. He pulled the bag labeled Parker and checked the contents. Found his coat and his pants.

"You can't be out of bed." A nurse had appeared in the doorway to the alcove. She was white-blonde, and rail-thin, with the type of pasty skin that always burns and never tans. She looked clean and alert, as if just starting her shift and plenty capable of handling a fat man in a paper-thin smock who had an implant driving his heart. "You shouldn't be moving at all."

"I shouldn't be a lot of things, but right now, I need to get out of here." Saul pulled his coat from the bin and felt around. Found the Encanto in his side pocket. With the porous stone between his fingers, his confidence rocketed.

The elevator dinged behind her. She marched toward him. Blood pounded through his head, probably thanks to the pacemaker. He felt more present than he had in months.

And then the elevator opened, and his confidence fell. Two large orderlies emerged, shoulder to shoulder.

He had hoped for a security guard who would remove him from the premises. A favor, really. But orderlies. Orderlies knew how to subdue unruly patients. Orderlies had syringes filled with sedatives.

And these orderlies didn't look like pushovers, either. The nurse must have called her top guys. They looked like bouncers at a biker bar—the younger one probably was. And the older guy, he might have been a Hell's Angel back in the day, back before some bad situation gave him the whim to do something good with his life. He scowled at Saul, then his face relaxed as his body tensed. Like he knew that once he forced Saul back into bed by whatever means necessary, preferably with violence, he'd feel better. His good deed for the day.

Almost, Sort-of Normal

As Ashley descended the stairs, she clutched the rail, feeling a little disoriented, as though her head was still clouded with the fog of sleep. Her dad should have been here by now, but there was still no word. The sound of laughter echoed up from below, filling the house with a sense of life that had always been missing before.

She followed the sound to the den. Mindy was spasming on the floor while Gray hovered over her, pretending to tickle her without even touching. Marta stood by the window, rocking Tyler in her arms. The ocean made glamorous emblems of light jiggle on the ceiling above them all.

"Stooop," Mindy said, struggling to breathe through the laughter.

"Gittcha, gittcha, gittcha!"

She laughed so hard she almost choked.

As Ashley approached, she admired how Gray was so in tune with Mindy, so in sync that they could play without words. She wanted that for herself. No way could she have lived Gray's life, but maybe she could be a part of it now? In a way, she was already. Reaching down, she ran her fingers through his hair.

He reached up and squeezed her hand without looking. "Claire."

She pretended not to notice his mistake, because it was her mistake, too. She hadn't meant to touch him.

Mindy stopped laughing. "Where's Mommy? Is she coming?"

"No…" He glanced at Ashley, but she had no idea what to say.

Gray said, "Gittcha, gittcha." He wiggled his fingers toward Mindy, but she rolled away and sprang to her feet. "You said we could go to the beach." She tugged at his arm.

He pretended to let her drag him along the floor, saying to Ashley, "I told her we couldn't go without you."

Mindy took Ashley's hand as well. "Come on, already."

Her little hand felt warm, but it seemed to trigger something sour at the back of her mind. Maybe some lingering uneasiness after so much time spent out of her body?

"Go," Marta said. "Mister Tyler and I will have lunch ready when you get back."

"Did my dad call the landline by any chance?" Ashley asked.

Marta shook her head, mirroring the disappointment which must have been apparent on Ashley's face.

"Please let me know when he arrives."

"Of course," Marta said.

Ashley led Mindy and Gray to the side door, hoping the ocean breeze might clear the cobwebs from her head. Mindy bolted ahead down the narrow stairs to the sand.

"She hasn't been to the beach since before Tyler was born." Gray almost stumbled down the stairs trying to catch up with Mindy.

Ashley ran after them. Down the beach, an off-leash black lab with a frisbee sprinted ahead of its owner.

Mindy stopped at the shoreline, glancing around and then up at Gray with wide eyes.

The lab pranced up to them, the half-chewed frisbee in his mouth as though it was his most prized possession. He lowered his head and presented the frisbee to Mindy. He dropped it on the sand at her feet.

"I think he wants you to throw it," Ashley said.

Mindy tentatively picked up the slimy disk. The lab bounded off, and when she didn't throw it, he doubled back. She giggled and sprinted in the opposite direction. The lab leaped after her.

"I have to tell her some version of what happened," Gray said, his brows furrowed. "I don't want her to be scared when the police show up."

"I don't think they'll find us here. My dad used some kind of holding company to pay for this house."

"Should we call them? They're going to have a lot of questions about all those bodies at your house."

"What would we say?" She needed to protect Gray as much as herself. After all, she'd been in his body when she killed Sammy.

He gazed out at the ocean and sighed. "I have no idea."

"Let's wait for my dad."

"What if he doesn't show up?"

"I don't know. I guess I'll call a lawyer or something." But which lawyer? Don could, of course, find one for her, but he'd try to sensationalize the death of August Grant at her house when she wanted as little attention as possible. Plus. she didn't need an agent anymore. She was done with acting, and she was done with Don managing her life.

The wind cut through her shirt. She shivered. Mindy had doubled back, and the lab was bounding around her. It had the same black fur as the dog that had tried to kill her last night. But that hadn't been a dog at all—dogs had kind souls. That had been Wayob.

Mindy fell in the sand, giggling, as the lab yanked the frisbee from her hand. He leaped a few yards and stopped, inviting her to chase him.

Ashley had been Mindy's age when she and Rexi played on this very same beach, when she threw his ball into the waves, and he fetched it back again and again for hours.

When Mindy didn't follow the lab, he pranced back and crouched just out of reach, chewing the frisbee on his front paws as if it was the best thing in the world, his hind quarters raised to leap away the instant Mindy showed any interest.

Ashley had to laugh. She hopped down from the bank of powdery sand at the high-tide line and stood beside Gray.

The lab's owner, a darkly tanned man with a tangle of sun-bleached hair and red shorts, apologized as he approached the lab and grabbed his collar.

"No worries," Gray said. "He made her day."

The man smiled at Mindy and took off jogging down the beach, his lab prancing along beside him, the frisbee in his mouth.

As Mindy carved her name in the sand, Ashley turned to Gray. "It almost seems sort of normal."

"Yeah." He gazed wistfully out across the waves.

As she imagined a world in which the four of them could somehow be a family, a pelican landed nearby on the sand bank. Mindy stomped toward it, but the pelican remained motionless. It glowered at Mindy until she finally got too close, and then it spread its wings and flew away.

—

Nothing felt normal to Gray; he had just agreed with Ashley because he was grateful. They were, at least, back in their own bodies, and Mindy was happy. He watched as she sang to herself and pulled a strand of kelp from the waves.

He touched the obsidian snake in his pocket. If Ashley had noticed him fish it from her pants while he was dressing, she hadn't said so. He wanted to hurl the damn thing into the ocean, but then what if it washed ashore? What if he buried it in the sand, only to have some kid dig it up? It might still do something even without the stone attached. He wanted to crush them both. Rosa's grandmother had told him to destroy the Encanto, and he would. He would also destroy Wayob. But Ashley's father had the stone, and if he didn't show up soon, they were going to have to go back to her house and look for it, which wasn't going to be easy if the cops were still there.

At least he knew that Wayob was back in the Encanto now, because he'd drawn a swirl of blackness and he and Ashley had returned to their own bodies. It had happened just like Rosa said—they had let go, thanks to Ashley. He never could have done it without her. Now he was himself again, and he could finally be the father that Mindy and Tyler needed. They were more important to him than anything, always had been. But the experience he'd shared with Ashley had meant something, and they both knew it. He would always hold a special place in his heart for her, even after they parted ways.

"Thanks," Gray said.

Ashley turned to face him. "For what?"

For making love to me, he thought, but instead he swept his hand along the shore. "For all this."

"It's nothing."

"It's not nothing. You saved my life."

She jabbed her foot into the sand and twisted it deeper. "I can't believe I killed Sammy."

"That wasn't Sammy; it was Wayob."

"It was both of them," she said, "but only Sammy died."

True, but what choice did she have? He hugged her. "I meant it metaphorically, but you literally saved me, too."

She pressed herself against him. She trembled slightly, and they stood like that until they were swaying, rocking back and forth like the waves washing over the rocks. A knot of sadness rose up his throat. He tried to choke it back and couldn't.

Ashley rubbed his back. "It's okay," she said. "We'll be okay."

"It's not." A wave tumbled over his feet and the cold water seemed to be siphoned up into his heart. "When Claire died... I felt... relieved."

"Shhh." Ashley squeezed tighter.

He wiped his eyes with his sleeve. The clouds had completely dissipated and now the air felt thin, empty, no buffer at all against the stark sunlight bearing down on him.

"I'm horrible."

"You're not. It's not like you wanted her to die." She spoke with such conviction that he wished he could see her face without her seeing his own. She felt good in his arms, and he wasn't ready to let go.

The loss he'd felt when Claire died had crushed him, and now he had no idea what to feel. He certainly wished she were still alive. "I did care about her." But the Claire he missed, the Claire he still longed for, was not the woman who had died on Ashley's lawn.

"I know," Ashley said. "I know."

And she kept right on hugging him until he started to let go of the guilt, and in its place, he felt a new hope seeping into him.

From over her shoulder, he saw Mindy watching them from inside a circle of seaweed she'd strewn out on the sand, and now the hug felt inappropriately long. He let go.

In the wet sand of the retreating tide, Mindy started building a sandcastle, and Gray wondered what she thought about coming here to Ashley's fancy beach house without Claire. After lunch, he'd sit her down and explain, in some filtered way, that her mother was dead.

He sat on the ledge of sand, and Ashley sat beside him. For a while, they just stared at the waves.

"So, what will you do now?" she asked.

He gazed out across the horizon, as if some answer might be floating on the distant swell. "I was going to open a bar." He almost laughed at himself—a bar to generate income so he could afford to paint. It sounded like a whole lot of work he did not want to do. "But now Mindy and Tyler are all that matters." They were his sole responsibility. He had to find another software job, which would be hard with no recommendation, not that Brad would have given him one even if Gray hadn't quit without giving notice.

"A bar?"

Now Gray did laugh, as though this bar idea was just a whim, not the vehicle for all his hopes and dreams.

"You should paint," she said.

"I was going to set up a studio in the bar's back room, but that's not going to happen now." What had made him believe the bar would be successful enough to cover him and his family, in addition to rent, the liquor licenses, and the bartenders, who would want medical, dental, and paid vacations? How many newly opened bars had he frequented, without considering the failed dreams behind the ones that closed in their place?

"I could help you," she said.

He considered how, with just a couple tweets from Ashley York, his bar would have a line out the door. But how long would that last? Even if she made frequent appearances, the novelty would wear off. "I don't really want to open a bar anymore. Even if I had the money."

"Yeah, no. I'm talking about your paintings. I can get you a gallery show."

Gray's heart swelled into his throat. "I would have to finish one first. I'd need several for a gallery show."

"I've seen what you can do, and I want to commission the works."

It was a generous offer. Too generous. Could he even paint with the pressure and expectations hanging over him? He watched a woman paddling out on a surfboard fight her way over a wave.

"I need to do this on my own."

"No one gets anywhere all on their own."

"Your father did." The words came out sounding more bitter than he had intended. He didn't like hearing that he needed help. Maybe it was true, but he didn't want help.

"That's the legend, right? Evan York, self-made man. It's bullshit. The media loves the one-man-all-on-his-own persona, and it's not like he ever discouraged it, but the truth is that my dad had people—tons of people—who helped him all along the way. On his own, he would have gone bankrupt, probably several times."

But the investors behind Evan York probably had different intentions than what Ashley was proposing. "If we hadn't..." Gray paused and chose his words carefully. "If you didn't know me, would you still be offering to help?"

"Look, Gray." She shook her head. "You have to take whatever breaks come your way."

He had no doubt that her father would, but he didn't want handouts.

She smiled. "You don't see it, do you? Your work is amazing! The world deserves to see what you can do. Don't be so nervous." She glanced at her feet, twisted them in the sand. "And it's not because of anything with us. If someone showed me your work and told me how you're struggling, I would have wanted to help. I enjoy helping, and I'm going to spend more time doing it."

Gray felt the urge to kiss her, not romantically but with gratitude, and he probably would have if Mindy wasn't right there, seemingly focused on her sandcastle but no doubt soaking in every word. And something about the stark light on the beach—kissing Ashley felt wrong. Had he taken advantage of her? She was ten years younger than him and probably reeling from the shock of all that had happened—she'd killed a man after all—and afterward, all he'd considered was himself.

"Let me just think about it, okay? This is a lot to process." Maybe if he created the paintings on his own first, without the influence of Ashley's money... and then once he had enough completed works he was happy with, if she still wanted to sponsor his gallery, they could take it from there. It might take years while working a full-time job and looking after Mindy and Tyler, but maybe that would be okay. Maybe this was how it had to be.

"I get that." She lay back in the sand and closed her eyes.

A wave crashed into the shore, and then another. Water surged up the beach and breached the low wall of Mindy's castle, washing it down to a wet mound of sand which, after the wave retreated, she began to reinforce.

"The sun feels so good," Ashley said. "You should relax."

Although he liked the idea of lying back in the sand, he felt like if he looked away from his future he might lose sight of it in the waves, the foam and the ripples, the sparkles of sunlight.

—

Ashley luxuriated in the warmth of the sunlight on her skin, soaking it in. She felt good about helping Gray; she'd find some way to persuade him to accept it. With her resources, she could do so much for him. LA was full of people struggling to get somewhere, and she wanted to help them all. It would be so much more satisfying to help others than whatever hollow joy she might have gained from acting.

Like when she rescued Andrea from the double shifts as a waitress at Providence and gave her an easy job with time to focus on acting, a chance to succeed.

But if Ashley hadn't hired her, she would still be alive. The thought ripped through Ashley like an icy wave.

And there was something else. Something pulling her back into the darkness behind her eyes. When she tries to open them, she can't. Her lids won't open. Something inside her has hold of her lids. She tries to tear her eyes open with her fingers, but her arms are like jelly. They can't seem to reach. The thing claws upward as she sinks into unconsciousness.

She tries to cry out, but there is only the sound of water. A wave smashing over rocks, hissing over the sand. She could sleep. Sleep. She wants to sleep yet at the same time she needs to stay awake. She is of two minds.

She forces herself to stand, unsure of her body, unsure even of whether she's actually moving or merely dreaming. But the ocean—it must be real. She just saw it. That must have been only seconds ago. If she can make it to the water, she might... what?

Another wave crashes. Closer? She cannot tell. It feels like she's swaying, drunkenly. A half-conscious passenger riding on her own unsteady legs, which are plodding like tree trunks through sand.

"Where are you going?"

It's Gray's voice, far away, beyond the dark tunnel she's trapped in. Although she can't speak, his voice spurs her on. She doubles her effort to keep moving.

"Ashley?"

Splash, plunk. A chill so cold her feet sting.

As she trudges into the water, her eyes come open and everything is blinding-white light.

Tears streamed from her eyes, but she held them open as she stood there and tried to steady herself. What just happened? Had she fallen asleep that fast, that hard?

She was in the water up to her hips with a wave rolling toward her. She turned back toward the shore. Gray and Mindy were staring at her, their mouths hanging open.

As her feet splashed free from the water, a wave crashed behind her and sprayed her back. She ran up the beach.

Gray had a curious look on his face, as if trying to decide if he should be worried or what. And what could she tell him? Had anything really even happened? Anything to worry about? How could she explain a dream that made no sense to her? She needed time to think... coffee, dry pants.

"I just needed to cool off," she said. The truth, in a way. "I'm going up to see if there's any word from my dad."

She made her way across the sand to the house.

—

Gray kneeled beside Mindy in the sand. No point in putting it off any longer.

"Can I go in, too?" she asked, beaming up at him. A tangle of hair blew across her face, and she swept it away without noticing how much sand was on her hand. "Please, Daddy?"

Gray was tempted, and it wasn't just procrastinating. If they had swimsuits, he'd take her out in the waves. "I need to talk to you about your mother. Would that be okay?"

Mindy turned to her castle, picked up a stick, and began etching a face on the side.

He scooped up some wet sand in his hands and began fortifying a wall. "Your mother, she... she had an accident."

Mindy added a frown and scribbled on hair with increased intensity. "Did she go to the doctor?"

"No. It's really sad. Your mom..." He had to keep it simple, blunt. He had read somewhere that kids were more resilient than adults, and Mindy was more resilient than anyone he had ever known. *Just tell her.*

"Mom died."

Mindy scraped away Gray's fortification and pointed him to a patch of sand off on its own. "Build here." She went back to carving her sandcastle with the twig.

When he had read her a story about a pet canary who died, she'd asked all kinds of questions. Did she understand it could happen to people too?

"Do you know what it means, that she died?"

Mindy nodded without looking up. "It means her body stopped working. She can't walk or eat or see anymore."

A lump welled up in his throat. He couldn't cry now. He had to be strong. "It's okay to be sad. I'm very sad. But you should know your mother is not hurting."

"So is Ashley going to take me to daycare?"

"No, I'm going to take you from now on, but you can stay home for a while."

"Can we live here now?"

He inhaled. "It's nice of Ashley to have us here, but we're just guests. Later, we'll go back to our house. Then, in a few days, we'll have a funeral. That's where we get dressed up and people will come to say nice things about your mother. Grandma and grandpa will be there."

"Will Mommy be there?"

Her ashes would be there. He wanted to say she would be there in spirit, but saying so might undo the sense of permanence Mindy needed to understand.

"No. She's gone forever. But we'll be thinking about her. And I could use your help. I'd love some of your special drawings of Mom, if you want to make some for us? Or, if you'd rather not, that's fine too. Whatever you want, okay? We can talk more about it later."

"Did Mommy die because of Ashley?"

"Of course not." Claire had died because of him; she had come to Ashley's to help him. He sat back and studied Mindy. Now she was etching what looked like a person riding a fish, maybe a dolphin, into the side of her castle. Her reaction was no different than if he'd said Claire would be gone for an hour instead of forever. "What made you ask that about Ashley?"

Mindy looked toward the house. "She hit herself."

He followed Mindy's gaze, but Ashley had gone inside. He got to his feet and offered Mindy his hand. "Let's go see if she's okay."

"Then can we go in the ocean?"

"The water's freezing."

"No it's not. I put my feet in ten times already."

"Okay, maybe after lunch." He tried to sound cheerful, but if she had really seen Ashley hit herself, then something was seriously wrong.

—

Ashley's hopes shot up when she saw the voicemail on the laptop in the kitchen. She had signed into her AT&T account to forward the number from her broken iPhone to the landline. *Must be from Dad.* She clicked the play icon.

"Gray?" a woman's voice said. "This message is for Gray… It's Claire. I'm in the hospital, at Cedars-Sinai. I'm… Just give me a call when you get this or come over here. Don't bring Mindy, yet, okay? … I love you."

Ashley felt double-bad now. She'd practically torn Gray away from Claire, and now it turned out she had been alive the whole time. He would go to her, she knew. He would have to.

She looked out the window. He was still down by the water with Mindy, crouched over her castle, so completely unaware. The thought of him leaving triggered something inside of Ashley. Something ugly.

She doesn't feel like herself.

Suddenly, Gray was standing. She had been watching him the whole time but somehow she'd missed him stand up, as if time had skipped a beat. And now he was leading Mindy by the hand toward the house.

When she glanced back at the screen, the message was gone. Her mailbox was empty. She would never—she just wouldn't delete the message. She refreshed the page and checked again. It was gone, definitely gone.

She had to tell Gray.

Or did she?

———

Gray found Marta on the lower deck where she had prepared a big smorgasbord for their lunch. Tyler was strapped into his booster seat, and she was feeding him avocado. He had surprisingly less mess on his face than usual. Gray kissed his head and watched Mindy spoon more macaroni onto a plate than she'd ever eat, but he was glad to see her hungry and decided not to press her to take some broccoli or carrots. Not today.

"Where's Ashley?"

Marta shrugged. "I was going to ask you."

He left Mindy with Marta and went upstairs to find her.

The landline in the charger by the fridge was ringing, and, seeing no sign of Ashley, he decided to answer, because he knew she was anxious to hear from her father.

As he removed the handset, the door by the stairs flung open and Ashley lunged out. "Just hang up. It's a wrong number."

He might have hung up, if she'd given him a chance, but she rushed toward him with such an intense look on her face that it confounded him. As he moved back, he heard the voice on the other end: "Gray?"

Ashley tried to grab the phone, but he turned sideways.

A week ago, he'd have said it was impossible—Claire was dead—but now it was hard to know what was and wasn't possible. Could his mind be tricking him?

His legs felt weak as he pressed the phone to his ear. "Claire? Is that really you?"

He braced himself against the counter. It was her. It really was her. His mouth opened but no words came out.

Ashley bit her lip, brows lowered. She looked dismayed. Had she known that Claire was alive?

"Yeah," Claire said. "It's me. Good to hear your voice."

He clenched the phone, his voice almost in a whisper. "How are you calling me?"

"I had the number in my call history."

"No. I mean... I thought..." He had seen her die, hadn't he? He should have checked her pulse.

"You thought I was dead? Well, too bad."

He laughed into the phone as tears streamed down his cheeks, and he sank to the floor, laughing and crying all at once.

Saul's Plan

The nurse got up in Saul's face and demanded he return to his room as the two burly beefcakes approached from either side of the counter. He grabbed a couple of syringes, bit the caps off. Held them up. "Sorry, but I'm leaving."

That stopped the nurse and slowed the orderlies.

With his other hand, he pulled his clothes out from the bag, and couldn't believe it when he discovered the Beretta Nano still in his pants. If Hernandez had known about it, she'd have taken it, for sure. Irresponsible to leave a loaded firearm in a semi-public place.

He shoved the syringes in a coat pocket, withdrew the gun from his pants, and checked the safety. It was on.

The nurse stared at the weapon, her face stark white. Behind her, the orderlies came to a stop.

He felt ridiculous standing here in a smock with a gun. He held it by his side. "Get out of here."

She backed up slowly, squeezed past the orderly on the right, and took off down the hall. The orderlies remained where they were. The older guy scowled at Saul, challenge flickering in his eyes. These were men who had seen guns before, but Saul knew he wasn't worth the risk of taking a bullet.

"Step back."

The younger one stepped back. They both raised their hands.

Without averting his eyes, he grabbed his clothes and stepped past the orderlies without incident.

"Don't bother following me. If I see you again, I won't be so friendly." He backed into the elevator.

As the elevator descended, he dropped the gun into the other coat pocket and stepped into his underwear. He pulled on his pants, donned his coat over his bare chest, and discovered the buttons had been torn off, but it was still better than the smock. He withdrew the syringes from the pocket to inspect them. They were EpiPens. *Uppers*. He chuckled. *Useless*. He shoved them back in the pocket and slipped his shoes on without socks.

He exited the elevator on the second floor and sent it down to P3, a little misdirection. A stairway led down to a side exit. He pushed open the big metal door and walked out into stark sunlight.

His eyes took a moment to adjust. The alley behind Cedars led to San Vicente, where cars flowed in and out of the Beverly Center. As he approached the intersection, he reached into his pocket and felt the porous stone. It seemed lighter than it should be, and cold. It anchored him into the world. He had the Encanto; he would stop Wayob.

He crossed San Vicente and hurried to a Prius Yellow Cab at a fifteen-minute meter. The back passenger door was locked. The driver buzzed down his window. He had a high and tight haircut and a real estate magazine spread open on his lap.

"I need a ride to Hollywood," Saul said.

"Don't we all?"

"You're a taxi, right?"

"I may drive one, but it does not define me."

Saul looked around for another option. Saw none. "Great, so open up."

"Look, buddy, it's not like there's a dress code, but—" He pointed at Saul's hairy chest, the bandage over his heart exposed by his open jacket. "I can't give free rides."

Saul fished two wrinkled twenties from his pocket and waved them toward the window.

The cabbie popped the locks. "Hop in."

Saul held his jacket closed as he climbed into the back and recited his address. He could use some fresh clothes. A sweatshirt and jeans. From here on out, he was done with suits.

His stomach growled. Last night's near-death experience had the side effect of jump starting his diet, but now he had to eat. In order to take on Wayob, he needed fuel. *Double cheeseburger. Chili fries.* Not going to happen. From now on, he was going to eat healthy. Maybe a salad. *With ranch and bacon and cheese.*

The cab rolled through a high-end stretch of Santa Monica Boulevard where the restaurants served farm-to-table fare. His stomach rumbled. At this point, plain spinach would suffice. He told the cabbie to pull over and promised another twenty if he'd wait.

Saul heaved himself out of the cab and up the sidewalk to the Green Grotto Juice Bar. He ordered his first-ever smoothie. It was green alright, but sweet with bananas and dates and a whole list of healthy-sounding stuff like bee pollen and hemp. The long description on the menu failed to mention the calorie count, but at this point he was too hungry to care. He gulped it down. He wanted more. It took all his will power to leave without buying the vegan chocolate-chip cookies.

Back in the cab, he felt his stomach get to work on the proteins and the sugars. Now he could concentrate. He took out the Encanto. It was a little bigger than a billiard ball, but it weighed almost nothing. The bottom and top were flattened slightly, and there was a tiny hole in the center. He angled it toward the late-morning sun pouring in through the window. The hole remained dark.

He returned the stone to his pocket and held it there. Closed his eyes and counted down from fifty. Meditating on the abyss he'd seen in Wayob's mind.

The fear.

Although Wayob seemed immortal due to his ability to change bodies, he was also afraid—almost consumed by fear. He was afraid of people getting close. And his fear could be used against him.

Firing Squad

In the conference room on the top floor of the PAB, Hernandez sat facing Chief Decker across the long table. The LAPD's top brass flanked him on either side, all staring at her. Decker rubbed his bald head and got to his feet. Behind him, outside the glass, City Hall towered through a thin haze slowly evaporating in the midday sun.

"Don't you find it suspicious?" he said.

Saul would have called this a firing squad. They were looking for a scapegoat for the massacre at Ashley York's. With August Grant and Evan York among the bodies, the news had exploded on all the networks, and the LAPD had to show progress before the FBI started meddling in the case. So, Decker had called Assistant Chief Gamela, who had called Deputy Chief O'Connell, and so on, passing Decker's demand for a suspect like flaming shit down the chain, until Lieutenant Levy had called Hernandez... but Hernandez had no one to call.

The fact that Garcia, who Hernandez had been partnered with for the investigation into the deaths at Ashley York's, hadn't been called into this meeting made it clear whose blood they wanted, and who they wanted to spill it.

Decker leaned on the table, waiting for her answer. His enormous sloping belly pressed against his blue button-down and the mile of belt that held up his gray slacks. Saul might weigh as much as Decker, but he carried it better. It was distributed heroically across his frame. Saul looked strong; Decker seemed incapable of standing for long.

"Hernandez?"

All she had to say was *yes*. All she had to do was toss even just a few grains of suspicion on Saul, and her future in the department would be secure, and so would the paycheck she, her son, and her mother all depended on. If she didn't align herself with the top brass now, all bets were off. She cringed inwardly. What choice did she have?

She recalled the stricken look on Saul's face when he learned about the pacemaker, and how, despite the setback, he was more determined than ever to stop Wayob.

Fuck. She couldn't stab him in the back. "Parker went there to stop the carnage," she said, "and he would have, if not for his heart."

Lieutenant Delrawn exhaled with disgust. The top brass all shifted in their chairs, rolling closer to the chief's end of the table. Decker shook his head and passed a photo to Cobb, the sallow-faced commander of IA. Cobb restrained a smug little smile as he passed it to O'Connell who passed it to Malone, who passed it to Levy, who had to wheel her chair several feet to reach Hernandez. Without making eye contact, Levy slid the photo to Hernandez and rolled back.

It was a wide-angle black-and-white of a garage, shot with an infrared camera. Outside the open bay, a figure stood with a gun. It was, unmistakably, Saul. Also recognizable was the panicked-looking blonde in the passenger seat of a Mercedes. Although Saul wasn't aiming the gun at Ashley, she had a terrified look on her face.

Hernandez should have been notified about the footage. This was her case. She should have seen this image before Decker or anyone else in the room.

Decker said, "That's the front page of the *LA Times* tomorrow."

She smoothed the emotion from her voice as she spoke. "Who leaked it?"

"If it was an officer, they'll be disciplined, but that's not your concern. What you need to worry about is our position on this."

"What do you mean, 'our position'?" she asked unnecessarily. Saul was either a villain or a hero—the gun left no middle ground—and she wouldn't have been called up here in front of the firing squad if they wanted to make him a hero.

Malone said, "We've got big things in store for you, Detective. Just stick to the script."

"The script?!" Her voice rose louder than she'd intended.

"The facts," Decker said.

"Like the press conference," Malone said, "after you arrested Rydell. We put you out front and center, and you handled it cool as a cucumber."

She glanced from Malone to Levy, who had made the press conference seem like her idea at the time. Levy glanced down.

"You want the facts? Ashley York will clear this up once we find her." Though Hernandez was worried that it might not happen in time. If anyone could afford to stay hidden, it was Ashley York.

"Our narrative sure as hell better match hers," Decker said. "People believe what she says. Once she learns that Parker is a suspended detective, she'll probably blame the LAPD. The rogue officer angle, I'm thinking, we can agree on. It could justify her fleeing the scene."

Hernandez flattened her palms on the table, wishing she had the nerve to flatten Decker's nose. She inhaled. "I don't see how. According to my witness, Ashley killed Johnson."

Although Claire Wilson, after all she'd been through, hardly counted as a reliable witness, and her husband's prints were on the knife that had been wedged between Johnson's ribs as well as on the gun that ultimately ended his life.

Somehow, Hernandez had to convince Garcia to sit on the info until she could reach Ashley York. But then who had leaked the photo to the *Times*? What if it *was* Garcia?

"Self-defense," Lieutenant Delrawn said.

She glared at him. "You think?" She didn't report to Delrawn—he needed to butt out. "Kind of seems like overkill to me."

"No jury will convict her," Decker said calmly. "YouTube took down the video of the execution Johnson performed, but everyone knows about it. It's probably all over the dark web. There's no DA that will file against her, and she probably has a whole team of lawyers explaining this to her even as we speak."

Hernandez stood. "Seems like you've got it all figured out then. Sacrifice a good detective who had nothing to do with it. Doesn't speak well for the LAPD." She turned toward the door. "Not sure what you need me for."

Levy spoke up, uncharacteristically bold. "If Parker is innocent, then where is he?"

Hernandez felt the heat rush into her cheeks. Did this question mean Saul had left the hospital? She shouldn't be surprised. She spun back to face her direct supervisor. "Maybe he's trying to do something instead of sitting around figuring out who to blame."

"He's a man on a mission, alright," Levy said. "He threatened a nurse at Cedars with a bunch of syringes."

Hernandez wanted to laugh. Of course the nurse wouldn't have let him just walk out of there.

"I'm sure you would have done the same," she said calmly, knowing full well that Levy wouldn't. No one else would have left the hospital right after having a pacemaker attached to their heart. "We've got a missing girl and possibly other victims, and probably a killer still on the loose." Not that she could expect anyone here to believe her. That was the problem with Wayob: no evidence.

"If Saul is so desperate to conduct an unsanctioned investigation, as you imply, then why bother telling his landlord he's leaving."

"Seems to me he's running. And he's partially my responsibility, since I let you persuade me to release him."

"Are you kidding me? Johnson was on a rampage. The body count would be higher if not for him." She had no idea if this was true, but it could be. He might have scared Wayob away, possibly saving Ashley York and Wilson in the process.

"Sit down, Detective," Decker said. "We can't put this all on Johnson, and you know it. According to your own report, he died before Evan York. The thing I'm wondering is how a guy like York ended up locked in a confined space with a deadly animal. Parker collapsed right outside the guard booth, right?"

Not even Johnson can be pinned on Johnson, she thought as she sat down again. *You'd blow a gasket if I told you.* "Maybe he was trying to let him out?"

"So," Decker said, "where is Saul?"

She shrugged. "No idea." Hopefully he was making more progress than she was.

"You would tell us, right?"

Below the table, she rolled the fabric of her dress pants into her fist. "I would want to."

Decker sat. He leaned forward without breaking eye contact. "You'd do well to consider your situation here."

"My situation?"

"Right now, this is just about your former partner; you don't want to turn it into something else." He leaned back.

She swallowed. The threat was clear.

"How many bodies do we have?" Decker asked.

"Four at Ashley York's," she said.

"No, I mean since Parker went haywire. It started with Rydell, right?" Decker began counting on his fingers. "You had him cold for the murder of Bob Jaggar, but Parker didn't follow procedure, did he?"

"It's not like that," Hernandez said. "Saroyan was nearly killed in the MDC. Parker put Rydell in the holding cell because he wanted him alive."

"Yet Rydell managed to hang himself," Decker said, "with his own shirt."

"Parker wasn't in the building at the time. I checked the logs."

"What happened in the interview?"

She shrugged. "Rydell went crazy." He'd said he was Wayob, though neither of them had believed him at the time. Twice they'd had Wayob in custody, and twice he had escaped.

"You saw this yourself?" Decker asked.

Levy knew she'd skipped the interview, and when Hernandez glanced at her, she looked down. High brass would understand; hell, they probably expected lieutenants to back up their subordinates. But not Levy. *Coward.* She had betrayed Hernandez's confidence, and it made her look weak. No wonder she never made captain.

Hernandez pushed her bangs back off her forehead. "No, I wasn't there. But that reflects on me, not Parker."

"Not only did he conduct the interview on his own," Decker said, "but he didn't even record it. Seems irregular, don't you think?"

She shrugged. "He tried to record it. The camera filled up."

Delrawn snorted, and Cobb chuckled, exposing his terribly narrow *u* of upper teeth. No way to convince them, and Levy, who knew the truth, only slouched down in her seat. *Chickenshit.*

Decker opened the folder in front of him. "And then we've got Sadie Wu."

Hernandez might have been fooled into thinking Saul had killed Collins, but she never doubted him about Wu. She'd seen how shaken up he was after her... murder. And it *was* a murder and not a suicide, because however the hell Wayob was doing it, he had forced Wu to eat that gun—he'd killed a girl with her whole life ahead of her, and why? To mess with Saul?

"Where are you going with this? You don't think Parker killed her."

"I wouldn't have thought it, except now both officers assigned to investigate are dead." Decker curled his ring finger and pinky—Arcos and Carter—two more deaths. His tally at four so far. "It's no secret how Parker felt about them."

"He's got a hell of an alibi for those two," she said.

"And that is?"

"Me. We had lunch at Langer's. No way he could have offed Carter in time to meet me there."

Decker's mouth opened, but she knew what he was going to say.

"Parker had nothing to do with Arcos either," she said. "He was in El Monte, cuffed, in the back of my car." Although technically she'd arrested him shortly after the time of death, there was no way he was involved. No way at all.

Decker flipped a page in the folder and studied it as if he hadn't already seen it before the meeting. "There's that damning photo of Collins on his phone. How do you explain that?"

She shook her head and exhaled. "You'll never believe it, but if you give me some time—"

"Doesn't matter what I believe; it's what they believe." He motioned to the wall of windows behind him, City Hall and the sprawl of LA. "Your partnership was just an assignment, but think about me. The LAPD is *my* responsibility. I'm going to look like a blind fool. I'm asking for your help here. We're all in this together, Hernandez."

She combed back her bangs. The moment of truth. "I am trying to help." *And trying to save Rosa's life.* She didn't give a damn about the headlines and politics. "Parker is the best detective in Homicide Special. If you're looking for a scapegoat, maybe go with Arcos and Carter."

Cobb glowered across the table at her. "Arcos and Carter gave their lives to the department. They were good men."

She glared back. "Good for what?"

"Maybe you'd like a demonstration?" He crossed his arms and leaned back. "If you're not going to help us, I'll open an investigation. Maybe it was more than carelessness when you released Parker; I'm thinking you knew where he'd go." He smirked. "And how did he end up with a gun in the hospital? You were there, right?"

Total bullshit, of course, but even if she could prove it, Cobb would find some other way to have her fired.

She unclipped her badge from her belt. "Go ahead and take it." She flung it across the table. It slid on the lacquer more easily than she'd imagined and her heart leaped after it. She should have thought about Rumi.

Cobb clawed for her badge, but Decker snatched it away, his hand the size of a baseball mitt. He held it up in the sunlight glaring in off of City Hall and seemed to study it.

How would she pay for Rumi's college now? But it was too late to back down. She straightened her shoulders. "A job is a nothing compared to a life."

No one said a word. The room grew hot. She wanted to take her coat off but forced herself to sit still.

"I need my best people on the case," Decker said.

A wave of relief washed through her, and she steeled herself against it. "Then you need Parker."

"What if I give you until tonight to convince me? Once the article hits the *Times*, I have to contain the damage."

"We've got lives at stake here—real people dying—and you're worried about public opinion?"

"Where do you think my budget comes from? I need officers to take down bad guys. I can't spare one man at the cost of many more."

She crossed her arms and repeated the words of Tony Blair: "*Sometimes it is better to lose and do the right thing.*"

Decker laid his palms on the table. "And always, where there's smoke there's fire."

She couldn't dispute the proverb, but Decker was wrong about Saul. The whole situation pissed her off. "Saul is the fire because, like Benjamin Disraeli said, 'Courage is fire, and bullying is smoke.' So think about what kind of signal you're sending." Hernandez swept her arm along the table. "You and all your goons here, too afraid for your own asses to actually do anything useful."

Decker stared at her and blinked. O'Connell scowled. Malone gave her a dark look and Levy actually glared at her.

Then Decker rocked back in his chair and roared with laughter, holding his shaking belly. Hernandez found her feelings transformed by his laughter—by his ability to become genuinely jolly in a heartbeat. Now she understood why the mayor's office had reappointed him as top dog of the LAPD time and time again. A laugh like that could quell the tensions in City Hall.

The others joined in but their laughter sounded fake, all except Cobb, whose laughter was genuine and sinister.

As Decker stood, his laughter rumbled to a halt. "You certainly have fire, Hernandez. I'll give you that." He glanced at his subordinates lined along the table.

They too halted their laughter and resumed glowering.

"I'm going against good advice here," he said. "Don't make me regret it." With a flick of his wrist, he sent her badge sliding back across the table.

Cobb watched it sail by, his eyes wide. They all watched, all seeming to wish they had balls to snatch it. The heavy metal made a pleasant percussive sound on the lacquered wood.

"Keep your badge, Detective," Decker said.
She told herself not to reach for it... and then grabbed it greedily.

Shera's New Alpha

Saul parked his Prius outside the KOK. It was a low-slung building with slatted windows punched into concrete walls.

He whistled as he approached, feeling more like himself now that he was wearing a pair of jeans. The handful of ibuprofen he'd taken had tamped the pain in his chest down to a dull ache. Maybe the electronics in his heart weren't so bad; he hadn't felt this good in months.

Inside the narrow lobby, chains in the ceiling supported fluorescent fittings that threw a flat glare onto the concrete. A counter blocked the entrance to the kennels. Behind it sat an officer with a thick crop of brown hair buzzed down to a whitewall, who was eating a burrito half-wrapped in foil. His eyes were narrow and nervous as he plopped the burrito down on a paper plate and swallowed.

Saul's mouth watered. *Carnitas.* The smoothie was now fast approaching the back gate. He needed a snack—something substantial, and soon—to settle his stomach. Once he dealt with Wayob, he'd have to treat himself to a 4x4 from In and Out: four patties, four slices of cheddar. One last hurrah before beginning his diet in earnest. His stomach churned. *Need meat now.*

"You must be Parker," said the officer. Officer Marisco, according to his name tag.

"One and the same."

"Detective Hernandez wants you to call her."

By now, she must have heard about his little breakout from the hospital and anticipated his next move. But if she believed in Wayob, like she said she did, then she had to accept that Saul had to do what needed doing.

"After I see the dog."

Marisco wrapped the foil around his burrito. "She said you'd say that. But you don't want anything to do with Cujo, trust me."

Saul shrugged. "No choice."

Marisco led him into the kennel, where German shepherds paced their cages with nervous energy. The aisle between the cages led to a double-wide doorway, which was open. Outside, a dirt track encircled a fenced-in field.

"What did it do?" Saul asked.

"It's a she. She tried to kill me, is what she did. She should be put down, and I've never said that about any other dog. Usually, when a dog hurts a human, there are extenuating circumstances, but it's always the dog who goes down for it, you know?

"Anyway, I thought she'd appreciate a walk, but I practically had to tackle her just to get the leash on. I thought she might snap out of it once we got moving. Since she's Ashley York's dog and all, I assumed she was probably trained. So, I got the leash on and she walked beside me to the door. Then, all of a sudden, she darted between my legs and cut to the side. And she was booking hard, I'm telling you—it was deliberate. The leash caught my leg, and I nearly bonked my head on the doorframe when I fell."

They stopped near a plaque of the police motto, *To Protect and Serve*. The cage across from it contained the black dog: Wayob. The dog looked from Marisco to Saul. Those black eyes that Saul would never forget seemed to lack the burning intensity from last night. Now they were almost eager, yearning. The dog jumped up on its hind legs, placed its front paws on the chain-link fence, and tried to shove its muzzle through. Saul sprang back.

The dog's tail wagged. Its whole body wiggled. It came down and leaped up again, sniffing and whimpering at Saul.

"Hard to believe with the way she's acting now," Marisco said, "but I'm telling you, I've worked with hundreds of dogs, and any one of them, after the leash came free, would have bolted out the door. But not this girl, oh no. She was on me. She leaped on my chest with a look in her eyes that was like... so evil. I could feel it. She locked her jaw on my throat. I thought I was going to die. She didn't break the skin, but I couldn't breathe. And she just held me there like that. I'd almost passed out by the time Shy pulled her off. If it wasn't for him, I'm telling you, the bitch is a straight-up killer. I'd put her down myself, if she wasn't Ashley York's dog."

The dog sniffed the air, whimpering through the fence, her tail whipping and butt shaking.

Marisco rubbed his cheek. "I guess it's hard to believe."

"Oh, I believe you." Last night, Saul had felt the same way when Wayob glared down at him from the guard booth with those burning black eyes.

He thought he'd know Wayob now, regardless of whose body he possessed, and if this was Wayob in the dog then he was acting uncharacteristically friendly. So unless Wayob was a better actor than Saul had imagined, or the dog's brain was somehow limiting Wayob's personality, then this wasn't Wayob.

"This the guy?" a voice behind them said.

Saul turned as an officer trotted in with a German shepherd. He was tall and black with the sort of dark skin that had spent a lot of time in the sun. His gray curls were cropped close and receding back from his forehead.

"Yup," Marisco said. "Check it out. Cujo is acting all nice now."

"One second." The officer ushered the German shepherd into the kennel by the door.

"The thing I don't understand," Marisco said, "is why Ashley York would want a dog like this? Guess she's not going to want it back now that it killed a guy."

Saul held a hand tentatively to the fence. The dog sniffed and tried to lick it.

"She's faking it," Marisco said. "I'm telling you."

"I'll have to take my chances." Saul tried to sound fearless, assuming Wayob had no problem following their conversation from inside the dog. "I've got a few pounds on you." He patted his belly. *More like a hundred fifty, but not for long.* "Can I borrow a leash?" *And maybe a taser.*

The other officer approached, sweat glistening on his forehead. He blew out a lungful of air and held out a hand. "Ronnie Shy, chief trainer." He spoke with a kind demeanor.

"Parker." Saul shook his hand.

"So you're taking Cujo, as Marisco calls her?"

"I've got orders," Saul lied.

"Good," Shy said. "She shouldn't be here. We only house K-9 officers, but someone in the upper echelon was afraid of the blowback if we sent Ashley York's dog to animal control."

"All citizens are created equal," Saul said.

Marisco laughed sarcastically. "We should put her down like animal control would have."

"Not a good idea," Saul said.

"Do you intend to handle this dog alone?" Shy asked.

"I can manage." Saul wished he had some kind of tranquilizer instead of the useless EpiPens he'd grabbed at the hospital.

Shy nodded skeptically. He grabbed a leash and a muzzle from the rack by the doorway. "You should have seen how my K-9s went nuts when we brought her in. I've never seen anything like it, and I've been around dogs my whole life."

Saul glanced at the other cages. Seven or eight German shepherds stood watching with what seemed more like neutral curiosity.

"Yeah, they've calmed down now," Shy said. "But I'm telling you, they'll rest easier once she's gone." He cautiously opened the door to the cage.

Marisco unsnapped his hip holster and gripped his Glock.

Too bad that bullets were useless against Wayob, and Saul did not care for another demonstration. "Don't you have a taser or something?"

"Relax, guys," Shy said. "I've got this." Shy slipped in and shut the cage behind him.

The dog continued wagging its tail. Perhaps involuntarily. Perhaps Wayob had no control or idea it was happening at all. It tried to leap on Shy.

"Back!" Shy shoved the dog's neck.

The dog fell back. The tail stopped.

Shy approached slowly, the muzzle in one hand, the leash in the other. "She hates to be touched."

The dog came forward, peering up eagerly at Shy as if to say, *Touch me, please, please.*

Shy quickly grabbed the collar. Twisted the dog around. Slipped the muzzle over its nose.

The tail resumed wagging, as if the muzzle meant nothing and the dog was just glad to have Shy in there with it.

"Weird." Shy led the dog out by the leash. "You should have seen her before."

The dog tried to jump at Saul, but Shy yanked her back.

"Doesn't even seem like the same dog," Marisco said.

"Sit," Shy said.

The dog sat.

"Meet us out front. I want to run her for a bit." Shy clicked his tongue and started toward the back door.

But Saul didn't want to explain why he was loading the dog into his personal Prius. "I'll just take her," he said. "I'm sure you guys have better stuff to do."

Shy didn't look back as he continued through the double doorway and into the sunlight. The dog trotted along beside him. Marisco shrugged and jogged after them.

With no chance of catching up in his current condition, Saul cut through the lobby to the front. He stood away from his Prius, by the K-9 cruisers, for a nervous few minutes.

Shy came around the side of the building with the dog prancing right along beside him. Marisco followed.

"If I didn't know better," Shy said, "I'd say this was a different dog."

Saul reached for the leash. "You're like the dog whisperer."

Shy glanced at the Prius and came to a halt. "Whoa, is that your personal ride?" He drew the dog up close by his side, just out of reach.

"Long story," Saul said. "I was planning to do something else today."

Shy squinted at the Prius, as if still deciding whether or not to let Saul take the dog. Marisco had his hand resting on the Glock holstered at his side, and he seemed punchy. Probably looking for any justification to put down *Cujo.*

"You covered for damages?" Shy asked. "She ain't acting up now, but she might." The dog sat on its haunches, tongue lolling out.

Saul exhaled—Shy was going to hand over the dog after all. "Least of my worries."

"Marisco, mind taking her in your cruiser?"

Saul's gut constricted. His pacemaker hammered into action. He needed Wayob alone, isolated with no place to go.

Marisco smiled. "Can I meet Ashley York?"

"Unlikely," Saul said. "She's got all kinds of handlers and middlemen." He didn't know where she and Wilson had holed up after the bloodbath, but fortunately he no longer needed to reach her; he had the Encanto.

"I'm on call, anyway." Marisco kicked the gravel. "I'm already pushing my thirty-minute leash just being here."

On call, Saul knew, meant a trial. The leash was the window of time allotted for Marisco to return to court when summoned before the judge issued a bench warrant.

"Right," Shy said. "Almost forgot. I'd take her myself, but I'm short staffed and behind on training."

"Not a problem." Saul considered requesting to borrow a K-9 cruiser. Putting a cage between him and Wayob on the long drive ahead would provide some peace of mind. But Shy would need a badge number for the log, and he might expect to see an actual badge.

Shy held out the leash. "Try walking her. Let's see how it goes."

Saul's fear of the killer possibly hiding inside that black furry body was overcome by his need to know. He took the leash and hoped that Wayob would reveal himself. The dog leaped ahead of Saul and turned back. It crouched with its front paws spread, wagging its butt in the air. Every muscle engaged as if to say, *play, play, play.*

"Guess she likes you," Shy said.

No, she doesn't, Saul thought, *not if she's Wayob*. He studied the black dog that was no longer acting like Wayob, no longer like Marisco and Shy had described. Dread weighed heavily on Saul's shoulders.

The dog tilted her head and cocked her ears. Peered up at him. It was the same eager expression as two days ago, the first time he'd seen her in Ashley's guard booth. She had leaped up and put her big black paws on the window, and Johnson—before he was Wayob—had rubbed the back of her head. What had Johnson called her?

She wasn't Wayob now. Not anymore. Saul wished she was, because not knowing where Wayob was, was worse.

It was one thing to guess something, but he had to put it to the test. He had to make sure.

He kneeled on the gravel and faced the dog.

"Whoa, careful," Shy said.

Saul heard the snap of Marisco's holster. If the dog so much as twitched, Marisco would shoot, Saul knew, and he couldn't let that happen. He moved into Marisco's line of fire.

"Relax," Saul said. "I think her name is Shera."

At the sound of her name, her eyes widened. Every muscle seemed to vibrate with life. An amazing performance, if this was Wayob.

Saul unstrapped the muzzle and braced himself.

"Don't," Marisco said.

The dog's mouth snapped open. And out came the tongue.

———

Shera tried to lick the big man, the man who knew her shame, trying to show

666

him she was herself now, but he held her back. She lowered her head.

Big man yelled to the other men, the one who smelled of smoked pork and the one who smelled of sweat. Men could share thoughts through voices, Shera knew.

The pork man yelled back, angry. Shera felt ashamed. Ashamed all over again for this morning, for the fact that pork man would never understand that Shera had tried not to attack him. She had fought the will of the bad one and failed. She had tasted the flesh of pork man's neck and nearly his blood, but the bad one—who Shera feared but did not understand—did not want pork man to die. The bad one had not meant to make Shera kill the man last night; he'd lost himself in overwhelming fear.

Shera barked. The men stopped yelling. She barked again, wishing she too could share thoughts through speak sounds. She needed to make them understand, but how?

Now pork man was pointing at Shera, pointing with the metal thing. The sweaty man yelled. Big man moved swiftly toward pork man. Shera could tell how it pained him.

Pork man yelled again, and big man shouted back. Sweaty man moved cautiously toward Shera. She wanted to run, but running away always got her in trouble.

When they had jogged around the building, sweaty man had called her a good girl, and she wanted to show him—to show them all—that she was a good girl. So she summoned all her courage and forced herself to stay, despite how much she hated harsh voices. She sat still: a good girl.

The big man snatched the metal thing from pork man. He turned back toward Shera and shouted, not at Shera but at the sweaty man, shouted at both men. What was he doing?

The sweaty man froze. He lifted his hands.

Now Shera understood: big man was protecting her. He knew her shame, and yet he protected her like an alpha. Turning his back on the other men, he kneeled and offered Shera his hand.

Shera smelled hunger and something bitter… pain? She smelled the scent of last night when she lost control. When the bad one made Shera kill a man. She had not known she could kill a man. Yet big man, even after witnessing the horrible act, here he was now offering his hand to Shera. Did he understand?

Shera's heart swelled. Barking wouldn't do. Howling, useless. Shera could and would nuzzle big man, but in this moment she had to give him everything, offer herself completely. She rolled onto her back. Exposing her belly and her neck. Vulnerable. She put it all on the line. Full submission.

For a long moment nothing happened. However big man chose to react, she would accept it, remain submissive regardless. Big man could not know Shera's sorrow, how the bad one had forced her to tear out the man's throat last night—the bad one who lived in the dark place and hid inside other bodies, and who had only anger and fear. Shera had wanted no part of it, yet all her struggling had amounted to nothing. The bad one had forced her jaws to the man's throat. Forced her to taste his blood, to suffer the bad one's revulsion at the very act he'd willed Shera into doing. Bad one confused her.

Her belly hair prickled, and then she felt it: big man's hand—rub, rub, rub. Strong, comforting joy spasmed through Shera.

Big man understood.

Shera popped up. Big man rubbed her head. The man who knew her shame like no other. Now sweaty man was there beside big man, holding his hand for Shera to sniff. He spoke with kindness in his voice.

Shera nuzzled big man. He laughed. His whole body shook, and she loved him. She burrowed her head under his big arm and his scent overcame all others. She felt home, and now she committed herself, completely. Her new alpha.

"Back." Big man laughed as he pushed her back, in a friendly way that meant not now, not right now, but soon they would play.

Big man stood. He handed the metal thing, smelling of harsh oil, back to pork man, who returned it to his hip and stepped back. He watched Shera warily.

Big man opened the door to the traveler. Old scents from the big man's many rides spilled out. He unlatched her leash.

"Get in," big man said. "It's okay, girl."

Better than okay—Shera loved rides!

She leaped into the traveler. Big man tossed the leash in and shut the door. He spoke to the other men, who seemed subdued now, and then walked behind the traveler. Was he leaving her here? Trapped and alone?

After a long moment, finally, big man opened the other door. Her heart swelled. She and big man were pack now. They would stay together. Shera would protect pack with her life.

As they drove, the glass beside Shera opened. She stuck her head out the window and sniffed the air rushing by: joy. Oh, how alive she felt with the wind in her face, the smell of travelers and people, of rabbit, coyote, and a distant he-dog. So many smells all at once. Above the road, above the trees, the burning yellow light moved along with them.

How much her life had changed. Last night, before the bad one found her in her sleep, Shera had thought of the soap-smelling Black man as her new alpha, but she had learned from the bad one that he had died too—and oh how she missed him. He had fed Shera and let her sleep in the house near the woman who smelled like lavender, who did not like Shera. And now the woman would never like her, because the bad one had made Shera bite her last night when she was wearing the skin of a man. (Until last night, Shera had not even known that people could change skins.) Shera had fought not to bite the woman but she had failed, and the bad one had wanted worse. He had wanted the woman to die by Shera's teeth, and Shera's teeth would have killed her too if not for the stone ball. The stone ball that the bad one wanted more than anything, so bad that he had killed the man. But the man had outsmarted the bad one by locking Shera—with the bad one trapped inside her —in the small room.

She loved the wind, yes, but more than the wind, more than all the smells in the world, she loved her new big alpha. She pulled back from the window and shoved her head between the seats. She and big man were pack. Shera licked his arm. She would guard big man against pork man, against all other men, against the bad one. She would guard with her life.

But here in the traveler they were safe, for now. She reviewed her objectives:

Man safe.

Pack safe.

Shera safe.

In that order.

Shera tasted the air… Bad one was not near. But she would be watching, always watching, for the man who hid in others. Dog or man, it made no difference to Shera. No skin could hide bad one from her.

Rise of Wayob

In Malibu, upstairs in her dressing room, Ashley smiled at herself in the mirror. It looked forced and more than a little fake. Outside, a wave gushed over a rock like a crescendo of applause that abruptly died off.

What had happened to the sense of well-being that had risen inside her? She still wanted to help others achieve their dreams, of course, but something was nagging her. She wondered if Gray would understand this growing feeling of disconnection, but he was at the hospital with Claire, and had left her alone in the house with Mindy, Tyler, and Marta.

Ashley blinked, and blinked again, and her lids felt a little less open each time. She rubbed them, strained her eyes open but still she felt... outside herself somehow...

Something shimmered in the jewelry box on the dresser: teardrop diamond earrings she'd never worn. She took them out, and they sparkled, and somehow the deep shades of the Pacific glinted in the stones.

As she hooked one earring in her left ear, the other slipped from her hand. It disappeared into the shag carpet. She got down on her knees near the dozen or so pairs of shoes she kept here for her rare visits and combed her hand through the white yarn. From between the fibers, the diamond sparkled.

As she stood, the room swayed. She tried to stand still, but the walls wobbled and spun. And blurred out of focus.

When she searched for her reflection, the mirror seemed dimmer. A smudge distorted her face. She snatched a folded shirt from the shelf beside her and rubbed at the smear on the glass.

How can she help anyone else when she's in such a mess? When she needs to get away before the cops swarm in with all their incessant questions about the ones who died at her house. The ones he had to kill. He'd had no choice. Wayob wants to become anonymous, to rid himself of all the fans. Just to live in peace, alone, at her palace on the hill.

These thoughts are not her own, she realizes too late. Now she can only watch as Wayob laughs at her in the mirror, laughs with her face, but the smile is all wrong. His malicious laughter sounds fake.

And she feels him like a thousand spiders wriggling around in her head. Like this morning, when she thought she felt that bug on her face—that had been Wayob, she realizes, clawing his way in; and throughout the day, he's been digging deeper and deeper...

———

"I have control," Wayob says. "Finally. No longer must I endure your miserable existence, your sex act." He frowns at Ashley in the mirror. "Where is the Encanto?"

But of course, she cannot answer. Wayob shall find his answer in her mind. She must have it here, or Gray has it. Could they have switched bodies without it?

He must sit in order to concentrate. In the bedroom, his lip curls. The white blanket covering the bed recalls the abuse to which Ashley and Gray subjected Wayob, having to endure every moment of their carnal union and powerless to stop it.

Out on the balcony, cold sunlight kicks off the sea along with a harsh wind. He sits in a chair made from woven twigs and shivers as clouds line up on the horizon. It's never cold in the Encanto, never hot either. He closes his eyes.

He opens the connection between what he knows and what Ashley knows. He searches her memories for the Encanto, but finds only her recollection of Gray stuffing it into the trash receptacle the night before last. Wayob had already found it there. He'd almost had it then. He would have, if not for the repugnant old man who stole it.

A distant dog barks above the din of the ocean, as if intentionally to interrupt Wayob's concentration. Why must he always be interrupted?

He feels a sudden sense of vertigo, as though he is falling, but he knows he is sitting still, so he keeps his eyes closed and tries to maintain his concentration.

But again, the dog barks from somewhere on the far side of the house, and there is something about that sound...

Wayob's face stings. His eyes spring open. Did he just slap himself? His hand smacks his cheek, a finger grazes his eye. Colored dots swim across his vision. Ashley! She's slashing her way back in. No! She is standing up, and he is powerless to stop her.

———

Ashley leaned over the balcony, clutching the rail so hard the steel dug into her skin, but she didn't care. Her arms trembled as she tried uselessly to bend the rail. Wayob could see everything, all of her memories. She'd never felt more violated. And worse, with Wayob in her body, Gray wouldn't see him coming. She would rather die than be responsible for murder. Gray had Mindy and Tyler; she had nothing.

She should just jump. It must be thirty feet down. But the tide washing through the stilts beneath the house looked uncertainly deep. She might just end up paralyzed, like Claire, who Gray was going back to. Like he should.

As she went inside, she had this sense sort of like floating over her own feet. She hovered before the bedroom mirror, wondering if Wayob could see what she was seeing, and knowing that he could. She couldn't stand the thought of him back there, ripping through her mind. Nor could she stand the way his smile twisted her face. His horrible musical laugh. Without even realizing what she was doing, she slammed her fist into the glass. The mirror shattered, and she snatched up a long shard.

She managed to reach her throat with it before doubt—or was it Wayob?—seized her hand. The edge creased her skin just short of slicing through.

"It will do no good," she hears herself say. Wayob's words. Her voice.

She is transported back to her lawn, where Sammy is trying to speak as he coughs up blood. *This is just a memory*, she tells herself. At least it's her memory, which makes it less terrible than the anguish and pain she glimpsed inside Wayob as he probed her mind. She'd seen tribal attire, a stone temple. He must be a thousand years old, moving from one body to the next, like slipping into a new pair of jeans.

A black ocean surrounds her. She swims upward for a long, long time, trying not to panic while also panicking. She cannot see, cannot breathe, can't keep on going, yet she must.

A faint wavering light oozes up from the deep. Is the light moving, or is she? Can it be the surface? She has lost all sense of up and down. With renewed energy, she struggles toward the light. It expands before her.

Instead of sunlight or sky, it's her own face. It ripples in the mirror. As she reaches toward it, her eyes close, and then she falls into the darkness behind Wayob. She sees his memory of her father's blue Henley stained with blood, his eyes glazed over. He's dead. And now she has no one—no family. Alone in the world. Alone.

———

But Wayob is not to blame, and if it were worth the effort, he would explain it all to poor, poor Ashley, who thought she could stop Wayob by killing her dear, sweet Sammy, but it was all for nothing. Now she knows that killing Sammy is merely a setback. And now Wayob has her as his vessel. This time, he is firmly in control of her young body.

He touches her lean face in the mirror. Wayob has learned, from the mind of August Grant, that men desire her skinny body, but Wayob cannot understand why anyone would desire any physical contact from her or any other. Ugh. Ashley's long golden hair feels oily on Wayob's neck. If he cuts it all off, would that make him unattractive to such men? The thought of them touching him makes his skin crawl. If this is going to be a problem, he will have to find a new vessel. Once he has the Encanto, if it can be repaired, Wayob will probably be able to transmigrate into anyone.

So where is it? Probably still with the repugnant old man who killed Wayob in the vessel of Arcos, and who, by poisoning the air, must have killed himself in the process. He got his just desserts.

Before Wayob goes to his house, he should kill Gray, because if Gray tries to transmigrate into Ashley's body at this point, it could be disastrous for Wayob. Gray will not be suspicious of Ashley's body. And if he is, well, Wayob has Gray's little children here in Ashley's seaside lodge, like bait in a trap. Gray will come back for them. Will he not?

This reminds Wayob of Rosa. Poor Rosa, probably still in the trunk of her car where Wayob left it last night. Wayob should free her, for she is of no use to him now and he knows all too well the agony of being trapped alone in a dark place, but he cannot spare the time. He needs to kill Gray and secure the Encanto for himself. She can stand a few more hours. Hours are a pittance compared to what Wayob has endured. If Rosa could comprehend that, she would enjoy waiting the short amount of time, alone with no one bothering her.

Wayob hugs himself in the young body of Ashley York and laughs in the mirror, rocking back and forth. Things are finally going his way, and he deserves this after so many centuries of suffering. He had not meant to kill Ashley's father—had not wanted to harm anyone—but as it turns out, thanks to Evan York's death, his new vessel stands to inherit a fortune far beyond anything Wayob has ever imagined throughout all his endless years trapped inside the Encanto. He has seen inside enough minds to know people are greedy, and with so much wealth in his possession, who would dare stand in the way of Wayob?

Parker? Ha.

That dog barks yet again. Its harsh voice grates through the walls. That voice... Wayob knows it—has *used* it. It belongs to the ignorant mongrel that was Wayob's vessel.

How could it be here? Who released it from its cage? The mutt should be put down for killing a man; Wayob had heard the officer say so—though technically Wayob's intention had only been to stop Luna but the mutt is to blame. If not for the mutt's pathetic useless paws, Wayob could have seized the Encanto right then and there and spared himself hours of unneeded suffering.

The mutt barks louder. How has it found him here? The incessant barking reverberates in Wayob's head. The mongrel wants revenge. *Well, too bad, you cannot enter.*

Wayob scurries down the stairs to verify what he knows to be true. He whistles some annoying tune, over and over. When he stops himself from whistling, the melody goes on in his mind. Where did this miserable tune come from? *Stop it.*

He finds no windows facing the street side of the house, so he stands behind the front door and listens... But he's whistling that fucking tune again.

He will have to open the door to see outside, but what if the wretched mutt is there on the other side, waiting to rip out Wayob's throat?

Wayob swallows his trepidation and is reaching for the doorknob when his legs buckle and he falls backward. His tailbone smacks the floor.

As he tries to right himself, his head throbs. *It is Ashley, clawing her way back,* he thinks. But no, now he sees the attack was external: a giggling little brat topples on top of him.

He crabwalks back, trying to roll the miserable child out of his lap without touching her germ-infested skin. She giggles and clutches onto him with her sticky little hands.

"Get off," he says. "I am not playing." But she obviously thinks that he is. She clutches his leg as he struggles to his feet. He drags her across the floor.

"How would you like to go in the closet, little girl?"

She stops laughing, but instead of letting go she grasps onto his other leg. Now he cannot move forward, and he lacks the leverage to kick free. Wayob would prefer to be alone in a dark place over this.

A bell rings. The dark rectangle by the door brightens into a moving picture of what must be the view from the other side: cars careening down the highway, and on the steps is the mutt.

The sight of it, standing there with its teeth bared, sends a chill down Wayob's spine, yet this is nothing compared to the other surprise. Wayob would have expected anyone over the corpulent man who holds the orange rope attached to the mutt.

Parker.

How can it be Parker? Wayob watched him dying last night. And if they somehow saved his life then he should have been imprisoned. Even if Saroyan's body has not yet been discovered, Wayob reported Parker for the murder of Collins. Wayob had not meant to end her life while using Parker as a vessel, but her hands were all over him and he had nearly lost control in the labyrinth of Parker's mind.

Did the mutt lead Parker here, or did Parker lead the mutt? Wayob could have killed them both—he *should* have—because now here they are, ganging up on him, and right when his freedom is so close at hand yet still so brittle.

But Parker cannot know that Wayob is here in Ashley's body, can he? He should not know… and yet, Wayob realizes that somehow, he does.

Claire Versus Hernandez

Claire awakened, feeling a little groggy but rested, but then she remembered she was in the hospital and her legs were useless, and, just to add to her misery, she saw Detective Hernandez standing over her bed. The detective's arms were crossed, as if Claire was rude for making her wait, as if Claire hadn't just about died last night.

"Sorry to be sleeping," Claire said. "Guess I thought for what this room costs, I could take a little nap in private." She glanced at the clock—it seemed like decades since Gray said he was coming—but it was only 2:56 p.m. Hardly an hour had passed since she called him.

"I'm so sorry for what happened to you," Hernandez said. What she didn't say, but probably thought, was that if Claire had told the whole truth yesterday, if she had let Hernandez help, then no one would have died, and Claire would still have working legs instead of useless flesh-logs attached to her torso.

"You woke me up to apologize?"

"I didn't mean to wake you, but I do have a few questions."

Gray chose that exact moment to slide through the doorway, all nonchalant, with his hair ruffed up like he'd been through a wind tunnel.

Claire shook her head as he opened his mouth to speak. Although she wanted him here, his presence would only make things worse. No doubt Hernandez had a long list of questions for Gray, but Claire had her own questions, and she wanted to ask them first. He glanced at Hernandez, seemed to grasp the situation, and slunk back into the hall.

"Talk to Officer Blake," Claire said. "I already told him everything." The hospital blanket covered her shoulders, so Claire had to shrug more with her eyebrows.

"Mrs. Wilson, do you know where your husband is?"

"Should I?"

Hernandez stared at her. Seconds beeped past on the monitor, and she began to worry that she'd given something away. But she hadn't. She hadn't said anything.

Hernandez glanced behind her at the now empty doorway. She sat in the chair beside Claire, hands outstretched in her lap.

"Do you know where your children are?"

Claire tried to sit up again but couldn't. She needed to figure out with Gray how to tell Mindy and Tyler that... Was she really paralyzed for life? Was there no chance she could recover the use of her legs?

"Mrs. Wilson?"

"They're not at my house?" If Gray had taken Mindy and Tyler somewhere with Ashley, then she might have to tell him how wrong that was.

Hernandez shook her head. "We have a uniform at your house. No one's been there all day."

"I've kind of been out of it." Claire motioned at her useless legs. "But I appreciate your concern."

"I'm sure the children are fine," Hernandez said vaguely, like she thought maybe Claire knew for a fact that they were not. "I was hoping we could talk about last night."

"Like I said, I already told *Blake* everything."

"Right. He gave me the download. And you weren't entirely honest with us." Hernandez pulled a notepad from her jacket and flipped through it, as if she were having a hard time deciding which of Claire's many lies to address first.

Claire swallowed hard. Maybe she was still under the influence of whatever drugs they had given her, but her head felt clearer now than it had in months. The fog of her insomnia had finally lifted. She had hardly told Blake anything. She was sure.

"Ah." Hernandez finally settled on a page. "You stated that Ashley York killed her guard. Is that correct?"

"Yes, she saved my life."

"Can you explain why your husband's fingerprints were on the murder weapon?"

Whatever the reason was, Claire looked forward to hearing Gray explain it, but it didn't make him guilty. Last night, as she lay bleeding in the grass, she'd confused Gray and Ashley somehow, thinking she saw Ashley leaning over her in the haze of her dimming vision, but it had been Gray. Of course it was Gray, which meant Ashley had killed her guard. "You even bother checking for Ashley's prints?"

"We checked. Ashley's fingerprints aren't on the knife or the gun. Your husband's are on both."

It was Gray who stabbed the guard. Claire knew now. She had seen him do it. Although it had seemed like Gray kneeling beside her, she now remembered it was Ashley caressing her cheek, saying her name the way Gray said it. *Weird.*

Yesterday morning, when Ashley said that she and Gray had switched bodies, it had sounded like the most ridiculous thing. But... Ashley had known how Gray proposed. How? She'd assumed Gray had told her, but why? It made no sense.

The only thing that made any kind of sense—impossible as it was—was that Gray had been in Ashley's body. It explained last night. It explained the phone call yesterday morning. It could explain all his strange behavior over the past few days.

"Look," Claire said, "you've got it all wrong. The guard..." There had been something off about the guard too, the way he spoke.

"Sammy Johnson."

"Yeah, he fucking shot me. And he'd have shot Gray and Ashley too. Whoever killed him should get a medal."

Hernandez pushed the gray strand of hair off her forehead. "I agree with you there. The thing I'm trying to understand is why you said it was Ashley?"

Claire had no answer for this. Not one she could say out loud. She only hoped that the man in the hallway actually was Gray. She needed to tell him that she believed him now. She needed to tell him so much.

"I'm just trying to understand what happened," Hernandez said. "Let's back up." She flipped through her notebook again. "When we spoke yesterday, you said you had a date with your husband, is that correct?"

"Yes. I didn't mean like a romantic thing."

"You intended to go to Ashley York's."

"He was with Ashley. You saw the photos."

"Were you expecting a confrontation?"

Claire had no idea what she'd expected. But when she'd found that snake thingy in Charlie's dead hand, she'd known Gray was in trouble. "What the hell kind of question is that?"

"A reasonable one, I think. A woman discovers her husband is having an affair with a beautiful and very young celebrity, and she gets mad. Am I right?"

"They weren't having an affair."

"So, what was it then?"

"I didn't exactly get a chance to ask."

Hernandez clawed back that strand of gray hair, which had again fallen across her forehead. She turned to a clean page in her notebook, looked down at Claire, and furrowed her brows. "Do you carry a gun?"

Claire didn't, normally. "Guess you found my pistol?"

"We did."

Claire hadn't fired it, but only because she never got the chance. "Was it the murder weapon?"

"No. Johnson was shot with a Colt M1911A1, the same weapon that killed August Grant."

"*August Grant was involved?*" This thing was like an onion, layers upon layers of weirdness, and no better inside than out.

"Did you enter Ashley York's house?"

Claire shook her head. "August Grant was inside?"

"In the kitchen." Hernandez began writing in her notebook at a million miles a minute. Claire had hardly said anything. What the hell was she writing?

"So, we've established you went to Ashley York's with a loaded weapon. It may not matter whether you fired it or not. If you escalated the confrontation, you could be charged with second-degree murder."

"This is ridiculous!" Gray said, charging though the door. "August was dead before she even got there."

Hernandez sprang up from the chair and blocked him from reaching Claire's bed. "Mr. Wilson. You're a hard man to find."

"Well, here I am. You going to arrest me?"

"Should I?"

He held out his hands. "You think I killed Sammy."

"No," Claire said, wishing she could wedge her body between them. She struggled to sit upright and failed even at that. "Gray, don't talk to her."

Hernandez glanced from Gray to Claire. And she seemed to soften somewhat, or maybe she just resigned herself to the fact that she was not going to get anywhere.

The phone on her belt rang. She snatched it off, and, as she looked at the screen, her eyes went wide. She answered: "Yes sir." As she listened, her brows knotted. "You're kidding me." She fixed her gaze on Gray. "Hold on," she said into the phone then covered the microphone with her thumb. With her other hand she pointed at Gray. "I'll be right outside in the hall, so don't even think about going anywhere."

"I'll stay here too. Don't worry," Claire said to Hernandez's back as she turned and walked to the hall.

Hernandez closed the door behind her, and Claire fixed her gaze on Gray.

Saul Stabs Ashley

Saul rang the bell to the Yorks' Malibu property and waited. He stood close to the camera in order to keep his soon-to-be-gone belly out of sight. This time, he'd to stick to his diet as though it were a matter of life and death, and basically it was.

Shera tilted her head, her nostrils in constant motion as if rearranging the air.

"What do you smell, girl?"

She perked her ears and looked at him with giant watery eyes.

The video intercom lit up with Ashley York's face, her lip curled into a sneer. "Why did you bring that filthy animal?"

"She's not Wayob anymore," Saul said. "I thought you might want her back."

Ashley spoke slowly. "The… animal… belongs to me?" The pitch of her voice modulated.

Maybe it was Johnson's dog? Saul had only seen Shera at the guard booth. "May I come in? I'm Detective Parker with the LAPD." Saul tapped the pocket of his trench coat where he'd carried his badge before it was confiscated. "I'm here to save your life."

"I know who you are, Parker." She practically spat his name.

As Saul gathered his thoughts to explain how her impression of him was all wrong, the lock disengaged and the door clicked open.

"I'll be upstairs," she said. "Put the dog in the garage." The video went dark but the door remained locked for a solid minute before Saul rang again.

The electronic lock clicked open.

Inside, a meaty aroma met Saul on the stairs. Shera pulled ahead of him, her claws pattering on the hardwood steps, probably as intoxicated by the aroma as he was. In the kitchen, a big pot simmered on the stove. Beside it, a young Latina with thick curls flowing over her shoulders was kneeling down, drying the tears of a pale little girl with pink bows in her hair.

Shera barked and lunged at the end of her leash, yanking Saul toward the living room where an all-glass wall faced the ocean. Outside, sunlight reflecting off the waves blurred a figure into a dark vertical line. Ashley?

Saul pulled back on the leash. A low growl emanated from Shera's chest. Her head trembled, all her energy focused on the figure in the glare.

The woman stood. She wore a baggy shirt tucked into tight jeans, in her front pocket, the bulge of a phone. "Ashley said the dog has to stay in the garage."

Shera whimpered, and Saul patted her head. He could hardly object to the way she was acting.

The woman introduced herself as Marta and said the garage was by the front door.

As Saul led Shera back down the stairs, she calmed and wagged her tail. On the landing to the left of the front door was the door to the garage and beside it another flight of stairs descended to the lower part of the house.

Saul trotted Shera into the garage, dropped the leash, and left. Shera spun, leaping into the door as he closed it. The door shook in its frame. From the other side, she clawed the wood. She barked and howled.

"Sorry, girl."

As he started up the stairs, Marta started down from above, carrying the little girl, who was hugging Marta's neck. He backed down to the landing to make room for them.

"Ashley's waiting on the deck," she said. In one hand she held a baby monitor, a crying infant on the screen.

Anticipation charged through his artificial heart. He knew the answer but asked anyway. "Your kids?"

"Mister Gray's."

Finally. He'd found Gray Wilson. "Where is he?"

"The hospital."

Saul's heart dropped.

"He's fine," she said quickly, perhaps reading the disappointment on his face. "It's his wife. He thought she was dead, but it turns out she's in the hospital."

And Saul knew which one. *Damn it.* After his great escape, now he had to go back.

Shera clawed at the door and whimpered as Marta continued past him down the stairs.

He had the Encanto stashed in the glovebox, so Wayob should be after him now, not Wilson; and if so, then everyone near Saul was in danger. But how would Wayob know he had the Encanto? Did Saul have to activate it somehow? Could it summon Wayob?

Although he now believed the Encanto held some power over Wayob, he couldn't trust what he did not understand.

They could surround Ashley York and Gray Wilson with uniforms, as a precaution, until he found out who Wayob was. High brass would probably authorize the manpower for Ashley York, if Hernandez gave them a good reason. But then, Wayob could be one of the uniforms. It was a catch-22. Either way, he had to tell her. He had learned his lesson about holding back.

A door closed in some lower part of the house.

His phone was still booked into evidence, so he climbed back up to the kitchen and searched for a landline. The rich smell of the soup simmering on the stove made him feel dizzy. He found a charger for a cordless handset near the fridge, but the phone was missing. He pressed the button to locate it. No response.

His stomach growled almost louder than Shera. He glanced around. He just had to try the soup. He grabbed a wooden spoon from the holder on the counter and stirred the thick, brownish liquid, scooped out a spoonful which included a chunk of pulled chicken, and blew on it. He sipped from the spoon. Spicy tomato. Tortilla soup. He slid the whole spoon in his mouth. A warmth spread through his chest. He was suddenly ravenous. No one would notice if he helped himself to another spoonful, or five.

But suddenly, he felt a cold prickle through the hair on his neck. Out on the deck, the thin silhouette of Ashley York had moved closer to the window.

Saul dropped the spoon in the sink and started toward her. As he crossed the living room, he glanced at a sketchbook that was spread open on the floor by the couch. He halted. Marched to the book and snatched it up. Bold pencil strokes depicted what he had seen just a few hours earlier.

Deja vu.

The cages, the German shepherds, and the sign, *To Protect and Serve.* Unmistakable. A sketch from inside the KOK, where only officers were allowed, here at the Yorks' Malibu property of all places. The probability of this coincidence was basically zero.

He turned the page. The next two drawings, if you could call them that, were just dark scribbled swirls. The remaining pages were blank.

He flipped back to the KOK. The point of view of the drawing was low down. Maybe Shera's height. Or Wayob's, when he was in her body.

Remarkable. A charge jolted through Saul's gut. Luna had claimed that his mother had had the ability to see what Wayob saw.

Just outside the slider, Ashley stood on the deck, and she seemed to be watching him. Could she see past the reflection? The glare on the waves behind her had dimmed as a bank of fog advanced on the shore.

Saul slid the door open.

Ashley was whistling. It was the same tune Johnson had whistled when he blocked Saul from hiking onto Ashley's property: the *Mission Impossible* theme.

As he stepped onto the deck, Ashley moved back toward a teak high-top, its chairs pulled aside. On the left, a row of chaise lounges reclined in the sun.

He slid the door closed behind him and held up the sketchbook. "Who drew this?"

Ashley stared him in the eye. Her hair was disheveled, blown back from her face, and she didn't seem to notice the thin trail of mucus streaming from her left nostril to her upper lip.

"Parker," she said. "I made you a drink." She gestured toward the table where a glass of cloudy water sat by a lime and a knife, its handle carved from some kind of hardwood and stained dark. The blade curved to a narrow point. A knife for cutting meat.

He opened the book as he moved closer. "Did Wilson draw this?"

She glanced away and backed toward the rail. "Stay out of my face."

Is it me or the drawing she's avoiding? He closed the book and set it on the table. Ashley York was no doubt used to a high degree of coddling. He had come on too strong, asking questions before explaining himself, especially after last night when his gun went off by accident.

"How, may I ask, did you find me?" she asked.

Fifteen years ago, Evan York had sold this property for the price of one dollar to an untraceable shell corporation. The corporation had moved it to a trust. "Death and taxes."

Her brows furrowed.

"It was a simple search with the registrar," he continued. "You're the beneficiary of the trust that pays the taxes." Plus, Shera had alerted as they neared, so he knew this was the place.

"Ah," she smiled. "So, a mere coincidence I happen to be here. And for what reason do you mention death?"

"Bad joke: no one escapes from death and taxes." *Almost inappropriate.* "I'm sorry for your loss."

She scooted around the table. A smear of blood streaked the wood where her hand had been. Gray sky reflected on the blade. It was clean.

"Some do escape death," she said. Her lower lip quivered but her eyes held no emotion.

"You're talking about Wayob? How much do you know?"

"A lot more than you, I would say."

Why was she acting so evasive? "I guess you met Wayob in Johnson's body?"

"You could say that." She looked down. "Dear, sweet Sammy." In her left lobe, a diamond earring flashed in the sunlight. Her right lobe was bare.

"Then you understand you're in danger. May I borrow your phone?"

"No. I am more in danger with you here, you and that filthy animal. Just leave me alone." She studied her palm.

"What happened to your hand?"

She balled it by her side. "You have never cut yourself slicing a fruit?" She circled the table.

Saul moved around the opposite side to face her head-on, his back to the ocean. Clearly, he wasn't going to get anywhere by coddling her; and besides, he was bad at it. "Are you familiar with exigent circumstances?"

A muffled howl pierced through the house. Shera. Ashley flinched, glancing behind her. The windows reflected the clouds clotting the sky, the sun darkened to a dim red disk.

Saul continued, "The law grants me the right to search and seizure if I believe others are in danger." He reached inside his coat. "Give me your phone. I'm not asking anymore." If he drew on Ashley York, there would be repercussions, but repercussions came later. And he wasn't worried about later. Not right now.

"I dropped it." She glanced down to the right. "Behind you, over the rail."

She was lying, but why? He opened his coat and showed her the gun. "Go get it."

A smirk flickered on her lips. "Look." She started around the table toward him.

He didn't turn. No need. Behind the reflection, Marta appeared at the window. She slid open the door, the baby crying in her arms.

Behind her, Shera's howl echoed through the house.

"I am talking to Parker," Ashley snapped. "Do not interrupt us."

Marta's mouth fell open. She moved back a little. "But the dog is chewing through the door. We have to do something."

"Get it out of here," Ashley said. "The baby too. I want everyone gone from this place."

Marta glanced from Ashley to Saul. "But—"

"This mansion belongs to me, does it not? I wish to be alone."

Ashley seemed manic. Why offer him a drink just to order him to leave? And the way she was speaking, that lilting cadence. It ripped into Saul's gut and yanked down.

"Sure," he said. "We'll get out of here."

Marta did a double take. Even Ashley's brows tipped up in surprise. Then her lips began to curl—a smile which quickly vanished when he moved toward her. Ashley stepped back.

"Just a quick question," he said, "then I'll go."

She stared at him, eyes wide.

"What was your mother's name?"

Her face darkened. Went blank...

"Too slow," he said. He had felt something was off from the instant he heard her whistling, and now his last doubts had departed.

Wayob opened his mouth and said nothing. Closed it and grinned. The same smart-ass lip curl Saul had seen on Rydell, on Saroyan, and on Sadie Wu's face just before Wayob forced her to eat the gun.

Wayob lunged for the knife. *Almost too predictable.* Saul grabbed his arm, twisted it, spun him around and shoved him face down on the nearest chaise.

Wayob screamed, "You cannot contain me."

"Should I call the police?" Marta asked. Almost definitely she was talking to Ashley.

"I am the police." Saul pulled his cuffs out and clamped a steel bracelet on Wayob's wrist, his battery-assisted heart pounding against the left side of his ribs.

"You see how he tortures me?" Wayob writhed, his other arm still free. "Do something!"

"Show me your badge," Marta said.

Even if he had a badge, he wouldn't risk pulling it out until Wayob was fully secured. "Go inside," he said, hoping the baby would stall her from making some heroic blunder.

He pressed a knee into Wayob's back and applied more weight, the armrest jamming into his belly. Although he was worried about residual damage to Ashley's body, he couldn't back down. "Give me your arm."

Wayob groaned and eventually surrendered his other arm to be cuffed.

"I'll call for help." Marta hurried inside.

Saul stood Wayob up and ushered him toward the slider.

"You think this will stop me?" Wayob screamed with Ashley's voice.

Saul ignored him. As he marched him through the living room, Shera's yelping filled the house. She presented a real problem. It was risky to divide his attention. But irresponsible to leave her here.

At the top of the stairs, Wayob collapsed as if his legs had become jelly. Saul caught him under the armpits and carried him down to the landing by the front. The effort left him desperately out of breath, probably voiding the warranty on the new hardware pumping his heart.

Shera growled and her nose appeared from beneath the jagged shards of wood where she had chewed off the bottom of the door to the garage.

Saul had a theory. He sat Wayob down on the third to last step and zip-tied his ankles to the lowest baluster. Though he appreciated Wayob's lack of protest, the sudden cooperation, and the smirk, made Saul nervous. He zip-tied Wayob's cuffed wrists to another baluster. Despite being restrained on the hardwood treads, he still issued no complaints.

Saul squatted and extended a hand toward the splintered door. The growling ceased. Shera's nostrils swept the air. She sneezed.

He crab-walked closer, and she rewarded his bravery with a lick.

He glanced up at Wayob. "Guess it's you she doesn't like."

No response.

His eyes were closed. It might be difficult to sleep zip-tied with the treads jutting into his side, but maybe not impossible. And by sleeping, Saul knew Wayob could flee from Ashley's body to some other "vessel," as he called them. Since Wayob had freaked when he was locked in the solitary cell that time, Saul assumed there must be a proximity limitation—suicide must be a means of last resort. He didn't know what the proximity might be, but the neighbor's house seemed too close to risk letting Wayob sleep, and although it seemed logical that his vessel would be sleeping, Saul wasn't about to chance it on Marta and the kids.

He scrambled over and shook Wayob by the shoulders until finally his lids flicked open.

He flashed his I'm-so-smart-I-own-the-world grin. "Watch me sleep, fat man." He again closed his eyes.

Saul reached inside his coat. "I don't think so." He pulled out one of the EpiPens that he'd taken from the hospital and stabbed Ashley's leg. Wayob howled as though the tiny needle was a dull knife sawing through his flesh. Saul almost felt sorry for him. But then his screaming summoned big trouble from the stairway below, big trouble in a small package: Marta appeared with a baby monitor, an indignant scowl, and wielding her phone like an instrument of justice.

If she posted a video on the web, the fallout would be way worse than when he shot a Black man in self-defense, and this time he could forget about the LAPD backing him up at all. He was already on suspension and in a hole so deep he had to dig up just to hit rock bottom. Even the most impartial observer would believe he was torturing Ashley York. And what could he say to dispute it?

"It's just epinephrine," he said into the camera, as if he had some authority to restrain Ashley and administer medication. *Also known as adrenaline,* he thought. *Good luck sleeping now, you bastard.* "For allergies."

Wayob writhed against the jolt racing through his system. "You see how he tortures me? Help me! Call my law-man!"

Behind the door, Shera barked, and from the sound of it she, at least, would approve of Saul's actions. He descended toward Marta.

"I'm going to need that phone." He held out his hand. "Official police business."

She clutched it to her chest and set her jaw. "I never saw your badge."

He didn't have his badge, and now he never would, so instead he opened his trench coat and showed her the Beretta.

Wayob whined. "Ask him who killed poor Edward Saroyan."

Marta's eyes widened. She backed down a step and offered him the phone.

"I need you to disable the passcode," Saul said.

She did so and handed the phone up over the banister. He swiped through her recent apps and found Twitter. She had already posted the video, and it had already been re-tweeted twice. He deleted it, but deleted doesn't mean gone for good. He had learned that the hard way when Hernandez found the photo of Collins in the deleted folder on his phone. The best he could do now was to confiscate Marta's phone. He couldn't keep an eye on both her and Wayob, and Wayob was far more dangerous. Saul had to get him away from here, away from any potential "vessels." And he had to call Hernandez. He needed to tell her what happened, and not just to cover his ass; he wanted to hear her voice, to hear she was still on his side. If he had any hope at all of things progressing with her, he would have to admit to his mistakes and let her in.

He opened the settings app to make sure the passcode had indeed been disabled.

"Ashley has rights," Marta said. "Even if you are a cop, you can't treat her like that."

No point in explaining. "This is for her own safety."

"Look at his phone," Wayob screamed. "He killed a whore and took her photo."

"Her name was Jenna Collins," Saul blurted out. "Did you murder her just to frame me? Or was it something else? You were afraid of her, weren't you?"

"You killed her," Wayob said weakly.

Saul turned to Marta. She stared up at him like a deer in headlights.

"She's not herself right now," he said. "That's all I can say at this time."

Marta braced herself against the rail and took another step down.

"Are the children downstairs?" he asked.

She nodded slowly.

"I need you to go down there with them and shut the door."

She straightened. "I'll stay. Do you really think she killed someone?"

"No, it wasn't exactly Ashley." He glanced at Wayob. His eyes were closed. "I have to go. Keep this to yourself, okay? For Ashley's sake more than mine."

Marta's shoulder twitched as she glanced to the right. "Of course," she said, as if of course she wouldn't.

Saul opened the front door and faced his next challenge: the PCH. Beachgoers barreled south toward the city, retreating from the clouds that had socked in the coast. Afternoon commuters sped north. Traffic was already heavy, and it would get worse. Crossing to his parked car presented enough danger without Wayob, who might attempt to flatten himself under the wheels of any vehicle whose driver was distracted by the sight of Ashley York.

The smarter option would be to leave Wayob restrained here and go fetch his car. The problem was Marta. She might get the notion to set Ashley loose. Could he count on Shera to help?

He closed the front door, returned to the garage door, and tentatively cracked it open. He inserted his hand. Shera's cold nose tipped into it, followed by a wet tongue. He slid through the door and shut it behind him. She wagged her tail and whimpered.

After leashing her up, he opened the door. The low growl returned. She charged forward, but Saul jerked back on the leash, and her front paws came off the floor. She snarled at Wayob, exposing rows of bloody teeth, her gums cut up from gnawing through the door.

"Go ahead." Wayob sneered. "Let the filthy animal loose. I dare you."

"Don't worry, Shera," Saul rubbed her head. "We'll take care of Wayob. But not here, okay?"

She whimpered and backed up to Saul.

"What is your plan of action, Parker?" Wayob asked. "I am curious."

Saul ignored him and led Shera halfway down the lower flight of stairs.

"How dare you treat me this way," Wayob shouted. "I only meant revenge on you in equal measure, but this is too far; now I must end your life."

He tied Shera to a post.

"No one comes upstairs. I can count on you, right?"

Shera cocked her ears, looking up at him with dark, moist eyes that seemed to say she understood. She wagged her tail.

"Okay. Shera, sit."

She lowered her rear end toward the stair plank without quite resting on her haunches.

"Release me, and I shall do the same for you," Wayob said as Saul backed up the stairs. "You think I don't know of the small dingy abode in which you live with your pestering property-lord?"

Saul extended his palms up toward Shera, miming for her to stay. On the landing, he checked that Wayob was still secured by the zip ties.

"I will buy for you a palace such as Ashley's. Bigger even, with more servants. I will do this for you. Just let me leave in peace. I only wish to live Ashley's life and no others. I shall harm no one else."

Saul glanced back at Shera. Her tail was between her legs. "Stay," he said to her.

She whimpered but stayed there on the step with slack in her leash, at least until he stepped out the door.

He strode to the PCH and waited to cross. Cars careened past. Marta's video had probably gone viral by now. Although it might take months for the inevitable disciplinary investigation to reach its inevitable conclusion, Saul's career with the LAPD was over. And he was fine with it. Actually, almost relieved.

Gray and Claire

Gray knew he had to tell Claire everything. After all she'd been through, she deserved to know. Maybe now she'd believe him. When he tried to lock the door to prevent Detective Hernandez from barging back in, he learned it wouldn't lock. Probably a hospital policy.

"Where are Mindy and Tyler?" Claire asked, her head lifting from the pillow.

The one chair had stiff cushions the color of dead leaves. He pulled it a little closer to her bed and sat on the armrest. "They're fine."

She rolled her head toward him. "But where are they?"

He looked at his hands. They were his hands, but after all the time he'd spent in Ashley's body, the creases in his palms looked somehow different. Maybe if he told Claire what had happened from his point of view, she'd understand what he'd done.

"At home. With Belinda."

"No one has been there all day," she said. "The cops are watching our house."

He swallowed.

She waited, her eyes pools of blue, wide open and without a trace of anger.

"It's just. I wanted to start at the beginning, not where things ended up. It's hard to believe, but—"

"You and Ashley switched bodies. I believe you." She reached toward him. "You were in trouble, and I should have listened."

He stood and took her hand in his. "How…?"

"Because I know it was you holding me last night, despite what my senses told me."

"I thought I'd lost you." He squeezed her hand, and she stared back into his eyes for a moment, and then her gaze fell to her legs stretched out under the blanket, motionless. *Your fault. Your fault!* His throat tightened. His eyes watered. "I'm so sorry, Claire."

She withdrew her hand and worked the controls on her bed until a motor buzzed into action and elevated her back.

"Some idiot called my parents," she said. "They're flying in tonight."

Her parents lived in Ohio, and it wasn't until after he and Claire got engaged that she introduced them to him. The next time he saw them was the wedding, and then five years later when Mindy was born, when they flew out for a weekend and spent most of the time in a hotel. Whatever the deal was between Claire and her parents, now seemed like a bad time for her to confront it.

"You don't have to see them if you don't want to," he said.

"You don't get it." She closed her eyes and grimaced. "My dad drinks—more than you."

More than you, as if Gray's drinking was a problem for her, when he was the one who had to endure the headaches and the fatigue, the false sense of euphoria from the alcohol, which made him believe that with just a few strokes of his brush he'd have a masterpiece. And then the crash the next day when he saw what he'd painted, the crushing feeling of failure from which the Scotch had been his one and only escape. The cycle of drinking like circling a drain.

It had nothing to do with Claire—mostly, it happened out of her sight—except when things went wrong between them and he doubled down on the booze as a means of escape. And she knew the signs, the smell on his breath. If it triggered bad feelings about her father, then no wonder she'd said she was done after he told her about his ridiculous plan to open a bar; she knew the extent of his drinking. Of course she knew.

"I had no idea," he said.

"I guess I never told you that when I went to college, I decided I was done with my parents for good. Maybe I was afraid that if I explained it, I'd talk myself out of the idea. You can't get rid of them, you know? Your parents are always your parents."

He squeezed her shoulder. "Family."

"When my dad drinks, he gets angry. And my mom... she defends him—she's worse."

Gray swallowed. Sometimes he had wished Mindy and Tyler could see their grandparents more often, but now he wasn't so sure. "Does he get violent?"

"Not physically, which is worse in a way. I know that sounds weird, but when I was little, I'd provoke him on purpose. Sometimes I wished he'd just hit me."

"Psychological abuse can be just as harmful as physical." That's what Gray had read but never having experienced it, he wasn't sure what to say.

"I guess," she said. "At least if he'd hit me then there would be no denying it when he sobered up, and maybe then my mom would have had to admit there was a problem. But he only yelled. He would yell until his face turned red, and he shook his fists, but he never touched me."

"Still, sounds hard."

"Anyway, my dad drinks Scotch too—it should have scared me when I saw how much you drank, but it was familiar, you know? And you never got mad. I thought I liked the way you go all quiet when you drink. You seemed thoughtful. But now I see how it's almost as bad, because it just meant you went off in your head and created a whole new life for yourself without telling me anything about it."

She was confusing two different things. He had wanted to paint, even more so when he was sober. The drinking had just been a way to numb himself, to dull the dissatisfaction. "Drinking wasn't the problem—"

"I know what you're going to say. I know, and you're right. I was too tired to pay attention. I was too wrapped up in how exhausted I was to notice how you haven't been yourself for a *long* time. And it's because of me."

He shook his head. "It's not because of you—"

"Let me finish," she said. "Insomnia is no excuse for the way I acted. I want you to know I'm not going to be like that anymore. I can sleep now. The doctors found a hormone problem. Turns out my insomnia was caused by low estrogen. And I know it's only been one day, and maybe I'm still a little doped up, but even without the use of my legs, I feel better in my head. I feel like all I need to do is close my eyes, and I can sleep. To think all this time I could have been sleeping."

He leaned over her, stroked her hair back. "That's great they fixed your sleep."

"Things are going to change. Okay?"

He wished he could dive into the current flowing through her eyes. He wanted to pretend, just for a moment, that her lack of sleep had been the only issue, that she could know for sure—after such a traumatic night—that everything would be okay now. That the four of them could be a family.

"I stopped drinking." He decided as he said it. He hated being compared to her father. And more than that, from now on, he needed to stay grounded in reality. Drinking had made it so much easier to pretend things were better than they were, and all the pretending had only made things worse.

"You don't have to."

"It wasn't getting me any closer to what I want."

Time to face facts. He felt guilty for what he was about to say, but if he didn't speak up now then he never would. "The problem is us."

Her brows wrenched down. Her mouth twisted into a grimace. She slapped at her legs. "You don't want me anymore."

"I'm not saying that." He hated the hurt on her face. Hated that he had caused it, and that she'd think he'd leave her because of an injury. He wished he could take it back. A week ago he might have, but not now, not after everything he'd been through—he just couldn't. "It's just... it doesn't work with us."

"But it can now. It will. I can help. Forget the bar—I can get my job back."

Of course, his plan to open a bar seemed even more stupid to her than it did to him now. Still, it was more realistic than the physical requirements of her job. Did she not grasp her situation? "Claire, the doctor says you'll be in a wheelchair for the rest of your life." The words came out harsher than he'd intended, but she was living in denial.

She sniffed but held his gaze, and before she could respond, he continued, "Look, you don't have to worry. I'll get a new job."

"No," she said. "I can work a desk."

"Maybe we should talk about this later."

"I don't want to talk later." She took his hand in hers, her eyes searching his face with an intensity that was hard not to look away from. "I was thinking," she said softly, "maybe you could stay home with the kids."

Of course. She still held a grudge against him for convincing her to have children. "You don't want to be a mother?"

"I'm not saying that. I'm so grateful for Mindy and Tyler; I should thank you for talking me into it. But I feel worthless sitting around the house all day. And now it's going to be worse." Her voice cracked. "I won't be able to keep up with them." She rubbed her eyes with the back of her hand.

"You're not worthless." Had he made her feel that way? All the time he'd focused on his goals, taking her for granted.

"It's just how I feel, okay? I need something else... outside the house. I talked to my old boss—"

"When?" He couldn't believe what he was hearing. She had nearly died. And now she was worried about employment?

"Yesterday. You asked me to call, remember? I thought you threw away your ring."

Yesterday seemed like an eon ago. He'd almost forgotten. "The transfer station," he said.

"Right." She adjusted the pillow behind her head. "I knew Kwesi couldn't help, but I sort of wanted to hear how things were going at Hyperion. Turns out the guy they hired to replace me is terrible. Kwesi said if I go back, he'd offer me a promotion to senior wastewater collection manager."

"That's a nice compliment, but I thought you hated it there?"

She exhaled. "Nah. I just liked to complain. And I guess I didn't realize at the time how much I liked being around all the pipes and sediment pools."

He laughed. "And the stench?"

"It wasn't that bad." She smiled. "I kind of miss it in a way."

He nodded. "Sometimes you don't know what you have until it's gone." This was how he'd felt about her ever since that night in college when she took off, which she never seemed to come all the way back from, even after his proposal and their wedding. And then insomnia had consumed her. He thought he had lost her for good when she told him to leave.

She leaned toward him. Her eyes sparked with life. "With this new position I'll make more than you did," she said, as though she'd already accepted the offer. "Think about it: Tyler can go to daycare soon, and Mindy starts school next year. You'll have all that time at home to paint."

This was hard to accept. All of a sudden, she was okay with his need to be an artist, and not only okay but willing to support it? It sounded too good to be true. "But you talked to Kwesi before—" As Gray motioned to her legs, the guilt caught like glass in his throat.

"And good thing too," she said. "Now they'll be too afraid of a lawsuit to even bat an eye. My damn wheelchair will be fine."

"Are you angry?"

"Not at you."

Why not? She should be furious. "But you're paralyzed because of *me.*"

"No. I'm the one who went to Ashley York's with a loaded gun."

Why couldn't she just get angry at him? "But if I had told you what was going on—"

"You tried to; I wouldn't listen," she said. "That was you, wasn't it? In Ashley's body? After that asshole shot me, it was you who held my hand."

He nodded. She extended her hand over the bedrail toward him, but he couldn't accept it. He backed into the chair. He tried to cover his reaction by dragging the chair closer to her bed. He sat on the stiff cushion and slouched below her eyeline.

She twisted her head to the side and began lowering her back.

"I shouldn't have left you there," he said. "I thought you were dead."

She shook her head. "You had to get out of there. Ashley York had just killed a psycho. That was her, right—in your body?"

True. But once he was safe, he didn't have to go and sleep with Ashley. Someday he'd have to confess this to Claire, but not now. She couldn't handle it now. Besides, they had bigger problems.

"Yes," he said, "but the thing is, she didn't really kill *him,* the psycho." He leaned back and ran his fingers through his hair. He glanced around for something to sketch with, to make sure Wayob was still in the Encanto. But, besides all the equipment and the little table by her bed, the room was bare.

Her brows furrowed. "What do you mean?"

"The psycho who shot you was Wayob. He was in the body of Ashley's security guard, and he can become basically anyone who is sleeping." He expected disbelief, but Claire's eyes were wide and accepting. "If he'd thought to take your body after you passed out, I would have been a sitting duck."

"I wasn't asleep. The ambulance guys were all like, 'Don't go to sleep,' and I was like, 'No problem.'"

He chuckled. If anyone could avoid passing out after a shot to the spine, it was Claire.

"So wait," she said, "why was this Wayob guy trying to kill us?"

"He was mainly just after me, I think. He thought I had the Encanto. Where did you find it, by the way?"

"At Charlie's. I think he filched it out of our trash."

"Crazy." Gray pictured Charlie in his house across the street, watching from an upstairs window when they threw it away. Perhaps the sight of

Ashley York had piqued his curiosity? "How did he explain that?"

"He didn't. He was dead when I found him."

A chill like cold water poured down the back of his neck. "What?"

"It was weird," she said. "I found Charlie and this cop suffocated on carbon monoxide in his garage. His car was still running. It looked like the cop had been trying to take the stone from him before they passed out. Maybe he couldn't get the garage open, or maybe— Do you think this Wayob guy had something to do with it?"

"Almost certainly." Gray inhaled. Two more people who would probably still be alive if he'd left the Encanto alone.

"Well, don't tell Detective Tightpants I took anything from the crime scene. She's all over me about it."

Gray agreed, although it seemed like a small thing compared to their involvement in Sammy's death.

He followed Claire's gaze to the vertical window in the door. Behind it, Hernandez stood in the harsh light of the hallway, speaking into her phone. When he glanced back, Claire was frowning.

"So, you just bought it randomly at the Day of the Dead?" she asked.

"A fortune-teller gave it to me."

Her brows ratcheted up in a way that he knew. She was struggling not to say something.

"I ran into her randomly," he said, "on the way to the bathroom. She just put it in my hand, and when I tried to return it, she was so upset I didn't know what to do. She didn't tell me what it was or anything, just that I should destroy it." His throat tightened, causing his voice to go higher. "If I had just listened to her, none of this would have happened."

Claire reached over the bedrail and found his hand in his lap. She squeezed it. "But why would you believe her?"

"Her tears were real," he mumbled. Even after discovering the Encanto's power for himself, after enjoying a day in the life of Ashley York, instead of heeding the fortune-teller's warning, he'd used the Encanto again.

"So, what happens if you smash it now?"

"It will kill Wayob, I think. That's why I need to get back to Ashley's."

Claire rolled her eyes. "Don't tell me you lost it again."

He explained how Wayob was going to kill Ashley, and how he'd had to throw the stone to distract Wayob. "But I've still got the snake." He pulled the obsidian carving from his pocket.

She waved it away. "I wanted to tell you where I went the night before you proposed. Do you remember?"

"Do I remember!" The question had festered in his brain like a cancer growing throughout their marriage—sometimes with frustration, sometimes regret. Over the years his thoughts had returned again and again to the shadow of scraggly pine, cast by the orange light outside her dorm, where he'd waited in the cold mist all night for her return, his legs going numb on the stone stairway, the cold seeping into his heart.

"I don't know why I kept it from you. I guess I just wanted something for myself, you know? A little corner of my own—like I would lose myself if I told you everything. But now I see that I've been hurting our relationship by holding back." She swallowed. "I hate to admit it, but... when you tried to needle it out of me, I was only acting annoyed. I kind of enjoyed not telling you. Or I thought I did. It was a hollow, rotten sort of satisfaction, and the aggravation I expressed—that was with myself."

She paused.

He waited for her to continue.

She sighed. "I just needed some space, I guess. Remember that stupid argument—our first?"

Gray bobbed his head. He remembered her shouting, and him shouting back. "Do you remember what it was about?"

She shook her head. "It doesn't matter. I think I just... I needed to get away. I needed some space, and not just from you—from LA, and from that dorm. I never told you how much I hated living with all those girls, so I got in my car and just drove. And I kept on driving until I could see the stars.

"The desert seemed to go on forever. Eventually, I ended up at Barstow, and it was like two in the morning. So, I stopped at a greasy spoon and got a booth by the window and just watched the headlights speeding past on the fifteen.

"There were some guys there fueling up on their way to Vegas, and one them put some Enrique Iglesias cheese on the jukebox and asked me to dance. Don't worry, I turned him down—he wasn't nearly as cute as he thought he was—but it was kind of funny the way he slow-danced with himself while he lip-sang and kept beckoning me to join him.

"But I didn't. I ate a big mama plate of fries followed by a slice of chocolate cheesecake, with whip cream, and then I drove back, and you were outside my dorm with that hangdog look on your face, but by then I was too tired to explain. I felt guilty and a little embarrassed that because of our argument, I had driven out to Barstow and back.

"And then, every time you asked, it made me more and more want to keep it to myself. I thought it was you, but it was me. I was selfish and mean, and... I'm sorry."

He inhaled. After so many years of being so sure she'd slept with someone that night to now find out that she'd only driven out to Barstow for some fries —and here he had slept with Ashley. He shrank back in the chair, wanting to disappear.

Now there was no way he could tell Claire. Not now. Not ever. How could he? What would be the point? The way she was talking, she didn't want to split up now, after all. And he didn't either. There was something adorable about her story that made his heart swell.

"You're mad," she said. "Aren't you?"

"I slept with Ashley."

The words just spewed right out of him like vomit with no preceding nausea, a thing too big to keep inside himself. And he'd hardly even tried.

And why? Because deep down, it was still hard to trust this new truth. But if he didn't believe her, he should man up and say so. Throwing gasoline on a fire was a coward's way out.

She was blinking fast. Hadn't he hurt her enough already? Here he was, the idiot who had twisted the snake right after he was told not to, but this was worse: this time he'd known exactly the hurt his words would cause. He'd known all too well, and yet he was too selfish to swallow the secret.

And now that it was out there, he tried to soften the blow for himself as much as her. "I thought you were dead."

Still, she said nothing, her irises phosphorescent as she probed him.

He felt cornered there in the chair. He glanced at the door. Hernandez had turned sideways to the window, her neck arched down, looking at her phone.

When he glanced back at Claire, or tried to, the intensity in her eyes was too great. He focused on the dimple in her chin and attempted to explain. "That's how we switched back to our own bodies."

The corner of her mouth twisted slightly and, if he didn't know better, he might think she was smiling. She rocked herself sideways. Her blanket fell off. She clutched her stomach where the bandages bulged beneath the blue-checkered gown, and grimaced.

Was she so repulsed that she just had to move away from him in spite of the surgery she just had on her spine?

He stood. "You shouldn't be moving around."

"Help me scoot over."

"Want me to go?"

"No," she said. "I want you here in the bed with me."

"What?" He floundered, trying to understand.

She smiled for sure now, and her cheeks flushed. "I guess I slept with her too, didn't I?"

"You thought she was me." Although he still wondered exactly what had happened, he knew now he could never ask again.

She grabbed him by the shirt and pulled him toward her until his thighs bumped the bedside, and then she repeated the words he'd said to her when he proposed: "*I don't care about the past, only the future.*"

A deep numbness he'd been unaware of thawed inside his chest. He smiled, his heart thrumming for Claire, who he'd never wanted to leave, not really.

Her eyes glowed with all her will and passion, her restless intelligence. Her plan could work. He could paint while she earned the paycheck, and he liked the idea of spending more time with Mindy and Tyler.

"I miss you," she said. "I feel like I've been missing you for a long time, even though you were right there."

As carefully as he could, he climbed over the bedrail and squeezed into the small space beside her.

She pulled his hand to her chest. "I wish I could turn sideways so you could spoon me."

He wrapped his arm gently over her, avoiding the bandages, pressing his body against hers. "How about this?"

"Closer," she said.

He knew she was underestimating how hard it would be to adjust to the loss of her legs. Probably neither of them grasped the difficulty, how much help she'd need, but he'd be there for her. He would do all he could and more. And he would be glad to.

Second Sight

Hernandez clenched her teeth and rewatched the video of Parker injecting Ashley York with god knows what, finding it hard to correlate this image of the man wielding the syringe with the gentle Saul in the hospital this morning, the man she cared about so much. What the hell was he doing? Was he Wayob? Now she could forget about a statement from Ashley York to clear Parker of wrongdoing in last night's massacre. His actions seemed to defy any explanation that could put him on the right side of things with the high brass. So, her career was over, as was his freedom. Her top concern now was Ashley's life.

She flung open the door to Claire Wilson's room and was surprised, given the palpable tension in the air when she'd left, to find them cuddling in the narrow hospital bed like teenagers. She might have thought it was cute if she wasn't so worried about Saul—if he hadn't just turned her decision to release him into the biggest mistake of her life.

"Where's Ashley York?" she asked Gray. "I need to know right now."

"I'm not supposed to tell you," he muttered sheepishly as he rolled over and climbed out of the bed.

Claire grabbed the back of his T-shirt but he broke free without seeming to notice and stood awkwardly by the chair in the tight space between the bed and the beige curtain.

"Then I have to go ahead and arrest you," Hernandez said. "Hope you enjoyed your last time lying next to a woman."

He gripped the rail of the bed. Claire pressed a button, and the mattress raised behind her back. "You can't arrest him. It was self-defense, and you know it."

"I don't know anything," Hernandez said, knowing full well that whoever killed Sammy Johnson, or rather Wayob in Johnson's body, had been fighting for their lives. No DA would touch the case, but she needed a lever to pry out what this couple knew, because as much as she wanted to, she couldn't just draw her gun and insist. "What about when you broke into Ashley's house, was that self-defense?"

"I didn't break in." Gray almost smiled as he said it.

She assumed it was because it was Ashley in his body who broke into her own house. At least, that was Saul's theory. However, although Hernandez believed Saul in general, he wasn't necessarily right about everything, and she wanted to hear it from Gray. "Your fingerprints were on the rock used to break the window," she bluffed. The techs couldn't lift a print from the rock.

He studied his hands. "She forgot her keys."

"Uh huh. Look, I want to believe you, but then we've got the blood on your Doc Martins."

He blinked hard and swallowed.

"That doesn't prove anything," Claire said.

"Maybe not." Hernandez shrugged. "But I like Occam's razor. The simplest explanation is almost always the truth. Juries like simple explanations too. And we've got four bodies, one of them being August Grant. Someone needs to answer for them."

Gray slumped, his resolve weakening.

She unsnapped the cuffs from her belt. "Hope your kids are nowhere near Ashley."

His eyes widened. "What are you talking about?"

She pulled her phone and showed him the trending video of Parker, who was probably Wayob now, injecting Ashley York.

As Gray watched, his eyebrows knotted together and then widened. He touched his throat.

"Let me see," Claire said.

His eyes darted around the room. "When was this?"

"The video was posted twenty minutes ago," Hernandez said as she went around the opposite side of the bed to show it to Claire. "But it could have been recorded hours ago."

Gray pulled a small scrap of torn paper from his pocket, picked up the landline by the bed, and dialed.

Hernandez looked at Claire, but she seemed enthralled by the video, completely unaware of whatever Gray was up to.

"Where are they?" Hernandez asked Gray.

He hung up the phone without speaking. "Ashley's beach house, I think." He dashed to the door and peered out into the hall.

Hernandez wanted to reach Parker before anyone else, but with Ashley's life in imminent danger, every second mattered. She had to send some uniforms out to this beach house ASAP. "What's the address?"

Gray shut the door and stood in front of it. "I don't know. It's in Malibu, on the PCH..."

"That's twenty-six miles you've narrowed it down to. Don't tell me you forgot."

"So, wait," Claire said, lowering the phone. "Why would he drug her?"

"I'm not sure," Gray said, "but he could be Wayob. Maybe he injected her with a truth serum or something to make her tell him where I am?" He glanced at Hernandez. "You need to get some more police here. I don't know how to explain this, but—"

"I know about Wayob," she said.

His mouth fell open. He closed it. Tilted his head to the side, no doubt finding it hard to believe what she'd just said. "I don't know what he is, but I know he can control people, and Detective Parker is my partner, so you're coming with me."

Gray backed against the door. "We need to move Claire to a new room under a fake name."

"What about your kids? I bet they're at Ashley's, aren't they?"

"They're safer if I'm nowhere near them." His voice trembled. "They're probably fine."

"So, let's make sure. Okay? We'll get there faster together."

"Gray," Claire said. "Who's watching them?"

He picked up the phone, dialed again, and waited for an answer.

"Marta, it's Gray. Are the kids okay?" He nodded at Claire, but if he felt relieved, it didn't show.

Hernandez reached for the phone.

"I need some paper," he said as he handed it to her.

She spoke into the phone. "This is Detective Hernandez with the LAPD. Is everyone there okay?"

"Yes," Marta said, the fear almost palpable in her voice. "But he kidnapped Ashley York."

"Do you have any paper?" Gray almost shouted. "Wayob might already be in the building."

"Paper for what?" Claire sounded as frustrated as Hernandez felt. If Gray was Wayob's next target, then a hospital was no place for a showdown, and paper wasn't going to protect him.

He started toward the door.

"Hold on," Hernandez said to both Marta and Gray. Gray paused. She set down the phone, pulled out her notebook, ripped out a page, and shoved it into his hand along with her pen.

He spun the chair to face the little table by the bed, sat on the armrest, and began to draw as Hernandez gathered the address details from Marta. She told her to wait for the police and ended the call.

"I have to go," she said.

Gray was sketching something. "Hold on." He shot her a look. "I'm drawing where they are."

"What are you talking about?" Claire asked.

"I can draw what Wayob sees. Literally. It might help us figure out where he is."

"How can you draw what he sees?" Claire's voice cracked.

"I have no idea. I just can."

Is that possible? Hernandez wondered. She already believed Wayob could control another person, and she'd accepted the idea of body switching, so why not second sight? "How did you learn this?"

"It took me a while to figure it out, but I kept drawing things I hadn't seen before, and they kept turning out to be real. Like your partner: I thought I'd made him up when I drew him, but then a few days later he showed up at our house. It was weird."

"And you could tell where he was from the drawing?"

"He was in a small room with a big window, but I couldn't tell what was behind it."

The two-way in the interview suite. "Could it have been a mirror?"

Gray shrugged. "Maybe."

"When was this?"

"Sunday."

On Sunday, they had arrested Rydell. If Gray could see through Wayob's eyes, this confirmed that Rydell really was under Wayob's control when Saul questioned him. He hadn't strangled himself; Wayob had murdered him. Just like Saul had said.

If Gray could draw Wayob's location, then she could get to Saul first, maybe before he did anything worse. It was worth a try. "Okay, you're coming with me. You can draw on the way."

"It'll be faster if you wait."

She glanced at her watch. 4:54. She decided to indulge him. She leaned against the wall, watching over his shoulder as he drew, and the room grew quiet.

Pretty quickly she recognized Saul's burly silhouette in the sparse lines. The view was from the backseat, with Saul driving. In the front passenger seat, a dog with dark eyes, drawn like spirals, stared out from the page.

Wayob must have jumped from the dog to Saul. Except... "That's Parker." She tapped the drawing. "Are you sure this is from Wayob's point of view?"

"That's my theory." Gray studied the drawing.

The way he said "theory" didn't inspire much confidence.

In the video, Saul had acted like Wayob, but it was possible that Wayob was in Ashley's body, watching Saul from the backseat. She needed to focus on finding them.

"Where are they?"

"It's a freeway. I can't tell which one."

"Keep drawing," she said.

He sketched in the cars ahead of Saul with minimal angular lines. Five lanes of traffic.

"Is anything above the freeway?"

Gray nodded and seemed to lose himself in the drawing as he outlined a tall rectangle with a spire. And then, to the left, an unmistakable cylinder: the US Bank Tower.

Hernandez's heart pounded in her head. "They're on the 10 East."

Gray glanced toward the door. "They're coming here."

"No," she said. "From Malibu, you'd take La Cienega up to Cedars. They're almost at downtown."

"So where would they be going?" Gray asked.

She pulled out her phone. She could call in an APB on Parker's car—she *should*; it was procedure, and her duty—but *nowhere is safe from Wayob*. That's why Saul had confronted him alone last night. He had understood how useless it would be to take Wayob into custody in Johnson's body, like she'd have insisted at the time.

She returned her phone to her belt-clip. "Let's go." She motioned Gray toward the door.

"Why does he have to go with you?" Claire asked.

"He can help." Hernandez had to think about the greater good: stopping Wayob. She placed her hand on Claire's arm. "Keeping him safe is my job."

Claire pulled away. "He's not bait."

He looked up from his drawing. "I won't be safe anywhere until we get Wayob locked back in the Encanto, and nor will you. I can't be around you, Claire. And what if he goes back to Ashley's for Mindy and Tyler?"

She swallowed. "Then kill the fucker. I don't care what it takes."

He nodded slowly. "I will."

"Just don't die," Claire said to Gray. She looked at Hernandez. "If my husband comes back dead, it's on you."

"Don't worry," Hernandez said, but her words sounded hollow, and she had to stop herself from making a promise she might regret.

Claire bit her lip and narrowed her eyes.

Gray's voice caught in his throat as he said goodbye.

She followed him out of the room and, as she closed the door behind them, she glanced back at Claire, who was rubbing her legs beneath the blanket.

Into Darkness

Shera was barking from the stairwell again. Although Saul couldn't take her along to Wayob's final destination, he certainly couldn't leave her here at the Yorks' beach house. So, he untied her leash and led her out to the pristine garage where he'd secured Wayob in the backseat of his Prius. Without the standard d-ring installed in police vehicles, he'd made do with just the seatbelt and handcuffs.

When Shera spotted Wayob, a low growl rumbled in her throat. Saul rubbed her head. "Let me know if Wayob tries anything." He opened the front passenger door and unhooked the leash.

Shera leaped onto the seat and sat facing backward, watching Wayob.

Wayob's eyes remained closed, like he couldn't hear her growling. No way he was asleep. His arms were cuffed uncomfortably behind his back. Plus, Saul had given him an additional shot of adrenaline.

"That's good," Saul said. "Keep still or you'll have Shera to contend with." He petted her head as he whispered into her ear. "I can count on you, right, girl?"

She looked up at him with those intense eyes of hers, and he knew that he could. He stood back and she returned her gaze to Wayob.

He shut the door and called Pete at the Castle.

"Saul," Pete said when he answered. "What's happening?"

"Seen anything of note online?" Saul might have deleted Marta's tweet after confiscating her phone, but he couldn't keep up with all the platforms. She might have shared the incriminating video somewhere else.

"Like what?"

"I don't know. It's all rubbish, anyway."

"I hate social media," Pete said. "So, what's the deal with that bald jerk? It was kind of fun, giving him the runaround."

"He died."

Silence over the line.

Saul turned his back on the car. "His death has nothing to do with us, so don't worry about that, okay?" He ran a finger along an empty shelf mounted to the wall. The paint was layered on so thick that the wood felt like plastic.

"What happened?" Pete asked.

"Can I count on you for a solid? I'm in a hurry here."

"Of course, but—"

"I need the black bag from my locker and the Table of Death. I'll pick them up behind the Castle in half an hour."

"The Table of Death?" Pete said. "You've got to let me in on this."

Pete liked to be on the inside of things, which Saul ordinarily appreciated— he had the same need to know –but tonight it was a liability. Tonight, he needed Pete to stay back and not ask any questions.

"Tonight's no good," Saul said. "But tomorrow I can do an informal show in the Close-Up Gallery. If you assist, I'll show you the Table of Death inside and out."

"I'm going to hold you to that."

"I hope you do, Pete. I hope you do." If Saul lived through the night, he'd be happy to show Pete his secret variant on the trick. "But tonight I have to pick up the table alone. No one around and no one watching. Got it?"

"What's going on?" Pete asked. This time more slowly, more insistent.

Saul glanced through the windshield. Wayob's eyes snapped closed.

"You ready for the next part?" Saul asked.

"I guess."

"I have a dog I need you to look after. Just for tonight."

"A dog? What am I supposed to do with a dog?"

"Well, her name is Shera, and she's very well behaved, but if you don't want to keep her around then you can put her in a doggie hotel—a nice one— and I'll pay you back."

"I could keep her in the office behind the seance room, I guess. You'll definitely be back by tomorrow afternoon?"

"I should be. I'll text you from this same number when I get close. Wait *inside* the back door and I'll knock twice and hand you Shera. Under absolutely no circumstances should you even so much as glance out, okay?"

"Why not?"

"Sorry, I can't tell you—for your own protection. Promise me, Pete. It's a matter of life and death."

"I promise. Don't worry."

But Saul worried. He worried the whole way down the PCH to the 10, while beside him Shera remained transfixed on Wayob.

As they cut eastward, the marine layer banked up and swallowed the freeway behind them. Cold air gushed through the window. Saul buzzed it up.

Shera growled. In the mirror, Wayob had opened his eyes, and he had that smirk. The Wayob smirk. It looked the same no matter whose face he wore.

"You are a sworn officer of the law, Saul Parker," he practically sang. "'To serve and protect.'"

"You can save your breath on the pity party."

"Oh yes, clearly you have no concern for *my* safety, but I am concerned about someone else."

Saul said nothing. Whatever Wayob was talking about was probably a lie.

"So, you are breaking your oath?"

"No, I'm keeping it. You're not going to hurt anyone else."

"But, you see, I never wanted to hurt anyone. If someone is suffering, if they are being tortured, your job is to help them. Is it not?"

Saul groaned inwardly. Wayob was probably referring to himself.

"No," Wayob answered his own question. "I guess you are just a *de-tec-tive*. You just *investigate* who to blame for people who have already died. Well then, we shall just wait for her to die, so that you can investigate how it was your fault."

Saul stiffened. As much as he didn't want to entertain Wayob, what if someone was in danger? "Who?"

"I believe she calls herself Rosa. You are familiar with her father, Luis Luna."

Familiar? Saul clenched his jaw. Wayob had murdered Luis Luna. If Wayob was involved, then Saul had to assume Rosa was dead… but… what if she wasn't? "Where is she?"

"The place I left her, it is such a dark place. I am sure she would rather be dead."

Saul followed the cloverleaf from the 10 down to the 110. Would she be afraid of him, after having witnessed his arrest?

"Do you not hear me?" Wayob's singsong cadence collapsed into annoyance. "I have trapped Rosa where you shall never find her."

"So, go ahead and tell me if you want. You'll feel better."

"I propose an exchange."

Of course Wayob's proposed exchange would involve some means of escape—what good was anything without freedom?—but freeing Wayob would mean valuing Rosa's life above all the others he would harm, and Saul couldn't do that. In order to find her, he was going to have to return to the place he most feared—he would have to journey back into Wayob's mind.

He swallowed and began shoving his way through the lanes of traffic in order to make the 101 before the divider split the lanes.

"All I've got for you is another EpiPen," Saul said. Eventually sleep would override the adrenaline, no matter how much Saul gave him, but not yet.

"No," Wayob shouted. "Release me and I shall free Rosa. Time is running out for her, but I shall still find my freedom, either way. I can wait. Sooner or later, you must sleep, Saul Parker. I think you have learned this by now."

Saul cut in front of a Beemer. Its driver honked. Saul waved a hand in the mirror.

"Not going to happen," he said. "Once you find out what I've got in store for you, you'll wish you had told me."

"You cannot harm me in the body of Ashley York. Others will believe her word above yours—we both know this—and I shall be the one saying it."

"Too bad you've got no one to listen to you. Not now and not ever again."

"There shall be consequences for your actions. You know this, *Saul*. Why make things worse for yourself?"

Saul paired Marta's phone to his car system and dialed Hernandez. Although he didn't want Wayob overhearing, with a possible countdown on Rosa's life he had to call now, regardless of Wayob sneering over his shoulder.

Her line rang through the car speakers. A row of palms ruffled in the wind. The freeway snaked below a hill.

When she picked up, he spoke before she could: "Before you say anything, I need to tell you that something happened, and it might look bad—"

"Let me guess," she said. "Wayob's Ashley?"

"No," Wayob shouted with Ashley's voice. "Saul Parker is Wayob. He is torturing me. Help me. Help me, please."

"I haven't done anything to him," Saul said. "Not yet."

She sighed. "Parker."

"What happened to first names?"

"Where are you?"

A roiling gray wall of cloud charged toward him. In a matter of minutes, it would consume the freeway and the offices ahead, as well as the apartments, theaters, bars, and weed shops. And all the houses sprawled up to the scrubby face of Mount Lee, where the bold letters declared "*HOLLYWOOD.*" *Go big or go home.*

"Better for you not to know," he said. "Plausible deniability."

"I want to help," she said. "Just tell me where you are, please."

"He is driving toward Hollywood mountain!" Wayob said.

"We're leaving town," Saul said. Which was true, though not until after a pit stop at the Castle. "Turns out Wayob has Rosa locked up. I'm going to find her." *And trap Wayob*, but Saul had to keep that part of the plan to himself.

"Rosa shall not live much longer," Wayob said. "You hear me? Set me free or Rosa shall die."

Shera barked as if rejecting the idea before anyone else could consider it.

"It's under control," Saul said. "I have the Encanto."

Wayob straightened in the backseat. Saul restrained his smile. *Hook set.*

"The Encanto is broken," she said.

Doh. Aside from the tiny hole, the porous stone comprised a complete sphere. "In what way?"

"Wilson's here with me. Hear him out."

Gray Wilson came on the line and told him the obsidian dial, a black snake, had broken off from a dowel that fit into the stone. And according to Wilson's theory, it was required to lock Wayob inside the Encanto.

Judging from the laughter in the backseat, Saul indeed needed that snake.

He took the phone off speaker and held it to his ear, like he should have from the start. "I found this sketchbook at the beach house."

"Did it have a drawing of a German shepherd in a cage?" Wilson asked.

"It was the K-9 Officer's Kennel, where civilians aren't allowed."

"I can draw what he sees. Wayob must have been there when he was in the dog."

Saul tried to open his mind to the possibility. Luna had said that his mother saw through Wayob's eyes. Now, apparently, so could Wilson. It would be hard to believe if he hadn't seen that drawing. "How?"

"I don't know. But you've got a dog in the front seat and Wayob in the back, right? And a while ago you were on the 10, driving toward downtown."

It would take one hell of a coincidence for Wilson to know that. Plus the drawing of the KOK. Two unlikely coincidences were impossible for Saul to believe, so he believed Wilson.

He checked the rearview. Wayob's brows were raised. Probably listening for the first time in his life, but since he hadn't heard Wilson's side of the conversation, he was, most likely, unaware of Wilson's ability. Which could be useful, very useful in fact, so long as Saul kept it that way.

He asked Hernandez to take the call off speaker. Had to tell her how he felt. Might be his last chance.

"I…" He glanced in the rearview. Something about Wayob's smirk made the words catch in this throat. "Have to go."

He shut down the phone. "Guess you're happy the Encanto's broken?"

"You cannot stop me," Wayob said. "How many times must I tell you?"

"Guess we'll see about that." Saul exited onto Franklin.

"Let me go and no harm shall come to you. Or to Rosa. I do not want to hurt anyone, but I shall if I have to."

Saul pulled into an alley behind a 76. He climbed out and scanned the gloom. Shera watched him expectantly from the passenger seat.

When he opened Wayob's door, she whimpered. Saul snapped his fingers in Wayob's face. Then revealed the red handkerchief in his palm.

"Get away from me," Wayob said.

Saul hummed the *Mission Impossible* theme as he folded the handkerchief into a blindfold. "You're used to the dark, right?" He wrapped the blindfold over Wayob's eyes.

Wayob squirmed. "You cannot treat me this way," he screamed. "I am Ashley York. This is cruel and unusual punishment."

Saul glanced around the alley.

No sign of anyone.

He slammed Wayob's door. Folded himself into the driver's seat. And texted Pete: *there in ten*.

He angled the rearview on Wayob. "If you tell me where Rosa is, I'll remove the blindfold."

Wayob's laugh sounded more like a sob. "You think I am stupid? First you set me free, and then I shall set her free."

Saul powered on the Prius. He rolled out of the alley and turned west on Franklin. "Right now is as good as it gets for you, Wayob. You're going to spend the rest of your life wishing you could go back to just being blindfolded and handcuffed. So enjoy it while it lasts."

Wayob sneered. "Poor Rosa. She has gone without sustenance or water all night and all day. How much longer do you suppose she will live?"

Saul turned into the Castle and slowed up to the valet, Marco.

Marco hopped off the stool beside his little stand of keys and saluted. Black suit and slicked-back hair.

Saul buzzed down his window. "I'm just here to pick up something in the back."

"Right on," Marco said.

"Help me," Wayob shouted. "He is torturing me."

Saul smiled. "Pretty good, right? She's practicing her act."

Marco squinted into the back window, which unfortunately had no tint at all.

"You see how he tortures me! Help!"

As Marco stepped back, Saul prepared to gun it up the hill, but then Marco smiled. "Keep practicing."

Saul exhaled. He buzzed up the window and rolled forward. "I should gag you too," he said to Wayob.

"You would not dare," Wayob said.

Saul would dare, except that it would look wrong. Magicians used blindfolds; kidnappers used gags. Besides, allowing Wayob his little outbursts at least assured Saul he was still awake.

As Saul turned behind the Castle, he saw the Table of Death and the bag of restraints by the back door, just as he'd requested; but also, there was Pete, who, Saul should have known, was too curious to wait inside.

Pete waved and grinned sheepishly.

As Saul heaved himself out of the Prius, Wayob screamed. Saul slammed the door and stood in front of the back passenger window to block Pete's view so as to occlude Wayob, in Ashley's body, from Pete who, probably, had already seen him.

"Pete, you can't be here."

Behind Saul, Wayob slammed his head against the glass. Shera barked.

"The situation is absolutely not as it appears," Saul said. "You have to trust me on this."

"What situation?" Pete winked and wiggled his unibrow. "I figured you'd need help loading the table."

But as they squatted to lift it, Pete groaned. "My back's sore. Give me a second."

"I can probably handle it myself," Saul said. Not that he should be straining his new pacemaker any more than he had to.

"Nah, I can do it." Pete grunted as they lifted the table and turned it flat. Saul tried to steer Pete backward toward the car, but he protested, saying he couldn't walk backward with his bad back. All the while, Wayob kept slamming his head against the glass, as if trying to knock himself out.

"It's just an act," Saul said as he shuffled backward.

Pete strained to see over Saul's shoulder. "Weird."

In order to fit the table in the trunk, they had to rotate it a quarter turn and shove it in diagonally.

"So where's your performance?" Pete asked.

"Can't tell you that."

"I know, but gosh. How did you hook up with Ashley York? You could sell out the Palace of Mystery solid just on her name alone."

"You never saw her, remember?"

"I know but..." Wayob slammed his head against the window, and Pete winced. "Gosh."

Saul shut the trunk. "Pete, she's just acting."

"Seems so real."

Saul wished he'd moved Wayob to the center seatbelt where his head couldn't reach the glass. No way to do so now without exposing the handcuffs for Pete to see, which only would raise his suspicion when Saul needed to ease it.

"Marco could tell she was acting right away," Saul said.

"He saw her?"

"Couldn't be helped. Think we can trust him to keep it secret?"

"Sure, sure. I'll talk to him. Actually..." Pete said with an edge in his voice. "You know, I really should come with you."

Saul tensed. Pete furrowed his one fuzzy brow. "You'll need help setting up. And I've got to see this act. Come on. Please."

"Not ready for consumption. She wants to practice just us tonight." He clapped Pete's shoulder and steered him around the car. "You're the only one I can count on, Pete, and you're going to love this dog." He opened the front passenger door and grabbed Shera's leash just as she brushed past his belly toward Pete, who was opening the back passenger door.

Her paws tapped the pavement. She bounded into the air, tearing the leash from Saul's hand as she threw herself into Pete. He fell backward, and his phone smacked the pavement as he tried to catch himself with his hand. He landed on his butt, then Shera jumped on his chest.

As Saul reached to close the door, Shera spun, a blur of black fur. She launched off Pete and into the backseat where, on the opposite side of the car, Wayob thrashed, restrained by the seatbelt and cuffs. Shera snarled in his face.

Saul grabbed the leash and pulled her back. "It's okay, girl."

She backed out warily.

Saul shut the door. He rubbed her head.

Pete snatched up his phone and slid backward. "I just wanted a picture of Ashley York, was all." He got to his feet.

"Shera can be a little overprotective," Saul said. "She's Ashley's dog. She'll be cool, as long as you stay back from Ashley." He tried to hand him the leash, but Pete backed away.

"She'll be fine," Saul said.

"I don't have anywhere to put a dog."

"What happened to the office behind the seance room?"

"I'll just come with you and keep her off to the side. Plus, the Table of Death isn't safe, not even to practice, with just two people."

"You can't come, Pete." They had been over this twice. Why was he still insisting? It might be faster just to let him in the car and then force him out somewhere along the way, where he couldn't interfere. But that was too risky, and Saul couldn't do that to Pete. No, he had to quell Pete's curiosity as much as he could, and then get out of here. "It's too dangerous, and I don't mean the table. You just have to take my word on this."

Pete glanced at his phone and looked around. "Dangerous for you or for Ashley York?"

"Right now, it's you I'm worried about."

"I'll take full responsibility."

"No. Forget it."

Pete blinked rapidly.

"I'll make it up to you," Saul said. "I promise."

Pete started around toward Wayob's side of the car, and Saul chased after him. Shera pulled ahead at the end of the leash.

"Pete, I need you to take her inside."

"Sure, sure. I'm just going to take a couple selfies."

"Ashley's not cool with that."

Pete stopped in front of Wayob's door and tapped his phone. "Just through the window. I'm not going to post them or anything. You know how much I hate social media."

Saul didn't want to get physical, but he would if he had to. "I can't let you do that."

"How about we ask Ashley? I won't even show them to anyone. They're just for myself." He turned toward the car.

Inside, Wayob screamed for help. Shera growled right on cue.

"Gosh." Pete reached for the door, then glanced at Shera. He squinted through the window and rubbed his chin.

"Back away from the car, Pete." Saul wanted to shoulder him aside, but he was afraid of what Shera might do if he let her get any closer.

In the distance, a siren wailed. And then another.

Coincidence? No. No way.

The sound ricocheted between the stucco wall of the Castle and the hill behind it. Pete backed away. All his questions, the way he was acting—he didn't want a selfie; he'd been stalling.

He must have seen the video of Saul injecting Ashley York.

"I thought you hated social media," Saul said.

Pete shrugged. "I was curious."

There was still time. Saul could still escape—if Pete didn't report which way he went. "Go inside," Saul said. "Now."

Pete shook his head.

Saul dropped the leash and pulled his Beretta. "I'm not asking."

"You wouldn't." Pete took a step back and fiddled with his phone. "I can't believe you're pulling a gun on me."

Saul regretted it, but what choice did he have? He had to think about the greater good. "It's not about you, Pete."

A growl rumbled in Shera's chest. The sirens advanced from the south, where Hollywood Station was less than a mile away. No doubt Pete was recording, but Saul had no choice. He fired into the air.

Pete ran for the door.

"Lives are at stake," Saul shouted above the ringing in his ears.

Pete threw the door open and disappeared inside.

Saul wanted to make things good with him, but right now the problem was Shera. If she fell asleep, Wayob could escape. He'd have to bring her along. No way around it.

He unhooked her leash. She gazed up at him and whimpered, her eyes like dark pools glistening in the ambient glow of LA at night.

He opened the driver's side door and motioned her into the car. As she leaped in and scrambled across to the passenger seat, his shoulders eased back with relief. With Shera onboard, the long drive ahead with Wayob seemed less daunting.

As he squeezed himself behind the wheel, she licked his ear.

"Can I count on you to stay awake?" he asked her.

Her ears perked up, and she tilted her head as if the answer was obvious.

As he rolled toward the exit, she resumed her post, sitting facing backward in the passenger seat, glowering at Wayob.

Blue strobes washed the hillside. From the sound of the sirens, three cruisers at least.

Saul glanced in the mirror as the back door to the Castle flew open. Pete leaned out with his phone to film Saul's attempted escape.

As he prepared to turn onto Sycamore, a patrol car spun off Franklin and sped toward him, siren wailing.

Assuming the responding officers had coordinated their approach, the main exit to the Castle would be already blockaded, so reversing past Pete was not an option. To the right, Sycamore narrowed into the exit-only access road from Yamashiro, one way in and one way out, both ends easily blocked by the cops before his Prius could ascend the hill. But he had long passed the point of surrender, and there was no going back now.

———

The sunlight through the crack in the trunk's lid had faded to a haunting orange glow—a streetlight?—yet the heat remained. Rosa's insides were cooking. Her shirt, which had been soaked with sweat earlier, was now dry. The fabric sandpapered her skin as she tried to adjust her position in the narrow space between the back of the car and the boxes.

Her jeans were worse; the denim trapped the moisture from where she'd had no choice but to piss herself. Maybe she could work them down her thighs, but then what if she passed out again and someone discovered her like that?

The half-bottle of water in the trunk had saved her life, at least so far. Over the course of the day, she'd doled it out, but now it was down to the last swallow, which she was going to save in case someone came, because she could hardly even moan with her tongue swollen like a toad in her throat and her mouth dry to the point of cracking. She sloshed the water in the bottle and tried to drink in the sound of it.

Just ten more minutes. She could wait ten minutes. Ten minutes was nothing compared to how long she'd been trapped here, and if she could do ten, then she could do another ten. But her legs ached and she needed to stretch them, and she was so dizzy. She wished she could sleep but it was too hot.

Her father must be going crazy by now. He probably thought Wayob had killed her. And she couldn't die—she just couldn't—she had to tell him that she forgave him, and not just because it was Abuela's dying wish but because she understood now: Abuela's cancer might have been the catalyst, but his motivation for using the Encanto was to provide a better future for her.

Rosa imagined how, if she had a child of her own, she'd feel the same way, and determination swelled in her chest. Consequences be damned.

But she could not accept a future bought with Evan York's money, not the way her father had come into it. If she lived through this, she would have to withdraw from USC.

At least if her father reached Ashley and Gray in time with the description she'd texted of Wayob, her death might mean something. All her suffering would be worth it if Ashley and Gray had managed to force Wayob back into the Encanto and smash it with him inside. It would be worth dying just to know the bastard, who had destroyed her whole family, was in hell.

Would her father have admitted it was him under Evan York's coifed white hair, driving Evan York's black Tesla sports car? If he hadn't, then Rosa would, if—*when*—she got out of here. Ashley had a right to know that her own father had died in Rosa's father's body.

Her thirst compelled her to suck at the broken nail on her finger, which she'd cut trying to force the trunk latch. It tasted like rusted pipe.

The sound of tires on pavement. Approaching. Slowing down.

Stop. Please! Stop.

Shocks groaned as the tires dipped through what must be a pothole. The sound of an engine drifted by and then idled to a stop. The car must have parked right alongside her.

She kicked the wall of the trunk. Slammed her fists into the metal above her. The engine continued idling. No one got out. No one heard her. This was the third time. In LA, people stayed in their cars, yet she hoped without reason. *Get out of the car.*

She didn't care who found her. She'd be ecstatic to see anyone, so long as it wasn't Wayob.

She heard gears shift in the car beside her. She kicked and kicked. Maybe they had their window down? Maybe, if she screamed loud enough, they would hear her above the rumbling of their engine. This might be her last chance. She unscrewed the cap on the last of the water. Just a fraction for now. Only if the engine stopped would she risk finishing it.

She leaned on her elbow, lifted her head as much as she could before hitting the trunk lid, and, with the utmost restraint, she tilted the bottle...

Yet somehow, by the time the moisture reached her tongue, it was gone. Not even a whole swallow. Almost worse than nothing at all.

Her body shook as she began to cry but no tears came out. Her body understood what a waste it was. She was done with crying.

She tried to swallow the dryness in her mouth, sucked in a breath, and yelled, "Help!"

Her voice sounded like a toad croaking.

As though disappointed with her pathetic plea, the car kicked into reverse. Shocks squeaked through the pothole. Tires bumped up onto the pavement behind her. Brakes whined. Then the car sped away.

—

Saul's only option was a bad one, but it was all he had, so he reached across to Shera, grabbed her collar to hold her in place, and floored it. The Prius accelerated mildly, not even squealing tires as he turned up Sycamore. The patrol car followed after him. Two hundred yards and closing fast.

"What are you going to do now, Parker?" Wayob called out. Although still blindfolded, he had, of course, heard the approaching siren, and he'd heard the gun go off. He probably thought Saul had shot Pete.

Shera growled, transfixed on Wayob. Saul killed his lights and breezed past the *Wrong Way* and *Exit Only* signs for Yamashiro.

As he rounded the curve, headlights came at him in the darkness. Saul flipped his lights on and kept going. The road cut into the hillside, too narrow to pass, so the other car would have to reverse.

It flashed its high beams. It had the distinctive LED halos of a BMW. It honked and it didn't stop. It didn't even slow.

Saul drew the Beretta. The driver of the BMW laid into the horn.

Saul had to slam the brakes; they both did. Shera fell back against the dash and slipped off the seat. He had managed to stop just inches from the BMW. Wayob demanded to know what was happening, but Saul didn't care to answer.

Blue lights flashed on the hillside. The patrol car had seen him turn and would soon sandwich him here on the narrow strip of asphalt cut though the rocks and the scrub.

Saul revved the engine. The BMW honked. The glare on the windshield obscured the other driver into a vague shadow. A guy, it looked like, or a woman with cropped hair.

Saul held the Beretta out the window so whoever it was could have a better look. The BMW kicked into reverse, and Saul herded it up the hill.

The road widened into a viewing area, and the BMW reversed into it. As Saul passed, the driver buzzed down his window. He thrust out an arm clad in a dark jacket and flipped Saul the bird. Then he accelerated hard enough to squeal his tires as he took off downhill, oblivious of the oncoming strobes, or perhaps he simply couldn't wait to report Saul.

Saul rolled up to Yamashiro. The restaurant was built in a traditional Japanese style, with curved roof-lines and woodwork laced with gold. By the valet stand, a couple climbed into a Land Rover and pulled toward the exit, buying Saul some time perhaps, but not much.

Instead of driving the wrong way down the entrance road, Saul parked on the red curb opposite the restaurant, unfolded himself from the Prius, and jogged toward the valets.

As he approached, the older valet, a stocky man, limped off toward the lot behind the restaurant. The one who remained with the keys was a Korean with a baby face that looked fourteen but probably he was twenty-five, possibly thirty. Saul stood so as to block the man's view of the Prius and brandished his business card, wishing it carried the weight of a badge.

The valet's mouth opened and closed. "You're that guy."

So much for the easy way, Saul thought. Crazy how just one video could block his progress at every turn. He needed to learn how to use social media to his advantage.

The valet pulled out his phone and pointed the camera at Saul. Saul reached out and blocked the lens, while, with his other hand, he reached into his pocket and unscrewed the needle from a used EpiPen.

He leaned in close as if letting the valet in on a secret. "That video is fake." Saul slid the needle-less syringe up his sleeve and brought out his hand. Gestured with his empty palm. Released the valet's phone and snapped his fingers, making the syringe seem to appear out of thin air. He waved it back and forth such that it looked rubbery. "The syringe wasn't even real."

The valet's brows came all the way down but made only a slight dimple in his shiny forehead. Saul could practically see the gears turning, ever so slowly …

Precious time was ticking by. Saul needed the valet distracted long enough for him to switch cars and slip away unnoticed. "How about a hundred bucks for a two-minute task?"

The valet crossed his arms. "I'm listening."

Saul tried to picture someone unmemorable. For some reason, Carter popped into his head. "I need you to check the restaurant for a bald guy with a scraggly mustache. Possibly in a suit."

The valet held out his hand.

Saul gave him a twenty.

"He's not here," the valet said.

"I'm asking you to go check." Saul snapped his fingers and again produced his card, and again the valet was not impressed. Saul scratched out his phone number and wrote Marta's across the top. "This is Ashley York's phone." He showed him Marta's phone with the sequence of selfies of Ashley and Marta cheek to cheek.

The valet's eyes widened. "She's here?" He strained to see past Saul.

Saul glanced over his shoulder. Ashley York's platinum-blonde hair was dimly visible in the backseat, despite the shadow where Saul had parked. He stepped out of the way.

The valet squinted toward the Prius. "Can I meet her?"

Saul had to stop him with hand to the chest. "You don't want to do that. She's already going to be wondering what's taking so long. Just text us if you see the guy, okay?"

Now the valet took Saul's card. He squinted at it briefly, set his jaw, and glanced up at Saul and then down at his feet. "Keep your money. The thing is, I'm not supposed to go into the restaurant. But I'll do it on one condition. I need Ashley to retweet me."

Saul considered using his Beretta to convince him but decided to play the long game. "She'll do it tomorrow."

"Why not now?" the valet asked.

Saul pointed his thumb to the right, where a garden path led to a carved wooden fence topped with a thick red rail. The view overlooked the shimmering lights of Hollywood in the fog. Blue strobes washed up from below the hillside. Close and getting closer.

"Because right now we've got to get lost."

The valet frowned. "I thought you were a cop."

"I'm a detective, and that guy I'm looking for is a cop too." Saul found himself glancing right and down. "You hear about the murders at Ashley's mansion?"

The valet nodded. "Yeah, August Grant was killed by her security guy." A siren echoed up the hillside and then died down, followed by the sound of an engine revving. The couple in the Land Rover reversing. Time was dwindling, and dwindling fast.

"They think Ashley's involved, but she's the one in danger. If they find us before I find the guy..." Saul motioned toward the entrance where more blue strobes were approaching from below. "So, are you going to help us? It's now or never."

The valet glanced from the blue lights to Saul's Prius, where Shera guarded Wayob, who was sitting very still, probably trying to sleep.

"Fine," he said. "I'll text you my Twitter. If Ashley York doesn't retweet by tomorrow morning, I'm going to post your picture all over the place, and you're not going to like the caption."

"I'd expect nothing less." Saul thought he'd blocked the lens, but either way, it didn't matter; how could it be any worse than the video?

The valet finally started toward the ornate entrance just as the Land Rover reappeared, reversing slowly back up the exit road, blue lights blazing behind it. It swerved, and a rear tire bumped off the blacktop. It had only dropped a foot, but the big car halted, blocking the road.

Saul glanced around to make sure no one was watching. He snatched a key fob from the rack. The officer below the Land Rover bleeped the siren. Saul sprinted back to his Prius and folded himself into the driver's seat.

As he swerved past the valet stand, the Land Rover recovered. The sheer size of the SUV saved him from being spotted. He drove around the restaurant to the lot below. He hoped they would assume he'd driven out the entrance and not down here to a dead end.

He parked between a Lamborghini and a Tesla. Ducked down and waited a beat. On the seat beside him, Shera lay down and worked her head into his lap. Wayob was silent, his eyes still closed, but he wasn't sleeping, at least not yet, Saul knew, because he'd held his head upright through the turns.

No one had followed them, but the reprieve wouldn't last. The officers in pursuit would have called for backup by now, and soon both access roads would be blocked, and uniforms would swarm the restaurant and search the lot. Saul had ten, maybe fifteen, minutes at the most.

"Keep trying to sleep," he said to Wayob as he got out of the car. "I've got a little present for you when I get back."

Shera growled in approval.

Saul trotted the lot while pressing *unlock* on the key fob. Most of the cars valued higher than his net worth. Finally, lights flashed on a red Land Rover. For the first time, he was glad that so many people chose a car capable of fording a river in a city where it hardly rained. Standard equipment on a Land Rover included a hill-descent control system, probably never used on this particular vehicle and tonight he would put it to the test. Borrowing the car was a necessary evil.

He backed it up to the Prius. Shera barked as he got out.

"Quiet, girl."

The Table of Death was more awkward than heavy as he transferred it from the Prius to the Land Rover.

He couldn't risk the police recognizing Ashley York, so he forced Wayob into the Rover's sizable back cargo area, where he'd be hidden from view. Saul tied Wayob's feet and forced a handkerchief into his mouth. Forget about appearances. If the cops found who they thought was Ashley, it was all over. Wayob thrashed his head from side to side. In order to secure the handkerchief, Saul had to tighten it almost to the point of bruising Ashley's skin.

Shera stood guard and wagged her tail. No objections from her. He was a little nervous about leaving her in the cargo area with Wayob, so he ordered her into the footwell of the backseat. She complied, lay down obediently, and didn't seem to mind when he draped his trench coat over her. He tried to make it look as if his coat had been tossed there loosely. They wouldn't search his car without cause. Not in Hollywood. They wouldn't dare. Too many rich people and too many lawyers.

Before they left, he transferred the Encanto from the glovebox of the Prius to his pocket and put on his Merlin wig. The long gray hair would be the first and hopefully the only thing people would notice. He left the beard in his prop bag. The beard looked too Gandalf, and Gandalf looked suspicious. Saul was going for an old hippie, the sort of guy who cops found annoying.

He tightened his belt and sucked in his gut, but there was no hiding it. If they stopped him, under no circumstances could he get out of the car.

If a uniform looked twice, or looked like he might be thinking about looking, Saul would have to play offense, and he knew just how to do so from his early days as a patrol cop. He had learned to avoid the sort of personalities who got off on dramatic confrontation. They called them 5150s, referring to the California code for the involuntary psychiatric commitment. Hauling them in, though perhaps satisfying at first, rarely proved worth the effort. Their jabbering was a prescription for a headache, plus all the paperwork that usually amounted to nothing because after the seventy-two-hour holding period, they were released, even more belligerent than before.

Now it was his turn to become one: a guy who had nothing but time on his hands, was looking to attract attention, and would especially relish a confrontation with the cops. A guy best ignored.

He leaned into the Land Rover and stuck Wayob with another EpiPen. "One more for the road."

Wayob thrashed around, his screaming muffled by the handkerchief.

Saul shut the door, then used Marta's phone to call 911 and report the license plate of his Prius along with a fake sighting of himself waving a gun around on the Boulevard. That would divert some, if not all, of the backup that had been sent to Yamashiro.

He hoisted himself up into the front bucket seat of the massive vehicle. He actually fit behind the wheel. At last, a vehicle where he didn't feel stuffed in like a clown. As he adjusted the mirror, a man darted behind the car. Saul ducked down.

It was the stocky valet with the limp.

Saul checked the messages app on Marta's phone. The other valet, who he had made the deal with, went by the name Ted, according to his texts. Ted had texted three times already asking for Ashley's retweet, each message more insistent than the last, but there was no mention that the guy Saul had sent him looking for wasn't there.

Saul:
Tweet will happen tomorrow. Stay cool.

Ted:
The cops are back. What do I tell them?

Saul:
Tell them I'm in the restaurant. If they ask, you parked my car, but that's all you know.

Four spaces down from the Land Rover, a Maserati fired up. The valet with the limp backed it out and drove past Saul, either unaware or indifferent.

Saul waited for the Maserati to disappear around the restaurant before starting the Rover. Since it looked too clean for a belligerent hippie, he made a quick stop at the dumpsters behind the restaurant and gathered an armload of papers and cups from a recycle bin. As he scattered them on the backseat, Shera's head emerged from the coat and licked his hand. He scratched behind her ears, re-covered her, and spread crumpled napkins over the coat. How long could he expect her to stay hidden?

Although the exterior of the Land Rover would take too long to dirty up, at least it was a flamboyant shade of red. He got back in and sped to the bottom of the lot with the lights off. He nosed over the curb and barely felt the bump through the shocks and oversized tires. He engaged the HDC and descended the hill slowly, worrying the whole way that he'd bottom out in a pothole or lodge himself on a rock. Or that someone in the terraced houses snaked into the mountainside would feel compelled to report the suspicious activity to the blue strobes polluting their million-dollar view.

He bumped onto the blacktop of an exit-only road and turned south. As he rounded the curve, the intersection of Sycamore and Franklin came into view below. The one feasible exit. And a squad car was guarding it. Not exactly a roadblock, but the officers had a spotlight aimed to flood whoever came down.

He reversed until the hillside hid him from view, and then he waited.

Wishing for a visual on Wayob, he adjusted the mirror and tried not to think about what it would mean if Wayob had escaped—if he removed the gag and it was just Ashley York there with no memory of Wayob or of why Saul had abducted her. His stomach lurched. He had to remind himself that it wasn't just his freedom on the line, it was Rosa's life, and Hernandez's belief in him, and he would lose them all if Wayob slipped away.

A car rolled up behind Saul and stopped.

He rubbed his eyes. The officers at the bottom of the hill were a minor obstacle compared to what lay ahead for him, but at least the consequences for his actions would be his and his alone, and there was a chance he could still save Rosa. He would have to put his own life on the line in order to find her. In order to trap Wayob once and for all. It was the only way. Whether Saul lived or died, tonight it all ended for Wayob. Saul would see to that. Wayob had seen his last sunrise.

A second car eased to a stop behind the first car, and waited, almost ridiculously patient. What he needed was a self-important asshole in a rush.

As he adjusted his wig in the mirror, a third car rolled up and did nothing as well. Then a fourth car came around the bend and hit the horn. Saul eased forward and stopped again.

Honk.

Here we go. He turned on the radio and skipped through the FM bands. Found a station playing "Break on Through." Buzzed down his window and freed the voice of Jim Morrison into the cold night air.

On the way down to Sycamore, he stopped and started several more times until the fourth car was full on riding the horn and two more had joined in.

"Stay," he shouted to Shera as a reminder.

He shook his head to the beat and let the long gray locks thrash across his face as he rolled into the spotlight.

Black Canyon

A uniform stepped into the light and signaled for Saul to stop. He was on the younger side of thirty, his face long and placid. He was most likely bored to be stuck here instead of chasing the action.

Saul stopped even with the patrol car, and now he could see that behind the light, a second uniform was sitting in the patrol car with the door open, hopefully listening to Saul's bogus report on the feed from dispatch. The uniform in the patrol car had a vast, sloping gut sagging into his lap. Bigger than Saul's, though he had skinny arms and legs, so he probably weighed less.

As if the spotlight wasn't enough, the first uniform whipped out a big metal flashlight and shone it in Saul's face as he approached. "Turn down your music, sir."

Saul made a slow performance of finding the volume while the cars stacked up behind him. As he turned it down ever so slightly, Wayob thumped in the cargo area. But the bass was still pumping. Saul slapped the dashboard and bobbed his head.

The fourth car honked, its alto wail almost pleasant to Saul's ears.

The uniform glanced at the other cars then dusted his beam over the trash in the backseat, over Saul's coat in the footwell, Shera beneath it.

Saul held up the phone and aimed its camera. "So, what's happening, Officer?"

"No photos."

"This is video, man. We're live. You want to search my car without a warrant? What are you looking for, man? What do you think I've got?"

The horn of the fourth car drowned the officer's response. Then the third and the fifth joined in.

He swiped at his neck for them to cut the horns.

The guy in the fourth car yelled out the window, "This roadblock is illegal. What's your badge number, Officer?"

The uniform rolled his eyes and motioned Saul forward. "Just get out of here."

Saul heard the trash shift in the backseat. He mock bowed with a big flourish of his hand, which the uniform thankfully followed with his eyes.

"Your wish is my humble command."

The uniform grimaced. "Fucking Hollywood."

Saul pumped up the music. Rolled through the stop sign and turned past the Castle. A wet nose nuzzled his elbow as if to say, *All clear.*

"Not yet," he said. "Not yet."

Before he could check on Wayob, they had to lay down some distance.

—

The power had been disconnected from the Lunas' abandoned apartment, so Hernandez searched it with a flashlight. It was exactly as the uniform she'd sent this morning had reported: the spilled contents of Rosa's purse on the floor, along with the photo of her grandfather, the glass shattered from its frame.

She pulled the door closed and strode to the stairs, disappointed but not surprised. She hadn't expected any clues as to Rosa's whereabouts, but of course she'd needed to try.

The stairs down to the lot offered a bleak view of the underside of the freeway where someone had spray-painted *FUCK* along with a graphic illustration of male anatomy prepared for the act. It looked like it had been there for a while. Probably the whole time Rosa had lived here.

She opened her car door and slid in. In the passenger seat, Gray Wilson had all but blackened another page with dark angry lines. If the high brass knew she was counting on his scribble to find Parker, they would bump her out of Homicide Special. She might even find it funny herself, if she wasn't so desperate.

As Wilson looked up at her, his hand continued sketching, as if disconnected from the rest of himself. "Any luck?"

"No. You?"

"I don't know." He tilted the page toward her. "It could be that Wayob's back in the Encanto. I drew dark swirls sort of like this when he was before."

"You mean inside the stone? I thought it was broken without the snake."

"Not completely. Unless... Maybe Ashley and I didn't need the Encanto to return to our own bodies."

"How did it happen?"

"Well, we kind of..." His face reddened in the harsh light streaming in from the side of the Lunas' apartment. He rubbed his cheek.

It was so obvious that she hardly needed to ask. "You hooked up."

"It wasn't like that."

She wondered what it would be like to experience her own body from Saul's point of view. Would it feel like sex or masturbation? Or something else entirely? "Was it weird?"

"Claire already knows, okay?"

"Yeah, okay. You don't have to talk about it if you don't want to. I just want to know how this Encanto works, and if Wayob's not in there, then we need to know who he is now."

"You're afraid he's your partner?"

Good question. Saul had been himself when he called, and Wayob had all but confirmed that he had taken over Ashley with his strange way of speaking. But then again, it was strange that Saul had hung up on her. Plus, a lot could have happened since then. *Something* must have happened, because Saul would never shoot at Pete, and even if he did, he wouldn't miss. Whereas Wayob, from what she'd seen in the video from the surplus store, had very poor marksmanship.

At least Ashley was still alive when Saul had fled the Castle. "Wayob would have killed Ashley if he wasn't using her body, right?"

"I don't know," Gray said.

She sparked the engine and backed out over the uneven asphalt. Perhaps the shot had been a warning, which would mean Saul must have been desperate, because he knew better than that. Whatever had happened, there was more to the story. Pete was holding back.

"Where are we going?"

"To find Saul."

"You found out where he is?"

"No, but I know where he was, and I'm a detective."

It was a long way back to Hollywood, but at least the westbound lanes weren't as jammed, plus driving helped her think. Whatever Saul was up to, she had to get there in time to help. She should have stayed with him instead of following protocol. Just because the top brass had summoned her didn't mean she had to come. The threat of insubordination seemed so minor now compared to saving Rosa's life.

"Just keep drawing," she said.

"I am."

She glanced over and saw that he was. If Wayob had control of Saul's body, then Gray's ability was her only hope, but if Saul was Saul then maybe she could find him. She knew Saul. So where in the hell would he take Wayob, if Wayob looked like Ashley York? Not back to his place with his landlord always nosing around, that was for damn sure.

It made her smile to think that he was finally moving out of there. And a possibility blossomed inside her: they should move in together. She was getting ahead of herself, she knew it, but Rumi was old enough now that she didn't need her mother's help anymore. What Rumi needed now was a father figure, and maybe Saul's love of magic could drag him out of the video games and back into the physical world.

But this wasn't about Rumi, was it? This was about her. And about how tired she was of sleeping alone in her cold bedroom with the empty place beside her in the bed. The place where Saul belonged.

—

On his drive east through the vast sprawl of the Inland Empire, Saul stopped at an isolated Chevron. While the fuel was pumping, he glanced around for cameras. Saw none. He opened the back to check on Wayob.

Wayob didn't react. He lay there, limp, as if unconscious. Saul gave him a good shake.

Wayob groaned into the gag.

Saul slammed the door shut and jogged into the gas station for some water, snacks, and food for Shera.

He tossed the supplies into the backseat, drove a few miles down the road, then pulled off into the shadows. Checking again that no one was in sight, he got out and dragged Wayob out and put him in the backseat behind Shera, where he could keep an eye on him. He removed the gag and blindfold.

Wayob screamed, of course.

"Go ahead," Saul said. He'd gotten what he wanted: now he knew Wayob was awake.

He got back on the road and drove out from the urban glow. The 10 snaked through the narrow canyon between the San Bernardino and the San Jacinto Mountains. Vast jagged cliffs blotted out the night sky above the windshield. In the passenger seat beside him, Shera growled. Saul rubbed her back and glanced in the mirror.

Wayob had closed his eyes, but he wasn't asleep. He was faking. Probably. Maybe.

Unless the adrenaline had worn off, which Saul needed to happen but not yet. He jerked the wheel.

Wayob's eyes flicked open. "Do you mind? I am trying to sleep."

"You can sleep when we get there."

Wayob closed his eyes. "I can sleep right now."

Saul counted to twenty. He racked the wheel. The Land Rover swerved and rocked.

Wayob's eyes remained closed. "You will not harm us."

"And you know that for a fact?"

"I will come back in a new vessel. You have seen me do so. And once you are dead, who will stop me? So go ahead, kill us, Parker. I shall consider it a favor."

"You're confident you can still do that? With the Encanto broken and all?"

Wayob said nothing. Saul accelerated. An array of motionless wind turbines lined the freeway.

"I got the lowdown," Saul said. "Wilson's back in his own body. So now when you die, you'll be trapped back inside the Encanto."

"Not true." Wayob leaned his head back, eyes squinted shut. "Not true."

According to Wilson, Wayob couldn't be trapped without the snake-dial, but did Wayob know that too? He sounded *too* confident.

"I'm thinking I just shoot you," Saul said. "Take my chances."

"You would not dare, Parker. Parker, Parker. Saul Parker."

Wayob was right about that. Regardless of the outcome for Wayob, Ashley would die. Saul was just bluffing to keep him awake.

Rosa had said to destroy the Encanto, but this wasn't so easy, he realized. He couldn't risk Rosa's life in order to kill Wayob. First he had to find her, and there was only one way to really find out what Wayob knew.

When the memories of Wayob controlling his body first started to surface, it had seemed like a dream, and then like a nightmare, but it had all been real —and now he remembered more than just what Wayob had seen through his eyes. He retained memories that had nothing to do with him: a tropical canopy, a muddy river, and a bare-chested girl standing on the river bank. Sobbing... Wayob's memories.

Saul had the sense he could navigate the labyrinth. If he could somehow remain conscious while Wayob came into his mind he could find Wayob's memory of Rosa's location.

It must be the same for Wayob. That's how he'd learned where Ashley went to school; he saw her memories. But not her thoughts. The thoughts of those who produced the imagery were unknowable, like watching a movie. Any conclusions were filtered through one's own perception, not much more than a guess, really.

The trick was how to let Wayob into his mind without setting him free, which meant Saul had to restrain himself in such a way that he didn't know how to escape. It was going to be like jumping off untethered into an abyss: the abyss of Wayob's mind.

Shera growled.

Saul slammed the brakes.

Wayob face-planted into the back of the passenger seat. A satisfying smack of skin on leather. He rocked back, still refusing to open his eyes.

Saul scratched Shera's head and accelerated. By now the owner of the red Rover had had plenty of time for a leisurely dinner, perhaps followed by a stroll through the gardens of Yamashiro; maybe they were still there now, admiring the view. Or maybe they'd presented the valet with their ticket, and the valet had checked the number against the keys. And checked again. And come up with a loss. Then, after a search of the lot and probably some yelling and frustration, the owner would report it stolen.

Although the hill-descent control system had saved Saul's ass, Land Rovers also included a stolen vehicle locator as standard equipment. Under normal circumstances, the LAPD responded slowly and methodically to auto theft. The officer who took the report might not even enter it into the system until tomorrow. Except this was also a kidnapping—a celebrity kidnapping. Once they connected the Rover to Saul, the search would quickly escalate. They might have already swept the lot behind Yamashiro and found Saul's Prius, or the valet might have made the connection for them.

But the SVL relied on cell service. Once out of range, it would be useless, and with over twenty-five thousand square miles of wilderness in the Mojave Desert, most of which the Rover could traverse, the chance of them finding it before daylight, even with air support, was practically zero.

Ahead, at the edge of the horizon, the lights of Palm Springs shimmered against the night. Saul exited and tacked north onto 62, a narrow straight-ahead into the Mojave. There were no more houses or gas stations. No structures of any kind. Only rocks and sand and two lanes of asphalt that rolled across the immense desolate landscape. A small stripe for mankind.

No moon. Not a whisper of cloud. Saul exhaled. True darkness. The San Bernardino Mountains walled off the smog and the lights of LA. Above, a surreal multitude of stars dotted the sky. And beyond the pinpoints of light, an unknowable vastness. He felt far away.

"Where are you taking me?" Wayob seethed. His eyes glinted in the reflection of the headlights on the desert.

"Just looking for a spot to pull over. Any preference where I put the bullet?"

Wayob said nothing.

Saul dug his fingers through the thick fur of Shera's neck, her pulse practically vibrating in his hand. No chance of her falling asleep.

"Head or heart?" Saul asked, and waited for a reaction. But in the mirror, Wayob remained a vague outline of blackness against the rear window and the night sky beyond. The fear in his silence practically confirmed Saul's hunch.

"So, tell me, how do you move to a new 'vessel'?"

Wayob said nothing.

"You obviously have some control over it. Must be really hard to do."

Wayob snorted. "The vile priest never expected that I would escape the Encanto; you think he explained how it worked? Even if I knew, I would not tell you."

Maybe it was some kind of energy current that flowed below the rational existence where Saul had spent his whole life focused on logical explanations. Hernandez held the belief that all living things were connected, and science had basically proved her right. According to an article on quantum physics Saul had read, solid matter did not exist. Everything was energy, and energy moved through everything. He had no idea how in the hell Wayob moved from one body to the next, but this did not preclude the possibility of understanding. It was still physics. And physics had rules. There were limits.

"Shoot." Saul shook his head and laughed. "If I had your ability, I'd be gone. I'd be on the other side of the world. No one would find me."

"You think it's so easy? You think you could do better? The power of the Encanto only reaches so far. I doubt that with even a million years of effort you could transmigrate further than the throw of a stone, if you could even learn at all."

"I guess I should be impressed then that you managed to transmigrate all the way from the officer's kennel to Malibu. But if you're so smart then why pick Ashley York? Didn't you know I knew she was connected?"

"Yes, but if you knew how she was connected, then you would have no need to ask. Release me and I shall teach you true magic instead of the worthless tricks you have learned so far."

"If you still think it's magic then you don't understand it, either."

"I understand far more than you."

"Prove it. Surprise me."

Wayob fell silent. Shera growled.

"When I show you," Wayob seethed, "it shall be too late for you. I shall have my revenge."

Saul clenched his jaw. Wayob's attempt to frame him for murder had nearly worked, but the fact that he was now changing tactics so quickly made it clear he was out of options. He was trapped. Did he really think the Encanto was true magic? *Advanced technology is indistinguishable from magic,* someone had said, and Hernandez would know who that was.

Hernandez.

He had to tell her he loved her before venturing into the labyrinth of Wayob's mind. Why was it so hard to say it? They were just words.

He pulled off into a sandy turnout, shifted to park, and glanced over his shoulder at Wayob. "I'll be back to shoot you in a minute."

"I do not believe you."

Saul shrugged, climbed down from the Rover, and slammed the door.

He powered up Marta's phone.

As he wandered into the scrub, he gazed up at the radiant band of the Milky Way. The sky seemed impossibly close, and the stars were infinite compared to the few dots visible on even the clearest night in LA.

On the phone, the words *NO SERVICE* replaced the carrier icon. He held it up toward the stars and waited... No change.

Six years ago, when he'd driven out here with his wife—now ex-wife—she'd been on her damn phone the whole way. Back then, they had had T-Mobile; wasn't Verizon supposed to be better? He shoved the phone into his pocket. Scrambled up onto a boulder. Got to his feet and held it above his head again.

No bars.

He ran his fingers through his hair. It wasn't just about how he felt; he had to tell Hernandez where to find them in case his whole plan went sideways. If he died, there was still hope for Ashley. Plus, someone had to come and get Shera.

At least the lack of service meant that the Rover was probably off the grid. If he drove back to where he had service to make the call, he might encounter any number of officers who had been sent to wherever the SVL reported its last known location.

Even if no one was coming, he couldn't afford the time. And it was too late to turn back.

He climbed back in and continued north. The road banked up a long grade and then steepened. Arid wind gushed and whipped, as if trying to pry its way inside. Ahead were only stars, the high beams on the blacktop and the surrounding rocks and sand. The grains of sand were indistinguishable at this distance, a massive, unknowable number. Simple probability dictated that for any one thing that existed, the universe contained infinitely more. So there must be others like Wayob. Souls who could transmigrate from one body to the next. And other devices like the Encanto.

Did Saul need to find them?

Certainly, he would never again assume that anyone was who they appeared to be.

—

Thirty miles later, Saul turned onto Black Canyon, a dirt road near the western flank of Joshua Tree. It was the place he'd come to six years ago during the final month of his failed marriage, when his then wife had decided a camping trip would somehow save their relationship.

When they had arrived, the campground was empty and it was scorching hot, but then the temperature plummeted with the sun. They spent most of that night in the car with the engine running for heat, uncomfortable and sleepless. At four in the morning, they drove back to LA, arguing the whole way over who had wanted to go in the first place. If she hated camping so much, why plan the trip? That was a Saturday in late September, so he was fairly confident that no one would be around now in November.

Eons of erosion had unearthed immense boulders from the desert floor. Scattered between them, Joshua trees twisted up from the rubble and dry grass. After a few miles, the dirt road ended with a loop through a cluster of exposed campsites, each with a fire-ring and a picnic table. At the entrance to the loop, a metal box was stationed with a stack of envelopes for paying campground fees on an honor system. Not much chance of a ranger patrolling before dawn. No one was around for miles.

Saul pulled off into a spot where a two-story rock formation partially blocked the view from the road. He flipped on the interiors, scratched Shera's head, and turned to Wayob. "Now it's just you, me, and Shera."

Wayob's smirk looked almost childlike on Ashley's face. "You are wasting what precious time Rosa might have left."

"We'll see about that." Saul retrieved the Encanto from the glove box and waved it in front of Wayob.

His eyes widened. "It is broken. I told you. It is not of any use to you."

"Maybe not," Saul said. "But what can you do with it?"

Wayob said nothing.

Saul studied the porous white stone. The four-millimeter hole drilled through the top was the only place to attach the missing piece Gray had, but how did it connect? A groove traced the equator. He worked a thumbnail into the crack. It wouldn't pry apart. He shook it.

"Stop that," Wayob shouted.

Shera growled. Saul placed a hand on her chest to hold her back. "Or what?"

"Or you shall die. I could have killed you. You know this! I should have."

Saul tried twisting the stone apart on either side of the groove. "Can you really fit inside here? Seems too small." It budged, maybe a millimeter, and then it seemed to stick. More force might twist it open, if it didn't break. He decided to wait. No point in taking it apart now.

"Just drive back to the city," Wayob said. "I shall take you to Rosa."

"Your freedom for her safety, right?"

Wayob puppeted Ashley's head up and down. His eyes glistened. "This is our deal."

"So, what then? What's to stop you from killing someone else?"

"I will not. I swear, I will not. I just want to be free. You know this."

Saul held the stone in front of Wayob's face. A big part of his plan required Wayob to believe he held the upper hand. "Sorry, this is as good as it gets for you." Saul snapped his fingers and made the stone seem to disappear.

"You still have it," Wayob said. "I know you still have it."

"Maybe. Either way, you'll never see it again."

Saul let Shera out, gave her some food and water, and unloaded the Table of Death. It was too big to carry alone, so he dragged it through the sand, past the picnic table to a bus-sized boulder behind the campsite. Ordinarily, the table was used to stage a near-death escape from falling swords, but tonight he'd brought it for the shackles built into the corners: trick shackles that he'd secure with real locks.

He unfolded it and kicked out the metal legs, which were shorter on one end than the other, and then set it upright with its surface almost vertical, facing the headlights of the Rover. The ankle shackles were a few inches above the ground. Since Ashley was taller than average, Saul pulled in the slack for the chains at the top and clamped them in place.

Shera stood beside him, but her focus remained on Wayob, who was still restrained in the backseat of the Rover. Once Wayob shifted into Saul's body, she might go nuts, like she had at Ashley's beach pad. She had realized Wayob was in Ashley right from the start.

Saul tied her leash to a leg of the picnic table, out of reach from both the Rover and the Table of Death. When he stepped back, she strained to the end of the leash and whimpered. No doubt she could chew through it, but by then the ordeal would be over, one way or another. She stared up at him, her eyes forlorn and glistening in the starlight.

"Sorry, girl." In his new electric heart, he felt a spark of her pain. Wayob considered her a threat, and Saul needed him feeling confident.

Saul opened Wayob's door and unhooked his seatbelt.

"Do not touch me," Wayob shouted.

"Then get out nice and slow. No sudden movements."

Wayob slid out, hands still cuffed behind his back. He swiveled his head, and his eyes darted from the boulders to the stars to Shera. She pulled her leash taut and growled, hackles raised.

"There is nothing out here," Wayob said. "Where is this place?"

"Exactly." Saul grabbed his upper arm and steered him toward the Table of Death.

Wayob writhed, forcing Saul to tighten his grip. A bruise on Ashley's arm was the least of his worries.

"I do not deserve such treatment," Wayob said. "This is not fair."

"No, it's not fair. You deserve worse."

"Do you not see I have suffered enough? It was the odious priest who made me like this? He banished me to the Encanto because of his own deplorable behavior, because of what he made me do."

"Is that supposed to be a confession?"

As they shuffled past Shera, Wayob jumped away from her and nearly twisted from Saul's grip. He stumbled a few steps, turned toward Saul, and looked up at him.

"It was an accident." Tears rolled down his cheeks. "I killed her—is that what you wanted to hear? It was not my intention." As he spoke, a blast of hot air and spittle blew from his mouth onto Saul's neck.

"Who was an accident?"

"My bride. My beautiful bride. If you had been there... If you had seen what she did...with that priest." In the glare of the headlights, Wayob turned up the waterworks on Ashley's face. It looked genuine.

Saul recalled the bare-chested girl who, in Wayob's memory, was crying on a riverside in the jungle. She must have been this bride of his, his first kill, his first taste of murder.

"What about Jenna Collins?" Saul asked.

"Who?"

"Have you forgotten the woman you murdered with my body?"

"She... she... it was horrible. The darkness of the Encanto was nothing compared to her vile desires. I did not mean to kill her. She was a *whore*—did you know that?"

"She was a human being. What about Sadie Wu? Don't tell me she was an accident too?"

"You gave me no choice. You had cornered me. You have no idea how painful it is to die, but see how you are torturing me now? No one will blame me for escaping again, after all I have suffered."

"Keep walking." Saul steered Wayob on a wide arc around Shera toward the Table of Death. Where did it end? If not here, then how many more victims would Wayob slay using this sick logic of his to justify his murders?

Saul clasped the Beretta in his pocket. "Get on the table."

"Why?"

"We're going to be out here for a long time, and I'm guessing the handcuffs are digging into your wrists, am I right?"

He put his own wrist in a shackle and demonstrated the amount of movement allowed by the six-inch length of chain.

A grin flickered across Ashley's face as Wayob struggled to contain it. Obviously, he suspected a trick.

"Yeah." Saul popped the trick release and pulled his wrist free. "Trick clasps. Think you can figure it out?"

Wayob leaned back on the slanted table and offered only token resistance as Saul clamped the shackles above his ankles and chained his arms above his head. Undoubtably, once Saul let his guard down, Wayob expected to pop the clasps. But in order to do that he'd have to search Saul's mind for the trick open them, and even if he found it it would be useless because, careful that Wayob couldn't see, Saul slipped a padlock through each shackle.

"Don't bother trying to get free. You'll just hurt yourself. It took me months to master the trick shackles, and I had a teacher."

"I would not dream of it." Wayob's smile, once again, betrayed him. "How long do you intend to try this worthless waste of time."

"Depends on you. As you probably guessed, I don't have much life left." Saul unbuttoned his shirt and showed Wayob the bandage over his heart. "Take my body as your 'vessel.' I get hers." Saul stabbed his finger into Ashley's chest.

Wayob squirmed beneath the cashmere pullover as though Saul's finger were a hot poker, and Ashley's breast brushed Saul's hand. He withdrew, feeling a bit uncomfortable himself.

"That's my best offer. Other option is that I kill you. Your choice."

"Ashley York shall die. This does not concern you, Saul Parker?"

Saul inhaled. "Collateral damage. I don't see any way around that, do you?"

Wayob opened his mouth. Closed it and stared at Saul.

"After our little trade," Saul said, "we drive back to LA, and you take me to Rosa. If she's still alive, then I'll let you go. Deal?"

"Should I be surprised? The great Saul Parker desires youth, just like everyone else."

"Don't forget thin," Saul said truthfully, although he wanted to be a thin version of himself, not of Ashley York. Even if there was any chance Hernandez would actually go for him in Ashley's body, he couldn't imagine it working long term.

"It is you who forgets, Parker. The Encanto is broken."

"So then how are you here?" Saul gestured toward Ashley's body, her limbs outstretched and shackled to the Table of Death, Wayob's scowl on her face.

"I'm thinking," Saul continued, "that this snake is not so important. I bet we can use the Encanto without it. Maybe if I shove a paper clip in that little hole—"

"No!" Wayob's eyes widened. "I accept your pathetic body as my vessel. I just want to be free."

"Are you saying a paper clip won't work?" From Wayob's reaction, Saul began to wonder if it would.

Wayob glanced down to the right. "Do not tamper with the Encanto. You will ruin it. Just hold the stone and go to sleep. The snake is no matter."

"That's it? Just hold the Encanto while I go to sleep?"

Wayob grinned a toothy Cheshire. "This is all it shall take."

Saul had to restrain a smile. Good thing Wayob couldn't tap into Ashley's acting skills. Now Saul knew there was no risk of waking up in Ashley's body. "Any special way I need to hold it?"

"In your palm."

Saul pulled the Encanto out. Wayob's eyes locked onto it. He practically drooled.

Saul made an elaborate show of studying it in the palm of his hand. He closed his fist around it. "Like this?"

"Gentle. Gentle. You must be careful. This is my life—and yours." Wayob strained his wrist against the shackle. "Give it to me."

Saul rubbed his chin. "No, I think I get it." He turned his back on Wayob and started toward the Rover.

Shera wagged her tail between her legs. He patted her side. When he glanced up, he noticed an unmistakable blue flash in the distance. Not good.

He climbed onto the picnic table for a better view across the jagged terrain. About eight miles to the west, a chain of blue strobes bathed the hills. Three or four patrol cars at least. Saul held his breath as they strobed north.

Could be a coincidence. Could be they were on their way to take down a meth lab in Yucca Valley or Twentynine Palms. But on the very same night that Saul happened to steal a car, with a vehicle locator, and drive it down that very same road? No, they were looking for him.

The strobes continued past the turnoff for Black Canyon and faded into the darkness.

Saul exhaled. His breath like smoke in the cold, dry air.

But that couldn't be all. They were probably just deputies, maybe even a sheriff from San Bernardino. The LAPD would be a couple of hours behind, at the most, and they would send everyone they could spare. So would Palm Springs. This was a celebrity kidnapping.

Hopefully they would guess he was heading for the state line, Nevada or Arizona. That would buy him a couple more hours or so until the locater in the Rover failed to ping its location. Until heads were scratched and someone raised the possibility that Saul had stopped somewhere in the desert. Then they would fan out from the highways and search every road, and there weren't many, even though the Mojave stretched out over twenty-five thousand miles.

The edge of the picnic table felt like the rim of the abyss. And it was time to dive in. Now or never.

"You must bring me a blanket," Wayob said. "Please. I am not accustomed to such cold."

"It's above freezing." Saul stepped down from the table.

The Mojave sat above three thousand feet. As cold as it was now, in a few hours the sun would rise and the temperature would rocket, and then the Rover would become an oven. He trudged ahead toward its dark shadow and climbed in. Started the engine and racked the thermostat to seventy-five.

Hernandez would keep searching until she found him. He knew that. But he needed her here first. Anyone else would believe what their eyes told them: that Saul had splayed Ashley York out on the Table of Death like he had some kind of sick fetish. And Wayob would back up their assumption, so they would release him. And in the meantime, Rosa might die. But Hernandez had Gray Wilson, and Wilson had the ability to draw what Wayob saw.

Saul buzzed the window down and shouted to Wayob. "It's almost hot in the car now. After we switch bodies, you aren't thinking of leaving me here, are you?"

"I would not dream of this." Wayob twisted his head in the headlights. "I do not know of the way back."

Saul looked at Shera. "What do you think?"

She sat at the end of her leash and stared at him intently. His heart swelled. He could count on her to know who was who.

He shut down the engine and got out. "I'm going to trust Shera with the keys, just in case."

Wayob grimaced. "You are wasting time."

Saul squatted and clipped his keychain to Shera's collar, including the key to the padlocks on Wayob's shackles and to the handcuffs Saul was going to use on himself. He rubbed her head and held her gaze. "I can count on you, right?"

She leaned her head back and moaned a few notes, something between a whimper and a growl. She was worried. That was clear. He filled a bowl with water and left it by the table leg. At least when the sun beat down on her black fur and heated the sand like a stove, she could retreat under the table.

"I have to do this, girl."

Her jaw quivered. She looked up at him mournfully. He swallowed and turned back to the Rover.

In the driver's seat, Saul kept his movements below the dash. Wayob stared into the headlights with his superior smirk, as if he could see through the glare, but he had no idea.

Saul stowed the Encanto in the glove box along with the phone. He fished out a manual and a pen, turned to a blank page at the back, and wrote: *BLACK CANYON off HIGHWAY 62*. He sketched the route from the 10. He tore out the page and used the cap from the·pen to clip his rough map to the air vent in the center console.

Then he twisted the steering wheel until it locked, folded his coat into a makeshift pillow, and placed it on the wheel. He attached a pair of cuffs on either side. Using his right hand, he cuffed his left, but now the going got harder. He wedged the open cuff between the coat and the wheel and held it in place with his chin as he slid his remaining free wrist into it. Then, using his wrist to hold the cuff in place, he closed it with his chin.

And now he was trapped. The cuffs were real, and he had nothing within reach to pick the lock. He was now as helpless as Wayob.

The timer on the lights ran out, and they clicked off. Darkness surrounded him. And the darkness was nothing compared to the monster inside it, the monster to whom Saul was yielding himself.

He felt dizzy. The pacemaker slammed his heart against the inside of his chest. He laid his head on the coat between his hands and tried to focus on the clack of the engine cooling. The vast eerie absence of people. He belonged in LA, with the constant din of tires and engines that washed over everything, where his fears would be interrupted by the thunder of jets overhead.

The cuffs were too tight. His hands went numb. He closed his eyes and focused on his breathing. How the air filled his chest. And then he left his body. Dropping beneath the surface of all physical sensations, he counted backward from a thousand...

—

Wayob must calm down. Must be smarter than Parker. Must free himself from these chains. Wayob closes his eyes but cannot concentrate because he can practically hear Parker gloating there in the darkness of the car.

What have you done, Parker? You oaf. You cannot become the one who holds the Encanto. Or can he? What if he can? With all his manhandling of the wretched stone, Wayob could end up trapped inside, again.

No. No, no, no. The Encanto is broken. Wayob saw it himself. He held it, briefly, before the imbecilic old man interfered. Without the black snake, Parker cannot come to own the Encanto.

Calm down, Wayob. Listen. Breathe. It is so annoying to have to breathe; Wayob never had to breathe in the Encanto, but now he must in order to meditate on the sound of the mind of he who holds it.

He forces himself to inhale and exhale, practically hyperventilating but gradually, faintly, he begins to hear it... a familiar sound: the sound of Gray's mind.

Somewhere west. Somewhere closer than Wayob would have guessed but still quite far. Gray is still the owner of the Encanto, though Parker probably is holding the stone right now in his fat sweaty hand. Well, let him fumble with the stone in its broken state. Let him try all he wants, so long as he inflicts no further damage. Wayob shall have no problem transmigrating into Parker and taking control of his vile body.

Wayob cannot hear the emotions of others. No, the gloating that Wayob thought he heard was merely his own fear. There is no reason for Wayob to worry, for Parker has no understanding of the Encanto. Smart of Wayob not to explain, because now Parker's own ignorance shall be the key to Wayob's freedom. Smart of Wayob to let Parker believe he can take the body of Ashley York. *Ha. Fat chance, fat man.* Only the one true holder of the Encanto can transmigrate, aside from Wayob, of course.

But giving the keys to the mutt, that was a smart move, *Parker.* The mongrel hates Wayob. Somehow it knows Wayob is within Ashley. Wayob had to suffer its detestable stare for the entire tireless journey to this miserable place. Wayob shivers. He never had to suffer cold such as this inside the Encanto.

If the mongrel dog refuses to submit to Wayob, then Wayob will have to employ Saul's weapon to put down the miserable creature. Wayob will have no choice. He needs those keys to drive out of here. No one will blame him for ending the life of a mutt.

Wayob mires Ashley's body into a deep slumber from which she shall not awaken, while Wayob jaunts into Parker's body. Once there, he will find the trick in Parker's mind to unbind himself from these chains. Wayob shall make Parker lie down here in the dirt by Wayob's feet, and then remain asleep—the vessels always remain sleeping for quite some time after Wayob departs— while Wayob returns to Ashley's body, frees himself, and binds Parker to this loathsome table in his place. Then, by the time Parker frees himself from these chains, Wayob will be long gone in the lone vehicle, and Parker shall be trapped in the dungeon of his own flab and repugnance. *Ha!* Parker shall suffer the exact injustice he inflicted on Wayob. No less and no more.

—

Saul might be sleeping but he is still aware of something reaching into him. Spindly fingers. Spindly fingers stirring his thoughts. He has the feeling he could shove them out—and he wants to, desperately—but he resists the urge. He allows the fingers to probe around.

Then, all at once, another consciousness spills into his mind. An overwhelming weight coming down on him. And he is sinking. Even if he tries to fight, now he will lose. Wayob's invading psyche is drowning him.

Saul does not want this anymore. He tries to open his eyes…

Cannot.

He's disconnected entirely from his own body.

Darkness. So thick he can hardly move. Darkness so dense he feels he might choke, but he cannot, because Wayob has the reins on everything, even breathing. Saul feels the urge to just give in and drift off—maybe to wake up later, after Wayob is done with him. He struggles to stay lucid. Finds himself isolated, unable to fathom where his consciousness ends and Wayob's begins.

He imagines himself swimming upward. Imagines the movement, what it would feel like if swimming had any meaning at all with no connection to his limbs. The thought of moving up gives him hope.

Eventually, walls of a vast black canyon emerge from the murk. Below him, an infinite darkness. He could lose a lifetime down there. And he is so heavy. So easy to sink…

He feels the fatigue as he forces what he imagines are his legs to keep kicking, his arms to keep flapping in a direction which seems to be upward. After much effort, he reaches the rim of the canyon. Above it, across an arid wasteland, a ball of light hovers in the distance.

As Saul approaches the light, it becomes an immense, three-dimensional web. Bright streams branch out in all directions, channeled from a single source.

Wayob's core self.

Saul swims toward the brightest stream of neon green. He reaches out. He touches it.

A jungle. A river. The girl. Round face, bare breasts, her skin a honey brown. Dark hair flung over her shoulder in a way that reminds him of Rosa.

She pleads in a language Saul cannot understand. Her lascivious smile is universal. She places his hand on her breast.

Saul's hand jerks backward. Against his will, his whole body moves back. His experience of Wayob's memory is so immersive that it's jarring to learn he has no control. He can see details, the veins in the leaves, the canopy of vines and limbs which ascends to an unknown height. The sound of water flowing, punctuated by birds. The air tastes heavy and moist, alive with oxygen and vegetation.

The girl steps forward into a ray of dappled light filtering down through the green. Her fists coil. Tears glisten in her eyes. The mix of hurt and anger on her face is like a dagger in his heart.

She turns away and marches upstream along a muddy path beside the river.

He wants to run after her. But cannot. He is paralyzed right where he stands, watching her walk away. He sits on the bank. Water sloshes over stones. Glistens in the dappled light. Drips from leaves. The birds chirping around him are like sirens singing. He could stay here, forever, immersed in the song of the forest.

It's hard to remember that this is a memory. Not even his own memory but Wayob's, which Saul reached by grasping a green stream of light. In the back of his mind, he feels himself holding on. It takes all his strength to let go.

Lost in the web of light. If each thread is a memory, like the last one, it might take Saul a million years to find Rosa. But he has to try. He has to move faster.

He reaches for a stream of red-hot light.

Plunges into a nightmare.

In a chamber at the peak of a stepped temple made of stone, high above the jungle, he finds the girl with honey-brown skin on her knees, hair tied behind her back, giving head to a man in a massive headdress crowned with red and blue feathers, who must be some kind of priest. He clasps the back of her skull in his palms, guiding her up and down, his eyes bulging with pleasure.

Abruptly, Saul turns away, falls to his knees, and vomits. Below, in the jungle, monkeys howl.

The priest screams. Men in loincloths amass from the shadows of the chamber. Before Saul can run, they grab him by the arms and the legs. He struggles, but there is no escape. They drag him and then lift him onto an altar of stone. The jagged surface scratches the bare skin of his back.

Hands pin his limbs and torso in place. The priest stands over him and chants in a language Saul does not understand. After the priest disappears from view, the girl sobs from somewhere beside Saul. He tries to turn toward her, but the men hold his head firmly in place. Moss covers the ceiling above the altar.

The priest returns and places an object on Saul's forehead. He can't see it clearly, but it's about the size and the weight of the Encanto.

The priest resumes chanting. From under the object, something stabs into Saul's skull. His scalp burns.

The priest and the chamber fade away. The girl's sobbing seems to linger in the distance, then she's gone, too...

The pain in Saul's skull subsides along with the wounds on his back from the altar... along with all feeling, all sensation.

Darkness. Silence. Nothing more.

Saul tries to release the stream of light that plunged him into this nightmare... but cannot. All sense of Wayob has vanished. He's gone. This is not Wayob's memory. Not anymore. This is all Saul now. Alone. Trapped in the darkness. No sense of self.

If only he'd stayed by the river. Anything would beat this nothingness. Now he understands what Wayob meant when he complained that he'd suffered worse than Rosa, who may be suffering but at least could feel her own body.

Still, this does not justify Wayob locking her in the trunk of her Honda at that overlook on Mulholland, not even temporarily, not even to ensure his own freedom from suffering this nothingness ever again.

Saul must do something. But what? Without a body to move, what good is willpower? Without any way of communicating, what can he do? He is trapped here, alone. Alone with his feeling of failure looping around and around in the void.

—

Wayob, in Parker's body, strains against the metal bracelets. They dig into Parker's chubby wrists, causing Wayob to suffer a throbbing sensation and, at the same time, thousands of tiny pinpricks under his skin.

Parker, what have you done? You fool. Why shackle yourself to this wheel for steering, with no way to free yourself? He must have been so confident that not only could he transmigrate into Ashley York's body but that Wayob would adhere to the little deal they had agreed on.

Wayob kicks his feet around the floor well to no avail, his legs constrained by the massive flab on Parker's lower body, which is now Wayob's body. To be this close to the Encanto and unable to reach it is worse, way worse, than being chained on the hard table.

If only he could hold the Encanto. He had found Parker's memory of stuffing it in the little dash compartment opposite the seat beside him. So close, yet impossibly far away. Wayob yearns to study the groove in the rounded stone, which he saw in Parker's memory and which the odious priest perhaps never expected to be discovered. What if Parker were to shove his grubby nails into the groove? Could the Encanto be pried apart? Would it be further damaged? Certainly, Parker would ruin it if he could, if he knew Wayob still needed the dark current of the Encanto, which now works better than ever. Perhaps it is because the snake is absent. Or perhaps Wayob has always had a choice, and only just now acquired the skill required. Either way, he can now resist getting sucked inside the stone when the holder of the Encanto returns to his own body. As he transmigrated from Ashley's body into Parker's, he had again felt the Encanto's pull, and this time it was even easier to resist.

Perhaps without the snake, no one can ever come to hold it again. The Encanto works for Wayob now and Wayob alone.

Wayob has the feeling he could so easily drift out of this torture chamber that is the body of Saul Parker and shift into the Encanto, his own oasis away from all the suffering and the dizzying memories, a place where he can finally think. He can retreat there until he is ready to take a new vessel.

Parker. Wayob laughs. Parker must have restrained himself in order to torture Wayob. Thinking Wayob would... what? Give up? Cease to exist? There are no other vessels out here, sleeping or otherwise, Parker made sure of that. So what does he expect? Such a fool. Parker has no idea the extent of Wayob's recently acquired freedom. He shall soon learn.

But his wrists hurt. His back hurts. Even his heart hurts. He moans and gazes at the compartment where Saul Parker stashed the Encanto, as if he could hide it from Wayob. The Encanto is so close, and he is so sick of suffering. He can take a break and leave whenever he wants, can he not?

He can, but he is so close. Once he finds Parker's memory of the trick to the chains, he can return to Ashley's body, free himself, and take the Encanto. Then he will leave Parker and the mongrel dog to die in this awful place.

Wayob looks around, wishing he had some way to add to Parker's discomfort before he goes, but, of course, he can do nothing.

The pathetic directions Parker left on the dash puzzle Wayob. Did he expect to forget the way back to the city?

Seeing the crude sketch reminds Wayob of a drawing he saw at Ashley's palace on the beach. There was something familiar about it, which Wayob hardly had time to consider, understandably. Parker had arrived and ruined everything just when Wayob had finally made Ashley his vessel, after the torture of being trapped in her body all day with no control, seeing everything, and feeling everything—an agony worse than the Encanto, worse than these shackles binding him to the wheel. Ashley had been touching Gray all over— and between their legs—with no clothes between them. Wayob had transmigrated into Ashley at the same moment she had returned to her own body from Gray's, and somehow, in the process, Wayob became trapped under her mind. Wayob shudders to think how much more he might have suffered had he not gained control of her.

But the drawing. It suddenly seems significant. From the balcony overlooking the ocean, Wayob had watched Parker stroll through Ashley's palace as if he owned it, and Parker had stopped by the long, cushioned couch to pick up the drawing and study it. Why was he so interested?

Wayob closes his eyes. He falls back into the depths of Parker's mind. Dives into the labyrinth of his memories. They're less overwhelming now that Wayob has learned to explore them as though through a vast hallway of moving images. Before, when Wayob was first learning how to navigate the mind of a vessel, memories were like densely tangled vines of lightning. If he touched one, it forced him into the memory—to feel it as if he had been there.

Yes, much safer to observe a vessel's memories from a safe distance. And for this particular memory, Wayob can entirely avoid the blinding corridors of Parker's visceral recollections of the woman detective.

In a recent hallway, Wayob easily finds Parker's memory of the drawing: it is clearly a cage. The cage where they locked Wayob after he made the filthy mutt his vessel—but never again shall Wayob inhabit an animal. People are disgusting enough. The drawing aligns with Wayob's own memory, right down to the stupid saying on the wall, *To Protect and Serve*, as if the police believe in that. Parker attacks and harasses Wayob. Missing from the drawing is the rack of red-colored ropes the law officer used to torture Wayob, dragging him by the neck like a slave.

But that is of no import now. The question is, how could such a drawing end up in Ashley's palace by the beach? Ashley did not draw it. Wayob would have seen the memory.

It must have been Gray. Ashley had seen Gray drawing on many occasions.

Outside the car, the mutt, Wayob's former vessel, growls. Wayob wants to shout at the mongrel to shut up, but of course it will do no good. Foolish of Parker to leave it tied to the table where it cannot reach Wayob.

Wayob squints through the glass at the shadow where Ashley remains unconscious and chained to the table.

"Go ahead," Wayob says to the mutt through the open side window. "Bark all you want. It could take hours for her to awaken."

But Wayob can hardly concentrate. With all this noise, it could take him hours to find what he needs in Parker's mind. He had just realized something important. What was it?

He looks around. The foolish directions, Wayob now realizes, are not so foolish after all! Now he hears Parker's memory of Gray saying that he drew what Wayob sees. Has every holder of the Encanto had this ability? Probably. So, that was how Abuela knew to give the Encanto to Gray just before Wayob arrived to kill her. She saw Wayob coming. Wayob cannot believe he has just now discovered this. Of course, he did spend most of the last millennium trapped in the Encanto, thanks to the barbaric priest, so who could blame Wayob for not knowing? No doubt even the priest himself lacked a full understanding of the device.

Wayob stares at the directions. He is now and always will be the one in control. Not Parker. *Though I will concede you are a sneaky one, Parker.* Smart to send Gray directions, almost but not quite unwittingly, through Wayob.

Wayob closes his eyes and listens to the sound of Gray's mind. Growing closer. "Come on, Gray. I shall be ready."

But what if Gray travels with the woman detective, Hernandez? From her vividness in Parker's memories, Parker obviously cares about her, maybe even believes that he *loves* her. Like there is any such thing as love. Wayob, too, once believed in love, and then his bride betrayed him, and now he knows better than anyone how the human biology pollutes the mind. Inside the

Encanto, he experienced pure thought, free from hormones, pain, and hunger. Why, on top of everything, must he now experience hunger? The repulsive desire to masticate and to swallow. The never-ending process of digestion. The never-ending chain of messy filth it expels, the inescapable smell, the hundred-trillion organisms slathering around inside him, multiplying. Eating him alive. Wayob cannot concentrate like this.

"Focus, *Wayob*. Focus. Focus." There is not much time.

Hernandez, the woman detective. Parker's woman, who over the phone seemed to quickly determine that it was Wayob using Ashley York as a vessel. Was it just based on what Parker said, or did Wayob betray himself? *Well, Parker. Well, well.* Wayob shall learn from your memory. Learn all kinds of irrelevant details. When Hernandez and Gray arrive, they shall have no idea who is Wayob. *No idea.*

They shall set Wayob free, and Wayob shall take the Encanto for himself. He shall secure his future. Perhaps there is no need to kill Gray now that Wayob can no longer be forced back inside the Encanto. But will Gray leave Wayob alone? Wayob can shame Gray into shutting up with details of the physical act that he and Ashley engaged in. Wayob will start there and then maybe, after no one is watching, kill Gray, because after all, Wayob cannot have someone seeing what he sees.

But which vessel should Wayob take for the arrival of Hernandez and Gray? Clearly Ashley, with her youth and all the resources at her disposal, is the better vessel in the long term. And Gray, blinded by his own lust, shall believe whatever *Ashley* says.

But Parker has more authority. And, though it seems impossible anyone could think they *love* such a porker as Parker, hormones, no doubt, have polluted Hernandez into believing she *feels* for Parker—the same non-existent emotions he obviously believes himself to have for her.

Hernandez may be smart, but Wayob will be smarter. Wayob shall choose the opposite vessel of who she expects. But which would that be?

—

Two hours later, Hernandez skidded off the blacktop and onto the dirt one-lane to Black Canyon Campground. Gray dropped his pencil in the footwell and bent over to find it.

A Joshua tree sprang into the headlights. As she passed it, it seemed to transform into a contorted phantom, and she watched it in the mirror as it faded into darkness and the plume of dust behind her.

"Any luck?" she asked Gray.

He straightened and held up the pencil.

"I mean with your drawing."

He shook his head. "Your driving's not helping."

She plowed ahead into the darkness. Hours had passed since he had drawn Ashley York chained to a table, her arms and legs splayed out like an *X*. And since Gray had drawn Ashley, from someone other than her point of view, Wayob must be someone else. *Saul.*

But then, who had sketched the directions to the campground? It was hard to imagine Wayob doing so, especially if he knew about Gray's ability. Most likely, Saul had sent them a message through Wayob, which meant he was in trouble.

And now things were about to get worse. The LAPD was tracking the Land Rover that Parker stole. Hernandez had argued with Levy for permission to pursue him alone because too many officers would create confusion and Ashley might get harmed in the crossfire, but now the top brass had assumed control of the operation and it was too late to hold back the hounds.

Hernandez checked her phone. There had been no service since they exited the 10, which bought them some time since the Land Rover was off the grid, but not much since it also had a LoJack broadcasting its location using radio frequency, with a range of seven miles by land, ten by air.

As she fishtailed into the campground, Gray clutched the grab handle. Her headlights caught the reflectors of a vehicle: a cherry-red Land Rover, parked alone. *Thank goodness.* They had beat the LAPD.

The Rover faced a boulder the size of a house in front of which a table was propped upright, and chained to the table was Ashley York. Just like in Gray's drawing.

Hernandez's heart dropped as she slid to a halt behind the Rover. Through its rear window, Saul's massive shoulders and block-shaped head were unmistakable. She felt nauseous.

She ordered Gray to stay put. Drew her weapon and climbed out.

Fifteen feet from the Rover, a black dog strained toward her at the end of its leash.

Ashley shouted from the slanted table, "You have to help me. Detective Parker is Wayob."

Hernandez swung her Glock toward the open window of the Rover, and for the second night in a row, she aimed her weapon at the face she loved. "Hands up."

Behind her, the dog howled. But Wayob, in Parker's body, just sat there, eyes closed, head lolling against the headrest.

She tightened her grip on the Glock. "*I said* hands up."

No reaction.

She moved closer. She would know if it was really Saul from the things he knew—and not just their shared memories, but the way he spoke, the look in his eyes... but his eyes remained closed. He was unconscious. And both of his wrists were cuffed to the wheel—as though his last-ditch effort before Wayob took his body had been to trap Wayob there in the car.

Jesus, Saul.

"Don't!" someone shouted.

Hernandez swung her weapon toward the sound.

In the shadow behind the headlights, a figure froze. Gray. He was out of the car. "You can't kill Wayob," he said. "He'll just get away."

She lowered the gun. "I told you to wait in the car." She had no intention of shooting Wayob, especially not in Saul's body—not that she'd say so out loud while there was any chance Wayob could hear it. "Maybe you can draw more than a scribble now?"

Gray burrowed his right foot in the sand. "Maybe."

"We don't have time for maybe."

"No, you do not," Ashley said. "Let me free, now."

Hernandez turned toward Ashley. "How do we know *you're* not Wayob?"

"Ask me whatever you want." She spoke slowly. "I was slow to answer when Saul asked me my mother's name because she died in a hospital when I was five. Her name was Wendy, by the way."

Hernandez's breath quickened. The difference in how Ashley sounded now compared to over the phone in Saul's car was striking. Now she was completely devoid of that cadence Hernandez had come to associate with Wayob; her voice sounded flat, almost mechanical.

Ashley shook her wrists against the manacles. "Let me out or I am going to sue your asses."

Hernandez snorted. "Sounds like Ashley to me." Her tone was more sarcastic than intended, but she hated how wealthy people used lawsuits as instruments to bully people around.

"She's been through a lot," Gray said.

"See if you can open those manacles for her," Hernandez said to him. If the manacles had a trick release, she doubted he'd find it, but it was better for Ashley—assuming it was her—to think they were trying to help her.

Right now, her concern was Saul. He was breathing, at least, but his face was blank, just as it was last night when she found him behind the ambulance on that gurney. When she had thought he was dead. Then, after being granted another chance with him, instead of simply saying how she felt, she'd quoted Campbell. Why not use her own words for a change? Be direct. If she could just have one more chance, not only was she going to tell him, she was going to show him.

But now she was all on her own. There were no EMTs to bring him back from the dead, and a heart attack was nothing compared to Wayob.

She clenched her jaw. Transferred the Glock to her left hand. And shook Saul's shoulder.

———

Ignoring Hernandez's order, Gray retrieved the paper from her car and started toward the picnic table. The black dog pulled toward him at the end of its leash. *Maybe not*, he decided. The wound its teeth had left on his arm still throbbed.

He retreated to the Mustang and sat on the fender facing Ashley. She was chained to the table maybe forty feet away, her white pullover almost glowing in the headlights. Since his earlier drawing was focused on her, most likely she wasn't Wayob.

"You have to get me out of here," she said.

The desperation in her voice tore at his heart, but he had to be sure. Maybe

Ashley hadn't moved since his last drawing, but Wayob could have.

He used a copy of the Tao Te Ching that he'd found in the glovebox to prop up a piece of paper and stared at the blank white page. His eyes watered in the wind. His hands stiffened from the cold. If he could just draw, he would know who was who.

Hernandez had opened the door to the Land Rover and was taking Parker's pulse. "He's just unconscious," she said.

If Parker's body was unconscious with Wayob inside it, maybe it explained all the black blurs Gray had drawn.

The headlights shut off. Darkness fell over everything.

Hernandez clicked on a flashlight and aimed the beam at Parker's face. In her other hand, she held the gun pointed down.

Behind Ashley, beyond the boulder, the distant contours of the vast landscape emerged from the darkness, a world of shadows and stars. A row of jagged peaks on the horizon were rimmed by silvery light from the moon rising behind them.

Gray exhaled. He slid back on the fender, repositioned the book on his thigh, and centered the paper. It almost glowed in the starlight. He slashed a line across the page. Starting was the hardest part.

He sketched a pair of eyes, familiar eyes, floating on the page.

Hernandez threw open the door to the Land Rover and stood back, with both the flashlight and her gun aimed at Parker. Her silver bangs whipped back in the wind. She stepped up on the tread plate. What was she doing?

"Just wait a second," Gray said.

His pulse throbbed in his head. He sketched a square chin... big shoulders... Detective Parker. The perspective was almost head-on. Could be Ashley's point of view through the windshield, or Parker staring at his reflection in the mirror... or perhaps Gray had simply doodled Parker because he was already suspicious that Parker was Wayob.

Ashley moaned, her head craned back, looking up toward the stars. The dog watched her, intently.

Gray flipped the paper to start again. Indistinct shapes slid through his mind. A vague outline. When his pencil touched the page, the image faded. Pretty soon all he had was another scribble.

"Don't you care about me?" Ashley's voice reverberated from the rocks beside her. Her head was twisted to the side. She swiveled it forward and glowered at him. "How can you leave me chained up like this after what we did yesterday?"

"I have to make sure."

Hernandez stepped back from the Land Rover and peered at Gray. Ashley glowered. Even the dog was watching him.

The sky seemed to spin above him. So many stars, more stars than he'd ever seen before, and so close, impossibly close.

How could Wayob know that he'd hooked up with Ashley?

So that must be her chained to the table. Of course it was.

He slid off the fender. The wind stung his eyes. He wiped the tears away with his sleeve.

He trudged toward Ashley. Wind whistled through a fissure in the boulders. Something cold slimed his hand.

He jerked back.

It was the dog. She stood at the limit of her leash, ears cocked and head tilted up at him, gazing with big sorrowful eyes that glistened in the starlight.

This was like an entirely different dog from last night, when Wayob was in her body. It was Wayob who had wounded his arm, not this animal.

He reached out his hand.

She sniffed it.

Ashley hissed, "The keys are on its collar."

Gray kneeled.

"What are you doing?" Hernandez asked.

Gray pointed at Ashley, who was shivering in her thin sweater. "You said to let her out."

———

Hernandez was out of time. She could order him not to unlock the manacles, and damn the consequences if it turned out to be Ashley York chained to the table, but then what?

In the distance, the stuttered groan of a chopper swelled over the wind. LAPD, almost certainly, and soon they would pick up the signal from the LoJack.

So was it Wayob or Saul slumped against the seat? If there was any chance of awakening this big beautiful man, she knew how to do it. And then she'd know for sure if he was the one she loved or the one she loathed...

———

Gray slipped the keys from the dog's collar and turned toward Ashley. The dog growled.

When he glanced back at her, she went silent and peered up at him, her melancholy eyes begging him, but for what?

He scratched her chin. She licked his hand and wagged her tail. Maybe she just wanted attention. Maybe she was like his mom's terrier, who howled like crazy whenever he got shut in another room.

He approached Ashley again. Wind sliced through his shirt. The dog barked, ferociously.

He had to shout to be heard. "What happened between us..."

Ashley grimaced.

He had to tell her that what they'd shared was a one-time thing, never to be repeated, that he had been desperate to feel something, anything, other than the guilt and grief over Claire. Ultimately all of this was all his fault.

Mucus ran from Ashley's nose. Hair blew across her face. Her arms trembled. She shook the manacles. "Hurry up."

Behind him, the dog barked.

Gray tightened his fist on the keys. The metal dug into his palm. "If I had known Claire was alive, I wouldn't have… Even when I didn't know, I still shouldn't have." No matter how right it felt.

She blinked rapidly. Her lashes caught in her hair. "Let me out. I can fund your artwork for the rest of your life."

The lump moved from his throat to his chest. She'd already offered to be his patron. Was she reeling it back in now and making it conditional? "I'm letting you out, regardless."

The wind gusted, as though trying to blow away the approaching helicopter. Ashley closed her eyes.

Gray moved closer and chose a key that looked like it'd fit the padlocks on the shackles. As he reached down to unlock it, his fingers brushed her hand.

She flinched.

All the muscles of her face tightened. Her mouth twisted. Then, suddenly, she smiled. A smile which failed to reach her eyes. Too narrow. Not Ashley's smile. The difference was subtle… but huge.

Gray's legs felt weak. He stepped back, unsteadily. The Milky Way tilted above him. The helicopter droned closer. He didn't need a drawing, not anymore—now he knew where Wayob was.

—

Saul awakened into what seemed like a dream: Hernandez's lips pressed to his. She was kissing him, but the kiss was awkward, too awkward for him to be dreaming, and therefore better—this was happening. Why she was kissing him, he had no idea. It almost felt forced. But he for sure had a million reasons to kiss her back, and so he did. And when he started kissing her in earnest, she dove into it. Into him.

Something metallic mashed the stitches over his heart, which at the moment he hardly cared about. Hernandez withdrew what turned out to be her Glock. She dropped the flashlight, its beam of light bouncing around the SUV.

The world felt different, rearranged. He closed his eyes and tried to understand. He found some of Wayob's memories tangled in with his own. Some part of himself had been lost in the black canyon between their two minds, and this was preventing him from being all here with Hernandez, in his dream come true.

The spell was broken by the deafening chop of helicopter blades hitting the vortices of their neighbors. She withdrew. Wind and dust tore through the open door behind her.

He asked, "How did you know it was me?"

She smiled. "Wayob hates being touched."

She unsnapped the universal cuff-key from her belt and unlocked his cuffs as the chopper's search lights swept the boulders behind Wayob. It was just a matter of time until they were surrounded. But Saul still had a play.

Outside, Gray Wilson stepped back from Wayob as though startled by a snake, and then the beam of the chopper found them all. Light poured into the Rover. Hernandez freed his wrists. Before Saul could say anything, her lips returned to his, her arms around his neck. However much time they had, it was enough for this moment. This moment was all that mattered.

More than anything in the world he wanted to fully surrender to this, but he couldn't—not now. Rosa was locked in the trunk of her car, and now he knew where to find her, but they had to act fast.

———

Despite the agony in his every muscle and bone, Wayob feels only a surge of relief when the woman detective flings open the door of the giant car. She will shoot Parker, like he deserves.

But, no... inexplicably, she climbs into the vehicle on top of him and presses herself into his sagging chest.

She drops the light but this does not spare Wayob from having to watch. A massive helicopter rumbles over them, churning dust into Wayob's face, as if it wasn't already windy enough. The helicopter aims its blinding spotlight through the windshield as Hernandez and Parker smash their faces together. Their lips join, mingling saliva, infecting each other. *Kissing*. It's like deranged cannibals attempting to suck each other's insides out.

And Gray hardly seems to notice. He stares at Wayob as though enchanted by Ashley's body and the physical acts he has in mind, which Wayob must pretend to want in order for Gray to keep believing that Wayob is Ashley. At least Wayob's great effort to talk like Ashley has paid off. It is not so hard. All he has to do is find snippets of her words in her memory and say them again in the same way. In fact, his tongue already knows how. The hard part is containing his distaste for the way Gray is staring at him.

Gray approaches him. What if he wants to suck faces with Ashley? Wayob cannot bear to imagine what Gray has in mind for Ashley's body—with Wayob trapped inside it.

This is too much; it really is. His arms hurt. His legs hurt. He shivers. It is unreasonably cold, yet he would rather freeze than be suffocated by Gray's body. Wayob closes his eyes.

He can hardly concentrate with the noise grinding on his nerves. He is exhausted from all the suffering, the endless physicality in this body of Ashley York. With his mind, Wayob searches and searches hard, but of course, no potential vessels sleep within reach. Parker made sure of that. The only available vessel he finds in proximity belongs to some puny reptile, imbecilic, incapable of containing all that is Wayob. Hard to believe, but yes, it is somehow worse than the filthy mongrel dog.

And now, in addition to everything else, the idea of *thirst* wells up from the back of Ashley's mind. And there is no water, and Wayob hates swallowing. Worse than that, a pressure swells in his abdomen. A need to soil himself, which, if he gives into it, will only worsen his situation, to have to lie in the filth and yet still endure that insatiable sick look in Gray's eyes, which he can feel on his skin even with his eyes closed.

Suddenly, Gray rakes Wayob's hand with a bony, awful finger. From the pit of his stomach, a scream rises, which Wayob must swallow back. His body feels "icky," as Ashley would say. Wayob wishes he could just slough out of this dirty skin (the one redeeming quality of a reptile).

"Eyes open," Gray shouts above the din of the machine, "Wayob."

Wayob? Gray must be guessing. Wayob opens his eyes, blinded by the light of the awful machine. How long can it hover over his head? If not for the light and the restraints, Wayob could fake a seductive look, like Ashley has practiced in the mirror, but in this moment it takes all Wayob's effort just to not grimace. "Gray, please, okay? I am Ashley."

Parker suddenly appears beside Gray, rubbing his wrists, which are now free from the shackles. Why did Hernandez release him?

"Good work," Parker says to Gray. "Keep it up. Wayob hates being touched."

What makes them all think that it's Wayob in the body of Ashley York? How can they know this? Wayob *performed* so well.

"Well, so what?" Wayob shouts. *No sense in continuing the arduous charade.* "If you torture me more, I shall tell the world what sadists you are. You shall be punished for this, all of you."

"You think they're here for you?" Saul Parker points up at the monstrosity hovering above them. "They only care about the Rover. Once Hernandez drives it out of here, you and I will be all alone."

Behind him, Hernandez climbs into the massive car.

"Good," Wayob screams. *Just be quiet.* He can almost hear the peace of the Encanto, where he can hide without being trapped now that it is broken. If he could just get there.

The helicopter has stirred up so much sand that the air is almost toxic. Tears stream down Wayob's cheeks. "You want this body of Ashley York? Well, you can have it."

"That's not possible," Parker says. "The Encanto is broken, and you know it. All I want is revenge." He goes to the mongrel and releases it. It lunges toward Wayob and snarls.

"Shera, not yet," Parker says.

For some reason, the dog halts. It sits at Wayob's feet and stares up at him, as though it is contemplating how to tear out Wayob's throat. An evil growl rumbles in its chest, somehow audible despite the din of the machine overhead.

The woman detective starts the Rover and revs the engine. The discordant combination of sounds grates through Wayob's head. It is more than he can endure, and yet Wayob must endure more, because Gray still has that awful lustful look in his eye.

Hernandez lowers the window and shouts. "Use my laptop in the Mustang. Show Wayob some pornos. I know how he digs 'disgusting acts.'"

"Good idea," Parker shouts back. "He has a real thing for fellatio."

Fellatio? Has Parker seen Wayob's worst memory, the deplorable act Wayob's bride performed on the abhorrent priest? Parker must have seen it while Wayob was searching his mind for a means of escape—what a horrible waste of time that turned out to be—and means to use this knowledge to torture Wayob.

A torture beyond tortures, beyond what Wayob endured in the Encanto. Not even the black-hearted priest would have dared go this far. Truly, this is more than Wayob can endure. "Just leave me alone, and I'll go."

"Deal." Parker throws a sheet over Wayob, as if all this time he was merely waiting for Wayob's request.

"Parker, you fool." Wayob laughs, glad now for the ruffling sheet and the horrible engines to drown out his outburst. Once Parker learns what he has done, it shall be too late.

Suddenly, some mechanism drops Wayob back. Wooden sides appear from slots in the sides of the table, which Wayob is still chained to, transforming the table into a box with Wayob at the bottom of it. Even better.

With the sheet protecting him from the light of the helicopter, Wayob closes his eyes, already feeling the pull of the Encanto. The glorious nothing. Once inside the Encanto, Wayob shall be untouchable, disembodied with no needs.

He hears the massive car drive closer. Apparently, the woman detective has not left yet, which is fine by Wayob. Eventually they all will leave. Wayob can so easily wait. Soon enough they will succumb to their animalistic needs, their desire to masticate and swallow and digest, and then Wayob shall ride along with them, unseen in the Encanto, when they return to civilization; and there he shall be free to choose, from among the multitude, a new vessel.

Right when he feels himself start to drift, someone jerks the table, probably Parker. Without warning, Wayob is violently flipped over.

The weight of his own body causes the manacles to dig painfully into his wrists and ankles. Dust churned up from the helicopter chokes the air that Wayob must breathe. He tries not to inhale, but this body refuses to obey. He coughs, which causes him to inhale more dust, which forces him to cough more. Sand lodges between his teeth, his mouth too dry to do anything about it.

"Hurry," Hernandez says. "They've got to be close now."

Wayob hears movement above his back. The door to the massive car slams, and then its engine fades as it drives away. The awful din of the helicopter departs, along with its wind and light. Yet still Wayob is subjected to this agony of hanging face down in the chains.

Eventually—and with no warning, of course—the harsh mechanism in the table flips Wayob back over, and he is lifted to his previous upright position. But does Wayob receive the mercy he deserves? No, of course not. Gray is standing over him with a twisted, sick look in his eyes.

More than ever in Wayob's centuries of suffering, he wants to glide out of Ashley and into the dark current of the Encanto, away from all this pain and into its infinite nothingness. But Wayob cannot concentrate with Gray wiggling his fingers maliciously at him. Gray's hands approach.

———

The beam of the helicopter swept away. As Gray's eyes adjusted, the darkness gave way to starlight, the moon rising above the ridge line. Detective Parker's diversion had worked. The helicopter had assumed that the empty box they loaded in the back of the Land Rover contained Ashley and chugged after it. Now Gray, Parker and Shera were alone here with Wayob in Ashley's body.

Gray leaned over Wayob and wiggled his fingers.

Wayob bucked against the table. He jerked the chains on his arms and legs but had no way to avoid Gray's slowly approaching hand. Gray wondered if the threat was worse than actually touching him, like when he threatened to tickle Mindy and she writhed around on the floor laughing uncontrollably. It hardly seemed to matter if he touched her at all.

Wayob contorted Ashley's face into a mask of pain and started crying.

Gray clenched his jaw. This was the bastard who shot Claire in the spine. He deserved to suffer if that's what it took to scare him back into the Encanto, where he belonged.

Beside Gray, Shera barked as if in approval.

"You know it's Wayob, don't you?" Gray had heard of dogs barking at ghosts, and now he believed it. All the barking and growling earlier had been her attempt to warn him.

"I think Wayob gives off some kind of psychic energy," Parker said. "And I think Shera recognizes it from when Wayob was in her body. Hell, maybe she can smell it."

Gray turned toward Parker. The blue light from his phone made the furrows on his forehead seem deeper. Wind ruffled through his thin hair.

"I really thought he was Ashley," Gray said. "I almost let him out."

Parker dropped a hand the size of a mitt on Gray's shoulder. "Don't beat yourself up. Wayob used Ashley's memories against you."

Gray shivered. "He can read minds?"

"I think he can see the memories of the person whose body he's in. But if he could see thoughts, he wouldn't have fallen for my little trap."

Wayob sneered. "You think I am trapped?"

Parker glanced toward the distant chop of the helicopter, which now seemed to be growing louder again, then looked back at Wayob and spread his hands wide. "If you can get out of here, then by all means—"

"I cannot do anything with you treating me like this."

"Good," Parker said. "We're just getting started here." He shoved his phone in Gray's face. "Which porno should we show Wayob first?"

Gray wasn't sure he wanted to see but couldn't help a quick glance. On the screen was just text:

Give me the snake so I can fix the Encanto. Don't let Wayob see.
Keep touching him and take it up a notch!
Make him flee to the Encanto.

"Oh my god," Gray said as he slid a hand into his pocket and clutched the obsidian snake that was like the key to the Encanto. He was more than ready to smash the damn thing now, little good that it would do, because it wasn't just the Encanto that Rosa's grandmother had wanted him to destroy; she'd wanted him to smash Wayob inside of it.

"You cannot make me watch that filth," Wayob said.

Parker unbuckled his belt. "You're going to do a lot more than watch."

Wayob grimaced.

Gray wasn't too interested in seeing Parker's pants come off, either. He palmed the snake and took Parker's phone. "Check out this one," he said, typing out one of the few things he'd learned about the Encanto on the screen: *Counterclockwise resets it.*

He passed the phone back to Parker and palmed him the snake.

"Nice!" Parker said. "I'm going to tape his eyelids open. I'll be back with the tape." He strode toward Hernandez's car, leaving Gray alone with Wayob in the pale light of the moonrise.

Take it up a notch? Gray already felt weird about what he was doing. Did Parker expect him to come onto him? Gray had limits.

And what if Ashley was aware? She'd probably want Wayob out of her, regardless of what Gray had to do.

A helicopter rumbled in the distance, getting closer. A new one or the first one returning?

This is just a means to an end, he told himself. He owed her for the moment they had shared, which had centered him at first but now tasted like acid in his throat. He never should have touched her, despite what they had felt at the time, despite how badly they had needed to feel like themselves.

The grind of the approaching helicopter drowned out whatever Wayob was saying.

Gray spoke into Ashley's ear, imagining that only Ashley could hear him, imagining her here with him now. "I'm sorry."

He leaned forward.

Everything blurred to white.

Blinding light.

Wayob screamed.

Gray froze in the spotlight. But he'd come too far to stop now. It was his fault that Wayob had escaped from the Encanto, so it was his responsibility to force Wayob back inside it, regardless of what it might look like to whoever was watching from the helicopter.

He gulped down air and forced himself forward... leaning onto the table, on top of Ashley and Wayob.

Wayob screamed, "Get off me."

Gray wedged his arms in behind Ashley's back and hugged her body to him, imagining her deep down inside of Wayob, imagining his hug drawing her to the surface.

He ignored whatever Wayob was saying, refusing to feel guilty for what had happened between him and Ashley. It had been inevitable, a magical, one-time thing never to be repeated. However the real Ashley might feel about it, it hardly mattered to him, because Claire was fine with it.

For the first time, he finally felt as though he could talk to Claire, really talk to her. All this time he had blamed her for the obstacles he'd put in his own way. He was the one who had persuaded her that they should buy the house in Silver Lake despite it consuming most of his salary. And he'd convinced himself that she *wanted* to be a full-time mother, even after she said she'd rather work.

Beneath him, Ashley's body shuddered and bucked. "Why do you torture me?" Wayob screamed. "I have done nothing to you."

Gray clenched his teeth. He grabbed Wayob's shoulders, pulled himself up, squared him in the eye. "You really think that?" Gray had used the Encanto, true, but if not for Wayob, no one would have died. And Claire would still be able to walk.

"I shall make you wealthy beyond your wildest dreams," Wayob said. "I can bestow you with the fortunes of Ashley. Just get off me."

"I think you should know what it's like. Memories are nothing like the real thing." Now all Gray felt was anger over what Wayob had done to Claire.

"You shall not dare," Wayob said.

"But I shall. I'm going to eat your face off."

—

In the Mustang, Saul had to hurry. By his estimation, around the time Hernandez reached the two-lane in the Rover, a second chopper must have joined the chase, because the first had returned here. And it arrived just in time to discover what looked like Ashley York chained to a table with Gray on top of her. No doubt whoever was in the chopper was raising all kinds of alarm. A whole circus of officers—LAPD and probably FBI as well—would come charging into the campground now. Just a matter of time.

Saul had to focus. He had to ignore the voice in his head screaming *bad idea* as he grasped the Encanto on either side of the seam and began to twist.

At first, the stone refused to budge. Then, near the seam on the upper hemisphere, a small crack appeared... and before he could reduce the pressure, the crack fissured. The two hemispheres came apart. The crack became a chip, which spun into the floor well. Cosmetic damage, he hoped.

Both halves of the stone were hollow. In the lower half, a set of gears, chiseled crudely from volcanic glass, were lashed with what appeared to be human hair. The gears drove a set of three needles carved from bone. On their tips was a brown substance that Saul recognized at once as dried blood. At the bottom of the hollow was a dark gelatinous mass.

A shaft had been broken off, and it appeared designed to turn the gears, which in turn levered the needles through the mass. And that would... do what, exactly?

Saul had no idea and no time to consider it. The chopper was lowering. If it was landing, that meant backup was fast approaching.

Wind and dust poured in through the window. Saul buzzed it up.

Gray backed away from the Table of Death, where the unconscious body of

Ashley York lay in chains.

A strange new feeling for Wayob welled up in Saul: pity. Strange to actually feel sorry for Wayob, but pity was a long ways from compassion.

Shera crouched on her haunches, her gaze focused on Wayob—or was that just Ashley now?

Gray chased a piece of paper to the edge of the campsite, where it caught in a thicket of tumbleweed. He snatched it out, sat at the picnic table, and began to draw.

Saul studied the Encanto. If Wayob had left Ashley's body, then he had to be in the stone now, because, as he'd basically admitted, there was nowhere else for him to go.

The most Wayob could have observed from Saul's memories earlier was the seam on the side of the stone. There was no way for him to know that Saul could open it and reset it. Hell, Saul wasn't sure himself. But it was time to find out. If Wayob was in there, Saul had to lock the device before Wayob realized it was being tampered with and bolted back into Ashley's body.

Gingerly, Saul gripped the nub of the broken axle between his thumb and forefinger and turned it counterclockwise.

After a quarter turn, the gears tightened. Saul continued. Slowly. The quills raised and rotated into alignment with small holes in the bottom of the stone. Below the gears, something clicked. The axle tightened to a stop.

He did not dare to force it.

As he reassembled the Encanto, the stone felt surprisingly cold. Was it "locked"? How could it be? Maybe it harnessed some kind of dark energy capable of constraining Wayob's spirit—perhaps in the empty space of the upper hemisphere, or maybe in some other plane of existence. But Saul had a feeling the dried mass and the blood had something to do with it. For now, he just needed it to work; later, he could worry about *how.*

—

After the heat dissipated from the trunk, Rosa felt some relief, but that only lasted for maybe an hour, and then it grew cold. She shivered there in the cramped space for some unknown length of time. And now she knew she was in trouble, because although she still sensed the chill, her body had stopped shivering and she felt almost nothing at all. She crunched the empty plastic bottle and flung it limply at her feet. Still, she wished the night would just go on forever, because if the sun rose, so would the heat, and then she'd die for sure.

Her muscles ached, but it was too much effort to roll over against the box of dishes. Her eyes were dry, and they burned from straining to see in the darkness. Her lids came down against her will. She was passing out.

It was almost a relief to finally end the longest day she'd ever endured, aside from maybe the death train up through Mexico, which she was starting to remember for the first time in her life—those days and days of cooking in the sun on top of the train. She couldn't have been much older than two. Abuela's hair was just starting to gray, and she still had her sight. Rosa's father had tried to defend her from the men, but there were too many. Whatever Abuela had endured on the long journey must have been worth it to escape Guatemala, which she refused to speak of ever again. The army was after her, Rosa knew that much from her father, and they had Abuela's husband, who Rosa couldn't remember, aside from the black-and-white photo which Wayob had ground into the floor when he kidnapped her.

Tires hissed on the pavement. An engine slowed through what Rosa had decided was a curve in the road, yet still her pulse kicked up. She opened her mouth. She tried to call out but could not. No sound came out.

The engine revved. The car sped away.

As she drifted off, Rosa thought of Abuela, the way her whole body shook on the rare occasions when she laughed—or more like cackled—and how it was so loud the neighbors had knocked on the wall. The last time Rosa remembered her laughing was the Fourth of July, when they picnicked at Will Rogers, and a toddler on the blanket beside theirs struggled to fit a giant slice of cantaloupe into the impossible little *o* of his mouth. It had made Abuela cackle until tears rolled down her cheeks. "Como eras de niño," she'd said to Rosa's father. His face reddened but he laughed. They had all laughed, the toddler's parents too, and they shared their cantaloupe as the fireworks started.

Abuela wouldn't want Rosa to give up. Rosa could not disappoint her. She promised herself that if she ever got out of here, she'd graduate USC. It didn't matter where the money came from—this was Abuela's dying wish. Rosa would get her law degree and, somehow, help others like herself, other Dreamers who wanted to work in the country where they grew up. She would make Abuela proud.

As darkness overtook her, she pictured the fireworks on the last Fourth of July.

Streaks of colored light.

—

Oh man, that kiss, Hernandez thought as she sped down the empty desert highway in the spotlight of the chopper. Her heart swerved. *That kiss.* A current had seemed to surge from inside Saul and through her whole body.

Why had it taken the need to find out if Saul was really Saul to cut through all the bullshit? What a small thing her career seemed like now, compared to how she felt in his arms. Why had she waited so long for something so right?

She tightened her grip on the wheel.

On the horizon, a cacophony of blue strobes appeared. Ten squad cars, at least. No way around them. And by now their orders superseded whatever she might say. She racked her brain for some way to buy Saul more time.

No easy task.

And Rosa had waited too long already. The thought of her locked in a trunk weighed heavy on Hernandez's heart.

She checked her phone. No service still.

Keeping one hand on the wheel, she started a text requesting a patrol officer, code three, at Rosa's location. She hoped she could send the message before reaching the roadblock.

No. Hope was not enough. She *had* to.

In the upper corner of her phone, one lonesome bar of service flickered on. She hit send and waited for the swoosh of the message going out while the blue strobes ahead were closing in and closing fast.

To the left, beyond the cone of light from the chopper, the moonrise cast long shadows across the irregular landscape. And one shadow was moving. A mountain lion leaped onto the blacktop and faced her, eyes glowing green in her high beams, no fear of the Land Rover plowing toward it. She had no time to stop. The immense cat cemented itself solidly on the double yellow. She swerved right.

The majestic head of the lion traced the arc of the Rover as the right tire dropped off the blacktop and slammed into the wheel well. The Rover spun out of control and hit what was probably a boulder from the sound of metal crunching. The massive vehicle gave way like an aluminum can crushing all around her. She was thrown sideways. An airbag deployed and punched her in the face.

Darkness.

———

Gray blinked through the dust churned up by the helicopter and kept drawing. He drew a spiral and traced over it, over and over, around and around, until a blotch of solid darkness covered the page.

Shera startled him from his trance by launching toward the Mustang. She was going to greet Detective Parker, who had unfolded himself from the car. With one hand, he shielded his eyes in the spotlight. In his other hand was the white stone. It was still missing the snake-dial, so if Wayob was in there, he wasn't trapped.

Shera leaped up onto Parker, and he reeled his arm back, and for one crazy moment Gray feared he might throw the Encanto, as if it were a toy for her to fetch. But instead, he pushed her off and held it down near her muzzle for her inspection. She backed away, lowered herself to the ground, and then crept closer again. She sniffed and sniffed again, and once satisfied, licked Parker's hand.

He rubbed her head. Then he held up the Encanto. "I reset it."

"Without the snake?" *Was that possible?*

Parker approached the table. "I took it apart." He set the stone by Gray's scribble and tapped it twice. "Shera seems satisfied that we've got Wayob trapped in there."

"But how can we be sure?"

Parker studied Gray's scribble and furrowed his brow, as if the dark blotch really took any time to consider. His box-shaped head would be fun to paint again, now that Gray knew who he was.

"This is what Wayob's looking at, right?" Parker asked.

Gray shrugged. "I don't know. It's all I've been able to draw tonight, aside from your directions, so I can't say for sure this is what he's seeing."

The helicopter ascended again.

Parker smiled. "It worked."

Gray cracked his knuckles. "What worked?"

"I blindfolded Wayob earlier."

"But Ashley wasn't blindfolded when we got here."

"I took it off on the way."

"And yet... I tried drawing after we arrived, and still I drew nothing."

"Maybe he knew what you were up to. Are you sure his eyes were open?"

The turbulence from the helicopter caught the paper. Gray grabbed it before it blew off the table, smoothed it flat, and reconsidered his sketch. The blotch had a circular texture, less chaotic than the scribbles he'd made on the way here; it was more like the infinite-seeming black nothing that he'd painted back when Wayob was, almost certainly, inside the Encanto.

Parker approached Ashley. She was still unconscious and shackled to the table. He leaned over her and frowned. He glanced back at Shera, who lay halfway between the picnic table and Ashley, her muzzle on her outstretched legs.

"What do you think?"

She lifted her head. Her eyes darted around in the spotlight.

Parker began unlocking the manacles on Ashley's arms.

Gray inhaled sharply.

The sirens howled as they neared, out of sync like a tone-deaf choir.

"You think that's a good idea?" Gray asked. "It's probably her, but—"

Distant sirens wailed above the chop of the helicopter's engine.

"I've got it covered." Parker tapped something heavy in the side pocket of his trench coat, probably his gun. "If Wayob's still in there, he'll go for the Encanto."

Gray grabbed the paper and pencil and slid down the bench to distance himself from the weapon.

"Think of something to ask her," Parker said. "Something you know she knows and Wayob does not."

Gray knew things about her life, but Wayob probably did too; he seemed to know just as much as Gray, certainly enough to fool him into believing that Wayob *was* Ashley.

"I've only known her for a day," Gray said, a little embarrassed to admit that they'd slept together.

Parker rubbed the stubble on his chin. "When you were in her body, were you able to see her memories?"

He shook his head. *Was that even possible?* "No. It was more like I was wearing her body. On the inside, it was still all me."

Still, seeing the world through Ashley's eyes had given him a different perspective. He had learned about himself. Like the way true art, the sort he yearned to produce, struck a chord in the viewer's heart and made them think differently.

"Every man is an island," Parker said as he kneeled to release Ashley's legs. "Guess even the Encanto can't change that."

Shera sat right beside him. He rubbed her neck. Her tail thumped, kicking dust up into the wind from the rotors.

Ashley's eyelids fluttered open.

Parker stood back and waited with a hand on the pocket of his trench coat.

She leaned forward and rubbed her wrists, squinted in the spotlight, and then spoke slowly: "Her name is Shera."

Parker frowned. "She's your dog, right?"

Ashley wiped the dust streaked with tears from her cheeks. "She was Sammy's." She slid off the table, and her eyes found Parker's. "I'm not Wayob anymore, okay?"

Gray hunched over the paper to block the wind. The sirens were minutes away, maybe less. Below the blotch he'd drawn, he placed his pencil to the page... and in his mind's eye, he already saw the spiraling blackness. Wayob *was* in the Encanto.

"Grab the laptop," Parker said to Gray. "We'll cue up some smut for Ms. York."

"If you still think I'm Wayob, then why unchain me?" she shouted above the drone of the helicopter as she turned sideways, lifted her leg onto the table, and massaged her ankle where it had been shackled.

"One last test," he said. "Just to be sure."

She dropped her leg and spun toward Parker. Her eyes glinted in the spotlight. She grabbed his lapels and pulled him down toward her. Parker allowed himself to be pulled close, as if resigned to whatever came next.

She leaned forward and gave him a loud kiss on the lips—more sound than actual contact. The way a niece might kiss her favorite uncle.

Parker staggered back, and Gray almost laughed at his visible surprise.

"You brilliant, beautiful man," she said. "Thank you, thank you, thank you." She cast her gaze toward Gray. "You too. What you did, that took guts."

Gray's throat constricted. His voice came out high. "Not really."

Moisture welled in her eyes. "No, I mean it. You drove him out of me."

A desire surged through Gray: he wanted to paint her, especially her eyes and the way they had softened at the corners when she kissed Parker. He grabbed the pencil and leaned over the page to do a quick sketch. Darkness swirled over the image of Ashley in his mind. A spiraling, black nothing. That was all he could draw. Maybe all he'd ever draw, so long as Wayob remained trapped in that awful stone. But what if he destroyed it? Like he should have done from the start.

"How much do you remember?" Parker asked Ashley.

"Everything," she said. "It was like I was a prisoner inside my own body. All I could do was watch and listen while that bastard pretended to be me. It was..."

"Identity theft," Parker said.

"Torture," Ashley said.

The sirens grew louder. The white, porous stone glared harshly in the helicopter's spotlight. It blurred as Gray's eyes teared up from the wind and the dust. His heart pounded in his head. The light narrowed to a beam, which seemed to focus on the Encanto. Smashing it would kill Wayob, and Gray was fine with that. He just had to act before losing his nerve.

As he snatched the Encanto, he heard his name. Muffled by the din of the helicopter, her voice almost submerged beneath the sirens, Ashley shouted, "Gray, what are you doing?"

"What I should have done from the start," he said. What Rosa's grandmother, with tears streaming down her cheeks, had begged him to do.

If only he'd listened.

The porous stone was phosphorescent. It almost burned in his hand.

The beam swept away as the helicopter followed after it.

Gray held the Encanto above his head, and it seemed to hover there. Up above the sky. Up where the stars streamed together in the Milky Way, like if he let it go, it would just drift off into space…

He felt lighter, like *he* was floating, the Encanto pulling him to the stars.

It had so fully captured his attention that he failed to notice the huge hand approaching until it was lit up by blue flashing light. In the interval between flashes, the hand disappeared. Blue light. The hand—Parker's hand—clamped over the Encanto, engulfing it.

An interval of darkness.

The stone vanished.

Parker's voice boomed. "Better let me take that."

Gray swallowed. He had to let go.

Epilogue

December

Saul mopped the sweat off his brow, and Shera tugged on her leash, pulling his arm to its limit. It seemed as though she was more determined than him to reach the peak, though probably it was more about catching up to Ashley, who had let him keep Shera in exchange for visitation rights.

As he huffed up a near vertical stretch of trail, a pair of male voices approached from behind. "They should just make a digital August Grant," one was saying.

"No way," said the other. "Yoson An will make a way better Quantum Man than August Grant ever could have."

When Saul summited what looked like the peak, he discovered another long stretch of trail ascending ahead of him. His stomach sank. It was steeper, and more uneven, than before.

"Heel, Shera." He pulled her back beside him and leaned against a rock outcropping as the two men hiked past. Both pale, mid-twenties. Beer guts and hipster beards. The shorter one wore cargo shorts and a camel pack, and he thanked Saul for letting them pass.

Sprigs of grass peppered the mountainside. One more rain would color in the whole landscape with that just-sprouted shade of green.

Across a narrow valley to the east, a lone wisp of cloud clung to the face of Mount Lee. Saul was above the peak, looking down at the wide stretch of blacktop that led to a razor-topped fence surrounding a profusion of broadcast towers. The slope obscured the *H* in the Hollywood sign.

Shera sniffed the air. Her tail wagged. Her whole rear end jerked from side to side. Saul followed her gaze down the trail that had nearly killed him. Below the switchback, a head of raven hair with a shock of white bangs bobbed above the bank. Hernandez smiled broadly. She still had the cast on her arm, and her tank top offered a rare view of the mustang pony tattoo on her shoulder.

"I thought you had a doctor's appointment," Saul said.

"Didn't take long. The cast comes off in two weeks."

He chuckled. "So now you're going to risk breaking the other arm?"

"You think I trust you with two women? I've got to keep my eye on you."

"Fear not, my lady. They left me in the dust."

"Oh, so now you like me because I'm slow?" She squeezed past him and made a show of marching ahead up the trail.

Shera bounded after her, jerking the leash taut.

The rear-view of Hernandez in her yoga pants provided ample incentive for him to keep pace, and he silently vowed that soon he'd be in shape enough to do so. "Hold up, Hernandez."

She stopped and turned to face him. "How many times do I have to tell you?"

"Right. Rhonda." Somehow, living together had been an easier adjustment than using her first name. "So, you took the afternoon off?"

"Didn't have to. Turns out my new partner does paperwork."

"Sounds like you got an upgrade."

"Nah," she said. "He's an idiot. I'd like my old partner back."

"Too bad Levy will never agree to that."

"Actually, she will. I had a long talk with her this morning."

"It'd take more than just talking for her to reinstate my badge. What did you have to promise her?"

"It's more what I promised not to do."

"You threatened to quit?"

She shrugged.

"You tell her we shacked up?"

"Well, I didn't exactly mention that, but yeah, I think she knows." Hernandez turned back to the trail and started power walking.

He had to lean forward and use his hands to maintain his balance while ascending the incline. His pacemaker banged his heart against his chest. *Stop or die.* He leaned on a rock to catch his breath.

As much as he missed carrying a badge and working with Hernandez day to day, he was still done with the LAPD. Though it was flattering that she wasn't yet ready to accept it.

Shera tugged him forward, almost choking herself against her collar to reach Hernandez, who was waiting a few yards ahead again.

"Partners or not," she said. "We need you back in Homicide Special."

"A lot of people would be happy if I never came back. Especially Levy."

"Doesn't matter what anyone else thinks. You're good for the department. You're the only one with the guts to do the right thing, regardless of how it might look."

"Not true. You're the one who stood up to the top brass when it appeared I had abducted Ashley York."

She combed back her shock of white. "That's what I'm talking about. They were more worried about finding a scapegoat than finding the truth."

"They'll never believe the truth," he said. What they did believe, and only because Ashley York had thankfully said so, was that the video of Saul injecting her and the whole abduction had been a publicity stunt. "If things had gone sideways, it might have ruined your career as well. You should have thrown me under the bus. I knew what I was getting into. You could still make a real difference with the LAPD, if you don't step in the shit."

"But I wasn't worried about me. I was worried about you." She half-smiled. They had discussed this many times. "I still am."

"You mean like how am I going to pay my half of the rent with no job?"

She shook her head. *"Do what you love and the money will follow."*

"Like getting high and watching TV?"

She snorted. "If that's what you were into, I wouldn't be so worried. I'm more afraid you'll end up doing something dangerous."

He patted his stomach, ten pounds lighter than last month and he was just getting started. "For me, just getting out of bed is dangerous."

"You know what I mean." She continued up the hill.

He lumbered after her, lagging further and further behind.

For him, *love* had nothing to do with it. He was compelled. And now his eyes were open. Almost certainly there were others out there, bodiless souls like Wayob, who had perhaps succeeded where he'd failed in taking another's life and living it as their own, manipulating the general assumption that things are the way they appear.

Up ahead, standing on what Saul prayed was the peak, was Ashley York. She held her phone up to film their ascent, which for Hernandez was only three more steps. Hernandez waved at the camera, then stood to wait beside Ashley. They cheered him on, and he felt his cheeks redden. He exaggerated the struggle, hoping they wouldn't realize just how hard it actually was for him and that he might not have made it without Shera, pulling his weight like she was a sled dog.

But he did make it. And it was the peak. He leaned forward and braced his hands on his knees to catch his breath. The top of the mountain was relatively flat. Four other hikers, including the two hipster-beards, were pretending to mill through a grid of stones stacked into cairns while ogling Ashley with staccato glances. Behind them, a windswept pine known as the Wisdom Tree stood alone on the edge of the opposite cliff. Strung from its branches, an assortment of keys dangling on shoelaces swayed in the breeze. At the base of the tree an ammo box contained the hopes and dreams of all those who had made the climb before and taken the time to write them down. Rosa knelt beside it, tossed her hair back over her shoulder, and added her pages to the collection.

Ashley drew near, and Saul had to hold Shera's collar to stop her from leaping on her. Ashley knelt to pet her.

"Sorry we didn't wait for you," she said, although they'd previously agreed he'd arrive late in order to give her a chance to try and persuade Rosa one-on-

one to accept her help. Secretly, he'd been glad for the excuse not to have to maintain their pace on the climb.

"Oh, I would have caught up." He winked. "If not for Hernandez slowing me down."

Hernandez slammed her fists into her hips.

"Rhonda, I mean." Why was it so hard to use her first name?

He nodded toward Rosa. "Any luck?"

"She agreed to an internship." Ashley held up her hand. "A paid internship."

Saul slapped it.

"Plus," Ashley said, "now I can sponsor her green card."

"So, you're keeping InGenetic?" Hernandez asked.

According to recent headlines, Pfizer was now competing with Johnson and Johnson to purchase Evan York's biotech darling, and the offer price had soared above fifty billion.

"Her green card could take a year," Ashley said. "Besides, Dad would have wanted me to. I can do more good with the corporation than with just the money alone."

Saul nodded. With Ashley at the helm, InGenetic would morph into something vastly different. Probably a change for the better.

He spun in a slow circle and took in the view of the LA basin as it rolled down to the Pacific. The sun hung low, its reflection white-hot on the water. From here the waves looked like ripples licking the Santa Monica Mountains, which ran along the coast to the Palisades where the ridge line cut inland and divided the city. They stood on the third summit from the last before the slope gave way to the roofline of Glendale. To the east, beyond Glendale and Pasadena, Mount Wilson ascended like a wall into a row of rolling clouds.

Rosa closed the ammo box, her face shadowed with intense emotion. She got to her feet and, upon seeing Hernandez, smiled and hurried toward them through the cairns to give her a hug. Then, as if out of some obligation to politeness, she swung her arms limply around Saul and withdrew. Still upset with him, obviously.

"I moved the Encanto," he said. "It's in a vault now."

She rolled her eyes. "I don't care where it is. The fact that it exists is the problem."

"I thought you'd be happy."

She glowered at him. "I'll be happy when it's destroyed."

Saul rubbed the scar on his palm. The damn thing had pricked him when he took it from Gray.

"That would make me judge, jury, and executioner." He had gone too far with Brown and did not care to repeat the mistake.

Hernandez gave him a knowing nod.

"I'll do it," Rosa said.

"Trust me," Saul said, "you don't want that on your conscience. Wayob was human, after all, or at least he was at one time."

Rosa glanced from Ashley to Hernandez. "Then it's the humane thing to do."

"I don't know about that," he said. "I think Wayob might like it in there." But, regardless, he wasn't going to risk destroying the Encanto. If Rosa's grandmother had known for sure what would happen when it was destroyed, the knowledge had died along with her.

"You'll be tempted," Rosa said. "Abuela told me what it's like. You'll let him out again. And if you don't, then someone else will."

Saul was curious what it would be like to awaken in someone else's body, but he wasn't tempted to find out. Not now. His life was beginning again, and he wanted to live every day of it.

"Temptation, I've got a handle on," he said and patted his belly, which he hoped the others could see was getting smaller now that he'd cut out bread and sugar, which, after a month, he hardly missed anymore. He still had a long way to go, but he'd get there. Living with Hernandez had cured his addiction to food, and he felt better than he had in years. "Anyway, I had the Encanto encased in Lexan so no one can use it again, ever."

"What's Lex-an?" Ashley asked.

"Bullet-proof glass," he said. "Polycarbonate. Tell her, Hernandez."

Hernandez pressed her lips tight together.

"I mean Rhonda. Sorry."

The corners of her mouth curved upward as she shook her head. "*Saul* showed the stone to me," she said to Rosa. "It's sealed in a glass cube. There's no way to open it."

"It's unbreakable," he added. He had challenged Hernandez to bust it open, but she refused to even touch it.

Rosa balled her hands into fists. "So now it's impossible to destroy?"

Saul nodded. "You'd need a two-ton truck." The one downside was that now he had no way to learn how it worked. But maybe Hernandez was right— maybe some things *were* better left unknown. Whatever technology held Wayob within the Encanto, it was perhaps more than the world could handle at this point.

"So, where is it?" The intensity in Rosa's voice left no doubt of her intention, which was why Saul had worked with Ashley to place the Encanto out of reach for all of them.

"In the US Bank on Figueroa," Ashley said. "Access requires consent from all four of us, plus Gray as well."

"You agreed to this?" Rosa shouted at her.

Ashley glanced at Saul.

"Think about it," he said. "It's under lock and key with state-of-the-art security and guards around twenty-four-seven. It's way better than any prison we could have found for Wayob."

So long as the rule of law continued to exist, no one would gain access. Ashley had set up a foundation funded in perpetuity to which she'd transferred ownership of the Encanto along with the other Mayan artifacts her father had collected, all of which were in the vault.

Rosa sucked in a breath. She would come around. Eventually, she'd realize, like Saul had, that this was the best way to handle it. Now that the damn thing was out of the apartment, his nightmares of Wayob's terrible musical whispering had finally ceased.

Ashley waved to the hipster-beard in the cargo shorts, who was pretending to photograph the view even though it was obviously Ashley's picture he was taking.

He glanced behind him to see if she meant someone else.

"No, you." She held up her phone. "Mind taking our picture?"

The four of them lined up along the cliff, with Hollywood behind them. The dull sound of engines and tires on the 101 washed up through the Cahuenga Pass. Shera obeyed Saul's order to sit but would only look up at him, despite his pointing at the camera. He gave up and straightened his back, sucked in the sweaty bulge beneath his shirt, and put one arm around Hernandez.

"Looking svelte," Ashley said to him without a trace of sarcasm. She tossed an arm around Rosa.

Saul chuckled. "You're kind."

Hernandez lifted her arm with the mustang tattoo and flexed her bicep. "She was talking to me."

After hipster-beard took several photos, he returned Ashley's phone then whipped out his own, stood beside her and extended his arm.

She ducked her head and stepped away. "Uh, no thanks."

"I'll tag you on my feed," he said. "I've got over ten thousand followers."

"I don't do social media anymore."

"My bad. I thought you were Ashley York."

She laughed politely. "I'm still figuring out who that is."

But Saul had a feeling she knew exactly who she was. He'd heard about all the offers she'd turned down after their so-called "kidnapping stunt."

After the other hikers left, the four of them remained. Saul was in no hurry to begin the descent. As the sun sank into the Pacific, the great monoliths of stone and glass from Century City to downtown shone red in the fading light.

Beside him, Rosa blew out a long breath. "Some city."

"It sure is," he said. "It sure is."

"Look, I'm still grateful," she said.

"For what?"

"There's no way I'd let Wayob take over my body. Not to help someone I hardly knew." She put an arm around him, and this time she actually squeezed.

Saul patted her hand on his shoulder. "You never know."

"No, I know."

Hernandez winked at him. "You never know what you'll do until push comes to shove."

He nodded.

"Totally," Ashley said.

The breeze quickened into a cold wind, but the four of them remained. They watched the shadows reach across the city, engulfing the streets and lower buildings into darkness. Somehow, Wayob traveled beneath the shadows, through a darkness deeper than night. An abyss Saul had peered into. For now, he decided to call it magic. Might as well, because until he understood otherwise, the Encanto effectively worked like black magic. But if black magic existed then so did good. Just as shadows required light, there must be good magic too. *Good magic...* now that was worth searching for. Worth living for.

———

The shadow of the roofline crept across the deck and up onto the table where Gray had set his coffee down. Coffee had replaced Scotch as his new beverage of choice, and he was still adjusting to the taste. Maybe he'd take cream next time, or sweetener.

Across from him, Claire had angled her wheelchair toward the setting sun, her eyes closed, the wrinkles around her eyes and mouth smoothed away as she basked in the glow.

Gray used his finger to smudge the lines in his sketch. His pocket buzzed, but he ignored it. He wished there was time to set up an easel and paint her portrait before the last rays faded from her face.

At least he could paint now, and he had been, profusely, ever since that insane night in the desert, ever since Saul took the Encanto. After that, he'd painted no more black blotches, no point of view other than his own.

His pocket buzzed again.

Claire's eyes opened. "Who is it?"

Gray pulled out his phone. Ashley had texted a group photo from the hike. He tapped back a thumbs up and showed Claire the photo. "Saul made it to the top."

When she smiled, the skin crinkled at the corner of her lids. Her eyes, Pacific blue, shimmered in the warm light. "Tell Ashley to stop texting my husband."

He opened a photo of his painting, the first work he'd ever completed to the point of signing his name. In the painting, Claire stood before a mirror with Tyler in her arms, her eyes focused and full of passion. On the opposite side of the glass, Mindy mirrored Claire's pose, her arms wrapped around a doll, like a reflection of Claire's younger self (Mindy looked more and more like her every day). Gray had nailed the likeness of Mindy and Tyler, but somehow Claire had turned out different than he'd intended. There were no wrinkles around her eyes—those wrinkles that were like scars from all her sleepless nights—and without them she looked younger. He had a feeling that he'd painted her more like the way she saw herself in the mirror.

To his surprise, the portrait made her smile, and she'd insisted they hang it in the living room. So far, no one else had seen it. What if it wasn't any good?

He swallowed and texted the image to Ashley.

His phone swooshed out the message... No taking it back now.

"You sent her the painting," Claire said.

He checked the angle of the screen. No way she could have seen it.

"You stared at your phone forever," she said.

"You mad?"

"Of course not. It takes guts to put yourself out there."

Gray nodded. He had to get past this fear of his, which probably had a lot to do with why he'd never finished a painting before. In order to be successful, he was going to have to show his work in public. He was going to have to suffer through other people's opinions, their critiques, and all the judgment.

He sipped his coffee. Cold and definitely too bitter. Maybe different beans would taste better? Maybe coffee was like Scotch in that the taste took time to acquire. He did enjoy the surge through his system, and the caffeine seemed to cut through his trepidation and give him confidence. People *would* like his stuff. And if not, then so what? He would paint something else. Keep trying. It wasn't like he could ever give up.

"When do you start the mural?" Claire asked.

"Next month." He realized there was no point in researching the shell corporation that had commissioned him to paint a three-hundred-foot mural on the side of a building, because there was only one person who would have hired him supposedly based on the few sketches that he'd posted on Instagram. "I'm pretty sure it's Ashley who commissioned it."

Claire shrugged, as though she'd guessed this already. Of course she had. "Doesn't matter. It's still a great opportunity for you."

"True." It might not be fine art, but it *was* art, and he was getting paid for it. He rubbed his neck. "How many people do you think drive down Wilshire every day?"

"Don't worry," she said. "They're going to love it." She slurped her tea, her face half hidden behind the bowl of her favorite mug. Its handle had broken off years ago, but she refused to get rid of it.

"I start work January first," she said.

"So soon?"

Her face tightened. She ducked her eyes into the rising shadow from the roofline—he'd said the wrong thing and he knew it. Even as he said it, the words had felt wrong in his throat. "What I mean is you don't have to start right away; I didn't expect to be making money this soon."

She clunked her mug on the table, her face raw with resolve. "But I *need* to."

He swallowed. Did she realize how hard it was going to be? What if her insomnia returned?

She crossed her arms. "I don't care how hard it is. I'm doing it."

He nodded slowly. He understood. She needed that sense of accomplishment that comes from overcoming a struggle, and as much as she'd let him, he'd help her.

As she leaned her head back into the sunlight, he wanted to paint her even more than before, her face framed by satin hair, the last rays of sunlight glowing in her eyes, and a feeling surged inside him, as though he were seeing her for the first time.

"I love you," he said. "I love you now, and I always have, and I always will."

She tilted her head. Her brows knotted... then rose. "I love you too."

The sliding glass door rocked in its track. From inside, Mindy, who was head height to the handle, was trying to shove it open with both hands. She had red lipstick smeared all around her mouth, giving her the look of a drunken clown. She grunted and the door gave a few inches.

Gray stood to help her. He'd been meaning to clean out the track, which was gummed up with dirt and dried leaves.

"I can do it myself," she said.

Gray reached for the handle. "I know."

"No," she shouted.

So Gray stepped back to let her try. She leaned against the door, but she was too small to add any meaningful force. She jutted her jaw out and managed to groan the door a half-foot further open, enough for her to squeeze through the crack. "Tell Belinda I don't have to eat if I'm not hungry."

With Claire going back to work, and his mural, they would have to count on Belinda more than ever now. Better not to undermine her authority.

"If she made you something," he said, "it would be polite to try it. You don't have to eat it all if you're not hungry."

"But it *smells*."

Gray struggled not to laugh, which he knew would further anger Mindy. He hid his smile by taking a sip of coffee.

"What did Belinda make?" Claire asked.

Mindy frowned. "Slimy orange worms."

"But you love macaroni," he said. Belinda prided herself on her homemade sauce and took offense if no one ate it.

Mindy stared down at her bare feet. They were caked with dirt as though she'd been playing outside, but she hadn't left the house all day. Had she?

"How did you get so dirty?"

She didn't seem to hear him. She climbed on the side of his chair and leaned over his sketch. She ran her fingers over it, then turned over her palm and rubbed the spot where the Encanto had pricked her. It had healed, and Gray had hoped that she'd forgotten, but of course the things that hurt you are hard to forget.

"What happened to it?" she asked.

"It healed up."

"No. The snake thingy." It was hard to take her seriously with all the lipstick around her mouth.

"Uncle Saul got rid of it." Gray still wished that he'd destroyed it when he'd had the chance, but at least no one would ever touch it again.

Mindy's brows furrowed.

He glanced at Claire, and she shrugged. "Mindy, have you been in Belinda's purse?"

Mindy blinked. She wiped her mouth, smearing crimson across her cheek. When she saw the lipstick on her hand, her eyes widened. "I didn't..."

Claire remained calm. "Go wash your face, and then if you try Belinda's macaroni, we'll have dessert after she goes home."

"I don't want dessert. I wanna be left alone."

"*Estingtay imitslay*," Claire said to him.

He nodded. Mindy was testing the limits, all right, and soon she'd understand Pig Latin if they kept using it in front of her.

"You think I don't know what '*mits-ay*' means but you're wrong." She spun with her elbows up, her hands balled into fists, as if outrageously offended. She stomped back inside.

He managed to contain his laughter until she was out of earshot, and then Claire laughed along with him, and they continued laughing until their laughter had nothing at all to do with Mindy anymore. It felt good hearing Claire laugh, and to laugh together like this.

He scooted his chair around the table to be beside her. He combed her hair back with his hand and held her neck like it was a porcelain vase. She gazed at him, and the world seemed to sway. It was the ocean in her eyes. It was rocking him. He kissed her, full on the mouth. Felt her pulse hammer away beneath the skin of her neck.

They kissed, and continued kissing, as the shadow from the sunset settled over them. From somewhere in the backyard, a cricket began chirping.

When he stood, he felt dizzy. He inhaled. The moist, cool air which had drifted in with the twilight carried the smell of ocean. He could almost taste salt. He exhaled and squeezed Claire's shoulder. "I'll go talk to her."

As he stepped inside, the ocean scent was overridden by the smell of cheddar. The living room was empty. So was the kitchen. A covered pot sat on the stove, but the stove was off.

On the way to Mindy's room, he heard Belinda in the nursery making goo-goo sounds with Tyler, and then the stuttered sound of Mindy sobbing.

She was in the bathroom with the door closed. And she wasn't sobbing, not quite, it sounded... guttural, staccato. Chuckling? Certainly, he had never heard Mindy laugh like that before.

He pressed his ear to the door. Her chuckle climbed to a wail.

He knocked. "Mindy?"

She went quiet.

He knocked again and tried the knob... Locked. Usually they had to remind her, insist actually, that she even close the door when using the bathroom.

Gray knocked again. "Mindy, we don't lock doors in this house."

Giggling erupted. She was delirious. If he didn't get some food in her soon, he knew she was going to crash, and then there would be tears.

But the door remained locked, and she kept right on laughing.

Panic seized him. He reared back to kick open the door, and right then Belinda's squat frame emerged from the nursery.

He dropped his foot and straightened as if it was no big deal. And, he thought, he probably *was* overreacting.

Belinda's eyes, which were already too small for her head, narrowed. "What's going on?"

He shrugged. "Mindy's got the giggles."

"What's she laughing at?"

Good question. "She's five."

"She begged me to make macaroni and then she wouldn't eat any of it."

"I'll talk to her," he said. "Mind giving us a minute?"

Belinda frowned. "She's upsetting Tyler."

Gray stared at Belinda until she stepped back into the nursery and shut the door.

He knocked on the bathroom door. "Mindy!"

She continued laughing.

He pounded on the door again. *Please be okay.*

Her laughter grew.

The carrot cake. She must have gotten into the carrot cake. That's why she wasn't hungry. He pictured the tracks left by her little fingers in the white frosting. In order to reach it, she'd have had to push a stool across the kitchen and climb up on the counter. It wasn't like her, but what else could explain the way she was cackling? It lacked all sound of fun. It sounded sharp, almost… malicious.

What in the hell was she laughing at?

"Stand back from the door."

He kicked below the knob. The door bowed but remained intact. On the third try, the knob splintered free from the wood, and he shoved his way in.

Mindy was standing in front of the mirror, her back to him. She fell quiet, entranced by her reflection, lipstick smeared around her mouth like a wound. She pulled at the skin above her cheekbones, and her lower lids pulled away from her eyeballs, exposing a network of veins. She giggled.

Her eyeballs bulged in the mirror, and she kept right on laughing.

Acknowledgements

Thanks to my amazing editor Marissa Van Uden for reading so carefully and paying attention to every detail. Sharpening this work was no easy feat. Thanks to Robin Samuels for such thorough proofreading, and Jen Gregory for additional proofreading and the photograph of yours truly. Thanks to Donn Marlou Ramirez for the amazing cover design. Thanks to the Writers of Sherman Oaks for the two years of critiquing LA FOG, especially Scott Coon who read every single entry. Thanks to Damien Chazelle, James Lee Burke, Michael Connelly, and thank you, dear readers, for taking the time and supporting my work.